Gray Fisher Trilogy

The WAG and The Scoundrel
Tabula Rasa
Distractions

by
Debbie McGowan

Beaten Track
www.beatentrackpublishing.com

Gray Fisher Trilogy

First published 2021 by Beaten Track Publishing
Copyright © 2016, 2021 Debbie McGowan

Print ISBN: 978 1 78645 512 3
eBook ISBN: 978 1 78645 513 0

Beaten Track Publishing,
Burscough, Lancashire.
www.beatentrackpublishing.com

CONTENTS

Author's Note

The Gray Fisher trilogy is intended to be a stand-alone series within the Hiding Behind The Couch universe.

However, there are still some pre-existing relationships which are not explained in detail in this trilogy.

A short summary of relevant back-story is included at the end of this book (contains spoilers for anyone intending to read Hiding Behind The Couch).

Mini-Glossary

CID   Criminal Investigation Department – the police department which investigates serious crime; officers are known as detectives and wear plain clothes (office attire) as opposed to uniforms.

CPS   Crown Prosecution Service – the body responsible for processing offences and deciding whether they should go to trial.

DCI   Detective Chief Inspector – a senior CID officer; lower ranks are Detective Inspector (DI), Detective Sergeant (DS) and Detective Constable (DC).

Drink-driving   The term used in English law for driving under the influence of alcohol.

ISA   Individual Savings Account – a tax-free, usually stocks-related investment.

Met Line   The Metropolitan Line (aka 'the Met') – a London Transport Underground/overground rail route that runs between Aldgate, City of London and Uxbridge, Middlesex/Watford, Hertfordshire.

PC   Police Constable – uniformed officer.

PNC   Police National Computer – a system of databases used by law enforcement agencies in the UK.

Police Fédérale   Belgian Federal Police.

RTA   Road Traffic Accident – a collision involving one or more vehicles.

SIU   Special Investigations Unit – a fictional white-collar crime investigation unit of the Metropolitan Police Service.

The Met   The Metropolitan Police Service – the police service in London and Greater London (distinct from City of London Police).

The WAG and The Scoundrel

Three years after the death of his civil partner, DCI Gray Fisher is finally ready to make the break from the police. For too long, he has used his work as a means of survival; now, he's looking forward to a nice, quiet life in academia.

Investment banker Will Richards is a walking, talking contradiction. With his love of surfing and his farmhouse menagerie of rescue animals, he's far removed from Gray's idea of the perfect man, but that's 'not a problem'. Gray wants nothing more than friendship, and Will seems happy to accept that. After all, with his mum's illness and resigning from his job, he's got enough on his plate already.

Assuming, of course, he's telling the truth.

When former colleague, Rob Simpson-Stone, asks for Gray's help with a case of a destitute banker who faked his own death, Gray is understandably reluctant to get involved...until Rob reveals the identity of one of the suspects.

For Ronnie and Will...
and the everlasting smell of goat.

"Though I myself refrain from violence towards animals, I must admit that I am not fit enough to dissuade others from it. I know that we have a duty towards animals, but cannot make others feel it."

Mahatma Gandhi

1: One Night Downtown

Naomi Tanner was a willowy five foot ten with skin like smooth vanilla fudge, dark-brown hair straightened into a neat, page-boy style, a small nose, perfectly made-up eyes, well-plucked brows, expertly manicured nails, and a passion for haute couture. She was attractive, more than moderately intelligent, and completely out of place in The Blue Bell public house.

It was not where she had intended to be that evening. She'd only stepped in to dodge the sudden shower, which had quickly turned to torrential downpour. An hour and two glasses of wine later, it was still coming down by the bucketful.

The pub was busy, considering both its location and state of disrepair. The seating was lumpy and frayed, the tables didn't sit level, the carpet was threadbare...the nicotine-stained ceiling told the rest of the story. The Blue Bell hadn't been decorated in decades, but the regulars seemed happy, and Naomi was in no state to care. She swirled the red drip in the bottom of her glass, watching it snake and spread and coalesce once more. She was in a world of her own, a very different world to the one she had inhabited until three weeks ago, when Aaron left for good. Or so he'd said. But the wine, which had done little more than give her a headache, was nowhere near close to eclipsing the pain.

She didn't miss him. It was what she'd always wanted: no more ironing shirts, sending suits out for dry cleaning, tolerating nosey cleaners, hosting dinners, standing in badly aimed piss. Why would she miss any of that? No. It was better this way because behind the well-fitting, expensive suits and the successful career, he was a slob. A rich slob, admittedly, but what did it matter? He'd always claimed money could buy anything, happiness included. They both now knew it simply was not true.

Taking her empty glass back to the bar, Naomi drifted to a stop, entranced by the landlady flirting with her customers. To Naomi's mind, the woman was far from attractive, but what did she know? She'd always tried to look her best—essential, she believed, for the wife of a director—and yet there she was, a life repossessed while she sheltered in a back-street pub where a scraggy-haired woman in jeans and a man's T-shirt held court.

Life was topsy-turvy. A home worth twenty million, and now she was sofa-hopping. When had it all gone so wrong? She'd wanted escape, but not like this. What point was there to freedom when she had no means to enjoy it?

Still no luck in getting a refill of wine, although she'd had enough, Naomi wandered aimlessly out of the pub and up to the high street, her lack of speed at odds with others marching in both directions as they raced to escape the rain. She was already drenched. Where to next? Something to eat? She had nowhere to cook and nothing to cook with.

How difficult it all seemed. How utterly impossible. The life she lived came at a very high price—not her clothes, shoes, make-up. They were unnecessary luxuries, and she was out of foundation again, such use as the oily gunk from a chain store had proved to be. She'd slit the tube that morning and squeezed out the last dregs for nothing more than to have it wash away in the rain.

The life she *had* lived, she consciously corrected. It was all behind her now. Aaron had warned their luck was about to run out, and she'd tried to dismiss it as paranoia. He was working too hard, they were getting older...a mid-life crisis? No. She had thought herself to be in her prime, a much younger protégé to the delectable Miss Brodie—she was only thirty-seven, after all—but not anymore.

For this was not living; it was existing, and she'd had enough.

With a soul-heavy sigh, she paused and slipped off first one shoe—tipping out the rainwater—then the other, glancing along the high street and squinting at the commotion, the wet tarmac alive with the glisten of blue flashing lights. Police, ambulances, a fire engine; none of her business. Nor did she care that another fool in a big car had attempted invincibility, no doubt fuelled by alcohol. They were all the same, and she was done with them. She slipped her shoes back on, turned, and walked away.

2: Second Date

S TUPID NIGHT FOR a date, a Thursday. The restaurant was near empty, and Gray had the staff's undivided attention. He'd bought a drink; what more could he do? A couple passing by stopped to read the menu on the external wall. Gray willed them to come in, take some of the pressure off him. He didn't usually have that problem; light-brown hair, average height, average build, average looks—average everything—he blended in, and he liked it that way. But when there were only four customers...

He watched, dismayed, as the three business execs who had been sitting at the back of the restaurant came towards him and stopped to peer out at the rain. In his head, he begged them to stay. It didn't work, and now he was the only one.

"Would you like to order yet, sir?" the waiter asked.

Gray glanced at his watch: almost nine-thirty. *Should I assume I've been stood up?* "I'll give it another ten minutes, if you don't mind?"

The waiter bowed and retreated.

Gray took a swig of beer and sighed in anticipation of another evening alone...or for the lack of explanation and non-argument that would follow. It was too predictable, too *frustrating*. He was only going along with it because everyone insisted he shouldn't be single, but he rather liked being single. He got up when he wanted, showered and made coffee with no distractions, went to work, came home, wrote all night if the mood took him or, equally, headed out to a cinema to watch a movie of his choice.

Being single was seriously underrated, and generally by those who were not, as if to justify their decision to permit another to impose restrictions upon them. Gray had no desire to get into that situation again, although, with Jean-Michel, he had never perceived the restrictions an imposition.

The wail of sirens stirred him from his thoughts, and he watched an ambulance tear past. Two police cars followed soon after, and then a fire engine. *A nasty accident*...Gray's heart seemed to momentarily cease beating, paused along with his breathing. He exhaled, and his heart overtook itself, until he remembered: he wasn't on the job anymore, and he had no significant other.

Which strengthened his point. The single life was infinitely less painful. He was being a little unfair, perhaps, when he knew plenty of happy couples who would, in all likelihood, share wonderful, long lives together. But to his way of thinking, that 'perfect match' happened once in a lifetime, and it had already happened for him. It was three years and three months since Jean-Michel died, and Gray was finally back to something resembling normality, which wasn't to say he'd stopped missing Jean, for they were soul mates, lovers, partners. Only weeks before Jean's death, they'd talked about moving to Belgium, to Jean's hometown. They'd even looked at properties and had a survey performed on their house in England.

The night of the accident, they'd been at a wedding and chatted with the bride and groom about their plans, at that stage undecided on when they would properly put them into motion. The newlyweds were honeymooning in Paris, Berlin and Brussels but delaying their trip until Christmas, and that was when Gray and Jean made up their minds for sure. They would emigrate before the end of October; that way, their friends could visit them on their honeymoon.

On the way home, Jean was tired, his concentration lapsed, and he ended up on the wrong side of the road. The other car swerved and hit the driver's side. Jean never regained consciousness.

As soon as Gray had recovered sufficiently—physically, at least—to handle the move, he'd put the house on the market, and it had sold within weeks, but he'd no longer wanted to live in Belgium, not without Jean. So he'd stayed in England.

Now a fourth October was upon him, and he wondered if he'd ever stop mourning.

The door to the restaurant closed, although Gray only noticed when the waiter greeted the new arrival.

"Evening, sir."

"Hi." Will gave the waiter a wide, cheery smile and indicated to Gray. "I'm with him."

"Of course, sir." The waiter led Will over to the table. "I'll bring you a menu. A drink?"

"Just some water, thanks."

The waiter acknowledged the request with another bow and left.

"Glad you could make it," Gray said dryly.

"Yeah. Sorry. Trains." Will looked like he was waiting for Gray to say something else, but what was there to say? He could demand more of an explanation, he supposed, but wasn't it self-explanatory? Will shrugged. "You know how it is this time of year. Leaves on the track. Go figure!"

"Hmm." Gray eyed him dubiously, almost sure Will was lying, though he could think of no reason why he would. "I haven't ordered yet, by the way."

The waiter returned with the promised glass of water and menu. Will acknowledged him with a nod and a smile and took the menu from him.

"The set meal looks reasonable," Gray suggested.

"Sure." Will handed the menu back.

"Don't you want to check what's on it?"

"I trust you."

The waiter confirmed their choice and left them alone again.

Will sipped his water and looked around the restaurant. "Nice here, isn't it?"

"Yes." Gray took the opportunity to observe him while he was otherwise engaged. There was no obvious indication of deception, and he'd travelled in from home, so a delayed train was plausible.

Will finished his inspection and met Gray's gaze with a frown. "What's up?"

"Nothing, particularly. Although if I lived out of London, I'd allow a little extra time for my journey, especially at *this time of year*."

"Yeah. Sorry. It didn't occur to me."

"Or failing that, maybe a phone call to say I was running late?"

"Ah. Well. Funny story." Will stopped talking and adjusted his position. "Actually, not that funny, but I lost my phone this morning. I thought I'd dropped it while I was out with the dogs, and I've spent half the day retracing my steps, trying to find the thing. And then, would you believe, Fido found it? Monster got spooked by something, and Fido went rooting around—he's good like that. Intuitive, you know? They're like a proper little pack, looking out for each other. Anyway, my phone had fallen out of my pocket, into one of my wellies, and the vibrations were what had upset Monster. Bless. She's definitely getting better, though."

"Monster," Gray repeated, fighting a smirk of amusement. He thought it was a ridiculous name for a dog. He couldn't recall much of what Will had told him about the mutts during their previous interchanges, but it was polite to show an interest, so he hazarded, "Is that the little one?"

"That's what we call her, though she's not *the* littlest. That's Dotty Doris. Monster's the collie cross."

Gray wasn't a great lover of pets. He didn't really know one breed of dog from another, other than German shepherds, which he recognised from working with the police dog teams and customs officers, and both his sister and brother had one—remarkably, given that Becky and George had never met nor were they biologically related, yet their dogs were near identical—black, long-haired and great temperaments.

If Gray were ever to consider getting a dog, which was unlikely, he'd probably go for one of those, and only one, as opposed to the five assorted hounds Will shared his home with, along with chickens, a parakeet and who knew what else.

"Sirs," the waiter said. Gray and Will leaned back for steaming bowls to be set down in front of them, thanked the waiter, and picked up their spoons, quickly discovering the chicken and sweetcorn soup was too hot.

"Doesn't it bother you?" Gray asked in between blowing the soup and trying to slurp it without burning himself. At Will's puzzled expression, he clarified, "Didn't you say you keep chickens?"

"Oh! I see what you mean. I don't usually eat meat."

"You're vegetarian?"

"Yep."

"I didn't know."

"Not a problem."

"You could've said, instead of going along with the set meal. Beef in black bean sauce, Schezuan chicken, prawn satay..."

"Like I say, not a problem."

That irritated Gray, and the fact that it did irritated him all the more. What difference did it make to him whether Will discarded his dietary preferences? The man didn't seem to care about anything, like, for instance, turning up for a date on time, or how he was going to pay his bills and look after his precious menagerie since he'd given up his city career—the topic of conversation on their last 'date'. Will hadn't mentioned being vegetarian then either, so maybe it wasn't a big deal. Yet, to Gray, it felt as if Will was casting aside his morals to avoid disharmony, in which case, why have morals at all? Assuming that was the reason he was vegetarian, of course, or, indeed, that he'd had any morals to begin with.

To ease the silence, and because it was on his mind, Gray asked, "How's the job-hunting going?"

Soup dripped from Will's spoon onto his lip and down his chin, and his head jerked back in response to the scalding. He sucked his bottom lip clean and dabbed at his chin with a napkin. "Not bad," he said, recovering quickly. "I had an interview yesterday with the Royal Mail."

"Oh? For what?"

"Delivering post?" Will was amused by the question, if his cheeky grin was anything to go by. Despite Gray's vow to remain single, he found it quite alluring.

"Just because it's the Royal Mail..."

"I was kidding."

"With your qualifications, shouldn't you be going for something higher status?"

"Like postmaster?" Will's grin widened.

Gray laughed and shook his head. "You're telling me you want to be a postman?"

"No, I don't. But it's a job, and it's local to me, so no more getting up before dawn to walk the dogs, only to spend two hours on a packed train—"

"You'll be getting up at dawn to go on your rounds."

"And I'll have the afternoons to myself. Plus, I'll be free in the evenings. We'll be able to meet up more often. It's all good."

Gray raised an eyebrow, not so sure that it was 'all good' from his perspective. He liked Will. He was a genuinely nice, down-to-earth guy, but he was nothing like Jean, nor any of the other guys Gray had dated before Jean. At least, that was his impression, as he and Will hadn't really got to know each other properly. This was the third time they'd met up, and only their second date.

The first time they'd met, it was arranged by Josh—Gray's brother-in-law, who was the common denominator and responsible for the entire matchmaking debacle. He'd brought his family along, "for the safety of numbers," he'd said. More likely, he was ensuring Gray didn't stand Will up.

The second time was a cinema trip, when they'd gone to the late viewing because Will was delayed by an hour—no explanation offered—and then had to dash off to catch a lift home from a friend as he'd missed the last train. Following that, they were supposed to meet up again with Josh, George and their foster daughter Libby, who were in London doing the whole tourist thing but popped in to check Gray was 'settling in' to his new house. On that occasion, Will had cried off at the last minute, and Gray had been secretly pleased. He found it incredible that these people—essentially strangers until a few months ago—had accepted him as part of their family, and that was more important to him than dating. However, it meant, in spite of having spent a good eight hours in each other's company, he and Will had yet to have a proper conversation.

As if Will were tapping into Gray's thoughts, he asked, "Have you heard from Josh lately?"

"By lately, you mean since we all went out to dinner and you bottled out?" Gray's light-hearted teasing put a blush on Will's cheeks, and he tried to cover it by sipping his water, giving himself hiccups in the process. Gray chuckled.

"I'm glad you find it amusing," Will said dolefully.

"Because it *is* amusing."

Will returned to eating his soup, still hiccupping.

"Oh, come on. Surely you can see the funny side?" But it turned out Will couldn't. *A first time for everything.*

"OK." Will set down his spoon and clasped his hands. "Imagine you were in my situation. How would you feel?"

"Well, other than the bit about you hitting on George on his honeymoon, I don't really know what that situation was."

"Josh didn't tell you?"

"All he said was he'd invited you to dinner because you were a nice guy and he thought we'd get along. I've no idea what he was thinking." The last part Gray muttered under his breath but smiled at the same time so Will would know he was joking. Kind of joking—he really didn't know why Josh thought he and Will would get on. They were too different. Incompatible, in relationship terms. Still, that didn't preclude friendship.

In fact, Will seemed exactly the kind of friend Gray needed in his life—undemanding, easy-going and attractive, particularly in the more casual attire he'd worn this evening. His blonde-brown hair was long—or longish, it was hard to tell—and neatly tied back, and he was bare-faced, which Gray appreciated. He wasn't a fan of beards; they obscured individuality and intent, although since his 'retirement', Gray no longer shaved daily, preferring his reflection with stubble to without, and he hadn't shaved for their date.

It wasn't through lack of effort. Indeed, he'd pondered long over his wardrobe choices, at the same time wondering why. It wasn't like he was going out on the pick-up. In the end, he'd opted for chinos and a loose-fitting shirt, smart but not stuffy and, thankfully, not at odds with how Will was dressed. Tonight, Will's outfit consisted of well-worn blue jeans, biker boots and a long-sleeved tee that was fitted enough to show off his firm though not over-muscular physique. Will kept his fitness levels up for his two big loves: his dogs and surfing. That much Gray did know.

Their second course arrived—barbecued spare ribs and seaweed—and Will settled for eating the latter.

"I didn't hit on him, by the way," he said.

"No?"

"We were chatting about his dog, and I said I thought it was great that he was a rescue. Then we arrived at the hotel, and George showed me his ring..." Will screwed up his nose. "Let me rephrase that."

But it was said, and Gray was instantly helpless with laughter at the innuendo, which was childish. He wouldn't have noticed if Will hadn't drawn attention to it.

Will sighed and folded his arms, looking away across the restaurant, waiting for Gray to recompose. It took a while, but once he did, he reached over and gave Will's hand a gentle squeeze that was both apology and reassurance. He wasn't going to mock him further.

Will frowned. "I can't figure you out, Gray."

"In what sense?"

"You're so serious and restrained one minute, giggly and touchy-feely the next." Will leaned forward and held Gray's gaze. "You're an enigma."

Gray narrowed his eyes. "I'm going to get the waiter to swap one of the meat dishes for something veggie. The protein's gone to your head."

"It really isn't a—" Will began, but Gray cut him short by calling the waiter over and asking him to exchange the beef dish for stir-fried vegetables.

"Done," he said.

"Thanks."

"Not a problem," Gray replied, deliberately borrowing Will's words. "So why are you vegetarian? For animal welfare reasons or...?"

"Yeah. Pretty much. My mum's always been veggie, and I know too much about slaughterhouses. I volunteered weekends at an animal sanctuary through uni, and I've been taking in rescue animals ever since."

"No wonder you hit it off with George."

"You see, that's where you're mistaken. Not that I dislike your brother—he's a lovely guy. But, er..." The colour flooded Will's cheeks again. "Don't laugh, but I had a bit of a crush on Josh."

"You..." Gray started but trailed off as it sank in.

"It passed once I got back from Cornwall, and I'd never have acted on it, but there's something about him."

Gray could think of absolutely nothing to say. He hadn't anticipated that. Josh wasn't an eyesore, but he wasn't good-looking in any typical sense. He was five-nine, at a guess, very slim, and with his longer than average sandy hair and glasses, a little on the geeky side both in looks and conduct. As a therapist and academic, his understanding of the human condition was enviably impressive. In his work and with his closest friends, his 'people skills' were exceptional. Otherwise, he was aloof and standoffish. For all of that, Gray agreed with Will; there was something about Josh that made him special, which was a big part of why Gray had let himself be talked into a blind date in the first place.

For a while, the two men continued with their meal in silence, with Will's appetite seeming to pick up now there was something on the table he was happy to eat. Gray subtly watched him, trying to make sense of the man. On their previous encounter, he'd told Gray that the job from which he'd resigned was with one of the big city banks, and he hadn't been small fry either. Granted, he wasn't up in the highest echelons, so he'd been distanced from the bankers' bonuses scandal, but he'd also been working in investment banking for fifteen years. He'd taken a temporary sabbatical during the finance crisis before returning to the same job when investment picked up again.

"Why did you resign?" Gray asked, his curiosity running ahead of him.

Will shrugged. "Like I say, the commute is a pain, and I guess I got sick of the rat race."

"It's not cheap, living where you do, though, is it?"

"You'd be surprised. The house...it's a bit of a shambles, if I'm honest, but my grandma rented it back in the fifties, and the landlord hasn't been near in years. So I just pay the rent and keep my head down. So yeah, it's actually dirt cheap."

"Interesting. I expected you to live in some grand suburban detached."

"With the dogs? Are you kidding?" Will chuckled. "I'm not interested in status symbols. As long as we've got a roof over our heads and food to eat, we're good."

"And your surfing," Gray pointed out.

"Yeah, OK. But with promotion and all the big commissions that came with it, I was never into spending money for the sake of it."

Gray nodded as he took that in. In a way, Will's career trajectory wasn't that different from Gray's in the police, he supposed, although his own reasons for chasing promotion and then resigning were personal, and he was relieved Will hadn't bounced the question back at him. He wasn't ready to share yet. After he'd lost Jean, his career had become his lifeline, a way of getting through each day. He'd been head of an undercover unit working on fraud and embezzlement cases. He'd even been involved in an investigation of the bank Will had resigned from, not that Gray had been in any state to commit the finer details of that investigation to memory.

However, there was a stark contradiction between the world of high finance populated with shallow go-getters and the laid-back guy across the table, whose only indulgence was surfing. Add in the animal welfare and vegetarianism, and to Gray's mind, Will was far too 'new age' for investment banking. Perhaps everyone had those hidden sides to them, although with all the time he'd spent in undercover surveillance, he thought he might have noticed. As Josh had told him often enough, people are consistent in all aspects of their lives, so maybe Will was uniquely at odds with the rest of the world.

After their meal, they walked back up to the high street together, towards the Underground, and Gray felt a pang of disappointment that their evening appeared to be drawing to a close. It almost hadn't been worth Will making the journey, but either he'd picked up on Gray's mood or was thinking along similar lines, as he stopped outside a club and looked at Gray expectantly, hopefully even. Gray considered his schedule for the morning. He had a class at ten and research notes to write up. They could probably wait.

"OK," he agreed, not entirely sure it was a good idea. He hadn't been inside a nightclub in months—not since rehab. Until a couple of weeks ago, he'd have refused point blank, but he felt safe with Will, which worried him a little. He didn't want to depend on someone else to get him through, even if it was only an evening in a nightclub. Still, there was no point second-guessing, as they were already past the bouncers and on their way to the bar.

"What would you like?" Will asked.

"A beer, thanks. Any'll do."

Will went to order their drinks, and Gray stayed where he was, his attention immediately drawn to a group of guys dancing frenetically in front of a speaker. *High as kites.* He could see it a mile off. They were oblivious to their surroundings, other than the thump of the music, and he had to admit, it was entrancing. The sub-bass shook his insides, catching hold of him, drawing him in, until his pulse was racing and then synchronising with the thrumming rhythm, and he was falling under its spell... He couldn't stand it for long. Not sober, at any rate, and the alternative wasn't an option.

Will handed Gray a bottle of beer, and they moved away from the bar so other people could get through to be served. It was pointless trying to have a conversation, and they swigged their beers in silence, watching the other patrons doing whatever they were doing. Most were standing around, yelling directly into each other's ears and faking having heard what was said with hearty, physical laughs and nods.

A short while later, Will mimed smoking and headed for the back of the club. Gray watched until he was out of sight, his gaze drifting back to the guys who had been dancing earlier, now standing to the side of the dance floor, fidgeting restlessly. One of the bouncers approached and spoke to them. A couple attempted to argue back, flinging their arms wide and jutting out their chins. The bouncer shook his head and drove them towards the door, like a shepherd penning his sheep. It reminded Gray of the many nights he'd spent in the company of men like them, and it was liberating to realise he had no desire to be a part of that. It was a sign he was well on the road to recovery, though he knew the craving would never completely go away.

That didn't mean he was going after Will, who he was fairly certain had gone outside to smoke a joint. If he'd been a cigarette smoker, Gray would have smelled it on him before now, and cannabis fitted the new-age hippie profile. Evidently, Gray being an *ex*-copper made not a blind bit of difference to either Will's illegal activities or Gray's instinct to profile everyone he met.

When Will came back, he did smell of cigarettes, and Gray unconsciously wrinkled his nose. Will quickly found a piece of mint gum. "What do you want to do?" he asked, leaning in close and shouting at the same time as a trance track started, so Gray had no problem hearing him at all.

"I'm happy here," he said.

Will didn't look like he believed him, but two could play at that game. If Will wanted to stay a while longer, then whether Gray wanted to or not, that's what they would do. After all, hadn't they eaten meat tonight? But apparently, Will didn't want to stay. He quickly finished the last of his beer and indicated towards the door to the street. Gray followed, exasperated. He hated club-hopping. It was too much hassle.

Once they were outside, Will gave Gray a quick, nervous smile. "Sorry," he said.

"For what?"

"Leaving you on your own."

"It was only for a few minutes. Don't worry about it."

"A few minutes?" Will repeated in disbelief. "It was almost an hour."

"No way," Gray argued, but now he thought about it, he couldn't say with any certainty how long he'd been there, enjoying the opportunity to be a bystander.

"I'm afraid I need to head home," Will said. He sounded disappointed. "Or I'll have to catch the night bus, but it's been really good spending time with you tonight."

"Except for the hour you didn't."

"Yeah." Will looked sheepish.

"Not to mention the hour late."

Will took a breath and let it go again. "Look, if I tell you something, will you promise not to get mad?"

Gray laughed and didn't bother pointing out that no-one in their right mind would agree to something like that.

"The thing is, my mum's sick."

That wasn't what Gray had expected, nor a reason for him to get mad. "If you'd said, we could've cancelled."

"No, what I mean is...she has a brain tumour, and it's causing dementia, so she's in the hospice, but she took a turn for the worse this evening."

"Oh, Will. I'm sorry."

"It's OK. She's been sick a couple of years, and we've known for a long time it was incurable. She made us promise not to change our arrangements because of her. So I had to come, and truthfully, I'm not ready for tonight to end. You're great company, and I'd have been well up for stumbling in at four in the morning. But when I went outside, I called my uncle to see how things were going, and he was upset, which is why I was gone so long. I'm only telling you so you don't think I'm doing a runner. I'm not. I like you, as in *like* you, and...well, I accept you're not looking for a relationship, but if you ever decide you are..."

Gray didn't know what to say. His first instinct was to confirm that Will was right. He wasn't looking for a relationship, and he couldn't see that changing. But he also couldn't bring himself to be that brutal after what Will had told him, so instead he gave him a brief arm squeeze and said, "I'll bear that in mind. Take care."

3: 'S Class

PC Rob Simpson-Stone slid out of the passenger side of the S-Class Mercedes, trying not to hook his vest on the gear shift or cut his legs on the remnants of shattered passenger side window. He handed the wallet to Detective Chief Inspector Hedley.

"Where was that?" she asked.

"Under the steering column."

The DCI extracted a driving licence from the pocket inside the well-stuffed wallet. The accident looked like a typical drink-drive—too many double Scotches, by the smell of it—and the Merc had ended up half in and half out of a bus shelter. Luckily, no-one had been waiting for a bus, so just the one casualty: the idiot behind the wheel.

"Right, Aaron Tanner, let's see what we have here." The DCI checked through the rest of the wallet's contents—blood donor card, credit cards, a wad of twenty-pound notes, a card with next of kin's name and address. "Are you OK to deal with the wife?"

"Yes, Ma'am," Rob confirmed, frowning as he took the plastic card from the DCI.

"A problem, Rob?"

"No, Ma'am. Just..." Actually, he had a couple of problems. First, he still hadn't worked out why DCI Hedley had attended an ordinary road traffic accident, but irrespective of their long, affable working relationship, it wasn't his place to ask. He could, however, ask about the other thing that was troubling him, as it must have occurred to her too.

Rob tapped his finger on the card in his hand. "Thing is, Ma'am, much as it would make our job a lot easier if people carried this info around with them, they don't."

The DCI nodded in agreement. "True enough. There again, have you seen the car? It's spotless, inside and out. Maybe he's one of those OCD types."

"Yeah, maybe." Rob pushed the card into his pocket. "Do you want me to go now or wait for the tow truck, Ma'am?"

"No. You go, mate. You're on overtime as it is. Bastards." The DCI shook her head and left the rest of the complaint unsaid. It was always about funding, or the lack of it. The cutbacks implied they were wasters, snatching extra money for nothing, when the truth was, they were understaffed and bogged down in paper trails.

Rob returned to the patrol car, checking the address on the card. He knew vaguely where the road was—very well-to-do area, with big, detached properties worth tens of millions—but he still played it safe and typed it into his satnav. It took a moment to load the maps, and Rob set off, not thinking about the task ahead of him and instead planning what he was going to eat when he got home. Takeaway again, obviously, probably Chinese, as he'd had Indian last night, kebab the night before, pizza the night before that.

He could almost work out the day based on the kind of takeaway, and he was getting out of shape. He smiled as he recalled Lucas's remark at swimming the previous Saturday, about how cool it was having a dad who got in the pool with him. Most of the other parents watched from the side—Rob would be joining them if he didn't pack in the junk food, and soon. No way was he missing out on any more of his son growing up. He'd already lost most of the first seven years to undercover work, and a whole lot more besides. But things were back to normal...more or less. He and Zoë were on speaking terms, and he got to spend his days off taking Lucas to swimming lessons or the skate park or just sitting and doing homework.

And he was enjoying the job again, even the difficult duties like informing next of kin, which was nothing compared to what he'd had to do with the Special Investigations Unit. Granted, for the first couple of years, the job was mostly an excellent excuse for tearing up and down the country on his bike, and he'd be lying if he tried to convince anyone he hadn't loved that bit. But acting the part of being a criminal to catch one? That was hell on earth, especially given who the criminal was.

Lambert's dead. We're putting everything we've got into getting Folden.

Rob laughed to himself, though it was no longer in bitterness. Jess Lambert had been his first crush, the dream girl who broke his teenage heart and then broke it all over again when she died. No-one had delivered the news to him in a gentle, compassionate manner. They were more concerned with prioritising manpower and catching the rest of the fraud ring.

It would be the first time since Jess's death he'd be delivering the news to someone that their loved one was dead, although as he arrived outside the accident victim's residence, it appeared he wouldn't be doing it this evening.

The house was enormous, like the neighbouring properties, and fronted by tall, locked gates. Rob drove up to them and glanced along the driveway. There was an oldish compact hatchback parked in front of a double garage— not the sort of vehicle he'd expect to see parked outside somewhere like this, but nonetheless a sign someone was home.

"Great," Rob muttered, rubbing his hand over his hair and scanning the dark house. What was worse than telling someone their husband was dead? Waking them up to tell them their husband was dead. He dropped the driver's window, reached out and pushed the 'call' button on the gate's intercom. It rang through to the house for a full minute before it stopped automatically, unanswered. Rob pushed it again: same result.

Well, he'd tried, which was the main thing. It meant offloading it onto someone else, but he'd worked twelve hours already today. He needed food, and he needed sleep—he was almost tempted to skip eating and head straight home to bed.

He put the car into reverse and slowly eased it backwards, just as the intercom crackled and a male voice said, "Hello? Can I help you?"

Rob held in the sigh. *So close.* "Hello, sir. It's the police. Would it be possible to come in and speak to you?"

There was a moment's silence, followed by another crackle and a beep, and the gates slowly swung open. Rob put the car in first gear and drove up to the house; the gates remained open behind him—to his relief. These days, being locked inside anywhere gave him the heebie-jeebies, even if on this occasion it would only be with a grief-stricken widow, and...her bit on the side? Either way, Rob was about to change somebody's life drastically and likely very much for the worse.

The front door was already open, a man silhouetted against the light within. Rob stopped in front of him.

"Evening, sir."

"Officer?" The man automatically stepped aside to grant Rob access. Rob gave him a brief, sympathetic smile, at the same time trying to work out who he was dealing with. Tanner was thirty-seven, according to his driving licence, and the man in front of him appeared to be around the same age. A brother, maybe?

The man closed the door and turned back, frowning heavily as he checked out Rob's uniform. "What can I do for you?"

"I was hoping to speak with Mrs. Naomi Tanner."

"She's...not here. Can I be of assistance?"

"Can I ask your name, sir?"

"Aaron Tanner. Naomi is my wife, but we recently went our separate ways."

"Right." Rob was stumped. "Do you own a silver Mercedes, sir?"

"I did, until two weeks ago." Tanner stepped past Rob, motioning with his arm towards a doorway off to the right of the vast entrance hall.

Rob followed him into what turned out to be the living room, although it didn't look like it had been lived in lately, with a naked light bulb hanging from the ceiling, plain bare walls and a bare concrete floor. The only furniture was a small circular table.

"Can I get you a drink, Officer?"

"No, thanks. Are you decorating?"

Tanner laughed joylessly. "No. The liquidators seized my assets. I'm..." He put his head down and sighed. "I have nowhere else to go."

"You're squatting in your own house?" Rob asked.

"Yes," he nodded. "I'm afraid I am."

Rob raised an eyebrow but didn't comment. Tanner looked terrible—bloodshot eyes, lank hair, gaunt, drawn cheeks, and his faded T-shirt and threadbare jeans were too big—although he was still very much alive, unlike the guy who had been driving Tanner's Mercedes.

"Whose is the car on the driveway?"

"Naomi's, or it was. She sold it. The new owner is collecting it tomorrow."

"What happened to your car?"

"It was part of my directorship—on lease. As far as I know, the dealer took possession of it."

"As far as you know?"

Tanner shrugged. "Perhaps I should explain." He walked across the room to the small table, picked up a packet of cigarettes, lit one and inhaled deeply, letting the smoke go before he spoke again. "I was a director at Berringer's."

"The bank?"

He nodded to confirm Rob was correct. Berringer's was the latest of the small investment banks to declare insolvency, having tactically paid out to their shareholders before their remaining assets were bought up by bigger banks and they shut their trading doors for good. That was as much as Rob knew, and as much as he wanted to know. His old unit had investigated fraud and embezzlement, and he'd seen enough of the finance industry's shady goings on to last a lifetime. He'd also seen what happened to directors when it came to the final throes of companies going under. They lost everything, and they had a great deal more to lose than the average man on the street because they enjoyed the full trappings of the good life.

"Were you aware that your wallet was still in the car, sir?"

Tanner frowned and shook his head. "It's in my jacket." He walked past Rob, back to the hallway, opened a closet and reached inside. A moment later, he returned, holding up a battered brown leather wallet.

"Can I take a look?" Rob asked. Tanner willingly handed it over. Rob flicked through the contents—no credit cards or wad of twenty-pound notes in this wallet, though it did contain a photo driving licence and donor card, both bearing the name 'Aaron Tanner'. Rob glanced back at the man to check he was the person pictured on the driving licence, which he undoubtedly was. He closed the wallet and handed it back, utterly perplexed but too tired to think beyond getting the information he needed in order to leave and finally clock off for the night. "Do you happen to know the name of the dealership that leased the cars?"

"It's the Mercedes official dealership on the ring road."

"And you returned the car to them?"

"No. I handed the keys over to the liquidators."

"Right. Thanks for your help." Rob moved towards the door. Tanner followed him out.

"What's going on, Officer?"

"I'm investigating an accident involving the Mercedes. It's still registered to you, at this address." That thought brought another one with it. "Actually, Mr. Tanner, I need you to provide me with contact details. Do you have a mobile number?"

"Sure. Let me just check..." Aaron fished in his pocket and extracted a very basic phone. "Pay as you go," he explained, matter of fact, tapping at the keypad. He handed over the phone.

"At some point, they'll come and change the locks on this place, I'd imagine," Rob said as he wrote down Tanner's number. He handed back the phone.

"I'd imagine so. I'll be at my mother's. Thirty-two Drury Court."

Rob wrote that down too. "Thanks for your help, Mr. Tanner. Much appreciated." He moved off, towards the hallway. "Sorry about your marriage and everything."

"Thanks."

As Rob stepped out into the fresh air again, he turned back and gave Tanner a rueful smile. "Take care of yourself, all right, mate?"

Tanner lifted his hands in a hopeless shrug.

***

Rob waited until he'd ordered his special curry and rice before he called Martina Hedley to let her know what had happened with Aaron Tanner, in case the DCI got any ideas about him conducting further inquiries before he'd had a chance to eat.

"Interesting, that, Rob," she said.

"Why's that?"

"It's the second incident involving someone from Berringer's. Are you in tomorrow?"

"Day off. I'm in over the weekend."

"Balls. I'm off to Turkey for the week. Back in next Saturday. Catch up then?"

"Annual leave. I'm back in on the Tuesday."

The DCI laughed. "Tanner's double's not going anywhere. Pop in and update me when you get a sec."

"Will do." Rob ended the call, collected his paper bag of food and headed for home.

His flat was, as always, in darkness. No noise of family life, no toys cluttering the hallway. After a tough day, he was usually glad to have the place to himself, but not tonight. Seeing poor Aaron Tanner in what had to be a six-bedroom house, devoid of all his possessions, made Rob grateful for what he had. Even so, at times like this, he missed Zoë and Lucas so much it was physical pain.

His marriage had crumbled while he was working away, although to be fair, it had been rocky before he'd left. Being a police officer and family man wasn't a good combination; the job was too important, distracting. Like tonight, for instance: if he'd had to deliver the bad news and then go home to Zoë, he'd have been quiet and contemplative, and she'd have thought there was something wrong with 'them'.

That part he didn't miss. Rob was at peace now with how things were between them, and happy to be back on the beat. His only real regret was ever having agreed to the undercover job with the SIU, but even that sat much easier with him than it had six months ago. He'd more or less forgiven Gray Fisher for knowingly putting him in a situation where he couldn't refuse. There was too much at stake for that to be a possibility. The crimes of high finance were not, as the papers claimed, victimless. People lost money—vulnerable people, often going through the loss of a loved one or other emotionally difficult times.

Granted, not all the SIU's cases were as emotive as the Strang case had been. Perhaps Rob felt it more keenly because of how it had played out in the end. There again, Gray hadn't fared well either, from what he'd been told. He'd also heard that Gray had moved back to London—maybe it would be good to catch up sometime, go for a pint, now they no longer worked together, and find out if there was any truth to the rest of the gossip. *Yeah, definitely worth a catch-up...*

***

Rob awoke on his sofa at five in the morning, with a foil container in his lap, the dregs from the beer can pooled in congealed curry sauce, and a crick in his neck. He set the container aside and heaved to his feet, trudging his way to bed. He'd deal with the mess later.

4: Prelim

SINCE THE NIGHT out with Will, Gray had so many questions, and as always, it was the not knowing—the gaps he couldn't fill with logical explanations—that kept him awake. Why was Will lying to him? Was he lying to him? And if he wasn't, why did Gray think he was? He wondered if it stemmed from Will's resignation, which seemed improbable, seeing as what they did for a living was one of the first things that had come up in conversation the night Josh had introduced them. Will had said it flippantly, like it bore no consequence. I'm an investment banker, or I was until three months ago. There was nothing underhand about it; he'd been quite frank. He'd resigned from a top-paying city job to reinstate some quality of life.

On one level, Gray got it. Money was never the answer. Between insurance policies and gratuities from death in service, Jean had left him a wealthy man. He hadn't needed to work, yet he'd continued to do so because without Jean, his life wasn't merely lacking quality. It was lacking, full stop. They'd lived together, worked together, socialised together. Outside of Jean, Gray had *no* life, and if he hadn't stayed with the SIU and retained what little of his sanity persisted, he'd have done himself in. Indeed, he'd intentionally sacrificed his career to bring down a senior police officer, knowing that it might be the last thing he ever did, but it was a small price to pay for the liberty and happiness of those he held dear.

Will's decision was the direct opposite of Gray's. Holding down a job in the city and having any kind of life outside was impossible *without* the additional responsibility of caring for a sick relative, and Will seemed to have a good life. He had his house and his dogs; presumably, he had a supportive family. It was entirely reasonable that he'd want to spend his time with them, particularly when his mum's days were numbered. But what didn't make sense was the timing. Will said his mum had been sick for a couple of years, so why had he gone back to the bank a year ago after his sabbatical leave? And why resign? His employer had given him extended time off once; surely, they'd have been open to a period of compassionate leave?

The truth was, Gray could reasonably answer every one of those questions. The bank would be disinclined to grant further leave, with or without pay, when Will had already taken time out. Two years was a long prognosis, so there was no need for Will to resign until his mum's condition deteriorated. In short, there was nothing untoward about anything Will had said or done, which brought Gray back to his starting point: why was he so sure Will was lying?

So he was an investment banker. So what? Gray had met honest bankers— not many, admittedly, which wasn't to say they were all swindlers. When one's job was to investigate fraud and embezzlement, the sample was somewhat skewed, and Will didn't fit the profile. He didn't worship money and was more slacker than hacker. He wasn't competitive or confrontational, as illustrated by his willingness to eat meat in order to keep the peace. *Not a problem*.

But it *was* a problem to Gray. No matter how tough it got, the risks it posed, the people who might get hurt, Gray abided by his morals. Fairness and integrity were the values he held closest to his heart, both in his work and, now he had one, in his everyday life, although he appreciated it probably didn't look that way to the likes of Rob Simpson-Stone or Helen—the woman he'd married as part of his cover. Maybe his personal investment had led to some poor decisions on his last couple of cases, but he'd made them for the right reasons.

What it all seemed to boil down to, then, was Will's dismissal of his vegetarianism, which was an absurd reason not to trust him if taken in isolation. Yet, however hard he tried, Gray couldn't separate that one instance of Will taking the easy route from the complex whole. After all, if he'd done it once, he'd do it again, and a man who was prepared to compromise his morals...

"Ah, get doon of yer high horse, man," Gray chided himself and then laughed ruefully at the fake Geordie accent that leaked out. All that time in the guise of Newcastle-born Detective Sergeant Graham Farrar was difficult to leave behind, and his alter ego had a point. In principle, Will had only tried to avoid further conflict on their date; the fact he felt the need to do so was not surprising, given Gray had laid into him for arriving late.

But still...it couldn't hurt to do a little digging.

The phone rang out without switching to voicemail. Gray held on for the minimum time it took to establish nobody would answer and hung up. If there was one thing guaranteed to cause him stress—or one of many things—it was an incoming call that rang on and on when he couldn't or didn't want to answer, and he imagined the same was true of others. He'd try again later.

Or not. He accepted the call.

"Gray?"

"Hey, Dom. How's it going?"

"Not bad at all, mate. How are you?"

"I'm doing great, thanks. Not missing the work, that's for sure."

"I can well imagine. I've not had a day off yet."

Gray wasn't happy to hear that. "You've got a lot on?"

"Haven't we always?"

"No rest for the wicked, eh?" Gray joked, but Dom—his former second-in-command, now head of unit—had his every sympathy. "Don't suppose you're around over the weekend?"

"I will be."

"Can you spare a couple of hours for a pint and a catch-up?"

"Is there an agenda for this catch-up?"

"You know me far too well."

Dom chuckled. "Usual time and place?"

"Perfect."

***

The high street was an emotional obstacle course, a trail back through time to the year before Jean died, when Gray had traipsed these pavements on his way to meet his new team. He'd made the same arrangements for them as for his previous teams: none of that conference room, bored rigid and uninspired nonsense. Gray was well aware his gift did not lie in public speaking and only did it when he had to. If listening to himself made him miserable, there was no hope for anyone else. Instead, he'd invited them to join him at The Royal Oak for an evening of beer drinking and pool, no real office talk because, of course, it was a *public* house. The following afternoon, he'd conducted the formal briefing in a Northumberland Police conference room, temporary HQ for their investigation of Strang and associates: the SAP case, as it came to be known.

He'd stumbled upon the fraud ring by accident while running searches on another company engaged in insider trading and always just above the law. There was nothing he could get them on, so he'd broadened his search to include their trading partners. One of the names struck a familiar chord, and familiar was exactly the word for it.

Gray had always known he had an older brother. It had never been a secret in their house. In fact, Gray's mum bragged about it because she saw snagging a professional footballer—albeit for only a three-year extramarital affair—as one of her greatest achievements. Had the 'WAG' acronym been in use back then, she'd have fitted the stereotype perfectly. She was slim and pretty with bleached-blonde hair and otherwise not much going for her. She'd skipped school, hadn't even turned up for her exams, and then hopped from job to job—shop work, cleaning, bartending, and so on.

Then she'd met Jack Morley and fallen for him. Whether she'd known he was married, Gray wasn't sure, but she had known he was with another woman, and that they had a son who was six years older than Gray. In the end, Jack had abandoned them all. Mum had moved on—or gone full circle, seeing as her relationship with Becky's dad was an action replay—and brought her kids up on her own. She was a good mum, right up to the point when Gray told her he was gay.

As for Jack Morley, he was dead, and Gray didn't remember him, nor was he interested beyond mild curiosity. Or not regarding his father. Within weeks of joining the police, he was abusing his privilege to track down George Morley, his half-brother. By then, George was in his late twenties and living in Colorado on the ranch Jack had left him in his will. That was how Gray had tracked George down, through probate, and for all he tried not to let it, it hurt. He didn't expect an inheritance; he didn't want one. It was simply that both parents had rejected him. His sister had still been too young to face the repercussions of going against their mum, and the brother he didn't yet know was in the USA. In short, Gray had nobody. Cue wild ambition.

It was another six years before he met Jean-Michel, and by then, Gray's career had been soaring. He'd set aside his hope of one day making contact with George, postponing it to some indefinite point in the future, because with Jean at his side, Gray was no longer alone.

Three years was all they were given. Thank goodness his resistance at the beginning—when they'd gone from colleagues to madly in love in what seemed like the blink of an eye—had been short-lived, or they'd have had even less time. Their relationship was intense, passionate, all-consuming, and had they not worked together, they'd have both been reprimanded for taking time off.

It had been so different from Gray's previous relationships. Work was always his priority, and while there had been one-nighters here and there, plus a couple of longer flings, dating got in the way, so he didn't do it. He could remember, almost word for word, the conversation he and Jean had following a night spent together only a few weeks after they'd met, when they'd woken in a tangled mess, pillows askew or on the floor, the fitted sheet bunched up beneath them. Neither cared enough to move and fix it. They'd both recently turned twenty-eight, and Jean had remarked on how they were becoming too old to be 'boys'.

Smoothing his hands over Gray's chest—firm then, not so much now— Jean had joked about wrinkles and grey hair and reading glasses and all the other adornments of age, and Gray had realised. He wanted to watch Jean grow wrinkly and old, and he didn't care that Jean would witness the same happening to him.

The irony of falling in love. He'd have skipped work to spend time with Jean, but he didn't have to because they were on the same team. How grateful Gray was for that now. If he'd resigned or been fired, he'd have been left with nothing at all, and in the dim, fuzzy hell that followed the accident, his job was the only beacon bright enough to guide him out of the darkness.

He was warned. Occupational health told him he still needed to heal. He wasn't ready to return, psychologically or physically, but what else could he do?

And anyway, he wasn't healing. He was stuck in the same horrific loop. He slept only because the sleeping pills made him. He did physio only because he was too tired to fight.

His bosses agreed to a staggered return to work. Two days a week, then three, four, five, six, seven. He worked until he dropped, and with the sleeping pills, he dropped far too soon. He stopped taking them, but it still wasn't enough. As Dom said, there was always too much to do that couldn't wait until tomorrow. With a little chemical enhancement, it didn't have to.

Illegitimate son of a WAG and a scoundrel, disowned by mother, disinherited by father, widower, coke addict... Barely in his thirties, Gray had been losing at life. He'd been ready to give in, roll over and die. He'd stopped caring about his colleagues and lost interest in his work. Every day was another day of getting through, until one morning, shuffling confidential files as if they were playing cards in a meaningless game of Solitaire, the Strang case rose to the top of the pile, and he saw it again. *Campion Holdings PLC*: the trading partner that had given him his lead all those months ago, when Jean was still alive. Its location: George's hometown.

Gray figured the Fates were trying to tell him something. Maybe they'd known it all along. *One day, this case will save your life.* He'd stepped up the investigation and taken over the surveillance himself, with the intention of making contact with George: his one tether to the living.

Initially, Gray had approached a detective inspector local to Campion's and Strang and Partners—the law firm at the centre of the investigation—for assistance. Short-staffed, the DI declined but put forward Rob Simpson-Stone, a 'local lad' who was a serving Met officer with some covert surveillance experience. At that point, Gray had known one of the lawyers involved was a Jessica Lambert, but he'd had no idea she and Rob had attended the same high school. Nor did Rob let on until the case was over that he and Lambert had been lovers, on and off, since leaving school. And, small town that it was, one of Lambert's close friends—a Joshua Sandison, also subject to surveillance—was also a close friend of George. Closer that close, given they were now married.

So Rob hadn't been Gray's first choice. Indeed, had he been operating with any level of rationality, Rob wouldn't have been a choice at all, but all Gray saw was opportunity, and he wasn't wrong. Rob's insider status allowed them to bring down Lambert and her associates relatively quickly and with minimal collateral damage. This was high-level organised crime, and the operation was still ongoing, but with Rob's help, Gray's team had closed down a significant part of it. It was over for them.

Alas, the same could not be said for Gray's successor, whom he could see through the window in the pub's front door. Elbows resting on the bar, head bowed, a fresh pint in front of him, poor Dom Hooper was half-asleep, possibly more than half. Gray felt a surge of tenderness; it wasn't so long ago it would've been up to him to fix that. *We can manage without you for a couple of days. Why don't you go visit your mum or something?* Dom had always argued back, until eventually, a direct order was the only way to make him comply. Gray smiled at the memory—he'd almost forgotten the good times—and went inside.

Dom spotted him the second he walked through the door and was off his bar stool, hand at the ready. "Looking good, Gray."

The handshake turned into a hug, which Gray reciprocated, delighted to see his former colleague, although they were more than that. They'd trained together, and when Gray took the SIU job, he'd asked Dom Hooper to join his team. He was an outstanding officer and a good friend.

They released each other, and Gray observed the dark rings under Dom's eyes. "You look exhausted."

"Yeah. That'd be because I am, mate."

There was no need to elaborate when it would be the same old story. Eighteen-hour days, long-distance commutes or nights in cheap hotels, all to gather evidence and then watch someone else reap the glory. Dom had always taken it in his stride, which was why Gray had put him forward for the head-of-unit job.

"What are you drinking?" Dom asked.

"Lager, cheers. I'll get the next one."

Drinks poured, they adjourned to the table at the back of the pool room. The clacks and thuds of the game afoot, against the mishmash backdrop of music and televised sports, was an ideal sound screen for their conversation, which wasn't 'top secret' but shouldn't have been happening.

"That investigation we did into Kestra and Company a while back," Gray said.

"The bank that does all the energy technology stuff?"

"That's the one. Do you remember the name William Richards coming up?"

Dom blew air out of his mouth, vibrating his lips and puffing beery breath in Gray's direction. "Can't say I remember any of them, to be honest. Not even the CEO."

Gray laughed. "You spent plenty of time with him."

"Don't remind me. He was a nasty bastard, that one. So who's this William Richards?"

"He's...a friend of a friend," Gray said, but then it clicked who he was talking to. "Or that's all he was to start with. We've been out a couple of times, and, er... Something doesn't sit right, you know what I mean?"

"Yep." Dom nodded wearily. "I had the same trouble with Karen."

"Oh? Who's that?"

"No-one, it turns out. Two dates, a weekend in the Cotswolds, and she started asking the sort of questions that set the warning bells ringing, so I checked her out. Clean as."

Gray gave a half-hearted chuckle. "Is that our destiny, Dom? A two-date average?"

"Sad, isn't it?" The pool table became free. "Want a game?"

Gray nodded his agreement.

Leaving their pints where they were, they moved over to the pool table, where Dom set up the balls and Gray picked the two straightest cues from the rack. He handed one over, chalked the tip of the other and then offered the chalk to Dom, who waved it away, as always. He'd win, too.

"You know—" Dom paused to break and simultaneously potted a red, centre-right. "—I'm ninety percent sure it's us, not them."

Gray watched Dom take his second shot; the ball rebounded off the cushion and slowly rolled back almost to where it started. Gray took up position and bent over, aiming for yellow, centre-left. He misfired and clipped the cue ball, which rolled slowly and tapped the yellow ball forward no more than an inch. Gray tutted at his poor performance and moved out of the way.

"Only ninety percent?" he asked, tongue-in-cheek. He'd have set it closer to the sixty-forty mark, but he'd always thought Dom could be too trusting for his own good.

Dom shrugged. "Maybe that was a bit generous." Another shot, another ball potted. Dom circled the table and picked his next target. It was the best of a bad lot and it stayed up.

"Are you still seeing what's-her-name?" Gray asked.

"Karen. I dunno. She's not happy. I had to cancel on her for work, or we'd already be above average."

That was the other issue with relationships and working undercover. Dates were cancelled, important events missed, and every excuse was a lie.

"How's everyone else getting on?" Gray asked.

"Pretty well. We've lost a couple, gained a couple. One of the new lads came from your last case."

"I bet that went down well."

"Yep. DI Hartley's been on the blower to me Christ knows how many times asking how long the secondment's for because they won't give him an extra body."

"No surprises there." Gray made his next try and potted one. "Hallelujah."

"The yellows are too big for the pockets, Gray," Dom teased.

"Shut it, you. I'm only one behind." Gray aimed a second time. He missed by miles, but the ball rebounded off the cushion and found its way into a pocket.

"Jammy bastard," Dom muttered.

Gray laughed and lined up for his third shot. No such luck this time.

"So, d'you need me to have a gander?" Dom asked. He refrained from cheering when he took the lead again.

"If you wouldn't mind."

"Should be easy enough, seeing as we've got a file on the bank."

"Actually, Richards resigned."

"Still, it's somewhere to start." With ease, Dom potted another two reds, followed by the cue ball.

For all of one minute, Gray's hopes for victory glimmered, and then faded faster than a dying light bulb when another red went down. The last remaining red ball was a sitter; Gray put his cue back in the rack and watched the master put away the red and the black in rapid succession. He didn't even change position to do so. If there hadn't been others waiting, Gray might have been inclined to suggest another game, and he'd no doubt have lost that one too.

Returning to their table at the rear of the room, Gray downed his pint and went to get his round in. While he waited to be served, he anticipated a wave of misery would engulf him, but it didn't, and his resultant smile seemed to unnerve the bartender. Gray straightened his face, ordered the two pints and returned to Dom.

"I've missed this."

"Yeah." Dom held up his pint. "Cheers."

Gray tapped his glass against Dom's and took a good swig. The pool game was in full swing, and the young couple who were playing were both terrible. From the sound of their giggling and the kisses as they passed each other on the way around the table, they didn't care.

"I'll give you a bell if I find out anything," Dom said.

"Thanks." Gray kept his gaze on the girl and drew a sharp breath when she nearly put the cue through the felt. "Ooph!"

"Dear me," Dom muttered. He was also focused on the girl, but he was preparing to offer Gray advice. Gray glanced his way and raised an eyebrow to give him the go-ahead. Dom shrugged. "No lecture, but I stand by what I said. It's the job. We see the worst in people because we've seen the worst in people. This guy, William Richards, is probably a decent, ordinary bloke."

Gray sighed. "You're probably right. Still, I'd rather know what I'm dealing with."

"Fair comment, but your life's been on hold long enough, mate. Don't wait around."

5: Workout

ROB HAD ALREADY packed his panniers and was on his way up to let his neighbour know he was leaving when he got the call to tell him he wasn't going anywhere. Where he should've been going was back up north for his mum's seventieth birthday, but his aunty had surprised her with a long weekend at Lake Como, Italy. Rob was happy for them, but it would've been nice if his aunty had let him in on the arrangement beforehand.

Presumably, his brother hadn't known either, seeing as he'd answered their mum's phone when Rob had called the first time and hadn't said anything, although it would be typical JJ to have known about it for months and not think to mention it. Of course, their sister would've known about Mum's trip, but she and Rob didn't talk anymore—another casualty of the undercover work. Whatever, it was too late for him to change his annual leave and probably too late to rearrange the camping trip with his son they'd postponed in the summer, when Lucas got an ear infection. Still, 'don't ask, don't get', as his dad would've said. So, rather than cancelling his arrangement with Shammy—the Rasta on the floor above—to keep an eye on the flat, Rob backtracked to give Zoë a call.

"Alright, Zo? It's me."

"Hey. I can't talk long. I'm at work."

"Yeah, sorry. Just a quickie. Have you and Lu got any plans this weekend?"

"Nothing much. He's got a match after school, and Travis is taking us to Whipsnade on Sunday, but otherwise, no. Why?"

Rob ground his teeth to stop himself from saying what he was thinking. He didn't dislike Travis. He'd only spoken to the guy once or twice, but there would be plenty of time for that later, seeing as he and Zoë seemed to be doing the relationship thing for real. Rob was trying to be reasonable...no. He wasn't trying. He didn't want to be reasonable when *his* son and ex-wife were going on a family day out with another man. A pretend dad. An *imposter*.

"That his idea, was it?" he said, instead of the cusses threatening to shoot from his mouth.

"Rob, don't start. He's a good man, and Lucas likes him."

"I wasn't starting anything."

"And anyway, didn't you say you were visiting your mum?"

"Yeah. I was supposed to be. Aunty Cathy's taken her to Italy."

"Aw, that's nice, isn't it?"

"I guess. So, anyway, all I was thinking was I could have Lu for the weekend. Go down to the New Forest. What d'you reckon?"

"Ah." Zoë fell silent, and Rob could picture her with that frowny, crinkly-nosed expression she always got when she was trying to think and do something else at the same time, which he knew she was, as he could hear her tapping at her keyboard. "I can ask Travis to cancel?" she suggested. Rob could tell from her tone how she really felt about that.

"Nah, don't worry." He tried to sound gracious, pretty sure he failed. It would've been easier to let blood. "What about tomorrow after swimming?"

"We usually go shopping on Saturday afternoon, stop off somewhere for dinner on the way home."

Now she was being obstructive. "With Travis?"

"If he's not working."

There was no point asking if he was working tomorrow. Rob knew he wouldn't be. He'd be making time to take Zoë shopping and 'stop off somewhere for dinner'. Travis was self-employed—Rob had no idea what he did, but he begrudged him that freedom, the luxury to pick and choose when to work.

"All right, how about this," Zoë said.

Rob squeezed his keys hard. "Go on."

"If you pick Lu up from football later—"

"Won't Travis be doing that?"

"Rob."

He clamped his teeth together before he talked her out of letting him see Lucas at all. "Yeah, I'd like that."

"If you stop off at McDonald's on the way back..." Zoë left it trailing.

Rob laughed. "Give you a call? Will do."

"Awesome. Look, I'd best go. See you later?"

"All right—" Even now, after all this time, Rob had to forcibly stop the words leaving his mouth. *Love you, babe.* He hung up and spent a moment with the phone in his hand. His weekend was rapidly turning into a lost cause. So it looked like he had four days to himself, with a few hours of Lucas thrown in. He supposed that wasn't so bad. He could go to the gym and burn off some of the takeaways, or go for a run. He could even go out for dinner somewhere, instead of eating out of foil and plastic containers, or see a film.

"Or go slowly out of my mind," he muttered to himself. It was one thing having alone time after a long, hard shift at work, another entirely to fill four days off, when his mates were either working or up north. He'd been looking forward to getting the bike out on the open roads for a couple of hours, but it wasn't to be, and he wasn't one to mope. So, first up, he could go to the gym, which would kill a bit more time. If he showered afterwards, he could brave the supermarket and get some proper food.

The prospect of eating something other than sausage and chips, chicken tikka masala or special curry and fried rice was becoming more enticing by the second. Decision made, he popped up to see Shammy, who was surprised— or as surprised as he ever got, considering his perpetual state of ganja-induced rapture—but assured Rob he'd look after the place anytime. Rob returned to his flat, changed into his exercise gear, and jogged across the park and onwards the mile and a half to the gym.

The place was deserted, with a few retired people pounding the treadmills and a couple of younger women on the cross-trainers. Rob did a quick warm-up on a bike and then moved to the cross-trainer for thirty minutes, earphones in, weekday morning TV on the screen in front of him. It wasn't the kind of thing he would normally watch, but they were interviewing the widower of an actress who had recently died from cancer. In spite of every instinct telling Rob he should change the channel for his own good, he couldn't tear himself away.

On this occasion, his instincts turned out to be wrong. Listening to the poor, broken man try to hold it together and talk about his late wife's bravery and her legacy, Rob realised he'd got off lightly. Discovering the girl he'd crushed on since high school was a fraudster had been a hell of a kick in the teeth, but it was nothing compared to finding out she had cancer and only weeks to live. Yet he'd never been alone in his grief; he had Lucas—had a life ahead of him—and, like the actress, Jess's legacy was a good one. It was that final act of selflessness that redeemed her in Rob's eyes. He knew there were many who still despised her for what she'd done, but what point was there to holding grudges against the dead? What point was there to holding grudges at all?

If there was one person Rob should have hated, it was Gray Fisher, for recruiting him to get Jess in the first place. None of Rob's fellow officers had understood how low he'd had to go to get the job done, using his and Jess's friendship to establish trust and get as much information out of her as he could without arousing her suspicion. That had been the least of his worries, as it turned out.

Right back from their first physical encounter in sixth form, he and Jess had a connection, sexual chemistry, or whatever. It was the easiest way to draw her in, and things were already bad with Zoë. So Rob expedited proceedings, did the unthinkable. Slept with Jess. It wouldn't have been anywhere near as bad if he'd felt nothing—if it had all been an act—but he still desired her. She still turned him on. At the same time, he'd been desperate to salvage his marriage and felt as if he was cheating on Zoë.

The job had turned him into a cheat and a liar, and he'd let it. Going undercover meant spinning Zoë a yarn about being transferred to a different unit when the job didn't even work like that. His SIU colleagues gave him all the BS about thinking like criminals if he wanted to get inside their heads, but he'd been undercover plenty of times before, and he knew how Jess operated. She was ambitious and would stop at nothing to reach the top. The entire Strang case came down to that. She was clever—too clever—and she'd been showing off. That was all it was in the end. A display of her cunning.

Rob was at peace with that now. He'd done the job he'd been recruited to do; Jess never knew of his deception, and all 'her' money had gone to good causes. But if he could rewind time...

The first day he was back with the Met, Martina Hedley had come to tell him how pleased she was to have him on the team again. Over a celebratory pint, he'd told her about Zoë ending their marriage. Hedley had asked if he regretted taking the undercover work, and he'd replied without hesitation. It was the worst decision he'd ever made. He'd lost his wife and son, his home, his life, and watched his childhood sweetheart fade away. For all that Jess had done, she didn't deserve to suffer the way she had.

In fairness, Gray wasn't to know how it would turn out. He couldn't have predicted Jess's death nor realised that the friendship group he had Rob spying on was the one he'd shared with Jess until she and the others went off to university and Rob joined the army. They were once his friends as much as they were hers, and he'd almost lost them too.

With the next surge of adrenaline, Rob managed to put a lid on the stew of anger and misery sloshing around inside him and moved on to the weights, cranking them up to the maximum he could take. The burn was perfect, punishing, and he was really pumping. One of the women who had previously been hammering out a good pace on the cross-trainer took up position on the lat pulldown opposite the bench Rob was using and, when she thought he wasn't paying attention, gave him a thorough visual inspection.

Rob tried not to smile, but it felt good to have someone admire his physique. He wasn't arrogant—he hoped—or conceited, but he figured he must have something about him to have won Zoë's affection. More than once or twice, women had told him he was good-looking, and there were men who saw him as a threat. Sadly, some of those men were people he respected and admired, and his actions could well be construed as setting himself up as a rival.

Rob swiped sweat from his forehead—his bare arms and legs were beaded with the stuff, glistening under the gym's cool LED lighting—and glanced across at the woman, catching her with her mouth hanging open. She blushed and gave him a shy smile. He smiled back. She was attractive—toned yet shapely, a creamy complexion, pale-blue eyes and dark-brown hair tied back in a ponytail that bounced as she pulled down on the handles. Yes, Rob could have got well into her...if he wasn't still carrying a torch for Zoë. Sometimes he wondered if that would ever change.

At the end of the song currently playing on his phone, Rob put the weights back and moved on to the mats, ready to work on his abs. The next song didn't make it past the intro before it cut out. He unclipped his phone and glanced at the screen. Number unknown but local. He hit 'answer' and said, "Hello?"

The call ended, and the song faded back in. Rob's curiosity wasn't great enough to warrant calling back, not when it was probably a telesales company. Setting his phone to one side, he lay with his hands behind his head, knees raised, waiting to catch the beat and then keeping time with it, which was too slow, really, but he was in no rush. It was hours before Lucas finished school.

When Rob's mum and dad had separated, he'd made a vow, which, in retrospect, was naïve. He'd vowed that if he were ever to settle down with someone and have kids, whatever it took for them to stay together as a family, they'd do it, at least until the kids reached adulthood. His parents had stuck it out until he was fifteen, JJ was seventeen and Tanya was twenty, and in many respects, that made it worse. They'd heard the arguments and understood enough to know their parents' differences were irreconcilable. No affairs or anything like that. Luckily, they'd never married, so no messy divorce either, and Rob and JJ were old enough to choose which parent they wanted to live with. Tanya was an adult—officially—but she'd still lived at home.

Ultimately, both she and JJ made their own arrangements while Rob stayed with their mum and saw their dad at weekends. The three 'kids' hadn't been destroyed by the breakup and still had a good relationship with both parents, but where his brother and sister had remained in their hometown, Rob had left at eighteen for four years with the Royal Engineers, followed by eight with Warwickshire Police, which was when he met Zoë. Nine years younger than him, she was a 'Cockney'—not really, she was from Wembley—in the final year of her degree at Warwick University, and they'd moved back to London together after she'd graduated.

That was when Rob had made his first mistake. The Met Police weren't recruiting, but Scotland Yard had sent a request to other areas for a black officer with knowledge of Rastafari culture to work undercover. Rob knew the culture, but it wasn't his. His grandparents were from Barbados and Catholic; his parents were British-born agnostics. In high school, he was one of nine black/Asian pupils against 1,500 white pupils, and there were no black or Asian teachers. His friends were almost all white, mostly from Christian backgrounds. But for the sake of earning a living and buying somewhere to live, Rob was prepared to let his skin colour and working knowledge of Rastafari qualify him for the job.

It was part-time, and dangerous, completely at odds with the admin job he'd been given to make up the rest of his hours. He had to get close to a drug dealer and gain his trust, but Scotland Yard wasn't interested in the dealer. They wanted his suppliers, and when they'd gathered enough information to get them, Rob was debriefed and 'returned to normal duties'. A vacancy with CID came up—working under Martina Hedley—and Rob applied and got it, but by then, he had the undercover bug and continued to pick up assignments if he matched what they were looking for.

Two years after moving to London, Lucas was born, and Rob was torn. There were bonuses that came with some of the undercover jobs, and the extra money meant Zoë could stay at home with the baby. But every hour she spent with their son was one less for Rob, and inevitably, they argued about it.

Thus, when Gray Fisher came to him, Rob had been about to throw in the towel. He'd been doing it for Zoë and Lucas, but the longer it went on, the further he drifted from them. Gray told him it was only for one job, which would take a few months, and it was a level-one assignment, deep undercover. He'd be away from home, working as a courier for a law firm defrauding their clients. There was little physical danger with white-collar crime. Rob had said no; Gray asked him to think about it.

Rob immediately put it out of his mind. Working for the SIU meant a substantial pay rise, but there was more to life than money, and if their finances got too tight, they could always sell up and move out of the city. He and Zoë were getting on better, and he was spending more time with Lucas. They would've been all right. They would've made it, he was sure, if Gray Fisher hadn't come back and tried again, and this time, he wasn't taking no for an answer.

A few months turned into three years of living undercover, yet he'd had to use his real name—or not quite. He'd dropped the 'Stone' while he was working the Newcastle-to-London courier run, which kept him out of Jess's sights, and she'd died before the investigation concluded, so she never got to hear his testimony against her, read out by Gray in court. She'd also left a full written confession and documentary evidence that sealed the deal for the others. They went to prison, Rob received a commendation, was debriefed and returned to duty, and Gray...

The guy had been operating on self-destruct, and no-one had realised. He'd been no more ruthless or demanding than any of the other senior officers Rob had taken orders from over the eight years he'd worked undercover, but the only truly right decision Gray had made was getting out of the police, and from what Rob had heard, he was happy with his lot. Meanwhile, Rob struggled on, restless and lonely, hating his ex-wife's boyfriend for doing what he'd failed to do.

And his abdominal muscles were screaming for mercy. Rob tugged his earbuds out, groaning at the effort it took to sit up.

The woman with whom he'd exchanged smiles earlier advanced and indicated the next mat along. "I won't be in your way there, will I?"

"Nah," Rob said, getting to his feet. "I'm done, anyway."

6: Guinness and Black

"Graham Farrar."

Gray was on his way to give his Friday morning seminar and didn't have time to stop, but the use of that name, and that voice... He turned around, a grin already on his face.

"Rob. Hello!" Gray shifted the pile of books onto his left forearm to shake hands.

Rob pulled him in, releasing the handshake to pat him on the back. With the crash helmet under his other arm and full leathers, he was exactly how Gray remembered him.

"How are you, man?" Rob asked.

Gray nodded. "I'm great, thanks. You?"

"Not bad at all. You're looking well."

Gray had heard that a lot since he'd left the police, and on this occasion, he could return the compliment. "Likewise. What brings you to this neck of the woods?"

"Well, you, as it happens." Rob fell in step beside Gray, and they talked as they walked. "You're a lecturer now?"

Gray laughed. He wasn't kitted out with the necessary skills—or patience—to lecture. "Not quite. I'm on the PhD programme, which means I have to teach four hours a week—two seminar sessions with third-year undergrads."

"PhD? Bloody hell! I always said you were a smartarse, but I hadn't realised you were that clever. No offence."

"None taken. To be honest with you, it's just an excuse to read books."

"See, now that sounds like torture to me. Give me a copy of *FHM* and I'll read it cover to cover. Well, I say read..."

"Pity they don't do a Braille version?"

"Damn right." Rob chuckled a little uneasily. "Listen, I heard you'd had a rough run, health-wise. Are you better?"

Gray gave himself a mental kick. He was so used to acting the part, he'd automatically implied he, like most of the guys on his old team, appreciated a magazine full of 'tasty birds', which fitted with the man Rob had worked alongside in the SIU: Graham Farrar, the undercover officer with a wife. But the question about his health was a probe for information. Rob knew the truth and didn't want to ask the question outright.

"I'm much better, thanks, Rob. Who told you? DI Hartley?"

"Nope. Josh, as it happens. I went up to visit the crem a few weeks back, and he offered to go with me. It's a beautiful place, but...well...it's still tough. You know what I mean?"

Gray gave Rob a sympathetic pat on the arm. "I do, Rob. I know exactly what you mean."

There were few who knew the real Gray Fisher, the identity he'd buried to be the tough man at the helm of the SIU, and he sure as hell didn't want to elaborate in a busy university corridor...although maybe that was the best way to do it. Just get it out there.

"I lost my partner a few years back."

"Sorry to hear that."

"Thanks. He was killed in a car accident. I was with him."

"Jeez, man." Rob looked lost for words.

"I'm getting back on track now. It's just a case of giving it time, permitting myself to grieve, you know?"

"Yeah, I do. Funnily enough, me and Josh were having the same discussion about Jess—Jessica Lambert."

Rob's clarification was unnecessary. Gray had known how important she was, to both Rob and Josh, and he felt like a prize bastard for using that to get Rob onside.

Rob continued, "Josh says he feels like he's wasting his tears on her, but he meant a lot to her. He was the one person she really trusted."

"Did you tell him that?"

"Yeah." Rob frowned. "I think I did." He shrugged. "Well, whatever, I'm getting it back together now as well."

"I'm glad to hear it. Listen, Rob, I owe you a massive apology for bringing you in. I was out of order."

"You needed me."

"We couldn't have done it without you. That doesn't make it right."

"I'm sure I can find a way for you to make amends." Rob gave Gray a wink.

Gray laughed and shook his head. They were nearly at the seminar room, and he still didn't know why Rob had sought him out. "Is this a social call, or business?"

"Well...I was thinking only the other week, it'd be nice to catch up and have a pint, and then..." Rob stopped walking, glanced along the corridor and then back at Gray. "Look, is there somewhere we can talk in private?"

"Can it wait a couple of hours? I could cancel my class if it's urgent, but I'd rather not."

Rob checked his watch. "OK. I'll come back at twelve?" Gray nodded to confirm. "See you later."

"See you." As Gray watched his ex-colleague retreat along the corridor, he wondered what business Rob could possibly have with him. No point second-guessing, he entered the classroom and was met by twenty faces depicting varied states of eagerness. "All right, guys. Quills at the ready. We're looking at Jacobean tragedy today..."

***

Rob sidestepped a group standing near the bar and sent an easy, confident smile their way. He was an attractive guy, tall, with broad shoulders and an athletic build set off to full effect by his fitted black leathers. The light caught the small stud in his left ear—off-duty today—and his hair was longer than the last time Gray had seen him, although only just long enough to have coiled into short locks; it was a good look for him.

"Guinness and black," Rob said, handing over the pint of black beer topped with three-quarters of an inch of purple froth. His nose wrinkled in disgust, and Gray laughed. "I'm sure you never used to drink that."

"No. I usually had JD, but I can't take spirits anymore. Not since... I changed career."

"Yeah. What happened? I thought you were gonna be in the job till retirement."

Rob was in the process of taking off his jacket so hopefully didn't see Gray's incredulity before he got it in check. The assumption was odd, considering Rob had got out of the SIU as soon as the Strang case was over. Gray obviously came across as much tougher than he was, and he decided to treat Rob's question as if it were rhetorical. It may well have been, given he wasn't pushing for an answer.

"So, what's it like being a civilian for real?" Rob asked instead, although it took him a while.

"It's out of this world. No exaggeration. I get up in the morning, go to work, do some research, go home, have dinner, meet up with friends—all that normal stuff—and then I go to bed. And sleep? I don't know how I got through so many years on so little of the stuff." He did know, but that was all in the past too. No looking back—that's what his therapist said. Don't think about yesterday, or tomorrow. Deal with today. And it was working. His therapist also suggested he try Guinness with a dash of blackcurrant cordial, and what a heavenly nectar that turned out to be. Gray took a good glug of the thick, sweet liquid, letting it slide smoothly down his throat. He sat back and smiled in contentment.

"You seem happy," Rob observed.

"I am. And how about you?"

"I'm doing great. Back in uniform, just getting on with the job, really. Plus, I've fixed things with Zoë, so I get to see Lucas a lot more these days."

"How old is he now?"

"Nearly seven." Rob laughed quietly. It was tinged with regret, but he shook it off. "For his birthday, I'm taking him up to Aviemore in Scotland, snowboarding. He's been watching it on telly, and he's well into his skateboarding. I think he'll love it, and I'm up for having a go myself—I've only ever been skiing."

"I used to ski," Gray said. "With Jean. He was really good."

"Your partner, yeah?"

"He was, yes. In life and on the job—Police Fédérale, international cooperation. That's how we met, working a money-laundering case."

Rob smiled. "Sounds like a James Bond movie plot."

Gray laughed. "Nothing so exciting, I'm afraid, although there was this one time we were on a private jet, and the target sussed us. He ordered the pilot to ditch the plane in the Channel, but the pilot was one of ours."

"Nice one." Rob took a swig of his lager, keeping his eyes on the glass as he swallowed.

Gray's openness had created an uneasy silence between them. They'd got on well as colleagues, but they'd never been friends. Only Dom had known that the few weeks Gray had been forced to take off were for bereavement, not a holiday as he'd told everyone else. It was none of their business, even if, as officer-in-charge, it was Gray's job to know what was going on with each and every one of his team members. So he was aware that Rob's marriage had ended during the Strang case, and it was yet another burden of guilt he had to bear. Their undercover work had cost them both dearly, and whilst it was common ground, it was also too painful to put to any good use. But if Gray could make it up to Rob in any way, he would, and he had the feeling he was about to get his chance.

"You wanted to talk to me about something?" he asked.

Rob nodded. "Yeah. Berringer's bank. They went bust a few weeks ago?"

Gray knew the bank. He'd run a preliminary investigation on their investment practices a couple of years back, and it appeared to be one of those rare cases of all smoke and no fire. Allegations of overvaluing their assets turned out to be an accounting error caused by a new computer system, and by the time the SIU was alerted, it was already being dealt with internally by Berringer's. The company seemed fairly benign, as banks went. The glitch cost them a lot, which was likely the reason they'd gone bust.

"I take it your thoughtful silence means something?" Rob asked.

"Not really, or at least, I know who they are. Why?"

Rob frowned. "I don't know, in all honesty, Gray." He paused for a quick gulp of lager. "See, there was a fatal RTA last week, involving an expensive motor—a Merc S-Class—and at first, we thought it was just a typical Hooray Henry getting sloshed and losing control. The car was registered to one of Berringer's directors, and his wallet—or what we believed to be his wallet—was in the driver's foot well, with his address and next of kin's details, a load of cash—"

"Who's 'we'?"

"DCI Hedley and me."

Gray nodded. He knew Martina Hedley only vaguely; he'd had to clear it with her for Rob to have time out for the SIU. "I thought you said you were in uniform. How come you're working with the DCI again?"

"I'm not. She turned up at the RTA because she was in the area, and then it got complicated…"

Gray waited. Rob was one of those men who thought very carefully about what he wanted to say, which could sometimes come across as him not paying attention, but he was. Always watching and listening. It was how they'd managed to collect so much intel on the Strang case, because Rob Simpson-Stone didn't miss a trick.

"The thing is," Rob continued, "I went to deliver the bad news to the director's widow and instead came face-to-face with the guy who I thought we'd just seen carted off to the morgue. They both had photo ID bearing the name Aaron Tanner, and the guy at the house confirmed his wife was the next of kin detailed in the wallet found in the Merc. And he seemed legit. He said when Berringer's went under, they took his house, his car—everything—but the car was still registered to him, and the wallet contained credentials pertaining to him."

"Identity theft?" Gray suggested.

Rob shrugged. "That's what I thought, which is why I've come to you. The case has gone to CID, and I've been waiting for someone to come and ask me about Tanner, except Hedley's on annual leave, and when I looked at the file yesterday, no one had picked it up. Then this morning, I received four silent calls from the same number, which turned out to be some idiot repeatedly misdialling, but I did wonder if someone was trying to get hold of me about Tanner. So, I thought, seeing as I've got a bit of experience with identity theft and it's not stepping on anyone's toes, I'd see what I could piece together."

"Are you sure you're happy in uniform?" Gray asked. He made it sound like a joke, although it was a valid question.

Rob laughed. "Yeah, definitely. I'm just killing time. I was supposed to be up at my mum's for the weekend and had a change of plan."

"Have you considered taking up a hobby?"

"Like reading books, you mean?"

Gray tried to picture Rob Simpson-Stone sitting in a coffee shop, cappuccino in one hand, *Crime and Punishment* in the other.

"I do play footy," Rob contended defensively.

"I'm only winding you up, Rob. All right, so the guy you saw. Could he have been a male relative? A brother, maybe?"

"Nope. I've looked into all that this morning. He's an only child, and no kids either. Plus, he claimed he was Aaron Tanner, and his ID matched. I don't know if anyone's ID'd the body from the Merc yet, but he looked nothing like Tanner."

"His ID matched, presumably?"

"As far as we could tell. And I can't see any motive for nicking Tanner's ID. He's listed as a director online. His photo's on there, so everyone knows what he looks like, and he's worth nothing. Well, less than nothing, seeing as he's liable for some of Berringer's debt unless—" Rob stopped.

Gray could almost hear the penny drop. He nodded and finished the sentence for him. "Unless he's dead."

"Shit." Rob flopped back in his seat and ran his hands over his head. "The bastard faked his own death, and I gave him the heads-up we're on to him."

"You weren't to know."

"Odds-on, he's fled the country by now." Rob huffed, dismayed with himself. "You'd think I'd know better."

"Swings and roundabouts, Rob. You're primed for liars, and you find plenty, which makes you think everyone is bullshitting. That, or you over-compensate."

Rob was nodding slowly and quite deep in thought, for which Gray was glad, because his own words came back at him. He'd pretty much had the same speech off Dom Hooper, and Gray wished it changed how he felt. He still couldn't decide if Will was lying to him or if it was all in his head. Either way, he didn't trust Will, and whilst he could justify his scepticism as an old habit dying hard, it was no foundation for a friendship.

It was a terrible accusation to level, not that he planned on making it for real. Gray was appalled at himself, and yet, he could pull up countless records of people who had concocted illnesses and deaths of close relatives for their own gain. But was Will one of those people? Who in their right mind would use their mum having a brain tumour to excuse tardiness? No, like Dom had told Gray, and Gray had told Rob, too long with the SIU had made him unnecessarily untrusting. Will was a great guy. If he wasn't, Josh would never have set them up.

"There's nothing on Berringer's you can think of?" Rob asked, pulling Gray out of his downwardly spiralling thoughts.

"No, but I'll see what I can find out for you."

"You don't need—"

Gray raised his hands to stop Rob's protest. "I don't mind. I know a few people I can ask. And I owe you, more than I could ever repay."

"So it's a down-payment?" Rob said with a cheeky grin.

Gray laughed. "Exactly."

"Thanks, then." Rob picked up his lager and glugged half of it in one go. "I need to make a move soon. I'm going to Lucas's after-school match."

"I should get going too. I'm working this afternoon."

"You do all your teaching in one day?"

"No. It's, er...my other job."

"Yeah? Doing what?"

The question was bound to crop up sooner or later, which was why, despite Rob's prior unease at his openness, Gray had prompted it. When Jean died, Gray had walked out on his past—the life he'd shared with the man he loved, his family and good friends, who, even after all this time, had welcomed him back. They were still there for him, and he was finally recovering some semblance of normality. He went 'home' to see Becky every now and then; he met up with friends for coffee, dinner, a movie, and while all of it was still meshed with life with Jean, the pain was fading, being painted over by happier recollections.

But undercover work had fundamentally changed him, and not in ways his friends could understand. He had seen behind curtains, heard private thoughts, witnessed raw pain unmoderated in the absence of others. He had been a ghost, invisible yet all-seeing. It was a significant part of why he felt such a strong connection to Josh, who didn't need surveillance equipment to tap into people's psyches. Nor did Josh have the luxury of an off switch.

Through the small piece of history they had shared, Gray also felt that connection with Rob, and he hoped there was enough there to build a friendship. Plus, it would be interesting to see what Rob thought of his new job—Gray hadn't told anyone other than George and Josh. George didn't have an opinion. Josh said it was reactionary exhibitionism, a perfectly normal response to having spent so long lurking in shadows and behind pseudonyms.

The thoughts must have played out more quickly than Gray had perceived, because Rob was still attentive, waiting for his answer.

"I'm an extra in a soap opera," he said. He watched Rob's mouth open part way, but then he clamped it shut and nodded without a word. Gray started laughing. "It's for fun. I don't need the money, but if I don't do something, I'll skulk around the house on my own all day."

Rob gave a wide, carefree shrug. "Each to their own, mate. Right, I'm off." He got up and put his jacket back on. "Give us a bell if you find anything out, yeah?"

"Will do."

With a quick parting handshake, Rob turned and strode back through the pub. A moment later, Gray heard the rev of Rob's bike as it took off.

It wasn't ideal, sitting in a pub alone on a Friday afternoon, and Gray still needed to eat lunch, but he was struggling to find the motivation to get up and leave. He could've stayed where he was and caught the train straight to the TV studio, except he'd left his tablet at home, and if he was going to dine alone in public, he needed to be doing something or he'd look like a lonely fool. So really, there was no excuse to stay where he was, other than the company of unassuming strangers.

Not that he was lonely, as such. After almost two months in his new house, well-meaning relatives and friends were finally allowing him to go whole weeks without anxious phone calls or 'happened to be down your way' impromptu visits, seemingly satisfied that he was settled and ready to once more strike out as an independent adult, which he bloody well should be, at his age. Thirty-five next birthday—it was crazy to think how much he'd been through when he really wasn't that old. And he was content with everything he'd achieved since leaving the SIU. He was clean, he was working his way through his grief, and he was studying again—the dream he'd clung to through all his years in the police.

So where had this sudden dissatisfaction come from? Rob had asked if he knew anything, and he'd ended up offering his services. By accident? Or because—if he was completely honest—he missed the work? It was all a bit much to think about, and Gray didn't want to consider it too deeply, but he could help Rob and perhaps deal with both of the issues troubling him at the same time. He took out his phone and brought up Will's number, glancing at the clock above the bar. Coming up to one-thirty.

"Hello?"

"Will? It's Gray."

"Hold on. I'll get him for you."

Gray waited, at the same time wondering why Will hadn't answered his own mobile phone, or, in fact, where he was that someone else would answer it for him.

"Hey."

"Will?"

"Yep. Are you OK?"

"Fine." Gray pursed his lips to stop himself asking what Will was up to. It was none of his business. "Are you?"

"Yeah, not bad. Just heading out to visit Mum."

"Then I won't keep you, but I do need to talk to you about...a business matter. Are you free to meet up sometime? Sooner rather than later."

"This evening?"

"I guess, but it's not urg—"

"One sec." Will cut him off, and the line became muffled, indistinct voices that Gray couldn't hear clearly enough to make out the words. Dogs were barking in the background, followed by a scuffling sound, and then, "Any chance we can meet closer to here? Maybe halfway?"

"I'm happy to go all the way," Gray said. He felt the blood rush to his cheeks and was glad no-one could see him. Will cleared his throat, and Gray knew he was trying not to laugh. "I mean..." He tried to recover a modicum of sense. "Should I come to you? Would that be easier?"

"It would, thank you. If you can get the Met line to Croxley, text me, and I'll meet you at the station."

"Cool. Time?"

"About seven?"

"Good for me. See you, then."

"Bye."

Gray took his phone from his ear, the beep sounding to signify that Will had already ended the call before Gray had a chance to. He stared at the screen, a little perplexed by the way he was feeling. He wasn't attracted to Will. Well, that was a lie. He *did* think Will was attractive, but he didn't want a relationship. He'd called him on Rob's behalf, and to satisfy himself that Will was telling the truth. That was all it was.

And he didn't feel put out by another man answering Will's mobile phone. Not in the slightest.

7: And Other Animals

WHEN GRAY MOVED to London, giving up the car had been the hardest part. Wherever he'd lived in the thirteen years since he'd graduated, and regardless of how little he'd possessed in the way of home comforts, he'd always had a decent car. He loved cars, and while his own were never particularly showy, they'd been high spec, with big engines, big wheels and a hell of a lot of go.

He enjoyed driving. Long journeys at night on clear roads were best, even though they were the exact conditions the night Jean was killed. Gray had lost consciousness in the collision and had come round forty-eight hours later, by which point Jean's family had flown over from Belgium and already knew the results of the tests that determined Jean was brain-dead. At the time, the laws regarding same-sex partnerships were such that Jean's parents could have made the decision without Gray's consent, but they hadn't. They'd waited for Gray, and then Jean's mother had stayed with him while the doctors switched off the machine.

In Gray's memory, the scene looked like something from a TV drama, with a similar lack of emotional impact, perhaps due to the pain meds, perhaps because it was such an enormous amount of pain that his brain refused to acknowledge it. Hardly a day had passed without some well-meaning friend or colleague telling him it would sink in at some point, and he'd stacked up a fair number of promises they'd 'be there' when it did. But it had never hit him the way people said it would. He'd refused to let it.

Strange, then, that he should choose to replicate the conditions of the accident, and not just as a one-off. When he visited his sister, he always hired a car and made the return journey late at night. He'd told Becky it was to avoid traffic, but the truth was it kept the memories of Jean fresh, for there were many more journeys they had completed together successfully. It was those that came to mind when he was driving alone, replaying conversations, laughing and sighing and feeling every emotion again.

Alas, taking the Metropolitan line's rickety route through the North West London suburbs and out to Hertfordshire did not afford the same kind of stimulus, but it was a pleasant enough journey, Gray supposed, as he emerged from the station a little before seven, realising as he did so that he'd forgotten to text Will to say he was on his way. He took out his phone to rectify that and then put it away again.

Will was standing outside; there was no missing him. He was the one with the five dogs and dressed in scruffs, which set Gray's pulse speeding. It took him a few seconds to get past *God, he's hot* and rationalise his reaction. Will hadn't gone to any effort for Gray's benefit, which could mean he'd been tied up with his mum all afternoon, or he didn't care what Gray thought of him, or he saw no need to put on an act. The latter was the best fit for what Gray knew about Will so far and also the easiest to live with.

As for the dogs, they were a varied bunch of mutts, all very well behaved, patiently awaiting their next instruction. Gray stopped mid-step, unsure how best to approach. He looked to Will for guidance and received a wide, cheery grin.

"They're all friendly," Will said, qualifying it with, "Well, Monster's a bit highly strung." He pointed to a black-and-white dog, previously described to Gray as 'the little one' and not that little, in his unqualified opinion. "And Kenny can be a bit snappy at first." Will swapped all of the leads into one hand and patted a dog to identify he who was known as Kenny. Gray could hardly believe what he was seeing and continued to gaze in awe as Will explained to his dogs, like they were children who understood his every word, "This is Gray. He's very nice, but he's a bit nervous, all right? Shall we go home for some supper?" The five dogs, and Will, turned and walked away.

A bit nervous? It was true enough, but Gray took exception to being introduced as such, even if it was only to the dogs. He shook himself out of his stupor and jogged to catch them up, stepping off the kerb and walking in the road so he didn't get too close to snappy Kenny. He couldn't take his eyes off him, and not out of the fear he'd get chomped. "What happened to him?"

"Kenny?" Will asked and, assuming he was correct—which he was—went on. "We think he was run over. He was found in woodland half a mile from the motorway. He must've crawled to safety, and some kids found him and called their dad, who took him to their local vet, luckily for Kenny, as he's our vet too. If the RSPCA or warden had picked him up, he'd have been euthanised."

"Right," Gray said, still watching the dog trotting along beside the rest of them—with his two front legs. His back end was suspended in a harness attached to an aluminium frame with a wheel on either side, but he was having absolutely no problem keeping up with the others.

"He's named Kenny after the Paralympian swimmer, Dave Kenny—you should see this guy in the hydro pool. He's a fantastic swimmer, aren't you, Ken?"

The dog gave Will a brief glance and returned to facing ahead as they veered to the left and stopped at the kerb to cross. Gray had visions of Kenny rolling right off the pavement and was relieved—and amazed—when he stopped, just like all the other dogs.

"Incredible," he uttered as Kenny, along with the rest of their group, safely reached the other side of the road.

"Yeah," Will agreed. "He took to them really quickly. Off the lead, there's no stopping him, but I think we'll walk back the conventional way tonight." He glanced down at Gray's feet, which made Gray do the same. He was wearing boots, but they were built for fashion rather than cross-country hikes.

"Don't change your route on my account. I don't mind if they get a bit muddy."

"How about a lot muddy?"

Gray shrugged. "They'll clean."

Will looked unconvinced but took Gray at his word, and evidently, the dogs knew where they were going. They stopped at the end of a well-lit lane with a footpath signpost and stayed still for Will to unclip their leads. As soon as all five dogs were liberated, they went tearing off together, with Kenny, as the biggest, quickly making ground on the others. Gray could do little but watch in wonder. Will moved off again; Gray snapped out of it more quickly this time and fell in step beside him.

"I got the job, by the way," Will said.

"Congratulations."

"Thanks. Not sure when I start, though. They've given me some leeway because of the situation with Mum, so I guess it'll be a couple of weeks."

Gray nodded but could think of nothing to say, nor did he feel compelled to try, and the two of them walked on in companionable silence. Will's attention was on his dogs, who slowed down every so often, seeming to wait for the humans to catch up. The lane wasn't pedestrianised, but there were no pavements or cars. The boundaries on either side were formed by tall fencing that obscured from view all but the rooftops of the large townhouses. The properties in this part of the South East were worth a great deal of money, but the greater value of the place was what Gray was discovering right then: the quietness and the open space.

If Gray had not been so at peace, he might have worried about the fact that he was, in that moment, feeling more content than he had in years. It helped that Will was so calm and 'real'. He strode with confidence, his boots marking a firm, steady rhythm. It was too dark to make out detail or colour, but he was wearing loose-fitting cargo pants and a baggy pullover with a shirt underneath, one collar tip visible. His hair hung in a ponytail at the nape of his neck, and the long stubble on his chin, turned orange by streetlight, indicated he hadn't shaved in a few days.

This was Will 'at home', and he put Gray completely at ease. Gray had accompanied George and his dog on a couple of walks, which he'd enjoyed. But this? This was something else. He could see the dogs waiting at the start of a footpath up ahead of them, beyond that, woodland, and he felt his stomach fluttering with the effect of the feel-good chemicals.

They reached the dogs, and Will must have given them some kind of unspoken signal, as they all dashed ahead into the woods. Will and Gray followed at a leisurely pace.

"You're very quiet," Will said. He sounded concerned, but before Gray could reassure him that he was absolutely fine, if not a little wowed, Will looked his way, and that sassy grin bloomed again. "I don't think I've seen you look so chilled."

"I'm really enjoying this walk," Gray admitted. Will gave a deep, gentle laugh, completely unmocking, and Gray joined in. "I should go for walks more often."

"Yeah, well, it helps having these guys." Will nodded towards his dogs in the distance. "They're a reason to get up in the morning, put on my wellies and get out in the fresh air. Plus, it's nicer here than where we used to live."

"You've not been here long?"

"This is where I grew up, but I went down to Sussex for uni and stayed there. It was more convenient for getting into the city. I moved back last year, when Mum started to get worse, and it's great for dogs here. Lots of little animals to chase and smells to explore."

Gray took a good, long sniff. The air was much fresher than in the city, and the earthy damp of the woodland triggered all kinds of associated memories of his childhood, growing up in the countryside surrounded by miles of fields. Back then, he'd walked or cycled in all kinds of weather...except the rain. Snow, gale-force winds, flag-cracking sunshine, no problem. Traditional British downpour? Not a chance. Rainy days were for sitting in with a good book and a glass of pop.

Now that they were under the cover of the trees, the light from the street had been blocked completely, and Will extracted a torch from his pocket. Gray instinctively shaded his eyes with his hand. It was very bright, even though it was being cast on the ground ahead of them.

"Wow. And there I was wondering, is that a torch in his pocket, or..."

Will's heartwarming, deep laugh poured over Gray like melted chocolate, and he suppressed a sigh of contentment.

"We'll come out by the canal in a minute," Will said. "Not that it's much lighter there, although a bit spills from the estate and the business park."

"How far are we from your house?"

"Another ten minutes."

The undemanding silence resumed, just the occasional rustle of the trees, dogs snuffling in the undergrowth, and the now-distant hum of traffic. The only downside was that Gray could feel the mud squelching dangerously high up his boots, and if the conditions got much wetter, they'd be trashed. It served him right, he supposed, for not checking in advance, although he didn't own a pair of wellies; there wasn't much call for them in central London.

Fortunately, the canal bank was drier than the woodlands, and as Gray's eyes adjusted to the minimal light, he noticed slow, gliding movement on the surface of the water.

Will cast his torch beam that way. "Swans. They're quite well-behaved, considering."

"Considering?"

"They're swans. They're very protective, and powerful, but I've always found if you leave them alone..."

"You don't talk to them?" Gray tormented.

"Ha. I'm no Doctor Doolittle, but with any animal, it's fairly easy to tune in and figure out how best to behave around them."

"That's what George says too. You're a lot alike, actually."

"In what way?"

"Well, the affinity with animals, for one thing. He works on an educational farm, and before that, he worked on a cattle ranch in the States."

"That's cool," Will remarked unconvincingly.

"Farming doesn't sit well with you, does it?"

"No. I don't believe humans have the right to kill any species. All our knowledge, and the variety of food available to us, there's no need. But I'm not going to start preaching."

Gray laughed. "Preach away."

"George took to surfing well," Will said—a dilpomatic change of subject.

"That's not surprising. He plays football. I imagine that needs good balance and coordination."

"Yeah, and it definitely helps with surfing. I think he maybe got the bug a bit on his honeymoon. He always comments on my posts online. I should probably talk to him more often, but it's...awkward."

Gray didn't need to ask why. He'd been there too, which was a bizarre thing to have in common with Will—both being attracted to the same man—when in all other respects they were nothing like each other.

Will leaned close and said quietly, "This is what I mean about tuning in. See that?"

Gray didn't see anything yet and squinted into the dark, watching the dogs fall back. "What's happening?"

"These idiots coming our way. They go shooting in the woods at night, and we've had a couple of run-ins."

"Are they allowed to shoot there?"

"No, and no-one's been prepared to challenge them, but we're on it."

As Will finished speaking, the silhouettes of two burly men materialised on the path up ahead, accompanied by two large dogs. Both men were dressed in dark jackets with mufflers and woollen hats pulled low, concealing all but their eyes, noses and mouths. If Gray were ever asked to identify the pair again, he would've struggled, which was their intent. Their gun dogs were obedient— lurchers of some sort, Gray guessed. All he knew was they weren't Labradors.

As the two men passed by, one nodded solemnly at Will, the other clicked his teeth at the dogs and held out his hand to wheel-bound Kenny, who emitted a low, warning growl but kept moving. Gray glanced over his shoulder, watching the men continue on their way. When he turned back, Will's dogs had broken formation again.

"That's incredible." Gray was genuinely impressed. "They know exactly what's expected of them."

"Yeah, they do." Will's tone suggested he was smiling, but it was too dark to see. "Because humans and canines have evolved together, a lot of dog behaviour is sympathetic to ours. That's part of Monster's problem. She's very sensitive to changes in mood, and she's picking up on how stressed I am about Mum."

Gray didn't think Will seemed that stressed, although he was obviously going to be affected by his mother's illness. Assuming his mother was ill to begin with, of course. There it was again, that noxious thought. He really needed to kick it into touch. "How is your mum today?"

"Out of it. They think she's probably only got a few days, so they're keeping her comfortable and sedated, other than for visiting time, although I'd rather they didn't, to be quite honest."

"I'm sorry, Will." Gray's guilt cranked up a notch, and yet, however much he tried to pass it off as ex-cop paranoia, he still couldn't shake the thought that something was amiss.

"OK. This is us," Will said, taking a right turn off the path into what looked to be nothing more than a clearing in the undergrowth. Gray followed, swatting back branches and unhooking a stray vine of bramble that wrapped itself around his leg. Will stepped to one side and held open a rickety wooden gate, which he released behind Gray, leaving it to bang shut. Their arrival triggered a sensor, and the space filled with light. Dazzled, Gray took in the sight through the strobed still shots his rapid blinking afforded.

If he'd thought about it at all, which he hadn't, he'd have expected Will's home to look exactly as it did. They had entered a run-down farmyard full of broken mechanical parts; brown weeds tangled in the rusted remains. A dilapidated black lean-to with corrugated roofing rested against the left end of the back wall of the farmhouse, and a couple of moss-hued caravans were parked on the right.

"That's Jon and Micky's place," Will explained as they passed the first van, "and that's Tie's." He indicated to the second.

"People live in them?" Gray asked incredulously. The second caravan barely looked big enough for a person to stand in, let alone live in.

"Yep. Tie's a good friend of mine—an ex from long ago. Jon is Tie's younger brother, and Micky is Jon's girlfriend. And that's where the chickens live." Will pointed to the lean-to as he opened the back door to the house.

Gray dumbly followed him inside, wondering why the door was already open, soon realising that the caravans' inhabitants had free access to the farmhouse, and there was a man standing at the kitchen sink.

"Alright?" Will greeted.

"Alright, mate?" the man responded.

"Tie, this is Gray."

The man identified as Tie turned his head slightly and gave Gray a swift nod. "Good to meet you."

"Likewise," Gray replied, utterly transfixed, first by the man's appearance—he'd never met a white guy with dreadlocks before—and then by what he was doing in the sink. Suffice to say, he wasn't washing the dishes. "Is that, a, er..."

"This is Benjy." Tie lifted the drenched creature out of the sink. "He was a lab rabbit, weren't you, little mate?" Tie wrapped the large, white rabbit in a towel and carried him over to the table, gently setting him down and moving the towel over the rabbit's back with the flats of his hands. "He's got a skin condition, and we have to bathe him every two days to keep it under control."

Gray nodded. The whole situation was so alien to him it had rendered him speechless. While Tie was drying off his rabbit, Will was filling bowls with disgusting-smelling food, three of the dogs following his every move, the other two lapping thirstily from an enormous water bowl in the corner of the room.

"I'll make us a drink in a sec," Will said over the whinnying dogs and the squeaking of something else in a hutch against the far wall. "I'll have to feed the guineas first, though, or we won't be able to hear ourselves think!" He had to raise his voice for the last part, outdone by the crescendo of squeaks.

"I'll deal with them," Tie said, abandoning the towel-swathed rabbit.

Gray eyed the animal in fear.

Tie laughed. "Oh, don't worry about Benjy."

It was all well and good him saying that. Gray had visions of the rabbit making a leap for freedom and being instantly ripped to shreds by the hungry pack.

Will set down the dogs' food bowls, and four of the five started eating. Only Kenny wasn't doing so. Unclipping the harness connected to Kenny's wheels, Will lifted the dog's back end clear of the frame and supported him until he was on the floor. Kenny shuffled closer to his food bowl, the guinea pigs stopped squeaking, and the relative silence of multiple animals having their fill descended.

Will looked across the room and met Gray's gaze, offering him a reassuring smile. "And relax," he said.

Gray hadn't realised it, but his shoulders were hunched, and he was standing rigid. He wasn't even sure why he was so tense. Animals didn't frighten him, and Will's ex-boyfriend or not, Tie seemed a decent bloke. In fact, the entire place was devoid of pretence, and that in itself made Gray feel welcome. He consciously dropped his shoulders and accepted Will's gestured offer of a seat at the kitchen table, under the constant surveillance of the big, wet, white rabbit.

"We'll get out of your hair shortly," Tie said, reconvening the rabbit drying. All the while, the creature's enormous pink eyes remained fixed on Gray. At first, it was disconcerting, watching the twitchy nose and all those tickly whiskers. One of its ears stood fully upright, while the other flopped to the side, like it was broken or damaged, which Gray supposed it might be. In the background, he heard the kettle being filled.

"Coffee or tea, Gray?"

"Coffee, please," he answered, still watching the rabbit, which had once again been left unattended—or not, seeing as Gray was there to catch it, should it bother with anything more than nose-twitching. A moment later, Tie returned with a hairdryer, plugged it in and commenced blow-drying the rabbit's fur. More amazing yet was how it rolled onto one side and then the other to have its belly dried. Something wet touched Gray's hand, distracting him from his viewing. He glanced down to find Kenny peering up at him. Gray frowned, trying to figure out how the dog had made it from the other side of the kitchen, where he'd been eating his supper only a moment before. Another nudge of his hand: Gray got the message and stroked Kenny's head. His coat was sleek and soft, and he tilted his head to the side, pushing his ear into Gray's palm.

"You like that, hey?"

Will laughed, and Gray melted a little more. "He'd let you do it all day."

"I thought you said he was snappy."

"Only with people he doesn't like."

Gray continued stroking Kenny and subtly watched Will. He was leaning against the cupboard, arms folded, ankles crossed, looking handsomely laid-back, but beat. He stifled a yawn. Gray turned his attention back to Kenny again. "How does he get around without his wheels?"

"He shuffles and pulls himself along with his front legs."

"Doesn't it cause damage?"

"Nope. He's tough, and the floors are smooth. Plus, he's got plenty of fur to protect him."

Kenny must have realised Will was talking about him, as he shuffled away, as Will had described, walking with his front legs, his back legs dragging behind him across the tiled floor.

"Wow," Gray said, truly in awe. These people and their animals were like nothing he'd seen before. Not even George's bond with Blue came close. Kenny nuzzled against Will's leg, and Will crouched low so the dog could sniff and lick his face. OK, so that bit made Gray feel a little queasy, but *apart from that*, he was full of nothing but admiration.

"'Kay, dudes. We're outta here," Tie announced, scooping up the now dry and exceedingly fluffy rabbit. He paused and held out his free hand for Gray to give him five, returned the gesture, and then he was gone, leaving Gray and Will alone. Kind of alone, if the five dogs and however many guinea pigs didn't count, but Gray figured they counted more than he did.

Will finished making the coffees and brought them over to the table, sitting in the chair adjacent to Gray's. Kenny and Monster remained nearby; the other three dogs went off prowling. Kenny put his head on Gray's knee.

"You're a handsome chap," Gray said. Will stifled a chuckle. "What?"

"He's ugly as sin."

"No, he's not. Look at those eyes. They're like black onyx."

"And he stinks, don't you, Ken? You're a proper stinky git."

Kenny breathed out heavily—sighing, Gray liked to think—and peered up, blinking those big, soulful eyes. "Don't listen to him," Gray cooed. "He's just trying to put you down." As the words left his lips, Gray realised their other meaning. "Shit. Sorry."

This time, Will didn't hold back and let out a big, rich laugh.

Gray was pretty sure the chair beneath him was the only thing stopping him melting into a puddle.

"He doesn't understand a word you're saying. You know that, don't you?"

"I don't believe you." *Again with the big mouth?* "Dogs must understand some of it or they'd never follow commands."

"True, although it's more about tone and intent than words. Like this." Will looked down at Monster and affected a baby-talk voice. "You did bad things this morning, didn't you, girl? Pooed in Daddy's bedroom and stole Nev's breakfast." The 'little' collie cross was straight up on her feet, wagging her tail like mad, whilst Will continued to berate her in the same cutesy tone. "And you chewed up the chair again, hey? Oh, you are a little sod. Yes, you are."

Gray was laughing so much his sides hurt—something he hadn't experienced in a long time. "OK," he uttered eventually. "Point taken."

Will grinned at him and nodded towards Kenny. "He likes you, Gray. He doesn't usually cope well with strangers."

Gray looked down at Kenny and got the same doleful big-eyed slow blinks. "I like you too, Kenny."

"So anyway," Will said, "you want to talk to me about something?"

"Yeah, I do. Did you hear about the fatal accident involving the banker?"

"That sounds like it's going to end with a terrible punchline. I can't say I did. Why?"

"It's to do with a police inquiry."

"I thought you were done with the police."

"I am, but..." Before he went any further, Gray needed to be sure he could trust Will, and he wasn't. Not yet, but tonight felt different. He wanted to get to know this curious man—the investment banker turned postman with the ramshackle farm and menagerie—not talk about boring police work. Now there was a thought he hadn't seen coming. "Actually, forget I asked. You're right. I am done with the police."

"Fair enough." Will let it go, just like that, which did create an uncomfortable silence, but only briefly, as the phone started ringing. Will answered it, and Gray tried not to listen, not that Will said much. The call continued for a couple of minutes, during which Will listened and hummed in acknowledgement of what the other person was saying, and then scribbled something on a piece of paper and said, "Got it. Later." He hung up and gave Gray a quick smile. "It was about a job."

With that call, Will's demeanour changed, and he was even more cagey than he had been on their date. Gray had been on the brink of convincing himself it was all in his head. Now he was in no doubt: Will *had* lied. The question was why and in relation to what?

"So how would you like to spend the evening?" Will asked. "There's a decent little pub down the road. Fancy a pint?"

8: For She Had Eyes

R OB GOT BACK on his bike and turned to wave at Lucas, who was still standing on the doorstep and looking miserable. His team had lost by a whopping seven goals to nil, and Rob was gutted—for them, and because even primary school football mattered. He'd been on the team all through school himself, and he played on a team at work. He loved it and was proud Lucas was following in his bootsteps.

Zoë's only comment had been, "Never mind, sweetheart. There's always the next game." It had made Rob smile, briefly, until he remembered who else was listening. It had been a running joke in their relationship. When Rob was drowning his sorrows over a defeat, Zoë would raise her glass and say, "Never mind, babe. There's always the next game," to which Rob would protest, "You don't understand, babe. Every goal counts." They never got any further than that because they'd end up tickling each other, laughing, kissing, making love.

But the joke fell flat tonight, with Travis loitering in the hallway, pretending to ignore the banter. What a plonker. He was trying too hard, and Rob couldn't see it lasting. He wanted Zoë to be happy and, in principle, didn't have a problem with her seeing someone else, but Travis was the latest in a line of men who weren't up to the task. Or maybe they weren't up to Rob's high expectations, and in fact, it was he who was hoping someone might just step into his shoes so he wouldn't feel guilty they no longer fitted him.

Whatever, it was none of his business. He started the bike, and with one last wave—Lucas was *still* standing on the doorstep—he turned around and headed for home: his tiny apartment, which was all he could afford after the maintenance payments and the bike. And the takeaways.

Other than the ring road, there was very little traffic about, and as Rob zipped between the cars, his mind wandered to Aaron Tanner. After he'd left Gray in the pub, Rob had gone home and called the number Tanner had given him, expecting to discover Tanner had skipped the country. He hadn't, which put paid to the theory he'd faked his own death to escape liability for Berringer's debts, and put Rob back to square one. Someone had stolen Tanner's identity, but why? And why did Rob even care? It wasn't his case anymore.

They weren't that different, him and Tanner. They'd both lost everything because of their job—families, possessions, their lives—and Rob empathised up to a point, but working for the SIU had hardened his emotions. Those kinds of people, involved in high finance, worked to different rules and had values that set them apart from the rest of society. They were, almost without exception, ruthless, greedy, self-serving and competitive—all positive traits when it came to what they did for a living but hardly qualities for a harmonious social life.

When the real big money was involved, it seemed nobody was immune to its allure, not even lifelong friends he'd thought had everything they could possibly need. That was the hardest part of accepting what Jess had done. They'd known each other since they were four years old, although, being a typical football-and-mates lad, Rob had only thought of Jess as the swotty girl with glasses...until high school, when she'd blossomed into a stunning, curvaceous blonde. And she knew it.

He could remember the exact moment his view of Jess had changed, when she had ceased being the snotty little cow he was always paired with in class to stop him from misbehaving, and became a desirable young woman. It was fourth year of high school, a PE lesson, and as always, the lads were in their kits first, out on the field doing warm-ups. A good few minutes passed before the girls emerged from the building, each carrying a hockey stick.

Rob glanced over in time to see Jess clamp her stick between her thighs so she could tie back her hair. She was talking to one of the other girls, so natural, carefree, none of the usual attitude. She laughed and rolled her eyes, straightened her shirt over her breasts...man, they were something else. She'd had them before that day, but Rob had never really noticed them. They were big and pert, and as she tucked her shirt into her skirt, his eyes travelled down over her slim waist, wide hips, shapely thighs... She parted them to free the hockey stick, and Rob felt a hard smack on the back of his head. While he'd been ogling Jess Lambert, the rest of the lads had got into position and were ready for kickoff. He went and joined his classmates, but it was safe to say his eye was rarely on the ball that day.

From fifth year onwards, Rob and Jess had been an item on and off. It wasn't a relationship, as in they weren't boyfriend and girlfriend because she didn't want that. She was going to be a top lawyer—no time for boys getting in her way. She treated most of the lads the same, like they were good for one thing, with few exceptions. Rob liked to think he'd been one of those exceptions.

At the next set of lights, Rob stopped and lifted his visor to wipe his eyes. It wasn't like him to dwell on loss, but tonight, he was struggling to keep his head above water. The Berringer's case was playing on his mind more than it should. His involvement officially ended at the point when he'd attempted to deliver the bad news to Naomi Tanner, after which he should've signed it off to CID, but Hedley's holiday had left him in limbo. Hedley had said it was the second incident involving someone from Berringer's, and Rob was fighting to suppress his curiosity. He was done with undercover work, and it wasn't his case.

He was so absorbed in his thoughts he missed the lights changing to green, only noticing when they were changing through amber a second time.

"You dozy twat," he muttered and got his head back in the game. He was usually a focused and careful rider—a necessity on a 1000cc Suzuki. He had little opportunity to put it through its paces these days, not since the Strang case. Twelve months ago, the end had seemed a long way off and he'd been desperate for it to be over so he could go back to normal life. But 'normal' had taken on a whole new meaning, and there was little resemblance now to his life before the SIU. The nuts and bolts were still there; his job, for instance, and he was staying on top of it, refusing to let it become the be-all and end-all again. He was spending time with his son, going to footy, and he was no longer in mortal danger, living a lie, pretending to be a rip-off merchant. But he was bored.

Perhaps his mistake had been returning to regular duty 'on the beat', working shifts, filling out paperwork, kicking shoplifting teenagers up the arse. Almost a year down the line, he was struggling to get back into a routine when he'd been without one for so long. With his time in the force, and before that, in the army, it should've been second nature to work within a regimented structure. He knew where he was meant to be at any given moment on any given day. He could plan ahead, take time off...

Or perhaps it was only that he was missing getting out on the bike.

"Yeah. That's all it is," Rob confirmed aloud, and in an instant, his mind was made up. He knew what he was going to do with his evening, and there would be no beans on toast, pizza, Chinese in front of the TV. No lonely drinking in a crowded bar. At the next junction, he took a left and set off for the Western Avenue and out of the city.

9: Ale and Hearty

WILL'S LOCAL WAS a traditional real ale pub with a great atmosphere, friendly and busy but not overcrowded. There were signs and posters everywhere, advertising live music, quiz night, beer festivals—not the sort of place Gray frequented but in keeping with all he knew about Will so far.

"What are you having?" Will asked.

"I'll get these," Gray offered. Will didn't argue. "You'd better choose on my behalf, though."

Will picked out an ale; Gray ordered two pints of it and followed him over to a table. There was an old guy with two Jack Russells sitting at the next table along and a couple standing at the bar with a German shepherd.

"It's a dog-friendly pub," Will explained, unnecessarily. "I've brought my bunch up here a few times."

"Why not tonight?"

Will laughed lazily and put his hands behind his head. "I'm knackered, Gray, and they're hard work."

"You make it look easy."

"Ha. I don't know about that. They're good dogs, but they're all rescues, with their own unique challenges." Will paused and wistfully shook his head. "You probably don't want to hear all that rubbish."

"I'd love to." Gray was aware his prior disinterest had stopped Will from talking about his dogs as much as he'd like. Now he'd met them, Gray genuinely wanted to hear more, but Will still looked doubtful. Gray nodded and smiled in encouragement.

"OK. Well, you know Kenny's story. Doris came from a puppy mill. She's only five, but she's already had at least seven litters. Fido was abandoned at a farm out Hemel Hempstead way. He was there a while before anyone saw him, and he's got a few health problems as a consequence. Monster was a stray we picked up and no-one claimed her. She was in a hell of a mess. And Nev is just part of the homeless Staffie phenomenon. If you ever wanted to adopt a dog, you'd find hundreds just like him in need of a good home."

"Unlikely," Gray said, although he couldn't deny he was rather taken with Kenny. The dog had spirit. "What about the bunny? And the guinea pigs? They're all rescued too, I take it?"

"Yep. The rabbits are from a bioscience research facility down in Wiltshire, and whatever you're thinking about where they came from, you're probably right." Will gave Gray a meaningful look, but Gray had no idea what he was supposed to think. Wiltshire was a big county, and he knew next to nothing about animal research facilities or those who protested against them. It hadn't exactly been part of his remit.

"And the guinea pigs were from a pet shop. They've done the decent thing and stopped trading."

"Of their own free will?" Gray asked, not that he really wanted to know.

"Absolutely," Will confirmed with a wink. "Likewise for the battery farm the chickens came from."

"Right." Gray rolled his eyes. "So, five dogs, a rabbit—"

"Three rabbits."

"Three rabbits, and how many guinea pigs?"

"Just the four now. Some have been rehomed."

"So, five dogs, four guinea pigs, three rabbits, chickens...all you're missing is a partridge in a pear tree."

Will's amused laughter made the skin around his eyes crinkle, giving away his age—coming up on thirty-eight, Gray recalled—and his exhaustion. "No partridges in pear trees, but we do have a psycho parakeet on a perch."

Gray shook his head, but he was laughing too. "You never fail to amaze me." Will was the most contrary person Gray had ever met, and the more he learned, the greater his belief that Will's previous career in investment banking had been a mistake or the result of parental pressure. It was completely at odds with everything else about him.

In the aftermath of Gray's statement, Will kept his gaze politely averted, no doubt waiting for it to be rescinded or justified. It had been quite some admission, but Gray wouldn't take it back, not when it was true. In spite of his minor embarrassment, he was curious. "How did you end up working as a banker?"

Will shrugged. "I'm good with numbers. I loved maths at school so decided to stick with it—joint honours in maths and economics—and the banks came to uni for a careers day. I thought, why not? It's a good job, pays well. It was that or teaching. Or accountancy. God, that would've been terrible."

"Couldn't you work for an animal charity as a fundraiser or something along those lines?"

"I could if I agreed with the practice. It's a waste of money. The big charities that pay out for fundraisers spend a fortune on campaigns, and they pull in a lot more than they fork out, but the work they do isn't direct action. Like the RSPCA. They're rigidly governed by legislation, which is great for dealing with abuse and neglect, so long as there's evidence the law has been broken. But the research labs where Benjy was? They're legal. How do we stop them?"

"Why do you need to? If they're legal..."

"It doesn't mean they aren't cruel. The suffering they inflict is appalling, there's no need for it, and there's not a thing we can do to stop them, not in the short term. We pressure government to change legislation, and we educate so people know which products are cruelty-free, but in the meantime, what happens to the likes of Benjy?"

Gray had no response to that. He could see Will's point about animal research and did his best to buy products that hadn't been tested on animals, but he wasn't sure where he stood on medical research. Perhaps he was misjudging Will in predicting his opinion would become less radical over time, like Gray's had when he lost Jean.

Bereavement was a life-changer, and those old values he'd held so dear suddenly seemed so futile. Like, for instance, the importance of family. It had been easy to dismiss them for the past three and a half years and not feel anything, by blocking those feelings when they did surface. Yet before Jean's death, Gray's sense of rejection had been pervasive, and not a day had passed where he didn't at some point wish his mum would accept him for who he was.

After Jean, he hated her for that rejection, because even if she were to change her mind, it would not bring Jean back, and she'd missed out on meeting the man who made her son happy. The strength of that hatred was easing and no longer cut into him as it once had. Much of the homophobia he'd encountered over the years was down to ignorance. In most cases, addressing it directly dealt with the problem, and Gray still held on to the hope it would be the same with his mum, should he ever gather the courage to tackle her.

Of course, it was a different situation to Will's beliefs about animal research. What if that research could save Will's mum's life? Would he stand by his convictions and let her die?

The beer was going down very well, and it was Will's turn to buy a round, but Gray already had his wallet out. Will put his hand on Gray's arm to stop him, went to the bar and ordered another two pints, scraping around in his pocket for change to pay for them. Gray watched, guessing at what was occurring, as Will examined the coins in his hand and then shrugged at the barman, who said something to him. Will smiled and gave him a thumbs up. He returned to the table bearing two pints and a beguiling smile.

Gray narrowed his eyes. "Everything OK?"

"Yeah," Will said breezily.

Gray wasn't sure what to do for the best, so he let it ride for the time being. It would be his round again next time, and that would probably be it for the evening. He could only hope Will hadn't left himself too much out of pocket.

"You know, I was thinking..." Will kept his gaze on his pint as he spoke. "I kind of cut you off earlier, when you were talking about whatever it was."

"When?"

"Back at the house, when I said you weren't supposed to be doing police work. I didn't mean to criticise."

"It's fine. I didn't take it as criticism."

"How is it you're involved?"

"A friend of mine..." Gray wasn't going to mention Rob by name, but he was going to have to share how he knew him or else there would be nothing left to say. "We worked together in my previous job."

"Right. He's a cop."

"Yeah. There was a fatal accident involving the car of one of the directors of a bank that has recently gone out of business."

"Oh? Which bank?"

"I can't say, but the guy in the car had ID matching the registered keeper. When my friend went to deliver the news to the widow, he came face-to-face with the director instead."

"Hmm." Will chewed his lip in thought. "That's interesting, although I'm wondering why you wanted to talk to me about it, especially as I get the feeling you kind of don't want to talk to me about it."

"It's..." Gray frowned. "I shouldn't be telling you, or anyone else. My colleague—ex-colleague—shouldn't have mentioned it to me. But I figured you might know something about the bank in question, except I can't really tell you any more than I already have."

Gray felt awful. He was essentially admitting he didn't trust Will, when, in truth, he had no idea if he did or he didn't. There were too many unexplained occurrences, like the disappearing act in the club last week and the mystery phone call tonight. Gray wanted to qualify but had a feeling it would only make matters worse. Instead, he just said, "Sorry."

"No need to apologise," Will assured him, but after that, the conversation dwindled, and it was difficult to find something neutral they could talk about in place of their mutual secretiveness.

When they reached the end of their second beer, Gray glanced over at Will. "Do you want another?"

Will wrinkled his nose. "No, thanks. I've had enough. I need to be up early to walk the dogs. But we can always head back to my place for a nightcap?"

Gray was tempted. However, much as he enjoyed Will's company, things seemed to deteriorate when they were alone, or effectively alone. The pub was busy, but their conversation isolated them from what was going on around them. It was also getting late, and last trains were not fun to catch, so he decided to forego the nightcap in favour of a more pleasant journey home.

"I'll walk you to the station," Will offered, and Gray didn't refuse. He wasn't sure where the station was in relation to the pub.

"Is it on your way?" he asked, once they were en route.

"No. But it's not out of my way either."

"In that case, thanks." They walked on for a while, the silence not quite comfortable enough to let it be. "What've you got planned for the weekend. Anything nice?"

"Nope. I'm going to the hospice in the morning, and then my uncle will take over around lunchtime until he goes back up north for work on Sunday. I promised Tie I'd take him up to his boyfriend's tomorrow afternoon, and then I've got to put the van in for its MOT. I don't think it's gonna pass."

"Oh. Not good."

"If it fails miserably, we'll have to get shot, but last time, it only needed new front tyres. Until I start the Royal Mail job, I'm skint. I reckon between us, we could probably stretch to a wheel nut if we're lucky."

"Do the others work?"

"Yeah. When they can get it. Micky works in a nursing home, which is enough money coming in for her and Jon. Tie and Jon do agency work if it's there. The rest of the time, they're tinkers, picking up odd jobs like gardening, decorating—they've even had a go at laying tarmac."

"Laying tarmac?" Gray repeated with a chuckle. "I remember the Irish lads coming round to do that when I was young. Our next-door neighbours foolishly agreed to let one lot have a go. It was one of the worst decisions they ever made."

"Not the worst?"

"No. That was the pebble-dashing. And don't get me started on their conservatory."

"Cowboys, I'm guessing?"

"Cowboys and Indians, I'd say, the amount of noise they made, and it took months to finish. Then the council inspector said they'd breached building regulations, and they were made to pull it down again."

"Sounds like fun times," Will said.

Gray laughed, although he wasn't sure whether Will was being sarcastic or not. "We moved soon after, so I don't know what happened in the end. I remember my mum threatening if they put the thing up again, she'd knock it down herself."

Now Will laughed too, but it wasn't the same cheery sound Gray had heard from him earlier in the evening. He glanced Will's way to take in his facial expression. "Are you all right?"

"Hmm? Oh. Yeah. Just thinking. I haven't heard you mention your mum before, and it made me realise how much I talk about mine."

"That's understandable." Gray wasn't going to ask the question—*is your mum really ill?*—because...it was appalling to even have the thoughts he was having. But he did need some reassurance that he wasn't being led up the garden path, so he went for a slightly different approach. "You know, even though I'm a retired police officer, you don't have to cover up what you do."

"What?" Will seemed puzzled.

"The phone call earlier, and when you disappeared at the club? If it's animal rights stuff, you could just say...I don't know. That you're going to see a man about a dog, or something like that, if it makes it easier."

"At the club? I told you what happened, didn't I?" They'd reached the station, and Will drew to a stop at the entrance. "Did I tell you?" He looked confused, as if he couldn't accurately recall what he'd said.

"You said you'd called your uncle, and he was upset."

"Yeah."

Will's reaction should have left Gray in no doubt that here was a man struggling with tremendous emotional turmoil, as one would expect of someone whose mum was dying. Yet *still* a doubt niggled at him, and there was no reason for it. Well, other than the built-in sensor from years of undercover work. Will triggered it, and Gray couldn't explain why.

"It's been good to see you this evening, Gray."

Gray nodded. "I've enjoyed it." And he had. Especially meeting Will's dogs, which he would never have expected. "Give Kenny a pat from me."

"Will do. Right, I'll head off. Speak to you soon."

"Yeah. Night."

Will raised his hand in a lazy wave of farewell, and Gray did the same, watching a moment longer before going to the platform to wait for his train, pleased that one was due in two minutes. He was surprisingly tired, which he imagined had a lot to do with an hour wasted loitering on set, followed by all the fresh air and walking, plus a couple of pints—three, including the one at lunchtime. To top it off, he had nothing to tell Rob, but perhaps Rob's luck had been better.

The train arrived, and Gray picked the least full carriage, sitting at one end, trying to keep out of the way of other passengers. He was feeling antisocial and a little off his game, which wasn't his style. Not that he had ever been overly sociable, but he didn't mind people usually, and at other times he could fake it well enough to get by. Or he'd always thought he did a good job of faking it, until he worked with Josh. Gray let his thoughts drift back, feeling that flutter of what, these days, was regret and embarrassment for the way he'd fallen for Josh.

He'd never have acted on it, and he'd only told Josh in an ill-measured attempt to put his mind at rest after Josh had misread the signals and decided Gray had a romantic interest in George. It had taken extraordinary effort on Gray's part to convince Josh otherwise without telling him that George was his brother. Of course, he'd told them both eventually, but the time hadn't been right, not least because by that point, Gray had brought Josh in to profile suspects on a child abuse case.

It was incredible, really—that Josh could build a full and accurate psychological profile of a perpetrator, yet he couldn't see the obvious connections between his nearest and dearest. It had to be an unconscious blocking of the stuff Josh didn't want to see. That was Gray's theory, at least, but he was no psychologist, or else he'd have already figured out what Will was up to. Or maybe Will was innocent and Gray was looking for a get-out clause because subconsciously, he wanted more than friendship. It seemed unlikely when they were barely past acquaintance level, which left him with option one: Will wasn't being entirely honest with him. Gray wasn't sure which of the two he least preferred, but he'd had a nice evening. For now, that would suffice.

10: Annual Leave

I T WASN'T ROB'S intention to ride to Oxford, and in truth, he hadn't realised how long he'd been on the road until he saw Shakespeare's name plastered all over the tourist signs. He rode into Stratford, taking the route along the river to a quiet spot not far from the Royal Shakespeare Theatre and parked the bike. It was two in the morning, and Middle England was asleep, leaving perfect stillness and moonlight. Time and space to think.

Ending up in Stratford hadn't been entirely random, but he could've headed south instead of north. Nor could he lay the blame entirely on this being the route he had most often used between Newcastle and London. Each time he'd passed through, he'd told himself: when the Strang case was over, he'd take Zoë and Lucas on an extended holiday to make it up to them and see if there was anything left to rekindle. He'd hire a camper van, drive all around the UK, up to the Highlands and down to the Scilly Isles, stopping in Stratford at least once each way.

The town held a special place in his heart, for it was there that he and Zoë had met. He'd been on duty, and she'd been with a group of her fellow students, out for a day of 'history' before an evening at the theatre to see *Othello*, followed by post-play refreshments. Rob and his partner on the beat that evening had stopped to watch the five young women stagger out of a bar, using language that was a bit ripe for young 'ladies', especially as the young ladies in question were well-spoken, well-dressed and most certainly well-to-do.

As they'd continued on their zigzag trajectory to the next establishment, the heel came off one of the women's shoes, and she'd tilted sideways, lost her balance and fallen into the road, or she would've done, had Rob not swooped in to catch her. She had decreed him her hero—her very own Othello—and planted her wine-wet lips on his cheek. From that moment, he was a goner.

Rob strolled along the dark riverbank, transfixed by the water's silver-and-black shimmer in the sliver of moonlight that hung in the sky like a slash in a blackout curtain. He remembered the days that followed so clearly, they could have happened mere weeks ago.

Zoë was a snob, no two ways about it. Her parents were minted, and she was used to getting what she wanted. There was Rob, a thirty-year-old copper, on duty and in uniform, and there she was, a twenty-one-year-old student, blitzed on wine and insisting they were destined to meet. Rob couldn't deny he felt the attraction, but he couldn't act on it while on duty. Instead, he and his partner warned the five young women to take it easy, bid them good night and went on with their patrol.

The next day, the desk officer called him at home to let him know someone had been into the station looking for him: a Zoë Clifton. It hadn't occurred to him it would be the woman from the night before, but he called the number she'd left and recognised her by her voice. She asked him out on a date. There was no reason for him not to, so he said yes and asked her if she had a problem with bikes, to which she'd replied, "Oh my god, no way, no way! What do you ride?"

Back then, he'd had a Yamaha XJ600, bought when he'd left the army. It was a good runner, but it was old and battered and not really fit for carrying the gorgeous young woman who awaited him, stunning in black-and-white leathers. She admitted she didn't have her own bike, her parents wouldn't permit it, and the minimal wear and tear on her leathers was from tagging along with anyone and everyone who'd let her.

Needless to say, Zoë was convinced the planets had aligned to bring her and Rob together, and their date was spent tearing up the Oxfordshire countryside until she finally, reluctantly, admitted her arms were aching and invited Rob back for a nightcap, which meant what he'd hoped it would. The following morning, on more hours of sex than sleep, Rob worked his shift, went home, napped, showered and went to Zoë's for a repeat performance.

It was a while before they discussed the age difference. If it turned out to be a short-term fling, it didn't matter, but Rob was falling in love, and he needed to know if Zoë felt the same. His answer came in the form of, "Come home with me next weekend and meet my mum and dad," followed by, "Don't mention the bike."

"What's your dream car?" Mr. Clifton had asked.

"A Ducati 999," Rob *didn't* say, and came up with some guff about Porsches instead.

It didn't go down well when Mr. and Mrs. Clifton found out Rob was a biker. He and Zoë had put off telling them for as long as they could, as in, after the wedding ceremony and before they'd zoomed into the sunset on Rob's brand-new Suzuki, a wedding gift from his blushing bride and one and the same bike as he had ridden to Stratford that evening.

He took out his phone and snapped the river in front of him, the dark yet distinctive outline of the theatre on the opposite bank.

Guess where I am. Miss you Zo. x

He couldn't deny it. He still loved her. Coming up on three in the morning, the only thing stopping him from sending that message was the horrible vision of her reading it while Travis lay sleeping at her side.

Maybe one day he would tell her the truth, that he still loved her and would give anything for them to be together again. Until then, it was time he stopped being miserable and moved on with his life. Without looking back, Rob put on his helmet, climbed onto his bike and set off for home.

***

The DCI glanced up from her computer screen, surprised but pleased. "Alright, Rob?"

"Can't complain, Ma'am. How was Turkey?"

"Bloody wonderful. I'm sure you said you weren't in till tomorrow."

"I'm not, but I thought I'd pass on what I've found out."

"You know there's no money for overtime, don't you?" It was said tongue-in-cheek. Rob wasn't on Hedley's payroll.

"I know, Ma'am. It's just that…well, it's taking me a bit of time to adjust."

"So, what've you found out that wouldn't wait another twenty-four hours?"

"Enough to think it might be worth calling in the SIU. The bloke in the car with Aaron Tanner's ID—"

"We haven't been able to identify the body yet."

"I'm aware of that, Ma'am. I had a look at the file and spoke to the dealer. The Berringer's fleet came back in, as Tanner said, and his Merc had less than two thousand on the clock. It was bought for cash the day of the accident."

"Wouldn't you know it?" Hedley muttered.

"I didn't get any further on that score, but I did do a bit of internet research over the weekend."

"Rob, mate, you know annual leave? I think HR might have to set you some rules to follow."

"I wouldn't have bothered, only I was due to go up north and visit my mum, but she went away with my aunt—surprise trip."

"Fair enough. What've you got?"

Rob took out his phone and brought up the images he'd downloaded. "These are from a couple of techie-type websites that ran a feature on Tanner a few years back. Apparently, he was some kind of computer whizz-kid, still at uni when Berringer's started up, and the investors recruited him on a promise."

"Directorship in return for intellectual investment. Nothing unusual there." Hedley turned her computer monitor so Rob could see it. "Remember the other Berringer's director I mentioned? This is her. Carrie Duggan, a language specialist, one of four that the investors brought in, including Aaron Tanner. According to her mum, Carrie went overseas the week before Berringer's ceased trading. Mum hasn't heard from her since, which she says isn't unusual in itself. Carrie's into mountain climbing and all that jazz. But what's different this time is she left no contact details, which is why her mum called us. Carrie booked a flight to Toronto and arrived there, but after that, nobody's heard a peep from her."

Rob didn't see the woman's disappearance as conclusive evidence that something untoward had happened to her, despite what Hedley thought. "I'd probably want to disappear for a while if the company I worked for went bust. It's horrible watching all your worldly goods get carted off."

"It's not like they can't spare it."

"With all due respect, Ma'am, if you saw the mess Tanner was in…"

"My ISA bleeds for him."

Hedley's snipe sent Rob a clear message that defending bankers was not doing him any favours, so he backtracked to the DCI's earlier statement. "You said there were four youngsters brought in. Who were the others?"

"I'll let you know. Everyone's up to their eyes, as per, and that's as far as I've got—in between pointless meetings. But I can tell you the CEO is Frederick Berringer, son of Lord Berringer. He owns the Berringer superstore chain. He's worth billions."

"And what did Frederick bring to the table?"

"Not a lot, as far as I can tell. More likely, the bank was a job creation scheme for young Master Berringer, and Duggan, Tanner et al. get to do all the hard work while Berringer sits in the big chair and watches the money roll in."

"Are you going to pull him in for questioning?"

"He's on jury service."

"That's a pain in the arse."

"For him or us?" Hedley turned her screen back and tapped at her keyboard.

She had a point there. Rob had never done jury service, but he'd played the courtroom waiting game often enough to sympathise with the poor jurors.

"I doubt he had anything to do with Duggan's disappearance or the Merc driver's demise," Hedley said. She stopped typing and huffed. "That's another hour of my life I won't get back. They'll have me counting staples next."

"What makes you so sure about Berringer, Ma'am?"

"He's not the sort to get his hands dirty. If he did have anything to do with it, he'd have drawn on the services of others. We'll keep an eye on him just the same. At least we know where he is." Hedley shut the window on her computer and turned to Rob, studying him intently. "Are you serious about referring this to the SIU? You know better than I do how they work."

"I don't know, Ma'am." Rob wasn't sure how to play it. In the few minutes since he'd suggested it, he'd begun to wish he hadn't. With their resources, the SIU would probably have the case done and dusted in a week, which would be good for their performance indicators, such as they were ever pushed to provide any. But Rob owed them nothing. However, it was more that he wasn't sure if it fitted their remit, and without doing a bit more preliminary work, he wouldn't know.

"OK," Hedley said, settling back in her chair. "Here's what I'm thinking. Tell me if I'm taking advantage, but you're the best man for this investigation, and...to tell you the truth, I want you back on my team. The job's still there, Rob."

Talk about put him on the spot. Rob had no idea what to say, and Hedley forged on before he could come up with anything.

"If I clear it with Mr. Petridis, would you be willing to take the Tanner case?"

"As a detective, Ma'am?"

Hedley nodded. "Temporary secondment, with a view to making it permanent, should you feel it's appropriate at this stage in your career."

Rob was tempted—beyond tempted—and he hated himself for it. True, it wasn't undercover, but if he followed the investigation through, he was looking at working detective's hours, and he couldn't let Lucas and Zoë down. Not again. He needed time to think.

"I don't know if I can, Ma'am."

Hedley leaned forward and clasped her hands together, chewing her knuckle as she considered him. "I get where you're coming from. I do. But don't forget, there's a time limit on it. Petridis isn't going to let me keep you indefinitely, so the ball's entirely in your court. If you want to continue after the Tanner case, we'll do the necessary. If you don't, no problem."

"When d'you need an answer?"

"Well, seeing as you're not officially here today, I'll pretend we didn't have this conversation. Come and see me tomorrow."

"Cheers, Ma'am." Rob took his leave with a growing sense of despondency. It was win some, lose some, whatever his decision, and he was completely torn. An extra twenty-four hours was unlikely to change that.

***

Sod's law would have it that the second Rob set foot in the shower, his phone starting ringing. He'd had no more calls from the mystery number since the previous Friday, and aside from his mum and Zoë—both of whom would try again if it was urgent—no-one else called him.

After he'd left Hedley's office, he'd done the shopping he'd been threatening to do for more than a week, which had taken his mind off his decision for an hour, but it was a conscious effort to not think about Aaron Tanner and Berringer's, and the more he committed to not thinking, the worse it got. He'd painstakingly put the shopping away, cleaning out dregs in cereal boxes and combining the odds and ends of Cup a Soup sachets into one whole box so he had something to do. His plan, should the shower fail to relax him, was to clean the bike, and after that...he should probably cook something, seeing as he now had a kitchen full of provisions.

He wasn't sure why he was so keyed up about investigating Tanner's identity theft. Rob had made it out of sixth form with three A' Levels, but he'd never been the intellectual, problem-solving type. What he did best was the leg work, and credit where it was due, Gray had been spot on in working to his team's strengths. He'd used every one of Rob's—his love of riding, his relationship with Jess and, apparently, his level-headedness—to the SIU's advantage, and that was true for every member of the team.

Dom Hooper was a chameleon, a high-risk player who could blend into any situation. When he wasn't working—about once in a blue moon—he could be found at the roulette table. Then there were those with a financial or legal background, who infiltrated companies at a higher level, and the spies, often double agents whose details were never recorded on official documentation. For every case the SIU investigated, every officer was hand-picked for their specialist skills and knowledge.

Lastly, there was the man at the top: Gray Fisher, or, for the purposes of his last two cases, Graham Farrar. Gray was the intellectual, *a smartarse*, and Rob wasn't alone in thinking it. He didn't often bump into other team members, but when they met up for interim briefings, there were always those who would openly gripe about the pointlessness of the task they'd been given, convinced Gray was trying to keep them out of the way of 'the important work'.

What didn't help was Gray's management philosophy, which seemed to work on the basis that competitive people tried too hard, and trying too hard led to mistakes, therefore his team was more effective if he kept them in the dark. On the plus side, if they didn't know why they were doing what they were doing, they couldn't inadvertently leak it. But when the question 'What's the purpose of this, Sir?' invariably received a response along the lines of 'wait and see', it was safe to say that Rob wasn't the only one tempted, at times, to smack Gray in the face.

It all came together in the end, though, and that, really, was the proof of how good Gray was at his job. He delegated with precision, analysed the information as it came in and adjusted their targets as required, and then collated all of the evidence to pass it on to the CPS or whichever department the referral originated from.

Rob and the rest of the team didn't need to see the big picture to do their job, but Gray always had that vision in mind, and he loved the big reveal at the end. His briefs and debriefs were excellent, the former because it was a chance to get to know each other in a social setting, the latter because it was like watching the conclusion to a televised crime drama, if somewhat less dramatic.

When Rob's phone rang again, he took it as his cue to get out of the shower. He had no idea how long he'd been in there, and he knew what he was doing. Ten months down the line, revisiting his time with the SIU wasn't painful or spiked with the same toxic regret. For the most part, he'd enjoyed the job, and he was wiser now. Never again would he put police work before the people he loved. That didn't mean he had to refuse Hedley's offer, but he would need to stay vigilant to avoid slipping into old habits.

The missed calls were from Zoë, and he called her straight back.

"Hey, Rob. How are you?"

"Fine. You?" He didn't like her bright, chirpy tone. She was scheming something.

"Yeah, same. Did Lu ask you about taking him to the cinema?"

"No. He didn't mention anything about the cinema."

"Oh, well...there's a movie he wants to see, and, er, I thought you and he might like to do that tonight?"

"It's a school night, Zo."

"The movie starts at five."

Rob pulled his phone away so he could check the time. He had exactly forty-five minutes to get dressed, pick Lucas up and get to the cinema. He put the phone back to his ear and drew breath to tell her he wouldn't make it.

"Or there's a showing at six," she added helpfully.

"Why?"

"What d'you mean?"

"Obviously, you've got plans for this evening, or you wouldn't be asking."

"That's not fair, Rob."

"Yeah, whatever."

She sighed into the phone. "OK. Fine. Travis promised to take him, but he can't, and Lu's gutted."

Rob didn't know whether to punch the air and do a victory dance that The Mighty Travis had cocked up or find him and kick his arse. He punched the air and banked the arse-kicking for later.

"Tell Lu we'll catch the six o'clock showing."

He heard her repeat what he'd said, followed by a yell of "Yes!" from Lucas, which was all the payback he needed.

Zoë came back on the line, laughing. "Thanks, Rob." For once, her words held the affection of old, and he stayed quiet for a moment to relish the feeling.

"Right, I'd best get a move on. See you in a bit."

11: Nomad Naomi

GOOD MORNING, Ms. Silvestri. Will you require a paper today?"
Naomi stopped, took a second or two to compose herself, turned and walked back to the reception desk. "Yes." She offered the concierge her best smile. "Thanks so much."

The concierge nodded an acknowledgement, and Naomi set off again, towards the lift to her room. She regretted checking in under the name Silvestri. She hadn't thought it through in advance, and when put on the spot, it was the first name that came to mind. It could lead anyone who dug too deeply straight to her.

Two weeks ago, she'd checked into the Claremont Hotel with a change of clothes, her handbag, her make-up and a toothbrush. At some point, she'd put on all of the clothes and walk out without paying her bill. And go where? She didn't know. She was starting to feel like a common criminal, though she'd done nothing wrong, and now the man she loved—her only ally, the person who knew her best of all and loved her in return—was dead. Never had she been so lonely and afraid.

So many times, she had taken her phone in her hand and brought up the number of the policeman who had visited Aaron. So many times, she had been on the cusp of calling and telling him everything, but what would it achieve? The very best-case scenario, if she went public now, was a prison term for more or less every fraudulent act punishable by law. Chances were, they'd charge her for the murder too, and where was her alibi? Would the landlady even remember her being there, in that back-street pub, not two hundred yards from where he died?

In the papers, they'd reported that the body had not yet been identified, but she knew it was him. If not, then why hadn't he contacted her? She could have identified him, if only she could have gone to the police.

She was heartened that her picture had not appeared in the press yet. No-one had noticed the Tanners were missing, and that was good. It meant she still had time to get away; all she needed was the means to do so. She had a passport—or at least, *Naomi Silvestri* had a passport—but no money to buy a ticket. The liquidators had taken her phone, computer and tablet, and with them, all her contacts at home and abroad. So even if she could get hold of the money, she had literally nowhere to go.

There was no other option. She had to call him.

The phone rang out three times and picked up. She listened to the silence and established it was him, not his voicemail.

"Freddie, it's Naomi."

The silence continued. She was about to speak again.

"I'll call you back," he said and ended the call.

Her hand shook as she watched the phone within it, waiting for the screen to illuminate with the incoming call. Ten minutes passed by with no call. Twenty minutes. She walked over to the kettle and switched it on. It boiled. Still no call. She made a cup of Earl Grey; a knock came at the door. Her paper. She thanked the bellboy and returned inside, browsing absently, tears welling, spilling over. Finally, her phone rang.

"Where are you?" he asked.

"In a hotel."

"Which one?"

"I'll meet you at—"

"Damn it, Naomi, we're in deep enough already. Which hotel?"

She sighed, defeated. "The Claremont. Room 391." She would have to check out sooner than she'd hoped. "I need you to bring money."

He delayed in his reply; it was telling. "I'll see what I can do." Again, he ended the call.

With tears freely streaming, Naomi put on the rest of her clothes, patched her make-up as best she could, packed her toothbrush and the miniature bottles of generic toiletries into her bag, and walked away.

***

"Going somewhere, sweetcheeks?"

For a few seconds, Naomi kept walking, each click of her heels against the pavement an echoing boom in the silence of a side street packed with people, mute smiles and conversations, noiseless cars, the tunnel that closed in all around. Her steps slowed as she fought the urge to drop to the ground and submit. The black limousine kept pace.

"You called me." He knew she'd heard him.

"I changed my mind."

Under his breath, he muttered, "For fuck's sake," but said, "*Please* get in the car, Naomi."

"I don't need—"

"Stop here."

His command, directed at his driver, had the same effect on Naomi. The door opened, and he advanced. With her eyes to the ground, his tuxedoed presence fell into her peripheral vision and she couldn't see his face, but she smelled the alcohol as he came up close, murmuring hot breath against her cheek. "I haven't even been home yet, do you know that?"

She nodded, breathing through her mouth, afraid and repulsed and wishing she hadn't called him.

"I brought the money you asked for."

"It doesn't matter."

"Methinks the lady doth protest too much."

"I can't stay, Freddie."

"I didn't ask you to. Look at me." She closed her eyes, shook her head. "Naomi, please."

The words escaped in a whisper. "I'm scared."

"I know." He clasped her head to his shoulder, caressing her, trashing her hair. The lapel's braid dug into her cheek, and she pressed harder, revelling in the pain. His champagne sigh warmed her scalp. "I know." Leaning back, he hoisted her chin with his finger, forcing her to meet his gaze. She saw no kindness there, but then, she had not expected to. "I have the money and documents," he said.

"I only need money."

"I'm afraid the documents are part of the package. I don't plan on losing you too." Before she'd even formulated the thought to agree and double-cross him, he added, "Don't push your luck, sweetcheeks."

"I want out."

"It's not an option."

"Then I'd rather be dead."

He didn't argue. He released her, gave her one last hard look, and strolled back to his limo. It moved off slowly, joining the other cars, becoming noiseless.

12: Gatecrashing

IT WAS AS well Gray had steered clear of the spirits. The time was fast approaching two a.m., and the ten bottles of Belgian wheat beer—which he'd bought on the premise they'd last out the week and then finished in one sitting—had made him morose. But for once, his misery hadn't dumped him in the deep dark abyss of Life After Jean.

He pondered on that awhile, trying to decide if he felt guilty—which he didn't—and then whether he should feel guilty about not feeling guilty.

Guilt-free, ethereal, divine.

Two a.m. in the reality of a drunken Gray Fisher was a twilight zone in which he could communicate with the dead. Not all of them, thank goodness. There were quite a few he was glad were on the other side of the curtain, including his philandering father—a phrase he'd tried out in the full array of Scottish accents for it sounded much better than in English—but when a good dose of alcohol had softened the edges of the world, blurring the boundaries, Gray felt Jean's presence, he was sure of it, or as sure as he was of anything.

He'd talked himself hoarse, telling Jean all about Will and his dogs. Four days had passed with no contact. No phone calls, no text messages, and he wasn't online. Gray didn't know if that was atypical or not. What *was* atypical was that he was paying attention, hence his lack of frame of reference.

He was worried about Will, which was...promising, and his pleasure at being worried appalled him. But how could he not be pleased when his concern indicated that, in spite of his doubts on other matters, Gray believed Will had been truthful about his mum.

"I disgust me," Gray admitted to Jean, or to his semi-comatose common sense. He was still a long way from sober but not quite as far into drunk as he had been an hour ago, when he'd commenced his one-person séance. "It's so petty. Why do I care if he's lying about..." He didn't know what, or why. He had no logical explanation for the feeling.

It had to be some kind of mental illness—the remnants of his addiction maybe? Or post-SIU stress syndrome? Whatever the cause, he'd developed an unhealthy obsession with uncovering the truth, which was useful when he was on the job. Off the job, it was debilitating, infuriating. It was like a sixth sense, a reflexive deception detector that made it impossible to trust first impressions, or trust anyone at all.

"I'm not even sure I trust Josh and George, not one hundred percent. George...he's got plenty of motive to hate my guts. I'd hate my guts if I were him. And Josh..." Gray mumbled incoherently, effectively backtracking and admitting he probably did trust Josh, lest Jean take his mental infidelity to undead heart.

"I trust Rob, though." That was easy. The man was like some kind of moral automaton: key in the algorithm for 'the right thing to do' and run the programme. That wasn't to imply Rob was unthinking; nothing could be farther from the truth. For Rob, the decision was front-loaded, and once he'd analysed the situation and come up with a strategy, he worked with single-minded diligence, unceasing until his mission was accomplished.

As for Will, Gray wanted to trust him, wanted to be proved wrong. He shouldn't even be questioning Will's integrity, but there had been so many people in Gray's personal life who had let him down, abused his trust or been absent when he needed them, Jean included.

Gray realised his trust in Rob and Josh—and Dom, for that matter—came from their professional bonds, not personal. There were a few other friends he'd made contact with when he was in the process of moving to London, but there was a distance between them that hadn't existed before the accident. However, it wasn't losing Jean that had caused it, or not directly. It was Gray's coke habit.

With Josh...well, Gray's pride had taken a nosedive for a while there, and he still felt more than he should. He couldn't help that, and it wasn't as if it were some kind of teenage crush that made his foolish heart ache and yearn. He'd fantasised romancing Josh, breaking through the cool, passive exterior to the beautiful, vulnerable man beneath. They shared so many interests and could have done so much together. Read literature, discussed politics, visited galleries and museums, made love.

In all except the last regard, the dream bore no resemblance to Gray's relationship with Jean, who was no intellectual, yet they had fallen in love just the same. As Josh had said, love had less to do with similarity than compatibility, how two individuals complement one another, coming together to form a perfect whole. Josh and George were two halves of a whole, as Gray and Jean had been, and Gray had no intention of damaging perfection. Josh had eyes only for George, as it should be. Gray accepted the lesson he had learned from falling for Josh—that he could still feel, he was still alive—and got over it.

He laughed and shrugged, peering up 'at Jean'. "Yes, I'm a fool. And I still love you. And miss you. I miss...hearing your car pull up, the jingle of your keys, that awful song you used to hum under your breath. What was that? 'It started with a kiss'? No, it'll come to me. It'll come to me...

"And I miss your food, oh, God, I miss your food. Have you any idea of the junk I've been surviving on? I guess you probably do. I tried to make those croquettes. I had a craving for the taste, the texture. They weren't the same. I wish I'd asked you what went in them. I got the potatoes and scallions right, and salt, garlic...*mon Dieu*, they were a mess. A terrible mess. Although...I don't miss cleaning the kitchen when you're done." Gray hugged his knees to his chest. His smile faded. "I'm lonely, Jean."

***

Rob had left a voicemail, but Gray didn't see it until he stopped for lunch. Being able to leave his phone unchecked for hours at a time was a luxury he doubted he'd ever tire of, and he delayed returning the call, mainly because he had no information to pass on. He listened to the message again; it was short and appropriately cryptic—*"Alright, Gray? Any joy yet? Catch up with you later"*—yet rich with detail. First and foremost, it made clear that Rob was still investigating Berringer's bank, although whether it was out of personal or professional interest, it was difficult to tell. It wasn't a uniform officer's job—no time and not enough manpower—so if Rob was officially still on the case, he was working for Hedley. Unless...

"No, he wouldn't," Gray thought aloud, skipping over the bit that was too improbable to seriously consider: Rob was undercover again. He hadn't sugar-coated how he'd felt about working with the SIU, but even if he'd been more subtle in expressing how much he hated it and, by extension, Gray, it had been there in his tone, weary and resigned. Rob wasn't unique in that regard; there were a few officers whose 'voluntary' stint with the SIU was performed under duress. They'd been approached for their expertise and agreed for career enhancement. There was something inherently unethical about their recruitment, but Gray hadn't dwelt on it. Someone had to do the job.

What made Rob's voicemail distinct from every previous communication was that there was no reticence, no regret, and no doubt in Gray's mind that Rob was pursuing the Berringer's case of his own free will. It made the decision to help him sit easier. Whether it was with CID, the SIU or some other unit, Gray could legitimately forward an information request on Rob's behalf. He brought up Dom's number and made the call.

"You're missing me, aren't you?" Dom said. His greeting made Gray laugh.

"Always. Everything OK?"

"Not bad. I'm about to click send on this email. I got what you asked for, PNC records and all."

"Hold that button push. Can you dig out the file on Berringer's bank?"

"I can, but...am I right in thinking they were cleared?"

"They were. Unrelated. There's a drink-driving investigation allegedly involving a director, or ex-director."

"Gotcha. Give me twenty, and I'll send it through with the other stuff."

"Thanks, Dom." Gray ended the call, sent Rob a text message to let him know he was working on it and would forward what he'd found, and returned to his study with his lunch.

The article he'd been reading had been replaced by his screensaver, and he left it undisturbed to better appreciate his food. That was another thing he didn't miss about the SIU: eating while trying to type up a report, drive the car, make a call, climb the stairs, or whatever else was happening at the same time as he noticed he was hungry enough to pass out. Jean would've been furious with him, the way he'd abused his diet. Between the job and cocaine, Gray had lost two stone, and he'd been a little under his normal weight to start with.

He vividly recalled the horror of realising how dire his health was the day he'd brought Josh down to London to view a crime scene. One split second of catching his reflection in a shop window, and it hit Gray like a dive into icy water. He was sick. He'd messed up on the case, put the people he cared about at tremendous risk. He needed help. Rather than ask for it, he'd gone on a bender. A serious bender. Coke, crack and pretty much anything else he was offered. Even for someone as hell-bent on self-annihilation as he was, he'd had way too much. When the local police picked him up, he'd asked—more like demanded— they call Josh, not because of his feelings. He'd honestly thought he was going to die.

In some ways, that wasn't extraordinary. He'd had plenty of extreme highs and come-downs when he'd briefly wondered if that was it. What had differed on that occasion was the fear. He didn't want to die, and he'd been terrified it was too late.

So much for enjoying his lunch. He'd eaten the entire sandwich and not registered a single mouthful. Unlocking his screensaver, he found the point he was up to in his reading and tried to continue, but he was having the same trouble digesting the words. He checked his inbox again: no message from Dom yet. Back to the article, another paragraph read and re-read. He opened his browser, scrolled through his newsfeed, checked his inbox again—still nothing—and cursed his procrastination as he took out his phone. There was a text message from Rob that said '*cheers*'. Two below it was the last message from Will, sent the previous Friday. He hadn't noticed it before, and he clicked on it, smiling at the truth of '*we're outside the station – can't miss us*'.

"I should check in, make sure he's OK," Gray thought aloud and, to that end, clicked reply. He got as far as typing '*Hey, Will...*' and changed his mind. It was far easier to gauge intent from a phone call, plus...there was too much at stake.

The call didn't connect at first, and when it did, the poor signal chopped Will's greeting into "Oh-oh, he-ey."

"Hey. This is a really bad line. Where are you?"

"On the train. The hospice called to…"

The rhythm of the train's progress still reached Gray's ear. The cut-off had been Will's. "I'm sorry, Will. What can I do?"

"Nothing, really. Tie's with the dogs. My uncle Jim's on his way, but he won't get here in time. I've just got to do this."

"You're on your own?" Gray asked.

"Yeah."

Whatever Gray's doubts, they vanished in an instant at the prospect of Will facing his mum's death alone. "Do you need some company?"

"Thank you, but…you don't have to."

"No, and you don't have to accept, but I mean it. Tell me which hospice and I'll be there."

The train rattled on. Gray waited out the seconds.

"St. Michael's, North London. I'm not sure which route's best."

"It's OK. I'll figure it out. I'll see you soon."

"I'll tell reception to expect you. Thanks for this, Gray."

Before Gray could tell him no thanks were needed, Will had hung up. Gray grabbed his jacket and left straight away, checking the location on his phone en route to the station.

Three line changes and a five-minute walk later, he reached the hospice's reception desk. The woman behind it was speaking on the phone but acknowledged his arrival with a swift nod. She was very solemn, which was to be expected in a hospice, although she was wearing a vibrant red trouser suit and about a hundred silver bangles that tinkled tunefully as she put the phone receiver down and peered up at Gray. "Sorry about that. Can I help you?"

Gray stopped dwelling on the juxtaposition of her cheery attire and smile-less expression to answer her question. "Afternoon. I'm a friend of Will Richards. His mum's a patient here."

"What's your name, please?"

"Gray Fisher."

The receptionist smiled then. "Will's expecting you. I'll take you through." She came around to the front of the desk and led the way along a short corridor with doors off either side. She knocked on the last door on the right, opening it at the same time. "Your friend's arrived."

"Has he?" Gray didn't care for the obvious surprise in Will's tone, but he wasn't going to call him on it today.

The receptionist pushed the door fully open and retreated along the corridor. Gray watched her while he waited for the bolt of reality to work its way through his system. In his peripheral vision, he could see Will, and beyond him, the room, flooded with natural light and seemingly sparse in terms of furnishings. "You doing all right?" he asked, slowly turning to face Will and wishing he'd waited to ask the question. Understandable as it was in the circumstances, it was a killer seeing another man fall apart. "Hey, come here." Gray stepped into the room and pulled Will into a hug, their first proper physical contact.

"I stink," Will mumbled through his tears, puffing hot breath that penetrated both Gray's jacket and shirt. He had noticed Will was a bit on the sweaty side, but he didn't smell that bad. "I'd only just got back with the dogs when they called."

"What did they say?"

"Today."

Gray hadn't dared look past Will, but he did now, his gaze avoiding the bed to his right as he took in the picture window, reclining armchair, bookshelves and TV, light beech floor, bathroom off to the left, hoist, thick mattress warped into a flattened 'U', and finally, the woman lying upon it. Will's mum.

Her head was wrapped in a brightly tie-dyed bandana. Her face held the smooth serenity of unconsciousness. There were no machines attached to her—no machines at all in this strange room that was both clinical and informal. Nothing like the room in which Gray had watched the dark screens of disconnected monitors rather than witness Jean take his last breath.

Will moved away and tugged at his T-shirt sleeve, using it to wipe his eyes. He gave a quiet, self-conscious chuckle. "Sorry."

Gray shook his head and brushed a hand over Will's arm. There was nothing he could say, and he would be guided by whatever Will wanted to do. Will beckoned to him and walked around the bed, where there was a second chair, which he sat in, leaving the recliner for Gray.

"Mum," Will took her hand, "this is my friend Gray."

"Hello," Gray managed to squeeze out before his stoic determination wobbled, was rescued briefly by Will's cheeky, if not a little bloodshot, wink, and then completely obliterated by his next words.

"See? I told you I'd bring someone home to meet you before you popped your clogs, didn't I?"

Keeping his head bowed, Gray tried to pull himself together. As it should be, Will was focused on his mum, stroking her hand, watching her breathe. "I'm ready," he said quietly.

Gray swallowed a sob. His throat spasmed painfully. Tears escaped and ran down his nose. He tried for a stealthy sniff.

"There're some tissues over there."

"Thanks." Gray went to deal with his stupid face, still fighting for control over his tears. They had no right to flow. It was not his time to grieve, and though it was for Will he cried, it was a strong shoulder to lean on that Will needed most. From across the room came a sharp gasp. It was happening.

"See that button on the other side of the bed?" Will's voice was quiet and steady.

Gray turned only as far as was needed to see that part of the room. "Yes." He moved towards it.

"Can you press it, please?"

Keeping his back turned to Will and his mum, Gray lifted the plastic tab connected to the wall by a thin beige flex and pressed the button on top of it.

"She's gone," Will said.

"Has she?" He knew, of course. He made a slow about-turn and watched Will fall forward, still clinging to his mum's hand, pressing his lips to her skin as the sobs wracked his body, leaving him heaving and lost.

The door opened. People entered, one, two, three of them...and passed Gray by. He took a couple of steps back to keep out of the way. "Oops. Sorry."

The nurse startled but quickly recovered from her stood-upon toes. She smiled at him. "Are you Will's partner?"

"A friend."

"Ah. Sorry about this, but you need to step outside."

"Sure." Gray moved towards the door. "Is there somewhere I can wait?"

"The lounge—just the other side of the reception."

"Thanks." He retraced the route back to the reception area and through it, to a square room with sofas lining two walls, a TV and games console on the third, windows on the fourth. He sat on the closest sofa and rubbed his face, stretching his eyes open to stave off his sudden weariness. He should've asked the nurse to tell Will he was waiting, but she probably knew to do that. Better still, he should've answered yes to her question. At least there was nowhere he had to be on a Tuesday afternoon, so he could stay for however long Will needed him.

It wasn't a scene Gray wanted to imagine, but his mind went there anyway. If he were in Will's place, it would be different, less painful perhaps, because Gray had, out of necessity, already grieved for his mum to a certain extent. He still loved her and missed her, and he doubted he'd ever stop hoping she'd change, more so when he witnessed other people's losses at close quarters. He didn't want it to be too late.

That would be when it hit him hardest, when he had to accept they would never 'reconcile their differences', as Becky had put it, like he could compromise, but that was what they'd been brought up to believe. According to his mum, people chose to be gay or bisexual. They didn't have to be that way. When Gray eventually understood it was about more than 'making the right choice', he'd mustered the courage to talk to her, genuinely believing she might be a little bit shocked at first, but then she'd adjust and accept it.

Instead, she'd stepped up her efforts, thrusting articles from gossip magazines in his face that reported horrifying statistics on HIV and AIDS among gay men, or 'success stories' of people who'd 'grown out of' their homosexuality. He'd gone away to uni, glad to escape but also wondering if he might, actually, grow out of it. He'd managed one drunken fumble with a girl who had taken his lack of arousal personally and then slapped him hard when he'd apologised and said he thought he was gay. After that, he'd joined the LGBT and met other people who had been through similar experiences with their families, and he accepted once and for all it wasn't a matter of choice.

So there would be no meeting his mum halfway, not even if she were on her deathbed. She accepted him or she didn't, and he'd survived this long without her. He just wished he could stop caring, but he couldn't. He could, however, stop thinking about it. That *was* a choice.

There were magazines on the table in the centre of the room, mostly of the kind he'd been thinking about. He gave them a miss and checked out the bookshelf, shaking his head in dismay. Modern crime thrillers—same plot, different protagonist. He gave up and took out his phone. The email from Dom was at the top of his inbox, unread, but he was coming around to the possibility that his suspicions about Will were unfounded. He ignored the attachment titled 'Document 26', made a mental note to suggest Dom revisit the SIU manual on file-naming conventions, and opened the second attachment, more usefully titled—he'd created the file himself—'6429DGF_Berringers.zip'.

His phone couldn't decompress the file, and he had to download an app, which took a while. He wasn't sure how long it was since he'd left Will. He'd caught the 13:40 train, and it was coming up to four p.m. The app downloaded and installed. Gray clicked the zip file and chose the personnel spreadsheet from the preview window. The resulting list displayed all Berringer's personnel, ordered by last name. Gray scrolled through, scanning the names all the way down to *Tanner, Aaron*. He stopped and scrolled back.

"Not *William*. Huh."

"Who, me?" Will said.

Gray jumped an inch off the sofa. "I didn't hear you come in."

"Sorry. Everything's...done."

Gray put away his phone and stood up. "How are you doing?"

Will nodded blankly. "OK, I think. *Did* you mean me?"

Gray frowned. "What, the William thing?" His undercover skills appeared to have deserted him.

"Yeah. Did you think Will is short for William? Most people do."

"Erm, well, yes, but..." Gray motioned to where he'd been sitting, for no reason whatsoever.

"Listen, would you mind..." Will scratched his head and pulled a face when he caught a whiff of his armpit. "Better make it a quick one, but can we find a pub?"

"Sure."

"Thanks." Will moved towards the door. "For everything."

"Hey, it's fine."

Will offered him a watery smile. "It's not William, by the way."

"I gathered. What is it?"

"Take a guess."

Richards, Wilfred. "Wilbur?"

"Close."

13: Misfire

GRAY WAS SUFFERING the aftermath of his late-night solo beer-drinking, but he'd bought a pint for the sake of camaraderie, and he was making it last. Will was on his fourth, and the alcohol, on top of the situation, had made him chatty. It had also made it necessary for him to take increasingly frequent toilet breaks, the latest of which he returned from with a run-on statement of, "I really need to shower, I should go home, my dad'll want to know, I wonder if he's still got the same number."

It wasn't the first time Will had mentioned his dad, but he had only mentioned him, so all Gray knew was Will's parents had parted ways when he was young, and his dad travelled a lot. It sounded more like backpacking than for business purposes, though everyone had to make a living somehow.

"What does your dad do?"

"He's a nurse."

"A nurse." Gray was pretty sure he'd failed to hide his surprise, but Will didn't seem to notice.

"Yeah. Children's nurse. There's a new children's hospital being built in Johannesburg. If he stays, he'll be working there once it opens." Will picked up a beer mat and tapped the edge of it against the table, becoming quiet as his thoughts took over. It didn't last long.

"I don't think he's spoken to Mum since she was diagnosed. They didn't talk often anyway, but Dad can't help himself. You only have to hint you're sick— even if it's a common cold—and he's off. 'Take this, do that.' He's a know-it-all, and he got on Mum's nerves. He'll want to come to the funeral, though. I'll deal with that tomorrow. The hospice gave me a list of funeral directors and a booklet detailing everything I need to do."

"If you'd like me to tag along..." Gray offered.

Will smiled wearily. "If you don't mind. I've not done it before. When my grandma died, Mum dealt with the arrangements. Well, I guess the funeral director sorts everything out."

"They do," Gray confirmed.

"I couldn't cope with ordering coffins and stuff right now."

"No, they do all that for you."

"She didn't want a big fuss, she said. Whatever's easiest for me." Will noticed his half-finished pint and picked it up, nursing it without drinking any. He shook his head. "Sorry. What did you say?"

"About the funeral director?" Gray asked. Will nodded, for what it was worth. His eyes had that stoned-on-stress glaze, but Gray pressed on anyway. "They arrange everything for you."

"Right. Cool." He put his glass down again. "The tenancy agreement is already in my name, so there's no inheritance stuff to do. And I need to close her bank account. I'll have to register the death first, I guess."

After the ordeal of processing Jean's estate, Gray sympathised. The will had gone through without a problem. Under Belgian law, Gray and Jean's partnership was considered equal to marriage. However, providing the correct documentation to the banks, the police and everyone else had Gray at the point where he contemplated forgoing the inheritance in favour of keeping what little of his sanity remained.

"Hey, I owe you big time for today."

Gray smiled and squeezed Will's hand. "You owe me nothing."

"I wouldn't have coped on my own. It seems silly to say, when I've been doing it for so long."

"What about your uncle?"

"He comes and goes. He couldn't deal with it, when Mum started losing control of her body, you know? Soiling herself and needing to be fed. Until a couple of months back, she was still kind of with it, and she hated it, me cleaning her up. The carers were great, came and got her up in the morning, put her to bed at night. In between, it was down to me. Jim couldn't do it. And the worse she got, the less he was around. Which sounds awful when he's been really good. He got the shopping in, picked up prescriptions and things like that. What are your plans for the rest of the evening?"

Luckily, Gray had been paying attention, or he'd have missed the quick change. "I don't have any, beyond eating at some point. So if you need me to stick around, I'm happy to do so. Equally, if you want some time on your own, I'll head home."

"Thanks. I'd... OK, I know we're only friends, but it's years since I've been in a meaningful relationship and we're not even screwing each other." Will's previously pale cheeks turned blotchy pink. "That didn't come out quite how I intended."

Gray hid his amusement at Will's accidental admission, at the same time saddened by the implication. Will had been on his own a long time, and not by choice. He'd been honest about seeking a deeper level of involvement, and Gray hoped their friendship wouldn't stand in Will's way if the opportunity presented itself with someone else. He'd have told him as much, but now was not the time.

Will was back to gazing into his beer, so Gray cut to the chase. "What do you want to do?"

"I need to get back for the dogs. Takeaway at my place? There's a tandoori with a decent menu."

"That suits me."

"Great." Will rose from his seat, leaning a hand on Gray's shoulder as he edged past to take one last trip to the Gents'. The slow release was not imagined.

They walked to the station in silence, no awkwardness. Even in the circumstances, Gray appreciated the easiness of being with Will. He was quite something, the way he could work around whatever life sent his way. Regardless of what Will had said, Gray was an added extra. Will could have made it through the day without him. Not that Gray was intending to withdraw his support; rather, he admired Will's strength of character. That he'd been able to help him at all was a privilege.

"That's one of the many positives of having dogs," Will said once they were on the train. It was rush hour, and the carriage was packed, leaving them standing so close together Gray felt the press of Will's chest each time either of them took a breath.

"What's that?"

"It doesn't matter what else is going on, they need me. I have to be there for them."

"A lot of people would see that as a burden."

"Like you, for instance?"

The question caught Gray off guard, but it shouldn't have done. He'd been using his personal beliefs about pet ownership as a barometer for everyone else. Whenever Becky went on holiday, she had to put her dog in kennels, and George and Josh had taken their dog on their honeymoon. To Gray's mind, pets tied their owners down and created additional stress with their constant need for food and walkies and the expense of vet bills. Or that was what he'd believed before he'd met Will's pack.

"No," he answered, although enough time had lapsed for the question to have become rhetorical. "I did think that, and they are a burden financially."

"They more than pay their way," Will argued.

Gray smiled. "No argument there." He wasn't thinking ahead, but at some point this evening, when he went home, he knew Will's emotional needs would be met not by Tie, but by Kenny and the crew. They were there for him as much as he was there for them.

It was all quiet when they arrived back at the house—nothing like the last time Gray had visited. He looked to Will and shrugged in query. Will raised his index finger in a 'wait for it' gesture and called, "I'm home." All hell broke loose in an explosion like frontline cannon and gunfire as the five dogs came tearing into the kitchen, scrabbling to gain traction on the tiles beneath their paws, with the exception of Kenny, who skilfully speed-shuffled across the room and ploughed through the others to reach Will.

It was one of the most touching scenes Gray had ever witnessed, and hilarious. Will crouched low to receive the love and affection of his pack, and it took only one sturdy nudge from Kenny's big nose to topple him. Will sprawled with his back on the floor, and the dogs descended, two of them slobbering all over his face, one lying on his chest, and the little terrier—*Doris?*—had grabbed the stretchy band tying Will's hair back and was pulling it and growling. Through tears of laughter, Gray spotted Kenny coming his way. He knelt, rather than crouched, and stroked the dog's broad skull.

Just as it seemed the furore might die down, the squeaking symphony of the guinea pigs started. Will slowly sat up, keeping hold of Monster's collar as he did so.

"She'll leg it now if I let go," he said quite loudly, and Gray still had to strain to hear him. Once Will was on his feet, he released Monster. She bolted from the room, and Will sighed. "She'll be fine." Gray couldn't decide which of the two of them he was assuring. "Want to meet the guineas?"

Gray nodded noncommittally and followed Will across to the large hutch on the other side of the room. Will thumbed the wooden catch and slowly dropped the door.

"Oh!" Gray said.

"What?"

"I thought they were smaller."

"They're about average size."

"I mean *much* smaller."

Will reached inside the hutch and retrieved an empty flat brown dish. "Were you thinking of hamsters?" he asked on his way to the sink. "I wish they'd stop peeing in this."

Gray only half heard him, more concerned with the row of brown-and-white fur balls lined up along the front of the hutch. It was a three-foot drop to the floor, and they didn't strike him as the kind of creatures that could jump.

Will returned with the dish, now full. "Or gerbils maybe?"

"Maybe," Gray agreed absently. "Looks like the muesli Jean used to eat."

"Yeah." Will laughed. "It probably doesn't taste like it." He put the dish back inside the hutch, and the guinea pigs descended on it. Peace resumed, and Will exhaled in relief. "That's better. Would you like to hold one?"

"Erm..." Gray's instinct was to say no. They might've been bigger than he'd anticipated, but they were still rodent-like, and they were smelly—not in a bad way. It was an earthy, natural smell, but he wasn't used to it or animals, and they were skittish. He had visions of one of them leaping from his hands to its death.

"You don't have to," Will said.

"No. Go on."

Will seemed pleased he'd agreed, which, for a brief, few seconds, gave Gray butterflies that turned to whopping great moths at the sight of the twitchy nose coming towards him.

"Ah, oh." Suddenly his arms weren't under his control, and he contorted them into all kinds of peculiar shapes in a bid to find a safe way to hold the guinea pig that was now in his possession. It ran up his forearm and buried its nose in between his chest and elbow. In that position, Gray couldn't even shove it back at Will.

"Are you OK, Gray?"

"Yes," he answered tightly. He wasn't. However, he was determined to give it his best shot. Why, he wasn't sure. Will would have understood if he'd said no in the first place. His tenseness must have been obvious, as Will moved closer, hands ready to take the guinea pig from him, but Gray turned away. "No. I want to do this."

"What, it's like getting over a phobia?"

"Something like that." It was a phobia, of sorts, though it went far deeper, and Gray wasn't sure he'd be able to explain it if he tried. These animals were important to Will, and with his mum gone, his dad overseas and his uncle working up north, they were, for want of a better way to put it, all the family Will had left.

When Gray had told Jean about his estrangement from his mum, Jean had said whenever Gray was ready, they would face her together, find a way to get through to her. It was a completely different situation, yet Gray could see the parallels, and the fact he could see them was the reason he was afraid. To all intents and purposes, he was getting to know Will's family, accepting them, paralysis, twitchy noses and all.

Casting most of his caution aside, Gray used the tip of his index finger to stroke the guinea pig's back from head to no-tail.

"Has it...he?"

"She."

"Has she got a name?"

"Jeep Two."

"Jeep Two?"

"Yep." Will pointed to the other guinea pigs in the hutch. "Jeep One, Jeep Four and Jeep Five."

"What happened to Jeep Three?"

"One of the rehomes, along with Six to Ten."

"OK." Gray decided not to question the name. Then he changed his mind. "Why?"

"We didn't plan on keeping any of them, so we numbered them. GP—short for guinea pig—one to GP ten. It got shortened further from GP to Jeep."

Gray peered down at the creature snuggling in the crook of his arm. She'd calmed down, as had he. "Jeep Two. Does her fur grow like that because she was mistreated?"

"Nope. She's an Abyssinian. The rosettes are a mark of the breed."

"I thought guinea pigs were just guinea pigs."

"There're a few different breeds. Abyssinian, Peruvian, Silkie, which both have long coats, American..."

Gray laughed. "Yeah, I can't remember dog breeds. I've got no hope." The smile he got back from Will was warm and affectionate and bumped Gray's heart rate up a notch. Jeep Two wriggled and pushed her nose into Gray's armpit.

"I'd better put her back so she can eat her dinner," Will said, already moving closer. He slid his hand between the guinea pig and Gray's chest. The contact registered as more than what it was, but there was no indication Will had felt it, much to Gray's relief. "That's them done for the night. Tie's fed the dogs, so just us now. I'll have a quick shower and find the menu for the tandoori." Will moved off towards the door through which the dogs had charged earlier and called back, "Make yourself at home, Gray." He disappeared from view.

Gray glanced over at the kitchen table, and then at the sea of dogs he'd have to cross to reach it. He was still trying to figure out the safest route when Will returned, showered, changed and studying the takeaway menu in his hands. "I'll let you choose first." He stopped halfway across the kitchen and looked up. "You haven't moved."

"No. I..." Gray gestured to the dogs.

Will nodded in understanding and clicked his tongue against his teeth. "Come on, guys, shift out the way." He pointed to a corner of the room, and three of the four went over to where he'd indicated.

"Don't worry about me," Gray said. He felt mean for disturbing them.

"Oh, they're fine. They've got blankets."

Gray finally made it to the table and saw what Will had said was true. The corner of the room was a mass of blankets in all kinds of colours. The dogs circled a few times and lay down again. Will handed Gray the menu.

"Thanks. What are you getting?"

"Not sure. Chana masala, probably. I usually order a thali and share with Tie, but it's too much for one."

Gray scanned the menu and found the vegetable thali. Four dishes, with rice and bread—Will was right. It was far too much food for one person. "I'm happy to go with that." He closed the menu and handed it back.

"It's vegetarian."

"Not a problem." Gray grinned. Will smirked, aware he was being mocked.

"Are you sure?"

"Absolutely. It all sounds delicious."

"It's really good." Will took out his phone and dialled the number. It rang out. "I don't know where Tie's got to. He usually texts if he's going—Oh, good evening. Can I place an order for delivery, please?"

Usually, when someone broke off a conversation to deal with a phone call, Gray looked away. It was only ever an illusion of privacy when he could hear what was being said, but he'd offer it just the same. Not so this time, and for a while, Will didn't notice he was under surveillance. *Under surveillance. Ha.* Gray was outright ogling him. The physical attraction he'd already acknowledged was growing and transforming as Will's positive traits coloured Gray's gaze—his compassion, contentment, generosity. He had always considered Will good-looking in an unconventional sense, but now it was in his own right rather than in comparison to Jean.

"Yeah, that's everything." Will's eyes met Gray's, widening a little in response to Gray's attentiveness. "Thanks. Bye." He hung up without breaking eye contact. "You OK?"

"Fine. Are you?"

"Strangely, yeah, I am." Still holding. The unspoken questions played out in the subtle arching of his eyebrows, the singular quick blink. "About ten minutes, they said."

"That's quick."

"Yeah, they always are." Will rubbed his chin and staved off a yawn. His amusement was rising to the surface, lifting his cheeks. Still he didn't look away. "You want a drink? Beer? Something else?"

"A soft drink, if you've got one."

"Coke?"

"Great, thanks."

They were prisoners in this eye-to-eye communication from which Gray had no wish to escape, even though everything about the situation was setting off alarm bells. Whether Will was coping as well as he claimed—Gray thought he probably was—the timing was off. Each was permitting the other to see the desire, the willingness to take this further, and they were mature adults. Spending the night together would have as much or as little bearing on their friendship as they let it. Yet Will was emotionally vulnerable, and it tapped into Gray's nurturing side, the part of him that was a big brother and a team leader, rather than a lover.

It was, in the end, Will who broke the connection, but it was no more than a temporary cessation while he collected drinks, plates and cutlery. He set them on the table and sat on the chair adjacent to Gray's, at the same time lifting a leg to reach his socked foot and bracing as he rubbed at what must have been a tender spot.

"They don't smell," Will said, pre-empting a protest Gray hadn't considered. "I broke my foot a few months back, and it still aches if I walk on it too much."

"And you're going to be a postman?" Gray winked to make it clear he was teasing. Will laughed.

"I'll be in a van, but yeah. The foot's fine, really." The sharp intake of breath said otherwise.

Gray beckoned and indicated to his lap by way of offering to take over the foot massage. Will accepted and extended his leg, resting his heel on Gray's knee. It was hard to tell who was the most surprised by Gray's offer.

"How did you break it?" he asked.

"Someone stamped on it."

"On purpose?"

"Yep." Will winced, and his foot stiffened protectively.

"Sorry." Gray hadn't been pressing particularly hard, although he could feel a lump through Will's woolly sock. "You did get this seen by a doctor, didn't you?"

"I had it X-rayed, yeah."

That was as evasive a response as Gray had ever heard.

"I was told to rest up for six weeks."

"And did you?"

Will tilted his head from side to side and hummed.

"That's a no, then," Gray said, no judgement. He was as guilty as Will of ignoring medical advice. "You should probably go back to your GP. It's not healed properly."

"Yeah, I know. I can't afford time out for surgery, though." Will looked over at the pile of dogs asleep in the corner.

"Won't Tie help you out?"

"If he's still around. He's up in court next month." The doorbell sounded, and the dogs jumped to alert. A couple of them gave a small *woof*, but Will raised his hand, silencing them. "That's our food."

Gray released Will's foot, and Will left the room. Both times Gray had been to the farmhouse, they'd come in through the back door, straight into the kitchen. He hadn't given any thought to the rest of the house or the presence of a front door, but that was obviously where Will was, chatting with the delivery guy, personable as ever. Gray shirked the unexpected swell of jealousy by reasserting his position in his mind. Friendship, nothing more.

14: Offbeat

I T WAS COMING up to ten p.m. when the same mystery number called Rob's phone. He gave half a thought to blocking it—too much like hard work—and switched the TV to the news rather than doing what he needed to and getting his arse to bed. No earlies for him anymore, which meant a long day ahead. Petridis had kicked up a stink about Rob's temporary secondment to CID when there were already too few boots on the ground, which meant cracking on with the Berringer's investigation. A week, Petridis had given him, because the guy was stressed out and they were short-staffed. Rob was eager to make a start, but he needed a good night's kip first.

It seemed his mystery caller had other plans, however; Rob was nodding off when his phone rang again, or it didn't. He'd muted the volume. Instead, it vibrated off the bedside table, hit the floor with a clunk and shuddered away under the bed. Rob almost fell out stretching to reach it, by which point voicemail had kicked in, but enough was enough. He returned the call.

"Hello, who's this?"

"My name's Naomi. Are you PC Simpson-Stone?"

"Naomi Tanner?"

"That's right."

"Yeah, this is Rob Simpson-Stone. How can I help you, Mrs. Tanner?"

"It's about Aaron. He's in danger. Could we talk face-to-face?"

"Is he in immediate danger?"

"He's in hiding. He thought he'd be safe, but..."

Rob threw back the covers and sat up. "Where are you, Naomi?"

"Drury Court. Number thirty-two."

That was the address Aaron had given to Rob two weeks ago—his mother's place, therefore Naomi's mother-in-law's. It seemed an odd set-up. There again, Rob didn't suppose all marriages ended in acrimony.

"OK. I'll be with you in thirty minutes." He hung up and spent a few seconds staring at the screen. So it had begun: the antisocial hours, the late-night calls.

Back on with the clothes he'd not long taken off, Rob grabbed his keys and helmet and headed out, stopping at a petrol station to pick up a couple of energy drinks. He downed one and stuffed the other inside his jacket in case it turned out to be a long night.

Rob kept the revs low as he rode through the dead silence of the run-down housing estate with streetlamps too few and far between to be useful, though most residents were neither brave nor foolish enough to venture away from their homes after dark. He wondered how many people imagined somewhere grand when they were given addresses in Drury Court or Bellevue Plaza. It was not a good place for a lone copper, but Rob was back in his undercover mindset. It hadn't occurred to him to inform Hedley of what he was up to before he left, and he reasoned the kids here couldn't be any worse than what he dealt with on the job or in the army.

Nonetheless, on his way up the piss-stinky stairs in the block of flats, he sent both Hedley and Gray a text so they'd know where to start looking for him. He received a '*10-4*' back from Gray and an incoming call from Hedley, which would be a bollocking for going it alone. He let it go to voicemail. True, he should've asked for backup of some sort, but from what he'd seen so far, the Tanners weren't dangerous.

It took a couple of walks up and down the two corridors of the third floor to find number thirty-two. Tucked behind a stairwell and with no number on the door, it looked more like a bin cupboard than a flat. Rob wasn't a hundred percent sure it was the right place, but he knocked anyway and took a step back.

"Who's there?" someone asked from the other side of the door.

"It's Rob Simpson-Stone." Locks turned, a chain tinkled, and the door opened. "Naomi?"

"Yes. Come in. Please." She stepped aside.

Rob entered a small hallway and followed her through to the living room. Terrible judgement that it was, the furniture was good quality for a council flat, and the place was unusually well-kept.

Naomi perched on the edge of the sofa and picked up a packet of cigarettes from the side table, but then put them down again. Rob recalled Aaron lighting up in his presence and would have assumed Naomi was more considerate but for the absence of an invitation to sit down. She seemed barely aware of his presence at all.

"Mrs. Tanner..." It took a few seconds for his words to reach her; she was spaced out like she was on something. Eventually, she looked up at him. She was terrified. With caution—for her benefit—he approached and sat next to her. "Naomi, what's going on?"

"I think...Aaron's next."

"Next?"

"They're going to kill him."

That sort of fitted with what Hedley had said about Carrie Duggan's disappearance and the guy found in Aaron's car, who they still hadn't been able to identify. However, the Merc looked like a drink-driving accident, and Carrie Duggan was missing, not necessarily dead. Whether the threat to Tanner was real or in his wife's head, something had put the fear of God into her.

"Who do you mean by 'they'?" Rob asked.

She picked up the cigarettes, took one out of the packet and tapped it against her thigh. She handled the cigarette like a smoker, yet there were no signs—smell, ashtray, lighter, matches—to indicate she was. Whatever, she didn't seem any nearer to answering the question.

"Naomi, did you hear what I asked?"

She nodded. "I don't know who's doing it, but I know who's responsible." She set both the loose cigarette and the box back on the table and looked Rob in the eye. "Can we do this off the record?"

"Unfortunately not, but if you're worried for your own or Aaron's safety, we can see about arranging some form of protection."

"Protection?" she repeated with a disbelieving laugh. "It's too late for that." She clasped her hands over her face, only her eyes visible above her fingertips. As she blinked, tears trickled and dropped from her long, dark lashes onto her pink-painted fingernails. She stayed that way for several minutes, her silent weeping more heartrending for Rob than if she'd been sobbing her heart out. He'd seen people do both; one was no less felt than the other. But it was the silent weeping that always hit him the hardest.

"Look, Naomi, I'm sorry to push you, but why did you call me? To give me information? To ask for my help?"

She cleared her throat and mumbled unintelligibly behind her hands as she got up and left the room. A moment later, the honk of someone blowing their nose reached Rob's ears, followed by a toilet flush and Naomi's return. She remained in the doorway and smiled apologetically.

"Can I get you a drink, Constable—"

"Rob is fine."

"Rob. Would you like something to drink?"

"A coffee, but only if you're making one."

"I am, yes. I've been up for...it feels like weeks. I'll be right back. How do you take it?" she called on her way out.

"Just black, cheers."

While she was gone, Rob properly surveyed the room he was in. Based on Aaron Tanner's age, his mother had to be at least in her fifties, which wasn't particularly old, and there were older people with modern tastes, as well as younger people with traditional tastes, but the flat didn't fit. There were no photos, no ornaments or other trinkets. The walls were painted plain cream, and the floor was laminated, with a beige rug that was hard-wearing rather than decorative. Even the sofa he was sitting on, whilst comfortable, was plain and functional. In short, it looked like his flat: rented accommodation with no soul whatsoever.

"Coffee's on," Naomi said.

Rob waited for her to sit again before he restarted the questioning. "This flat, who lives here?"

"That's a good question. Usually, Aaron's mother, but she's gone to stay with her sister while he gets himself together."

"Right." It still didn't sit right with Rob, but it wasn't pertinent, so he let it go. "Both you and Aaron are staying here at present. Is that correct?"

"Yes, although we do our best not to be here at the same time. The business put us under a lot of stress, and we decided, for our own safety as much as anything, to go our separate ways."

"Are you both being threatened?"

"Well, that's just it, really. Neither of us has been overtly threatened, but we know the danger. It's only a matter of time."

That was too cryptic for Rob. "You'd better start from the top."

Naomi smiled again, a relieved smile. "I'll go pour that coffee first."

Rob sensed her trust in him, and it wasn't misplaced. He'd committed to the case, and he'd do everything he could to resolve it with no further casualties.

When she came back, Naomi set down the cups and fed the cigarette back into the packet. "I've given up," she explained. "I have this one cigarette left, and whenever I get the craving, I hold it between my fingers. It's working so far. It's been two weeks now, since the night—" She stopped. Rob could see her mentally preparing for what she needed to say. "From the top?" she asked.

Rob nodded.

"It's all about Berringer's bank. In the beginning, there were five of them went in as directors. Two got out at the first opportunity. The other three were Aaron, Carrie Duggan and Freddie Berringer. He's the son of Lord Berringer, one of the wealthiest peers in the country. The bank was, officially, Freddie's twenty-first birthday gift from his father, in return for which Freddie was to take full responsibility for the venture.

"His first task was to recruit his board of directors and other key personnel. He's very astute, takes big risks that pay off. He's also a sociopath and a sadist. He had a clear vision for Berringer's. Remember, we're talking sixteen years ago, and Berringer's was technologically as advanced as any investment bank today, and global. Carrie was Freddie's language specialist, and her ability has to be heard to be believed. Last count, she was fluent in more than fifty languages. She only has to come into contact with native speakers to add another language to her repertoire.

"Hector Laird-Browne was one of the two who got out, but not for long. He was in charge of trading. Again, his gift was astounding. He had an eye for patterns. He'd see movement on the exchange and intuitively know what needed to be done. I never really understood Hector's work, but something happened a couple of years ago, and the police were brought in. Freddie kicked Hector off the board. It was...Hector was..." Naomi's face crumpled.

Rob put two and two together. "Was Hector driving Aaron's Mercedes?"

Naomi nodded, unable to speak. Her reaction suggested there was more to her relationship with Hector than him being one of her husband's colleagues, and whilst it was insensitive to ask, Rob needed to know exactly what he was working with.

"Were you and Hector having a relationship, Naomi?" She nodded again. "When did you last see him?"

"In the morning, on the day of the accident."

"And what about Aaron? Did he see him after that?"

"No."

"You sound very sure."

"If Aaron had seen Hector, I would know, I promise you."

"Is Hector the reason you and Aaron separated?"

"No. We had his blessing."

Rob wasn't sure he believed her. From his meeting with Aaron Tanner, he'd had a clear sense of a man resigned to his fate. He'd lost everything, but he was at peace and ready to surrender. In Rob's experience, the most dangerous people were the ones who had nothing to lose. If they could, they'd seek vengeance on their way down, and they fought to the bitter end.

"Where is Aaron, Naomi?"

"He's in his bunker."

"Which is where?"

"I can't tell you, I'm sorry." It was a refusal as opposed to not knowing.

"But you know he's still alive?" Rob asked.

"Yes, very much so."

There was little point asking her if she thought Aaron had killed Hector. She was protecting her husband, which was understandable—if someone was taking out the directors—or she could be harbouring a murderer, but Rob didn't think so. However, he needed to tread carefully. He found Naomi attractive, and it would distort his judgement of her truthfulness. He backtracked.

"We haven't been able to identify the man in the car. What makes you think it's Hector?"

"I saw the article in *The Standard*, and I desperately wanted to come forward, but I couldn't. Maybe it wasn't him, but why hasn't he contacted me? I don't know what to think. The article said he was drunk."

"That's correct," Rob confirmed.

"And Hector didn't drink. At all. He was teetotal."

"Was there a reason for that?"

"He liked to keep his mind sharp."

"Would you be prepared to help us identify the body?"

She looked as if she might vomit, but she nodded her agreement.

"I know this is very difficult for you, but I need to understand why Hector would have been driving your husband's car. Aaron told me it had gone back to the dealer."

"It had, almost a month ago, and Aaron was devastated. He really loved that car. He's agoraphobic, and for a long time, he didn't leave the house at all. Mostly, we hosted business dinner parties, but he needed to attend board meetings, and sometimes investors demanded to see him on their own territory. In the end, it was the car that got him out of the house, and Hector knew how important it was to him. On the day of the accident, he'd told Aaron he was going to get the car back from the dealer."

"That would explain him being in the car," Rob said, "although the driver's blood alcohol was equivalent to having consumed a litre of spirits."

"No." Naomi was adamant. "He never touched a drop. Ever."

Rob paused to drink his coffee and consider. Very little of it made sense. From what he'd uncovered so far, Berringer's had been squeaky clean, and their technology portfolio wasn't politically contentious. There didn't seem to be any motive, yet Naomi was convinced Hector and Carrie had both been murdered and Aaron was next.

"Who do you think is responsible?" Rob asked. "Freddie Berringer?"

"He'd have paid someone to deal with them."

"Why?"

"They know too much. Freddie blackmailed them all into joining him. Before Berringer's, Aaron was a hacker, but he didn't do it for personal gain. People paid him to attack large corporations, which is why I don't believe the bank was a birthday present. One day, Freddie was paying Aaron to hack his father's accounts, the next, Freddie's got all this money to build his business. He knows what Aaron is, and he has enough evidence to send him to prison. It would kill Aaron within a week. Probably within a day."

"What about Hector and Carrie? How did Freddie buy their loyalty?"

"Carrie, I'm not sure. She's always kept away from the trouble. But Hector… He is—*was*—so trusting. Innocent. Freddie offered him the world, and Hector believed him. It was so cruel. To Hector, it was all a game, watching the numbers change, clicking the right button at the right time…just a game."

"Naomi, did Hector have a learning disability?"

"I suppose you could call it that, but he was a functioning adult who knew his own mind, so please, don't judge me or think less of him. I loved him so much, as did Aaron. They were close friends for a long, long time."

"What about the other director?" Rob asked. "The one who got out. What do you know about him?"

"Not much, I'm afraid. I haven't seen him in years. He ended up working for Berringer's main competitor. He obviously had something on Freddie, or he wouldn't have let him go."

"Could he be holding a grudge?"

Naomi laughed bitterly. "Everyone holds a grudge against Freddie."

"This guy who ditched Berringer's. Is it possible he's responsible for the murders?" Rob said 'alleged murders' in his head.

"God, no. They were all in it together, Aaron, Hector and Will. United against a common foe, as it were. If he was going to kill anyone, it would be Freddie, but Will's nothing like that."

Rob stifled a yawn. It was coming up to two a.m., and he was getting fidgety. "OK. I need to eliminate him from my inquiries." He took out his phone, ignored the missed calls from Hedley, and opened the notes app. "What's his full name?"

"Will Richards. That's Wilfred."

Rob typed the name into his phone and locked the screen. "Got it. Do you need me to arrange protection for you and Aaron? It'll be tricky to persuade my boss when there's no visible threat, but if you feel it's real, I'll give it a shot."

"Thanks, but we'll be fine." She shrugged. "I'm sorry for bringing you here on a false pretext. I can't stand the idea of Freddie getting away with it again, the way he always does, and when I saw the accident was being blamed on drink-driving, I had to say something. But Freddie doesn't know about this flat, so we're safe here."

"All right." Rob made a move. "I'll give you a call tomorrow, and we'll arrange for you to come and identify the body. Apart from that, just look after yourself, yeah?"

"We'll try. Thanks, Rob."

"No problem."

Rob waited outside the flat long enough to hear the locks and chain being secured and then returned to his bike, wondering if he was hyped enough to ride home or if he should chug the energy drink. He decided to save it for another day when he needed it more.

15: Dropkicked

IT WASN'T QUITE the first train, but it was early enough for Gray to question whether there had been any point to going home. He'd left Will's after ten—too late for the last train back into the city—and ended up paying a ridiculous amount for a cab when Will had two spare bedrooms and a sofa. Indeed, Will had gone to great lengths to outline the full set of alternatives, his intention, now Gray thought about it, most likely nothing more than paying back the favour. Or maybe Will had only wanted the company, but that wasn't how Gray had interpreted it the previous evening, so caught up in the internal hearing of Friendship v More he'd proved himself a poor friend.

That aside, he'd needed a few hours away to shower, read and reflect. Especially reflect. With concrete evidence that Will hadn't lied about his mum, Gray had still feigned ignorance of Will's full name. Will had been too distracted to notice Gray had questioned his name at all, or perhaps he'd assumed one of the hospice staff had used it. Either way, he hadn't attempted to change the subject or make excuses. Gray was doing his best to believe it was because Will had nothing to hide...and getting annoyed with himself for being so suspicious when he could have avoided all the speculation with a straightforward conversation.

Except it wasn't anything close to straightforward. Gray was wading into deep water, and he was dragging others with him. Dom shouldn't have sent him the Berringer's file nor conducted a database search on Gray's behalf. That he'd done so was an extension of trust and deference stemming from Gray being his former superior. More to the point, Gray shouldn't have asked. It was an abuse of their friendship that worsened the longer Gray delayed in passing the information on to Rob.

He had no ulterior motive. The information from the Berringer's files showed Will had been on the investor relations' payroll fifteen years previously and for less than eighteen months. No damning information, or not in that file; Gray was holding on to it purely because he hadn't found the time to contact Rob. Well, that, plus his mind kept skipping from *must text Rob* straight to *I wonder if Will got any sleep last night?* It was distracting and disconcerting, and a definite turning point. Gray kept catching himself thinking about Will, and it was more than a fleeting *I hope he's OK* or *I bet he looks hot in a wetsuit*. More like

Could I cope with early morning dog walks? and *How much would I miss eating meat?*

The unconscious mental leap from reluctant acquaintance to best buddy was irksome but not surprising. When he and Jean had laid bare their souls the morning they'd spent in bed, it had delighted them both to have found someone like them: a homebody who appreciated the mundane routines of sharing a house together and all that went with it. It was the flipside to the job, to the unpredictability and being constantly on the move, and their decision to emigrate to Belgium had also been a decision to quit the police and leave that life behind.

Back then, Gray had been more reluctant than Jean to give it all up. Before they'd met, his career had been the most important aspect of his life. Unlike others, who chased glory, he had only gone after the posts that interested him. He'd loved everything about his job, paperwork included, but Jean had wooed him with depictions of all the possibilities a leisurely life would afford. He could take up gardening or winemaking or reach the end of a novel before he'd forgotten the beginning. It was, ultimately, the latter that had sold the idea to him.

So, on the one hand, while Gray might have been jumping the gun with Will and thinking too far into a future that resided mostly in his imagination, on the other, his thoughts were still in the realm of companionship—something he'd sorely lacked since moving to London. A city bustling with life had no right to be so big and lonely a place—a fact that had evaded his excellent surveillance skills and entirely passed him by during the brief periods he'd lived there over the years. But then, working every waking hour left little time for loneliness.

As the train put Greater London behind it and picked up speed, the blur of suburbia gave way to greenery, creating an illusion of wide-open countryside even though it was barely far enough from the city to be commuter belt. That was the other draw, of course. Gray had grown up in a Somerset village where the buses ran twice daily, and everything closed on Tuesday afternoons and Sundays. His memories of childhood presented for his review an idyllic existence of days spent cycling or lying in a wheat field and reading. For a loner like him, there was no better way to spend a warm summer's day, even if it had resulted in a couple of near misses with combine harvesters.

Where Will lived was the best of both worlds. It had good transport links and shops that were open when working people could get to them, yet it was sparsely populated with fewer houses and more open space, although not so much in Will's back garden, Gray discovered when he opened the gate. The caravans had been joined by a rusty Transit van, complete with a chicken on the roof, neither of which had been there the night before. He was almost sure of that, as he had to turn sideways to squeeze between the vehicles.

"How...?" He was flummoxed, and a glance back at the gate confirmed it was nowhere near wide enough to get a big van through. *They must've lifted the fence.* Great theory, except it was held up by concrete posts that were only six feet apart. *Underground tunnel?* Ludicrous as that was, Gray still examined the earth for signs of a hatch, in the process nearly tripping over another chicken and losing his precarious footing on the muddy path. He made a grab for the corner of the caravan, missed and startled himself with the impressively loud thud of his fist against the fibreglass panel.

From inside the caravan came a muttered "Fuck's sake," followed by the door being flung open. The chicken legged it, and Jon—Gray assumed, they hadn't met—glowered at him.

"Sorry." Gray offered a grimaced smile.

"He's out with the dogs," was what he got in response. With a further muttering of, "I've only just got back to fucking sleep," the caravan door swung shut.

Not sure what to do for the best, Gray trudged back up the garden path and out of the gate, looking left and right in an attempt to psychically divine which route Will would have taken. He had no idea. The sensible option, which felt way too much like taking liberties, was to wait in Will's kitchen. *I could put the kettle on, make him coffee...* He still didn't like it but didn't see as he had much choice. Back through the ramshackle mini scrapyard, he walked on tiptoes between the caravans and Transit van—a glance through the window revealed it was kitted out as a rudimentary camper—to the back door. It was, as he'd anticipated, unlocked. Gray stepped inside.

There were many occasions in his time with the SIU where he'd snooped around houses, having intentionally waited until the occupants were away from the premises. Never had he felt so much like he was invading someone's privacy as he did now. It was intimate, misleading, as if he were claiming a right to be there that was reserved for close friends and family. Either he was intruding or he was staking his interest, and he wasn't sure which of those he liked the least.

He filled the kettle and visualised when Will had made coffee for them the previous week. At the time, Gray had been more concerned with the safety of Benjy the bunny than what Will was doing, thus hadn't noticed where he kept the mugs, which, inevitably, led to him opening no less than four different cupboards before he found them. And behind them, a well-used crowbar. He studied it for a few seconds, hating it for being so absolutely, undeniably there. *Could be for self-defence, in case of a break-in.* Unlikely, but still. He picked out two mugs from the mix 'n' no-match collection and shut the door. He didn't want to know.

Actually, that was an outright lie. He didn't want to *already know* and wished he'd given Will a chance to tell him instead of reading it in his police records.

The clues Will had offered had been far from subtle, and maybe, if Gray had asked the right questions, Will would have told him everything, unless, as Gray's gut instinct continued to insist, the lack of trust extended in both directions.

The kettle had boiled and Gray had yet to locate the coffee, which proved easier to find than the mugs due to the elimination process of having already searched four of the six cupboards. He made it as far as adding a spoonful of coffee to one mug before the back door opened.

"Alright?" Tie reversed in, holding the door open, and then did a double take. "Oh, alright, Gray? I thought Will was back."

"No," Gray answered, pointlessly, once again distracted by Benjy bunny, who hopped past Tie and commenced exploring the kitchen at his leisure. With the rabbit safely inside, Tie shut the door.

"Just popping upstairs. He'll be all right a minute." Tie was gone before Gray could protest.

Keeping Benjy in his sights, Gray cautiously edged along the wall to the fridge, concerned he might accidentally step on him and looking away for only as long as it took to locate the milk—soya, and he hadn't noticed it tasted any different. Perhaps the vegetarian lifestyle wouldn't be so difficult after all. He looked for Benjy again, panicking when he couldn't see him, until he felt light pressure on his foot. Resisting the urge to jerk out of the way, Gray peered down.

Benjy had both front paws on top of Gray's shoe and was snuffling at his jeans, yet Gray could barely feel it. The rabbit was a beautiful animal, white as fresh snow, apart from his nose, eyes and the insides of his enormous asymmetrical ears, all of which were pale pink. Gray was fascinated and a little sad he'd missed out on having pets when he was younger. It was probably the wrong motivation, but unconditional affection was a tempting notion. Unlike humans, animals were uncomplicated and honest. In a good home, like Will's, they had a worry-free life, and Gray was beginning to understand why Will, Tie and the others did what they did.

Much as he was enjoying the unassuming contact, Gray needed to get the coffee made soon or he'd have to re-boil the water. He carefully slid his foot out of the way and stepped off; Benjy hopped along beside him as he returned to the mugs and added a drop of milk to both. As an afterthought, Gray took out a third mug for Tie, spilling most of the coffee granules when he jumped and the spoon jumped with him as the door opened a second time to admit—

"Will! The dogs!" Without a thought to his minor—though rapidly fading—phobia of furry beasts, Gray scooped the rabbit out of harm's way.

"Good morning." Will grinned and shut the door. "This is a surprise." He stooped to remove his boots. "A good one. He'll be fine, by the way."

Gray was doubtful, but Will nodded in encouragement, and for once, Gray took him at his word. He crouched low enough for the rabbit to hop down onto the floor and then shut his eyes, waiting for the pack to pounce. All he got was a chuckle from Will that made him blush. He opened his eyes again and dealt with the coffee rather than look Will's way. "You weren't expecting me?" He'd said he'd come back in the morning, but he also recalled those hazy first few weeks after Jean had died and the number of times someone had said to him 'I did tell you such and such' yet his battered brain had retained nothing.

"I was," Will said, "but I didn't expect you to arrive at the crack of dawn."

"It's hardly the crack of dawn," Gray argued, aware it wasn't yet eight o'clock and that he was disagreeing for no reason at all. His early arrival didn't have to mean anything.

"I had you down as more of a night owl."

There was a fifty-fifty chance of Will getting that right through guesswork, but he hadn't guessed. He'd read Gray, and correctly. "The tungsten pallor gave me away, did it?"

Will smiled. "Something like that." He padded in socked feet across to Gray and picked up one of the mugs. "They're all the same, I take it?" Gray nodded to confirm. "Cheers." Will sucked a tiny amount of too-hot coffee from the cup and leaned back against the cupboard, locking his gaze on Gray. "What's up?"

"Nothing." Gray might as well have said 'I know everything' because his quick response made it clear he was lying, and all he had for cover was a change of subject. "What do you need to do first?"

"Not sure. The doctor said I need some bit of paper before I can register the death. D'you know what she meant?"

"Certificate of cause of death, by the sounds of it."

"Right. I'll give the hospice a call after nine and see if I can go and pick it up." Will's eyes turned glassy, and he lost focus. "It's weird. I'm glad it's over, but it's still..." He left the sentence trailing, sniffed and shook his head. As Gray knew only too well, the real grief wasn't allowed to kick in until the funeral was over, and Will was making a heroic effort to fight his. "OK. I'll get this lot their breakfast and make us something. Or have you had breakfast?"

"At the crack of dawn? You've got to be joking." Gray cracked a grin. Will offered a half-hearted laugh in response and squeezed Gray's arm on his way past, a silent gesture of thanks that Gray selfishly welcomed. It made him feel less like a home invader. "What do you usually have for breakfast?"

"Whatever takes my fancy. I've been on a croissant kick for a while, but I don't think I have any. Omelette?"

Gray nodded. "Suits me."

Will lined up five bowls and poured cereal into them, but it was like no cereal Gray had ever seen. "Chicken with yoghurt and berries," Will said in answer to yet another question Gray had only asked in his head.

"That's an...interesting combination."

"They seem to like it, although it's not something I'd buy. It was a free sample."

The second the bowls were on the floor, four of the five dogs got straight down to chomping, but it wasn't Kenny playing odd dog out this morning.

"You not hungry, Nev?" Will looked around the kitchen for the missing dog. Gray looked too and spotted him lying under the table. Will frowned and went over. "What's up, mate?" He held out his hand to the dog, offering up a nugget of the cereal, which Nev took but then dropped it on the floor. "He's a good eater, usually." Will straightened up again, his continued frown indicating his worry as he watched the dog, who was taking short, sharp breaths, and even those seemed a trial.

"What do you think's wrong?" Gray asked.

Will shrugged. "I'll see how he is when we've eaten. Looks like a trip to the vet after the hospice."

Those priorities immediately changed order when Nev went into a seizure. Will was pouring beaten eggs into a pan, and Gray took over the cooking, freeing Will to go to the dog's aid. The seizure didn't last long, but it was clear from Will's reaction that it wasn't a normal occurrence.

"I'm going to have to walk him there," he said. "The van's off the road."

"Do you want to get a taxi?" Gray asked. "I'll pay for it."

"It's not far." He kept on stroking the dog, all the while falling apart.

Gray switched off the heat under the pan and slid the half-cooked omelette onto a plate. "I'll call you a taxi. Is there a local firm?"

"Number's by the phone in the hall. Tell them it's to transport a dog. Some drivers won't let them in the car."

Gray moved towards the door.

"Thanks," Will called after him.

Gray nodded, no need to look to confirm Will was crying. He left to make the call, overwhelmed by what Will was going through, more so for knowing what he did about Will's past. Gray had been up half the night reading, not to prove Will was lying, but to better understand this man whose company he was beginning to crave. Will's conviction to the animal rights cause had put him in dire situations where he'd risked his life to do what he felt was necessary. He'd been mown down by a sheep transporter and, the moment he regained consciousness, arrested for causing actual bodily harm to the driver. The hospital confirmed the driver had no injuries, and the haulage firm offered to drop the charges if Will did. Instead, he'd handed his evidence to the police; the haulage firm was found guilty of multiple offences under The Animal Health Act and landed a fine large enough to put them out of business.

On another occasion, Will had required sixteen staples in his scalp when an abattoir owner assaulted him—with a cow bone, of all things. The prosecution tried to undermine Will's testimony by painting him as a good-for-nothing layabout when, in truth, he'd used his annual leave from the bank for a stint of working in the slaughterhouse to gather evidence of mistreatment. The owner was sent to prison for six months.

Many of the entries on Will's record were of that ilk—his involvement in the prosecution of animal abusers—but the greater majority were offences he'd committed, mostly minor: disturbing the peace, obstructing police officers, allegedly threatening behaviour. They were a smokescreen to obscure the more sinister work of animal liberation; Gray was almost certain of it and, strangely, unperturbed.

He dialled the taxi firm's number several times, but the line was engaged, and the noises from the kitchen indicated the dog was having another seizure. Right at that moment, Gray would've paid for a helicopter to get Nev to a vet. He couldn't even pull strings with the local police, although...the head of the SIU probably could. He gave the taxi company one last try. If he didn't get through this time, he'd call Dom. The phone rang out. Gray switched to surveillance mode to distract from the ominous silence in the kitchen.

The hallway was a nondescript narrow passage painted terracotta brown with a few prints on the walls—of flowers, not dogs, which struck him as odd until he remembered Will's mum had lived there. The wooden front door was directly ahead of him, scruffy stairs to his left. On his right was an open doorway, beyond it a big, comfy-looking sofa that was most kindly described as 'well used'. In short, the house was in a poor state of repair. Either Will didn't care, or he was living hand-to-mouth.

Finally, the taxi firm answered. Gray quickly explained the situation and was told a car would be with them in ten minutes. He returned to the kitchen, where the four healthy dogs and Benjy were lying in a protective circle around Will and Nev. Nev appeared to be unconscious.

"The taxi's on its way," Gray said.

"OK, thanks." Will remained on the floor with his hand resting on the dog's side. "I don't think he's going to make it."

There was nothing Gray could say, no comforting words or promises that didn't look set to be proved false. "Do you want me to deal with the hospice?"

"Will they let you?"

"With your permission. We could give them a call now. What do you think?"

"If you wouldn't mind. I need to..." Will bowed his head.

Gray found the number and called it on his mobile, handing it to Will. He explained, without going into detail, and responded to whatever they'd said with, "Yep, I'll give him my passport." He handed the phone back, and Gray ended the call. "It's in the right-hand drawer of the dresser," Will said, indicating behind him.

Gray squeezed past to reach the Welsh dresser. The drawer in question was crammed full of documents bundled by type—bills, bank statements, and so on—along with two passports. He took one out and opened it: Will's mum, though barely recognisable as the woman Gray had seen moments before she died. Will had inherited his looks from her, from the blonde-brown hair and dark eyes right down to the heavy brows and thicker-than-average lips. She was beautiful in a very natural way, nothing like Gray's mum. He closed the passport and exchanged it for the other, again opening it to check it was Will's. He smiled. "That's a great photo of you."

"Yeah, right," Will said drolly.

It wasn't an awful photo, but the super-serious expression and hair pulled back from his face made Will look like a thug. Gray put the passport in his pocket and opened his mouth, about to run through what he was going to do, cut short by the dog going into yet another seizure. Will's quiet reassurances were devastating, his voice trembling with anguish as he told Nev it would be over soon. Gray stayed close by, wanting to reach out and offer Will physical comfort but quite certain doing so would obliterate what little control he had.

The taxi arrived mercifully soon after. Tie came downstairs wearing only his jeans, helped Will carry the dog to the car and returned to the kitchen. He gave Gray a rueful smile. "Poor bloke."

"Yeah," Gray agreed. Will was having the week from hell.

"Are you staying to wait for him?"

"No. I'm going and coming back. I offered to pick up the paperwork from the hospice."

"That's good. Is there anything I can do?"

Gray shrugged. "Just look after this lot, I guess."

"Goes without saying."

"I made you a coffee. It's probably cold by now."

"Cheers." Tie picked up the remaining full cup and took a mouthful. He nodded towards the window. "I'm gonna see if I can get the van sorted. Jon was out in it last night and got pulled. Idiot." He took another mouthful. "So, you and Will. Mates or more?"

Gray was taken aback by the question.

"None of my business, of course," Tie said. "But we've known each other years."

"And you don't want to see him get hurt?"

"Well, there is that, although he's big and ugly enough to look after himself most of the time. He doesn't deal with death well. Mind you, who does? No, I was just being a nosey git."

"Fair enough." At least he was honest, and he came across as a nice guy, albeit a nice guy whose dripping dreadlocks had created a moat around him. "Are you going to be here later?" Gray asked. "There's a couple of things I need to do after I've been to the hospice, but they can wait. I don't like the idea of Will being on his own."

"I'll be here. You do what you need to. I'd best get on myself. See you later." Taking his cup with him, Tie went out to the yard.

Gray tipped the rest of his coffee away and rinsed his mug, flinching when Tie hammered on his brother's caravan and made a somewhat uncomplimentary demand he get out of bed. An argument ensued, with the pair of them standing between the van and the caravans. The two brothers looked nothing like each other, although they shared the same foul language. They were vicious with it too, and Gray hung back until they were done. He didn't much fancy getting caught in the crossfire.

The train was pulling into the station as Gray reached the platform. He hopped on board and sent Rob a text message to see if he was free to meet up for lunch. That was one thing to be thankful for: all of this was happening in reading week, or else Gray would've been teaching for most of the afternoon. Rob replied in the affirmative and asked when and where. Gray sent back '*12:30 – usual place*' and settled in for the short journey followed by the walk to the hospice, where the paperwork was done and waiting for him at the reception desk.

The text from Will arrived as Gray was walking back to the station and knocked him for six.

RIP Nev the Naughty :(See you later? x

16: Back to Basics

"IT'S YOUR FAULT, you know," Rob said as he approached Gray, who was standing at the bar with a glass of orange juice in front of him.

"What's that?"

"Me saying yes." At Gray's enquiring—and concerned—head tilt, Rob grinned. It wasn't a serious accusation. "Hedley asked me to take the case. I'm on secondment."

If Gray was at all surprised, he did an excellent job of covering it. "How are you doing, Rob? What are you drinking, by the way?"

"Coke, cheers. Yeah, I'm not bad. You?"

"I'm OK, thanks." Gray kept his eyes on the bartender, which wasn't that odd, given he was waiting to be served, but Rob picked up on something behind the automatic response.

"You don't sound so sure."

"Don't I?" He frowned, then shrugged. "A friend of mine's going through a rough patch. I guess it's on my mind."

"Sorry to hear that." Rob didn't push the issue. Gray had never been the kind to share personal information. Even admitting he had friends was more than he'd shared the entire time they were in the SIU, although he'd been frank when they'd last met. A little too frank in some respects, and Rob was glad Josh had given him the bare basics in advance. He wasn't sure how he'd have reacted to the news Gray was a widower and that his deceased partner was male. As far as anyone in the SIU knew—with the exception, possibly, of Dom Hooper—Gray was a typical arrogant pen-pushing senior officer who got the job done and was good for a few beers after work but didn't give a toss about anyone, including the wife he never went home to see.

Knowing what made the real Gray Fisher tick also made it easier for Rob to forgive him for what he'd done, or not forgive so much as understand. Rob had been a bit of a soft arse at high school, which, if nothing else, had kept him out of trouble. Then he'd joined the army and come out a different person. Conflict no longer bothered him, although he didn't go looking for it, unlike a few of his old army mates, who were always spoiling for a fight. To them, everyone was the enemy, and the smallest stirring of trouble could get blown out of proportion.

Life was a struggle, and they lost friends, spouses, family. They hadn't adjusted well to civilian life.

Truth be told, neither had Rob. He'd joined the police, which had helped him to decompress without losing the discipline and routine. What he'd seen in Bosnia would be a part of him forever, and it had been highly effective desensitisation, but with the police, he'd been able to keep it in perspective. He had a clear sense of who 'the enemy' was and could hold off on retaliating when it was nothing personal. However, if Travis laid a finger on Zoë or Lucas, Rob would kill him without a second thought. It wasn't mindless. Rob still believed in the sanctity of life, but he'd seen enough to know that taking one life could save a lot of others. He could kill, if he had to, and walk away with a clean conscience.

Likewise, Gray had made some heartless decisions because his baseline was his own suffering. He'd asked his team to do what he'd have no qualms doing himself, but his judgement had been skewed. No doubt his gratitude for Rob's work on the Strang case was real, as was his reaction when Rob told him, straight up, what he thought of him. He'd expected Gray to argue back—*horses for courses* and all that other BS that kept the SIU functioning—but he hadn't. He'd admitted to messing up. He'd even said he was sorry, and Rob believed him.

It wasn't the same as forgiving him. Gray had changed in the past year, for the better, and he was helping Rob with the Berringer's case out of sheer good will. But the SIU had cost Rob his family. Nothing could undo that.

"You've got something to tell me?" He hadn't intended the question to sound so brusque.

"I have," Gray confirmed, "though I'm not sure how useful it'll be to you. Shall we order lunch first?"

It wasn't a pub renowned for its cuisine, but they'd always done decent fish and chips, which was what they both ordered and then, out of habit, took their drinks over to the table at the back of the pool room. For once, there was no-one playing, but the mumbling TV and background music was enough to obscure their conversation. Their meals were brought over, and Gray picked up from where he'd left off.

"The bank you're investigating, we ran a prelim on them, so it's a snapshot only, and it's two years out of date, but there might be something in there you can use."

"They were cleared?"

"Yeah. There was an allegation of deliberate overvaluing of assets to gain majority control of the company." Rob must've looked clueless because Gray went on to explain. "It's what's known as a short and distort. In this instance, it appeared Berringer's had recruited rogue traders to spread rumours that the bank's share prices were about to crash so shareholders would sell.

"Normally, it's the rogue traders who benefit by cleaning up and sitting on the shares until they recover. We had it on good authority Berringer's was attempting to buy back shares from its own shareholders. Berringer's claimed there was a system error and a couple of short traders had jumped on it. We had someone look over the data and confirm that claim."

Rob wasn't up on the finance side of the SIU's work; he hadn't needed to be. Nor did he need to understand now to spot the deliberate mistake. "What kind of system error?" he asked.

"The information shareholders had access to. I don't recall the ins and outs, but they'd brought in a new computer system, and a glitch in the accounting subroutines overvalued Berringer's assets, which led to a surge in share prices and a subsequent increase in trading. The glitch was discovered and rectified within the hour, and the shares didn't take the expected nosedive. Or not until later. Unfortunately, our investigation played its part in that, and probably in Berringer's liquidating."

That was all Gray had to say, and he made a start on his lunch, seemingly untroubled by having contributed to a company going out of business. It was fascinating, the way he'd instantly switched back to SIU mode, where everything had received the same cool treatment. Maybe that was the only way Gray could deal with it, or maybe the cases hadn't got to him the way they had Rob and some of the others. Gray was the king of dry factual delivery, the long-and-winding debrief—Rob could almost hear Dom Hooper's piss-take of 'pub'll be open again soon', which was usually enough to shut Gray up. Much as they'd all appreciated how meticulous he was in his recording and reporting, it had sucked the life out of them faster than Dracula on speed.

Cold as he'd been, and in spite of the personal hell he'd been going through, Gray's work couldn't be faulted. His success rate was incredible. Yet, for all of that, Rob had serious doubts about the SIU's conclusions on Berringer's. "Who made the allegation?"

"One of Berringer's investors who sold out. You think there was something fishy?"

"I don't know. But I don't buy the technical glitch story."

Gray set down his fork and gave Rob his full attention.

"Aaron Tanner's a techie, and no ordinary techie either."

"That's right. He was recruited for his leet skills, I recall."

"Yeah, recruited isn't the word I'd use," Rob said. "I spoke to his wife last night. She's worried Aaron's in danger." That was finally what had swung the decision of whether to take the secondment, but Rob wasn't prepared to admit it aloud.

"What kind of danger?" Gray asked.

"She thinks he's next on the hit list. The dead guy in the car who had Tanner's ID turned out to be one of the other directors, who also happened to be Naomi Tanner's lover. Apparently, Aaron knew they were seeing each other. I'm meeting up with him later to see what he has to say. The other director who's missing—Carrie Duggan—Naomi reckons she's dead too."

"What do *you* think?" Gray asked.

"I think Freddie Berringer is a nasty piece of work. Whether he's capable of murder is another matter. Naomi Tanner's got it in for him."

"You think she's stitching him up?"

Rob shrugged. "Who knows. Whatever, I'm seeing the case through. I thought it might be one for the SIU, but the ID in the car turned out to be Aaron Tanner's old driving licence."

"Didn't you say it matched the guy in the car?"

"Yeah. I thought it did. Naomi showed me photos of Tanner in uni. He and Laird-Browne—the dead man—were the spit of each other, but Tanner's lost a lot of weight since."

"She obviously goes for the same type," Gray said.

"Ha, yeah." Rob was much the same. He was also aware of the similarities between Naomi Tanner and Zoë and its potential influence on his investigation. "I'm hoping to track down the other bloke Berringer brought in. According to Naomi, he got out early, but there's history there. He left Berringer's and went to work for their competitor."

"Who'd be a banker, eh?" Gray asked dryly.

"That's the trouble, isn't it? It's cutthroat, and there might be nothing to it, but I'd like to have a chat with him just the same."

A couple of lads came over to play pool, and Rob and Gray watched them in silence. There was nothing left to discuss, or no business, at least, and Gray looked eager to move on. He took out his phone. "You still got the app?"

"Yeah." Rob dug out his phone too and unlocked it. It took a minute or so to activate the encrypted NFC app they'd used with the SIU and accept the incoming files.

"The personnel list is in that lot, with contact info," Gray said. He stood and put on his jacket. "I don't know how current it is, but it was complete as of two years ago."

Rob got up and followed Gray past the pool table, acknowledging with a nod the men who had paused their game to let them pass.

Outside, Gray glanced along the street like he was looking for a taxi, but not, as he let two go past. "You got anything nice planned for the rest of the week?" he asked.

Rob shook his head. "Gonna crack on with work, see what I can find out. I'm back in uniform on Tuesday."

"Lucky you're a fast worker, eh?"

"You're not wrong." Rob held out his hand for Gray to shake. "Thanks for the info. I owe you one."

"You don't, but..." Gray paused. He was acting cagily, which wasn't like him. "What I'm about to ask—can we keep it between the two of us?"

"I guess." It was difficult to agree unconditionally when he didn't know what he was agreeing to.

"There's a name on that list. Wilfred Richards. If you find out anything interesting, will you let me know?"

Rob laughed, surprised, and hoping his agreement to keep schtum didn't come back to bite him. "Funny you should mention him. He's the one that got away."

***

Between leaving Gray and meeting up with Aaron Tanner, Rob had managed no more than a quick glance over the Berringer's files, and apart from the personnel file, they might as well have been written in Japanese for all the sense they made. Most of the information was appendices to a written report, which Rob was happy to trust matched Gray's verbal summary: there was an alleged computer glitch that led to shareholders ditching their investment, and Berringer's lost out.

The personnel list included information on other board members, but Rob wanted to talk to the founding five first, or those he could locate. The feeling he got from Naomi was that it was a personal feud between Freddie and his inner circle, and the bank had simply been a casualty, such as the sinking of a multimillion-pound business could be described as simple. Rob didn't need to know. At least one person was dead, and his priority was to establish whether it was murder. He'd worry about motive later.

Aaron had already arrived at their rendezvous point: the Science Museum café. Rob had offered to go to Drury Court again, despite the arse-kicking Hedley gave him for going there the last time, along with strict orders to either wait for backup or meet in a well-populated, public place. Aaron said if they could meet somewhere close to a Piccadilly line station, he'd cope with making the trip into the city. The Science Museum was the first location that came to mind. Rob had taken Lucas there during the summer holidays, and the pedestrian subway meant Aaron could get within spitting distance of the museum before he had to venture out into the open.

There were a few more people around than Rob had banked on, and he could've kicked himself for not realising the schools were out for half-term week. If he'd thought about it at all, he'd have made some kind of arrangement with Zoë. He wondered why she hadn't mentioned it the other night when she'd asked him to take Lucas to the cinema and he'd pointed out it was a school night. Then again, she'd have assumed he was working most of the week, which he had been, but he'd have found a way to fit in doing stuff with Lucas—*if he'd thought about it.*

He was still pissed off when he finally made it to the table in the far corner, where Aaron was sitting, his focus mostly on the newspaper in front of him, but it was a ruse, and he had seen Rob approach. Aaron was tense, his shoulders drawn too high, his jaw rigid, and the illuminated tabletop had washed much of the colour from his face. He glanced up at Rob and attempted a smile. Rob stopped dead.

He prided himself on being fairly unflappable. There was little got past him, therefore few surprises, or, at least, those of the variety that made him think *what the fuck?* In fact, he'd only ever had the one—when he'd found out Jess was the master criminal he'd been sent undercover to catch. Now, he was experiencing his second 'what the fuck?' moment.

"Naomi?"

Aaron's head moved from side to side, a feeble effort at denial from which he desisted soon after.

"I'm going to get a coffee," Rob said. He needed thinking space. "You want another?"

Aaron attempted to speak, but no sound came out. He cleared his throat and tried again. "No, thank you."

Rob nodded and went to order his coffee, completely missing the question from the girl behind the counter because he was still reeling. He apologised and ordered a latte, turning back to watch Aaron from afar. It wasn't obvious, even now he'd seen it and knew it for sure. Aaron and Naomi were the same person, except...they weren't. They were listed as two separate people on the electoral roll. They each had identity documentation, which meant nothing, as he knew only too well after working the Strang case. So he'd been right, after all. This *was* one for the SIU. A week ago, he'd have been glad to have someone to dump it on. But a lot could change in a week.

Rob paid for his coffee and took it over, sliding onto the bench opposite Aaron, unsure what to say. He didn't want to make accusations, but what it looked like was identity fraud, which was indictable. Maybe he'd jumped the gun. The more he studied Aaron, the less sure he was of what he'd seen. That fleeting glimpse of Naomi...had he imagined it?

"I'll do it the easy way," Aaron said. "Or not easy for me." He moved the newspaper to one side, revealing the documents hidden beneath it: two passports, two driving licences. "Take a look, Mr. Simpson-Stone, and then I'll answer your questions." Aaron pushed the documents across the table.

For a minute or so, Rob could do little more than stare at the photos on the two licences. Side by side, they looked like twin brother and sister, with similar-shaped features, the same brown eyes, coffee skin tone, narrow nose, slightly pointed chin. But then there were the eyebrows—Aaron's were thicker—and the jawline—Naomi's was less defined. However hard he looked at those photos, Rob could not merge the two into one. He examined the passports, same result.

"Aaron Tanner. Naomi Silvestri." He shrugged and made eye contact with Aaron. "It's listed as Naomi's legal name."

"Yes. It is Naomi's legal name. And mine."

"When did you change it?"

Aaron bit down on his lip. It was a nervous response rather than an attempt to distract or delay. "When I started work for Berringer's."

"So you're really Naomi?"

Aaron laughed, and it *was* Aaron, not Naomi. "I'm both," he said. "Right now, I'm Aaron. The woman you met yesterday is Naomi."

"OK." Rob had no idea what to think about that. "Let me try and get this in some kind of order. Your surname is Silvestri."

"Yes, it is. I changed it by deed poll."

"Because of your...gender identity?"

"Because of my previous career, although people don't see it as a career. It's a criminal offence."

"By legal definition," Rob agreed. "But don't you guys see it as some kind of moral crusade, a way of bringing down evil corporations?"

"Some of us. Until we get roped in and tied down."

"Freddie Berringer."

"Yes, but it's not quite as it seems."

"How is it?"

"Freddie's in love with Naomi. He offered to pay to get rid of me once and for all."

"He was planning to kill you?"

"To kill me and keep Naomi."

"How does that work if you're the same person?"

"Not the same person." Aaron's eye started to twitch. "We share the same body, and sometimes we're whole. She always knows what I'm up to and how I'm feeling. Sometimes I feel completely disconnected from her. At other times, we interlock. Aaronaomi. I can't explain it."

"Are you transgender?"

"No. That's what Freddie wants to believe."

"Ah, I think I get you, not that I'm saying I understand. When you say Freddie wanted to get rid of you, you mean he offered to pay for treatment."

"That's correct. Hormones and gender reassignment."

"But it's not what you want, is it?"

"No," Aaron confirmed with a sigh. "All my life, I've flitted between male and female. Sometimes, it's as if someone's swapped my brain while I'm asleep. Some days, I wake up absolutely certain I'm a man. Other days, I wonder if I should get rid of those parts that mark me as male, but I dismiss it quickly. I don't want surgery or therapy. I want the world to move on and understand we're all different, even those of us who are happy to be a man or a woman, both or neither, or all of the above, like me. How do I explain that to people? I don't fit in any of their boxes. Did you have one of those shape-sorting buckets when you were little?"

"Yeah, I did. It was passed down from my sister to my brother to me, and the star was missing. I hated that." Rob chuckled as he thought back. It was one of his earliest memories, when he was too old for the toy anyway, but it had infuriated him that he couldn't 'win' the game because of the missing star-shaped brick.

"That must've been so frustrating," Aaron said, and he smiled too. Rob noticed it again, that tiny flash of Naomi's presence, gone as quickly as it had appeared. "That's how I feel at times, like I don't fit in any of the holes. But then something inside me shifts, and I can slot through the square hole, or the triangular hole. Sometimes it's like pushing the triangular brick into the square hole, and I won't damn well go, however much I want to. I don't know if that makes sense to you." Aaron picked up the passports and driving licences and put them away, drawing out the action to give Rob time to process.

"I think it does. Let me see if I've got it." Rob hoped he'd followed the analogy correctly, or he was about to add further insult to injury. "Essentially, you're the bucket. You've got all the different-shaped bricks inside."

"I'm the bucket. I've been called lots of things in my time..." Aaron laughed. "Yes, that works for me."

Rob picked up his coffee and adopted a more formal posture whilst trying to keep the relaxed rapport. "I need to ask you some difficult questions, Aaron. Do you feel up to answering?"

"I'll do my best."

"Thanks. First of all, who knows about you and Naomi?"

"Professionally, only Freddie and Carrie—and Hector, of course. Personally, only my mum and Will, but I haven't seen Will in ten years."

"Do you know where he is?"

"No, sorry, I don't. I know he worked for Kestra until a few months ago. He kept his distance because of Freddie. He couldn't understand why we stayed when he'd shown us it was possible to escape. Freddie met his match in Will Richards."

"In what way?"

"Will doesn't care about money or reputation, or not in the same way as the rest of us. If he had to go to prison to take Freddie down, he would, but he's more a 'don't bother me and I won't bother you' kind of guy."

"You said Freddie forced you all to go in with him."

"*Naomi* said."

At first, the correction seemed pedantic, and Rob had to adjust his thinking again. It was hard. He'd never questioned who or what he was, and he could just about get his head around Aaron-Naomi by treating them as a split personality, which was effectively saying Aaron was mentally ill. Rob didn't believe that, but it was the only frame of reference he had. "Sorry. Did Freddie threaten to out you as Aaron slash Naomi?"

"No."

"He was going to report you to the police," Rob speculated. Aaron nodded to confirm. "It is *you* who's the hacker, isn't it?"

"Yes, it's me. Naomi could do it if she chose to, but she prefers to leave it to me. We're not as segregated as I imply. The skills and interests are constant. Some come to the fore when Naomi is dominant, and she isn't interested in technology to the same extent I am. I suppose part of it is gender role. On a fundamental level, we're the same person. In answer to your question about Freddie threatening me, he didn't. Not directly. He expects my compliance, even now, and it frightens me."

"Why do you think he killed Hector?" Rob asked.

"Jealousy, and to eliminate his competition. Hector and Naomi loved each other."

"What about you and Hector?"

"He was a wonderful, kind friend to me. So patient. It helped that Hector needed time on his own. He accepted Naomi couldn't always be there. They planned to move in together once everything had blown over."

"You too, presumably?" Rob said.

"Yes and no. Hector and I discussed the possibility of converting a house and taking a storey each—Naomi and Hector downstairs, me upstairs."

For a few seconds, that sounded like a reasonable arrangement, and then Rob remembered Aaron and Naomi shared the same body—a body he'd appreciated when inhabited by Naomi. Yet he wasn't attracted to Aaron. He wasn't even the sort of guy Rob would look at and think *if I wasn't straight...* He couldn't decide if that was an indication of his own shallowness or proof positive that Aaron and Naomi were two distinct people. Or three people. It was a bit mind-boggling. He settled for Freddie Berringer having a motive for killing Hector Laird-Browne— if Aaron's story was reliable—and moved on.

"What about Carrie?"

"Naomi may have overreacted. Carrie's father is an earl, friends with Lord Berringer. I'd say it's more probable she's keeping a low profile. She's no real threat to Freddie."

"But you are."

"Yes. As was Hector. And Will too. If Freddie's cornered, he'll lash out, but he won't kill me. He'll report my crimes and let the criminal justice system do his dirty work for him."

"We could get you protection, a reduced term."

Aaron shook his head. "A reduced term in a men's prison is a death sentence for Naomi. I'm sorry, Mr. Simpson-Stone, but I can't tell you any more than that."

It was exasperating to be so close to the information he needed yet unable to get to it, but Aaron was right. Prison would probably kill both Naomi and him.

"Thanks, Aaron. I appreciate what you've done today."

"No, thank you for listening and trying to understand." Aaron tapped the LED-lit tabletop with his finger. "Naomi would love this. Me, not so much."

Rob raised an eyebrow and smiled. "Yeah, it's been an illuminating meeting, that's for sure." He finished the last of his latte and got up. "My regards to Naomi."

"I'll pass them on."

"Cheers. You take care." Rob left the café and wandered the ground-floor exhibits, keeping Aaron in his sights. Aaron stayed seated a few minutes more and then made a dash for the nearest exit. Rob followed at a distance, across the street to the subway, but had to stop there. It was too quiet to pursue Aaron unnoticed, besides which, Rob believed him. He needed to locate Will Richards, and he was making no progress in that regard. His only other avenue was to talk to the man who'd dragged the rest of them into this mess: Freddie Berringer.

17: Saying it Wrong

AFTER HIS MEETING with Rob, Gray headed straight back to Will's, fighting himself all the way. Or not quite all the way, seeing as he left the train four stops early and walked around Pinner in an attempt to get his head together. As soon as Rob had said the guy he was chasing had gone to work for a competitor, Gray suspected he was talking about Will. He didn't know why. There was no reason to think that. People changed jobs all the time. But then Rob had confirmed it, and Gray couldn't get away fast enough. All the pieces were falling into place, except they were pieces of a puzzle Gray's copper brain had manufactured from a few shady actions on Will's part and his own search for reasons not to get involved.

Because really, what the hell did he think was going on? Will's mum had been sick: fact. Will was an animal rights activist: also fact. Will was a murderer? No, Gray didn't think so, yet Rob said he was involved in his case. Actually, that wasn't right either. Rob said there was history between Will and Berringer. That wasn't the same as being involved, and there was a simple way to find out, but Gray didn't want to.

Theirs was meant to be an easy friendship, a source of companionship and mutual support, regardless of how compatible they may or may not be, Will being up for taking things further and Gray's jaded determination not to. Never mind Will's criminal record or Gray's previous occupation as a senior police officer. He'd been OK with all of that. *Why couldn't he have worked for bloody Barclays or something?*

So Gray hadn't told Rob where Will lived. Aside from wishing to the point of denial that the connection between Will and Berringer wasn't there, he wanted to make sure Will was in the clear, which meant asking some blunt questions, but he could hardly do that in the circumstances. Or could he?

Gray stopped walking and looked back the way he'd come. He'd covered about a mile already and was closer to the next station than the one he'd left. He continued onwards, working through what he should say to Will, if anything. After all, if Will was involved, he'd be tipping him off that the police were on to him. It was a big if, aside from which, Gray didn't think Will would do a runner, not with the dogs to worry about and a funeral to plan.

Before he knew it, Gray was back on the train, still with no decision made, but maybe that was for the best. He'd play it by ear, see how Will was doing.

It wasn't all ex-cop paranoia at work. Will had worked for Berringer's, and he did have a criminal record. Admittedly, Gray hadn't trusted Will since the night of their date, which preceded Rob coming to talk to him about Berringer's and the fatal accident. The thought flipped a switch in Gray's brain. He'd heard sirens when he was waiting for Will. He took out his phone and searched for 'Mercedes accident Berringer's', knowing exactly what the results would show.

Gray wasn't that old, and he was far from wise, but he'd experienced the phenomenon of coincidence often enough to greet it with a certain amount of scepticism. Will had arrived at the restaurant approximately fifteen minutes after the accident, but it didn't mean he was involved.

He was trying so hard to convince himself of that, the train doors were closing before Gray realised he was at Croxley and bolted from his seat, squeezing through the gap and out onto the platform, where he almost lost his footing on the wet flags. It felt like it had been raining nonstop for days. Whether it had or not, Gray wasn't chancing his shoes on the woods and canal bank. The other route took longer, in part because he didn't know how to get directly to Will's from the station, thus had to take a detour past the pub they'd been to. Even then, he wasn't entirely sure he was heading the right way, but it gave him something to focus on rather than thinking himself further into a fix.

It was with some relief—and to the accompanying clang of heavy tools—that he approached the farmhouse back gate. Gray peered over the top to where Tie was poking in the Transit van's engine compartment and coughed loudly before he entered. Tie looked up, as did two of the half dozen chickens, and nodded in silent acknowledgement.

"Alright?" Gray said, slowing to a stop next to the van. "How is he?"

Tie ruefully raised an eyebrow and shook his head. It was bad, then. Gray patted Tie's shoulder as he passed by, bracing for what he was about to face. He knocked on the back door and opened it, calling "Hey" in warning as he entered. There was no sign of Will, but judging by the direction whence the dogs came at speed, he was in the living room. Gray's theory was confirmed soon after, when Will stepped into the hallway, a million miles away and unaware he had company. He walked with his head bowed and shoulders hunched, only noticing Gray when they were within touching distance.

"Oh, hey. When did you get here?"

"Just now."

Will half nodded in response and drifted across the kitchen to the kettle, which he filled and switched on. "Everything go OK?"

"At the hospice? Yeah, it was fine. The paperwork was all done when I got there." Gray held up the A4 envelope. "Shall I leave it on the table?"

"Can do. Oh, actually, no. I'll put it in the drawer." Will took it from him and went over to the dresser. "Doris'll nick it if I leave it on the table."

Gray looked down at the little terrier and then at the table. He couldn't see how that was possible.

Will closed the drawer and came back over, a fair attempt at a smile on his lips. "She can jump six foot in the air, that one."

"Wow. A kangaroo dog."

Will's smile grew. "She is. Coffee or tea?"

"Either." Gray didn't want a drink at all, but it was no big deal. Whatever Will needed to do to get through, Gray was happy to go along with it. Even he could feel how much emptier the house seemed without the big brown Staffie. Nev had been the second largest of the dogs and the most boisterous. It was so sad. "I just realised you don't have any cats."

"No." Will dropped teabags into two mugs. "Not at the moment, we don't. Nev wasn't good with cats, and we've got plenty of other people who'll take them in until they're rehomed."

"Like foster parents?"

"Yep."

"These are *your* dogs, though, aren't they?"

"They are. Because I suck at fostering. Monster was supposed to go to a retiree who lives on his own, but she'd settled, and...I get attached. It makes no difference to me whether I have three or five or even ten. They're pretty chill." Will stopped talking to deal with the kettle. He barely got the water into the mugs before he lost it and raised his hands to his face, muffling his gulps.

"Oh, dear." Gray went over and put his arms around him. "Come on." Will's head juddered against Gray's shoulder as he cried, his entire body jolting with each sob. Gray rubbed his back and whispered words of comfort, knowing all the while they brought none. For what it was worth, Will smelled a lot better than he had at the hospice, especially his hair, which was getting in Gray's mouth, but again, he wasn't going to protest. Will was six foot, maybe six foot one, to Gray's five foot ten, yet in his grief, he seemed to diminish.

It took quite a while for Will to stem the flow of tears, and when he moved his head away, his hair was caught around one of Gray's earrings. Gray had to remove it to untangle them and then couldn't get it back in again.

"Want a hand?" Will asked, still sniffling and swiping at his eyes.

Gray doubted Will would've been able to see to do it, but he'd found the hole, anyway, and poked the post through. "Got it, thanks."

Will stopped rubbing his eyes and squinted to focus on Gray's earrings. "Did your husband give you those?"

The question took Gray by surprise, though he wasn't sure why. "He did, instead of a ring. I get bad eczema." He held up his hands, inspecting the skin between his fingers. At its worst, it had cracked and bled, but it had been clear since he'd left the police.

"They suit you."

"Thanks." Gray self-consciously checked the other diamond stud was secure and rolled it between his finger and thumb. "My bling," he said and felt himself smile. He remembered Jean's voice murmuring the words, his hot breath on his earlobe as he caught the stud between his teeth and tugged. The memory was a good one, even if its erotic value had depreciated over time. But it didn't hurt anymore. "Shall we drink our tea?" Gray suggested.

Will nodded and handed him a cup. "It's probably cold, sorry."

"Don't worry. I'm sure I've drunk colder." Gray sipped and fought a shudder.

"Yeah, iced tea. You don't have to drink it."

Gray carried on just the same, watching Will over the rim as he tipped his cold tea into the sink, washed the mug and put it back in the cupboard, paused and did a double take at his own crowbar. It must have dawned on him that Gray had seen it.

"Interesting utensils," Gray said, trying to make light.

"Er, yeah." Will quickly closed the cupboard. "Did you get sorted what you needed to?"

Gray replayed what he'd told Tie and nodded. "Library books." The voice in his head called him an idiot. It was definitely on to something, although he could've said anything at all for all the notice Will was taking.

"Cool." Will nodded vacantly. "I spoke to my dad."

"How was it?"

"OK, until he asked about..." Will gestured to the dogs. "That was harder than telling him about Mum." He shrugged and rolled his eyes. "So, Dad can only take a couple of days off work, but the flights are overnight. He'll arrive the morning of the funeral and fly back the following evening. I need to call him again as soon as I've got the details."

"That must be exhausting."

"He'll sleep on the plane. He's used to it. And I still have to, er..."

Gray waited, but Will didn't get around to finishing the sentence. The back door opened. Tie came in and went straight to the sink.

"It's done," he said.

Will stared vacantly at the same spot on the floor.

Tie looked Gray's way. "Will?"

"Hmm? The van?"

"Lucky guess," Tie tormented. "I'll change my jeans, then sort the MOT on my way."

"OK." That was all he was getting out of Will.

Tie finished washing his hands and left again. Apart from Kenny's slobbering noises as he cleaned his bits and bobs, all was silent, but not for long. A grating sound prompted Gray to look out of the window. He watched Tie lift out the fence panel next to the gate and then heave the concrete post free, creating a space a little wider than the van. "Ah! So that's how." Tie drove the van through the gap and left it idling while he returned both post and panel to their previous positions. "That's brilliant!"

"What's that?" Will asked.

"The instant driveway."

"Huh?" Will came over to see, but everything looked the same as before.

"Getting the van out," Gray explained.

"Yeah. There're no parking spaces out the front."

"It wasn't in the yard the first time I came here, was it?"

"No. Jon's been using it. Illegally."

Gray nodded. "I'll keep that to myself."

"You can tell who you like. He's driving me nuts. I only let him and Micky stay as a favour to Tie. A few weeks, they said—five months ago. Tie did the same, but he's not as bad. At least he helps out. Micky's always working, and Jon just takes the piss. Shall we sit in the living room?" Will was already heading that way.

"Er...sure. Why not?" Gray followed, getting caught in the tide of dogs that came with him. He couldn't help but laugh at Kenny's speed-shuffling. It was comically awesome.

When Gray finally made it into the room after the dogs, Will was sitting at one end of the sofa, and Gray moved to sit in the chair, but Doris beat him to it. Gray swayed forward as he stopped. "Ah."

"You can always sit next to me," Will suggested, the last part lost to a chirrup from the corner of the room, where there was a large, bell-shaped cage containing a green-and-yellow bird.

"The psycho parakeet," Gray said, advancing for a closer look—anything to delay joining Will on the sofa.

"Don't put your fingers in," Will warned.

Gray nodded to show he'd heard and leaned forward, as did the bird. It was a funny-looking thing, like a big budgie with an extra-fluffy head. With its evil sideways glare, there was no way Gray would've touched it even if Will hadn't warned him first. "Does it stay in here all the time?"

"Yep. He has to. He's escaped a couple of times when I've cleaned his cage. Nightmare. He loves the dogs, though. Maybe he just hates me."

Gray laughed. "What's he called?"

"Paul."

Gray glanced Will's way. "Paul, did you say?"

Will nodded. "It's not that ridiculous. You've heard the rhyme 'Two Little Dicky Birds'?"

"I get it. Was there a Peter?"

"Yep. His brother. He killed him."

"Nice." Gray studied the bird. "He looks too innocent to commit fratricide."

"Don't let him fool you."

The bird hopped from its perch and clung to the bars directly in front of Gray's face. It was making a quiet noise, like it was whispering to him. "He says he's not guilty," Gray said and heard Will chuckle. "Can he talk?"

"A little. He and Peter were badly neglected by their previous owner, so he's not been in contact with humans much. He's picked up a few phrases—'Hello, Paul,' 'Want your dinner?'—stuff like that."

"Hello, Paul, want your dinner?" the bird repeated and then squawked in Gray's ear. He backed off.

"Does he swear?"

"Nope, but I don't swear often. He can bark, though." Will sighed. It was loud enough to make Gray look his way again. "He mimics Nev."

Gray frowned in sympathy and went to join Will, but at the opposite end of the sofa, which was a four-seater.

Will eyed the significant gap between them and tutted. "He might bite—" he nodded at the bird "—but I don't."

"I didn't want to invade your space."

"That's a pity. I was hoping if I put my feet up, you might..." Will wiggled his thumbs.

"Give them here." Gray shuffled a bit closer.

"I wasn't serious," Will said but lifted his feet up regardless and then groaned when Gray began circling his thumbs over Will's insteps. "My head's banging." He groaned again and slid down, bending his knees to compensate. His heels dug into Gray's thigh. Gray adjusted position, removed Will's socks and continued with the massage. He quite liked feet if they were clean and well-pedicured, which Will's were.

"Have you taken anything?" he asked.

"Not yet." Will closed his eyes and lay back against the arm of the sofa. Gray watched crinkles form across Will's forehead and around his eyes as he flinched in discomfort, and then disappear again as he relaxed. "I've got so many calls to make tomorrow. Registrar, funeral director... My uncle said he'd deal with the funeral director when he gets here, but that won't be till the weekend."

"Weren't you expecting him yesterday?"

"Yeah, and he was on his way, but when I saw Mum, I called and told him to stay where he was, or he'd have been forking out petrol money for no reason." Will put his hands above his head and stretched, his back arching off the couch and giving Gray an eyeful of bare belly. He probably should've tried *not* to look rather than marvelling at the smooth, hairless skin.

"Do you wax?"

"No. Why?"

"I thought you'd have a hairy belly."

Will's arm fell over his eyes, and his cheeks turned pink.

With effort, Gray shifted his gaze and his increasingly lewd thoughts. "Is Tie out for the evening?" If ever there were a question with an ulterior motive...

"Yeah, probably."

"Working?"

"Yep."

"What's he up to?" Gray recalled Will had said he did agency work.

Will peered from underneath his arm and said nothing. Gray scolded himself for asking the question and concentrated on massaging Will's feet, feeling his tension ease. Will's breathing deepened, and his knees fell to the sides; it wasn't long before Gray heard quiet snores coming from the other end of the sofa, and he continued with the massage a while longer before settling back for the duration.

It wasn't too bad for the first twenty minutes. That was how long Gray estimated had passed before he began thinking up ways of getting his phone out of his pocket without disturbing Will. He tried shifting to the side; Will stirred. Gray froze. Will recommenced snoring. Gray sagged and instead made a mental things-to-do list. He did, in fact, have library books that were probably overdue, but he hadn't so much as opened a cover. He'd check when he went home and renew them online. He needed groceries too, but that would require writing down. He tried to reach his phone again, but it was deep in his pocket, tucked around the bend of his hip. He had to face facts; it wasn't happening.

The afternoon turned to evening...

The dogs slept on.

Will slept on. And on.

The room became dark.

Gray heard the back door open and close, followed by the click of a switch. Light spilled along the hallway and illuminated Will's twitchy toes. Someone mooched in the kitchen cupboards. The tap ran, crockery clanged, a man belched. Gray hoped it was Jon, reasoning a thief would've gathered their loot before they made a snack. The back door opened and closed again, this time with quite a bang. Gray flinched. Will flexed his knees, the resultant shift of his feet removing the restriction in blood flow that Gray hadn't noticed until his lower legs started to warm up.

"Oh, God, Gray. I'm sorry."

"It's OK."

Will reached behind his head and switched on the lamp. He stretched and spoke through a yawn. "I'm so knackered." The yawn ended with a shake of the head. "Sorry."

"Sleep if you need to. Don't mind me."

Will shuffled into a sitting position, freed his hair from the elastic band and ruffled it with his fingers. "Headache's gone."

"That's good." Gray was preoccupied with Will's mane. He'd only seen it tied back and was surprised by how much of it there was, a golden halo with the lamp's backlighting. "How're you feeling?"

"OK. A bit...disconnected? I'll be all right."

"It's all right if you're not."

"Yeah, I know." Will crossed his legs and reached over them to affectionately squeeze Gray's thigh. "Thanks for being here. I'm really grateful, but if you need to go..."

"I'd rather you weren't on your own."

"I'll cope."

"Hmm. When did you eat last?"

"Oh! Good point." Will got up and left the room, with the dogs in hot pursuit. Gray heard their food bowls being filled and set down and went to join Will in the kitchen.

"Have you eaten today?" he asked.

"I can't be bothered, and yeah, I know. I need to eat something." Will wandered over to the fridge, opened it and peered inside for all of three seconds. He shut the door again.

"I could make us something," Gray offered. Will wrinkled his nose. "Thanks for the vote of confidence."

Will laughed, but it was a weary effort. "I didn't mean it that way. There's some veggie cottage pie in the freezer. Want some of that?"

Gray shrugged. "Fine with me."

"That's easy, then."

Fifteen minutes later, they were eating, or Gray was. Will managed a few mouthfuls and pushed away his plate. He looked like he was expecting a lecture, but Gray had been where he was. There would be no lecturing.

"What time's Tie due back?" Gray took out his phone to check the train timetable.

"Probably not till the early hours."

Gray put his phone away.

"You can go," Will said again.

"Do you want me to?"

Will frowned in consideration. "Honestly? No. I don't."

"OK. Well, I don't mind kipping on the couch. I need to pop home in the morning, though."

"Are you sure?"

"I'm sure. Just throw a blanket my way when you want to go to bed."

"I've got a spare room—two, actually."

"You told me yesterday."

Will frowned. "Did I? I don't remember. I feel like I've been drugged." He pondered on that a moment and then shook it off. "So, yeah. I'll need to make up the bed. Or you can share mine. It's a king-size, and there'll be a barricade of dogs between us."

Gray laughed, quickly dismissing how much he liked that idea. "The couch'll do me."

Will sighed—Gray interpreted it as relief rather than disappointment— and swallowed down a bit more of the cottage pie before he cleared the table. Between them, they washed up and took the dogs for a walk, which didn't feel any different to Gray, but he imagined it did to Will. The rest of the evening was spent in front of the TV, which was background noise to the meaningless conversation that existed only to distract Will.

A little before midnight, Will brought a duvet and said good night. Gray switched off the lamp and plumped a cushion to use as a pillow. The sofa was very comfortable and long enough to lie full stretch, but he was wide awake. He found his phone and checked his email: he was needed at the studio tomorrow lunchtime; a student wanted an extension on an assignment; Becky enquired whether he'd been abducted by aliens. He chuckled, sent a quick reply to let her know he was OK and locked his phone. Roll over, try again.

He heard Will use the bathroom at one a.m. and again at quarter to two.

He heard Tie come in and go upstairs at three o'clock.

He heard the murmured conversation that followed.

He didn't hear Tie come down again because Tie didn't come down again. Gray wondered if he and Will still slept together—in the biblical sense, as opposed to either side of a 'barricade of dogs'. If they did, they were very discreet, but it was none of his concern. He'd refused Will's offer of sharing the bed. He couldn't really grumble if Will now chose to share it with Tie.

Both Will and Tie were up at six, and Gray pretended he was asleep in an effort to avoid them as much as he could before it was late enough to catch a train. It wasn't that he felt like he was intruding; rather, the tense silence between the other two men had taken over the house. There was something going on, and this time, Gray was confident it was more than a figment of his ex-cop imagination.

When he heard the back door open and close, Gray took a chance and went through to the kitchen, but he'd misjudged. Tie hadn't left; Jon had come in.

Will offered Gray a tight smile. "Morning."

"Morning. Are you OK?"

Will's eyes flitted to Tie. "Not bad, thanks. Did you get any sleep?"

"Er...not a lot."

"Sorry about that." He didn't sound sorry.

"It's fine." Gray nodded too long. "Right, I'll erm... I'll get going, give you a call later, OK?"

"Yep." Will walked Gray to the door.

"If you need me..."

"Yeah, cheers, Gray. See you later."

Gray stepped outside and looked back in time to catch Will's solemn expression. The door shut, and Gray moved off, slowly, the heated exchange from within the house following him all the way to the gate.

18: Assets to Burn

BERRINGER HAD FAILED to answer or return Rob's calls, but the doorman to his Marylebone apartment building had been very helpful. Rob hadn't even needed to mention he was a police officer to find out Berringer hadn't been home for two weeks and his mail was being forwarded to a sub post office in Berkshire, in the town closest to the family estate. If Freddie Berringer was hiding, he wasn't doing a very good job of it.

The CPS had advised Rob not to speak to Berringer while he was on jury service, even though the investigation had no bearing on any of the trials going on at the Crown Court. Rob was already halfway through his seven-day loan to CID; with no time to waste, all he could do was ask around and see what else he could find out.

Berringer had been keeping a low profile since the bank went under, cancelling his entire social calendar bar one event: a fundraising dinner he'd attended with his father the previous Monday evening. The charity had posted photos on their website, in which Freddie was pictured with his arms around the shoulders of two young women and looking very much the worse for wear. The waiting-on staff from the venue said he'd been drunk when he arrived, and the photo was of him being escorted off the premises—'escorted' being the operative word, as it turned out the two women were from an escort agency.

It took a few calls and a threat to prosecute the agency for obstructing an investigation, but Rob finally got hold of the two women, who told him they'd spent the night with Berringer, but it had consisted of staggering from club to club and then to a hotel, where he'd passed out. At six a.m., he'd received a phone call and sent the women on their way. Soon after, according to the concierge, Berringer's chauffeur had collected him from the hotel. Rob was still waiting for someone to check the traffic cameras to see if he could figure out where he went in the two hours between leaving the hotel and turning up at the court. It was the only period he couldn't account for since the night of Hector Laird-Browne's death.

It was an afterthought, calling Aaron to ask if he'd heard from Berringer. Rob assumed he would've mentioned it already, so he wasn't surprised when Aaron said he hadn't—but Naomi had, and that pissed Rob right off. Whether they were distinct personas or not, whatever Naomi went through, Aaron did too. However, when Rob pushed for details, it became clear why Aaron hadn't mentioned it, and it made no sense. Why would Naomi ask for Berringer's help if she believed he'd killed Hector?

Except Naomi hadn't said that, or not in those words. She'd said Freddie was responsible for Hector's death, and Rob was trying to complete the puzzle with half the pieces missing.

A hand waved in front of Rob's face. He blinked it into focus and followed it up to Detective Sergeant Miller's inquisitive expression.

"You all right?" Miller asked.

Rob smiled and nodded. "Yeah. Just thinking."

"You stopping for lunch?"

Rob drew breath to say 'thanks, but no thanks' at the same time as the DCI shouted, "Yes, you are."

"Ma'am..."

"You've been staring at the same point on the wall for the past half hour."

"Actually, it was the bird shit on the window," Rob argued. Miller turned away to hide his grin.

Hedley glowered at him, though the smirk somewhat took the edge off it. Sometimes he wondered how he got away with giving her backchat.

"I can get you a bucket and a ladder if you're looking for work to do," she suggested dryly.

"I'm not slacking, Ma'am. I've hit a brick wall with the Berringer case."

"Right, so you can stop for lunch." She got up from her chair, logging out of her computer as she did so, and marched past. "That was a direct order, Constable."

Rob vented a sigh of frustration and muttered, "Yes, Ma'am." He walked with Miller up to the staff canteen, grabbed a tray and joined the queue.

"You're still set on going back to uniform next week?" Miller asked as they shuffled along the serving counter. None of the food looked in the least bit appetising.

"Yeah, I am." Rob pointed at the large pan of yellow something. "What's that?" he asked the young guy behind the counter.

"Kedgeree."

"You're not exactly brimming with enthusiasm there, Rob," Miller said.

The server was still watching him, awaiting instruction.

"I'll have some of that, cheers," Rob said, and then to Miller, "I want to conclude this case before I go back, but my prime suspect is on jury service, and I can't track down the other people I need to speak to." With a nod of thanks, Rob took the plate of kedgeree, set it on his tray and moved on.

"See if Petridis will give you a couple more days," Miller suggested as they joined the DCI at her table.

"Hmm." There was no point even asking, but Miller was right. Obstacles aside, Rob was enjoying the work, and he wasn't looking forward to going back to his normal job. But he was also aware he was having an easy ride. Everyone else was working on half a dozen cases at the same time, admittedly in teams, whereas he only had to worry about getting enough evidence to bring down Berringer or whoever the hell was responsible for killing Laird-Browne.

What also suited him was that Hedley, for the most part, was letting him go it alone. It was another after-effect of working with the SIU, where theoretically, he had been part of a team, but the reality had been three years of solo detective work, and whilst the team mentality of uniformed life was one of the biggest draws, these days, he had no patience for slackers.

"Any good?" Miller asked, jabbing his fork in the direction of Rob's plate. He'd eaten half the kedgeree without it touching the sides. He put another forkful in his mouth and paid attention so he could report back.

"Nah. Greasy, not enough fish. And what are these about?" Rob tried to spear a bullet-like garden pea, and it shot off across the table, landing on the seat between Miller and Hedley.

"You can do better, can you, Rob?" Hedley challenged. Another CID officer—DC Steven Tang—came to join them, shoving Miller's tray along to put down his own.

"Oy!" Miller said, shoving it back again and then snorting with laughter when Tang plonked his backside on the pea. Rob and Hedley joined in with the laughter.

"What?" Tang asked, frowning at them all.

"You're not a princess, then?" Rob asked.

"What are you on about?"

"Look under—"

Miller cut Rob off. "So when are you inviting us over for kedgeree?"

"Ha! I'm not bloody cooking for you lot. I might make it for Lu over the weekend, though." Rob liked that idea, and while he made a shopping list in his head, the conversation moved on. He needed to get out to see Berringer at some point over the weekend, but he was taking Lucas swimming first thing, come what may.

People started getting up around him, and Rob quickly downed his coffee, nearly spraying it out again when he caught a glimpse of the squashed pea on Tang's backside. He wasn't cruel enough to let the poor bloke walk around like that all day.

"Ste, mate." Tang turned back, and Rob nodded him towards the general area.

"Balls. I've not split another pair, have I?"

"You've peed yourself," Miller said, giggling like the big kid he was.

Rob shook his head. "I remember now why I moved to uniform." He got up and picked the offending item off Tang's pants.

"Cheers," Tang said with a dark look in Miller's direction, not that he cared.

Rob waited for Hedley to stack her tray in the stand. "Is everyone else out for the day, Ma'am?" They were down two female officers.

"Two separate rapes reported this morning."

Rob grimaced.

"Yeah. So, are you going to have enough for the CPS by Tuesday?"

"I doubt it, but I wondered if you were free for a drive out to Berkshire tomorrow afternoon."

"Business or pleasure?" She grinned.

"Always a pleasure with you, Ma'am," Rob said with a wink, hoping Hedley's missus never got to hear about his flirting. She was a chief superintendent.

"We're off to see Berringer, are we?"

"We are. He's holed up at the family estate."

"Oh, how super. I'll wear my best tweed togs. What time?"

"Leave at one-thirty? It's an hour's drive."

"One-thirty it is. I'll come over to you."

"You don't fancy riding pillion?"

"Next time, Rob." She patted his arm and walked off.

"That's what you said the last time, Ma'am."

"One of these days, I'll surprise you." With that, she disappeared through the doors, leaving Rob with a smile on his face and a glimmer of hope that he could conclude his investigation by Tuesday. And then what? He didn't know, but he had some thinking to do.

19: Scarpered

GRAY GAVE UP on sleep at something past four. He wasn't sure precisely when, as it was the power outage and subsequent ear-piercing screech of the house alarm that brought him to after at most an hour. It was still something past four when he'd reset the circuit breaker, and he went straight from the fuse box to the kettle to make a cup of tea and some breakfast, hoping it would ease the nausea and help him figure out what to do.

Most of the time, Gray liked his stove-top kettle. It looked old and well used, but it wasn't really. It was made of some clever super-conductive metal alloy and took as long to boil as a standard electric kettle. However, this morning, he needed to get to his tea more quickly than any kettle would allow. He was exhausted—physically and emotionally. The still solitude of the night had granted little more than the opportunity to reflect on his latest series of poor judgements. He shivered, almost feverish, his body seeking balance it could not achieve with the sleep deprivation, along with the dawning truth.

The kettle started to whistle, and Gray let it. He leaned back against the worktop and covered his face with his hands. "Oh, God. What did I do?"

The boiling kettle screamed. *You abandoned Will when he needed you most.*

He hadn't heard from Will since Thursday morning—two days ago—and for the first twenty-four hours, Gray refused to call him. He was tired and angry, but with time and distance, he'd realised it wasn't Will he was angry with. As if it wasn't bad enough that Will had lost his mum and a dog in the same week, Gray had effectively granted him the hat-trick. *Oh, that I should be so important in someone's life.* He didn't deserve to be, that was for sure. He'd let Will down, promising to help with the funeral arrangements and then sulking because Will had kicked him out of the farmhouse.

The kettle was still yelling, the jet of steam shooting from its spout accumulating in a thick layer of mist that completely obscured the ceiling. If Gray didn't do something about it soon, it was going to rain in his kitchen, which was apt, but he'd rather it didn't. He turned off the flame and finally made the tea he'd wanted so urgently before.

With the outside door open, the steam quickly dissipated, and Gray took in a good, deep breath of cool, early morning air. It was at this time of day the city air was at its clearest, and it gave him quite a jolt. He needed to fix things with Will and be there for him, as he'd promised.

Gray closed the door and returned to his bedroom to collect his mobile phone—not to call Will. He refused to acknowledge the possibility Will had done a bunk because he was guilty and knew Rob was on to him. There was no evidence Will was involved. If he had been, he'd have cut contact a week ago, when Gray first mentioned the accident and the investigation.

Will deserved an apology and an explanation, but Gray had to find him first. He typed a message—*are you awake?*—and sent it to Josh. Not twenty seconds later, his phone vibrated with an incoming call. He slid his thumb across the screen.

"Greetings, fellow insomniac," Josh said cheerily.

"Morning," Gray responded gloomily. Josh was far too chirpy for a time of day so ungodly.

"I sense you're not enjoying this gloriously tranquil hour."

"You could say that. I didn't wake you, did I?"

"No. I've been up for a while. I have a paper to submit by the end of today."

Gray gave a light laugh of disbelief. "There's no way you'd leave something like that to the last minute."

"Oh, it was written weeks ago, and I've read it through at least a dozen times, but it was on my mind. So, assuming this isn't just a courtesy call..." Josh let the sentence trail as a prompt for Gray.

"No. It's not," he said and then fell silent, knowing if Josh gave him permission, he'd pour out his soul. It was what he needed to do, which was, of course, why he'd called Josh—the only man he felt safe confiding in.

"Graham?"

"Yeah, I'm still here." He collected his tea, took a tentative sip and sighed. "I've done something selfish." The line remained quiet, and Gray visualised Josh at the other end, jotting notes while he waited for him to continue, but it was difficult to know where to start. Maybe with something else? He could ease into it, take a side road. "Rob sends his regards."

"Never mind Rob. You can tell me about him after you've told me what you needed to so desperately you risked waking me up."

"I knew you'd be awake."

"That's by the by. Come on, Graham. Out with it."

"Will's mum died, and then his dog died, and I kind of ended things between us. By accident."

"I see."

"I didn't mean it to come across the way it did."

"Kind of...by accident—what exactly did you say, or do?"

"It's a long story, but Rob's investigating a bank Will used to work for, and... Basically, I concocted some rubbish in my head, and when I went back to Will's, he was a mess—worse than with his mum—and I stayed over, on the sofa, because we're not there yet, or I'm not, and I realise now that when he said we could share his bed, he wanted the company, but I'm stuck in that place. I didn't want to send out the signal I was ready to try a relationship, when maybe I am, but until I'm sure, I daren't risk it.

"Then Tie, his ex, came home, and they slept together...probably slept together..." Gray felt so stupid. Restating it in context made it even clearer he'd overreacted and his conclusions were unfounded. "I don't know if they slept together, but Will was eager to be rid of me the morning after, and I decided it would be better if I kept my distance for a while."

"You thought Tie meant something more?" Josh asked.

"No, or...yes. Maybe. I accused Will of lying about his mum being ill. Not to his face, but I thought it. He turned up late for a date, and...I don't know. I can't make head nor tail of his intent or how I feel. I called him, and Tie answered his phone. It's all innocent, I know that now, or not innocent, but that's another story. And idiot me..." Gray sighed and rubbed hard at his head. He couldn't rally his thoughts.

"OK, Graham, just so you know, you're rambling, but I think I've got the gist. The date and the phone call came before his mum and the dog?"

"A couple of weeks back, yeah. But there's the case Rob's working on..." Gray figured he may as well own up now, to both Josh and himself. "I used it as an excuse to call Will the week after our date."

"Why?"

"I don't know. To catch him out?"

Josh didn't respond for a while and then said, "No, that's not it. You were testing the water before you jumped in. Is Tie the guy staying at the farm?"

"Along with his brother and his brother's girlfriend. But I think I... Oh, I don't know what I think."

"I do," Josh said. "You're jealous."

"No, I'm not."

Josh laughed. "Yes, you are. I used to do exactly the same when I called George at uni, and again when he was on the ranch. 'Why is this stranger answering George's phone?' 'Who is this Ray that George keeps talking about?' You, my dear brother-in-law, have a classic case of denial."

"Don't be ridiculous." Gray was fooling no-one.

"If not, why are we having this conversation?" Josh asked, then said, "Morning, Lib."

In the background, Gray heard Libby respond with a sleepy "Good morning" and ask who Josh was speaking to.

"Your uncle," Josh told her.

After a couple of seconds of silence, he heard Libby say, "At this time of day? Is he mental? Actually, don't answer that. I already know." Another quiet moment followed. "It's Graham."

"Gray?" It was George this time. "At five in the morning?"

Now Gray felt really guilty. He'd disturbed the Sandison-Morley household en masse. "Look, Josh, I'm sorry. I'll leave you in peace, and—"

"You'll do no such thing," Josh admonished.

"OK. Then I'll cut to the chase. Will's gone. I called him all day yesterday with no response, so I went up to the farmhouse, and Tie said he took off in the van."

"Where?"

"I've no idea."

"He won't be gone for long, though, will he?" Josh reasoned. "He wouldn't leave his dogs."

"He asked Tie to look after them."

"Ah."

"And now he doesn't have to worry about his mum, there's nothing to keep him there."

"He's not going to leave his dogs, Graham. Not permanently."

Gray wanted to believe Josh was right, but the way Will had been after Nev, and then with the argument or whatever it was on Thursday morning, he wasn't so sure. He'd been through feeling like that—the walking through fog, the anger, the desperation that made him run from the pain. It was why he'd spent so long undercover, avoiding anything and everything to do with Jean, including his own grief. There had been no reason for him to stay. His sister had family and friends to look after her, just as Tie and the others would take care of Will's dogs.

"So," Josh said, dragging Gray back from the brink of despair. His timing was impeccable. "If you knew where to find him, what would you do?"

"I'd apologise."

"That's it?"

"I need to tell him I'm sorry before I do anything else, and be honest with him, like I should've been two days ago, two weeks, even. The rest, I need to get my head around. I'll have to wait, hope he comes back at some point."

"And if he doesn't?"

Gray closed his eyes, trying to block out how that made him feel. He wanted Will to come back. More than that, he wanted to go and find Will, tell him he was sorry and admit he'd been wrong. He wanted something more; he just didn't know what.

"This van he took off in," Josh said. "Camper van, perchance?"

"No. A beat-up old Ford Transit, but with a mattress in the back. They use it for doing whatever it is they do."

"The animal rights stuff?"

"That, and if anyone needs a place to kip. I think it's kitted out with the full works—camping stove, mini fridge and what-have-you."

"OK." Josh fell silent. Gray waited, wondering if Josh was expecting him to say something else. As he was about to speak, Josh said, "I can tell you where he is."

Gray's hackles rose. He'd asked for Josh's help, or his ear, at least. That was not an open invitation for Sandison-Morley smugness, and since when was Josh an expert on relationships anyway? Gray gritted his teeth, determined not to let Josh hear how much he was winding him up. "You knew all along?"

"Knew what?"

"Why didn't you say he'd been in touch, instead of making me confess..." *that I have feelings for him. Damn it.*

"I haven't spoken to him, Graham, or I'd have told you. I'm merely deducing from what you've said."

"Oh." Gray's temper simmered down, leaving a mush of foolishness. "I'm sorry. I don't know what's the matter with me. I guess... I'm worried about him. He shouldn't be going through this alone, and it's my fault he is."

"Nonsense. He'd have likely taken off, regardless. But, if you're serious about going after him—"

"Where?"

"Cornwall."

"Surfing?"

"Obviously."

"It's the middle of winter."

"It's late autumn, but that's not going to stop a surfer, I can guarantee it. The going gets tough, they bugger off and surf it out of their system."

"You're sure that's where Will's gone?"

"Almost one hundred percent. There's a campsite up on the cliffs. He'll be staying there, or if it's closed, there's a hostel with camping space for hippies like Will."

Gray managed a brief chuckle at that.

"I'll send you a text message with the address of the hotel," Josh said. "It's on the beach, so it'll give you a postcode for the satnav."

"OK." Gray was grateful for the glimmer of hope Josh had granted him. "Thank you."

"No problem."

"I don't know what I'd do without you sometimes."

"I do, and it wouldn't be pretty. You take care, and keep me posted."

"Will do. Love to George and Lib. And Iris."

"I won't tell my mother-in-law she was an afterthought, but I'll pass it on. Bye, Graham." Josh ended the call.

Gray drank the rest of his tea, thinking, planning. The text message arrived with the name of the hotel and the postcode, but he already knew where he was heading. He'd been there before.

***

Gray didn't bother stopping at the hotel first. He drove straight into the car park overlooking the bay. There were only two other cars and the Transit van, to Gray's relief. A car rental and a 270-mile drive would have stung if it had turned out to be for nothing. *In denial?* OK, yes. He was glad Will was safe. Or relatively safe, as the ocean looked deadly. From where he was parked, Gray's entire visual field was taken up by the roll and swell of enormous, white-edged waves forging their way to shore. It was a striking view, but his only thought was how easily one could be overwhelmed by the power of those waves. He couldn't fathom what possessed a person to throw themselves at the mercy of nature like that, but was again reminded of how he'd felt after Jean. That recklessness, loss of hope—not even so much as that. It was a numb, grey nothing he'd sought to fill with his work and drugs, searching for something, anything, that would make him feel again. Perhaps he and Will were not so different after all.

The wind wasn't strong, although it was bitterly cold, which Gray had anticipated, and he'd brought a coat, hat, scarf and gloves. He put them on and zipped his coat right up under his chin before venturing down the slipway onto the beach. The tide was coming in rather than going out; that much he could tell from the dryness of the shoreline. Out in the midst of the rolling ocean were two surfers, some distance from each other, both standing with their boards at their sides and looking out to the horizon.

Gray was no stranger to surfing. Growing up near the southwest English coast, summer holidays had been filled with bodyboarding, bobbing around in a dingy and other pursuits that in adulthood seemed dangerous and irresponsible. But the risks were new, or rather, his perception of those activities as inherently risky was new.

His mum, for all her faults, had been a good mum—when they were kids. She'd taken them out to places; they'd gone on family holidays. She'd bought them just the thing they wanted for Christmas, and it had always been a surprise. They'd only ever scraped by because Jack Morley had left both his mum and George's to bring up his sons with no support whatsoever. Jack was, as Iris Morley so aptly put it, a fucker who cared for no-one but himself, and Becky's dad wasn't much better, but none of the three children had suffered for being part of a single-parent family. When Gray looked back on his childhood, he did so fondly—great memories of good times.

And then he'd had to go and ruin it, first by being gay, second by meeting the love of his life, and third by 'marrying' said love. He didn't really blame himself, but there were times when he'd wished things were different.

Both of the surfers were now up on their boards, and Gray watched on, slightly envious, as the two of them took off, traversing the lengths of the waves with ease, seeming to ride for many minutes before first one and then the other toppled into the foaming dark turquoise of the autumnal Atlantic. He thought the surfer on the left was Will, although it was impossible to tell for sure from a distance.

Between the insulation their wetsuits afforded and the adrenaline, the surfers were no doubt a lot warmer than Gray was, in spite of his many woollen layers. He shivered and banged his gloved hands together, turning his back to the wind. It was picking up and battered against his legs, which were not well protected in jeans. His boots were wet, and the tide was advancing quickly. The cold, salty spray added to his chilliness.

Glancing back along the bay, Gray homed in on the café. With the sky darkening, the glow of the lights inside was warm and welcoming. He could do with a hot drink and to get out of the wind, but he hadn't driven all this way for a beach-front cappuccino. He'd spent much of the drive thinking what he wanted to say—what he *needed* to say—to Will to make amends. He wanted Will to know how sorry he was, but this was not about his apology being heard. Will needed the support of his friends, and Gray was willing to be there for him. It was what had been missing from Gray's life when he lost Jean—his own fault, as he'd deliberately distanced his friends, unable to face their questions, support or love. It hadn't done him any favours; nor would it do Will any.

"Gray?"

He turned, startled, and met the vision of the wetsuited Will Richards, board under one arm, the other raised to sweep back his hair. It was already drying in the brisk wind.

"Will."

"What are you doing here?"

"I..." Gray's face attempted a simultaneous frown and smile. He shook off his confusion and volleyed the question. "What d'you think I'm doing here?"

"You came looking for me?"

"Well, yes."

"How did you know where..." Will rolled his eyes and mustered a smile—not his most convincing attempt, but it was there, nonetheless. "Doesn't matter. You came looking for me."

Gray shivered again, not quite sure how Will was able to stand there in skintight neoprene—which Gray was trying very hard not to attend to—and not be freezing his bits and bobs off—which Gray was also trying not to attend to. He cleared his throat. "Can we go to the café and talk?"

Will shrugged. "Sure."

The two men walked side by side, in silence, the wind too strong for conversation. It wasn't until they were climbing the steps to the café that the silence was broken, and even then not in any more meaningful a way than Will explaining he was going to put his board in the van.

"OK. I'll order the drinks," Gray suggested. "What would you like?"

"Hot chocolate, cheers." Will continued on his way.

Gray went inside and placed the order. There were other people in there, but it wasn't busy, as was to be expected on a wet and windy afternoon in November.

A further ten minutes passed before Will returned, minus his wetsuit and wearing entirely inappropriate clothing for the season: cropped cargos, skate shoes and a long-sleeved tee.

"You're a lot hardier than me," Gray remarked lightly, feeling a little self-conscious that Will had caught him staring. Strange, but in this environment, he was different—more confident, certainly, and somehow more attractive. Russet cheeks, ruddy lips, messy hair, fathomless dark eyes, so much vitality. He was extraordinarily handsome. Or perhaps Gray was seeing him in a new light.

"I'm surprised you're here," Will said with none of his usual light-hearted cheeriness—understandably.

"Me too," Gray replied, which was the truth. It wasn't his style to go chasing after people, however much he cared about them, and he did care a great deal about Will. It hurt to see him so down and to know there was no instant fix. In time, he'd work through his grief his own way. "I need to say sorry for... everything. I was out of line."

"No, you weren't. I kind of pushed you out. But it wasn't anything you did."

"I realised that—later. I overreacted and let you down. Though I'll admit to wondering if there's more between you and Tie."

"There's not."

Time to lay his cards on the table; Gray owed it to them both. "The truth is, Will, I'm attracted to you, but I'm struggling to trust you. And I know it's my problem, but until I've dealt with it..."

Will didn't respond for a few minutes. He toyed with his lip, his gaze flitting between Gray's face and the mid-distance. "Why didn't you say something before now?"

"Your mum, Nev...it's not the right time."

"For whom?"

"For..." Gray shrugged. "For me, I guess."

"But I already told you I was fine with you not wanting anything more than friendship."

"Are you?"

Will's eyes narrowed. "You question every single thing I say. Why?"

Gray was affronted, though he had no right. "I don't."

"Look, Gray, I kind of get why you're suspicious."

"It was my job to be."

"True, but I haven't helped matters. I should've been more open about what was going on—not just with you, with everyone. Like with Tie and Jon. It's difficult when people are relying on me, and they've been waiting for me to jump back in the saddle. That's what caused trouble on Thursday morning. They've been on at me for months. Then you questioned why I gave up my career—you weren't the only one, by the way—and I get it. To everyone else, it seems like I'm making crazy decisions, but it's hard, you know? Trying to explain you're doing it because someone you love is dying." Will swallowed back tears. Gray reached across and gave his hand a squeeze of reassurance.

"Hey, I'm sorry. I had no right to judge you. After Jean, I did the opposite."

"And it made you ill."

Gray nodded. "It did, yes. Some of us never learn from our mistakes. But can I ask you something? Not about work." Gray waited for Will's permission. "If you're OK with us just being friends, why did you take off?"

"Because I could." Will had slumped in his seat and pulled himself upright again. "And because I was ready to thump Tie."

"Did you sleep together?" Gray screwed his eyes shut. "Don't answer that." It wasn't so much an escaped thought as a question he'd hoped he could word more tactfully before he asked it.

"Gray."

He opened one eye and caught Will's smirk.

"Tie and I are ancient history."

Gray opened the other eye and pretended his cheeks hadn't turned fire-engine red. "It's none of my business."

"Er...yeah." Will's smirk turned into a grin. "Sounds like you want to make it your business."

"I just thought with him spending the night in—"

"The spare room," Will interjected. "He was expecting the police to turn up, and last time, they dragged him out of the caravan."

Gray pinched the bridge of his nose and laughed at himself. "Can we talk about something that doesn't involve me acting like an insecure fool?"

Will's smile was a good indication of how much he liked what he was hearing, but he saved Gray further embarrassment and changed the subject. "I haven't been down here in over a year. The last time was when I met George and Josh."

"Really?"

"Yep." Will pointed past Gray. "We sat out there, on the balcony, and drank beer. I think Josh'd had a few too many."

Gray smiled. "Can I let you in on a secret?"

"You're trusting me?" Will wasn't being sarcastic.

"I am. But whatever you do, don't mention it to Josh or George."

"Of course."

"I had them under surveillance."

"Surveillance?"

"The fraud case with Josh's friend?"

Will shrugged. He didn't know about it.

"Well, anyway, I followed them down here."

"You were watching them on their honeymoon?"

Gray nodded, ashamed. "I'm afraid so. But it was entirely professional."

"Oh, you sly dog." Will looked highly amused.

Gray cleared his throat. "You were saying..."

"Yeah, so, Mum started going downhill the week after I got back, and I had to find a job—beg for my old job—to pay for her carers. The doctors wanted her to go to the hospice, but she didn't want that."

"It was the right decision, though?"

"In the end, it was. She needed twenty-four-hour nursing, and she wasn't really aware of what was going on, as you might've noticed."

Gray nodded, yes. He wouldn't forget that visit in a hurry.

Will continued. "I'd always said I was going to catch some waves once it was over, although I didn't want to leave the others when they're grieving for Nev as much as I am."

"The dogs, you mean?"

"Yep."

"Wow. I'd never thought of that."

"So, I guess, if I'm honest, with Tie and Jon's antics, you disappearing on me was the final straw. I wouldn't have made it through this week without you, Gray. Truthfully. But I needed to get away for a couple of days to clear my head."

Gray could understand that. "You mean I drove all this way for nothing?" he tormented.

"It's still good to see you, and, if you'll forgive me for calling *you* to question, it does suggest you care, and I need that. So thanks."

"I do care about you, Will. More than I show." Gray felt himself blushing again and covered it with a grin. "Plus, I knew you'd be hot in a wetsuit."

"Oh, you noticed?" Will asked with fake coyness. It was the first time Gray had seen him flirt.

"I did. I just..." Gray was unsure if he could say the words out loud, but perhaps it would help if he told the whole truth. It wasn't that he was still grieving for Jean or believed no-one could ever replace him. No-one could ever replace him, but that didn't mean there was no room in his life for another relationship. Yet he was so terrified of having to go through the pain again, it seemed easier to avoid it to begin with. Easier, and getting lonelier with every passing day.

"Let's carry on being friends," Will suggested. "And if it goes further, it can be no strings. What d'you think?"

Keeping the friendship and the potential sex separate sounded like an excellent idea. The question was, did Gray really want to?

20: Dance with the Devil

M UM SAID YOU could come to the fireworks with us."
"Did she?" Rob tried not to let his surprise show, but it didn't matter. Lucas was already two body lengths away and splicing the water with helicopter arms. These past few weeks, his crawl had come on in leaps and bounds. He was still creating whitewater and bringing his arms forward too soon, but he'd only learnt to swim in the summer holidays, when he'd had Rob at the pool on every day off, before late shifts and after earlies.

It was a difficult balance to strike, and Rob wasn't sure of the wisdom of giving in so easily to his son's demands, but he had a lot of catching up to do. It would've been different if they'd still been a family under one roof. The opportunities to do things together were always there, like when Rob's dad had said, "Come on, let's get this mess sorted," and Rob had cussed under his breath at being coerced into tidying his room before he could go out with his mates, even if it had been done twice as fast with his dad's help. Those times had taken on a new value, now Rob was looking back from the vantage point of a dad on the outside.

Lucas had turned and was on his way back across the pool, oblivious to other swimmers dodging around him. His strokes were getting slower and longer, which improved his technique. He was no natural water baby, that was for sure, but as long as he was building stamina, Rob was happy. Strength was more important than speed. His panting son appeared next to him, grinning and proud.

"You did great there, Lu."

The praise made his grin wider still. "My arms hurt."

"Yeah, they will do, mate. When you bring them back—"

"Are you coming, Dad?"

So much for talking technique. "Where?" Rob asked. Lucas tutted and rolled his eyes. He looked the spit of Zoë, and he was just as astute. "Are you sure your mum said that?"

"Yeah." Lucas stretched the word for emphasis and gave Rob the kind of hopeful, pleading big-blinky-eyed look that instantly stole any hope he had of saying no. The boy was always one step ahead.

"I'll talk to her when we get back, all right? Do you..." There was no point asking if he wanted to swim a bit more; he was already scrabbling to get out of the water. Rob gave him a foot up and warned, "Don't run," as he got out himself and followed his floppy-legged son into the changing rooms. Another dad and his little girl passed them, and Lucas turned to stare at the girl.

"I don't need them anymore, do I, Dad?"

Rob glanced behind him at the girl's fluorescent-yellow armbands. "Oh? Why's that?"

"Cos I'm a big boy." Lucas grinned up at him.

Rob laughed and rubbed Lucas's head. "Come on. Let's get showered and dressed, eh?"

"Are we having soup from the machine?"

"Too right. It's the best part of swimming, soup from the machine." It was all the incentive needed to hurry Lucas along, and soon they were drinking dodgy chicken soup out of plastic cups, followed by chocolate bars and the walk to the bus stop, while Lucas gave him the mandatory drilling about when he would be old enough to ride on the bike, and why they made kids' seats if it wasn't safe, and why his mum thought it was OK for grown-ups to ride motorbikes but not OK for children.

"Your mum's right, Lu." There was little point in explaining the hundred reasons why Zoë—and Rob—believed it was too dangerous for a seven-year-old to ride pillion, but by the time the bus arrived, Lucas had moved on to football, and then back to the firework display.

"Last year, we went on the bumper cars and in the funhouse, and the rain melted my candy floss. Mum wouldn't let me have a hot dog, and I didn't want my burger. It had onions, and it was disgusting. The fireworks were well loud. Did they have fireworks when you were little, Dad?"

"Yeah." Rob gave Lucas a playful nudge. "Cheeky." He knew what Lucas was getting at. He'd mentioned it a couple of times since Travis came on the scene. Lucas had noticed the age difference and sometimes asked the kinds of questions Rob had asked not of his parents, but his grandparents. Forty wasn't old, but Rob only had to look in the mirror to see what Lucas saw. Greying hair, dark lines under his eyes—Rob looked his age, as did Travis, sadly, seeing as he was ten years younger.

So it seemed Travis had let Lucas down again, and Rob wasn't happy, which was to say he was up for going to the fireworks or doing anything else Zoë would permit. What he didn't like was being brought on as a sub when Travis was out of action.

Travis's car was still outside the house when they arrived back, not that it made any difference. Rob hadn't planned on staying; he needed to get home and eat before Hedley arrived for the drive out to Berkshire.

"Did Lu mention tonight?" Zoë asked as Lucas ran past her into the house and up the stairs. She turned briefly, shouted after him, "Put your swimming stuff in the hamper," and turned back to Rob, who was still standing on the doorstep. "Are you coming in for a coffee?"

"Thanks, but no. I've got to get off. Lu said something about fireworks."

"Are you up for it?"

"What time?"

"We're leaving here at five. Or you can meet us there at six."

"I'm working this afternoon, but I'll be back before five."

"Overtime?"

"Sort of. CID job." Rob spotted the partial eye-roll. "I'll be here at five, all right?" She still didn't believe him, and he didn't blame her.

Lucas came bounding downstairs and pulled up next to his mum. "You coming, Dad?"

"Yep." He ruffled Lucas's damp curls. "Laters, taters." Lucas scowled at the head rub, which made Rob laugh. He lifted his hand in a wave to Zoë and turned to walk to his bike.

"Don't be late!" Lucas called.

"I won't."

***

"Lord Berringer bought this place, did he?" Hedley tilted her head back and squinted up at the high ceiling of the enormous drawing room into which they'd been ushered on their arrival. There was very little furniture: a grand piano, a couple of high-backed chairs, a small, round table with ornately carved swirly legs and the upright sofa they were sitting on. It put Rob in mind of his visit to the Tanners' place, except there was no hardship here. The Berringers obviously chose to live like this, although given the size of the house, there was a possibility the room they were in was only used as a dumping ground for unwelcome guests.

"Yep," Rob confirmed belatedly. He'd been through Berringer's publicly declared assets, and the estate was listed as having been purchased in a private sale in the 1960s, as opposed to Lord Berringer inheriting it. He was a peer, rather than landed gentry, which meant Berringer's wife and children were commoners, with delusions of grandeur, it seemed. Given what Rob knew about Freddie Berringer, he didn't imagine he liked that much.

A woman appeared and strode across the room to them, her arm already raised to indicate she intended to send them on their way. "I'm afraid Mr. Berringer is indisposed this afternoon."

Rob looked at Hedley to see if she wanted to handle it. She gestured for him to do the honours. Rob turned back to the woman. "Where is Mr. Berringer, ma'am?"

She peered down her nose at him. "That's none of your business."

Rob shifted onto his hip and took his phone out. "And you are?"

"Sarah Garrett, the estate manager. I'd like you to leave now, please."

"Of course, Ms. Garrett." Rob and DCI Hedley rose from the sofa but remained where they were. "Can you let Mr. Berringer know we came by. Unfortunately, as we were unable to speak to him, there will be a warrant issued for his arrest on Mon—"

Ms. Garrett held up her hand and twitched out a smile. "Let me stop you there, Officer."

Rob nodded graciously and waited for her to continue.

"You didn't say you'd come to arrest him."

"We haven't. We need to speak with him in relation to an ongoing investigation."

"And if he refuses, you'll arrest him? It hardly seems fair."

Rob maintained his stance, waiting for her to capitulate, which she did with a dramatic sigh.

"I'll see if I can get hold of him for you." She left the room. Rob and Hedley remained standing. In the distance, a gun fired. It was the third shot since they'd arrived.

"What are your thoughts on hunting, Rob?"

"I don't have any, Ma'am. What about you?"

"I don't agree with it, but what do I know? I'm a townie."

"Yeah, likewise. I don't suppose there's anything wrong with hunting for food."

"Mind you—" she looked around the room again "—if they had a telly, they'd have something better to do than kill animals for fun."

"I doubt that, Ma'am. When did you last watch telly?"

"Fair point. But Christ, look at this place. It's miserable as sin."

Rob couldn't agree more. Berringer House was grand and stank of money, yet it felt more like a courthouse than a home. They'd heard voices and footsteps echoing in the hallway, so they knew there were other people around, but aside from the estate manager, they'd seen no-one, and Rob was getting restless. It was three o'clock already, it would take them an hour to drive back to London, and there was still no sign of Freddie Berringer.

"How long do you want to give him?" Hedley asked.

"I need to be away from here by half three, so...another fifteen minutes? I've got enough to arrest him."

"D'you think he killed the guy in the Merc?"

"Hector Laird-Browne. I don't know. He had motive. He's jealous, according to Aaron Tanner."

"Jealous?"

"Yeah. He's in love with Naomi."

Hedley nodded. "She's a looker, then, Tanner's missus?"

"Er, yeah. She's a very good-looking woman." Rob's cheeks started to burn. He wasn't sure how long he could cover for Aaron-Naomi. He might already be on a hiding to nothing, depending on what Freddie Berringer had to say, assuming the man ever showed his face. But it wasn't a lie. Naomi was beautiful.

"We could have a sing-song if either of us could play this thing." Hedley walked over to the piano and pressed a couple of keys. "Can you play?"

"Not the piano. I used to play guitar. Probably wouldn't have a clue now." Rob checked the time again.

"Are you worried he's done a bunk?"

Rob shook his head. "If he was going to, he'd have done it already." He was confident of that. If Berringer was true to form, he'd think he was above the law and no doubt sue them for harassment.

The steady thump of deliberate, heavy footsteps echoed along the corridor, getting closer, and a man marched into the room. Judging by Berringer's furious glare, Rob's analysis had been spot on again.

"You realise you've fucked up my entire fucking afternoon?"

Rob's scalp prickled. He looked the man over, giving himself a chance to cool it. Berringer was a typical toff—green jacket, navy sweater, beige pants tucked into boots—and he reeked of gunpowder. Rob worked his way back up to the smarmy round face and met the man's black-eyed stare. "Are you Frederick Berringer, sir?"

"You know damn well who I am."

Behind Rob, Hedley camouflaged a sardonic laugh with a cough. Rob breathed through his nose, clenching his teeth. There weren't many who could rile him this quickly, and he was sorely tempted to arrest the guy whether he thought he was guilty or not. "Mr. Berringer, I need to ask you some questions about an accident on Thursday, October the—"

"Yeah, yeah. Hector got smashed and then got smashed." Berringer smirked at his own joke. "It had nothing to do with me."

"Where were you on the evening of the accident, Mr. Berringer?"

"How the fuck should I know?"

"Do you recall seeing Hector Laird-Browne that day?"

"Again, how would I know? I'm a busy man, Constable...?"

Now Rob came to think on it, there was one part of working for the SIU he'd really enjoyed, and that was being able to smack someone and claim it was to keep his cover. However, he couldn't do that with DCI Hedley standing a few feet away. Next time, then.

"All right, Freddie, this is how it is. We suspect you were involved in Hector's death, and we *are* going to question you about it. So you can either cooperate now, or we'll take you into custody for the rest of the weekend and you can cooperate on Monday morning. Your choice."

Freddie gave a wide shrug. "You've got nothing, or you'd already have me in cuffs." He held out his hands, wrists together, and attempted to stare Rob down.

It was a step too far for Rob. He had a date with his son, and any patience he'd had for dealing with jumped-up idiots like Berringer had been lost within the first few weeks of the Strang case. They were like cockroaches.

"Do you want me to call it in, Rob?"

"Yes, Ma'am, if you wouldn't mind. Frederick Berringer—"

"All right. For fuck's sake. There's no need to make a scene." Berringer pulled out the piano stool and perched on it with one elbow leaning on the piano lid. "Ask away."

"Did you see Hector on the day he died?"

"No."

"Were you and Hector on friendly terms?"

"Decidedly not."

"Why was that?"

"He was involved with Naomi Tanner, and it was...an unfortunate distraction for Aaron."

Rob narrowed his eyes. "Were you jealous of Hector?"

"God, no. Why on earth... Oh, hang on. You've talked to Aaron. What did he tell you? I've been in love with Naomi since our undergraduate days? Well, it's true." Berringer gave another flamboyant shrug, accompanied by a wide, fake grin. "I wouldn't kill for her, though. She's not worth that much to me. Besides, when Carrie gets home from her jaunt, we're getting married."

"Is that Carrie Duggan?" Rob asked.

"One and the same. Yes, I'd heard her mother had reported her missing. She's not."

"When did you last speak to Carrie, Mr. Berringer?"

Berringer pondered for a few seconds and then raised his finger. "Interestingly, it was the day poor Hector died."

"You said you couldn't remember what you were doing that day."

"I lied."

Rob knew some unsavoury characters. A lot of unsavoury characters, any one of whom he could call up and ask to have 'a chat' with Freddie Berringer on his behalf. Berringer got right under Rob's skin. He didn't give a shit about the people whose expertise he'd commandeered, even though they'd lost everything while he was still living it up at Mummy and Daddy's expense. Rob decided, right then, he was going to find a way to punish Berringer, even if he wasn't involved in Hector's death.

"I have just a couple more questions for you, Mr. Berringer. What happened to your business?"

"Why don't you ask your fraud squad?"

"I'm asking you, sir. In your own words…"

Freddie swivelled to face the piano—with his back to Rob—and began to play. "We were fucked over."

"By?" Rob had to shout to be heard over the increasingly loud music. He didn't recognise the piece, but clearly, he wasn't the only angry person in the room.

"I couldn't possibly say."

"But you do know who."

"I couldn't possibly say." Freddie slammed several keys at once, and the noise erupted like shattered glass, ricocheting off the walls. Freddie leaned on his elbow again and gave his face a hard but weary rub. "What do I need to say to make you go away?"

Rob met Hedley's gaze. She raised her eyebrows. It was his call. He unlocked his phone: 15:28. "One last question. Why did Will Richards resign?"

"I wondered if we'd get around to him. He has a vendetta against me. Did you know that?"

Rob could well imagine every person who'd had the misfortune to come into contact with Freddie Berringer had a vendetta against him, but that was beside the point. "Why did he resign, Mr. Berringer?"

"It was trivial. A clash of personality."

"It must have been quite some clash for him to relinquish his ten percent share of the company."

"You can bet your arse it was some fucking clash. Why don't you talk to him about it?"

Before Rob could ask whether Berringer knew Richards' whereabouts, another man stormed into the room. He was older, in his sixties, and wore a conspicuously expensive tweed three-piece suit and knee-high leather boots. He also had a rifle over his shoulder.

"What the hell's going on?" he demanded, of Freddie rather than Rob and Hedley.

"Nothing to worry about, Dad. They're leaving now." Freddie turned to Rob with a fixed smile that dared defiance, but Rob had no intention of rising to it. Not today.

With a nod to Hedley, he moved off towards the door and said, without looking back, "We'll be in touch." Apparently, Freddie realised it wasn't in his best interests to argue.

***

"You made it, Dad!" Lucas held up his fist for a bump.

"Yeah!" Rob said, as if his being on time was unworthy of comment. In his defence, not once had he let Lucas down by turning up late or not turning up at all. It had to have come from Zoë. That or Lucas had overheard the screaming rows they'd had when he'd gone home during the Strang case, or any of their subsequent snappy interchanges.

Don't let him down, Rob.

When have I ever let him down?

Just the once—for three years.

Zoë was right, and it killed Rob to think of how many times Lucas must have asked her when his dad was coming home. Lu had been too young to understand, and even before the SIU, the parenting had fallen to Zoë. It was what she'd wanted—a house in the city, a decent kitchen, a bit of a garden—and it didn't come cheap. It was old ground, and there was little point re-covering it. Rob had let her down, but he'd kept every promise he'd made to Lucas, and the job would not come first again.

Zoë handed Lucas's coat to Rob. "There's no parking, so we're going to have to get the train."

"Right?" Rob wasn't sure why she was telling him that. Zoë didn't have a car, and they couldn't go on the bike. "Come on, Lu." He held the coat open for Lucas to poke his arms in and then helped him tug his sweater sleeves down. "You're supposed to hold them, mate. Where are your gloves? In your pockets?" Rob lifted a pocket flap to see. Lucas shrugged him off.

"In my bag," he said and ran off up the stairs.

"And where are *your* gloves?" Rob asked Zoë and gave her a cheeky wink. She waved them in his face. "Good girl." That earned him a slap with a glove, thankfully without the hand inside it.

"I don't know where Travis has got to," she said, stepping past Rob and peering out of the front door. "He was only buying bottles of water."

Rob's heart sank right to the bottom of his gut. "I didn't know we were waiting on him."

With an intentionally audible sigh, Zoë turned back. "You need to give him a chance, Rob."

"Yeah, actually, I don't."

"He loves me, and he loves Lu."

"That's great. I'm happy for you, and him. It doesn't mean we have to be best buds."

"You could at least talk to him."

"I do."

She glared.

"Look, Zo…" He tried to find a tactful way to tell her how he felt, ideally one that didn't involve admitting he wanted to punch the guy's lights out. In the end, he'd do what was best for Lucas and Zoë because he loved them. "I'll try, all right?"

Zoë rubbed his arm affectionately. "Thanks, Rob."

Lucas came racing back downstairs with his gloves, and once Travis arrived, the four of them set off for the station, with Lucas walking next to Rob, and Zoë and Travis in front. Lucas's constant chatter throughout the walk, the train ride, and then the walk at the other end was a welcome distraction, and Rob had to wonder if he was savvy enough to be doing it on purpose.

The park where the display was being held was massive, with over half the space taken up by a travelling fair. On the dodgems, Lucas and Rob shared a car; Zoë and Travis had one each and seemed happy to engineer constant collisions while Lucas and Rob went around and around the mini arena. Watching Zoë and Travis flirt made Rob want to hurl, and he was glad when the cars powered down so they could move on.

Next stop, the teacups, with the four of them sharing one cup. With Lucas between Rob and Zoë, and Travis on Zoë's other side, it was impossible to avoid catching sight of Travis's lovey-dovey expression as the ride sped up. Rob let it wash over him and got on with enjoying the evening. He even managed a civil conversation about whether Travis wanted his hot dog with or without onions.

The firework display was spectacular but short—not short enough to save Rob's shoulders from the pains of carrying a seven-year-old. When the final explosion of what was probably about two grand's worth of fireworks had died away, Rob set Lucas down on the ground.

"You're getting too big for that."

Lucas grinned up at him. "Can I have some candy floss?"

"Haven't you eaten enough already?"

Lucas vigorously shook his head.

"OK. Come on." Rob checked Zoë knew where they were going, and he and Lucas set off for the candy floss stall.

"Dad?"

"Yeah?"

"Why don't you like Travis?"

"I do like Travis."

Silence. It was the first time he'd lied to Lucas, which felt bad enough without suspecting Lucas had already sussed him.

"Dad?"

"Hmm?"

"You and Mum got a divorce, didn't you?"

"Yeah." Rob wasn't sure where Lucas was heading with that, or if he should encourage him, but he was curious. "Why?"

"Travis wants Mum to marry him."

"Does he?"

"He didn't say nothing."

"OK." Through gritted teeth, Rob ordered and paid for four bags of candy floss and handed one to Lucas on the way back, which Lucas offered to Travis.

"Cheers," he said, taking the bag and ruffling Lucas's hair. Rob wanted to punch him. "I love candy floss."

Zoë shot Rob a threatening glance, but he wasn't going to start a fight.

"Are we ready to head home?" she asked.

Lucas was too busy stuffing his face to care, as was Travis.

"When you are," Rob said.

They ate the rest of the candy floss on the way back to the station and caught the next train. Lucas leaned sleepily against Rob's side while Rob stared at the dark window, his eyes straying every so often to Travis's and Zoë's pensive reflections.

When they arrived back at the house, Rob grabbed his helmet from the hallway and stepped outside, making it clear he wasn't intending to stay. "See you later, Lu."

"You're not coming in for a drink?" Zoë asked and then, without waiting for him to answer, added, "We need to talk."

It looked like Lucas was right.

21: Dinner

N O MATTER HOW much Gray tried to ignore it, the more he thought about Will's mum, the greater his need to try to fix things with his own mum. The last time they'd spoken was when he and Jean first got together, and Gray had gone to tell her, thinking if he was in a long-term relationship, she might find it easier to accept. He was wrong. The conversation had ebbed away to awkward politeness, and Gray had felt the same shame rising up around him as he'd felt when he first told her he was gay. He couldn't live like that—didn't have to live like that—so he'd cut contact, other than to invite her to the partnership ceremony. She didn't even reply.

So why was he so determined to try again now? That she had asked Becky if she'd seen him—and not just the once—was a big part of it. Surely, it was more than simple curiosity or wondering if her daughter was still defying her? There *had* to be something there. She was his mum, after all.

Seeing as he had the rental car for a couple more days, he thought he might as well put it to use. He called Becky to check Mum wasn't planning on going anywhere tomorrow—which she wasn't—and then shoved away the nervousness and gut-churning to get ready for dinner with Will.

They were eating in the hotel's restaurant. As Josh had predicted, Will was staying at the campsite up on the cliff, and he'd left the van there and walked back so he could have a few beers. He was already sitting in the bar when Gray came down from his room.

"You OK for a drink?"

"Yeah, cheers." Will held up his glass as evidence.

Gray ordered a pint for himself, watching Will in the mirror behind the bar. He was taking in his surroundings as if he'd never been anywhere so grand before, yet his investment banking career must have involved a few high-price jollies along the way. Gray re-joined him with a frown of bemusement.

"Great place, this," Will said, swivelling on his stool to take in the dark bay through the floor-to-ceiling windows extending the full length of the room. It was a sizeable hotel, built into the cliff side, and with luxury in mind. On the floor above the bar was an infinity pool that shared the same view of the ocean, and the top-class rooms also had that vista. Gray hadn't booked into one of those, as he'd not anticipated spending much time in his room, thinking he'd deliver his apology, eat dinner alone, stay the night and drive home, but Will had suggested meeting up, and Gray was delighted. He was trying not to let it show, in case it gave the wrong impression, although he was also beginning to accept it wasn't the wrong impression at all.

"How's the case going?" Will asked.

That was something else Gray hadn't anticipated, but maybe Will had only brought it up as small talk to distract from his mum and Nev. It had the added advantage of rescuing Gray from thinking himself into a hole again, even if it did mean digging another. He hadn't intended to have this conversation with Will until they were back home and he was sure Will was in a fit state to deal with Rob's questions.

"It's going well, so I'm told. There're a couple of leads the Met are following up, and they look like they might prove fruitful."

"Are you allowed to talk about the undercover stuff?"

Gray shook his head, trying to come across as nonchalant. He was still hoping Will would volunteer the information. "Not really. But it's not undercover stuff. Why? What did you want to know?"

"Did they shut your unit down when you left?"

"No. One of my team was offered the job on my recommendation."

"Right." Will frowned, puzzled. "Why haven't the Met passed this case to them?"

"Because the SIU deals with organised crime—fraud and embezzlement—not some drunk guy who died in possession of fake ID that turned out not to be fake at all. Apart from that, there's nothing on Berringer's. They're squeaky clean."

"That's got to be a first. A bank with no dodgy dealings."

"You think there's something Rob's overlooked?"

"Not necessarily." Will took a swig of his beer and held it in his mouth for a long time. He swallowed but stayed quiet, mulling something over. Gray knew that look by now. Will held strong opinions on many subjects, animal welfare being at the top of the list, and the non-verbal cues were there. He had something to say about Berringer's. Gray's chest tightened. *Shit.* Mentioning the name of the bank had been intentional, a baited hook to entice Will into talking. However, mentioning Rob's name was not.

How could he have slipped up so easily? It wasn't as if he was being probed for information, or maybe he was. *No.* Just more evidence of old habits refusing to die. But it had never happened to him before, and he was disappointed in himself. All his training and experience, and in a split second of carelessness, he'd revealed Rob's identity. Not that it mattered, seeing as Rob wasn't undercover, and sooner or later, he was going to question Will anyway.

The more Gray thought about it, the less certain he was he had been careless. If Will was untrustworthy, by the time they were back in London, the news of the investigation would have reached Berringer's ears, and it would take little to piece together that the Tanners had talked to the police. The entire case would collapse. Except Gray was certain it wouldn't come to that, and his reasoning, now he'd done some instead of relying on flawed gut instinct, was that he didn't make careless mistakes. He wasn't perfect by a long stretch, but his errors had always been due to poor judgement and plans gone askew, not slips of the tongue, which meant, on an unconscious level, he did trust Will.

But was he big enough to admit it? They'd been sitting in silence for many minutes, and whilst Gray had zoned back in, Will had not. He still had the same brooding expression, although it disappeared when he realised he was under scrutiny. Rather than ask outright, Gray raised an eyebrow in query. Will sniffed and rubbed his chin in a gesture of reticence. The long, reddish whiskers stood out where the pressure of his fingertips turned the skin white.

"I went to uni with Freddie Berringer." He picked up his beer and held the glass aloft, his gaze on it rather than Gray. "We didn't get on."

"Oh? Why's that?" Gray asked.

"He's filthy rich and enjoys all the privileges his social position affords."

"Blood sports?"

"Yep. He's a master of foxhounds, and he'll tell you the change in law destroyed British cultural heritage rather than the truth of it attempting to end centuries of unnecessary torture and killing of animals to satiate the needs of bloodthirsty men. He'll also claim he no longer hunts foxes and he believes in animal welfare. The video footage we collected suggests otherwise. We're waiting on the CPS to process the case. He'll get off with it again, because they're all part of the same club."

"Again?"

"Last time, his lawyer argued they were chasing a trail and only came across the fox 'by chance', but there's no trail without a fox, and they didn't call off the dogs."

Gray was less surprised by the tangential conversation than by how interested he was to hear more about the most important aspect of Will's life. "So you hunt activists still have plenty to deal with?"

"Hunt saboteurs, yep. In some respects, it's nowhere near as crazy as it used to be. We were out all season, whatever the weather, and all we could do was come between the hunt and the animal, trying not to disturb the peace. Hunts bought the support of farmers so they could cross their land, while we had to stick to the highways. The local police weren't exactly impartial either. We were hooligans spoiling for a fight, according to them, but it's not true. Keeping animals *and* humans safe is paramount."

"How do you stop hounds from getting to a fox? I mean, short of shooting them with tranquiliser darts?"

Will laughed. "Have you ever seen a pack of foxhounds?" Gray couldn't say he had, or not outside of pictures on pub walls, but the question was rhetorical. Will continued. "We deter them—use anti-mate spray to cover the fox's scent—or we call them on hunting horns at the same time the hunt does, which confuses them. They're driven by their natural instincts. Foxhounds were bred from deerhounds, so they'll track deer scent in preference to fox. Deer urine works a treat."

Gray blew out his cheeks, which made Will laugh more.

"We've had some great times out on hunts, Gray. And I can kind of understand the whole adrenaline rush the hunters get, because we experience it too, chasing them. But it's the violence that goes with it, and going back to where we started, Freddie Berringer is a king-sized tosser. If I thought I'd get away with it, I'd happily murder the bastard."

Gray swallowed a whole lot more beer than he'd intended but managed to utter, "Are you serious?" before the coughing fit erupted. Will waited it out before confirming what Gray knew.

"I worked for him. Not for long. His father's Lord Berringer, one of the super-rich and worth a few billion. He provided the start-up capital. Freddie brought the four of us in early on. Two of us got out at the first opportunity."

Time to go out on a limb. Gray might not yet be up to saying it verbatim, but he could prove his trust through his actions. "What can you tell me about Aaron Tanner?"

"Aaron? Wow, I haven't seen Aaron for such a long time. It wasn't him in the car, though, was it?"

"No."

"I thought not." Will averted his eyes. "That was why I was late." Gray waited for him to elaborate. "For our date. I came out of the station, and the road was blocked, so I had to walk the long way around. When I reached the other side of the accident, I recognised the car. One of Berringer's exec fleet. They were putting the driver in a body bag, but he was too big to be Aaron."

"It was Hector...can't remember his surname."

"Oh, no. I hoped it was a chauffeur. Well, I don't wish anyone dead, but... I'm wondering if I should keep an eye out for the Grim Reaper here." Will gave a quiet chuckle, but he was visibly shaken by the news.

"You know what they say about these things coming in threes," Gray said and then asked, gently, making it clear it wasn't an accusation, "Why didn't you tell me the truth about why you were late?"

"Because of Jean-Michel. I didn't know if it would bring back bad memories."

The revelation made Gray's throat constrict, and for a moment, he couldn't breathe. He was such a fool. A stupid, paranoid fool.

"Do you know what happened?" Will asked. "To Hector?"

Gray had to think how to breathe; he gasped for air, triggering a return of his coughing fit. Will was almost on his feet, set to come to his aid, but Gray waved him off. "I'm OK." Will hovered briefly, but Gray nodded to confirm it and took a few careful sips of his drink. "Sorry. I do know, yes. He was over the limit."

"Drink driving? Are they sure? Hector was very anti-alcohol when he was younger."

"I can only tell you what I've heard."

"God, that's awful. I can't believe he's dead. He was a great guy, and a good friend, the same with Aaron. I loved working with them, and I'd have stayed if it wasn't for Freddie. He's a nasty piece of work—thinks us proles should know our place. And he's ruthless."

Gray didn't want to plant ideas in Will's head, so rather than asking if he thought Berringer could've killed Hector, he said, "I'm surprised you took the job."

"He didn't give me any choice." Will glanced at the people sitting closest to them. He was checking he could speak without being overheard. "You're not under some lifelong obligation to report crime, are you?"

Gray laughed. "It's an oath, and it doesn't apply anymore, although all of us have a civic duty. But I can keep your past misdemeanours to myself, if that's what you're asking."

"How about present ones?"

Gray pursed his lips. He couldn't answer, or he could, but neither of them would like it.

"OK." Will leaned forward, reducing the distance between them. "When I was at uni, someone blew up the bioscience labs, and before you ask, it wasn't me. I've never been involved in anything like that. I don't agree with terrorism. It doesn't help the cause. But I knew who was responsible, and I knew what they'd planned to do.

"There were a few of us students involved in small-scale activism. We held protests outside the bioscience building, but mostly it was away from uni—hunt sabbing, forming human blockades to stop animal transportation, attending rallies, stuff like that."

Will smiled, absorbed in his reminiscing. "I was more of a liberal back then. I wanted nothing to do with the attack on the labs, but we knew what they were planning, and they asked us to set off the fire alarm and make sure the labs were evacuated. We thought the staff would take the animals out." The smile was gone now, in its place a volatile mix of fury and distress.

"We watched them, the vile abusers, all pile out, laughing and chatting like it was a tea break. I heard someone calling us lunatics, saying they hoped it was a false alarm, to which someone else said it would backfire because we'd condemned all the animals to a horrific death. We couldn't believe what we were hearing, and we went back in, three of us, undergraduate students. We didn't know how long we had, so we just went in there and grabbed what we could. Rabbits, rats, mice, guinea pigs—there were so many, Gray. So many. It took forever, and all the while, we're waiting for the explosion.

"I remember thinking, at least if we get all the cages out, dying won't be in vain. I was twenty, for Christ's sake."

Will's agitation had grown to the point where his fidgeting was rocking the table. Gray pushed his knee against the pedestal to stop their drinks from slopping. "You didn't get them all?"

"Almost. We had one massive cage left, and we needed to take the rabbits out of it, which was why we'd left it till last. Then we heard someone yell at us to get out of the building *now*. We were out of time. It would've been quick. It would. I can't think about those last few seconds and what—"

Will looked Gray in the eye. There was so much pain and anger, Gray wanted to reach out to him, but Will was too tense.

"That was the moment my radicalism was born." Will uncurled the fists that had formed while he'd been talking and cracked his knuckles. "Freddie knew I was involved. I wouldn't have got much time for my part in it if I'd given names, but there was no way. It was our own stupid fault. We should've realised what they'd meant by 'evacuate'."

Unable to find words to elucidate his feelings, to Will or himself, Gray took a chance. He reached across the table and wrapped his hand around Will's. What he had shared with Gray was the key to trust and understanding, a floodlight allowing Gray to see Will with clarity for the first time—his motivation, his passion, his humanity. It made Gray feel unworthy and question all the 'good work' he had done for the police. Next to Will's heroism, it was trivial.

They put a hold on their conversation whilst they moved to the restaurant for dinner, where they ordered wine and their first two courses. The restaurant was very proud of its fish and game menu, further narrowing what were always limited choices for vegetarians, and Gray felt indignant on Will's behalf, although Will shrugged it off.

"My appetite's pretty lousy at the minute, so it's not a problem."

"Even so, only two options from eight starters and one of eight main courses? Any other minority group being discriminated against to this extent, it'd be breaking the law."

Will shook his head and laughed at Gray's naivety. "If I was vegan, like Tie and Jon, I wouldn't be able to eat here at all."

"What the hell do you eat if you're vegan?"

"Oh, there's loads. Vegetables, pulses, and if you're any good with herbs and spices, you honestly wouldn't miss the meat and dairy. Mushrooms have great textures. Much of what I eat at home is vegan."

Newborn trust or no, Gray wouldn't have doubted the veracity of Will's statement, not that, as a meat eater, he had any right to dispute it. With Jean, he'd had the chance to sample many varieties of mushrooms and other fungi. Jean loved cooking. On his days off, he could invariably be found in the kitchen, where he'd stay all day, preparing their dinner for the evening and drinking way too much wine. Their kitchen had been a wonderful room, with bunches of herbs and garlic hanging from racks, rows and rows of spices, sauces, oils, pots and pans everywhere. Aromatic chaos.

Until recently, cooking anything more elaborate than a shepherd's pie had caused Gray painful flashbacks, but they were less traumatic these days. His grief counsellor had asked him to write down all of the things he'd stopped doing when Jean was killed because it was easier to avoid than face up to his feelings. Nighttime driving was the first item he'd tackled, followed by dining out. He could finally listen to favourite songs again, in moderation, and classical music was bearable if he steered clear of Vaughn Williams. In short, there was less left on the list to do than had been done, but cooking for one was hard enough, never mind for one who had been left 'reluctantly single'.

"Are you all right?" Will asked.

Gray smiled, aware it was not his most convincing attempt. "I'm fine, thanks. I was thinking about Jean."

"OK." Worry flickered across Will's face. He clearly regretted having asked the question.

When Josh had first introduced them, he said he'd told Will that Gray had lost his partner but kept the details to a minimum, and on the one hand, Gray would have preferred that his identity was not first and foremost that of a widower. It felt too old, like he was embarking on his twilight years when he wasn't yet halfway through his working life. On the other hand, Josh had saved him the trauma of telling Will. While it was relatively easy to say to a passing acquaintance, "I lost my husband," telling a friend or someone he cared about was as hard now as ever.

But Gray could feel a change taking place within. At its most fundamental level, it was that thinking or talking about Jean no longer made him wish he had also died in the crash. He wasn't getting better as such, because he was losing the memories and he wanted to hold on to them, but he could rationalise now. Over time, everyone forgets, and doing so didn't betray Jean or deny how much they'd loved each other.

"Good memories," Gray thought aloud, and this time, he smiled with feeling. "I was remembering what we used to eat. Jean was a fantastic cook, and he loved mushrooms. We ate veggie quite often—or veggie and cheese, at any rate."

"Very French."

"Close. He was Belgian, but he was very French in his diet, and his love of wine...in everything, really. Although he hated reading, whatever the language. He'd ask me to read to him, and I'd be coming to a good part and notice him watching me and smiling. I'd look at him and say, 'What?' and he'd shake his head and motion for me to continue. Or he'd stop me and ask me to re-read something that he found amusing or sad." Gray felt his eyes filling but pushed on. "And then he'd cry and tick me off for being cruel and telling him sad stories." He tried to blink away the tears, laughing to cover his loss of composure.

Will offered a kind, sympathetic smile, although tonight wasn't supposed to be about Gray, and he tried his hardest to thwart his sudden tearfulness.

"How long were you together?" Will asked.

"Three years. It's crazy. He's been gone longer than that, and I feel it, stretching into eternity. The days are all the same—get up, realise he's gone... I still miss him so much." Gray held Will's gaze, needing him to understand why he was so resistant to the idea of a relationship. He didn't just miss Jean; he missed having someone who knew him, knew all his faults and loved him anyway.

He was under no illusion that Will could be such a man. Gray didn't buy into hopes and dreams—he'd seen far too much of the other side of human nature, the cheaters, the liars, the fraudsters—but Will was like a breath of fresh air. Of course, Gray knew the intricate details of Will's animal rights activism, but in all other respects, he was a gentle, law-abiding citizen. A handsome one at that, although Gray imagined he didn't look an especially good catch himself right at that moment. He was exhausted and miserable, and he needed a haircut, and to get a grip.

"I'm sorry. I didn't come all this way to burden you with my grief."

"You're not, and in any case, it's helping me keep things in perspective. It's not fair you lost Jean-Michel. It's not fair we lose anyone, but my mum... She was sick a long time, and—I feel bad thinking it—*that* was a burden. I'm glad she's gone, for her sake and ours. Is that awful?"

"No," Gray answered assuredly. He'd watched, from an emotional distance, terminally ill people fade, and his heart had gone out to their loved ones. It was a terrible but necessary ordeal.

Will didn't look convinced. "It's so much harder losing Nev than Mum. God, that sounds bad. Talk about having all the wrong priorities."

"I'm sure a lot of people feel like you do. I don't know, maybe it hits you up front, when the terminal prognosis is given, so you do a lot of the grieving early on."

"Yeah, maybe."

Will looked so downhearted, and Gray wished he could give him a foot up, but as it had been with losing Jean, Will needed to find his own way back to the sunshine. He had good friends, and his animals. And if he'd still accept it, he had Gray's friendship too. But there was one last thing Gray had to do to clear the decks.

"I want to come clean, Will. I already knew you worked for Berringer's, but I kept it to myself. I'm sorry."

"Yeah, well. It's not easy, is it? Living a secret life."

Gray nodded dolefully. "You can say that again. Are you OK?"

"About you holding out on me?" Will fought a smile, and the resulting cheeky smirk sent Gray into a bit of a fluster. Will laughed. "I said I was, didn't I?"

"You did."

"I take it your friend Rob needs to talk to me about Freddie?"

"He does."

"I'm cool with that. Can it wait till we get back to London? It'd be good to just chill out together while we're away from the hassle."

"Yes," Gray agreed, to everything.

22: Where the Heart Was

CHEF'S RECOMMENDATION WAS a grilled artichoke and bean curd starter, followed by a main course of haricot bean and root vegetable medley. Given the indulgent quantities of garlic in both, it was as well Gray had opted to go veggie for the evening in moral support...or something like that. After dinner, he and Will returned to the bar, where the view through the panoramic window was of blackness occasionally interrupted by the dotted lights of distant passing ships, or the close-to erratic trail of a dog-walker's torch.

Gray and Will watched the relative nothingness with no recourse to conversation. Around them, the other guests' chatter created a low, pleasant hum of company. Gray inhaled deeply, letting the breath escape as a contented sigh. He supposed he should have felt embarrassed for being so open about his feelings, yet there was no judgement on Will's part, now or ever.

"When are you heading back to London?" Will asked some time later—Gray wasn't clock watching, so it could have been anything between five minutes and an hour.

"Tomorrow. How about you?"

"Same. We could convoy."

"Convoy?" Gray repeated. The use of the word in relation to their two private vehicles amused him more than it should or, indeed, more than it normally would. "Another artefact of your secret life?"

"Yeah." Will grinned sheepishly. "I meant we could..." He thumbed twice, which was in the direction of the ocean, and gave up trying to explain. "You know what I mean."

Gray laughed. "Yes, I do, and I'd really like that, but...I'm taking a mini detour to stop by at my mum's."

"I could be your chaperone."

Gray's laughter turned rueful. "And I'd really like that too. If you need the company, feel free to tag along. But I don't want to put you in a difficult situation. My mum and I don't get on. She's homophobic."

"Oh, Gray." Will reached over and rubbed his arm, which seemed a bit of an overreaction until Gray realised thinking about his mum had seen off his prior relaxed posture so that he was hunched forward in his seat. He forcibly loosened his shoulders and tried to shake the feeling, but it wasn't easy.

"It's a long time since I visited her." He scrubbed at his palm with his thumb, keeping his eyes focused on it rather than Will, who remained attentive. He was a good listener, but Gray had no right to dump all his baggage on him. He tried for a quick recovery and conclusion. "The last time we spoke was when I first met Jean."

Will's sympathetic expression darkened. "So, basically, since Jean died, you've been on your own."

"In my private life, yes. Which is why I threw myself into my work."

"Makes sense."

"Do you think so?"

Will frowned and shook his head as if clearing it of thoughts. "Sorry. I was stuck on you not seeing your mum for what, six years?"

"Somewhere around there."

"It's crazy. But yeah, it does make sense. You loved your job. It was your sanctuary."

"I guess."

"It's interesting," Will said. "I never really enjoyed my job. It was all right, but it was just a job, and it got in the way of the important stuff, like looking after my mum. I've been pretty lucky. That's the only real tough time I've faced in my life."

"Or maybe you deal with it better."

"Hmm...I'm not sure about that. Tie called me a prima donna."

Gray looked Will up and down. "I don't think so."

"Oh, you haven't seen me lose my rag. It takes a lot, but Tie knows how to push my buttons. Like this court case. There's a guy picking up strays and selling them to research labs. Tie was caught on camera trashing the guy's pickup. It was impulsive—we usually plan stuff like that—and Tie should've known better. He lost his job when his boss found out he was being charged, and he's skint, which is nothing new, but this time, I can't afford to bail him out. He said he'd sort the van a month ago, and he only dealt with it because I kicked off."

"You know, Will, I don't think kicking off is melodramatic after the week you've had."

"Still, I'm usually better at keeping my temper. What about you? Are you hotheaded?"

"The total opposite. But Jean..." Gray gestured an explosion and mouthed *boom!*

"What is it they say about opposites attracting?"

"Josh seems to think it's more to do with complementing each other, the way you sort of slot together. Their strengths compensate for your weaknesses and vice versa. I forget now, how moody Jean was. He broke the door—twice—slamming it on his way out." Gray could see the scene in his mind's eye. The first slam had cracked the glass pane; the second had shattered it. At least Jean had repaired the damage he caused...except for the last time.

"Hey." Will's voice tugged Gray back to the moment.

"Sorry. I am *really* bad company."

"No, you're not."

Gray was doubtful, but Will looked genuine.

"I get the feeling you haven't talked about him much."

"It was easier to bottle it up. To start with. Now, I realise I do need to talk about him."

"It's been tough without him, hasn't it?"

Gray nodded. "The worst time of my life, and I've been through a few things where I thought it couldn't possibly get any worse. Finding out my dad was dead before I had the chance to meet him wasn't nice, although, as you know, he's George's dad too. He remembers Jack, and not fondly. His mum had nothing good to say about Jack either, so I'm OK with that.

"Then there was telling my mum I'm gay. She properly shrieked and screamed at me, and then reverted to acting like the conversation had never happened. I suppose she was trying to convince herself that it hadn't."

"I don't know what to say, Gray."

"It's all right. I wish I could forget about it, or at least let it go, but I can't. I have to keep trying."

Will nodded his understanding. "I got lucky with my mum. She was brilliant."

"You seemed close, the two of you."

"Yeah, very, although she wasn't there much when I was little. She was a feminist and a bit of an old hippie—CND and all that jazz. She was part of the Greenham Common protest and very politically active, a huge influence. She taught me how important it is to stand up for what we believe and to think about the future—not just our own, but our kids'. That's what the women at Greenham Common were about—ensuring a better future for the children. Never mind that I got dumped on Uncle Jim while she was off saving the world for me. I'm not complaining. I learnt more about numbers in the bookie's with Jim than in the entirety of my formal education."

"How times have changed," Gray mused.

"They certainly have, and not always for the better. Like this place." Will nodded towards the window and the bay beyond. "All these restaurants and holiday apartments. It's hypocritical, I know. I've been coming here since I was a teenager, and it's the surfing that's made it what it is. I feel very strongly about natural preservation, but that was the other thing my mum taught me. Pick your battles. You know what Gandhi said—the greatness of a nation can be judged by the way its animals are treated—I think that's also true on an individual level. Like Freddie Berringer. He's a..." Will drew breath but, on this occasion, left the name-calling to Gray's imagination.

"We weren't going to worry about him until Monday," Gray reminded him.

"Yeah, good point. It's a bit harsh, but I really hope he's in it over his head this time. It couldn't happen to a more deserving person." Will picked up his glass, which contained about an inch of beer, and took the tiniest sip.

"You want another?" Gray asked.

"It's late, isn't it?"

"...ish. I'm having another."

Will was considering, or acting the part.

"Do you want one?" Gray asked again.

"Yeah, but you'll have to let me pay you back sometime."

"Whatever," Gray said dismissively and set off for the bar.

One of the wonders of it being November was getting served quickly, and he was back at their table within a couple of minutes. It had been more than enough time to contemplate what he was about to say without delving too deeply into what it might mean. "If you want, you can stay in my room. It's a twin."

"Hmm." Will finished off the inch of beer and exchanged the empty glass for the full one.

"Hmm?" Gray repeated, aware his cheeks were starting to glow, as were Will's.

"How close together are these twin beds?" Will asked.

Gray shrugged. "As close together as you want them to be."

Will nodded slowly. His blush was quite something to behold. "I appreciate your offer," he said but didn't elaborate on whether he was accepting it.

It left Gray floundering for a change of subject that wouldn't take them too far from the point. Maybe it would be better to let Will get away with not answering at all. "So, you sleep in the van when you come here?"

"Yeah, or a tent in the summer. I'll have to show you inside the van. It's nice when it's tidy. It's a pit when Tie's had it."

"What do you sleep on?" Gray knew already.

"A mattress. It's a bit damp, but it's bearable."

"Good, good." Gray nodded along with the words. Will was smirking at him, and he'd had enough to drink to make him pushy. "Well?" he asked.

"Won't they charge you for an extra person?"

"I paid for the room."

"So you were hoping to get lucky?" Will gave him a cheeky grin. Gray couldn't be bothered to explain he'd booked a double for the extra space but they'd given him a twin instead.

"Yes," Will said, finally putting him out of his misery. "Whenever you're ready."

That put the ball firmly back on Gray's side of the net. He was sure it never used to be this complicated pulling someone. "Let's finish these drinks," he suggested.

"Sure."

Now came the decision of whether to knock back his pint or take his time. It wasn't as if there'd been no-one since Jean, although there'd been no-one worth more than one date, maybe two. Hook-ups with strangers were easy to walk away from. In fact, Gray had never had sex with anyone he considered a friend first, but Will had already offered him the no-strings get-out clause. With that thought, the beer couldn't be gone soon enough. Gray chugged his, catching a glimpse of Will through the bottom of the glass and discovering he'd already finished.

Gray led the way to the stairs, only speaking once they were standing outside his room. He was having a problem remembering which pocket he'd put the key card in. "So what's your special power?"

"Huh?"

"Berringer's. Rob said they recruited an elite four."

Will chuckled. "Take a guess."

Gray found the key card and let them in, switching on the light as he passed by but getting no further into the room. Will caught his hand and pulled him back. Gray didn't resist, but he did delay looking up. In the enclosed space, he could smell Will's aftershave, and his brain automatically called it—*not the same as Jean's*—but it was a fleeting acknowledgement that he cast aside in favour of doing as Will had suggested.

"Data analysis?"

"Nope."

"Accounting."

"Nope."

Gray tried to come up with something else. It was tricky when the space between them appeared to be shrinking of its own accord. They were so close each puff of air that escaped one entered the other, and arousal was making Gray giddy. "Were you the board's eye candy?"

"How could you tell?" Will put his hands on Gray's hips, holding firmly, as if he expected him to bolt when he kissed him. Had the intention to back out been there in the first place, it was wiped out by that kiss. Dry lips and beard stubble made for rough contact and a startling contrast to the first touch of tongue against tongue. Gray mirrored Will's hold on him and used it to walk him over to the beds, which were already butted against each other, and not by Gray's doing.

He'd only been in his room long enough to shower and change for dinner, and the clothes he'd travelled in were still on the end of one of the beds.

The kissing was a bit out of control, and Gray was trying to pull Will's T-shirt off without getting in the way of his own shirt's unbuttoning. His craving for skin contact was on a par with his past craving for cocaine.

"Can I just..." He batted Will's hands away. "OK. Get this off."

"Bossy!" Will laughed but lifted his arms and assisted in removing his T-shirt. Gray slid his hands up Will's chest, over his shoulders and down his arms, releasing an enormous sigh.

"You're a hands-on kind of guy, huh?" Will's eyes glistened with amusement.

"Hands," Gray kissed Will's shoulder, "lips," and nipped at his shoulder blade, "teeth..." He flicked with the tip of his tongue over the stubble and back to Will's mouth, at the same time shrugging off his now-unbuttoned shirt. They still hadn't made it to the beds.

"What do you like?" Gray murmured between kisses.

"This is good for me. Slow build."

"Slow build to what?"

"I'm easy."

Gray smiled into the kiss. "Are you?"

Will's answer was to push Gray backwards, without breaking the kiss, until he was lying with his back to the mattress and Will on top of him. He didn't want to ruin the moment by asking bluntly if he needed to get out a condom and lube. He was also too turned on to care what they ended up doing and decided to go where Will led and deal with the condom later if need be.

Gray shivered at the light touch of Will's fingers walking down his belly and then gasped and arched into his grope. "We should get naked."

"Good idea." With ease, Will popped the buttons on Gray's jeans and moved away to remove his own. Gray couldn't take his eyes off him. He was imperfectly handsome. His chest, disproportionately broad in relation to his shoulders, was covered in hair, in contrast to his bare belly, and his legs were hairy too. He was also more modest than Gray, who had stripped off so quickly he'd almost given himself denim burn, yet Will returned to the bed still wearing his boxers.

"Are you shy?" Gray asked as Will flopped down next to him and shuffled closer.

"Not really, but I wanted to warn you about my tattoo."

"Right?" When Will said no more, Gray prompted, "Is it rude?"

Will laughed self-consciously. "Nothing like that. I'm not embarrassed by it, or no more embarrassed than I am for putting someone's name there in the first place."

"It's not on your..."

Will winced at the suggestion. "No, I'm not that brave. Stupid..." His deep frown put his eyes in dark shadow. Behind his jest, he was worried what Gray would think.

"Hey, you must've loved him enough at some point to put his name down there." Gray propped up on one elbow and brushed his palm down Will's side, coming to a rest on his hip. "Can I look?"

Will nodded and shut his eyes. Gray hooked the waistband of Will's shorts with his thumb and pushed them down an inch or so, revealing the top of a line of swirly purple text. A bit further and he could make out the first letter: 'S'. The last letter had a long tail that trailed under the fabric, but the light was too dim to read the rest. Gray gave Will a gentle shove so he rolled onto his back.

"Shelley? As in Percy Bysshe?"

"Who?"

"The romantic poet."

"OK, that really would be a weird tatt to have around your todger." Will grinned. He seemed a little less uptight.

"So that would be Shelley as in...a woman's name?" Gray guessed.

"Correct."

"You're coming out to me."

"I am."

"OK." Gray pulled Will's boxers down further.

"You're not bothered I'm bisexual?"

"All I'm bothered about right now is seeing this." Gray yanked Will's boxers out of the way, revealing all of the tattoo. "Oh, I like that." He traced the path of the 'y's tail as it looped and swirled away, forming a heart before it terminated at a pot of ink and a quill.

"She's a journalist," Will explained. "She's freelance, but the big dailies commission a lot of her pieces."

"You're still friends?"

"Yep. Still friends, and...are you ready for this?

"Go on."

"We have a daughter."

"Wow." Gray fell onto his back and stared at the ceiling. He was fine with the tattoo, and finding out Will was also attracted to women, but Will being a dad? That didn't fit at all. "I tell you what. It's as well I got out of the job when I did. My profiling skills have gone to the dogs." He rolled back again and steadily met Will's gaze. "Sorry. I'm surprised."

"Yeah, I got that."

"How old is she? What's her name?"

"Suzannah. She's fourteen."

"Do you have a photo?"

"Yeah, but...we were gonna..." Will pointed down at their lack of arousal.

"If it happens, all well and good. We'll take it as it comes, even if *we* don't."

Will tutted and laughed at Gray's terrible innuendo. "You really want to see a photo?"

"I really do."

Kissing him on the way, Will clambered over Gray to retrieve his phone from his jeans, climbed back over and resumed his previous position. He unlocked the screen and scrolled through his photos. "Yeah, this one's recent. Her birthday, in August." He turned the screen towards Gray.

The girl pictured had waist-length, blonde-brown hair that had more blonde in it than Will's, but they shared the same kind of sun-kissed complexion and similarly proportioned facial features. His daughter had a smaller nose and a narrower chin, but there was no mistaking the genetic association. "God, she looks like you."

"Yeah, poor kid."

Gray elbowed him in the ribs. "She's beautiful."

Will had the soppiest smile on his face. "Cheers," he said. "Want to see more? You can say no. It's boring looking at other people's photos."

"It's not when they're this important."

Will handed over his phone. "Just scroll through."

Gray did so, pausing at each photo, still astounded by the likeness. A couple of the photos were of Will and Suzannah on a fairground ride and another of them sunbathing. Side by side, they were even more alike. Gray moved on.

"That's Shelley," Will said of the woman in the photo.

Gray zoomed in. He could see now that Suzannah had characteristics of both parents; while she was a similar height and build to her mum, she had her dad's colouring. Shelley's hair was dark brown, maybe black. It was hard to tell because it was wet, and both Shelley and Suzannah were wearing wetsuits. "Ah, she's one of you crazy people."

"Speak for yourself." Will returned the elbow in the ribs, which tickled and made Gray squirm away, laughing. Will waited for him to stop before he explained, "That was a couple of years back, at Fistral Beach. Shell and I met in California the year after I graduated. Her dad's American, and she was over there visiting her grandparents. She'd never surfed before, so I offered to give her lessons."

"Does she live in the States?"

"No. Leeds. That's where she's from. She moved down to London when we were together and then moved back when we broke up. I get to see Suzannah a lot, though, and she's started coming down on her own. She stayed with me for the summer holidays, which was hard work—six weeks keeping a fourteen-year-old entertained— but she loves the animals and she helps out. Shelley's bringing her down for the funeral."

The funeral. Somewhere between arriving in Cornwall and now, Gray had forgotten it was only four days since Will's mum had died. He'd talked about his dad, and about his uncle, but he'd said nothing about Suzannah. "Why didn't you mention her before?"

"I wasn't sure how you'd feel."

And Gray wasn't sure why that mattered, or rather, he understood why it mattered pursuant to a relationship, and Will's admission reasserted his interest. But it was part of the bigger issue, the one that left Gray questioning whether the aftermath of his career meant he'd always assume people were up to no good, or whether Will intentionally kept things close to his chest. "You're very guarded."

"Am I?" Will looked taken aback—as was Gray. He hadn't meant to say it out loud.

"I mean beyond the secret life of a freedom fighter for animal kind."

"Yeah, I suppose, but you're also very suspicious. Like, *all* the time."

Gray opened his mouth to protest but instead grimaced in acceptance of Will's point.

"Think of it from my perspective," Will continued. "We've known each other for less than three months, and you used to be a cop, the enemy."

"You're mis-apportioning blame."

"Not at all. The police work for the state. The state is run by the ruling class, which means the police, essentially, are the paid guards of the ruling class."

"So you're a communist?" Gray said.

"Anarchist," Will argued. "If we had a government of the people, I'd maybe feel a bit happier about accepting conventional law and order."

Gray handed Will's phone back and yawned. He was ready for sleep, never mind sex, although they'd wandered a long way from their starting point. But they were talking honestly, agreeing to disagree. It was a very different first night from the one Gray and Jean had spent together, which involved sex of athletic proportions. And a good thing it was too. Gray needed that distinction, even though he'd already reached the conclusion he'd been wearing his widower's weeds for long enough. The trouble was, they'd fitted him too well, and at some point, he'd moved on from grieving for Jean to mourning his grief. As the connection between Will and him grew stronger, he felt a different kind of affection blossoming. He couldn't pin it down, but there would be time for that later.

A snore sounded beside him, and Gray sighed. *That's one thing they do have in common.* "Come on, sleepy. Let's get this duvet over us."

Will lifted his bottom, so Gray could extract the duvet, and then rolled onto his side, facing the other way. With the covers over them, Gray spooned behind Will and closed his eyes.

23: The Morning After

GRAY WAS STILL in the same position, with one arm trapped under Will, the other draped over him, when he awoke to dull daylight filtering through the pale curtains.

"Morning," Will said without moving.

Gray wriggled to free the stiffness in his shoulder and pressed closer to Will's back, inhaling the scent of sleep and last night's cologne. "Good morning."

"I was gonna go surfing."

"You still could."

"Depends how far past six it is."

"I'd say it's closer to eight."

"Ah. I've missed it. Never mind." Will groaned and pushed back against Gray, confirming the arousal was mutual. "Don't suppose you brought an extra toothbrush, did you?"

"You're not getting up." Gray squeezed Will tighter. Will's deep laugh vibrated Gray's chest and also made him hump a little.

"I prefer minty morning kisses." Will looked over his shoulder and grinned. "Everywhere."

"Oh my word. And I thought I liked you before." Gray returned the grin. "Yes, I have an extra toothbrush. I like minty morning kisses too. See? Match made in heaven."

"Just give me the toothbrush before you get yourself in hot water."

Gray rolled to the side of the bed and tugged the duvet over his lap while he dug the toothbrush out of his jacket pocket. "It's a disposable. Is that all right?" He held it up to Will, who was already on his way to the bathroom. His boxers stretched like a tepee over his erection. He nodded at the array of other items Gray had pulled from his pocket: a travel pack of wet wipes, a sample-size aftershave and a lip balm.

"What's that? A morning-after survival kit?"

"Not of the sort you're thinking. I've never been into overnighters."

"Me neither." Will took the toothbrush and disappeared into the bathroom. "Although I did have one once where he made me an epic breakfast." He raised his voice over the running water.

"Did he?"

"Yep. I miss bacon."

That was one thing Gray wouldn't miss, should he ever permanently go veggie. Bacon, ham, gammon and most of the cold cuts, he'd eat them if there was nothing else, but he preferred his meat thick and hot. *Jesus, Graham. One-track mind this morning.* With the duvet still wrapped around him, he shuffled through to the en-suite, pausing in the doorway because there wasn't room for the two of them in there. "Hey."

Will gave him a frothy grin in the mirror and spat in the sink. "I'm done," he said, casually tossing the used toothbrush into the bin. Turning sideways, he edged past Gray, planting a kiss on his tightly closed lips, and scurried back to the bed. "Hurry up. It's cold."

Gray shook his head, mostly with a sense of disbelief at what was unfolding. The notion of their friendship and sex remaining two unrelated entities was fast slipping away, as was his resolve to keep them separated.

"I can't hear much brushing of teeth going on in there."

"Now who's being bossy," Gray muttered and got to it, making sure he was ready to receive minty kisses 'everywhere' before returning to the bed, where he covered Will with both his body and the duvet and shivered at the contact with Will's cool, bare skin. "I'm pleased to see you're feeling less bashful this morning."

Will responded by lifting his head from the pillow and enveloping Gray's mouth in hot spearmint that was sweet in contrast to his cool-mint toothpaste. As it had been the night before, their kisses were messy and out of control. One moment, Will was biting Gray's lower lip, the next, Gray had captured Will's tongue, laughing as he held it in his teeth and Will feigned fighting to break free.

Will rolled, taking Gray with him, and pinned his hands to the pillow. Wisps of Will's hair had escaped the elastic band, tickling Gray's face, and he screwed up his eyes, although he wanted more. He tugged his hands free and grabbed Will's head, pulling him down into another kiss while he removed the band and gripped handfuls of hair to keep Will in place and...well, just because. He'd never been with anyone with long hair before, and it was such a turn-on, he was thrusting up against Will with no concern for making it last. It was a tremendous joy to have physical contact with someone again. He'd missed it and, for the moment, didn't care if all they did was kiss and hold each other. That said, his disappointment was only minor when Will started working his way down under the duvet.

"I was enjoying that."

Will scooped his hair back and offered a wicked grin as he descended, hot breath, tongue, teeth, taking Gray fully into his mouth and then pulling back with a tantalising drag of dry lips. They were less so on subsequent ascents, each coming more quickly than the last. Gray's hands found their way to Will's hair again, and he twisted it around his fingers, torn between guilt and delight at the mess he was making. Will's head bobbed, and Gray thrust carefully but was tempted to speed up and let go.

Before he reached that point, Will released him, and Gray vented a sigh. "That was close. Oh-ohhh..." He closed his eyes and groaned in what was pure ecstasy at the heated suction that surrounded and lifted his balls. "Oh, you're good at this," he breathed.

Will's laughter sent ripples of sensation in every direction, and then he was making his way back up the bed again. "Thanks," he said with a cheeky smirk, rutting against Gray and kissing him hard.

Gray let him continue a bit longer before he pushed Will off. Eager as he was, he remembered what Will had said the night before about the slow build, so he took his time, kissing his way down, paying attention to both nipples, the bare skin around Will's belly button, smooth as silk against Gray's lips in contrast to the wiry profusion of dark hair below it as he finally reached the full expression of Will's arousal. He hadn't been kidding about loving the slow build, and Gray obliged further, at first using only the tip of his tongue to explore and tease, but there was only so long he could hold back.

If he could get away with it, he was going to suck Will off; the mere idea of that powerful pulsation against his tongue sent him into erotic overdrive.

"Gray..." Will's voice was a husky, urgent warning, which Gray heeded but increased his speed. The tattoo, blurry up close, was a timely reminder of Will's virility, and Gray had seconds to decide. Will's groans were not of complaint, so Gray kept going, smiling at the spasm that stretched his lips and groaning in unison as Will climaxed.

He didn't swallow—he'd never been able to do it without gagging, which was as far from sexy as it was possible to get—he let it dribble from his mouth as he withdrew and crawled back up the bed, aligning their bodies and using Will's ejaculate as lubricant for his own orgasm, which built quickly, briefly turned him rigid, blew his mind and screwed up his eyesight, and finally left him flopped like warm jelly on Will's heaving chest.

"Yep, it was worth missing the surf," Will said.

Gray bit his nipple in retaliation. It was about all he could reach until he found the energy to move. "We should go for breakfast."

"We should. What time's checkout?"

"Eleven-thirty, but I need to be away by eleven." Gray slid to Will's side, suddenly despondent.

"Do you have to go?"

"She won't be expecting me. It's safe to say she won't be pleased to see me. But yes. I do. Being there with you and your mum...it gave me pause. She might've changed her mind and be worried about making contact. She probably hasn't, but I won't know unless I go see her."

Will turned onto his side and rested his hand on Gray's hip. "The offer stands, OK? If you change your mind."

"Thanks." Gray would've been happy to forget about his mum and stay right where he was for the rest of the day—the week, even. He imagined Will shared that sentiment. He was still looking Gray in the eye, but his focus had drifted. "What are you thinking about?"

"What I told you last night. How much should I say to your mate?"

"As little as you can without committing perjury. He'll have looked at your record."

"Won't he want to know why I went in with Freddie and the others?"

"He will, yes, and I suggest you avoid telling him. If there's any suspicion you were involved in blowing up the lab..."

"Yeah, I know. Counter-terrorism measures. It's not like the good old days." Will's comment sounded flippant, but Gray knew it wasn't. "We were interrogated."

"That's a strong word."

"And accurate. It was horrendous. But the police must've figured none of us had the knowledge or skills to build a bomb. God, it really brings it home, using that word." Will absently brushed his fingers up and down Gray's side, creating a soothing yet tickly sensation that gave him goosebumps. "I never told my mum about it. She'd have been mortified if she'd known the kind of people I'm involved with."

"*Were* involved with," Gray intentionally miscorrected.

Will chuckled. "She believed peaceful protest was the only solution to conflict."

"Do you believe that?"

"I take it as my starting point. She was still going to Greenham Common when I was at uni, and she used to stop off to see me on the way home. Her car..." Will's expression was both grimace and grin, and he squeezed his eyes shut. He looked astonishingly cute.

"What was it?" Gray asked.

"A Reliant Robin."

"Ah-oh. That's..." Gray held back a laugh. "That's a very collectible car these days."

"It was a terrible car," Will said. "Dangerous, ugly..."

"I wouldn't go that far." They were both laughing now.

"She took me down to Greenham Common in it a few times. Very hairy. They tip over. Did you know that?"

"Like cows?" Gray hated himself the second it was out of his mouth. "Not that I in any way condone cow tipping."

Will narrowed his eyes but let it go.

"What's there now?" Gray asked, keen to change the subject.

"Greenham Common? Well, it's not an airbase anymore. It's an industrial park, but there's a commemorative garden. It's kind of amazing. Like a mini modern Stonehenge, with a metal sculpture of flames in the centre, which my mum hated because it's too hard and angular—masculine, she said. My favourite part's the fountain. It's a spiral, with the words of one of the camp songs inscribed into it. 'You can't kill the spirit'..." Will's breath caught in his throat, and a tear trickled from the corner of his eye down over the bridge of his nose. "Sorry. Don't know where that came from."

"Hey. No apologies."

"I owe it to her to live how she would want me to."

Gray reached up and brushed the wet trail away with his thumb. "I think you already do, Will."

"Maybe." It took a few minutes for Will's sadness to subside. "So, do you want the shower first, or...?"

"You can go first if you want." Gray shuffled closer and kissed the tip of Will's nose, or that was what he was aiming for, but Will moved, and their lips met instead. "After," Gray murmured as he rolled and Will came down on top of him.

Showers, breakfast, visiting living mums, saying farewell to mums who had passed... All of it could wait.

24: Seething

A FIVE-MILE RUN, A workout and a cool shower later, Rob felt no better. His anger was misfiring, hitting anything in his sights, and he didn't know what to do with it. It wasn't Gray's fault, even if the call from Will Richards indicated the two of them were involved. That, or it was a massive and unlikely coincidence that they both happened to be travelling back from Cornwall at the same time. What pissed Rob off the most was the wasted hours of searching social networks for Richards' location when Gray had known it all along. Or maybe he hadn't. Either way, Gray wasn't the cause of Rob's anger, merely an amplifier.

Though he hated to admit it, nor was Travis. So this was it, the end, officially. Zoë was remarrying. They were done, over, finished. Of course, they'd been that for more than a year, but Rob had been clinging to the shot-in-the-dark chance she would change her mind, and he was furious with himself for not dealing with it. He'd reasoned it through—Lucas liked Travis, Zoë loved Travis, and he seemed to love her, the guy was supportive—but it made no difference.

The worst of it was, Rob was no longer sure he wanted things back the way they had been. For as much as he loved Zoë and missed her and Lucas, the problems had started a long time before he'd left. If not the job, it would've been something else. But Rob should've fixed it back then instead of joining the SIU. He should've talked to Zoë about the impossibility of trying to pay for everything and have family time.

He should've asked her what she needed from him. It was a scary question to ask; she might've said 'nothing'. Now, she really didn't need anything from him, other than doing his share of the parenting, but that wasn't a chore, and it wasn't for her. They owed it to Lucas to remain on friendly terms, just as Rob's parents had done when their relationship fell apart and he'd stopped believing in fairy tales. Love wasn't even happy, never mind forever after, which was probably as well because he still loved Zoë. But he loved her enough to want her to be happy.

It didn't help to know that.

It was Sunday, and he couldn't go any further with his investigation until he'd spoken to Richards, which might prove to be a dead end, and then he'd be stuck. But was there even a case to investigate? Hector Laird-Browne had been drunk behind the wheel, and the only physical evidence indicating it wasn't a simple case of drink driving was Hector having Aaron Tanner's ID in his possession, which could be explained by his involvement with Naomi.

The entire case came back to what Naomi had told him, which Aaron had corroborated, and Rob knew how that would look in court. The defence would, at best, discredit Aaron and Naomi's testimonies by claiming they lacked mental capacity, and if they were considered competent, they would be treated as one witness. Freddie Berringer had reason to want Hector dead, and not necessarily out of jealousy. Someone had it in for Berringer and—as he'd so 'eloquently' put it—had fucked him over.

Rob's guess was it had something to do with the 'technical glitch', and whoever was responsible for that had also reported Berringer's to the SIU. With Hector dead, Carrie missing, and Freddie and Aaron refusing to talk, Rob's only hope now was that Will Richards could give him a lead. Or else...he'd got nothing.

Out of sheer boredom, and because he had a duty to at least attempt to understand, Rob opened the SIU report on Berringer's bank, but he'd only vaguely followed Gray's 'in simple terms' explanation. The words 'as can be seen in table 1.2' didn't help at all when table 1.2 was fifty lines of figures with an accompanying line graph.

"Jess Lambert, where are you when I need you, eh?" Rob closed the file and tossed his phone onto the sofa. His brain didn't do maths, and it was a stopping block he really didn't need with only two days left to work on the case. He was certain Hector's death was linked to the impetus for the fraud investigation. Aaron Tanner was a tech wiz and struck Rob as very particular; there was no way he'd have let a computer glitch pass him by, especially one of such magnitude.

Rob picked up his phone again and loaded the article he'd bookmarked and read several times already. The technobabble wasn't easy to decipher, but behind it all was gushing praise for Aaron, as the author recounted the projects he'd worked on. All of them were either for Berringer's or for one of their customers; he'd worked with pretty much every investor on the Berringer's portfolio, and there were links to different awards for innovation, growth, best use of technology and so on.

With each link visited, Rob became a little more indignant on Aaron's behalf. It wasn't his name tied to the awards; it was Berringer's, and if Rob hadn't known Aaron and Naomi inhabited the same body, he'd have been arresting Aaron on suspicion of murder. He had plenty of motive for framing Berringer, but Naomi loved Hector, and neither of them stood to benefit from Hector's death. However, they were capable of calling in the SIU and making sure there was something for them to investigate. But then, Freddie would've reported Aaron's hacking activities to the police, and he'd have faced imprisonment. There was no way Aaron and Naomi would risk it.

Which put Rob back to square one. Again.

A couple of the websites had photos from awards ceremonies, where Aaron was nowhere to be seen, although Naomi was in one of them, standing between Freddie Berringer and Hector Laird-Browne. That was another thing Rob was still struggling to make sense of. He could see the evidence, right there in front of him. Aaron didn't have a public presence, Naomi did, almost as if he had to become her to deal with the outside world. But that contradicted what he'd seen. Worse, it denied Aaron and Naomi's existence. Naomi was more than a costume Aaron put on so he could leave the house. She was a real person, with real fears, and those fears only partly coincided with Aaron's.

When Rob's phone started vibrating in his hand, he jumped in surprise, not least because it was from the mystery number that he now knew was the landline at Aaron's mother's apartment. He accepted the call.

"Hello?"

"Mr. Simpson-Stone?"

"Hey, Aaron. How's it going?"

"Not great. Freddie's been in touch."

"When?"

"He phoned half an hour ago. I don't know how he got this number."

Rob stopped pacing, not that he remembered getting up or starting to pace in the first place. "What did he say?"

"He asked me to meet him at his apartment."

"You or Naomi?"

"Either. He said it didn't matter."

"Did he tell you why?"

"No. But if he's got the phone number, he knows where I am."

"Who else has this number?"

"Nobody, as far as I know. Naomi tried to get hold of Carrie, but she made the call anonymously, I'm sure of it."

"I thought you were staying somewhere else."

"I am. I only came back to shower."

"Are you sleeping rough?"

Aaron didn't answer.

"Do you need somewhere to stay?"

Again, he gave no answer.

"OK, Aaron, don't leave the flat, I'll get a car out that way."

"I can't stay here."

Rob was at a loss what else to suggest. There wasn't enough evidence to support arranging a 'safe house', and the alternative was a hotel, which neither Aaron nor Hedley's budget could afford. That left only one other option, and it was one Rob shouldn't even be considering, but Aaron's plight struck a chord with him. He had no idea why he empathised as strongly as he did, other than perhaps his first impression of the parallels between Aaron's and his own situation. Knowing they were completely different hadn't made him care any less.

"What about bunking in with me for a few days?"

"I don't know..."

"I'm going to be out and about, so you and Naomi will have the place to yourselves. It'll give you a bit of breathing space."

"It's very kind of you, Mr. Simpson-Stone." Aaron fell silent.

Rob hoped he was considering the idea, and also that he'd hurry up, because his phone was beeping to alert him to another call. He was about to tell Aaron he'd call him back when he got his answer.

"Yes, please."

"Great. Can you make it to Kilburn? I'll meet you at the station."

"What time?"

"An hour?"

"I'll be there."

"See you then. Bye."

Rob waited long enough to hear Aaron say 'bye' back, hung up and went straight to the other call, recognising the number from Will Richards' earlier call.

"Hey, is that Rob?"

"It is. Will?"

"Yeah. I just thought I'd let you know I'm back home. I had the feeling you wanted to see me sooner rather than later. I'm around this evening. Tomorrow, I'm going to be in and out all day, arranging a funeral."

"I'm sorry for your loss, but I need to talk to you today if possible." In his head, Rob quickly ran through the logistics. "Whereabouts do you live?"

"Croxley."

"That's not so far." Rob could probably be there in less than half an hour in the lighter Sunday traffic, but he wanted to make sure Aaron was sorted first. "It's going to be about eight o'clock. Is that all right?"

"Perfect. I'll text you the number and postcode."

"Cheers. See you later."

***

Three trains had come and gone, still no sign of Aaron or Naomi. Rob tried calling the mobile number Aaron had given him, with no success. He'd considered calling back the landline and had second thoughts. If Aaron had changed his mind, no problem, but Rob would rather see for himself that he was safe and well. The fourth train arrived Aaron-less, and Rob returned to his bike, sending the same text to Gray Fisher as last time, to let him know where he was going, but not to Hedley.

It was terrifying to think back now to the undercover work, when he'd been involved in deals gone deadly and armed hostage situations with only a text message to cover him. On that basis, his assessment of the risk in going to Drury Court on his own was low to none, but Hedley wouldn't appreciate him telling her how to do her job any more than she'd appreciate him defying a direct order, let alone why he was doing so.

The estate was rough, and the time of day—coming up to five p.m. and going dark—meant the gangs would be out in force, although it was better than when he'd first joined the Met. In his first year, there were three teenage murders on the estate, and the papers had called for a public inquiry into the police failure to investigate. The truth was they had investigated, but there were limits to what could be done when violence was commonplace and there were no witnesses, or none willing to come forward.

Ten years of redevelopment, knocking down the tower blocks and replacing them with houses and smaller apartment blocks, had made it a bit less of a no-man's-land. Relations with 'the community' were on a firmer footing, and the media had stopped slamming the police. Nevertheless, Rob stood more chance of coming away unscathed as a black guy on a hefty bike than as a bobby, so when he spotted the group of younger teens watching him park outside Drury Court, he acknowledged them briefly, to take away their anonymity, and passed them by. If they touched his bike, the whole neighbourhood would know about it.

Even though he'd been there once before, he still had trouble finding Aaron's mother's flat. He knocked and waited, not expecting anyone to answer and successfully hiding his surprise when a woman's voice asked, "Who is it?"

"It's Rob. A friend of your son's."

The chain rattled and the door opened enough for him to glimpse the left side of the woman's face.

"He's not here. What do you want him for?"

"Do you know where he's gone?"

"Sorry, I don't. Are you a police officer?"

Rob delayed answering for a few seconds, trying to figure out which response would get him the furthest. "I'm here as a friend."

The door twitched open another couple of inches, and she looked him over. "I'm worried Aaron may be in trouble with the police." Her tone was offhand, and her statement was as ambiguous as Rob's.

"He's not in trouble, Mrs. Tanner. When did he leave?"

"Over an hour ago. He took an overnight bag."

"Did he say where he was going?"

"No. He never does."

The door was already closing, and there was no point pushing for more. "OK. Thanks for your help." As Rob turned away, he heard the door click shut followed by the rattle of the locks and chains.

Outside, the kids had moved closer to the bike and were actively admiring it.

"Alright?" Rob said as he approached, already putting on his helmet. He clicked the alarm fob and straddled the bike. The gang watched in sullen silence as he rolled back and started up. Unable to resist the opportunity to show off, he revved a couple of times and made a lot of noise as he departed at speed, only slowing when he emerged from the estate onto the main road.

All he could do now was head back to Kilburn and see if Aaron had made it, but he wasn't optimistic. Another half hour wasted on going up and down the high road, he gave up and returned to the flat with no idea what to do next. Or not as regards finding Aaron, but he could bring his meeting with Will Richards forward, assuming the guy was agreeable. He made the call, and five minutes later, he was on his way to Croxley.

***

Standing at the front door of the run-down farmhouse, Rob had to check he hadn't mistyped the postcode. After seeing Aaron Tanner's and Freddie Berringer's residences—or former residences—it didn't strike Rob as the kind of place an investment banker would reside. But the address was correct, so he approached and knocked. The racket of dogs barking erupted from within, and something large hit the other side of the door. Someone shouted, "Come in here!" The barking stopped, and the door opened.

"Will Richards?" Rob asked, surer than ever he'd got the wrong house. The guy, long-haired and dressed in cut-off jeans and a baggy T-shirt, looked nothing like the image in Rob's head. Neither had Aaron Tanner, but he was a behind-the-scenes geek, whereas Will Richards had been frontline, dealing with the bank's investors.

"Yep, that's me. Rob, isn't it? Come on in." Will stepped aside.

Rob accepted his invitation, peering past him to get a sense of what he was walking into.

"The dogs are locked up," Will said.

Rob nodded tacitly and followed Will into his living room. Everything was at odds. The house, the décor, the man, his career, all those dogs...

"Can I get you a drink?"

"I'm fine for now, thanks."

Will gestured to the sofa. "Please, sit down."

"Cheers." Rob did so. "It's an interesting place you've got here."

"Yeah." Will glanced around the room. "It was my mum's. I haven't had a chance to redecorate." He smiled apologetically.

"I wasn't judging," Rob said.

A moment of uncomfortable silence followed before Will sat in the armchair and gave Rob an expectant shrug. "Gray said you wanted to talk to me about Berringer's."

"I do, yeah."

"I don't know that I'll be much help. I only worked there for eighteen months, and it was fifteen years ago."

"That's OK. I'm trying to get a picture of the setup."

"Right. So, you want to know about the early days. How much do you know already?"

"I've spoken to Aaron Tanner. He mentioned Freddie Berringer recruited four of you to come in as directors."

"Yes, he did. Our intellectual investment in return for ten percent once the bank went public."

"You worked for free?"

"No. He paid us excellent salaries and bonuses. The shares were to keep us sweet. Aaron and Hector were in hot demand, and Freddie wanted to ensure their loyalty."

"Are you aware Hector is dead?" Rob asked.

"Yes. Car accident, I heard."

"That's correct," Rob confirmed. Will was being intentionally vague, but there was no sign of the fear that gagged Aaron and Naomi. "To go back to what you said about ensuring loyalty, according to Aaron, money wasn't the only incentive Freddie used."

Will sat back and rested one foot on the other knee. If Rob hadn't been trained to look for clues in people's behaviour, he'd have missed the change in Will's demeanour, as he still looked at ease, but it was forced.

"Aaron told you about the threats."

"He told me Freddie coerced you all to get you on board."

"Not just to get us on board." Will scooped his hair back and held on to it, his agitation increasingly apparent in his actions. He sat forward again and met Rob's gaze head-on. "If I admit to criminal activity—"

"Off the record," Rob cut in. The stuff he'd turned a blind eye to with the SIU made it an easy reassurance. However, getting Will to believe him might take a bit more doing.

"How's Aaron?" Will asked. It was only broadly pertinent and an intentional sidetrack, but Rob figured Will's concern was genuine.

"That's a good question," he answered honestly. He needed to show his trust first if he wanted Will to open up. "He was supposed to meet me this afternoon, but he didn't show."

"Does he still struggle with social anxiety?"

"I don't think that was the problem on this occasion. Since Hector's death, Aaron's been keeping a low profile, hiding from Berringer."

"Freddie or Charles?"

"Freddie." Rob thought it was an odd question, although now he was thinking back to what Naomi had said about Aaron hacking Lord Berringer's account.

"Is that what Aaron told you?" Will asked.

"He thinks Freddie is responsible for Hector's death."

Will shook his head. "There's something not right." He seemed to be thinking hard about what he wanted to say.

Rather than tell him what he already knew, Rob waited, interested to see if the trust extended both ways.

Eventually, Will asked, "Have you met Naomi?"

Apparently, it did. "Yes, I have. Can I ask what you meant about something not being right?"

"I don't think Freddie killed Hector. He's a lot of things, and he is a killer—"

"He's a hunter."

"Exactly. You've seen my criminal record—" Will paused for Rob to confirm it, which he did with a nod "—so you know I'm involved in direct action."

"Yes, and I noticed a couple of incidents occurred on the Berringer estate."

"He hunts with dogs and believes it's his birthright. We have a case with the CPS—a third case—and he'll probably get away with it again. Even if he doesn't, what's a couple of grand in fines to the Berringers?"

"Freddie thinks you have a vendetta against him," Rob said.

"Too right, I do. He's a manipulative, power-crazed sadist, and I will take him down."

Rob was surprised by Will's angry admission. He didn't seem the kind to get angry. "It sounds like it's about more than the way Freddie treats animals."

"Yeah, you could say that. He's greedy and controlling, and he doesn't care who he hurts to get what he wants."

"Yet you don't think he killed Hector."

"No. Why would he? Hector was his top analyst."

"Are you aware Hector and Naomi were in a relationship?"

Will's eyebrows rose to an almost comedic height. "Really? I guess I should've expected that. They were always close, even back in uni. But I still don't think—" Will shot up from the chair and dashed for the door, but not soon enough to halt the in-pouring of dogs—four, Rob counted—and a rabbit, which would've been surprise enough without the call of, "Hi, honey. I'm home!" followed by the appearance of one grinning-turned-sheepish Gray Fisher.

25: Underlying

R OB." NOW GRAY understood what people meant when they said they wanted the floor to open up and swallow them. Until that moment, he'd thought it no more than a cliché, but his joke, intended to distract from his misery so Will wouldn't notice, had exploded in his face.

"Evening, Gray," Rob offered in greeting. He looked none too impressed, while Will was averting his eyes and trying his hardest to stay serious.

"You didn't waste any time," Gray said. It sounded like an accusation, but it wasn't.

"Er, no." Will put his head down, explaining with great restraint, "I called Rob on the way home, and..." He shrugged, still fighting his laughter. "Did it go OK?"

"Not exactly." Gray was grateful for Will's cryptic enquiry. At some point, he'd tell him what had happened at his mum's, but he wasn't ready to go into it now, especially not with Rob present and clearly aggrieved.

"So you *are* together," Rob said.

"No!" Gray and Will replied in unison and then stared at each other with what Gray envisaged were matching narrow-eyed expressions that asked, *Or are we?* But no. They were friends who happened to have shared a bed for a night and a quick session of morning nookie. They weren't a couple. He didn't think.

"Where are you up to?" he asked in a poor and frankly unconvincing effort at deflection. He should've taken some tips from the dogs and Benjy; while the human commotion had been taking place, they'd sneakily found spots to sit or lie and were behaving impeccably lest anyone notice they were still there.

"I was going to make a drink," Will said. "Want one, Gray?"

"Please. Coffee for me."

"Rob?"

"Yeah, I might as well. Just black coffee, cheers."

"Be right back." Will gave Gray a quick smile on his way out of the room, leaving him at Rob's mercy.

Gray had a fairly good idea why Rob was pissed off, aside from that being his usual state of mind where Gray was concerned. This time, however,

Rob couldn't accuse him of putting the job before people because he'd done the exact opposite.

"If you've got a problem with me, Rob..."

"You could say that."

"Then we should clear the air."

"This isn't the SIU."

"No. It's more important."

Rob's laughter was scathing. "You've changed your tune. Do you know how much time I've wasted trying to locate Will Richards? You're as self-serving as ever."

The accusation hit him hard, and Rob was right...up to a point. "I'm sorry. It wasn't for me to share."

"What the fuck did you think I was gonna do? I'm investigating a murder, for Christ's sake, and Will is a key witness."

For the briefest moment, Gray considered pointing out Rob was exaggerating. At best, Will had information that might contribute to solving the case. But taking on Rob and his bottled-up anger was not on Gray's bucket list. One murder was enough to contend with.

"I really am sorry, Rob." Gray listened to check Will was still in the kitchen and said quietly, "His mum passed away last week, and he doesn't need his past indiscretions coming back to damn him. Can't it wait?"

"No." Rob's response was uncharacteristically heartless, and he couldn't even meet Gray's eyes.

"Look, Rob, I know you only have a few more days to nail this, and—"

"Aaron Tanner's missing."

"Ah, hell. Since when?"

"This afternoon. He was supposed to meet me, and he didn't show. He said Berringer had been in touch."

"Have you called it in?"

"How can I? All I've got is a potentially suspicious fatal accident that's already been recorded as drink driving and two missing persons, one of them for less than three hours."

"The other one's still not shown up?"

"No. I saw Berringer yesterday. He says he's been in contact with Duggan since her mother reported her missing, but no-one else has seen or heard from her."

If it had been anyone other than Rob, Gray would have concluded there was no case. But Rob had a knack for picking up the smaller details that bypassed everyone else or were discarded as irrelevant. Nonetheless, Gray was struggling to see how he'd got from A to B. "When you came to me originally, it was because of the fake ID."

"Which wasn't fake."

"That's what I mean. Where did the rest of it come from?"

Rob shrugged and slapped his hands down on his thighs. It was an act of angry surrender. "You're right. Everything I've got's based on Aaron and Naomi's say-so, and the fact they're shit-scared of Berringer. There's no point even trying for witness protection—I offered to put them up while I get to the bottom of what's going on, because that technical glitch that brought down Berringer's is bullshit. Tanner's as meticulous as you are. There's no way it would've got past him."

"Unless he caused it."

"No." Rob sounded confident. More than that, he sounded adamant, and while Gray was no longer his boss, he had managed people long enough and been there often enough to know when personal feelings were starting to impinge on objectivity.

"Do you think you might be a bit too close to the Tanners?"

"Yeah, probably. It was never a problem on the Strang case, though, was it?"

"I wasn't accusing you of shoddy work, Rob. All I'm saying is sometimes an outside perspective can be beneficial, especially when you're flying solo and you've nobody to bounce ideas off." Gray mentally braced, fully expecting Rob to lose his cool, but he didn't. He sat back and held out his hands, inviting— more like challenging—Gray to say more.

He needed to choose his words carefully. The last thing he wanted was to call Rob's detective work to question, but on the basis of Rob's evidence, Aaron Tanner was a suspect. Rather than state it, Gray asked tentatively, "Wouldn't putting Berringer's out of business have brought an end to Aaron Tanner's contractual obligations?"

"He could've walked at any time. Contractual obligation isn't the problem. Berringer was holding Aaron to ransom."

"OK. Say, for argument's sake, Tanner intentionally created the system error. If Hector knew what he'd done, would he have reported it to Berringer?"

"Unlikely. If anything, Aaron and Hector would've been in it together."

"Which Berringer could've known about—"

"This is all assuming Aaron sabotaged the system to start with, and there's no way. You'd have to meet him to understand. He's terrified of ending up in prison, and Berringer's got plenty on him already."

"OK." Gray could see the reasoning, and it was logical, but he still felt Rob had overstepped the personal mark on this one. "What do you think's going on?"

"I can tell you what's going on," Will said.

Gray hadn't heard him come back into the room. From the way he was leaning against the wall with his arms folded, he'd been listening for a while.

He wearily met Gray's gaze. "I'm sorry, but you're wrong about Aaron." He looked at Rob. "And Freddie's not responsible either. Or not directly."

"Who is?" Rob asked.

"His father."

"To what end?"

Will shrugged. "Same as always. To gain the upper hand. That's all they do, Freddie and Charles." His lip curled in disgust. "The bank, bringing us in, stealing investors—it's all part of their power struggle. Do you have any idea how many jobs I've left to avoid the Berringers' romp around the city? They're not even doing it for money. It's sport—a hunt, if you will. And while we minions are slogging our guts out, wooing investors and throwing god-awful dinner parties, Freddie and Charles sit back, enjoying the entertainment and planning their next foray. That was why I got out of Berringer's bank as soon as I could."

"He didn't report you," Gray said, remembering now that they'd broken off their conversation the night before. Will had only explained how he'd been strongarmed into joining Berringer's but not how he'd escaped scot-free.

"No, he didn't." Will turned back to Rob. "If you pursue this, I'll deny everything."

"I can't make promises, Will."

"I knew the Berringers from hunts before we started university, and I'd had a few run-ins with Freddie." Will's eyes flitted in Gray's direction; he was only giving Rob half the story. "He had photographic evidence that would've put me in prison, and he used it whenever he needed my compliance. Aaron... he was always broke at uni, and Freddie had paid him to write some computer programmes—"

"I know he was a hacker," Rob said.

"All right, then. Freddie paid him to hack into his father's business and then threatened to report him unless he went in on the bank. He'd already signed Hector up, but when Hector found out what Freddie had done to Aaron, he backed out. Actually, he went nuts and attacked Freddie, put him in hospital. The next thing, Freddie's demanding to see me. In short, I had to convince Hector to change his mind or Freddie was going to hand me over to you lot, and the only way Hector would do it was if I joined them."

"How did you get out?" Rob asked.

"I just walked. I decided I'd rather do time than spend any longer being bossed around by Freddie, but he didn't want me there in the first place. It was only ever an uneasy truce."

"Hector resigned too, didn't he?"

"Yes, he did."

"Yet Freddie still didn't turn you in."

"No."

"Any idea why that is?"

Will closed his eyes. Creases formed across his forehead, giving away how difficult it was for him to talk about it. "I persuaded Hector to go back. If I'd known where it would end..."

"You said Freddie didn't kill Hector."

"He didn't. He could lose Carrie, Aaron and the rest of us, but without Hector, Freddie's worth nothing."

"You didn't kill him either, Will," Gray pointed out.

"But I sacrificed Hector for my own liberty, because the only way to beat people like the Berringers is to play them at their own game."

"Explain," Rob said.

"We were on to them. We had enough to bring Freddie down, but we needed hard evidence, and we weren't going to get it if we were in prison."

"Who's 'we'? You, Aaron and Hector?"

"No."

"The Animal Liberation Front?"

"If you like. You need to understand the extent of Freddie's cruelty. Not just the hunting. The way he treats his hounds, horses... Those images never go away. And you know the injustice of it? If he was found guilty, he'd get six months for animal cruelty. But they're all in it together—barristers, judges, politicians—and Freddie thinks he's invincible."

"And that was enough to keep him quiet?" Rob asked doubtfully.

"No. That would be the video clip where he beat a hunt sab to death. Or not quite. He beat him unconscious, and he died later."

"You're withholding evidence of a murder."

"By all means, come back with a search warrant, turn this place upside down. You won't find anything."

"Stored digitally, by any chance?" Rob asked.

Will shrugged and said no more.

"All right, let's leave that for now. I need you to look at something for me." Rob took out his phone, unlocked it and handed it to Will. "This is the report from when Berringer's was investigated a couple of years back."

Gray pursed his lips, knowing his opinion on the sharing of a confidential SIU file—which shouldn't be in any of their possession—would not go down well with Rob or Will, although if he wanted to put a halt to proceedings, he'd need to act quickly. The way Will's thumb was working, he was a fast reader.

"Wow, talk about cross the 'T's and dot the 'I's. It's thorough. Who put this together? You?" The question was directed at Rob, who thumbed in Gray's direction. Will nodded, impressed, and returned to reading. Gray's heart leapt, and he inwardly cheered at the compliment. It made Rob's continued iciness a little easier to bear.

"Yep." Will handed Rob's phone back. "It's exactly the sort of scam Charles would pull to get one over on Freddie."

"So, if we wanted to prosecute Charles Berringer, how would we go about finding the evidence two years on?"

"System logs?" Will suggested.

"If they survived liquidation."

"Why Charles and not Freddie?" Gray asked.

"He killed Hector Laird-Browne."

"You know, Rob, I've always admired your detective skills, but where the hell did you pluck that from?"

"Will said it before. Freddie's nothing without Hector. That's all the motive his father would need."

"Jeez. And I thought I had parent problems."

"Aaron will have backups," Will said.

Rob nodded. "Yeah, he will. I need to find him." He was already on his feet.

"That's easy. He'll be with Freddie."

"For real?"

"That's what he's always done. Dogs stay loyal to cruel masters."

"I think Aaron's got more sense than that."

"More sense than dogs?" Will looked at his sleeping pack. "I doubt it."

Rob smiled. "Thanks for your help, Will."

"No problem."

"I'll catch up with you later, Gray."

"See you, Rob." Gray stayed where he was while Will saw Rob out. The front door closed, and Will went straight upstairs. When he came down, he had his jacket on and his shoes in his hand. He sat to put them on.

"Where are you going?"

"I need to speak to Aaron."

"It's police business."

"The police are going after Hector's murderer." Will stood to zip his jacket.

"Will..."

"Freddie's not getting away with it again, Gray."

"Then you should've given Rob your evidence."

"That's what I plan to do."

26: Hunters

THE LIGHTS WERE on in Freddie Berringer's Marylebone apartment, but the doorman was evidently under strict instructions to lie through his teeth. Rob turned to DCI Hedley in defeat. Behind her, the two DCs awaited their orders to either do something or go home. Rob's hands were tied. He didn't know for sure Aaron was with Berringer, and even if he was, he'd come here of his own free will.

"It's your call, Rob."

"I haven't got time to wait for a warrant, Ma'am." That counted for Aaron's sake as well as his own, and he needed a workaround. If they went in there without good cause, Berringer would have them for wrongful forced entry.

A sharp draught blew through the foyer. The external doors swung open, and Rob heard someone say, "Excuse me, please." The two DCs stepped aside.

"What the hell?"

The doorman squared up to the new arrivals. "Good evening, gentlemen."

"And a good evening to you, sir." Will rubbed his hands together. "Gosh, it's a cold one, isn't it?"

"Indeed it is," the doorman agreed. "Can I help you, sir?"

"Yes, I believe you can. I'd be grateful if you could let Mr. Berringer know Will Richards is here to see him."

"Sir—"

"Please?" Will offered the doorman a demure smile and pointed at the antique intercom phone on the high-sheen wooden counter.

With a disgruntled sigh, the doorman made the call. A moment later, he hung up. "Number three, first floor." A buzz sounded from the security door across the foyer.

"Thanks ever so much," Will said, leading the way through the door and holding it open.

Rob looked at Gray, who merely shrugged and gestured for him to go ahead. He stepped past Will but then held back while everyone else came through the door.

"Mr. Fisher," Hedley greeted.

"Ma'am."

"I wasn't aware Rob had called you in."

Rob was all set to correct her mistake, but Gray's stealthy headshake warned him off. In the absence of a better plan of action, Rob went with it, and he and Gray followed the others up the stairs to the first floor.

The door to apartment number three opened as they approached, and Will paused, looking back for instruction.

"Do come in, Will," a voice called. Rob recognised it as Berringer's.

Will moved off again, and Rob caught a glimpse of Gray's ashen face. He would never have sent an untrained man into an unknown situation. They had no way of knowing whether Berringer was armed. But this was Rob's case, not Gray's, and not Hedley's; it was time he stepped up to the plate. He edged past Hedley and the other officers to reach Will, who had drawn to a halt inside the doorway of a vast room containing a long dining table, around which were eight chairs, three of them occupied. Freddie Berringer was seated at the head of the table, with Aaron to his left, and at the far end was Rob's other missing person: Carrie Duggan.

"Late as always," Berringer muttered. He picked up the whisky tumbler in front of him and tilted it from side to side, rattling the ice.

"Sorry about that," Will said. He sounded cocky. "I didn't receive an agenda." He went straight past Berringer to Aaron, who was on his feet and almost threw himself into Will's embrace.

"That's Aaron Tanner," Rob whispered for Gray and everyone else's benefit.

Both Will and Aaron were emotional, possibly to the point of letting tears loose, until Berringer broke up their party.

"We have business to attend to, gentlemen."

Aaron obediently resumed his seat, and Will pulled out the chair next to him. He sat and put his feet up on the table. Rob beckoned the other officers into the room.

"So what's happening here?" Will asked Berringer.

"We're discussing a new venture. You want in?"

"Not on your life."

Berringer's eyes strayed to Rob and the others. "Oh, really. This is a little O-T-T. I'm not an *animal*." Berringer grinned viciously and stared hard at Rob.

It sent a chill of recognition down Rob's spine. He'd seen good men turn into crazed killing machines. He'd seen the fear and pain in their eyes, and the hopeless remorse when they realised what they'd done. But that was not what he saw now. His mind flashed back to the end of the Strang case and the hostage situation. Folden was going to kill Josh merely because he got in the way. Rob had talked Folden out of it, somehow; he forgot now. What he'd never forget was the coldness in Anders Folden's eyes—the same coldness he saw in Freddie Berringer's. Naomi was right; Berringer was a sociopath.

"I'm not staying," Will said.

"Indeed not. I've already called security."

"Oh, really, Freddie." Will mimicked Berringer's condescending tone. "That's a little O-T-T." He swung his feet back down to the floor and leaned forward, resting his elbows on the table and steepling his fingers. "Let's say, for argument's sake, I did want in. I'd need some reassurances first. For instance... should I expect you to sabotage your own company?"

Freddie picked up his glass, emptied it in one gulp, and slammed it down again. "Now why would I do that?"

"I'd have thought that was fairly obvious. To stop your father getting his hands on it."

Freddie swirled the empty glass, peering into it as if he expected it to refill itself. Or perhaps he was waiting for someone to come running along with the bottle. Still with his gaze fixed on the glass, he wafted a hand in the direction of the police officers. "I owe your friends a debt of gratitude." For all that he was acting like he didn't give a shit, the last three words were spat out.

"You called the police on your father." Will made it a statement rather than a question, and Freddie didn't deny it. "And they did what you asked them to. You can't really complain. That was low, though, Charles going after *your* bank like that. Still, you know what they say...like father, like son. It's no wonder you're so warped."

"At least I know who my father is."

Will laughed, although his eyes gave away his anger. He got up and moved to stand behind Berringer's chair, with his hands on Berringer's shoulders. Leaning close, he spoke directly into his ear. "I'm going to get you."

"Yeah, yeah. Haven't we had this conversation already?"

Will gave Berringer's shoulders a pat, firm enough to make him jolt, and released him. "Aaron, tell me you're not going to let this piece of scum use you again."

"I've got nothing left to lose, Will." Aaron's eyes darted to Rob and then to the tabletop. He looked gaunt and ghostlike and not at all like someone who was there of their own free will.

Berringer peered up at Will and smirked, but Will wasn't paying attention to him. His eyes were fixed on Aaron.

"I won't let this happen. I refuse to lose another friend."

Berringer gave a loud, bored sigh and flapped his hand dismissively. "For fuck's sake, I didn't kill Hector. Why would I? It's preposterous. Hector was my...friend."

"Oh, shut up! Friend? Hector was your most valuable asset. But Daddy took Freddie's toys away, didn't he? And now you want retribution. That's why you've brought Aaron here tonight—another innocent person you're going to destroy to get one up on your father. You both need to be stopped."

"And I suppose you're the man to do it."

"Nope." Will looked over at Rob. "But the police might want to speak with you."

Berringer gave a mocking laugh. "Sticks and stones, Wilfred."

Next to Rob, Gray was tense, ready to spring into action, and Rob was ready to restrain him if he had to. They needed to hold back until they had enough to arrest at least one Berringer.

"What about you, Carrie?" Will asked. "Have you told him?"

Rob had been keeping a subtle eye on her, and until that point, she'd quietly watched what was going on, trying not to draw attention. Now, she smiled at Will and gave a few exaggerated blinks. "Tell who what?" she asked.

Will raised his arms in a faux-hopeless shrug. "You know what? You deserve each other." He switched his attention back to Aaron. For what seemed a very long time, Will didn't speak, yet his eyes never left Aaron's. There was a connection between them like fizzling lines of current; whatever they had shared in the past still bonded them. Gray bristled at Rob's side.

***

See, now, this is jealousy. Gray acknowledged it without dispute. His feelings for Will were on the move again, and he was prepared to go wherever they took him.

"Aaron..." Will glanced back at Gray, and it set his heart pounding. He knew what Will was doing. "Have you still got it?"

"Yes."

"Will you come with me?"

Aaron swallowed so hard Gray heard the gulp.

"We'll be sent to prison."

"We won't." Will sounded confident, but it was by no means certain. He and Aaron had committed major crimes that carried lengthy sentences, and while Gray had magicked away a few offences in his SIU years, even he would have struggled to conceal acts of terrorism.

"He's lying to you, Will." Freddie sneered and rose to his feet, getting right up in Will's face. "Naomi destroyed it."

Will held his ground, refusing to look at Berringer. "I understand if you can't do this, Aaron, but I'm going to tell the police everything."

Freddie's cackle cracked through the air. "Oh, you're fucking hilarious as ever. They're not going to charge me. No evidence, no crime. Even if there was, who's to say it was anything other than self-defence? You brutes have no respect for life. You claim you do, but you're no better than we are. How many animals have died at your hands?"

Will clearly had a whole lot of Zen going on. He and Berringer were nose to nose, and yet Will didn't so much as flinch, never mind hit him. Gray would've been more than happy to oblige.

"Do your *friends* know the kind of man you are, Will Richards?" Berringer leaned his head back, nose in the air, and regarded Will with disgust.

"They do, as it happens. More to the point, they know the kind of man *you* are, so back off. Better still, make a run for it. We'll even give you a head start, you know? A fair chance to go to ground."

"Is that supposed to scare me?" Freddie shoved Will in the chest, and he stumbled into the table but stayed on his feet.

Gray was torn, desperate to go to Will's aid whilst also understanding his need to make Freddie suffer, with the added advantage of, bit by bit, drawing his confession from him. Everyone was a winner, but these situations could turn ugly very quickly. Gray marked the positions of the police officers, the exits...and realised what he was doing. He couldn't help it.

"See, the thing is, Freddie, the two people sitting at this table are the closest you have to allies. Not even friends. And, actually, not even allies. You've got nothing. You *are* nothing. Even this place..." Will cast a cursory glance around the room. "That has to sting, living in an apartment owned by your father, but at least you still have a roof over your head, unlike Aaron and Naomi.

"And poor Carrie. She would've lost everything too, but she knows how to manage risk, don't you, Carrie?" Will looked her way as if he were inviting her to respond yet didn't give her time to do so. "And work? Have you any idea how hard Carrie works, Freddie? No? I'll tell you. Before Berringer's went under, she had two jobs. Imagine that. Holding down two city jobs. It takes a special kind of person to do that, doesn't it, Carrie?"

She was halfway to the door and with no intention of saying goodbye. DCI Hedley intercepted.

"Who do you think she works for, Freddie?" Will asked. "Go on, take a guess."

Freddie smirked, but he'd lost his swagger. "You're bluffing, Richards, and it's utterly futile. I can see through your bullshit."

"Tell him how long you've worked for Charles, Carrie." As Will turned to her, he made eye contact with Gray. It was for only a fleeting moment, but Gray had it again, that feeling Will wasn't all he claimed to be, the proof of which was playing out before them, and suddenly it clicked: the reason he'd been so convinced Will had been lying to him. The story about his phone falling into his welly and spooking Monster, whilst undoubtedly true, had been intentional misdirection to stop Gray asking questions, and he'd fallen for it.

It was no wonder Berringer had used Will to chat up investors. He was a professional confidence trickster, and right in that moment, there was no way to gauge whether he was bluffing or not.

"Next you'll be telling me she murdered Hector," Freddie said. His tone was bombastic; he was so sure he was right.

"Of course I didn't kill Hector!" Carrie snapped. "He was the only decent man among you."

"Do you know who did?" Rob asked.

"It was Charles." She sighed, like it was a reluctant admission when, in fact, she was saving her own neck. "He met with Hector in secret. They had lunch, and Charles got him drunk. He was courting Hector to work for him, said he could have anything he wanted. They went to the Mercedes dealer together, to get Aaron's car back." Carrie shrugged. "You know the rest."

Freddie rubbed his hands over his face, laughing like it was some kind of joke. "You'd better watch out, Will. He'll be *recruiting* you next."

Will stared Freddie down. "I'll never toe the line for a Berringer." His voice was low and menacing, not dissimilar to Kenny's warning growl at the men who'd passed them on the canal bank, Gray thought.

"We'll see," Freddie said. With a devilish grin, he reached for his pocket.

In the slow-motion split second that followed, a collective gasp went up, Tanner cried, "Freddie, don't!" and Will dived, not for cover but between Berringer and Tanner. It was a protective reflex, which sparked Gray's own, overriding his common sense and propelling him towards Berringer, but Rob beat him to it. He kicked Berringer's feet from under him and slammed him face down on the floor.

"Keep your hands where I can see them."

"Christ! I was getting my fucking keys out, you imbecile!" He went for them again, and Rob's boot intercepted, flattening Berringer's fingers. Berringer cursed like a man possessed, but he didn't try to break free. "In the safe, in the bedroom," he said, still far too smug for Gray's liking. "There's an envelope containing photos you boys in blue might find interesting."

"Gray, can you deal with that?" Rob asked.

"Certainly." Gray reached down and tugged the keys from Freddie's pocket, successfully resisting the urge to kick him in the kidneys.

A detective followed Gray along the hallway, into the grandiose master bedroom—no four-poster, but the circular bed had to be eight foot in diameter—and stood by while he unlocked the safe.

"Is the SIU taking over the case, Sir?" the DC asked.

Gray nodded and said nothing. Hedley didn't know he was no longer in the job, and Rob's investigation was almost over, but Charles Berringer's sabotage of his son's company, which was built on funds Freddie embezzled from his father in the first place, was definitely one for the SIU. As for the stalemate between Will and Freddie... Gray found the envelope and opened the flap—to check that it did indeed contain photos—and then closed it again. He didn't need to see to know Will had told him the truth.

"Are you taking these, or shall I keep hold of them?" Gray asked.

"You might as well keep hold of them, Sir."

Gray shoved the envelope inside his jacket before the detective had second thoughts. They returned to the dining room, where Freddie was still on the floor. Carrie Duggan and the other officer had left.

"We're waiting for a special escort," Rob said. "I've been led to believe the suspect's father may assist him in absconding from custody." Rob looked over at Will. "They might appreciate a joint cell. Keep each other company. What d'you reckon?"

Will grinned. "That's very thoughtful of you."

"Excuse me, Rob?"

Gray looked around to see who'd spoken. He didn't recognise the voice, but then Aaron Tanner approached. Except he no longer looked or sounded like Aaron Tanner.

"Do you need to go?" Rob asked.

Tanner nodded. He was frantic, like he was having a panic attack.

"Find a hotel, and call me, OK?"

"I will. Thank you." Aaron moved towards the door.

"Do you want me to come with you?" Will offered.

Gray glared at him—without meaning to—and Tanner looked startled.

"I'm not going to steal him. We tried that once before."

Tanner's words left Gray speechless and Will red-cheeked.

"You haven't told him?" Tanner asked.

"No," Will confirmed. "Not because he's a police officer. For personal reasons." Will shrugged and offered Gray a nervous smile. "We're not there yet—the past conquests bit, I mean—or we weren't, but I guess you're going to hear it anyway." Will chewed his lip in thought. He looked pained. "Aaron...is Naomi. We were seeing each other for a while back in uni."

"Right." Gray processed the words 'seeing each other' and returned to the first part. "You're...gender-fluid? Is that the right term for it?" Will's expression was pure astonishment. "What? I read a lot."

Will raised his hands in an exaggerated shrug.

"Aaron is," Tanner agreed. "But I'm not."

Before Gray could respond, though he'd got nothing, Hedley said, "I'll oversee Berringer if you want to deal with Tanner."

"Thanks, Ma'am." Rob beckoned for Will and Tanner to follow him out of the room. Gray loitered in the doorway, keeping an eye on Hedley and Berringer and an ear on Rob and Tanner, such good as it did him. He couldn't hear a word Rob was saying. A couple of minutes passed, and Rob clapped Will on the back and said, "Nine-thirty, yeah?"

"Yep," Will replied and headed back to Gray while Rob and Tanner went in the opposite direction. "You all right?"

"I'm fine. Are you?" Gray gestured Will to the side to let two more police officers pass into the room. They hoisted Berringer to his feet, patted him down and escorted him out.

"I am," Will said finally.

"I trust you're done for the night?" Hedley asked, ushering Gray—and Will—out of the apartment.

"Definitely," Gray answered. "How about you?"

"God, yes." She closed up behind them. "See you in the week. Good night."

"Night," Gray called, but she was already down the stairs and out of sight.

Gray put his arm around Will's waist and steered him onwards. "So...busy day tomorrow."

"Yep. Are you going to be around?"

"For as long as you need me."

"Thanks."

"Not a problem." Gray grinned and let Will go ahead down the stairs. His relief that the evening hadn't ended in violence was rapidly turning to exhaustion. "So what's this about you and Tanner?" He yawned out the words.

Will stopped suddenly, and Gray walked into his back. "Do you really want to know?"

"Did you date them both?"

"Naomi, mostly. Aaron and I were friends first and foremost. It would've been too complicated."

Gray leaned forward, resting his chin on Will's shoulder. "I like complicated."

"I'll bear that in mind," Will said and moved off, leaving Gray to find his own footing.

Epilogue

SINCE JEAN'S DEATH, Gray had attended four funerals, all of them cremations. Will's mum's funeral, like Jean's, was a burial, but that was where the similarities ended. Jean's funeral had taken place in midsummer, on a humid, rainy day culminating in a rainbow that had obliterated their magic, possibly forever. There was flag draping and saluting, the entire day procedural, which had suited Gray. He couldn't have got through it any other way. The wake that followed consisted of quietly muttering groups, lingering awkwardly in a hotel reception room, eking out their paying of respects and leaving in twos and threes, until, finally, only Jean's family, Becky and Gray had remained.

It was a day Gray had not dared to dwell upon until that moment, as he walked across the cemetery, pulling his coat tighter though the light breeze was not enough to lift the frost-crisped leaves from the ground and created barely a rustle among the trees marking the boundary. No church service or family all in black today. The small gathering of mourners around the plot up ahead were loudly attired yet quietly sombre. As Gray approached, the girl—though she was more a young woman—to Will's right tapped Will on the arm and nodded in Gray's direction. *Suzannah*, Gray unconsciously whispered. Her mouth curved upwards, just a little, in response.

Will turned as Gray reached his location. "Hey. Thank you for coming."

Gray nodded. What could he say?

You're welcome.

I wouldn't miss it for the world.

Glad to be here.

"You're Suzannah."

"Yep. And you're Gray."

"That's right."

"Dad's boyfriend."

Will nudged his daughter with his elbow. "I totally did not call him that."

Suzannah homed in on Gray, her eyes moving as she examined his face, then his attire, then his hair, and back to his face. Her gaze was piercing yet playful. "He totally did," she said.

Gray smiled. "It wouldn't surprise me. He's totally like that."

Will looked affronted, briefly, but the moment of fun passed as the minister appeared before them, or Gray assumed that was who she was. She seemed official in a laid-back kind of way, dressed in a plain, pale-blue dress, navy jacket and matching flat shoes. Will leaned close to Gray and said quietly, "I'll introduce you to Shelley after."

Gray glanced past Will and Suzannah and exchanged a nod of acknowledgement with the woman he recognised from the photos on Will's phone. Behind her, two older men—Will's dad and uncle, presumably—held a murmured conversation. Tie, Jon and Micky stood next to them. Gray took a step back to join them; Will touched his arm to stop him.

"Stay, please," he whispered.

Gray hadn't intended to stand with immediate family. He didn't think he had the right, but Will's request bestowed it upon him, so he stayed where he was.

The minister began to speak, introducing herself as a 'celebrant', which Gray found rather odd, although it was, by far, the least disturbing realisation he had in that moment. Before them was the hole in the ground and the covered mound of removed earth, but no coffin.

He looked around the people gathered—most were tuned only to the celebrant's words—and met Tie's gaze. He gave Gray a wink and tilted his head forward and right. Gray subtly shifted his eyes in the indicated direction, containing his reaction—he hoped—to the sight of the coffin, carried by four women dressed in vibrant yellow ponchos printed all over with a pink emblem. As they neared, he saw it was a combination of the peace and female gender symbols.

The women lowered the coffin onto a cloth next to the grave and moved to stand behind the celebrant rather than joining the rest of the mourners, of whom there seemed to be twice as many as the last time Gray looked, and still more were drifting across the cemetery to their location, all of them older women. As the celebrant paid tribute to Will's mum's life, the women formed a circle that extended around the grave and the gathered family and friends.

After Will had told him about his mum's activism, Gray had read up on the Greenham Common peace camp, becoming a little star-struck when he found a photo online that included Will's mum. At Greenham Common, the women had formed a human chain to 'embrace the base', and it was what they were doing now. They joined hands and stood, resolute, many with tears rolling down their cheeks, and as the celebrant finished speaking, a quiet chant began.

> *You can't kill the spirit*
> *She is like a mountain*
> *Old and strong*
> *She goes on and on and on...*

The chant continued in a round that grew bigger, louder, until it seemed to entirely fill the air, yet it was so gentle—*peaceful*. As the coffin was lowered into the grave, Gray let his tears fall, moved in such a profound way he couldn't have explained the feeling if he'd tried. Will's hand found his, and Gray peered sideways at him, noting that everyone else had joined hands, and all of them were singing. It was such a beautiful, perfect tribute to Will's mum, and in that moment, Gray could honestly say he was glad to be there.

***

"Alright, Rob. What are you doing here?" Gray shuffled out from behind the pub table and shook Rob's hand.

"Alright, Gray. Sorry to bother you when you're... Crap. Sorry." Rob glanced around the packed pub. "Sorry," he said again and headed for the door through which he had just come. "I'll catch up with you later in the week."

"Hold on. I'll come out with you." Gray glanced over at Will, who had taken over the game of scissors, paper, stone that Gray had been losing to Suzannah. "Won't be a sec."

"OK," Will and Suzannah said at the same time. Gray laughed to himself, still astounded by their alikeness, and went outside, where Rob was leaning against his bike. "What's up?"

"Nothing bad. But seriously, Gray, it can wait. I didn't realise the funeral was today."

Gray looked back at the pub, astounded Rob had figured out it was the funeral when none of them were particularly morbid or wearing black. He turned to face Rob again. "Did you sort something out for Aaron...Naomi...?"

"Naomi, currently, and yeah. They're back with Aaron's mum for the time being. Aaron's starting a new job next week, working for an online investment company from home."

"That's got to be better for them."

"Yeah, I guess." Rob scratched his head. The perpetual frown deepened. "Zoë's getting married," he said.

The Guinness and black churned in Gray's stomach. "Oh, Rob, I'm sorry."

"Yeah, well. It was bound to happen at some point."

"I really hoped you'd get back together. And yes, it would've made me feel better about everything, but I know how much you miss being with them."

"It wasn't your doing, Gray. Things were already bad between us. Maybe if I'd stayed around, we'd have sorted it, but probably not."

"Thanks, Rob. I'm grateful for what you're trying to do."

"So, anyway, I had an idea. It's a bit out there, but..." Rob fiddled with the unfastened buckle of his jacket. "I'm thinking about going freelance."

"Freelance...detective work?"

"Yeah. You know, the white-collar stuff. I reckon there's a lot of call for it. Like Berringer's, for instance. Not that I fancy saving the necks of the likes of Freddie, but he could've avoided having the SIU romp through his HQ if he'd called in a private firm."

"You're setting up as a private detective."

"That's what I'm thinking, yeah."

"Hmm." Gray nodded. "Not a bad idea, that, Rob."

"Cheers. Glad you think so." Rob picked up his helmet and gave the lining a thorough examination. Gray decided to help him along.

"And the other bit?" he asked.

"Fancy coming in as a partner?"

Gray's surprised expression was completely faked. He'd figured out where Rob was heading as soon as he'd explained what he was planning to do. "We'd have to come up with a snappier company name than Simpson-Stone and Fisher or we'd sound like bloody lawyers. And I know what you think of them."

"Ha, yeah." Rob put his helmet down again to zip up his jacket. "So, er... Does that mean you'll consider it?"

"I'll consider it," Gray confirmed.

"Excellent. I'll leave you to get on." Rob held out his hand, but instead of shaking it, Gray pulled him in for a hug.

"You're one of the best, Rob. Don't you forget it."

"Likewise," Rob said. They released each other. Rob put on his helmet, climbed onto his bike and started it up. "I'll be in touch."

Gray waved and watched Rob rev and pull away before returning inside, where Will, Tie and Jon were in their coats, all three wearing black woolly hats.

"Where are you off?"

"To see a man about a dog," Will said. "Two men, actually. And two gun dogs."

Gray nodded. "Enough said."

The three of them moved towards the door.

"Be careful," Gray called.

With a grin, Will departed.

Gray returned to his seat, trying not to think, or worry, or write horror stories in his head. A light tap on his arm snatched back his wandering, catastrophic attention. Smile at the ready, he turned back to Suzannah.

"One, two, three..." she said.

He went for paper, and she chopped his fingers clean off at the knuckles.

Tabula Rasa

After years of working for the police—both as a beat bobby and undercover—Rob Simpson-Stone is moving on with no regrets. It may be too late to rescue his marriage, but his relationship with his seven-year-old son, Lucas, is back on track. Rob's grown-up nieces might be a taller order, but he's prepared to do whatever it takes to prove they no longer need to worry that one day he won't come home.

Fate, however, has different ideas.

When Rob fails to arrive at his leaving do, his former boss/new PI business partner Gray Fisher can't understand why nobody else is worried Rob is MIA, never mind that Gray is pointlessly missing out on a night in with Will.

As the reasons behind the night's events unfold, Gray's past recklessness threatens to catch up with him, putting those he holds close in danger and forcing both Rob and Gray to forge reluctant alliances.

For Julie, Bill and Kirsty:

You worked miracles.

"The hero surviving his own murder, his own suicide, his own addiction, surviving his own disappearance from the scene..."

Allen Ginsberg

Prologue

THE RICH MIXED aroma of chargrilled meats and beer began its daily takeover as the evening rush hour petered away, such as it ever did in London. Gray turned the corner into the street where the restaurant was located, observant, alert, briefly assessing the pedestrians ahead and every vehicle along the short stretch of wet tarmac. No agenda, no motive; habit reinforced by more than a decade of service.

A motorbike roared past, horn tooting a second later to announce the arrival of the guest of honour: former Constable Rob Simpson-Stone. The right indicator flashed, and the bike turned into what Gray knew to be a dead-end alley, an access-and-delivery point for the restaurant and hotel between which it fell. Less than a minute later, when he arrived at the neck of the alley and peered down it, he saw the bike parked at the far end, but no sign of Rob.

Must've missed him. It was no big deal. Gray wasn't concerned about walking in on his own. There was a good chance he'd know most of those in attendance—one that increased in likelihood when he stepped through the doors and discovered the restaurant had been entirely taken over for the evening by the Metropolitan Police. A few heads turned, and eyebrows rose here and there in recognition before they returned to their drinks and conversations. Laughter erupted to Gray's left; another new arrival excused their way past; a hand raised in a wave at the bar—Martina Hedley, standing alone. Gray went over to join her.

"Evening, Ma'am. How are you?"

She'd never been his superior and laughed at his formal address. "Evening, Gray. I'm well, thanks. You?"

"Fine." He squinted, his eyes struggling to adjust to the bar's blue LEDs. "Do we order drinks or wait for them to come to us?"

"I gave up waiting and ordered mine. I'm surprised Rob isn't here yet."

"He passed me on his bike about three minutes ago."

"Oh? He hasn't come in."

Gray saw the bartender heading his way and stepped up, ready to order. "He'll be making sure his pride and joy is secure for the duration."

Martina's eyebrow arched doubtfully. Irrespective of Rob's apathy for the evening's frivolities, both knew he was a stickler for punctuality.

"He'll get here sooner or later, I'm sure," Gray said.

"I'd bloody well hope so, seeing as it's his leaving do."

***

Rob barely got his helmet off when the bag came down over his head and he was dragged forcibly to the ground. Before the panic had a chance to set in, he was up on his feet again. His back slammed against the wall, a heavy weight across his chest forced him to take shallow breaths, pinning him in place. One of his assailants—he could hear two sets of boots—gave a warning *shhhh* and then nothing else happened.

A minute later, someone said, "Clear." The pressure on Rob's chest eased, exchanged for a strong grip around his upper arms as he was marched back along the alley to the street and manhandled into what he assumed—from the height he had to step up and the heavy sliding door—to be a van. The door screeched shut, and with a painful jolt, Rob was thrown onto his side as they took off into the early evening city traffic.

30 Minutes Earlier

1: Jock

LEATHERS OVER SLACKS and shirt, helmet in hand, Rob was at the door and ready to leave when his phone buzzed in his pocket.

Leave it, answer it, leave it... If it was important, whoever it was would call back. It stopped. Rob opened the front door a couple of inches at most before it started up again. With a grunt, he pushed the door shut and partially unzipped his jacket. There was a time when he could've ignored a ringing phone—the number onscreen was unfamiliar to both him and his address book, cold caller, more than likely—but he wasn't prepared to take the chance.

"Hello?"

"Hello, Shaz?"

"Sorry, mate, you've got the wrong number."

"Nah. I don't think so."

"There's no-one here by...hold up. Jock?"

"Yeah. Alright?"

"Bloody hell. It's been a while. How did you get this number?"

"Rang your landline. Your missus gave me your mobile."

"Fair enough." It wasn't like Zoë to give out his number without checking with him first, but he'd worry about that later. "How're you doing, man?"

Rob caught the microsecond pause before Jock—aka Corporal Harry 'Jocky' Wilson—answered, "Yeah, I'm doing all right. You?"

"I'm doing great. I thought you were still OS."

Jock barked out a laugh. "Where the hell have you been? I've been back five years. Forty-five and retired. Not bad, eh? Bought a gaff down Brighton way. The kids hate it, of course."

"Still just the two?" Rob remembered only because he'd heard Jock's second kid had been born the day after Lucas, seven years ago. He'd never met Jock's family—had hardly spoken to the guy since leaving the army.

"Yeah. You had any more?" Jock asked.

"No, unfortunately. Zoë and I are divorced."

"Sorry to hear that."

"Cheers." Rob braced, hoping Jock wouldn't ask him what happened. Most people didn't, but Jock wasn't most people.

"So...still got flat feet?"

Rob chuckled, relieved to be let off the hook so easily. "Ask me again in five hours. I'm just heading out for my leaving do."

"Bollocks. My timing's good as ever, eh?"

"Why? What's up?"

"There's a few of us getting together this evening for a pint and catch-up."

"Crap. If there was a way I could get out of it..." There wasn't, or Rob would've taken it. He hadn't wanted a leaving do to start with, and much as he and Jock weren't exactly on friendly terms, he was well up for a couple of pints with his old army mates. "How long are you gonna be out, d'you reckon?"

"Not sure. Depends who's got wives and kiddies to get home to."

"Right." Presumably, Jock had left his down in Brighton for the weekend.

"We're meeting at Euston. Are you anywhere nearby?"

"Yeah, at the Quarterhouse. Five minutes away."

"How about this, then? I'll text you where we are. If you make it, all well and good. If not, I'll call back tomorrow, and we can sort something else."

"Perfect," Rob said. "Have a good one."

"You too, mate. Bye." Jock ended the call.

Rob saved the number and put his phone back in his pocket, this time making it out of the door and onto his bike, but his thoughts were still on the conversation as he rode into the city. He hadn't heard from any of his old army mates in over five years because he'd been off the grid. Even before that, when they did meet up, it was with some reluctance that they invited Jock. He was one sadistic bastard and a racist to boot, but they'd had to work together, so they'd got on with it, although Jock's attitude was one of the reasons Rob had come out of the army when he did.

Given the way things were between them, there had to be an ulterior motive for the call or someone else would've made it, and Rob's curiosity was threatening to get the better of him. For the time being, he put it out of mind and focused on his riding.

Even though it was past rush hour, the roads were chaos, and he was beginning to regret not getting the train, but the bike would stop people buying him drinks all night. He needed a clear head; he was off up north first thing. He hadn't been home since Christmas, and in the three months that had elapsed, he'd become a great-uncle. Never mind that he'd had no idea his youngest niece was pregnant.

Traffic was backed up from the junction, and Rob could've got past it, but instead, he settled behind a bus and let his mind drift again. With the prospect of a couple of weeks of proper holiday, he was well up for some quality family time and a bit of R and R before he set the wheels in motion for his new venture. Of course, there was no guarantee it would take off, or, if it did, how long it would take to get fully established, and he was prepared for the possibility of failure. So long as it was moving in the right direction, he'd stick with it, but he had a backup plan just the same. As soon as he got back from his mum's, he was going to sign on with an agency as a security officer, pick up a few hours of paid work, maybe get up to speed on mechanics.

But first, this leaving do he'd said he didn't want. A sit-down meal and a restaurant to themselves was not Rob's first choice for a decent night out—but that he'd been given a choice at all. A couple of pints and a curry, he'd have been happy, and he'd planned an early exit strategy, which was pretty pointless now he was expected elsewhere.

What it is to be popular. Except popularity didn't come into it. True, Rob wasn't short of friends, some of them amongst his colleagues—or former colleagues—and his army mates, but there was always a performance to getting together—who could drink the most, stay conscious the longest, come up with the best bullshit for how perfectly bloody wonderful their life was. Most of them were single and made out it was their choice to be so or saw nothing wrong with acting as if they were. What happens on a night out...

Rob wasn't a fuddy-duddy, however much Zoë's fiancé made him feel like he was old enough for the hill to be a distant blur in his mirrors. Difficult as it had been for Rob to accept it, Travis was good for Zoë and Lucas. The guy seemed to have endless energy and time to burn it off on family outings—a luxury Rob's work could never afford, or, at least, one he had never permitted himself to take. Still, if he heard 'we went there with Travis, didn't we, Mum?' one more time... well, he'd grin and bear it, for Lu's sake, same as every time before.

Finally, Rob made it through the junction and put his foot down. A few hours of socialising, a good night's kip, then he could forget about posturing coppers and *Stepdad of the Year* in favour of a few nights out with his old mates, a few nights in watching telly with his mum, and if he could be arsed, he'd catch up with Jock and the others when he got back.

2: Not Leaving Yet

"DO YOU WANT me to come with you?" Will yawned the question.

Gray put down the iron and flipped to the next section of shirt, briefly glancing at Will's face onscreen. "You, in a room full of police officers?" He picked up the iron again.

"I've done it before."

"Have you?"

"Well...it was a courtroom. But I was quite civil."

Gray looked up and had to laugh. Will's grin glowed white in his stubble-darkened, mud-streaked face. He looked anything but civil. He was also knackered.

"You should go shower before you nod off," Gray advised.

"I'm all right yet. Tie's picking up food on his way home. Which means hummus again."

"There's nothing wrong with hummus."

"Every now and then, but we've had it every night this week."

"You know what you could do? It's a bit radical." Gray checked his shirt to make sure he'd pressed all of it, switched off the iron and tugged his T-shirt over his head.

"Get the train to your place and wait for you to come home from your party?" Will's tone was decidedly sultry.

Gray emerged from inside his T-shirt and covered the camera with his hand.

"Rotter."

Laughing, Gray successfully got his shirt most of the way on with his hand still covering the camera, only moving it when he had to in order to fasten his buttons.

Will scowled. "I was enjoying the view."

"I'm sure you were. But I need to go or I'll be late."

"Yeah, OK. What were you gonna suggest?"

"Suggest...oh. That you go shopping instead of sending Tie?"

"Think I'll put up with hummus. I'll leave you to it. Don't forget to enjoy yourself."

"Forget in the next half an hour? Unlikely. I'll give you all the gory details tomorrow."

"OK. Later." Will ended the call, leaving Gray free to finish getting dressed and ruminate over turning down Will's offer.

He hadn't set out to mislead Will, but somewhere along the line, he'd had a bit of a wobble and implied going to Rob's leaving party was a chore he could do without—hence Will's offer to go with him. It would've been a first for them—accompanying each other to an official function—but that wasn't why he'd put Will off. Plus-ones were rarely welcome at police socials, and even though this one was being held in a restaurant with a nightclub attached, the culture would be rife. Gray remembered it far too well—the all-consuming nature of the job that made it difficult to switch off.

Hopefully, tonight would be different because Rob had never been a typical copper. Work or play, no mixing the two unless he was under orders, and he was leaving because he'd had enough. He'd tried going back in uniform and a stint in CID, but he couldn't settle in his old job. So, he'd resigned to set up a private investigation agency...and asked Gray to go in with him.

It sounded far more thrilling than it would no doubt prove to be, and that suited Gray just fine. Only thirty-five and he'd already had his lifetime's worth of excitement. It wasn't so long since he'd been out every night of the week, getting drunk, getting high...it hadn't been fun. But he was past all that now and dealing with his problems like a functioning adult instead of an out-of-control lunatic with a death wish. If it were anyone other than Rob, Gray would've given tonight a miss in favour of lounging on his couch. Or Will's, along with at least one dog. The image popped into his mind of Will flopped full length of the sofa at the bottom of a dog pile, pitta bread in one hand, hummus in the other. It was a surprisingly alluring vision.

In the hallway, putting on his jacket, the *should I, shouldn't I?* debate started up again. Gray would've liked to have taken Will along, but no. He wanted the company, worried he'd be left standing alone at the bar all night—selfish reasons, in other words, none of them valid when Will would need to get a cab home and be up early for work. Another time.

Finally settled to the decision, Gray checked he had his phone and wallet, and set off for the Underground station. It was a bit lazy, seeing as it was only two stops, and he could almost have walked it in the time it took for the journey and getting through the stations at both ends. An eternal lift ride at Russell Square was followed by the realisation that Rob's leaving card was still on the coffee table, along with Gray's packet of gum. The card could wait until he saw Rob next; the gum couldn't, not that Gray was planning on getting up close and personal with anyone tonight, but garlic and conversation was not a good combination, and he did like his garlic—Jean's legacy.

There was a metro supermarket just around the corner from the station, which Gray had shopped in a few times, although, as usual, the powers-that-be had taken it upon themselves to switch the stock around, and Gray found tins of soup and baked beans in the aisle where the confectionery had previously been shelved. Rice and pasta now resided where the tinned goods used to be, and he eventually found the chewing gum—not even in the same place as the chocolate and sweets—on the top shelf in an aisle he couldn't ever recall walking down before, which meant it was probably once the home-baking aisle.

Typically, his usual brand presented an empty box, and as he considered the alternatives, a woman passed behind him, her trolley brushing his hip. She didn't notice, too absorbed in the heated discussion she was having via a headset.

"Yeah, I mean he's literally dropped off the face of the planet."

Literally? Flat Earth member?

The woman rounded the end of the aisle and disappeared from view but continued talking at a volume Gray could hear.

"We were together for eleven years, for Christ sakes, John. I can't just let it go."

Intrigued for no reason other than his enquiring mind had yet to break the habit of latching on to snippets of potentially useful information, Gray moved slowly along the aisle and eavesdropped the entire conversation.

"No forwarding address, no new number—nothing... Nope. Passport's still there... Oh, yeah, I know his Facebook profile is still live, but he hasn't logged into it since—of course he's not been kidnapped! ... It's not in the least bit comforting. Yes! ... No, I really would rather he'd upped sticks and found someone else. I don't hate him *that* much. I still..."

The woman stopped talking as they emerged simultaneously from the other end of their respective aisles. She gave Gray a self-conscious smile and, dropping her volume to almost a whisper, said, "I miss him."

Gray could've gone straight through the self-service, but it would've meant ditching the free entertainment—it was turning into a real tearjerker—so he queued at the checkout behind the woman and turned side on, his eyes on the activity of other shoppers, his ears still trained to her conversation. 'Kidnapped' was an attention grabber, although it didn't sound like a kidnapping. If anything, it sounded like a good deal of the cases he'd worked undercover—fraudsters and embezzlers who changed their identity and ditched their old life for a fresh start, with the sole intention of doing it all over again. The social networks were littered with ghost profiles that made it easy to pinpoint when someone 'went missing', but if they knew what they were doing, the trail ended there.

Of course, the more likely scenario was that the woman's partner had, as she said, found someone new. Without his passport, he couldn't have gone far, and leaving it behind indicated he intended to return at some point—unless he couldn't.

The woman continued her phone call all the way through loading her shopping onto the conveyor belt, packing it back into the trolley and paying for her purchases, but by then it had moved on to gossip, and Gray tuned out, wondering how it was he so often made the subconscious slip back into his old way of thinking. He'd been out of the police for almost a year; with his PhD well underway, his teaching, and weekends with Will, he had more than enough to occupy his mind. Yet at the mere hint of 'a case', off it went, sifting information for vital clues, which wasn't necessarily a bad thing when he'd be needing those skills soon enough, although not to find missing spouses. He and Rob still had to hone the fine print, but they were in agreement about limiting their commissions to corporate and commercial investigations.

Twenty minutes later, Gray made it out of the store, shoved a piece of gum in his mouth and the overheard conversation out of his head, and set off for the restaurant. It was less than a ten-minute walk from his current location, and as he walked, the streetlights switched on, bleaching out the blue-grey late-March dusk. Gray squinted painfully; his eyes were hyper-sensitive to light and took a long time to adjust, if they adjusted at all. The surgeon had been optimistic it was temporary, but almost four years on, he'd concluded he was stuck with it.

It was one of the more minor but no less inconvenient consequences of the crash—not too bad if he planned in advance. A cinema trip meant wearing prescribed tinted glasses or prosthetic lenses for 3D, and he always wore his glasses when driving—even at night. Sunlight didn't cause any problems; his 'photophobia' was specific to artificial light, and fluorescent and LED lighting was the worst.

Thus, Gray wasn't one hundred percent sure it *was* Rob's bike that passed him as he arrived. The horn toot suggested it was, but judging by the way Martina was searching the restaurant, she was concerned her would-have-been protégé wasn't going to show.

"Are you all right for a drink?" Gray asked.

Martina held up her glass, which contained about an inch of dark liquid. "Double brandy and Coke," she said, reaching into her pocket. Gray raised his hand to stop her.

"I'll get these. Ice?"

"Please."

"Who's next?" the bartender asked and homed in on Gray. "Yes, sir?"

"A pint of Guinness with blackcurrant and a double brandy and Coke with ice, please."

"Guinness and blackcurrant?" Martina queried.

"It's my tipple of choice these days," Gray said, distracted by the murmurs of conversation across the room. A few other people had noticed Rob arrive on his bike, and the question kept cropping up of where he'd got to.

Martina wrinkled her nose. "To each their own."

Gray had to recap to figure out she meant his drink. "They wouldn't have pulled a stunt, would they?"

"For a leaving do?" Martina's tone implied she thought that was a ridiculous suggestion. "I'm not sure they'd pull one on Rob even if he was getting hitched. He doesn't take practical jokes well."

"Really? That surprises me." Gray somehow kept his face straight. It wasn't so much that Rob had no sense of humour. OK, it was. Even away from work, he was serious and intense, and when he did crack a joke, it was hard to gauge whether it was appropriate to laugh. Gray had always assumed it was because he hated the undercover work, but from what Martina was saying, it was a personality trait.

The bartender set their drinks on the counter, and Gray handed over Martina's.

"Thanks," she said, a little contrite. "Sorry to snatch and run, but I need to catch up with my boss while he's in a good mood."

Gray laughed, understanding all too well. "No problem. See you later."

Martina edged past a group of men standing a few feet away and disappeared into the growing crowd. Gray paid for their drinks and took up residence on a barstool. Perhaps his worries about spending the evening alone hadn't been unfounded after all.

As he'd predicted, there were a few other familiar faces, all engaged in conversation, but he was quite happy watching for the time being. And it was just ordinary watching, he was relieved to find, not the obsessive vigilance that had contributed—possibly on a par with Jean's death—to his craving for mind-altering substances as a means of shutting off. But he didn't do that anymore—ten months clean and counting. Like anyone else, he had bad days when it was harder to resist, but on the whole, it was getting easier every day.

The evening moved swiftly along, and after another half an hour, the staff had no choice but to ask everyone to take their seats, still with no sign of the guest of honour. Gray took out his phone and started typing a message, but he abandoned it, unsent. Rob would be inundated by now—or not. No-one seemed overly concerned by his continuing absence. However, Rob was never late without just cause.

"Sir?" A waiter smiled at Gray and pointed him towards the tables.

"Yes, of course." Gray moved away from the bar, but rather than find a seat, he headed for the exit, phone held out in front of him as if he were going out to receive a call.

"Gray! Over here!"

He mouthed, "Won't be a sec," at Martina and dodged outside. It had gone completely dark, but his eyes had barely adjusted to the light inside, so he continued unencumbered to the mouth of the alley and squinted into the gloom, making out a few dark objects of various shapes and sizes—bins and boxes. But no bike.

3: Hostage

A s soon as the van's inertia would let him, Rob pushed himself upright, resting his back against the chilly side panel.

"You fuckers," he muttered. He could've taken the sack off his head himself—he wasn't cuffed—but he waited for someone else to do the deed, and grabbed them by the wrist, twisting their arm the wrong way.

"Ow, you bastard." John 'Bish' Garvey shook his hand and flexed his fingers. "My good arm, that."

"Aw, mate." Rob was loving the familiar banter already, even if they had, effectively, kidnapped him. "What the hell is this?"

"Rescue mission," someone called from the cab—Tonka, or 2nd Lieutenant Yvette Parker if you fancied losing your balls.

"Correct," Bish corroborated. "Jock told us you were looking for a get-out from this police do."

Rob sighed, long and loud. "Attendance isn't optional."

"I disagree," Tonka said.

"You realise they'll have half the Met out looking for me within the hour?"

"Only if they notice you're missing."

Rob smirked, taking the insult on the chin. This was madness, but he wasn't kidding about the search party. "Where are we off, Ma'am?"

"That's on a need-to-know." Tonka's reply was half-masked by the crunch of gears. "Christ, Bish, this is a bag of shit." More crunching ensued. Bish cringed and thumbed towards the driver's seat, mouthing, "Women drivers."

Rob shook his head and laughed. "Where is Jock, by the way?"

Tonka eyed the rear-view mirror. "Behind us."

Rob leaned forward and peered through a small crack in the paint covering the back window. "You let him ride my bike?"

"It was him or me." Bish grinned and waggled the stump that was all that remained of his right arm.

"If he trashes it, I'll rip off the other one and beat you with the soggy end."

"You and whose army, Shaz?" Pre-empting the smack around the head, Bish ducked, and Rob's fingers spliced thin air.

"All right, I'll come willingly, but—"

"Like you've got a choice."

"*But* I'm only staying for one. I need to at least put in an appearance tonight."

"We get the picture. Your police mates are more important. We're not offended, are we, Ma'am?"

"Not in the least."

"You soft gets." Rob took another glance out the back window; they were in Camden, heading for Hampstead Heath, Rob guessed—Tonka came from over that way—with the Cyclops eye of the bike's headlamp still on their tail. It was a forty-minute round trip; if he stayed for a pint and chinwag, he could be at his leaving do a little after nine. True, he'd be over an hour late, but with any luck, they'd only just have realised he was missing by then.

The sketchy view, front and rear, changed from lit roads to dark trees, and Rob caught sight of light reflecting off water—one of the bathing ponds, he thought—before the van veered right. Half a minute later, they stopped. Tonka got out and slid the side door open. It was Rob's first decent look at her, and he wasn't quick enough to hide his shock. From the state of her, she hadn't slept in months.

Tonka faked a cheery grin. "You getting out, or what?"

"Or what," Rob said but shuffled on his backside until he could jump down onto the tarmac beside her. "Good to see you, Ma'am."

She hauled him in for a hug. "You too, Rob." As she released him, she murmured, "Need your help."

He gave a subtle nod to confirm he'd heard and turned his attention to Jock, who was fighting to get the kickstand down on the bike. Rob went over and had it sorted in a matter of seconds.

"There's a knack," he explained in answer to Jock's grunt and held out his hand for his helmet and keys. Jock compliantly handed both over. "And my phone?"

"Ain't got it."

"For real?"

"Yeah, for real. You calling me a liar?"

"Come in, lads," Tonka called, already on the move. "That heap of scrap can stay out on the road. Maybe a neighbour'll get it towed for you, Bish."

"They bloody well won't," Bish muttered as the three of them followed Tonka, pausing for her to open wide double gates, beyond those a significant detached house that shone blinding white in the near-daylight illumination. While they waited for her to unlock the door and turn off the alarm, Rob sized up the property. Tonka must've been in her late fifties by now and hadn't long retired. She'd been in thirty years, so she'd have been on a damned good pension, although Rob doubted it would be enough to afford a house like this on her own.

He continued his surveillance as she beckoned them inside. Sometimes he wished he'd stayed in the army, or stayed single, at least, then he wouldn't be living in a crappy one-bedroom flat and handing over seventy-five percent of his salary. He honestly didn't regret marrying Zoë or having Lucas, but he had to wonder at the injustice of it when all his mates seemed to be so much better off than he was.

For all that Tonka's house was impressive, it wasn't his kind of place. It was one of the Scandinavian-style 1970s builds with an open-plan ground floor and too much pine and bare brickwork. Windows like a department store front ran the length of one wall; two oversize white sofas at right angles squared off the living area; beyond those were the dining area and kitchen, with a steep, open-step, spiral staircase tucked away in the corner.

Tonka strode across to the kitchen and opened the fridge, saying, "Beer?" as she withdrew four bottles, popped them open on the lip of the countertop, and distributed them.

"Cheers." Rob swigged from the bottle and rotated on the spot to take another look at the place. The other two men carried their beers over to the living area and sat, one on each sofa. "You live here alone?" Rob asked.

"More or less. My brother lives here too, officially, but he's away at present. You're not impressed, are you?"

"Well..." Rob frowned. He hadn't realised he was being that obvious.

Tonka laughed. "Don't worry about it. It's not to everyone's tastes. It was our aunt's place, and I'm not that attached myself, but it's a nice area and it's a hassle to move."

"I know what you mean." Rob was in much the same situation, or not as regards living in a nice area. He'd seen a couple of better flats in the paper for the same rent, which was going to be a stretch without a regular salary coming in. Ideally, he wanted something a bit bigger so he could have Lucas over more often, but on his income, he'd have to move so far out of the city he might as well go back up north.

"Shall we sit?" Tonka suggested.

"Sure," Rob agreed. This was nothing like he'd expected when Jock said they were meeting for a reunion, but he wasn't going anywhere until Tonka told him what was going on.

Seeing as Jock had parked himself smack bang in the middle of one sofa, Rob opted for the other one, sitting at the opposite end to Bish.

Tonka perched on the arm next to Rob. "You're leaving the police, then?"

"Yeah. I've had enough—not of the job itself. I still like the work, but I'm done taking orders."

Tonka spluttered air into the neck of her beer bottle. Rob scowled, but he had to admit, he'd been a defiant little shit when he first joined up. He soon learnt.

"Have you got something else lined up?"

"Pretty much. I'm going self-employed. Private investigations."

"Told you he was a dick," Jock said—predictably.

"Actually, you said I was a black c—"

"All right, lads," Tonka warned, though it was more a command, which they obeyed without hesitation.

"Sorry, Ma'am," Rob said. He knew better than to let Jock get under his skin.

Tonka nodded her acceptance of his apology and stood up. "You haven't seen my new car, have you?"

"Not that I know of." Ignoring the lewd remarks from the other two men about the two of them going for a quickie—it was never going to happen, but that didn't stop the wind-up—Rob trailed Tonka across the room to the staircase, behind which was a door leading to the garage. She flicked a light switch and stepped aside for Rob to come in far enough that she could close the door behind him.

"Whoa! You finally got one?" Rob edged along the garage wall, eyeing up the gleaming white paintwork and sleek curves. He wasn't into cars, but who wouldn't get a bit hot under the collar for a Lamborghini Aventador? "You get out in it much?"

"From time to time. You remember Siggy?"

"Yeah. 'Course I do." He remembered her very well, seeing as she'd been a constant presence when their unit was stationed in Germany. She owned a hotel a few miles from the base; they'd spent many evenings there. "You're still in touch?"

Tonka nodded, an uncharacteristically sappy expression softening the lines of age and sleep deprivation. "It's a good excuse to give the car a run out," she reasoned.

Rob smiled. "Couldn't agree more." He walked back to Tonka and checked the door to the house was closed. "You said you needed my help."

"Yeah." Tonka's eyes strayed briefly to the car and then met Rob's gaze. "You know Ethan's being discharged?"

"I didn't." He felt the effect of the adrenaline surge brought on by Tonka's question at the same moment she sensed it in him. Her jaw tensed, and her pupils, already dilated to compensate for the dimness of the garage, almost filled her irises. Rob turned away and stared at the far wall.

"It's been a long time," she said.

"I'm aware of that, Ma'am."

"They can't keep him locked up indefinitely."

"Why not? If he was a civilian—"

"It would've made no difference."

"Of course it fucking would!" Rob's shout echoed back at him in the bare-brick box; he quickly got his temper in check. "That Marine in Afghanistan who went down for murder—first case of its kind, they said, but we both know that's not true."

"What Ethan did—"

"Wasn't a mindless execution?"

Tonka tugged her hair back in frustration. "It was mindless, I'll give you that, which is why he's spent the last eighteen years locked up, but it's not in the same league as torturing an enemy soldier for fun."

"No, it's worse."

"I've got to say, I expected you to be more sympathetic, Rob."

He laughed in disbelief. "Sorry, Ma'am, I've got no sympathy for wife beaters."

"You know it wasn't like that." Tonka's tone had changed, trying to plead with his common sense, but he'd heard it all before. Sergeant Ethan McGrath had gone home on leave and caught his wife in bed with another man. He'd battered his wife and killed the bit on the side. He was charged with manslaughter and admitted to Brookhurst secure hospital. The official diagnosis was PTSD, but Ethan's anger issues had been there long before he saw action.

Rob cut to the chase. "What do you need?" Before Tonka's relieved smile had fully formed, he added, "I'm not agreeing to anything."

"Just hear me out, OK?"

He shrugged and nodded; he could agree to that much.

"We all know how hard it is to adjust to civilian life, and that's without a criminal record and a mental illness. If Ethan stands any chance of surviving in the outside world, he needs a fresh start."

"You're talking about a new identity."

Tonka unblinkingly held Rob's gaze but didn't answer.

"Much as I hate to disappoint you—"

Her short, brutal 'ha' cut him off.

"I've never let you down before," Rob said, hurt by her insinuation.

Tonka patted his shoulder. "You're right. I'm sorry."

"Even if I was still in the police—and willing—it's well outside my jurisdiction. In any case, it's there to protect victims and witnesses, not to hide madmen in plain sight."

"And to rehabilitate young offenders," Tonka argued. "Those lads who killed that kiddie up in Liverpool, for instance—"

"In very special circumstances, yeah. I'll give you that. But they were no more than kids themselves, and whether they've been successfully rehabilitated or not, the public are on a witch hunt."

"We're getting a bit off track, here, Rob. I'm not asking you to pull strings—"

"I wouldn't have done it anyway."

Tonka's eyebrows rose and her lips thinned in annoyance. "Ethan's not a common criminal. He has a mental illness, but it's under control."

"Until the next time he loses it and batters someone to death. Mental illness or not, he's dangerous—"

"Now, look," Tonka shouted him down. "With respect, you haven't seen him recently, Rob. He's a different man, trust me, or go visit him and see for yourself. If he wasn't, I wouldn't be doing this, but if we don't do something…well, they might as well throw away the key now. He's got to live with the consequences of what he did, which would be hard enough without being a veteran with a criminal record and a psych diagnosis. All we're doing is giving him a chance at a normal life."

Tonka waited for Rob's response, but she'd only given him the 'why', not the 'what'.

"Go on," he said.

"I know someone who'll give him a new identity."

"Ma'am…"

"You're going to tell me it's against the law? I know. Incredible how that same law doesn't apply to child killers who tortured for their own entertainment, eh?"

"It's a whole other situation."

"Ethan lost his temper for good reason, and he handed himself in."

"Because he wanted out of the army."

Tonka threw out her hands in a wide, angry shrug. "You know what, Rob? You've changed. I mean, you always were a stickler for the rules, but this?"

"Of course I've changed. The shit I've seen…" A few choice images flashed across Rob's mind, and he quashed them like always. Since Bosnia, nightmares were par for the course, and working undercover had done little more than add some variety, a bit like his own personal Freeview horror channel, but he'd never lost control, never taken a civilian life. "Out in the field, you tell yourself it's because there's a war going on, that people wouldn't do those kinds of things in a normal situation, but it's all lies."

"Money," Tonka said. "That's all I'm asking for."

"How much?"

"We need to raise another hundred and twenty-five grand. We've already got three hundred and seventy-five—"

"Half a million? Fucking hell. I might need to rethink my exit strategy."

"We're running out of time, Rob. Can you help or not?"

Rob ran his palm over his scalp, under immense pressure. He could raise the money, but it wasn't going spare. While Hedley and Petridis had wrangled him a decent settlement from the Met, that was all he had until the business started paying. If it started paying.

"What about compensation? Has he put in a claim? And he's got his disablement pension, hasn't he?"

"When he's discharged, yeah, but only if he's still Ethan McGrath, former REME…"

"Sorry, Ma'am. I've spent the last four years digging through the dregs of society, and I'm not prepared to play a part in you joining their midst. Because it will come back to get you later. You know that as well as I do."

"Not if we get it right."

So complacent, but she had no idea the resources the likes of the Special Investigations Unit had at their disposal.

"I've just resigned from the police. I've got no income." Rather than risk further conflict, Rob opted for an emotional appeal, but she was giving him the silent treatment and wouldn't even look at him. He could imagine what she was thinking: he had the luxury of walking away from a well-paid career while Ethan would be lucky to get a job paying minimum wage. If she was that bothered, she had half a million sitting in her garage. "I really am sorry, Ma'am."

"So am I, but I understand."

"What're you gonna do?"

"Doesn't matter." She stepped around him to reach the door to the house, paused and gave the Lamborghini a longing look.

"Yeah, cheers for the guilt trip," Rob muttered. She didn't take it back. He followed her inside, where he downed his beer and picked up his helmet and keys. "Who's got my phone?"

Bish and Jock looked at each other and shook their heads. They were sticking to their story.

"Crap. I must've dropped it. Ah, well. At least…" He was going to say 'I'm getting my money's worth on my insurance' but thought better of it, although he wouldn't have put it past either of them to have nicked it for a laugh. He'd have to wait and see if any practical jokes were in store. "I'd best get off."

"All right, mate," Bish said. "Good to see you again."

"And you. Jock, behave yourself."

"Always do." He stayed facing forward, his focus on the label he was peeling from the empty bottle in his hands.

Rob drew breath to suggest they arrange a proper get-together sometime soon, but there was no point. He'd let them down, and it would be a long time before they forgave and forgot, if they ever did.

4: Guest of Goner

I T WAS DIFFICULT to raise the alarm...without raising the alarm. Gray had tried to collar Martina on her own, but instead she'd insisted he join her table and introduced him to her tablemates: six other senior officers, one of whom was Martina's wife: Chief Superintendent Erica Dunleavy. It went without saying that Erica was one of those people who took command in every situation, and it was some fifteen minutes later, after he'd answered her questions pertaining to who he was and how he knew Rob, before Gray had a chance to tell Martina that both bike and owner were nowhere to be found.

It was when Martina said, "He's a sod," as if she were describing an errant kitten clawing at the curtains that Gray realised he needed to up the urgency factor a notch or two.

"Ma'am, I'm not convinced he left of his own volition."

"Ma'am?" Martina repeated in amusement. "We're the same rank, Gray. Or we were."

And that she'd had quite a bit to drink.

"Sorry, old habits," Gray excused, though he'd done it on purpose, hoping to tap into some far corner of her brain that still recalled she was a police officer.

"We'd best go and investigate, then," she suggested and pushed her chair from the table at the same moment as a waiter arrived with the starters.

"It's all right, Martina. You stay there. I'll go and have a poke around and report back."

"OK, Gray, you do that." She pulled her chair in again and picked up her glass but didn't drink from it, momentarily lost in a daze. Her wife cast a slightly concerned look in Gray's direction. Martina was evidently taking Rob's leaving pretty hard.

A couple of officers were outside, having a smoke, both pausing to eye Gray in suspicion. He gave them a swift smile as he passed them and rounded the building, slowing as he moved along the dark alley that stank of piss, as they always did, a make-do public convenience for late-night revellers caught short and nocturnal animals alike. At the halfway point, Gray tripped over a box and skidded on something he didn't want to think about. He took out his phone and activated the LED, blocking the dazzle with raised hand and squinting at the mute blue patch on the ground ahead of him. Flattened cardboard pulp, ring pulls, cigarette ends, a couple of used condoms, bins... He reached the end of the alley and turned to look back towards the street.

He could see tyre tread in the mush of muck and rubbish, and a few boot prints, potentially from more than one type of boot, but there was nothing to indicate a struggle had taken place. Switching off the LED briefly, he brought up Rob's number to try calling him again, but the signal was sketchy, and his phone abandoned the call. Gray moved back along the alley, watching his screen all the while, cursing when he tripped over the same box as before. He kicked it hard in revenge, sending it three feet into the air, and watched in satisfaction as it collapsed on impact. There was a sudden and bright blue glow in the gloom. A dropped phone? Gray was almost certain it was and backtracked to investigate.

The screen was locked but displayed multiple missed calls. By this point, it wasn't really necessary to establish ownership; nonetheless, when Gray reached the street and the signal picked up, he called Rob's number again, sighing in resignation when his name appeared, attached to the incoming call on the phone from the alley. Maybe he was wrong about the absence of a struggle—that or Rob had dropped it intentionally as a clue. Or he'd just dropped it making his getaway and Gray's imagination was running amok. Whichever of those it was, he returned to the restaurant and made a beeline for Erica.

"Can I have a word?"

She set her cutlery and napkin aside and edged around the table to reach him. "What's up?"

Gray turned so he was facing the window and away from the guests. "I think something's happened to Rob, Ma'am. He drove past me at approximately 1950 hours, and I saw him turn into the alley to the side of this building. When I got here, his bike was there, but he wasn't, or not that I could see, and I assumed he'd already come in. He hadn't, as you know, and when I went to check again at around 2010 hours, his bike was gone. I wondered if he'd popped to the shop or something..."

Erica looked doubtful.

"Yeah, I know," Gray said. Rob didn't smoke, and he didn't drink much either, so it was a silly theory to start with. He held out the phone. "I found this in the alley."

"Rob's?"

"Yep."

"That's worrying." Erica took the phone from him and activated the screen. It asked for the PIN number. "That's not a lot of use, is it?" She handed it back. "Right. Let's see...who looks sober?" She scanned the room and spotted her target. "Theo?" She beckoned him over.

"Yes, Ma'am?"

"Do you know each other?"

Gray and Theo Petridis did a kind of mixed nod and shrug. They'd both been Rob's boss at some point, so they'd corresponded, but that was the limit of their familiarity.

"Gray, can you tell Theo what you've just told me?"

"Sure."

"Great." Delegating done, Erica returned to her wife's side.

"Must be nice up there, huh?" Theo muttered.

"Yeah," Gray agreed with a chuckle. He thought it was wise not to mention he'd been on his way to the upper echelons before he met Jean. He'd left ambition behind when he'd fallen in love and hadn't been tempted to pursue it a second time, not even when he found himself single again. "All right. Short version: Rob's gone missing, along with his bike."

"What makes you think he's missing and hasn't just ditched the party?"

"Why would he have ridden all the way here to ditch the party?"

"To cover up that he was going to?"

Gray couldn't decide if Petridis was being facetious or the guy really thought Rob would pull a stunt like that, although... "It's a possibility," Gray admitted reluctantly. In a gathering of this size, Rob could claim to have been there all the time and they'd be none the wiser. "But wouldn't he at least have put in an appearance so he had eyewitnesses to corroborate he was here?"

"Or one ultra-reliable eyewitness."

"Hmm..." Gray wasn't buying it.

"Do you have any reason to believe he's in danger?" Petridis asked, looking Gray in the eye—the left one—as if by doing so he could telepathically glean what that reason might be.

"If you mean, is Rob's involved in any undercover cases at the moment, I wouldn't know. I left the police last summer."

"Lucky bastard. I've got another five years before I can afford to go."

Gray grimaced sympathetically. There was real envy there, as was always the case with officers in their forties or fifties who discovered Gray had got out at the tender age of thirty-four—unless they knew what he'd been through prior to penning his resignation.

"I could get the patrols to keep a look out," Petridis offered. "Will that do you?"

Gray checked the time: coming up on nine o'clock. "He could be well out of the area by now."

"Or sitting it out in a wine bar down the street."

Am I overreacting? Rob had put away some bad people over the years and hadn't exactly been 'undercover' on the last case they'd worked together. If he'd been recognised... "All right, let's give it another thirty minutes."

"If you're sure." Petridis was already moving away.

Gray nodded. Half an hour would make little difference. He returned to Martina Hedley's table, where his starter—mushroom paté and pain rustica, which, thankfully, was cold to begin with—had been covered with a napkin while everyone else was almost finished with their main course. He speed-ate one slice of the yeasty bread and caught the attention of their waiter.

"Your main course, sir?"

"Please."

The waiter nodded and strode away.

"What's happening?" Martina asked.

"We're giving it a bit longer to see if Rob turns up."

"I'm sure he will."

"Yeah," Gray agreed dubiously. Martina patted his hand. She'd switched to drinking water and seemed a little less intoxicated than earlier. The waiter returned and exchanged Gray's half-eaten paté for his main course: a mock-fish Thai curry with beautifully fragrant rice that set his mouth watering before the plate touched down. "Thanks." Gray sniffed deeply, filling his nose with the scent of spicy coconut and citrus.

"That smells incredible," Martina said. "What fish is it?"

"It's not. It's made from soya beans and seaweed."

"Are you vegetarian?"

"No, but I eat a lot of veggie stuff."

"It's a healthier diet."

"It is," Gray agreed.

"So, you're going in with Rob on this investigating business, I hear."

Gray was kind of relieved she hadn't passed further comment on his choice of meal, although the change of subject was unexpected. It wasn't a secret as such, but Rob generally kept his cards close to his chest. "He told you?"

"I think I interrogated it out of him. I wanted him back on my team. He could've made DI by now."

"Yeah, it's the paperwork he doesn't like. Luckily, I do."

"A perfect match!" Martina picked up her glass and raised it.

Gray passed on drinking the last of his pint—still his first, thus tepid and stale—and poured some water into his wine glass. "Cheers," he said.

The desserts arrived, and the half-hour mark came...and went. Petridis was involved in a loud political debate which Gray didn't want to interrupt, although that conversation sounded a lot more interesting than the one at Gray's table. Senior police officers seemed incapable of talking about anything other than targets and cutbacks. He quietly excused himself and took a detour to the Gents' on his way outside for a breather, and to further contemplate the possibility he was making a mountain out of molehill.

The traffic had dwindled to the usual nightly array of buses, cabs and pedestrians; they paid Gray no heed. That was London: a city crammed with nine million people, all of whom ignored each other. It was part of what had drawn him to buy a house there, the anonymity. That and the awful hours he kept, although even in London, it could be tricky to find a decent cappuccino at three in the morning.

"You all right there, mate?" One of the officers he'd seen earlier had come out for another smoke.

"Yeah, thanks." Gray offered half a smile and returned to staring across the road. A black cab stopped to let out its passengers and pulled away again. Smoke drifted in front of Gray's face; he held his breath until it had passed, yet still inhaled some.

"How d'you know Rob?" the smoker asked.

"We worked together on a couple of cases a while back."

The smoker nodded slowly and took another draw on his cigarette. "He's a good bloke."

"Yeah, he is. No idea where he's got to tonight, though."

"I expect he's caught in traffic." The smoker checked his watch. "Blimey, it's getting on. Didn't realise." He stubbed the half-smoked cigarette out on the bin, saying, "See you," on his way back to the door. The noise of chatter bloomed briefly, and the door closed again.

Two hours to get from Kilburn to Euston? It should've taken half an hour, tops, and in any case, Rob had arrived on time. There had to have been an emergency of some sort, and Gray had Zoë's number saved, but he was reluctant to call when all it might achieve was to have two of them fretting.

The door opened again, and the other smoker gave Gray a nod as he passed, stopping a few yards away to light up and take out his phone. Gray watched him and made a decision: he'd call Zoë when the guy went back inside.

Two cigarettes later, by which point Gray had realised it wasn't a particularly warm evening, the other officer left at last, and Gray made the call.

"Damn it." Voicemail. "Hi, Zoë, it's Gray Fisher. If you happen to hear from Rob, can you let him know he left his phone behind? Take care." Gray ended the call, hoping he'd been cryptic enough to not worry her, and returned inside, on a collision course with Theo Petridis, who raised his thick silver eyebrows in query. Gray shook his head. Theo squeezed Gray's shoulder as if to say 'there, there' and then, with phone clamped to ear, he strode back to his table.

"Gray, come and sit," Martina called. With nothing more he could do for the time being, he obliged. "Do you need another drink?"

"No, I'm fine, thanks." Gray topped up the water in his wine glass and sipped absently, casting his mind back to the Strang investigation. It had begun in London, when Gray's preliminary research into a corrupt legal firm tied them to a larger scheme to defraud will beneficiaries of their inheritance; Strang, Folden and the other lawyers involved were now in prison. However, the corruption extended upwards through the criminal justice system—the SIU investigation was ongoing—and Rob's infiltration had relied on his pre-existing association with Lambert—one of the lawyers—who was dead, but her friends on high were not.

"You think something's happened to him." Martina's observation broke into Gray's thoughts. Now he'd worried her too.

"I'm missing a perfectly decent night in for no reason here," he complained, trying to make light, though it was true enough, and if Rob had just decided to give it a miss, he'd be hearing about it later.

Martina's laughter was a little forced. "Had a better offer, did you? Who's the lucky man?"

"Nobody you know," Gray said evasively. "How long have you and Erica been together?"

"Twelve years."

"Fifteen," Erica corrected, barely breaking from the conversation she was having and to which she immediately returned.

"That's what I said, fifteen years." Martina winked at Gray. "Sometimes it seems like only yesterday. Other times, it feels like forever."

Erica glanced witheringly at her wife.

Gray smiled, appreciating the glimpse into their relationship. He and Jean had barely reached the point where infatuation evolved into easy familiarity, but even in the darkest months after Jean's death, Gray hadn't coveted or envied others for having that. Rather, he celebrated it, hoping that one day it might be within his reach again.

"Will Richards," he said.

"Will Richards..." Martina frowned in thought. "Is he on the job?"

"No, he's not."

"Why do I know that name?" She shook her head. "Too much alcohol."

Gray hoped his smile covered his astonishment. She'd seen the two of them together at Freddie Berringer's apartment the night the Berringers were arrested, and she was taking over from Rob in handling the witnesses. She had to be seriously tanked up to have not made the connection.

She shrugged. "Oh, well. It'll come to me."

Gray really hoped it didn't, or not until the party was over. "Think I fancy a drink after all. You want one?"

"God, no—thank you."

Gray confirmed no-one else needed a refill and went to the bar. He sent Will a text message: *Rob was a no-show.*

Another customer arrived and stopped next to him. "Alright?"

Gray nodded. "Yes, thanks. You?"

"Yeah."

"Who's next, please?"

Gray's phone buzzed. He gestured for the other guy to queue-jump and read Will's reply: *Bummer. Any idea why?* Gray responded: *Your guess is as good as mine.*

The bartender served the other guy's drink, the price of which made him mutter, "How much? Fucking hell." He paid anyway and picked up his glass but stayed where he was, surveying the restaurant, then homed in on Gray. "Dave Miller," he said and held out his hand.

"Gray Fisher."

"So *you're* the one Petridis is moaning about."

"Quite possibly."

"Whatever you said, it worked. He's got Traffic keeping an eye out for Rob."

"Good to know."

"Yes, sir?" the bartender prompted.

"Pint of Guinness and black, please." And this time, Gray was determined to finish it. The bartender poured the beer and left it to settle while he served someone else.

Miller sipped his Scotch and sniffed. "Waste of time, if you ask me."

Gray was fed up with hearing that—or words to that effect. He turned Miller's way, noting the confident pose, the ingrained arrogance. "I'm asking," he said.

"Rob told Hedley he was doing a flit after shift."

"You heard him, did you?"

"One of my colleagues did, yeah."

Hearsay, then. Gray would be asking Martina to substantiate what Miller was telling him, although it did sound like something Rob would say.

Gray's drink arrived in front of him. He paid—on that point he agreed with Miller, the prices were extortionate—and picked it up, already moving off. "Nice talking to you."

"Yeah, likewise."

Gray glanced back at Miller, who'd already downed his Scotch and was ordering another. Heavy drinking was an occupational hazard, one which Gray had side-stepped only to pursue another, so he was judging no-one. He returned to Martina. "Dave Miller's one of yours, isn't he?"

She nodded. "He's a DS. Why?"

"No reason. I was talking to him at the bar. Do you get on all right?"

"Mostly. He can be a bit of a wanker at times."

"Can't we all?" Gray asked rhetorically.

"What's he said?"

"That someone heard Rob tell you he wasn't coming tonight."

Martina leaned sideways and glared past Gray at Miller. "Where the hell did he get that from?" When Gray didn't answer, Martina homed in on him, her eyes narrow and dangerous. "Rob didn't say anything of the sort."

Gray held up his free hand. "Look, I'm merely trying to figure out whether Miller's spreading gossip or if there's some fire to go with that smoke. I'm worried about Rob, yet nobody else seems bothered. Is there something I'm missing?"

Martina pursed her lips, contemplating Gray for a moment and, in the process, confirming his suspicions weren't without merit. She sighed. "All right. You want the truth? I'll tell you, but you're not going to like it."

"Go on," Gray invited.

"Most of us would've been more surprised if he'd turned up tonight. Every social, it's the same—he says he'll try and make it, but he never does. We still invite him, because we enjoy his company, and...he wasn't always like that."

"It's since he worked for the SIU," Gray cut in before Martina could say it.

"Yes," she confirmed.

The food and beer in Gray's belly turned to concrete. It was like being told a friend had only months to live.

"In all other ways, he's no different," Martina said—for Gray's benefit, he was sure. "He gets on with everyone and has a laugh...well, he's always been a cool operator, and he's a bit more serious than he used to be, but he's still the same Rob on the job." She chuckled at her accidental poetry, and Gray managed a smile.

"But he doesn't socialise anymore, is what you're saying."

"Exactly. Did you know he started our footy team and coached them?"

"I didn't."

"Yeah, and they were bloody good, too. And he used to organise trips to the TT Races, the Grand Prix..."

"Why bother putting tonight on if you were all so sure he wouldn't make it?"

"Because he promised me he'd be here." Martina turned away to reach her glass. She was unsteady, but Gray didn't think it was the alcohol. Her pride had taken a hit.

"He wouldn't have let you down on purpose," he consoled. Martina stopped mid-sip, eyebrows arched like a silhouetted seagull flying above her glass. "He arrived here. I saw him."

She swallowed her emotions and nursed her glass. "Then where is he?"

"On the M40." Petridis appeared at Gray's side. "Traffic spotted his bike at High Wycombe, northbound carriageway."

**

"Dom, me ol' mucker. How's it going?" It was the worst Cockney accent ever, and it made Dom Hooper cackle.

"Bloody hell, Gray, don't give up the day job, will you?"

"Damn cheek! I don't know...you think someone's your friend..." Gray grumbled against Dom's continued throaty chuckle. He was smoking again— not surprising. Laid-back as Dom Hooper was, leading the SIU was unbelievably stressful, as Gray knew all too well.

"Aside from speaking with a dodgy accent—"

"When in London..."

"—how are you doing?"

"Very well, thanks, although this isn't a social call."

"Yeah, you've never called me socially."

"I have," Gray protested and searched his memory for an example. He didn't find one.

"Don't worry about it. I know you love me anyway. So, how can I help you this fine Friday evening?"

Gray was still reeling from the revelation. Fourteen years, he and Dom had known each other as colleagues and friends, but Dom was right. Gray had never called 'just for a chat' or to see how he was. It was a poor show on his part, but he'd deal with that later. There were more pressing matters to attend to. "Don't suppose you've still got access to that insurance underwriter? The one who does all the mobile devices?"

"Aspects, you mean?"

"That's the one."

"Let's have a look."

"It can wait," Gray said.

"If it could, you'd be all tucked up in bed by now instead of calling me."

Gray had no defence, so he stayed quiet, the silence punctuated by noises from Dom's end of the call—clicks and taps of a keyboard, the flick of a cigarette lighter, a long inhalation and then, "Yep. I'm in."

"Excellent. Can you look to see if there's anything for Rob Simpson-Stone?"

"That's ominous."

"We'll see."

"OK. Simpson, Simpson, Simpson, Simpson-Atkins, Simpson-Pettigrew— why would you bother? Ah, here we go. Simpson-Stone, L. Damage claim last year. His niece?"

"Possibly."

"And another... Yep. Simpson-Stone, R. Phone reported as lost or stolen at 21:26. Phone and SIM blocked. Why? What's happened?"

"Rob's leaving do was tonight," Gray said. "I saw him arrive, but he didn't make it inside. Traffic cameras picked up his bike heading north on the M40, and they were going to pull it, to make sure it was Rob, but lost sight of it in Oxford. I guess he could've stopped off somewhere…Stratford, maybe." Gray was speculating aloud. "Anyway, I found his phone in the alley where I'd seen his bike, but if he's reported it…"

"It's logged as reported by the owner."

"Does it say whether a replacement handset's going out?"

"One's been approved. No shipping info, though. It must be on a separate system for the courier."

"That makes sense. At least I know he's alive. Thanks, Dom."

"Anytime, mate."

"Listen, I'll do better."

"Ha. Yeah, all right."

"I'll give you a call next week—socially," Gray promised, which set Dom off laughing again. "And stop smoking."

"No problem, boss. Catch you later."

"Bye." Gray hung up, undecided whether the use of 'boss' was out of habit or sarcasm. Either way, he *would* do better.

5: Dodgy

Rob's guilt rode pillion all the way to Stratford-upon-Avon. He'd been on his way back to Euston, following a diversion around roadworks that took him within five minutes of the flat. At the junction where he should've turned left with the rest of the diverted traffic, he'd turned right and gone home. He'd stayed long enough to call his mobile phone company and leave Hedley a voicemail to say he was safe and would explain everything later, then he'd packed his panniers and hit the road.

He didn't stop in Stratford, but the brief detour off the slow-moving motorway went a long way towards clearing his head. It was quiet for a Friday late evening, not too cold, though not yet warm enough for people to sit outside. As Rob neared the river, moisture in the air hit him like hard rain, and the drop in temperature made him shiver in spite of his leathers. He slowed down and breathed deeply, intoxicated by the smoky mix of moss and new leaves that filled his nose while memories of Zoë filled his mind. They were so powerful that, for a moment, he felt her warmth pressed to his back, her arms gripped around his waist. Alluring and no longer painful, the sensation tempted him to circle back so he could feel it all over again, but he was ready to move on.

His route out of town took him past where his life as a beat bobby began: Stratford-upon-Avon Police Station. It somehow felt more fitting to revisit his time there than to spend his last night on the job with relative strangers in a soulless restaurant in a soulless city. His colleagues at the Quarterhouse would have finished eating long ago—Rob hadn't eaten since lunch—and the serious drinking would be underway. He realised, now it was too late, that he should've gone back if only for one pint. He'd let everyone down, not least Martina Hedley, and there would be no opportunity to make amends.

Rob was pleased, in a way, that he'd lost his phone—he still wasn't ruling out a prank—not that he expected a shedload of missed calls. At most, he anticipated a couple from Hedley, maybe a voicemail to tell him he was a let-down. Gray Fisher would no doubt also call at some point to give him grief for inviting him and not bothering to turn up. He'd apologise; he owed them that much, and he was sorry for wasting their time, but he wasn't sorry he'd missed his leaving do. Most of the people he'd worked with before he joined the SIU had moved on, and those in attendance were only there for a night out. It made no odds to them whether Rob showed or not.

The self-pity faded, along with his bad mood, as he headed away from Stratford towards the open road, and disappeared entirely after his pit stop for overpriced fast food. He was big enough to admit that the issue was him, not everyone else. After so long working alone or in the limited and exhausting company of false acquaintances, Rob was out of practice with socialising and still sore about the divorce. Almost eighteen months down the line, he needed to get his shit together, but he didn't—couldn't—think about that now.

With a bit more throttle, his worries were instantly wiped out, lost to the all-consuming joy of the ride. The new tyres bit into the tarmac as Rob leaned low around bends, zipping past cars on his side of the road, headlights approaching on the other side a short-lived blur sucked into the darkness as quickly as they'd appeared. He'd needed this: a few hours of just him and the bike.

As always, the journey was over more quickly than Rob would've liked, although it had started to rain, so it was no bad thing that he was almost home— or his mum's place, at least. She'd moved there after he'd joined the army, yet it still felt like home.

It was coming up on two a.m. as he turned into the road, keeping his speed down and the revs low so as not to disturb the neighbours. His mum would hear him regardless of how quiet his approach and whether she was asleep—he wasn't ruling out the same kind of parental telepathy that had got him up to Lucas the night he'd vomited in his sleep.

Rob parked up and let himself in with the key his mum kept in a planter, against his advice, though only a fool would risk running the gauntlet with Linford the giant—even for his breed—Rottweiler that belonged to his mum's partner, Harvey. Both dog and owner were fierce-looking softies, and the dog greeted Rob at the door—no barking, but he was snorting in his excitement and couldn't have wagged any harder if he'd tried. Working around the slobbery loving, Rob unzipped his jacket and just about got his boots off before the light came on.

"It's me, Mum," he called as she appeared in silhouette at the top of the stairs.

"I know. I heard the bike." She was on her way down. "I wasn't expecting you until the morning." She arrived in front of him and hugged him while his hands were still inside his jacket sleeves. He wriggled out of them, letting the jacket fall to the floor, and hugged her back.

"I missed you," he said.

"Hmm." She released him and turned towards the kitchen. "Didn't want to miss out on breakfast, you mean?"

"Added bonus." He'd have picked up his jacket, but Linford was in the process of turning it into a makeshift bed. That jacket had been through far greater trials, so Rob left the dog to his scuffing and circling and went to join his mum, who had already filled a pan with milk and set it on the lit stove. Rob collected the cocoa and sugar from the cupboard and then stood by, watching her expertly mix the sweet paste. The adrenaline was wearing off, leaving him at the mercy of the aches and pains of the ride and the aftermath of three months of working without a break. He yawned and stretched, catching the tail end of her question.

"...be at a work's night out?"

"I didn't make it—I was abducted," he said, hoping his weary tone conveyed that it wasn't a serious attempt, although if his mum had known half of what he'd been involved in over the past ten years, he wouldn't have used the word at all, not even in jest.

"Oh?"

"By the REMEs. An impromptu get-together." He wasn't covering for his mum's sake, or even for his ego. There was little point in staging an abduction simply to get at Rob's very limited funds, and Tonka hadn't tried that hard to persuade him. Surely she'd have realised he'd refuse to help Ethan, which meant either she was desperate and Rob was a last resort—the Lamborghini said otherwise—or there was more to it than she'd told him. Either way, he couldn't see her parting with the car when it had been her lifelong dream to own one.

Chocolatey steam warmed his face as a mug appeared in front of him and his mum ruffled his hair, bringing him back from his thoughts.

"Thanks, Mum." Cupping his drink with both hands, he sipped carefully and sighed in contentment, feeling all the stress and strain ebb away.

"Go on to bed." She pointed towards the stairs.

"I will in a minute. I just need to get my gear in—"

"Where are your keys?" She held out her hand for them.

Rob put down his mug and went out to the hallway, where Linford was curled up into a surprisingly small ball and was snoring and drooling all over his jacket. Rob tugged a corner out from under the dog and fished his keys from the pocket, both his hand and the keys drenched in slimy dog spit. With a grimace, he dried off on his T-shirt and took one step towards the front door before the keys were snatched from him.

"Bed, now!" his mum commanded as she disappeared outside. It was a direct order, and Rob knew better than to disobey. He retrieved his cocoa from the kitchen and went upstairs, to the spare room, set his drink on the bedside table, stripped to his boxers and made a quick trip to the bathroom. By the time his mum came up, he was under the duvet and fighting to keep his eyes open.

She put his panniers in the corner of the room. "Don't spill that on the bed," she warned without looking his way. Rob downed the warm cocoa in one. His mum took the empty mug from him and turned off the light on her way out.

"Night, Mum."

"Night-night, sleep tight." The door clicked shut behind her.

Rob slid down the bed and rolled onto his side, smiling at the way his mum still bossed him around like he was an eight-year-old flouting bedtime. He turned forty-one in a few months, but he'd never be too old to appreciate her pampering—it wasn't so long ago he'd feared he might have lost it forever.

His niece Lois had graduated from law school during the Strang case and started working for Jess Lambert, which was a good career move, on the surface. Lois wanted to specialise in family law—Jess's area of expertise—and she knew Rob and Jess were old friends, but it also meant Rob's investigation started with snooping on his niece to see if she was involved in the fraud scheme. He'd thanked God she wasn't. However, it put her at greater risk of getting caught in the crossfire.

To guarantee Lois's safety, Rob had kept his cover with his family, on the premise that if they didn't know anything, they couldn't accidentally let something slip. Then came the sting operation—a fake reunion to draw Jess and her associates out into the open—but Lois was too close to the target. She'd seen her Uncle Rob cosying up with her boss when he'd claimed he was trying to save his marriage, and when she called him on it, his choice was to either come clean—and blow the entire investigation—or dig himself in deeper.

Deeper he went. No training could've prepared him for dealing with his mum's sense of betrayal, and it had been an enormous relief to own up once the investigation was over even if some of his family—his sister, mainly—thought he'd stayed quiet because he didn't trust them. Everything he'd done was to make it easier for them, which had made it a lot harder for him.

More than a year on, his sister was still keeping her emotional distance, and Amber—Lois's younger sister—wasn't talking to him at all, which was why no-one had told him Amber was pregnant. He knew not to force it. Maybe, in time, they'd get back some of the closeness they used to have. For now, he'd settle for being allowed to call in and see her while he was home.

***

"Quarter to one? What the hell?"

Rob had expected to wake up the following morning to an empty house. Well, he got the empty house right.

Laughing in disbelief that he'd slept for ten-plus hours and felt bloody awesome for it, he wandered down to the kitchen to raid the fridge, noting the package—complete with a handwritten note addressed to him—on the counter on his way past, but his requirement for fluid was more urgent. He opened the fridge and contemplated which of the milk and OJ he'd get in the least trouble for swigging straight from the container. He opted for OJ and gulped down half the two-litre carton in one go. "I'll get some more later," he thought aloud and went to attend to the package.

The note was brief—*Something you're not telling me? Mum x*—but it made sense once he'd examined the printed label on the box: his replacement handset and SIM. Now he'd find out what had—or hadn't—happened to the old one.

Downloading the data didn't take long; Rob wasn't big on social networking and mostly used his phone for texts and calls. Those were the first things he checked—no outgoing calls or messages after 7:30 the previous evening. If Bish and Jock had it, they'd have cracked his PIN, so he could safely conclude he'd dropped it in the scuffle in the alley.

It took a bit longer for the incoming messages and voicemails to arrive; while he waited, he considered all the data that would need to be rewritten or wiped to give someone a fresh start. The half-a-million fee Tonka had spoken of sounded a bit steep, but now he thought about it, there was a lot of work involved—hacking into government databases, credit companies, amending medical records, or those that had been computerised.

It would need someone like Aaron Tanner, with the know-how but with fewer scruples—and there was the other thing. Tonka had a good upbringing, came from a respectable, fairly well-to-do family. What was she doing, getting mixed up with organised criminals? How had she established contact? Rob contemplated calling Aaron-Naomi on the off-chance Aaron could give him a lead on who Tonka might be dealing with, while also aware it was an excuse. Since the remand hearing, Naomi had been on Rob's mind more than she should've been.

His messages finally finished downloading and were much as he'd predicted: quite a few missed calls, mostly from Martina and Gray. He sent both a text message to confirm he was alive and would explain in full when he got back from his mum's. Gray replied with a simple *OK – thanks for letting me know*. Martina, on the other hand...

"Afternoon, Ma'am."

"Where the hell did you get to?"

"Something came up."

"An emergency?"

"Of sorts. It was out of my hands."

"I can't believe you sometimes, Rob."

"I know. I'm sorry, Ma'am."

She didn't say anything else for a while, then, "Is everything all right?"

"Yeah. Everything's fine."

"And Lucas and Zoë? They're OK?"

"As far as I'm aware."

She paused, waiting for him to say more. When he didn't, she asked, "Are you at your mum's now?"

"Yeah. For two weeks."

"Right."

"Anyway, I'd best—"

"You're really not going to tell me?"

"It's a long story."

"I've got time."

Rob laughed. "I haven't. I promised my niece a visit today and I overslept."

"Then I'll let you go. Just tell me this much. Are you in trouble?"

"No, Ma'am."

"You realise I'm not your boss anymore?"

"I dunno about that."

She chuckled, but Rob realised from her questions that she'd moved past being angry to worried. He was going to have to give her something to put her mind at rest.

"It's to do with an old army buddy," he said.

"Gray saw you arrive at the restaurant."

"Yeah. I got called away."

"If there's anything I can do to help..."

"I doubt it, Ma'am. Martina. But cheers, anyway. Listen, how d'you fancy going for a pint when I get back?"

"Will you show up?"

"Scout's honour."

"Yeah, OK." She didn't sound like she believed him. "I'm going. Have a good rest."

"I'll try."

"Take care, Rob."

"And you. Bye."

The call ended, and Rob realised he was smiling to himself, no longer worried that leaving the police had cost him Martina's friendship. On with the next mission: repairing his previous balls-up.

He called Amber's number, wondering what excuse she'd give him this time, assuming she answered at all. After a few rings, it went to voicemail. Rob hung up and tried again, deciding if she didn't pick up, he'd leave it, but as he moved his phone away from his ear, he heard the call connect.

"Hello?"

"Amber. It's Uncle Rob. Alright?"

"Oh, hi. Yeah, I'm good. How are you?"

"I'm good too. What are you up to?"

"Just putting the shopping away. Can I call you back?"

"It's only a quickie. Will you be in later if I pop round?"

"What time?"

"Whenever suits."

"Erm..." She tailed off, and Rob heard quiet rattles and bangs and cupboard doors closing. "We're having dinner with Kyle's parents."

Rob bent so he could read the clock on the microwave—almost half past one—not that it mattered. He'd got the message. "Never mind. I'll give you a ring during the week, yeah?"

"I come over to Nan's on Wednesday anyway."

"OK. I'll see you then." He was gutted, but he kept his tone light.

"Yeah. Bye...Rob."

"Catch you later, turtle." The pet name tumbled out of his mouth before he could stop it, and the few seconds of silence before she hung up were like waiting for a retaliative punch that didn't land. If she ever spoke to him again, he'd tell her he was sorry, promise not to call her that anymore—he shouldn't anyway, now she was twenty-four. And a mum.

It was hard to get his head around; his baby nieces were both grown women with family—in Amber's case—and careers of their own, but he still missed being part of their lives. He'd always been closer to Lois than he was to Amber; he was just a kid himself when Lois was born—well, an impressionable teenager—but the first time he'd held her, he'd known he wanted to be a dad someday. She was so tiny and beautiful, all long lashes and soft, dark curls, and the smell of her... Baby talc and milk. He could've got high on it, although he'd been happy to take his sister's word for it that Lois didn't smell too clever at WTF-o'clock in the morning with a full nappy.

Apart from that particular privilege, which he'd got to experience firsthand with his own son, Rob was one hundred percent the besotted uncle, unlike his brother, who'd only shown off his nieces to impress girls. According to JJ, being 'dad material' was a surefire route to getting a girlfriend, but JJ hadn't been pursuing Jess Lambert, who'd had no interest in babies—or being a girlfriend—then or ever. It was a pity that infatuation couldn't be knocked on the head by common sense, not that Rob had had much of that, either.

Amber had always been the more affected of the two girls, but he could bide his time with that one. With the other...

"Alright, Lois?"

"Uncle Rob? I was just thinking about you! What are you up to?"

"I was going to ask you the same thing."

6: Saturday Skirmish

THE TRAIN JOURNEY to Croxley had become routine to Gray, so much so that, regardless of how absorbed he was in his music or reading, he could gauge, by the distance between stations, the variations in speed, the curves and the number of passengers embarking and disembarking, when it was time to get up from his seat—assuming he got one at some point.

His choice of entertainment for today's trip was an eclectic selection beginning with *Bolero*, detouring into a couple of dance anthems he'd fallen in love with in his formative years, and culminating in *Rhapsody in Blue*, to which he quickly abandoned his reading material—an academic paper that was all the more droll against the soundscape of musical acrobatics. Gray leaned back with eyes closed, imagining his journey as one and the same as that which had inspired Gershwin's busy composition. In what seemed like no time at all, he sensed the familiar pattern—the rock from side to side when they passed over the points, the slight bend to the right, the brief dulling of light caused by an overhead bridge, deceleration... The piece ended a few seconds after the doors opened.

Gray popped the earbuds from his ears and left them dangling from his coat front until he was out of the station. It had been raining when he'd left home, heavily enough to have warranted forking out for a cab had it still been raining. For the time being, the downpour was holding off, although the sky was thick with dark clouds; Gray decided to chance it anyway.

It was a lovely walk—in appropriate footwear, which he now owned—a twenty-minute amble through woodlands and along the canal bank, and he was early, as per usual. He was also past justifying his perpetual punctuality as a hangover from the job. Admittedly, he hated being late, but between Will's early morning rounds and Gray's midnight-oil burning, they rarely saw each other during the week, and by Saturday lunchtime, Gray was embarrassingly eager for their time together.

Of course, it would have been far less embarrassing if, when pressed, he hadn't attempted a long-winded explanation about timetables and delays. In the face of Will's obvious amusement, Gray had given up without reaching his point, because he didn't have one...aside from the truth, though he suspected Will had been fully aware of that from the outset.

Pausing to tuck his trousers into his socks, and to marvel at how little he cared if he looked ridiculous, Gray stepped through the kissing gate into the woods and greedily inhaled the rich, moist air. Spring had arrived in its full verdant glory, a sensory overload of colours and scents to the accompaniment of blackbirds' songs and the drumbeat of accumulated rainwater, released by the canopy to nourish the tight furls of newborn bracken far below. Gray tucked his earbuds into his inside pocket in favour of listening to nature's overture; human music had no place here.

He was surprised to see so many people out walking their dogs and envisaged, being the only one without a dog at his side and in spite of his walking boots, he stuck out like a sore thumb. He smiled politely at everyone he passed whilst fastidiously ignoring their four-legged companions. Granted, he was much less nervous around dogs these days, but even with Will's mutts, there were moments when he was certain one of them was set to rip a chunk out of him, apart from Kenny—the biggest and, allegedly, least friendly of the six—who had taken an instant shine to Gray, and he to Kenny.

"Ouch! What..." A sharp bang on the calves made Gray's knees buckle, and he tumbled forward, grabbing a tree trunk to steady himself. When he turned back to see what had hit him, he laughed in amazement.

"Hello, mate!" Almost as if his thoughts had conjured him into being, there was Kenny. Hobbling a little, Gray greeted the big dog on wheels and glanced through the trees, spotting the rest of the pack heading their way, with Will, in his postie's uniform and wellies, trailing behind, his focus on his phone.

Gray sent him a text message—*nice togs!*—stifling his laughter at Will's confused frown, but as always, Will caught on quickly, and looked up and smiled. Gray smiled back, blushing at the fluttery feeling Will's presence evoked.

"You're early," Will said when they met at the midpoint.

"So are you," Gray observed and fell into step at Will's side.

"There was hardly anything to go out. What's your excuse?"

"Do I need one?"

Will shrugged with overplayed nonchalance. "You created an expectation. I'm merely offering you the opportunity to fulfil it."

"Oh, you know how it is." Gray played along. "No margin for error with the later train..."

"Leaves on the track?"

Gray's laughter almost concealed the catch in his breath when Will's hand found his, interlocking their fingers. "Leaves, twigs...entire trees in places..."

"Same every March."

"Terrible service," Gray agreed. He glanced sideways at Will's delighted grin. "What?"

"It's still a nice surprise. I like this."

"Me too," Gray admitted, to himself as much as to Will. He sighed, contented. No, more than that. Happy. Hand in hand in the woods with this unconventional man and the company of his motley canine crew, it was easy to let go. Their relationship was still new, the bond still flexible enough for Gray to walk away, not that he intended to. The strengthening emotional connection between them delivered blissful moments that Gray had to consciously grasp to avoid poisoning them by association. He could fall in love with Will if he let himself. He thought he wanted to, but it was hard to push aside his fear.

Perhaps he should follow Kenny's example. Run over by a car and paralysed, wheel-dependent and utterly fearless, the big mixed-breed dog romped ahead of the rest of the pack, weaving at speed between trees, tongue lolling in joy. He paused to sniff at a tree trunk and manoeuvred closer, in his mind cocking his leg and making his mark before he bounded off again.

"Did you figure out what happened to Rob?" Will asked.

"Not exactly."

Kenny hit a raised root and flipped upside down, wheels spinning in the air. Without a second thought, Gray dashed to his aid and got no thanks at all from the dog, who raced off as soon as he was upright. Gray supposed that was thanks enough.

"Remember when that used to freak you out?" Will murmured, his chin heavy on Gray's shoulder.

He smiled at the reminder. At the start, everything Kenny did freaked Gray out—the shuffling around the house and thadumping down the stairs with his back legs dragging behind him, capsizing in the woods, falling into the canal. Even Kenny's hydrotherapy sessions in a doggy lifejacket with a therapist standing by gave Gray palpitations. And while he was caught up in all that worry for nothing, that big old dog had thadumped his way right into Gray's heart.

"We've made good progress, haven't we?" he said.

"For a dog who doesn't like people, and a people who doesn't like dogs, I'd call it outstanding progress."

"Outstanding..." Gray side-stepped, laughing when Will jolted forward at the sudden loss of chin rest. He caught Will's hand and they moved on.

"What did you mean by 'not exactly'?" Will asked.

"With Rob? I got a text from him on the way here—he's at his mum's, which I'd already guessed. He said he'd explain when he gets back."

"You undercover cops and your secretive ways."

"Hmm. Says he with the mysterious bruises on his knees."

"And leet observational skills..."

"You never did explain why you were covered in mud when I called yesterday."

"Fell down a rabbit hole."

"See, this is what happens if you follow rabbits."

Will coughed the word, "Cats."

"A cat hole, then, surely," Gray argued.

"You know absolutely nothing about small mammals, do you?"

"Not true! I can name at least—" Gray tallied in his head "—five different species."

"Prove it."

Gray laughed, no intention of further making a fool of himself when it was a cover for his probing to see how much Will would tell him—no malice intended, just simple curiosity. Will was a risk-taker who often acted with little regard for his own safety if the life of another—animal or human—was at stake. That was who he was, and whilst Gray had no desire to change him, it would take time and significant effort to come to terms with that aspect of their relationship. In the five months they'd been seeing each other, they'd established a good level of trust, and they talked quite freely, although Will omitted the more dangerous elements, and for Gray's benefit. Gray had already lost too many people he loved, but he also acknowledged that his future happiness depended on his willingness to take risks—emotionally as opposed to with his mortality.

Still, exercising a little caution couldn't be a bad thing, particularly as he wasn't the only one doing so; Will's two newest pack members had hung back while the four old paws went tearing off through the trees in pursuit of unseen quarry.

"Damn it." Will let go of Gray's hand. "I bet it's that fox again." He strode away in the direction the dogs had taken, calling back a command to, "Stay there," which could have been for the two newbies or Gray, or both. In any case, the dogs were so close they were leaning against Gray's legs, and Will was no longer in sight.

"Good dogs," Gray said, trying to sound firm and assertive. The larger of the two—an Irish-cream-coloured bull terrier of some kind—gave a brief wag of its tail in response. The other was a scruffy little brown thing with its ears back and its tail curled between its legs; it looked at least as nervous as Gray felt being left in charge. Assuming he had been left in charge, of course; the bull terrier—called Bailey, possibly—was standing guard, square and alert with its nose in the air.

Gray listened hard, trying to interpret the rustling sounds coming from within the trees. The rustling became louder and Kenny reappeared, bouncing his wheels through the undergrowth as he made a beeline for Gray at the same time as another dog materialised from nowhere. For a few seconds, the three big dogs circled each other, the two that weren't Kenny with tails held high, wagging stiffly. Gray noticed Kenny's hackles go up, and then it all kicked off.

"Shit!"

The little dog bolted off down the path. Gray saw it from the corner of his eye, but his attention was on the frenzy of teeth and spit and a racket like hell hounds baying for souls that had him frozen to the spot. He wasn't a dog person; these weren't his dogs, but he had to do something. The question was what.

"Kenny, here!" he shouted, wishing rather than believing that the dog would obey, and he didn't, or not exactly. The command made him pause, and in that split second, the other two locked onto each other in a horrible tumbling, yowling mess. "Kenny!" Gray yelled again. This time he meant it, and the dog came close enough for Gray to grab his collar. He dragged Kenny a few feet away from the other two in case he changed his mind and re-joined the fracas.

It seemed forever before Will arrived, along with someone else, and the pair of them waded straight into the scrap and somehow broke it up. There was blood and a whole lot of foamy saliva, and Gray was shaking so much he could barely keep hold of Kenny.

"Sorry about that," the woman holding the unknown dog panted breathlessly. She'd already clipped a short lead to its collar.

"Not your fault," Will said. It was a relief to see the fight had left even the chilled Will Richards a little ruffled. "Is he OK?"

"I think so. Are yours?"

Will was still checking Bailey over. "He seems to be. How's Kenny?"

It took Gray several seconds to process the question, and several more to act on it. He lightly ran his hand over Kenny's back and visually inspected his head. "His ear's torn."

"Badly?"

Gray shrugged. "I don't think so." The tear was about a quarter of an inch in length and had already stopped bleeding.

Keeping hold of Bailey, Will checked the injury. "Just a nick. A clean with saltwater and he'll be right as rain." He straightened up, still holding Bailey, and made eye contact with the other dog's owner. "I'll give you my mobile number, just in case."

"I'm sure he'll be fine, but I'll give you mine too."

The rest of the dogs had returned from their adventure and were milling around but keeping their distance. In the background, Gray half heard the conversation over his 100-decibel racing pulse. He'd never witnessed a dog fight at close range before, and he hoped he'd never have to again. It was terrifying. Unfortunately, committing to a relationship with a man who insisted on taking in every stray, friendly or otherwise, meant this was probably the first of many, which left Gray with only one option, and his heart would've sunk at the prospect, had it not been bouncing around his chest like a rubber ball.

Soon after, the woman and her dog departed in the opposite direction to Will's house, and Will rounded up the renegades.

"I hope Holly knows her way home," he said breezily, though Gray saw the worried frown. "Poor little girl got used for bait."

That was more than Gray wanted to know.

"At least she got out of the way," Will mused. Understandably, his attention was on getting his dogs home safely—Gray was eager to get there himself—but the silent walk along the canal bank stretched on and on. It was only when they reached the gate to the farmhouse—where Holly was scratching to be let in—that Will looked directly at Gray and did a double-take. "Are you all right? Did you get bitten?"

"No, no. I'm all right." Gray nodded and smiled to back up his mostly true claim.

"You're shaking," Will observed, his worried frown renewed.

"Adrenaline does that," Gray dismissed. He followed Will and the dogs through the gate, closing it behind him, which wasn't easy with his hands so unsteady, but he did it and floated, lightheaded, past Tie's caravan and into the very welcome sanctuary of Will's kitchen.

"Sit down," Will instructed.

"Do you need a hand with Ken—"

"Sit!"

Gray raised his hands in surrender but quickly lowered them to his sides and went to sit at the kitchen table.

"All right. Kettle first..." Will filled it and switched it on, then beckoned to Kenny, who complied immediately. Will's voice dropped to a comforting murmur as he explained what he was doing and why, as if the dog understood every word.

Gray's concentration drifted. He hadn't felt this spaced out since he'd stopped taking drugs, but he caught the phrase 'sweet tea' and smiled. It was his mum's cure-all for everything from a bumped knee to that time a car clipped his back wheel and threw him off his bike. He was obviously made of tough stuff, because he'd escaped serious injury then, too, and the sweet tea had seen off the shock. If his mum had been there after Jean's accident...

"Here you go." A cup of tea appeared in front of him. "I've put sugar in it, OK?"

"Thanks." Gray tried his luck with gripping the handle, but he was still too shaky. He left it for the time being. "I need to talk to you," he said. Will was already on his way out of the room.

"Hold on. Just taking my wellies off."

Gray glanced down at his muddy boots. There was no way he'd manage those laces.

Will returned, made it halfway to the table—"Wheels"—and backtracked to free Kenny from his harness. He gave the rest of the dogs a visual once-over before he sat, with his tea, opposite Gray. "Holly and Monster are holed up in the living room," he explained. "I'm a bit worried."

"It must've given them both quite a fright," Gray reasoned.

"They'll be fine—you know how Monster is. I meant about you needing to talk to me."

"Oh! It's nothing bad. Sorry."

"Phew!" Will rolled his eyes, but his dramatics did little to conceal his genuine relief. He was so laid-back and confident in general, it was easy to overlook his insecurity when it came to interpersonal relationships. Whenever they talked about previous loves, Will was mostly open and honest, until it came to the breaking-up part, which he'd gloss over with humour or change the subject. He'd been hurt badly, more than once, and part of Gray's reluctance at the beginning came from needing to be sure he wouldn't add to that tally.

"We're good," he said. His words prompted a smile from Will that was gratitude and happiness rolled into one and did strange things to Gray's gut. Will had the most gorgeous smile, wide and heartfelt, all sparkly eyes and dimples. Between his looks and his gift of the gab, the investors Will used to sweet-talk would've stood no chance.

Those sparkly eyes widened, the smile became a grin, and Gray realised he was staring with his mouth hanging open. He cleared his throat self-consciously but didn't look away.

"What did you need to talk about?" Will asked.

"It might be wise for you to clue me in on how to stop a dog fight."

Will laughed. "Yeah. I wish I knew."

"You did it."

"I took a chance, stuck my leg between them, which was stupid, especially in shorts, but I'd rather I get hurt than the dogs. Anyway, you were awesome, getting Kenny out of the way."

"That was luck."

"I disagree. You intervened at exactly the right moment—your training kicking in?"

"Training?"

"Police. Stopping a dog fight's no different to breaking up a Saturday-night pub brawl."

"A riot more like..." Gray tried his drink again. He was still dithering a bit, but it was wearing off, and he managed to swallow a mouthful without spilling it or dribbling.

"The other dog wasn't neutered," Will said. "That won't have helped." He sipped his tea and stared into space—no doubt figuring out how to persuade the woman to get her dog seen to. He zoned back in and smiled at Gray. "Any better?"

"Getting there." He blew out a long, quivery breath and diverted his attention to the dogs, all snoozing and none the worse for their adventures.

"So, now the excitement's over, what do you fancy doing today?"

"Sleep?" Gray suggested. He was kidding, although it might take more than a few teaspoons of sugar to keep him conscious once the adrenaline rush had passed.

"We can do that if you like. We've got the place to ourselves." Will's wicked grin made it clear sleep was low on his list of priorities. "Why don't you have a lie-down?" he suggested. "I'll join you after my shower."

7: Reconnecting

"I'M NOT SURE how I feel, coming second to my sister." Lois gave Rob a tight hug and kissed his cheek. "Love the aftershave. What is it?"

"The stuff you bought me for Christmas." Rob hadn't paid any attention to the name.

"Oh, well, that explains it. I have excellent taste."

Rob laughed at Lois's boast, but he had to agree. She was dressed down for the weekend—long baggy sweatshirt, leggings and flat pumps—but Beyoncé had got nothing on her. OK, he was a bit biased. "What d'you fancy doing?" he asked. "We could go to the park..."

"Feed the ducks and play on the swings?" Lois grinned as she looped her arm through his. "I don't mind. It's so nice to see you, Uncle Rob. I've missed you."

He gently squeezed her arm against his side. "Missed you more."

"Have not."

"You don't know that."

"I know everything." Lois strutted, pointing her toes like a proper little madam—the way she used to when she was a five-year-old who really did think she knew everything and would throw the biggest wobbler if she was proved wrong, not that she often was. No tantrums today, though. Just a big beaming smile—Rob imagined he had one to match.

"I'm gonna take you out somewhere special while I'm here," he said. "Belated birthday treat—"

"You don't have to," Lois interjected.

"I want to. Not tonight, though."

"Why? What are you up to tonight?"

"Only the pub. You can tag along if you like."

"On one of your lads' nights out? Think I'll give it a miss, thanks."

"Your loss."

"Dodgy lager and pool followed by an even dodgier kebab..."

"How can you possibly refuse?"

"Like this. No, thank you, Uncle Rob. I'm washing my hair. But you can have one for me."

"I'll hold you to that," Rob said sincerely. His relationship with Lois was back to how it used to be, and that was definitely worthy of celebration.

While they hadn't consciously made the decision to go to the park, they ended up there anyway, bypassing the playground, which was teeming with kids. Another bunch were playing football—Rob and Lois stopped abruptly when the ball flew past their faces. A boy of around seven or eight sprinted after it, puffing and panting, and then back again with the ball tucked under his arm.

"He reminds me of Lu," Lois mused. "How's he doing with his footy?"

"Not bad. His coordination's still all over the place, but he's getting there."

Lois unlinked arms to buy 'duck food' from the vending machine. "I'm surprised you didn't bring him with you."

"He's in school."

She tutted. "Of course. I keep forgetting how old he is. He'll always be four in my head."

"I used to do that with you and Amber. I still tell people you're twenty-one."

"You won't hear me complaining."

"When you're nearly thirty..." Rob teased.

"Hey! I've got another three years yet!" Lois went to bop him on the head with the bag of grubs, but he successfully dodged out of the way—the first time. The second, she hit the target. The bag popped. "Oops!" Giggling, she stretched on tiptoes. "One there," she said and rubbed his head vigorously with her knuckles.

"Watch it, you," Rob warned—not seriously. He was having too much fun to worry whether a few dried grubs had landed in his hair. To be on the safe side, he confiscated the bag and only gave it back when they reached the pond. "Incredible," he said. He'd been coming to this park for thirty-five years, and the pond had always been exactly the same: murky green with a few flowerless water lily plants, a fair bit of rubbish and way too many ducks.

"D'you remember the last time we did this?" Lois asked.

Rob nodded. He remembered it vividly, but he stayed quiet, hoping she'd tell the tale.

"You were home on leave. I used to love that—sitting on the windowsill and watching for your bike. We could hear it from miles away." She smiled up at him. "And then you'd bring us here and let us play for ages, but we knew. Once we'd fed the ducks, it was time to go home." She threw some grubs to the three young drakes paddling patiently, awaiting their reward. "Amber always sobbed her heart out when you went back."

"Did she?" Rob hadn't known that.

"Yeah. Mum had to turn the news off if there was anything about soldiers dying, because Amber would freak. It was weird. She was so little, she shouldn't have understood stuff about war and fighting, but she did, and she was scared you'd be killed."

"Your mum never told me."

"No. She swore me to secrecy, said it would upset you if you knew. But now you're out of the army *and* the police, I guess it doesn't matter anymore." Lois turned to face him and held his gaze. She wasn't breaking the secret; she was sharing it so he could see Amber's perspective.

"Thank you," he said, but the words only half sounded. It felt like there was hot food stuck in his gullet—his guilt for Amber's suffering—and he was pissed off his sister had kept it from him, but what good would it have done to tell him? Short of entirely changing his career path, he couldn't have made it any easier for Amber. Still, he was hopeful he could fix things with her, now he knew where she was coming from.

"So, anyway," Lois turned back to the ducks and threw the rest of the grubs into the water, "you met up with Jess—the last time we came here."

"Yeah." Rob glance over his shoulder at the bench where he and Jess had sat and talked while Lois and Amber had played on the slide. He'd had to abandon the conversation to go and push the girls on the swings. Then they'd fed the ducks, he'd dropped the girls home and gone back to Jess's place for the night.

"She didn't like us much, did she?" Lois asked with a coy smile.

Rob laughed. "She wasn't a fan of kids at all. There was this one time, I reckon you were only about a year old, and I'd promised your mum I'd babysit. It was a couple of weeks after I'd got up the nerve to ask Jess out. Of course, I forgot about the babysitting, so I asked her to come with me. She ditched me for the night—went to the pictures with Andy Jeffries."

"What a cow!"

"I dunno about that. I mean, with Daisy dying and everything, it was a bit insensitive of me to ask in the first place, and we were all right afterwards. Well..." He shrugged. "Sort of all right. We were never girlfriend and boyfriend as far as she was concerned. Are we ready to move on?" He wasn't trying to change the subject. The ducks didn't seem to believe they were out of food, and quite a crowd had gathered on the bank.

Lois linked arms with him again, and they strolled back the long way, past the tennis courts and flowerbeds, pausing to visit the animals. There was no way they were the same ones as had been there when Rob was a kid, or even when Lois was little, yet there had always been the same combination of rabbits, guinea pigs, finches and peacocks, and they watched for a long time, hoping the peacock would display his tail. He wasn't in a showing-off mood, though, and all too soon, they were passing the playground once more.

"Guess I'm too big for the swings now," Lois said with an airy sigh. "Being *nearly thirty* and all."

"You took that to heart, eh?" Rob glanced sideways at her, and she turned up her nose. "How old d'you think it makes me feel?"

"You're not old," Lois argued.

"Hmm. You haven't met Travis, have you?"

"Zoë's fiancé?"

"Yeah. Nice guy."

"But you don't like him."

Rob weighed it up, as he'd been doing ever since Zoë and Travis got together. "I don't *not* like him. It's tricky, you know?"

"Yeah, it must be." Lois frowned, briefly lost in her thoughts. "You still get to see Lu a lot, though?"

"Not as much as I'd like, but I think that'll change now I'm my own boss. I'm a bit of a dope, really. If I'd thought about it, I could've left it a couple of weeks, come up for the spring break and brought Lu—assuming the mighty Travis isn't jetting them off to the Maldives." Postponing his trip hadn't even occurred to Rob, because he was still in the salaried job mindset of 'being on leave'. "I'm up again in three weeks, anyway, for Josh's fortieth birthday party."

"You could bring Lucas with you then," Lois suggested.

"And get your nan to babysit?"

"Or me."

"You?" Rob asked in disbelief.

"Yes, me! Don't you trust me?"

"Of course I trust you. I just figured you weren't really...the babysitting kind."

"I babysit Leila every week while Amber's at salsa."

"I stand corrected."

"Too right. Just because I'm a career woman..." Lois grumbled.

Rob was pretty sure she was faking her disgruntlement. In case she wasn't, he said, "Sorry. I shouldn't have assumed."

Lois held her scowl a little longer but then relented. "No, it was a logical assumption to make. Jess thought I was nuts when I told her I wanted kids at some point—most of my uni mates thought so too—and now Amber's got Leila..."

"You're broody," Rob said with a grin.

Lois shook her head, laughing at herself. "Just you wait—you'll see. Guaranteed, within the year, you'll be remarried and giving Lucas a baby brother or sister."

"I doubt it, unless you've got someone in mind for me."

"You're not seeing anyone?"

"Nope."

"Have you been looking?"

"Not really." He'd been cramming in the overtime to get a bit of extra money in the bank, which hadn't left much opportunity for looking, but since the divorce, he wasn't interested. Apart from Naomi Silvestri. He'd found her attractive the first time they'd met, but she was a witness for the prosecution against the Berringers, so it was a no-go, or it had been. Whatever, he hadn't seen or heard from her since Frederick Berringer's remand hearing.

"I think you were right about Jess, by the way," Lois said. Rob sensed a consolation coming.

"In what way?"

"Why she was anti-kids. It was as much about losing her little sister as being a career woman." Lois leaned her head on Rob's arm and sighed. "I miss her."

"Yeah, me too."

"She was fun to work with. I learnt so much. And she used her contacts to find me a job—the legit ones, I should point out."

Rob didn't comment. There was no need for Lois to know the SIU had continued watching her after Jess had died, but he wouldn't lie to her if she asked.

"Do you still love her?"

That was marginally better, he supposed, and he'd been expecting it. "Yeah, but not like when I was younger and an idiot."

"An idiot? Not my Uncle Rob?" Lois's tone was jokey but also a bit defensive.

"Oh, yeah, your Uncle Rob. Mind you, I wasn't the only one. Most of us lads had a crush on her at some point or another, although she was pretty intimidating."

"How do you mean?"

"How to explain... She was a bit snobby and sarcastic. I didn't blame her, with a bunch of spotty morons ogling her all the time. She was just stunning, Lo, and clever—unobtainable, really—so, when she said yes, she'd go out with me, it was like getting pole position on the starting grid."

Lois shoved him in the side. "A woman isn't a prize to be won!"

"Fair comment." He'd deserved that and decided to nip the conversation in the bud before he dug himself a deeper hole by admitting that when Jess had 'dumped' him, he'd accused her of leading him on. It was only when Josh had given him an earful—which was brutal but what he'd needed to hear—that he'd accepted he'd misread the signals and concocted more than was there.

After that, Rob and Jess hardly saw each other from one year to the next, but the chemistry had remained as potent as ever—even that last time, when Rob had been laying the foundations for the sting operation. Of course he'd still cared, and he'd hated the deception, but the infatuation, his belief he'd been in love, was a thing of the past.

"What about you?" he asked. "Any romance in your life?"

Lois laughed. "No, and I intend to keep it that way."

Rob patted her hand. "Wise girl. I mean woman," he corrected all by himself, although it wasn't sexism this time. She'd always be his little niece, and he'd kill to protect her. Amber too.

They reached Lois's apartment block, and she stepped around him to open the door. "Are you coming in for a coffee?"

"No, thanks, but can we take a rain check?"

"Sure."

"Cheers. I'm gonna head back, give your nan a hand with whatever's on her list of tasks for the day."

"Saturday..." Lois pursed her lips in contemplation. "Beds and bathroom."

Rob laughed. "I'll report back—let you know if you're right."

"I am," Lois asserted smugly. "I'd lay money on it."

"Yeah? How much?"

"Let's see... Loser buys the next bag of duck food?"

"You're on," Rob said. They shook on it and hugged again. "Thanks for this afternoon."

"No, thank you. It's been fun, plus you saved me from the huge pile of paperwork hogging my sofa."

"It's the weekend."

"Hypocrite much?"

"Right, that's it. I don't have to stay here and take your insults." Rob moved off backwards. "Let me know what evenings you're free and we'll go for dinner or something."

"Will do." She waved, and he waved back, watching to make sure she was safely inside before he jogged to his mum's place, chuckling to himself at the line full of bed linen wafting in the back garden and almost choking on his laughter when his mum appeared at the top of the stairs with a spray bottle of bathroom cleaner in her pink-rubber-gloved hands.

She frowned suspiciously. "What's funny?"

"Nothing, Mum. I'll do that for you if you like."

"For me?"

"You know what I mean."

"Hmm. Well, anyway, you're too late." She disappeared from view.

"Will that washing be dry?"

"Not yet. A cup of coffee would be nice, though."

"OK." Rob went through to the kitchen and prepared the coffee maker, waving at Harvey through the back window. He was planting bulbs, with Linford's 'assistance', which involved a lot of pouncing and dashing around in circles, followed by a bit of digging, a telling-off, and more dashing around in circles.

Rob's regret for not bringing Lucas resurfaced. Lucas loved dogs and had been pestering for one for a while. Zoë refused on the basis there was no-one home during the day, except that wasn't true. Travis worked from home more often than not, but for once, Rob wasn't going to hold it against him. A dog was a big responsibility and would put an end to Travis's impromptu family weekends away.

On second thoughts, a bit of gentle encouragement... He took a couple of photos with his phone and emailed them to Zoë. She wouldn't thank him for it.

It was only after he'd sent the email that Rob noticed he'd missed a few calls while he'd been at the park. He hadn't felt his phone vibrate.

"Yeah, that might help." He'd forgotten to turn on notifications when he'd run through the setup but did so before checking the call log: three missed calls and a voicemail. Rob deleted the voicemail without listening to it. Whatever Jock had to say, he wasn't interested.

8: Feasting

GRAY MANAGED TO swallow a few more mouthfuls of tea before the sweetness made him shudder; he tipped the rest down the sink. On the plus side, he was no longer shaking and got his boots off with relative ease. Leaving them in the hallway, next to Will's wellies, he went upstairs to the bedroom. He was not alone.

"Pick a side, Benj." Gray tentatively shuffled across the mattress, under the false premise that he could claim the space, and instead ended up lying diagonally with his legs on the bed and his body hanging off the edge. Through the open door, he saw Will emerge from the bathroom with towels wrapped around his lower body and his head, the rest of him shimmering with water droplets. He stopped in the bedroom doorway and smiled.

"You made it."

"I did. There's a rabbit in your bed."

Will bent forward, letting the towel drop from his head into his hands, and rubbed briskly at his hair. "You're not talking about sex toys again, are you?"

Gray laughed. "A rabbit, Will. Really?"

Will straightened up with a grin. "I'm told they're very satisfying."

"I'm sure they are," Gray agreed distractedly. Will had dispensed with both towels and held his arms out in a wide, unavoidably naked shrug. "What?" Gray asked.

"Am I getting dressed, or are you stripping off?"

"You choose," Gray suggested breezily. From where he was lying, Will's preference was perfectly clear—getting clearer by the second—but there was still a large white lop-eared bunny in the way.

"Come on, Benj, off you get." Will knelt on the edge of the bed, scooped the poor creature from his comfy resting place and set him on the floor.

"Aw. We could've worked around him," Gray said, although his guilt for Benjy's eviction was short-lived, lasting only as long as it took to get his fingers in Will's tea-tree-scented tangle of blonde-brown hair. The warmth of Will's damp skin permeating Gray's clothes was an instant trip switch for his arousal.

"I'm going to the barber's this week," Will murmured against Gray's lips.

"So you keep saying."

"Just a trim."

"Hmm-hmm..."

"You're not stripping off."

"No hands."

Will moved away, or tried to, but Gray grabbed his head and pulled him back in, taking control of the kisses. Will didn't resist, instead changing tactics. He unfastened Gray's jeans and pushed them down as far as he could. Gray kicked them off the rest of the way, sat up briefly to remove his socks and then whipped his shirt over his head.

"Better?" He hardly got the word out before his yelp of surprise at the coldness of Will's wet hair against his chest. He braced in preparation for what he knew would follow. Will's teeth clamped onto Gray's nipple and tugged lightly, pulling the surrounding skin taut while Gray held his breath so he didn't vocalise his response. He'd not yet decided if it was one of pain or pleasure.

That was only the beginning; Will attended to Gray's body as if it were a multi-course feast—a lick here, a nibble there—leaving virtually no spot untouched by lips, teeth or tongue. It always progressed the same way, and more than once, Gray had quipped, 'I thought you didn't eat meat,' but he wasn't feeling playful today. Will's touch, combined with the post-adrenaline comedown, left him both hyper-sensitive and in a state of deep relaxation; the paradox was like jet fuel to his libido.

"Can you, err..." Gray formed the phrase *cut to the chase* in his mind. He couldn't say that.

"Get on with it?" Will guessed. He reached Gray's belly button and circled it with the tip of his tongue.

"Well...yeah, basically."

"Not a problem."

Gray clamped his lips between his teeth and studied the ceiling. There were times Will's perpetual agreeableness irritated him. Like now.

"Don't you care?" he asked. It was an excellent example of cutting one's nose off to spite one's face, or one's penis to spite one's groin, seeing as Will had acted decisively but had to release him to answer.

"About?"

"Me hurrying you along."

Will shrugged and went back to it, although really, he'd only skipped a few courses. He was certainly making the most of the dessert, so to speak, interspersing long, slow sucks with licks and nips, nudging Gray closer to the edge but not quite close enough for him to go over.

"It's not an ice cream," Gray muttered.

"Nope. It's better," Will mumbled with his mouth mostly full. Gray drew breath to protest further, but changed his mind. Two could play at that game.

Without warning, he rolled sideways, taking Will by surprise, and pushed him onto his back. "Your turn," he said.

"OK."

"No. Not OK."

"It's not?"

"No."

Will looked hurt, and Gray partly rescinded. "I mean, it is...normally."

"You're bored," Will stated.

"I'm not. But I'm craving a bit more...something today."

"You're jonesing for adrenaline."

Gray raised his eyebrows. "Did you make that up?"

"Nope. I get it all the time when I'm surfing, especially if I screw up. What you want is something...a bit more...like this?" In a flash, Gray was flat on his back again, and Will was on top of him, kissing him so hard his head submerged into the pillows. He tugged the corner of one and threw it on the floor—remembering Benjy after the event. Lifting, with the intention of checking he hadn't accidentally suffocated a rabbit, Gray gasped and stopped breathing. Will's mouth clamped to his neck. *I'm too old for hickies...oh, so what? I own polo necks.*

The weight of Will's body, coupled with his hard rutting, made it virtually impossible for Gray to move, which was for the best. He was teetering on the edge again, and he still wanted more. With difficulty, he slid his knee up between Will's thighs, which gave him enough leverage to roll them onto their sides. They both reached down at the same time, firmly grasping each other.

"Don't you want a turn?" Gray asked.

"Yeah, but..." Will's breathing juddered.

"Next time..." Gray increased his speed, smiling as Will's body went rigid, his erection swelling in Gray's fist as ejaculate like rapid-cool lava hit Gray's abdomen, triggering his own orgasm that left him jolting with aftershocks for several minutes after. It had definitely been worth the risk to speak up, not that it was much of one when Will was so easy-going—about most things. Certainly worth pushing a bit further...

"Can we go out for dinner?"

Will opened his mouth to respond. It would've been a refusal, Gray knew, so he pressed on while he had the advantage.

"The food last night was excellent, but I didn't exactly get a chance to appreciate it."

"I'm skint, Gray."

"I'll pay."

"But—"

"I'd be happy to."

Will propped up on one elbow and studied him awhile. "You're changing it *all* up today, huh?" His tone had switched from defensive to amenable, neutralising potential dissent. It was an impressive tool in his professional negotiation skill set, but Gray was growing wise to it. Next would come the redirect. "What did you have to eat?"

"Mock-fish Thai curry and jasmine rice. I know what you're doing."

"Not steak?"

"I don't always have steak," Gray argued. In fact, he couldn't remember the last time he'd eaten steak. It had become a bit of a hobby, trying to find restaurants that served good vegetarian or, better still, vegan food for future dates, such as he and Will went any further afield than the local pub. Between what Will sent to Suzannah's mum and however much he 'donated to animal welfare', he rarely had funds to spare, whereas Gray was in the privileged position of being able to say 'it's only money'. He didn't care if it was always on him—there were so many other things Will contributed to their relationship—but Will did care.

"What's the occasion?"

"I just want to take you out to dinner."

"For no reason?"

"It's my mum's birthday."

"Is it?" Will asked doubtfully.

"On Monday." And not really an 'occasion'.

"Did you send a card?"

"Yeah, and a gift voucher." For cruelty-free cosmetics—not the gift he'd have chosen before he met Will. "I almost didn't bother."

"Do you usually?"

"Every year. And every year, I go through the same argument in my head. It's not as if I expect her undying gratitude. I'd settle for knowing my cards get there, but she doesn't even mention them to Becky. She could put them straight in the bin for all I know."

Will bent to kiss Gray's shoulder. "You're a good son."

"Debatable," Gray said. He appreciated the support, even if there was an ulterior motive, but he hadn't lost sight of his objective. He shuffled closer— so close their noses were touching. "I want to buy you dinner. Is that so bad?"

Will kept his poker face, but the emotions played out in and around his eyes— amusement, a little bit of admiration—"I need to get me some new tactics."

Gray laughed. "You really do."

—finally settling on submission. "OK."

"And for you to be happy about it," Gray added.

"So many demands," Will lamented with an overly weary sigh. Gray gave him a shove, and he fell back, laughing. "I can do that."

"Good." Gray closed his eyes, wondering how long he could bear to lie there, naked and sullied. It was such a peaceful afternoon, not that it would've mattered if the dogs were going loopy, or Tie was trooping in and out. The farmhouse was one big, rustic chill-out zone. Even so... "Are you planning on washing those towels?"

"I wasn't. Why? Ah. I'll get some tissue. Be right back."

Will sprang up from the bed far too energetically for one in a post-coital state and padded away to the bathroom. A moment later, the toilet flushed, but Gray didn't hear him coming back over the din of several sets of paws thumping their way up the stairs. A length of loo roll fluttered down onto Gray's belly; he did the fastest clean-up ever and yanked the duvet over him in the nick of time, grunting as Fido landed on his midriff.

"God, you're heavy," he spluttered, rolling his head from side to side in an effort to avoid Doris's tongue-based display of adoration. Meanwhile, Kenny yapped at the bottom of the stairs.

"At least they waited until we were done," Will said. "Are we staying up here for now?"

With no other body movement capability, Gray stuck up a thumb. Will left again, returning a moment later with Kenny. He set him down on the bed and slid in next to Gray.

"Did you just carry him up here naked?"

"He's always naked."

"I meant you, you..."

Will grinned.

"And if Tie had come in?"

"He's not here. Anyway, he's seen it all before."

"Thanks for the reminder."

"He wouldn't care. We could be watching TV starkers and he wouldn't notice."

"I'll take your word for it. Where is he, by the way? Releasing goldfish into a river somewhere?" Will and Tie's most recent campaign had brought down a guy selling goldfish and other animals as live food.

"We didn't release them into a river. They went to—"

"A safe tank?" Gray suggested, already chuckling at his own joke. "You know? Like a safe house."

Will turned his face away. "I'm not telling you anything anymore."

"The piscine witness protection programme..."

"Mock all you like. We put the guy away, didn't we?"

"You did," Gray agreed. In the continued absence of mobility, he sought out Will's hand and lifted it to kiss it.

"Watch it or I'll start thinking you approve."

"I do, most of the time. But I don't much fancy the idea of spending every Monday afternoon visiting you in prison."

"Why Monday?"

"Whatever day. You know what I mean."

"You worry too much, Gray. Most of what we do is legal."

"Such as?"

Will flashed him a grin and winked. "So, what time are we heading out for dinner?"

"Give me one example."

"Do I need to dress up?"

"Just one."

Will rubbed his chin. "I should shave..."

"Where did you say Tie was again?"

"Community service. I'm gonna go shave." Will was gone before Gray could claim the victory. Kenny immediately shifted into Will's space and rested his chin on Gray's chest, peering at him with sad brown eyes.

"Don't worry," Gray whispered, stroking Kenny with one hand and Fido with the other—and pretending he hadn't noticed Will come back into the room. "If it comes to it, we can all look after each other."

Will left again with the towels and without a word.

Gray's legs were going to sleep, and the rest of him wasn't far behind. He let his eyes close and his thoughts take over. They went straight to his mum and, by extension, Will's mum. On Mothering Sunday, he'd gone with Will to visit his mum's grave and somehow—the tears had a lot to answer for—agreed to reciprocate the visit at some yet-to-be-determined point in the future. That was two weeks ago, and he'd been waiting ever since for Will to bring it up again. He'd half hoped the conversation would veer that way earlier, because unless Will pushed for it—which was only slightly more likely than him turning carnivore—it wouldn't happen.

Unfortunately, thinking about his mum had Gray so worked up that he was able to truthfully answer no, he hadn't fallen asleep, when Will returned from the bathroom clean-shaven and with his hair neatly tied back.

"I take it you're not getting back in?"

Will eyed the abundance of dogs.

"Your own fault for letting them on the bed in the first place." Gray attempted to extract himself from under Fido, getting one foot on the floor.

"Don't hear you complaining."

"Err..."

"Usually," Will amended. He collected boxers from a drawer, socks from another. "What time do you want to leave?"

Gray shuffled on his bottom, freeing his other leg, and sat up. He checked the time, surprised to discover it was almost half past four. Saturdays always went far too fast. "When we're ready?" he suggested. The sooner they left, the sooner they could get back for a pint in the local pub, or even have an early night.

"Works for me." Will perched on the end of the bed to put on his socks. Gray gathered his clothes from the floor and got dressed, watching out of the corner of his eye as Will did the same—the watching and the dressing—both fighting a smile and then giving up when their paths crossed. Will put his arms around Gray's waist. "I could get used to this."

"I already am." Gray kissed him and edged past to collect the pair of ordinary boots he'd stowed in the wardrobe.

"I'll go sort dinner for this lot," Will said on his way out of the room.

"OK. You want me to bring Kenny down?"

"If you don't mind."

"Not a problem," Gray called after him.

"Hush, you."

Laughing, Gray beckoned Kenny to the edge of the bed and scooped him up—one arm around his chest, the other around his back end—the way Will had shown him months ago and which was now second nature. He carried Kenny downstairs to the kitchen, where the rest of the dogs were already eating. Will was at the hutch, filling the guinea pigs' food bowls. Gray lowered Kenny to the floor; the dog shot off as soon as his front legs touched down, his back end landing with a thump that made Gray cringe.

Will closed the hutch and frowned, nose wrinkled in thought as he stared out of the window. "I'll leave the chickens. Tie should be back before it goes dark. Are you ready?"

"Yep."

9: Call of Duty

ROB WAS ALMOST grinding his teeth in anticipation by the time he and his mum were done in the kitchen. He carried the pan of curry chicken over to the table and put it down as he sat. His mum arrived with the flat breads, shouted Harvey and moved the curry out of Rob's reach.

"Aw, Mum..."

"It's not all for you."

"But it's too far away."

"You've got long arms. *Harvey!*"

"I heard you the first time." Harvey closed the back door on his way in and made a speedy stop at the kitchen sink to wash his hands.

"The dog, Harvey..." The poor guy barely got his bum on the seat. With a gruff grunt, he pushed his chair back and glared under the table. Linford got up and skulked off to his bed. Harvey pulled his chair in again and looked over the array of food appreciatively.

Rob watched on, hawk-like, vaguely aware of his phone vibrating in his pocket and with no intention of answering. It was a definite no-no at mealtimes in his mum's house, and in any case was probably only Jock. Right at that moment, all Rob cared about was his mum's curry chicken.

"Most of the seedlings are in now," Harvey said. He carefully scooped with the ladle and waited for it to stop dripping before he moved it to Rob's mum's plate. "If the weather holds, I'll get the rest out tomorrow."

"Did you remember the canes for the sweet peas?"

Rob followed the empty ladle's progress back to the bowl.

"I'll do those tomorrow."

Down it went, scoop, up...

"You forgot, you mean?"

"I wanted to get everything into the ground first."

A piece of chicken tumbled over the edge and landed with a splat. Harvey frowned at it.

"Come on, I'm starving here, man," Rob complained, to which Harvey chuckled and dragged it out a *little bit* longer.

At last, a mound of hot, spicy chicken and chickpeas landed dead centre of Rob's plate; he had to sit on his hands to stop himself from digging straight in. He was virtually drowning on his own saliva, but Harvey didn't have any food on his plate yet. Fond as Rob was of the guy, if he didn't get a move on...

"For goodness' sake, Robert, turn off that phone."

"Sorry, Mum." He took it out, switched it to silent, noted the most recent missed call was from Zoë, not Jock, and put it back in his pocket. Nothing was coming between him and that curry, and as soon as Harvey was loaded up, Rob impolitely grabbed a couple of flat breads, scooped up as much curry as he could and crammed it into his mouth without blowing on it or even checking whether it needed to be blown on. It was so hot it made his eyes water. He put up with it, groaning in pleasure at the delicious sweet-spicy flavours mingling in his mouth.

"Could you pass the bread, please, Harvey?" Rob's mum requested with a stern glare in Rob's direction, the impact of which was diluted by her obvious delight that he was enjoying her cooking so much. As if that would ever change.

"Delicious," he mumbled, holding his hand in front of his mouth. She raised an eyebrow in disapproval. He reloaded his bread, greedily eyeing the pan to check there was plenty left for a second helping. After that, he ate and half listened to the conversation about bedding plants, quite sure if he keeled over right then, he'd die the happiest man alive. Certainly the fullest.

"No leftovers for supper tonight," his mum laughed, removing the scraped-empty pan after Rob's third helping. "You want dessert too, I suppose?"

"I wouldn't say no," he answered with a grin. He got up to help, but she shooed him back to the table. Harvey gave him a knowing nod.

"So, how's life treating you these days, young Robert?"

"Not bad, thanks, Harvey. How about you? You're looking well."

"Ah, you know..." Harvey nodded, but his usual wide smile was missing. He leaned closer and said, "Prostate, you know?"

Rob frowned, not sure if he'd interpreted correctly and hoping he hadn't.

"Cancer," Harvey confirmed.

Rob's pulse rate shot up. "Sorry to hear that." His voice didn't sound like it was coming from him.

"It's common in men of my age. And they can treat it."

"Yeah?" Rob poured a glass of juice, avoiding eye contact. He was lucky. He'd known relatively few people who'd been diagnosed with cancer. Not so luckily, all of them had died from the disease, but that didn't mean it was a guaranteed death sentence. He just needed to keep it in perspective.

"Lois has a copy of my will," Harvey finished as Rob's mum returned with three dishes topped by mounds of white fluff. Lemon meringue pie—Rob's favourite—which seemed a bit frivolous in the aftermath of Harvey's news.

"You haven't been telling scare stories again, have you?" She winked at Rob and scowled at Harvey.

"Cancer is scary," Harvey argued.

"Ignore his rubbish." Rob's mum set his dessert dish in front of him and kissed his head. He smiled up at her, appreciating her attempt to make light of Harvey's doom and gloom. The man was right. Cancer was terrifying, but, as Rob's mum had pointed out the night he'd broken down over Jess, so was riding a motorbike and he did that voluntarily.

"I made that especially for you..."

"Sorry, I was miles away." Rob put a roadblock on his trip to Miseryville and tucked in; within two spoonfuls, he was well on his way back to normal operations, the only trouble being it went down too quickly. "That was spot on, Mum."

"There's more."

Rob rubbed his bloated belly. "Can I save it till later? I'm stuffed."

"If I don't get to it first," Harvey said.

"Don't you dare!" Rob's mum admonished. "I'll cover it and leave it in the fridge for you, Rob."

"Favouritism..."

"If you want it—"

"No, no. It's all yours." With a firm pat, more of a lean, on Rob's shoulder, Harvey heaved to his feet and left the room, whistling Linford on his way to the front door.

"Thanks, Mum," Rob said.

"Always a pleasure cooking for you."

Between them, they cleared the table, and Rob got a good start on washing the dishes before his mum noticed. She kept shoving him with her hip, but he refused to surrender his position in front of the sink, and she eventually gave up in favour of making a pot of coffee. With all the dishes dried and put away, Rob stepped out onto the patio. His mum frowned at him by way of asking what he was up to.

"Returning Zoë's call. That's who phoned before."

"I hope everything's all right."

"She'll have forgotten I'm up here. I'm sure it's fine." In case it wasn't, Rob pulled the door to and moved a few feet away before he made the call. "Alright, Zo?"

"Hey, Rob. Having a good break?"

"Give me a couple more days and I'll let you know."

Zoë laughed. "Like that, is it?"

"I haven't had much chance to chill yet. Anyway, you called?"

"I did. Someone came to the house asking for you."

"Who?"

"No idea. He didn't say."

"Didn't or wouldn't?"

"I'm not sure I asked."

"OK." Rob always asked, but then he was a copper. Ex-copper. "Did he say anything else?"

"He asked if you were in. I told him you weren't but I'd pass on a message. He said to let you know he was disappointed you weren't in."

"Not a debt collector, then," Rob thought aloud.

"I didn't realise you were struggling."

"I'm not. I'm running through the possibilities."

"If we need to rethink the maintenance payments..."

"I'd tell you, I promise, but thanks. Did you get a good look at him?"

"I did. He had scars—a lot of them—all over his face, wide cheeks, broken nose... I know it's stereotyping, but he looked like a squaddie."

She was bang on the money with both the description and the career. It was Jock again, which lent a different meaning to 'disappointed you weren't in'. Rob wasn't happy Jock had involved Zoë.

"Who is he?" she asked.

"REME. Same bloke as rang you yesterday."

"Sorry?" The second syllable was a high-pitched squeak. She didn't know what he was talking about.

"He called me last night, said he got my number from you."

"Err, no!" And now she was pissed off. "The only call I received yesterday was from Gray to say you'd left your phone behind. I take it you've spoken to him?"

"I ordered a replacement. I didn't realise he'd picked it up."

"Apart from that, no-one called. Even if they had, I wouldn't give out your number."

"I did think that."

"Yet you believed the guy?"

"No—I'm sorry, Zo. He caught me on my way out, so I didn't give it much thought—I didn't get to my leaving do, by the way."

"Because of Moonface?"

"Ha, yeah." Funny she'd called him that. It was the same name Rob had used whenever Jock gave him shit, which was often. He wasn't surprised Jock had gone this far, but it was Tonka's show, and he hadn't expected heavy-handed tactics from her. "I'll give him a call now. I wouldn't mind but he knows we're divorced. He's a pain in the arse."

"Rob, if there's something going on—"

"Nothing you need to worry about." He hoped. "I'll let you go. Love to Lu."

"Yeah, same to you and yours."

"Take care, Zo." Rob hung up. "Might as well get this over with." He found Jock's number and made the call. It was answered right away. "Jock. It's Rob."

"About fucking time. Been calling you all day."

"Yeah, I've been busy. Listen—"

"You told her to do one, didn't you?"

"Who?"

"Tonka."

"Never mind that. How did you get my number?"

"I told you, your missus—"

"No, she didn't. Who gave it to you?"

"A copper at your nick. He mistook me for one of your colleagues. I wasn't going to correct him."

Rob clenched his free hand into a fist and pressed his knuckles to the brick wall until he felt it. "And Zoë's address? He gave you that too, did he?"

"Nah. It's on your army record."

Of course it was, because Rob hadn't updated it.

Jock pressed on. "What happened with Tonka?"

"I told her I couldn't help."

"Help?"

"With Ethan."

"What the fuck are you talking about?"

"He's being released, isn't he?"

"Not that I've heard. Is that what she told you?"

"She said…" Rob paused, only for a second. He hated Jock, and for good reason, but when they were serving together, Rob had trusted him as much as he'd trusted Tonka or Bish, or even Ethan, to have his back. And he still trusted him. "She said she'd found someone who could clear Ethan's record before his release date—no medical or criminal history, give him a clean slate."

"Aww, what a lovely bedtime story," Jock said, sickly sweet. "I've got another one to tell you if you're into fairy tales. You didn't fall for it, did you, Shaz?"

"Fuck you," Rob muttered, but there was no venom behind it. "Right, your turn."

"Yeah. Well, as it happens, me and Bish went down to see Ethan a few weeks back. He didn't mention anything about a new identity or whatever blag Tonka gave you."

"She might not have told him," Rob speculated. "Didn't want to get his hopes up."

"No offence, mate, but that's bollocks. Ethan's been on lockdown. He attacked a nurse or guard or something, so unless they decide he's sane and transfer him to a prison—there's more chance of Bish's arm growing back, in my not-so-humble opinion—that mad bastard's going nowhere."

"Is this a wind-up?"

"Not this time, I swear."

Rob ran his hand over his head, pressing on the tension spots forming. His holiday was quickly turning to shit. "What's going on, Jock?"

"Ain't a clue, mate."

"Did she ask you and Bish for money?"

"Yeah, but without the bull about Ethan, because we'd have seen straight through it. She told us she'd had a tip about a sure investment and wanted to share the good fortune—some property company that buys derelict houses in Eastern Europe, does them up and flogs them for four times what they paid out. They were looking for capital in return for stocks and shares."

"She's not involved in investment, is she?"

"No, but her brother is, which is why me and Bish were ready to hand over our hard-earned dough."

It made less sense the more Rob heard. Tonka was trying to get a large amount of cash together, that much seemed clear, but why hadn't she given him the same spiel as the others? Of course, if she'd known he'd worked for the SIU, it was reasonable she'd assume he knew a thing or two about investment. The fact he knew next to bugger all was by the by. But *none* of his army mates knew about the SIU—he hadn't seen them to tell them and wouldn't have done so, anyway—which meant either she'd found out through other means, or she hadn't wanted him to part with his money in the first place and the whole setup was...what? A means to scam Bish and Jock?

"How much did you give her?" Rob asked.

"Nothing in the end. After you left, she ripped up our cheques, said it wasn't enough without your share and she'd go in on her own."

"She was planning to go through a fund manager," Rob thought aloud.

"What's one of them?"

"Someone who invests on your behalf to spread the risk." And he'd already said too much. "What's your gut feeling?"

"All is not as it seems, Shaz. All is not as it seems."

He could almost see Jock's hideous moon-faced grin. "Yeah, I got that. Do you think she was trying to rip us off?"

"I dunno. Maybe she wants to buy a Lambo for the Kraut—hers and hers matching pair?"

"It's a possibility."

"See, now that *was* a wind-up."

"Likewise," Rob said dryly. He obviously needed to turn down the sarcasm dial on his sense of humour.

"I think she's in bother," Jock said.

"Agreed."

"Looks like you've got your first PI case, then, eh?"

"Yeah, once I'm on my feet, I might consider mates' rates."

"We'll pay you," Jock cut in quickly.

"Jock—"

"Me and Bish already talked it over last night. Well...as long as you're cheaper than two hundred and fifty grand." Jock laughed, and Rob joined in. It wouldn't cost them even a tenth of that, and while it was nice to know money was no object, Rob wasn't sure he wanted to be at Jock's beck and call.

"Before we jump the gun, I need to do some preliminary work—"

"Already one step ahead of you, Shaz. She's gone. The neighbours heard the car—they reckon it was about four, four-fifteen this morning."

"We don't know she's gone for good, though. Let me try talking to her first."

"Yeah, good luck with that."

"Number not recognised?" Rob guessed.

"I can see why you became a dick now. You catch on quick, considering."

"Considering what? That you need my help so it's in your best interests to stop being a knob?" Rob would normally have let it go, but he was stalling for thinking time. He'd heard enough to believe Tonka was having the kind of money trouble that came with threats to life and limb, and he'd have done some digging around with or without the incentive. However, he and Gray had timed the official launch—when the website, phone line and advertising went live—for Rob's scheduled return, and while he'd be a fool to turn down the money, if he agreed to do this, he'd have to cut his holiday short, and he'd miss the opportunity to sort things out with Amber. That was more important to him than getting his business off to a good start. There again, it wasn't just his business.

"Right, Jock, I'm gonna talk to my partner. If he thinks we're ready to take a case, it's a goer. Fifty percent of the fee up front—"

"If it's not a goer?"

"I'll point you towards someone else who might be able to help, which would be a better option for you—a cheaper one, for sure."

"Don't worry about that. You know me and Bish run a security firm, I take it?"

"I didn't."

"Yeah. We've got some big contracts—a couple with pharma companies. And you know how Bish is. He's always had a soft spot for Tonka. Me, I don't give a toss, but Bish is the brains behind this operation, so if it keeps him sweet..."

Jock was worried about Tonka, whatever he said, but he'd never admit it, not to Rob. "OK. I'll be in touch in a couple of days, let you know our decision. How's that?"

"I look forward to it."

10: For Dessert

G RAY AND WILL made it through the starters on mundane small talk, with nothing more contentious than Gray pointing out hummus was among the vegan menu options and then mercilessly mocking Will for choosing it after everything he'd said. For the main course, Will opted for the three-bean chilli with soft tacos and rice while Gray made a second attempt at the mock-fish Thai curry—now he stood some chance of tasting it on the way down. That was when the conversation took a slight nosedive.

"Aaron wants me to go with him to visit Freddie Berringer." Will put it out there like a 'nice wine' bland statement.

Gray stopped mid-chew. Will remained relaxed, or appeared as such, but it was hard to tell. Maybe he believed what he'd said was inconsequential.

"Why?" Gray asked.

Will bobbed his fork from side to side, weighing up. "I say Aaron. It might be Naomi. But if it's Aaron on the day, he won't cope with the security frisk."

"That only explains why they want you there."

"They have unfinished business."

"Berringer's remanded in custody precisely because he'll interfere with witnesses."

"I'm sure Aaron and Naomi are aware of that."

Gray wasn't being intentionally obstructive, or he was a bit. He had yet to fathom the dynamics of Will's relationship—past and present—with Aaron-Naomi. "You'll be monitored," he pointed out.

Will smiled placidly. "You're telling the wrong person. My lips will be firmly sealed for the duration."

"This could jeopardise the prosecution's case."

"Only if we...*they* talk about it. How's the soya and seaweed?"

Message received. Gray cut a piece from his mock-fish, lifting it to his mouth with an unnecessary flourish. He chewed and hummed in pleasure, perhaps more than his meal warranted. "Delicious. How's the chilli?"

"Almost as good as my mum's." Will looked around him, his gaze slowly passing over the wall décor, the paintings, the lighting sconces, and flitting past Gray to take in the same on the other side of the restaurant. "Very upmarket. Expensive?"

"Not overly so." The absence of prices on the menu suggested otherwise, but unless they switched to drinking Champagne, the bill wouldn't be extortionate. "So you're definitely going?"

"I told Aaron I would. Are you advising me not to?"

"It's not my place."

"In your professional opinion," Will pushed.

"I would be very concerned if my key witness visited the defendant in prison. Not only for the witness's safety, but for how the jury will perceive it."

"Like you said, we won't be alone."

"You won't. You need to be careful, Will. Both of you. All of you. When is it?"

"Well, funny thing...I thought you already knew."

"How would I?"

"Friends on the inside?"

"I haven't got..." Gray stopped short of finishing the automatic lie. "I didn't know. Why did you think I did?"

"It's a week on Monday."

"Oh—what I said earlier. Pure coincidence, believe it or not."

"Or an unconscious tell?"

"From you? Unlikely. But if it came to it, I'd spend every Monday afternoon visiting you."

Will grinned. "You say the sweetest things."

"You're easily pleased." Gray tried to keep a straight face against Will's suggestive taco nibbling, then closed his eyes and shook the image from his mind. "On a serious note..." He opened his eyes again; Will gave his full attention. "Don't lay a finger on Berringer—don't even shake the man's hand."

"Not a prob—" Gray raised his eyebrows. Will sighed and stopped being flippant. "Understood," he said.

"Everything all right?" the waiter asked.

"Yes, thanks," Gray responded. The waiter bowed and continued on his way.

Will leaned closer and whispered, "Are we being too loud?"

"I don't think so. They're just giving us our money's worth."

"Do they offer a personal massage with the dessert course?"

Gray laughed. "Now there's an idea."

"You know...I've never been comfortable with these kinds of places. I'd say it was down to social class, but our backgrounds aren't that different. Or they weren't when we were kids."

"We didn't go out for dinner much," Gray agreed, "unless you count fish and chips at the seaside."

"Fish and chips..." Will's expression took on a nostalgic quality. "My uncle used to get them for us after we'd been to the football. We didn't tell my mum."

"Would she have been mad?"

"No. But she'd have felt guilty on our behalf and given Uncle Jim an earful."

"I've always assumed he's veggie too."

"He's pescatarian, which is pointless. If you're going to eat one dead animal, you might as well eat them all."

They'd had this conversation several times before, the most recent being when Gray had brought a selection of goat's cheeses for their Saturday supper and hadn't thought to check whether his choices were from humane farms, never mind whether the rennet was vegetarian. It was a foolish mistake, but he only made it the once. He wasn't sure when it had happened, because it was more than simple respect for Will's values. Somehow, they'd become Gray's values too. Or perhaps, on an unconscious level, he'd always shared them.

He also understood Will's discomfort with living it up at someone else's expense. It wasn't so long ago it had been beyond Gray's means to dine out whenever he felt like it, when top-class restaurants and hotels were hostile territories where the language and culture were entirely alien.

Thinking back to the night Will had confronted Freddie Berringer, he'd slipped into his former merchant banker role with far greater ease than Gray had ever managed with any of his assumed identities because, contrary to Will's claim, their backgrounds weren't that similar. Will's parents were politically minded, educated people who fully supported their son's endeavours. Gray's parents had essentially left him to fend for himself, and whilst he hadn't earned his wealth, nor asked for it, he sure as hell wasn't going to squirrel it away in favour of living a humble existence of deferred gratification. But it was losing its appeal.

"I shouldn't have made you come here tonight."

"You didn't make me do anything."

"I hit you with it at the optimum moment."

"Yes, you did do that, but I'm enjoying it—the food, the company—it's all good."

"I'm sorry, Will."

"Hey, where's this come from all of a sudden?"

"I was thinking about money. Jean's money. I don't know what to do with it."

"In relation to investment?"

"Some of it is invested, but it's not that. It's...I don't know. Like a poisoned chalice that never empties. I bought a house that feels nothing like home. I've got all these gadgets I use once and put back in their boxes. I get cabs when I could use public transport, eat out instead of cook, force you to come along with me—for what purpose?"

"Because you can?"

"That doesn't mean I should. I could put it to better use, invest in a worthy cause. Look at all the good things you do with your money."

"I've got a daughter and moral obligations. I don't have any choice. But if you'd seen me when I was younger...it was like water running through my fingers. I didn't mean to put you on a guilt trip."

"You didn't. You got me thinking. Do you want dessert or...can we just go and drink good old working-class beer?"

Will laughed, a deep chuckle laced with amusement and so much more. It was like savouring a bite of a rich chocolate torte, and it was all the dessert Gray needed.

"Waiter, can I have the bill, please?"

***

They'd been at Will's local less than half an hour when Gray's phone rang. He frowned at the display. "That's unexpected," he said and hit the green button. "Evening, Rob."

"Alright, Gray? Haven't caught you at a bad time, have I?"

"No..." Gray made eye contact with Will. "You've caught me at a great time, actually. I'm in the pub."

"Fair enough. I won't keep you long, then. We might have our first case."

"Do you know the meaning of the word holiday, Rob?"

"It came looking for me not the other way round. A sort-of mate of mine. Ex-forces. That's why I didn't make it last night—I'll give you the full gory details when I see you—but if you're up for it, we'll be starting this week."

"Shouldn't be too much of a stretch. Is there anything you need me to do now?"

"I don't think so. I only called to check you were OK with it before I said yes."

"I am if you are."

"Good stuff. I'll let you go—I'm off to play pool with the lads."

"Dan and Aitch?"

"Yep." Rob felt the familiar scalp prickling at Gray casually name-dropping Rob's mates as if they were his mates too. "And Josh'll be there to kick my arse again," he added, on safer ground. At least there was good reason for Gray and Josh to be acquainted.

"Is he any good?"

"I'll give you a tip. If he ever challenges you to a game, insist he's designated driver."

Gray laughed. "Noted. I'll see you when you get back."

"You will. It'll be less than two weeks, unfortunately, but I need to take care of a couple of things first. Enjoy your evening."

"You too, Rob. Bye." Gray ended the call and put his phone down on the table.

"Is who any good?" Will asked.

"Sorry?" Gray picked up his drink, exhaling against the beery air and wishing it was cooler. If he'd answered instead of being evasive...in fact, he wasn't sure why he was being evasive, other than that Will had asked a direct question which implied he'd thought the matter was of no consequence. Thanks to Gray's response and the terrific blush accompanying it, Will now knew otherwise, although he wasn't pushing for more information, but it was time Gray actively demonstrated his commitment to their future together.

"Josh," he said.

"OK." Will shrugged. "I didn't realise you had history with the guy, but you don't have to explain."

"It's more than that. Or less... Or maybe it isn't. I'm not in the best place to judge."

"Or making much sense," Will teased lightly. He finished the last inch of his pint and got up. "Another?"

"Please." Gray glugged the rest of his ale—a fair bit more than an inch—and handed the empty glass over.

Warm fuzzies. The beer, on top of a couple of glasses of wine earlier, multiplied Gray's gratitude for the brief reprieve. Will was giving him a choice: change the subject, knowing he wouldn't be pushed for an explanation, or continue his confession.

He watched Will at the bar, chatting with the other punters, smiling, laughing, light touches of palm to forearm or shoulder, such easy interaction, such a charmer. Gray still had moments of uncertainty—was Will stringing him along? Would his honesty be reciprocated? It was impossible to ever know for sure, but it was a gamble Gray was prepared to take. He wanted to tell this man the whole truth and nothing but the truth, so help him.

The bartender beckoned for Will's attention, indicating the logos on the counter mounts. Will pointed at the yellow one, second from the left; the bartender collected a pint glass and began pulling the pump. Will glanced back at Gray and mouthed, "Wheat beer?" Gray nodded his approval. He'd yet to see Will choose a dud.

A couple of minutes later, Will returned to their table, deposited the beer, said, "Little boys' room," and walked off.

"Don't leave me to think about this too long," Gray muttered under his breath, worried he'd lose his nerve before Will came back. Dragging one of the pint glasses closer, he gazed into the cloudy pale liquid. He was partial to *weissbier*. Very partial. As in drink-too-much-too-fast partial. He took a tentative sip and pushed the glass away. Then picked it up again.

"They're keeping at least one wheat beer on permanently," Will said, sliding back into his seat.

"That's dangerous." And great news that had Gray grinning.

Will chuckled. "I thought you'd be pleased."

"You might have to ration it unless you fancy carrying me back to your place every Saturday night."

Will looked him up and down with a smirk. "The idea has a certain appeal."

"Stop it!" Gray ordered, not seriously. Being mentally undressed was not helping his alcohol blush at all. Conversely, it wasn't making it any worse. "I was going to tell you something, remember?"

"Yes, you were. Like I said, you don't have to."

"I'd like to." Perhaps 'like' was the wrong word, but it was right for where they were up to in their relationship. "As long as you're not going to get jealous."

"Me?" Will looked a little affronted.

"Well, the way you are about Naomi and Freddie..."

"Jealousy has nothing to do with it. Anyway, you were saying?"

For all that Gray was curious, he didn't push it. They had plenty of time ahead of them for discovering all of each other's dirty little secrets. "I told you I had Josh under surveillance, didn't I?"

Will nodded and grinned. "While he was on his honeymoon."

"Right, and for a long time before, but that was, err..." Gray fidgeted, rubbing his hands together and then clasping them tightly. "OK, promise you won't laugh."

"Hey, you laughed at me."

"Did I?"

"When I told you I had a crush on him."

"I'm pretty sure I didn't. I was stunned."

"Stunned? I..." Briefly, Will lost focus—replaying events, Gray envisaged. "I thought you were trying not to laugh."

"If I laughed at all, it was at the sheer audacity of him pushing us together when we both..." The heat in his cheeks notched up a couple of degrees.

Will's eyes narrowed. "You too?"

Gray sighed. "Me too, and it wasn't just a crush."

Judging by Will's careful attentiveness, Gray could have skipped past the confession to the explanation, but in for a penny...

"It started out innocently enough, or in relation to Josh, at least. I picked up a fraud case involving a company in his hometown—not because of him, I should add. I had no idea he existed at that point. I'd found out George was my brother years before and never done anything about it. Yes, I'd planned to track him down while I was there, but that would've been the extent of abusing my position. I'd already done the preliminary work on the case and had Josh's name on my persons-of-interest list—he was a friend of one of our targets—but I wasn't aware he and George knew each other.

"I also had no idea how big the fraud operation was, which was foolish at best. I put together a small team to conduct surveillance, go in undercover, and I..." Gray's throat tightened. This was a harder admission than the one he'd set out to make. "It was after the accident, and I was a mess—mentally and physically. I went back to work too soon, and I insisted I was fine, but I wasn't. I was reckless. I didn't protect my team the way I should have, and they were incredible, faultless. Especially

Rob. He hated the case...hated me...I don't blame him. But he did the job, saw it through right to the bitter bloody end."

Gray paused to drink some of his beer and gather his thoughts, all the while aware of Will watching him and waiting. The guy had seemingly infinite patience—one of his greatest yet most frustrating qualities—and would leave Gray to reach his point in his own sweet time. However, he hadn't intentionally sidetracked. He re-centred and forged on.

"It took nearly three years to nail our targets, and I should've been elated the case was over. We could all go home...but home to what? In those three years, I'd lost Jean, grieved for him, and—at the risk of vomiting poetic cliché—discovered my heart wasn't broken beyond repair. I'd developed feelings for Josh, and while I was cut up over never seeing him again, it was also liberating."

"You were healing," Will said.

Gray nodded but didn't answer, caught up in reliving the emotional resurgence of those last few weeks of the case. The nod became a self-conscious headshake and laugh. "I was so relieved the numbness had passed, I was like a kestrel on an updraft, observing without examining too deeply what I was doing."

"Very poetic," Will complimented.

"Not clichéd?" Gray prompted optimistically.

"You're the literature professor. You tell me."

Gray's confession was on the horizon, and he felt OK making it, but sensed Will was trying to divert the conversation. He decided to cut to the chase.

"I was in love with Josh, but, of course, he wasn't in love with me, mostly because he didn't know he had an admirer. It wouldn't have made any difference if he had known. I fell in love with him from afar, which sounds crazy. But when you watch someone's every move, hour after hour, day after day, in company, alone... Like you said, there's something about him."

"Blonde hair, blue eyes..."

Perhaps he'd been wrong about Will feeling uncomfortable, because his expression had turned positively dreamy. Gray dipped a finger in his beer and flicked it at Will's face, making him blink.

"Cheers for that." Laughing, Will dried off on his sleeve. "I can't believe you'd waste an extremely decent wheat beer to make your point."

"Hmm. I could always invest in hair bleach and blue contact lenses," Gray muttered. Will was still laughing. "That wasn't what I meant. I'm not that shallow."

"Shallow?"

"Yes, shallow. There's more to the man than his blonde hair and blue eyes." Gray huffed at Will's continuing amusement at his expense. "OK, I'll admit I find him physically attractive, but it goes beyond that. He's complicated, intelligent, funny, quick-witted, honest—fascinating. *I* was fascinated. I wanted to uncover the real Josh Sandison, get inside his head, pin down his motivations. I *needed* to know if he was involved in the fraud scheme, and that was all it was, at first. But over time, my fascination transformed. It was no longer professional, and I didn't notice it happening. Not until it was too late."

"At least you realised eventually," Will comforted. Gray averted his eyes. "Huh. You kept watching?"

"Worse. I made a move on him."

"Gray!" Will was aghast, and hamming it up, which went some way towards easing Gray's embarrassment, but he wasn't proud of what he'd done. Nor could he honestly blame it on bereavement or the drugs. He had no excuse.

"Obviously, I couldn't just ask him out on a date. He was with George—married even—and he'd have dismissed it as a joke. He'd probably have told me to fuck off. In fact, he did tell me to fuck off on a regular basis, but that was after I...asked him to come and work with my unit as a profiler."

"Very cunning," Will said with way too much admiration.

"Low, is what it was, Will. Low. I'm ashamed."

"Did he fall for it?"

"Hook, line and sinker. He was a damned good profiler too. Anyway, I did own up in the end, and for his benefit. I guess I always knew, deep down, that I didn't stand a chance. It just took a while for my heart to get with the programme. When I told Josh how I felt, he was surprised, which I didn't expect, because he'd already figured out everything else about me. The first time he made me, I was talking to George—a completely innocent conversation, I hasten to add. George intervened in a dog fight, funnily enough, or not funny at all, but interesting it's come up today. He beat up a guy who'd set his dog on someone else's. My colleague went with the ambulance, and I arrested George—he wasn't charged. But that was what we were talking about when Josh saw us."

"What happened to the dogs?"

"The one that did the attacking had to be destroyed—it was very aggressive. The other dog lost a leg, I think, but it made a full recovery."

"Nice one, George."

"Yeah, I've got to say, I prefer your rescue methods to his."

Will sat back and puffed out his chest. He couldn't have looked more proud if he'd tried.

Gray shook his head. "I really shouldn't have told you that."

Will grinned and relaxed again. "I ruined your flow. Please, continue."

"So bossy," Gray muttered playfully. This had been nowhere near as difficult as he'd anticipated. His feelings for Josh hadn't seemed like a burden, yet he felt so much lighter for sharing. "How are we doing on the jealousy front?"

"All clear so far," Will confirmed with a smile of reassurance that appeared to be the genuine article.

"Good because that's not why I wanted to tell you."

"I know. It's the same as me telling you about Shelley and Suzannah. Josh is an important part of your journey."

"Yeah, he is." Gray met Will's gaze and for a moment was lost in it and the wonder of being with someone who understood where he was coming from. "Where was I?"

"The dog fight..."

"Right. A few months after that—you can fill in the blank—"

"Gray Fisher, licensed to stalk?"

Gray sniffed sharply but continued. "This is what I mean about Josh being clever. He noticed a tiny discrepancy in Lambert's will—she was our target and a very close friend of his—and he started poking around. He was interfering with our investigation, so I went to warn him off, and he almost blew my cover. He had me completely sussed from minute one—where I was from, that I was a widower with one sibling—I have no idea how he does it."

"Yet he fell for your con?" Will was right to question it.

"He was suspicious of my intent. He just didn't see it for what it was, and... well, I can't really explain without betraying confidences—"

"Then don't." Will cut him off, and Gray was grateful to be saved from his dilemma. He wanted to share and felt comfortable doing so, but it wasn't his place.

"In conclusion, Josh is a very skilled pool player, according to Rob."

"But can he play poker?"

"It wouldn't surprise me. His poker face is almost as impenetrable as yours—perhaps you could take him on sometime."

Will looked Gray over with the same sultry, bordering on predatory, expression as before. His fingers walked up Gray's thigh. "There's only one man I'm interested in taking on."

Gray caught Will's hand before it crept any closer to places it shouldn't be in public, and grinned. "You say the sweetest things."

"I'm a professional," Will murmured. "Luckily, because you're really not that easy to please."

11: Eight-Ball

"Centre pocket." With the cue extended behind him, Rob leaned back and gave it a measured jolt with his left hand, tapping the white ball into the black. Down it went.

Aitch puffed air loudly and handed his cue to Dan. "This calls for some serious commiseration."

"Agreed. Your round, I believe." Dan grinned. It was Aitch's second defeat in a row, and they'd only played two frames.

"Yeah, all right. Same again?"

"Nothing for me, thanks," Josh said.

"Are you driving?"

"No, but I've got work to do when I get home."

"Fair enough." Aitch collected the empty glasses on his way to the bar.

"You're up next," Dan said, chalking the cue and holding it out to Josh, who waved his hand in dismissal.

"I'm useless at pool when I'm sober."

"Aitch, mate, buy this man another pint."

"Dan!" Josh protested, but Aitch was already ordering it. Josh blinked helplessly at Rob.

"Don't bring me into this," Rob said. "They're sods for it, but while they're getting you hammered—"

"They're leaving you alone," Josh finished, and then shouted, "Rob needs one too, Aitch."

"Oy! I've got to be up at the crack of dawn."

"For?"

"Footy." Rob gave Dan a glib grin and got one back.

"Are you playing?" Josh asked.

"Apparently."

"Oh, well, we're all in the same boat, then."

"You don't play, do you?"

"Not even drunk."

Dan offered Josh the cue again. Reluctantly, he took it and gestured to Rob to break. "Who are we playing tomorrow?"

"The Vets," Dan said.

"What kind of vets?" Rob asked. He took the break, leaving a ball in prime potting position.

"Not your kind. Vets and veterinary nurses from all different surgeries, and they're a decent side—mixed."

Josh paused from lining up his cue and glared at Dan. "Was it necessary to qualify?"

"Huh?"

"They're a decent side *in spite of* having players who aren't men."

"That's not what I said," Dan protested.

"You implied it."

"No, I—"

Josh took his shot with a little too much vigour, which shut Dan up, although the ball rebounded off the pocket. Josh sighed and retreated to his seat.

"I thought George was coming," Dan tried as a neutraliser.

"He is. Actually..." Josh checked his phone. "I wonder where he's got to? He was only dropping Libby off at a friend's. I'll give him a call. Won't be long." Josh went outside.

Rob circled the table, trying to find a decent shot. Josh had left the cue ball against the cushion and touching both a stripe and a solid. Whichever way he went, he was going to foul. "Charlie Davenport still plays for the Lions, I'm guessing?" he asked and took the shot.

"She does," Dan confirmed, the 's' merging with his sharp intake of breath as the cue ball went down. "I reckon you'd get away with taking another." He tilted his head in the direction Josh had gone.

Rob laughed, pretty sure Dan was joking. In the thirty years they'd been friends—and before that when they were sporting enemies—he'd never known the guy to cheat, which begged the question, even though Josh had just come back in, "How d'you get away with having a woman on the team?"

"Short answer? We don't. The FA told us if we didn't lose Charlie from the squad, we'd be disqualified. She offered to leave, but we'd be crap without her. So, we were gonna quit, disband the senior team and just continue with the youth team—under-18s mixed-gender is allowed—but the rest of the league took our side against the FA."

"Including the Anchors." Aitch delivered Josh's and Rob's pints. Both mumbled less than heartfelt thanks.

"Blimey. Who'd've thunk it?" Rob said. The Blue Anchor was a notoriously rough pub that attracted all kinds of rogues, including those from the police station directly opposite, which happened to be Aitch's station.

"Yeah, we're an independent league now." Dan nodded at Josh. "It's your shot, by the way."

Josh glanced around the pub, insinuating the question 'what's the rush?' and he had a point. It was dead for a Saturday evening, or maybe it wasn't. Pubs in London were always chock-a-block, and Rob was out of touch. Nonetheless, Josh got on with it and potted the first ball of the game. He didn't have the same luck with his second and extra shots.

"Still sober, then?" The question came from behind Rob and startled him.

"Alright, George?"

"Rob." They shared a very businesslike handshake. "Everyone OK for a drink?"

"My shout," Aitch said. "What're you having?"

"I'll get..." George started to protest, but Aitch stared at him until he backed down. "Lager, thanks."

Aitch clapped him on the shoulder on his way to the bar.

Rob bent over the table, lining up his next shot as George edged past to reach Josh. He could see them in his peripheral vision and hear them talking—more interrogation than conversation.

"Did you get caught in traffic?" That was an accusation on Josh's part. Rob gently tapped the cue ball, sending it on a slow roll across the table.

"Roadworks on Moss Lane."

One down. Rob changed position. *Far-left pocket.*

"Why didn't you go through town?"

"I thought the back roads would be quicker."

Two down. *Far-right.*

"OK. If you say so."

Three down...and snookered. Rob tried for a rebound, but hit nothing. "Josh, you're up, mate."

Josh nodded to show he'd heard. "You can tell me later," he said to George.

"Tell you what?" George had the puzzled frown to a tee, but he wasn't fooling Rob or Josh, and as soon as Josh's concentration shifted to the pool table, George made eye contact with Rob. It was either beseeching or threatening, the former, hopefully, although it was tricky to tell with George. Outside of Rob's field of vision, a ball dropped and rolled back to the reservoir.

"Damn it."

Josh's cuss gave Rob a welcome excuse to divert his attention back to their game and his opponent's predicament. "Trick shot?"

"If this were a magic wand." Josh waved his cue and then crouched, putting him eye level with the felt. "Impossible." The white teetered on the edge of the pocket, a hair's breadth from the black, with two stripes forming a curved wall.

"Forfeit?" Dan suggested.

Rob pressed his lips together, trying not to laugh at Josh, whose flared nostrils, just visible over the lip of the table, made him look like a basking hippo.

Josh straightened up again and held out his hand for his drink, which George duly delivered and Josh downed more or less in one go. He handed the empty glass back and moved in for the kill. He was right; it was an impossible shot. Still, Rob prepared for defeat. Josh and Dan's one-upmanship was a reassuring constant that had reared its head at every social event, every night out, since the start of high school. Losing a game of pool to their point-scoring was a small price to pay for the privilege of a night in the pub with his best buds.

The loud clack of balls signified, for all his determination, Josh had failed to clear the wall. The white flew upwards, hit the table lip, bounced, and landed some six feet away, directly in Aitch's path. Pints in both hands, he drew to a sudden halt and peered down at the ball. Josh went to retrieve it, mumbling an apology.

"No worries." Aitch followed him back to the pool room.

Josh set the cue ball in the D and stepped away from the table. The remaining three striped balls—he must've potted one by accident—were well spaced, and within minutes, Rob had cleared the table under Josh's watchful scowl.

"Rematch when we've had a couple more pints?" Rob suggested. He heard Dan mutter 'hypocrites'. Josh glowered at him.

"You're on," he said. He handed his cue to George and set off for the Gents', while Rob gave his cue to Dan and went over to join Aitch on the barstools at the end of the room.

"Where's Tash tonight?" Rob asked.

"Working till ten. Overtime for honeymoon spends, she says. She's gonna join us after."

"Good stuff. And are you all set for the wedding?"

"Yeah." Aitch picked up his pint and frowned into it. "I think so." His frown deepened. "I dunno, mate, to be honest."

Rob laughed. "Leaving it to the expert, are you?"

"Yep. We both are."

"Oh?"

"Adele's new company."

Both men looked over at Dan, as if he were accountable for his fiancée's business. He didn't even notice.

"Adele's a wedding planner?" Rob asked. She'd been working in a fitness centre, last he knew.

Aitch nodded. "Weddings, bar mitzvahs, conferences, psychic nights—you name it, she'll event-plan it."

"Shall I break?" Dan suggested.

"Yeah, sure," George said, on his way over to Rob. He leaned in to speak, keeping his voice low. "Can you do me a favour? Don't mention the party to Gray."

"Sure," Rob agreed easily. He doubted it would come up in conversation.

"Josh didn't invite him and Will," George explained. "It's a long story."

"Fair enough."

"Thanks." George darted back to the table in the nick of time and quickly eyed up his shot. Josh returned from the Gents' and joined Rob and Aitch in watching the game. No shots wasted, it was a very efficient frame that lasted less than ten minutes. Dan won and for once kept his gloating to a minimum as he thrust the cue in Josh's direction.

"Someone else can play," Josh said.

"We've all had two games already," Dan argued. "Plus the pool Mafia's just arrived."

Rob glanced over at the bar, where a group of younger men were supping and keeping watch on the pool table.

"In that case, another game it is." Josh took the cue from Dan and strode over to the table, which George had already set up. Josh chalked his cue, his expression dead solemn, whilst George's morphed into a grin. He moved the triangle out of the way and, as Josh was about to break, said, "Go easy on me."

The balls scattered. "Go easy on you... Pfft! You always beat me at pool."

"Not true," George claimed and went on to pot four balls in a row. He missed the fifth and groaned in disappointment. Josh immediately swooped in and systematically potted one ball after another until only four solids and the eight-ball remained.

"Victory is mine!" The wide grin that accompanied Josh's pre-emptive gloat gave Rob a flashback—of the good kind—to nights at the snooker hall with Zoë, before they had Lucas. They were evenly matched, but it was never about winning; it was about doing stuff together. Somewhere down the line, they'd stopped or forgotten how, and they'd blamed each other or Rob's job or Zoë being stuck at home with a baby, when maybe it was because neither of them was prepared to put the effort into their relationship. Or maybe they just weren't compatible anymore.

When Josh and George's game was over—Josh scraped a win in the end—the five of them moved to a table in the main room. Dan bought the next round and came back with a box of dominoes.

"How old are you? Seventy?" Aitch ribbed him but still accepted his tiles. Three games later, he was so set on beating Dan he didn't notice Tash arrive—nor did anyone else, for that matter—until she pushed her way into the space between Aitch and Rob.

"Alright, mate?" Rob greeted her.

"I will be," she said and held her pint aloft. "Cheers." She took a good, long swig and sagged on her stool. "God, that was the shift from hell."

"Yeah?"

"Oh, nothing out of the ordinary," Tash dismissed. "How's your holiday going? Getting plenty of time to relax?"

"Ha, I wish!" Given he'd slept the first ten of the twenty or so hours since he'd arrived, Rob couldn't grumble. He'd spent time with Lois, and he was having a great evening, but it was all the messing around in between that had worn him down and rose to the forefront of his mind whenever his concentration drifted.

"What d'you reckon? Curry? Kebab?" Dan asked, stashing the dominoes away and ignoring Aitch's pleas for 'best of five'.

"We could go to the Turkish place on the high street," Tash suggested. "Aitch has been promising to take me there ever since it opened."

"It opened two years ago," Josh said.

"Yep."

"We're never off at the same time," Aitch justified.

"We are."

"All right. Never off at the same time *and* free of obligatory nights with the family."

"We're not *obliged*, Aitch."

"My vote's with Turkish." George neatly cut off Aitch's wade into hot water.

"Mine too," Josh said.

Dan nodded. "That's four votes. OK with you, Rob?"

"Absolutely." He wasn't going to let on he'd eaten before he came out.

"Turkish it is. I'll—"

"Oy!" Aitch interrupted. "Don't I get a say?" He made a grab for the dominoes, but Dan whipped the box out of his way and got up to return it to the bar staff. Aitch stuck out his bottom lip. "I was gonna suggest we stay for another, give you a chance to catch up." He blinked, martyr-like, at Tash, who took it as a prompt to guzzle the rest of her beer. She set the empty glass down firmly.

"I'm done," she said and rose to her feet. The others followed suit.

"Fine. Whatever..." Aitch muttered, shuffling after them.

"Watch it or I'll bench you for unsportsmanlike behaviour," Dan warned. Aitch curled his lip, but there was no real hostility from either man, and as the six of them left the pub and walked into the town centre, Aitch and Tash put their arms around each other. Ahead of them, Josh and George walked hand in hand. Dan and Rob strolled a few yards behind the two couples.

They chatted casually about business and football; it was easy, comfortable, just as Rob had imagined. Selfishly, he was glad Adele didn't come on lads' nights out, and that Andy had cried off. If either had been with them, Rob would've been walking on his own and playing the sad, single mate when that wasn't how he felt. Seeing his friends' strong relationships right in front of him, on top of his earlier epiphany about where it had gone wrong with Zoë, he was confident he had a handle on getting it right the next time around. Now all he needed to do was put himself out there.

***

The restaurant was intimate yet buzzing at the same time. The minimal light from patterned lamps and candles was mostly absorbed by the dark walls. Up-tempo Turkish pop music competed with conversation, laughter and the sizzle of the open grill. Every table was taken, and they had to wait at the bar for one to become free, which happened as soon as they ordered drinks. They took them over, and once they were settled into their seats, the waiter gave them menus and recommended the shared-platter starter: calamari, grilled halloumi, wings of fire and garlic mushrooms.

"Something for everyone on there," Aitch asserted.

"Except Josh," Dan said loudly enough for him to hear.

Rob made a point of examining the lamps suspended from the ceiling. On this occasion, Josh didn't take the bait, claiming he liked everything on the platter—a statement that led to George snorting his drink out of his nose. His eyes were still watering when the waiter returned for their orders, and then again ten minutes later with an accomplice who assisted in filling every spare inch of the table with food.

It was, allegedly, a platter for six and could've fed twice that, but the beer and pool had given them an appetite, and they cleared the lot. Unfortunately, all that food on top of four pints of lager, on top of three servings of curry chicken plus lemon meringue pie, left Rob with zero space for his main course. He could hear his mum's voice in his head—*eyes bigger than your belly*—as he shoved the delicious-looking, mouth-wateringly aromatic chunks of chargrilled lamb around his plate.

"Are you OK, Rob?" Josh asked. He was watching him intently, and Rob suspected he'd been doing so for some time.

"Yeah, just stuffed. You?"

"Yes. It's delicious, but..." He put his fork down and picked up his napkin. "Too spicy for me." He wiped his hands and discarded the napkin, his attention back on Rob. "So...what's troubling you?"

The conversations with Jock and Zoë earlier were niggling, but Rob didn't feel overly troubled by them, or he hadn't until Josh mentioned it, and considered fobbing him off.

"Sorry." Josh grimaced. "You can't take me anywhere."

Rob laughed. "No worries. To be honest, I think I'm making something out of nothing. One of the blokes I was in the army with went to see Zoë earlier. He was looking for me, he said, but we spoke yesterday, so he knows Zo and I aren't together anymore. There's a situation involving our old CO—no idea why they've involved me in it—but that's why he was trying to get hold of me."

"Your detecting is obviously legendary."

"Ha, yeah. I did wonder if it was because I'm a copper—*was* a copper—and they thought I could pull some strings. What I can't figure is why he hassled Zoë, but I've spoken to him now, so hopefully, he'll leave well alone."

Josh's eyebrows rose, only for a fraction of a second—an unspoken invitation for Rob to elaborate.

"I dunno, Josh. There's something off, but I can't put my finger on what. Still...not much point worrying. I can't do anything from up here."

"Why don't you ask Gray to keep an eye on Zoë?" Josh suggested. "Treat it as a trial surveillance run for the new business."

Rob was doubtful. "He's not gonna agree to that."

"Oh, he will."

"For real?"

"It's like the sniff of the barmaid's apron to an alcoholic. He can't help himself. As soon as he gets a hint of a case..."

"I probably shouldn't feed his addiction."

"I'd say it's more a...passion." Josh grinned. "Joking aside, if he can't help, he'll tell you, but I think he'll be happy to, and it'd put your mind at rest, give you a chance to enjoy your holiday."

Rob considered his plans for the coming days—the morning's football match, sorting stuff with Amber, meeting his great-niece, dinner with Lois—and all the 'take it as it comes' down time he'd been looking forward to for months. He'd already had to cut it short—the last thing he needed was to be stressing over Jock and ruin what time he had.

"Yeah, all right," he said. "I'll ask him tomorrow."

12: Sunday Love

As Gray came to, he rolled and stretched his arm above his face, hitting something solid yet soft. At the grunt, he opened one eye and squinted up at Will, standing beside the bed. "What are you doing?"

"Taking the dogs out."

"You woke me up."

"Not on purpose. I was trying to figure out if you were already awake. Then you hit me."

"I didn't hit you. I stretched."

"The net result's the same." Will rubbed his chin and looked pained.

"And it wasn't that hard."

"Are you coming with us?"

Gray's eyes closed again. "Depends. Are you planning on getting back into bed afterwards?"

Will chuckled. "If you want me to."

"Mmm."

"OK. See you in a little while."

Gray rolled onto his other side, flipped the pillows and sank into them. A Sunday morning lie-in was *the* manifestation of heaven on earth—sleep-warmed bed, duvet-muted mumblings of activity familiar and comforting, and nothing Gray needed to worry about. The curtains wafted as the external door opened and closed behind Will and the dogs. An hour of glorious, peaceful sleep and then maybe some sex, cuddles, a bit of breakfast—any or all of the above. Gray wasn't fussy. With the bed all to himself, he scissored his legs, breathed deeply, let go...

"Huh?" He jolted awake again. "Tie?"

"Sorry, mate. I'm just checking to see if Benjy's in here." Tie's dreadlocked head bobbed out of sight. "I think he might've followed the dogs out." His voice resonated against the side of the bed. "Nope, not under here."

Gray skimmed his hand across the mattress, up to the pillows and back down again, in search of furry obstacles. "Yeah, he's here." The cunning little chap had burrowed under the duvet and snuggled up against Gray's thigh, and he hadn't felt a thing.

"Thank fuck for that." Tie popped back into view. "Last time he escaped, he was gone overnight. I didn't think we'd see him again. Here, I'll get him out of your way."

Gray pulled back the duvet, bracing against the cool draught. One-handed, Tie scooped up his bunny, said, "Cheers," and stalked out of the room. Gray released the duvet and rolled onto his front, hiding his sudden blush in the pillows, not that anyone was there to see it. Will was right; Tie didn't actually care if they were naked.

***

"Alright, Rob? We're in here." Dan's head poked out of a double doorway in the middle of the vast red-and-grey back wall of the stadium's stand.

Rob slung his bag on his shoulder and walked over. "I was expecting a kick-about in a muddy park."

"We've gone up in the world, though for the time being, we've only got access to the bar, one shower room and the pitch. The rest of the building's being renovated."

Rob followed Dan into a dark, windy passage with the football pitch ahead of them, to the left and right the closed doors of the changing rooms. The smell of sand and salt gave away the building work taking place.

"Didn't this belong to Comco Glass?" Rob asked.

"Yep. Till last year. It's part of Campion Community Trust now."

"And the Lions' home ground?"

"Got it in one. I'll give you a quick tour if you like."

"Great."

At the end of the passage, Dan veered to the left and took Rob clockwise around the perimeter of the lush green pitch.

"Astroturf?"

"Nope. The groundsman's worked here for years and he's top notch."

"No kidding. You could play cricket on that."

"You don't play cricket, do you?"

"Now and again."

"Well, you might get a match here at some point. Once the work's done, it'll be a multi-purpose stadium."

They reached the end of the pitch, and Rob stopped to take in the view through the net. "It's bigger than I thought."

"Yeah. It's got a 6,000 capacity, which is madness, or it was when Comco owned it, but the trust's got ambitious plans. Concerts, farmers' markets, car auctions...it'll have a retractable roof by this time next year. And there's a conference suite too, or there will be."

"Nice." They continued on their circuit. "So Campion's son's doing all right?"

"Very well," Dan said. "He's a funny kid, doesn't say much outside of discussing Trust business. I must admit, after what happened at Black Hole, I expected him to throw in the towel, but it had the opposite effect."

"That's good to hear." In a way, Rob wasn't surprised. The SIU had kept tabs on Jason—Campion's estranged son—as soon as it was known he'd inherited his father's millions, because he shouldn't have, and the fraudsters had been livid. It would have pissed them off less if Jason had blown the lot on sex, drugs and rock 'n' roll because in the end, it wasn't Rob's closeness to Jess that had given the SIU their win. It was that Anders Folden—Campion's murderer—couldn't stand to see *his* money wasted on 'childish pet projects', and he would've killed Jason too, to get his hands on it.

They arrived back at the tunnel, and Dan turned to face Rob, stepping closer so he could keep his voice low. "Are you still involved in the investigation?"

Rob frowned, caught short by Dan's apparent insightfulness. "The fraud ring? No. Why d'you ask?"

Dan tugged at his chin as he scrutinised Rob. "Daft question, really. You wouldn't tell me if you were. Why I asked... Comco originally put the stadium up for auction, and an undercover officer approached me and Andy about making a joint bid. We didn't know who or what he was at the time, of course. The auctioneers were bent—did a lot of business with Jess's cronies—and your lot shut them down."

"Who told you they were connected to Jess?"

"Not to Jess specifically. Her lawyer mates and a few other crooks in high places. Andy reckons they're all still out there."

"Well, I can tell you the ones we caught are locked up," Rob said evasively.

"And the rest of them?" Dan pushed.

Rob shrugged. "You know more than I do, by the sounds of it." Dan gave him a smug grin. Rob laughed. "No, I'm not involved in the investigation. I bowed out after Black Hole. A year playing best buds with a psychopath..." He still had nightmares where Folden had him trapped in a doorless room like a giant lead box. He couldn't escape and no-one could hear him banging on the walls, and all the while Folden was laughing like the lunatic he was. "I was ready to quit the police then."

"Fair enough," Dan said. "Right, we're in here." He pulled a door open, and warm, beery air spilled out, the voices and laughter carrying with it.

Rob peered in at the players from both teams, all getting changed together in the fully kitted and stocked bar. "That's got to have helped win over the rest of the league, eh?"

"Put it this way, it didn't hurt."

***

"I bet you didn't even miss the bacon," Tie said as he picked up the empty plates and took them to the sink.

Full English breakfast, veggie style. It wasn't too shabby, and no, Gray hadn't missed the bacon. He didn't really like it. Black pudding, however... "You're right, Tie, I didn't. Hey, I'll do the washing up." He took over at the sink.

"OK. Thanks. I'll be off, then. Only another forty-four hours to go..."

"Have fun," Gray said.

Tie offered a grim smile and left by the back door.

"That's gone quick, hasn't it?"

"Which?" Will asked.

"Tie's community service."

"Not for him." Will came over and picked up a tea towel. He stood by, waiting for something to dry, and fidgeting. "Can I ask you something?"

"What?"

"Have you actually gone veggie?"

"More or less." Gray tried to think when he'd last eaten meat. He couldn't remember.

"Is that *for* me, or *because of* me?"

"Both, I suppose." Gray glanced sideways at him. "I'd hate to contaminate you."

"I can see where you're coming from," Will leaned close. "You get it stuck in your teeth..." Closer still. "And then we kiss..."

Gray nodded seriously, going cross-eyed in his attempt to stay focused on Will's face, then grimaced. "That's disgusting."

Will left a slow kiss on Gray's lips. "We don't need to worry about it...now you're veggie."

Gray smiled. "Very true." The decision was easy yet as momentous as his admission the previous night—a long-term commitment to change his lifestyle for Will. It was unconditional, but at the same time, he couldn't help wondering what Will would do for him in return.

***

"Not a bad result, that," Dan congratulated the men on his team—Charlie had gone for a shower with the other women players. They'd drawn 2:2 against the Vets, who'd played a lot dirtier than Rob expected of those involved in the care of sick animals. He'd been fouled several times, and George got a boot in the shin from his own vet—the opposition's goalkeeper. For all of that, there were no sour grapes as the men from both teams bundled into the showers once the women were done.

"You're coming to the Red Lion, Rob, aren't you?" Josh asked when they all made it out to the car park a little after one p.m.

"Yeah, I'll come and have a quick pint."

"A quick pint?" Aitch repeated as if Rob were suggesting the impossible.

"My mum's making roast beef and Yorkshire pudding."

"I think I'll come round to yours," George said.

His teammates stared at him in horror.

"They put on an excellent roast dinner at the Lion," Josh contended. The lads all nodded and murmured their agreement.

"All right, I'll come," Rob said. "I'll drop the bike home and let my mum know." Somebody made the sound of a whip being flicked; Rob didn't catch who.

"D'you want a lift back?" Dan and Andy asked at the same time.

"Yeah, cheers," Rob accepted and left them to figure out who was giving it while he put on his helmet. A flip of a coin selected Andy, who followed Rob to his mum's. As if the neighbours didn't stare enough at the bike already, now they had a 1960s red Mustang to ogle. Rob popped inside, dumped his bag in his room and told his mum he wouldn't be there for dinner on the way back out. Yes, it was cowardly, and he hoped she'd save him some for teatime, but he didn't dare ask.

"Top motor," he said as he climbed in beside Andy.

"It's not bad, is it?" Andy checked his mirror and pulled out. "But look at this." As they stopped at the end of the road, Andy rocked the steering wheel from side to side.

"There's quite a bit of play on that."

"Yep. I've checked everything and adjusted the gear box. I'm at a loss what else to try. Any ideas?"

This was good—quite possibly the longest conversation they'd ever had and a decent neutral subject for breaking the thirty-five years of ice between them. "It could be the ball joint on the control valve," Rob suggested.

"Where would I find that?"

"You have to get underneath the car. I can have a look when we stop."

"Nah, you can't be lying on the floor in a pub car park."

Rob laughed. "I've done worse."

When they reached the pub, Rob made his offer again, and Andy rejected it again.

"I'll take it in to Len's mechanic."

"Len's your mum's husband, isn't he?" Rob said without thinking.

"Yep. He imports classic American cars. But you probably know that."

"I think Dan told me." It was better Andy didn't know how much his privacy had been compromised during the Strang case. Rob held the pub door open for him and then for another guy who'd followed them into the car park. The guy nodded in thanks and edged past the other players all standing around the bar.

"Not a supporter, then," Rob muttered under his breath.

"Rob!" Dan shouted. "What're you drinking?"

"Just a lager, cheers." He watched the guy dodge into the Gents' and glanced back out of the doors to the car park.

"Did you leave something in the car?" Andy asked.

"Hmm?" Rob zoned back in. "No, sorry. Old habits…" He hoped.

13: Spyware

"WELL, WELL, I didn't think I'd be seeing you again, especially not this bright and breezy of a Monday morning."

Gray scanned the building's outer wall and around the aluminium roller door, searching for a means by which he'd been 'seen'. The last time he'd come here, over two years ago, the camera had been disguised as a power box under the alarm, but neither of those items were present this time around.

The raucous chuckle coming through the intercom cut off suddenly, and the door began to rise. Gray stared dead ahead into the gloom gradually revealed by the shutter, along with a waft of stale cigarette smoke and warm electronic components. The shutter clanged home, and Gray stepped inside.

"Morning, Paddy."

"Good morning, yourself, Mr. Fisher. Come on through. Cup of tea?"

"I'd love one, thanks." Guided only by the dark silhouette against the square of yellow light twenty feet ahead of him, Gray walked blindly along the windowless corridor, his breaths shortened by the sense of history that struck him every time he visited Paddy's store. The building was a WWII gunnery partly repurposed into warehouses in the 1950s with many of the structural relics—long wooden workbenches and tables scarred by the heavy metal-cutting machinery they once bore—left in place.

"Milk no sugar?" Paddy asked as soon as Gray set foot in the tiny room that doubled as an office and, by the looks of it, these days, a bedsit.

"Yes, thanks." *Tobacco and feet.* He resorted to breathing through his mouth and focused on the custard-colour paint flaking off the brick wall beyond where Paddy toiled with skeletal back turned. When Gray had taken up position as leader of the Special Investigations Unit, DI Paddy Stewart was his antagonistic second-in-command—a pallid-skinned, chain-smoking stick of a man who'd worked undercover in Northern Ireland during the late 1980s and had been on a final written warning for most of his long career. He'd done plenty to get him summarily dismissed, had anyone been fool enough to follow through with further disciplinary action. What Paddy didn't know about surveillance wasn't worth knowing.

DEBBIE MCGOWAN

In the end, it was poor health that had got the better of him, and he'd finally retired to concentrate full time on the 'hobby' that had subsidised his smoking and gambling—and at least three ex-wives plus assorted children—leaving the way clear for Gray to bring in Dom Hooper as his 2-IC. It had also subsidised the SIU's overstretched budget on a regular basis. Paddy's wares were cheaper than the official suppliers and probably knock-offs, but Gray didn't ask questions, then or now.

Given the overall grubbiness of Paddy's cell, Gray was pleasantly surprised by the clean, chip-free mug he was handed, three-quarters full of muscular-looking tea.

"Sit down, sit down." Paddy led the way over to a pair of threadbare office chairs, pale blue with rusted chrome tubular legs. Gray wasn't heavy but perched carefully just the same. Paddy retrieved a tobacco tin from his breast pocket. He flipped the lid open and liberally sprinkled leaf onto a crumpled cigarette paper. "How's life treating you, Mr. Fisher?"

"Better." A smile slipped out with the word.

Paddy glanced up from his rolling and nodded his understanding. They'd never had a conversation about Paddy's fiancée who was killed in The Troubles, nor about Jean's death, yet each was aware of what the other had lost— the uncommon bonded by the common.

"And you, Paddy?"

"Fair to middling. You know how it is." He held the rolled cigarette lengthways to his mouth and licked as he looked up and around him. "Third wife got the house, so this is me." He picked up his lighter and flicked it open, paused as if to consider asking Gray if he minded the smoking, then lit up anyway and disappeared, like CancerMan the Magnifico, in a cloud of dirty-blue smoke.

The cloud drifted towards Gray, and he held his breath until it had dissipated to a slightly less noxious density. He exhaled into his mug and then inhaled the steam under some half-conceived notion that it might be safer than the cooler yet equally damp air in the room. All it did was make his eyes water.

"Down to business, then." Paddy propped the cigarette in the corner of his mouth and stretched sideways, snagging a notebook from his desk. "Unless I'm mistaken and this is a social visit?"

The words resurrected the pang of guilt. After speaking to Rob yesterday— a call which had stopped Gray languishing on Will's sofa for the entire day— it looked increasingly likely that Gray's next call to Dom would not be social after all. "No, it's not," he said. "I'm going into the PI business."

"Aye. You can leave the job, but it never leaves you."

Gray covered a sigh with a slurp of the tea and almost coughed it back out. It was even stronger than he'd anticipated.

Paddy hacked out a laugh. "Put hairs on your chest, so it will."

How that could possibly be construed as a good thing, Gray didn't know. Since he'd turned thirty, he'd had no problem in that regard. Keeping the hair on his head? Now that would be a boon. In every photo he'd seen of his dad, his shaved scalp showed male-pattern baldness, likewise for George. It didn't bode well. His eyes strayed to Paddy's full head of fuzz like nicotine-stained grey candy floss. Perhaps going bald wouldn't be so bad.

Paddy frowned and ran his hand over his hair, flattening it in places. "Right, so, what d'you need?"

"For now, enough kit for twenty-four-hour street surveillance—a couple of static cameras, sound-activated recorder that can be left in situ—I'll be back when I've finalised the rest with my business partner."

Paddy nodded as he scribbled, brushing aside the ash that dropped onto the page. "That's easy enough." Leaving his cigarette balanced on the edge of the desk, lit end outwards, he groaned his way to his feet. "You might as well have a peruse while you're here, see what else takes your fancy. Bring your tea with you, why don't you?"

Gray left the tea and followed Paddy from the room, halfway back along the dark corridor, where Paddy expertly unlocked by touch a reinforced steel door. With a creak worthy of a 1950s submarine movie sound effect, the door opened, white fluorescent light flooding the corridor. Gray squinted on instinct—he'd thought ahead and put in his lenses—and stepped into the treasure trove.

To a surveillance geek like him, Paddy's storeroom was more enticing than a bank vault full of gold bullion. The room was stacked, floor to ceiling, with boxes and plastic crates overflowing with equipment, some of which he recognised as ex-SIU. Cables dangled from shelves; aerials poked out of the edges of split boxes; small black boxes were positioned at intervals around the perimeter of the room. Not surveillance equipment—rat poison. Gray shuddered, recalling a morning he'd arrived at Will's and bumped into Tie on his way out to release a rat from the humane trap they kept in the chicken coop. Gray couldn't imagine his newfound respect for animalkind would ever extend to rats. He shook off the shivers and returned to the task at hand.

Contrary to how it seemed, there was order to the chaos, and Paddy had already located the items Gray had requested.

"A couple of options for you, Mr. Fisher." He handed over a junction box similar to the one that had been on the front of the building on Gray's previous visit. "That's your best bet if you need to cover just the one property. Ninety-degree view angle, motion detection, about forty-eight hours' battery life—I've got others with higher spec if you can get them up on the streetlights."

"Best I don't upset the local council on our first job. Can I view remotely?"

"Via wi-fi only, but there's a memory card on-board."

Understandably, Rob didn't want to worry Zoë, so connecting it to their wi-fi was out of the question. Fitting it was the other challenge: the only time he knew for sure nobody would be home was when Travis went to meet Lucas from school. It gave Gray about half an hour—hopefully long enough to screw a junction box to the front of the house.

"OK. I'll take one of those. What else?"

Paddy opened his hand, revealing a tiny black camera, less than two inches in diameter. "Line-of-sight transmission."

"No good," Gray said. He'd have to be sitting in a car outside Zoë's house—which he was going to do this evening—but he already had a camera for that, and with a more than decent zoom range. "I think one will be enough. What about the audio recorder?"

Paddy waved a brown-tipped finger in the air and held it there while he fished in his trouser pocket and extracted what looked like a pen drive. "Something like this? It's waterproof, so you can hide it in a plant pot or stick it under a windowsill."

"Perfect. How much?"

"Will you be needing a receipt?"

"No, I wouldn't think so."

"In that case, a hundred quid to you, Mr. Fisher."

Gray took out his wallet, thumbed the appropriate number of notes away from the rest, and the two men exchanged cash and goods. "Thanks, Paddy. Much appreciated."

"Always a pleasure, sir." He was already manoeuvring Gray towards the exit. The slam of the store's metal door and rattle of keys accompanied Gray to the end of the corridor, where he peered back through the gloom, waiting for the aluminium roller to rise.

"See you, Paddy. Take care." He received no response as he stepped out into the blinding daylight and filled his lungs with the fresh March air, pollution and all.

***

As Rob had predicted, Travis—Gray assumed from the description 'a stocky Rio Ferdinand in his heyday', although he'd had to look up who that was online first—left the house a few minutes after three. He was in running gear, which may or may not have been unusual, but Gray was taking no chances. As soon as Travis cleared the corner, Gray was out of his unremarkable hired hatchback—not his kind of car, but he was aiming for inconspicuous. The cordless drill dug into his chest as he strolled across the street, hi-viz vest over his jacket, defunct seven-inch touchscreen tablet in his hand. A man in a hi-viz jacket and carrying a tablet rarely roused neighbours' suspicions, and it gave Gray a buzz to find he still had the knack.

The house next door had a real junction box to the left of the window, with cables running up to the first floor. Next to it would have been perfect, rendered invisible by its symmetry, except the angle wasn't wide enough to take in the front door. Gray weighed up the space next to the gas meter under the bay window; it would be too low to capture the face of anyone taller than about five and a half feet, but the rest of the front wall was a clear expanse of well-pointed brickwork. If the motion detection was sensitive, it might pick up visitors before they reached the house. That was the best Gray could do, because there was nowhere else for it to go. Checking he was still clear, he opened the gate and walked up to the house.

DIY had never been his forte, but he knew his way around a drill, and it was only one hole. He positioned the end of the bit against a horizontal line of mortar, gave the trigger a gentle press to get a key, and then went full throttle. The bit cut straight into the mortar with virtually no resistance. Gray eased it out and affixed the back box, giving it a gentle tug to make sure it was secure before he attached the battery, switched on the camera and situated the front cover.

A quick check of the monitor app on his phone showed all was as well as he'd expected; he was five foot ten and appeared headless if he stood at the front door while all of him was visible at the gate but not clear enough for accurate identification of an unknown visitor. However, Rob had sent Gray photos of their targets, both of whom had obvious distinguishing features, and for one of them—the guy missing half an arm—didn't rely on a clear shot of his face.

Next, the sound recorder: there was a small gap between the top of the junction box and the bottom of the bay window casing, but as he took the recorder from his pocket, he caught movement in his peripheral vision. Travis was back, and alone. Gray stuffed the recorder and drill inside his jacket and blew the mortar dust on the ground to disperse it. He pushed against the front of the gas meter and turned towards the street.

"Afternoon, sir," he said with a nod, stepping past Travis. "Just taking a reading. All done."

"Again? It was only read a couple of weeks back."

Gray stopped at the gate. "Was it? I bet I've misread my jobs sheet again." He pressed the power button on his tablet and frowned. "Damn. Battery's dead. I'll check when I get back to the office. Sorry to bother you, sir."

"No problem." Travis jogged the rest of the way up the path and unlocked the front door without a second glance.

Given he'd returned without Lucas and he seemed to be in a rush, Gray predicted he'd be back out again in a couple of minutes, so he continued his meter-reader performance—checking house numbers, stopping at any with no cars outside and no visible signs of activity within. He was peeved he'd partly blown his cover, if not a little exhilarated by the near miss, but Travis didn't strike him as the suspicious sort. If it had been Rob, he'd have been demanding ID and making phone calls. Even so, Gray thought it best to steer clear of the car until he was confident Travis wouldn't see him getting into it.

Sure enough, Travis came out again a few minutes later, still in running gear, but this time with a gym bag over his shoulder. He set off in the same direction as before and didn't even look Gray's way. Travis cleared the corner a second time, and Gray went back to the house. He pushed the voice recorder into the space above the junction box and checked it was out of sight but didn't hang around to test it; he'd used the same brand many times, and it was highly reliable.

Back in the car, he stowed the drill and his hi-viz vest in the passenger foot well, sent Rob a text to confirm surveillance was in place, and started the engine.

He got the seat belt halfway across his chest before the realisation hit him of what he'd done. He'd been out of the police for almost a year, yet it had come so naturally to him, as if he'd never been away, and it was more than his actions. It was the mindset—the easy lies, the thrill of hiding in plain sight, and the mix of fear and excitement at being discovered. In less than fifteen minutes, he'd scrubbed out everything he'd achieved since leaving the SIU.

He stared across the street at the house he'd rigged. Zoë and Travis's house. He was spying on Rob's ex-wife with only Rob's say-so it was for Lucas's and her safety. No warrant, no consent. As for the information he'd planned to tap Dom for: once again, he was abusing his former position as Dom's superior, and worse, abusing their friendship.

He should've said no when Rob asked, and not only to spying on Zoë. No to the partnership. No to undercover work. He wasn't a detective anymore; he was a postgraduate student and an actor—precisely because living in the shadows had almost destroyed him once. He was a fool to have ever believed he could do it all over again with no fallout.

***

"Hey."

"Gray? Everything OK?"

"Yeah." He picked up a green bean from his discarded dinner and wrote his signature in the roux sauce. The skin wrapped around his bean pen and smeared everything. "Still at work?"

"Still at the office," Dom confirmed. "I'm not sure this constitutes work. We're investigating an online casino. They fix bets so new members have a sixty-percent win rate in the first twenty-four hours then refuse to pay out on a bonus play-through rule. I signed up last night—trying to spend two grand at five quid a pop is harder than you'd think."

"I can quite believe it." Harder still, Gray imagined, given Dom's recreation of choice was a night at the casino. "Are you having fun, though?"

"Oh, yeah," Dom said drolly. "It beats trawling double-entry books."

"Handwritten?"

"Yep. Thirty-seven years' worth."

Gray sighed. "If only I'd stayed a year longer." He was half serious about that; some of the accounts ledgers he'd analysed over the years were so rich he could've written a company profile based on that information alone.

"Do I sense regret?" Dom asked.

"A little," Gray answered honestly.

"Well, any time you're up for a consultancy..."

"Yeah, I'll keep it in mind." In the absence of something to say, Gray listened to the rapid click of Dom's mouse and tried to discern what he was playing. "Slots?" he guessed.

"Roulette."

"Ah, of course."

"Yeah. Time for a break." The clicking stopped, replaced by footsteps across carpet, a door opening, passing traffic... He was out on the fire escape. "So," Dom lit his cigarette, "what can I do for you?"

"Nothing."

"Nothing?"

"Social call."

Dom drew in deeply and talked through the exhale. "Bloody hell. I am honoured. Mind, I'd rather meet up for a pint. I should be out of here in the next hour."

"I'm tied up this evening..." Gray hesitated over saying more, but this was Dom, the closest thing he had to a best friend. "Rob asked me to keep an eye on his ex's place. A couple of old army buddies are giving them grief."

"What kind of grief?"

"I'm not sure. From what Rob said, it sounded fairly benign..."

"You think he's spying on her?"

"It crossed my mind, but for what reason? They're already divorced."

"Custody of Lucas?"

"I don't think so. Rob seems quite happy with the arrangement. Well, not happy, but you know what I mean."

"Yeah, I do. That's why you agreed, isn't it?"

"Agreed to what? The surveillance?"

"The surveillance, the PI agency..."

"What are you talking about?" Gray's arms erupted in goosebumps.

"You still feel responsible for Rob's marriage ending."

"I *was* responsible, Dom."

"No, you weren't. Even Rob said—"

"Rob let it go for his own peace of mind, but we both know the truth."

"Then you need to do the right thing."

"Which is?"

"Back out."

"I can't."

"Why? Because he'd never forgive you? It's the wrong reason, Gray."

"Story of my life." He laughed bitterly, too angry to defend his actions without resorting to snipes. He squashed the bean flat with his thumb and listened to Dom slowly killing himself. That was his fault too.

Eventually, Dom said, "Look, mate, you've got to do what feels right for you."

"I am—"

"*Whatever...*" Dom interrupted forcefully, "I'm here for you."

Gray released the rest of his protest as a breath. They were agreeing to disagree. "Thanks, I appreciate it." He meant every word. "And the same goes here. I'll leave you to get back to spinning the wheel."

"All right. Behave yourself, Gray."

"I'll try."

After he hung up, Gray cleared the table, symbolically clearing his mind. He and Dom had argued plenty of times before—about the job. It had never been personal, and it would be easy to blame it on the 'social call' when the truth was Dom had hit the nail on the head. Gray was trying to make amends, still trying to fix what he'd broken. And maybe it was the wrong reason—did that make it a bad one? He didn't think so.

In light of what was going on, Rob was curtailing his holiday. Once he was back, they could meet, thrash out a code of conduct, clarify data collection methods, learn some new techniques so they could stay above the law. Of course, all of that rested on Gray following through, and he needed to seriously consider, in the meantime, whether he had enough right reasons to do so.

At the very least, he'd see through the surveillance on Zoë's place. It wasn't illegal if they were preventing a crime from being committed, and he had reason to believe that was the case. Whatever doubts he had over his own motivations, the one thing Gray knew for sure was that he trusted Rob without reservation.

14: Baby

"DID YOU WANT a beer, Un...Rob? Is there beer in the fridge, Kyle? Excuse me, please, I need to get the lamb out of the oven."

Rob stepped aside, and Amber bustled past, pulling oven gloves onto her hands. She dropped the oven door and wafted the hot air away from her face. "*Kyle?*"

"What?" He appeared in the doorway, wailing baby in his arms. He shushed her, rocking from side to side; it was difficult to know whether it was to comfort the baby or himself. Rob's heart went out to him, and to Amber. Both parents had dark circles around their eyes and looked ready to flake at a moment's notice.

"Is there beer in the fridge?" Amber repeated. She poked the lamb joint with a fork. It spat at her.

"Well, I haven't drunk any in...let's see—" Kyle studied his daughter "—how old are you now? Eight weeks?"

"Oh my god." Amber threw a glance Rob's way. "There's beer if you want it."

"Err...thanks." He went over to the fridge. He didn't care one way or the other about beer, or roast lamb. "Anyone else want one while I'm here?"

"Breastfeeding," Amber muttered.

"Night duty," sighed Kyle.

Rob extracted a bottle from the four-pack, glad for the twist-off lid. He'd rather have been handed an armed grenade than ask for a bottle opener. "Can I get you anything while I'm here?"

"Please," Amber said. "Orange juice. In the door."

Kyle didn't answer—probably didn't hear the question.

"She's got a hell of a pair of lungs, eh?" Rob had to raise his voice.

"She never stops," Amber complained desperately. She tugged off the gloves and slapped them down on the counter on her way over to Kyle. "I'll take her to the bedroom." Extracting the baby from Kyle's arms, she trudged out of the kitchen and disappeared through a doorway on the right.

Kyle shoved his hands in his pockets and gave Rob a watery smile. "Think I might have that beer after all." He collapsed onto a dining chair.

Rob collected a second bottle from the fridge and joined Kyle at the table. "There you go, mate."

"Thanks." He opened the bottle and tipped it to his mouth, holding it horizontal, his eyelids drooping further with each gulp. Finally, he put the bottle down and gave several exaggerated blinks. "She misses you."

Rob glanced towards the open door. "I miss her too." He could hear the baby's intermittent crying, so Amber would also be able to hear their conversation, but it was the truth. He'd seen more of her this evening than in the past three years, and he and Kyle—whom Amber had married the previous summer—were essentially strangers.

"Thanks for coming tonight. When Lois suggested I invite you, she said you might refuse."

"To be honest, I thought about it. I don't want to force Amber into seeing me if she doesn't want to."

"If she didn't want you here, you wouldn't have got through the door."

Rob smiled. "That's my girl." He could see her in his head, in her Spiderman outfit, leaning her full weight against her bedroom door to stop him going in because he didn't know the password. She'd have been about six years old at the time, and he'd had no idea what he'd done to upset her. He knew now, though.

The two men drank their beer companionably while Rob tried to figure out his best approach. He didn't want things to get heavy tonight. Amber was too tired to fight him; he was fairly certain he was in for an earful when she finally broke her silence. He'd take the blows, say sorry again for the pain he'd caused, but for tonight, all he wanted was a chance to get to know her again, and to meet Leila. If she was prepared to stretch to that, it would be more than enough.

A pan lid rattled on the stove, and Rob drew breath to ask if it needed turning down, but Kyle had nodded off, still upright with the bottle in his hand. Knowing there was a strong likelihood whatever he did would be wrong, Rob left the guy to doze and dealt with the pan. The potatoes inside were turning to mush, leaving him with no option but to drain off the water. He put the pan to one side and watched Kyle for a moment. The baby had stopped crying and all was quiet, but the dinner wouldn't survive without intervention.

As Rob was gearing up to giving Kyle a gentle prod, Amber slipped out of the bedroom and tiptoed back into the kitchen, closing the door behind her. When she saw Kyle, she gave a long sigh that seemed to drain her remaining energy.

"I can finish making the dinner if you like," Rob offered quietly.

"You're a guest." She plodded to the stove and lifted the pan lid. "Thanks."

"No worries. And I don't mind. Have a sit-down."

She swayed, and for a second or two, he thought she was going to take him up on it, but then she shook her head and pulled a drawer open. "I can't."

It was like an invisible force was moving her around, a puppet that would collapse in a heap on the floor if someone cut her strings. Stubborn, always so stubborn. Rob took some relief from recognising the family trait. They weren't so different, the two of them.

"Come on, turtle. Let me help." He edged closer to where she stood in front of the stove, staring in despair at the potatoes.

"But we invited you round for dinner."

"Yeah, and I really appreciate it, but I'm not royalty...or your nan."

She almost laughed at that. "Get the masher?" She thumbed at the rack of utensils behind Rob. He unhooked the potato masher and awaited further instruction. "If you can sort the spuds..."

"I can do that." He went over to the fridge for the milk and butter.

"I'll just do some peas and carrots from the freezer. I was going to do fresh veg, but...screamy baby." She shrugged.

Rob closed the fridge and smiled in sympathy. Lucas had been a little tyke too, but he wouldn't share unless she asked. His sister had driven him mad with her knowledgeable-parent quips—listening to her extol the benefits of demand feeding was at least as exhausting as putting it into operation—and she'd no doubt been handing out more of the same to Amber and Kyle. "Peas and carrots in here?" he asked, nodding at the freezer door.

"Yeah. Bottom shelf."

He dug out the two bags and took them over.

"Sorry. It's a bit crap." She tipped both bags into the same glass bowl and stuck it in the microwave on full power.

"Nah, it's great. You can't beat home-cooked food."

"Microwaved peas and instant gravy?"

"Beats chippy teas seven days a week," Rob said and then wished he hadn't, but apparently, his cholesterol levels were not a cause for concern. Arms folded, Amber leaned against the counter, chewing her lip. He kept mashing, adding more milk and butter, smoothing out the bumps and trying to ignore the eyes-burning-holes sensation.

"This PI thingy, what'll you be doing?"

"Investigating white-collar crime."

"Same as you did in the police?"

"Along the same lines, yeah."

"So it's still dangerous?"

"If we discover a crime's taken place, we'd have to advise the client to report it to the police—"

"That doesn't answer my question."

The mash was as smooth as it was going to get. Rob used a knife to scrape the masher clean; Amber took it from him and rinsed it under the tap, then she was back to watching him.

He exhaled through his nose and gave a reluctant nod of confirmation. "It won't be as dangerous as what I used to do for the police, but yeah, it might get dodgy sometimes. People don't like being caught out, and there's no telling how they'll react. But I can promise you, I won't intentionally put myself in harm's way. Well, unless it's to save Lu, or you or your sister...or Leila..."

She laughed, but there were tears too. "At least this time you didn't tell me you just fix bikes."

"It wasn't a lie."

"In a warzone," she pointed out. Her gaze drifted towards the bedroom. "I want you to meet her, for her to grow up with you in her life, like I did."

"Fun times," Rob said.

"Yeah, the best. But I can't cope with her asking all the time when Uncle Rob's coming to visit again, which she will. And I don't want to have to tell her one day that you're not..." There was no laughter now.

"Hey, come on." Rob took her in his arms, and she clung to him, sobbing—from exhaustion as much as anything. The microwave pinged to indicate it was done, and again a minute later. It woke Kyle, who squinted at them, trying to get his bearings. On the third ping, he got up and squeezed past to rescue the veg.

Still sniffling, Amber withdrew and muttered something about tissues as she left the kitchen.

Kyle watched her go and raised an eyebrow at Rob. "Is everything OK?"

"I hope so." Now he understood the cost of getting to know his great-niece.

By the time Amber returned, Kyle had made instant gravy and Rob had carved the lamb. Amber served up to save carrying everything to the table, and over dinner, they kept up neutral chatter about Kyle's nursing and Amber's plans to complete her dentist foundation training after her maternity leave. They were also hoping to sell the flat and buy a house, a point of conversation on which Rob could swap like for like and which inevitably veered into comparing house prices in the North and London.

"You must be a calming influence, Rob," Kyle said as they cleared the table afterwards. "This is the longest Leila's slept since she was born."

"Blimey. No wonder you're both shattered."

"Shattered doesn't come close."

"Night off tomorrow, hun," Amber said and explained for Rob's benefit, "Lois babysits for us on a Tuesday so I can go to salsa and Kyle can play squash with his dad. She's usually tearing her hair out when we get home."

"Yeah, she mentioned she looked after the baby for you." He still couldn't quite believe it, and it must've shown, because Amber grinned for the first time all evening—the first time in his presence for years. It sent warm tingly waves over him. He wanted to hold on to that feeling. "Listen, I'm gonna get going, let you two enjoy the peace while it lasts." He was already up and moving towards the hallway. Amber followed him out.

"OK. See you at Nan's on Wednesday?"

"Unfortunately not. Something's come up—I'm heading back first thing."

"Oh, that's a shame." She looked genuinely disappointed. She frowned; familiar thinking crinkles formed on the bridge of her nose. "Do you want to say good night to Leila?"

"And get blamed for disturbing her? Not likely."

Amber laughed. "If you're sure..."

"I'm sure. And anyway, I'm up again in a couple of weeks. I can meet her then. She might even be awake." He winked to emphasise he was kidding.

"Ha. She might." Amber hugged him. "It's lovely to see you, Uncle Rob."

"For me too." He kissed her head and released her to put his helmet on even though he wouldn't usually do so until he reached the bike. He wasn't sure how much longer he could keep up the cheery façade. "You both take it easy, yeah?"

Kyle had joined them in the hall and stepped forward to shake Rob's hand. "Thanks for coming," he said. He held the door open for him. "See you soon."

"Count on it." Rob gave them a final nod and walked away. The quiet click of the door shutting behind him was like the inaugural tick of a stopwatch, a countdown until it would be too late to give Amber the assurances she needed and he missed the chance of ever knowing Leila.

***

"Rob, it's gone nine o'clock." His mum deposited a cup of coffee on the bedside table and left again.

"Crap." Swinging his legs off the bed, he sat up and grabbed his phone. "I swear I set the alarm." If he'd been at home, his body clock would've beaten the alarm by a long shot. At his mum's, he slept like the dead. Too much stress or not enough? Either way, his plan to be on the road before seven had gone out the window.

"D'you want some breakfast before I go to work?"

"It's all right, Mum, cheers. I can make it myself or get something on the way."

"I'm leaving in ten minutes..."

That was code for 'I expect a kiss goodbye' and was enough to propel Rob from his pit to the bathroom for a quick shower. Even then, he had to race downstairs in a bath towel to catch her in time. His mum's coat was prickly against his bare chest and arms as he hugged her.

"Thanks for letting me stay, Mum."

"You didn't get to see your dad or JJ."

"I'll call them later and explain."

"OK, dear." She freed herself from his clutches. "You'll be careful, won't you?"

"I will, Mum," he promised.

She turned and picked up her bag. "And don't forget to phone me to say you're home."

"I won't."

Without looking, she cuffed him around the head.

"Ow!"

"That's for rolling your eyes."

He laughed but didn't deny it. "See you in a fortnight."

"A fortnight," she repeated with a nod. "I'll get a list from you of what Lucas is eating these days."

"Chips, crisps, chocolate—"

"He'll get no junk food here." With that declaration, she was out the door and off to work.

Rob went back up to his room to drink his coffee, in no rush to leave and stop-start his way through the tail end of school drop-off traffic, instead browsing social networks and reading random web pages—the kind of stuff he didn't normally have time for unless it was part of an investigation. Scrolling through seemingly endless ads, he quickly realised he wasn't actually interested in making time for it. He ditched his phone in favour of getting dressed, packed his panniers and carried them down to the hallway.

Linford opened one sleepy eye as Rob passed by on his way back from loading up the bike and followed him at a distance into the kitchen. Quarter to ten: a bowl of cereal, another coffee, and then he'd be on his way. Or that was the plan until his phone rang.

"Morning, Gray."

"Hey, Rob. Sorry for calling so early. I've downloaded the surveillance video from last night. We need to meet ASAP."

"OK. I'm heading back in about half an hour, so I can be with you by... two-thirty?"

"I'm working this morning, but I should be home by then. Want me to come to you?"

"Nah, I'll come to you. Is there anything I need to know now?" Gray would understand what he was really asking: were Zoë and Lucas in danger?

"Nothing that can't wait. I'll text you my address. Take it easy."

"You too, mate." The call ended. Rob chucked his phone aside and analysed the conversation. He'd already told Gray he was heading home today, so whatever the video had picked up was urgent enough for Gray to ensure Rob didn't change his mind.

Dispensing with the spoon, Rob tipped the bowl of cornflakes to his mouth. They hadn't even had time to go soggy, and he was still chewing as he cleaned up and pulled on his leathers. "In a bit, Linford." He patted the dog on his way out and fired up the bike, planning his route home on the move. The motorways were his quickest option, providing they were clear—he should've checked on his phone before he left.

"Phone. Shit."

Luckily, he'd only reached the end of his mum's road. He switched his indicator to turn left instead of right, raising a hand in apology to the driver of the car behind him, and rode around the block, leaving the bike at the kerb while he went back in. The dog watched in seeming bemusement but didn't bother getting up to greet him or see him off.

With a quick route check—contraflow between junctions five and six of the M6, otherwise clear roads all the way—Rob set off once more. He indicated right, checking his mirror as he moved towards the centre line and noting the car turning into the other end of the road, too far away to pose an immediate threat.

Rob pulled out and took the main drag into the town centre, taking a right at the crossroads, then right and right again, which brought him to an out-of-the-way petrol station which was nothing close to the cheapest, but that didn't concern him. He didn't need fuel; he'd filled up over the weekend. What did concern him was the blue Mondeo, presently idling in the supermarket car park across the street—the same car he'd cut up when he'd gone back for his phone; the same car he'd seen in his mirror, and in the pub car park on Sunday after the footy.

"Right, mate, let's see how well you can keep up."

15: Rescue

GRAY WAS PREOCCUPIED with unsticking the zip on his rucksack and didn't see Will, in his postie uniform complete with bulky post bag, until he was within a few feet. Nor had Will noticed Gray, his attention captured by whatever was in his hand—too small to be his phone—and they both back-stepped in surprise. Will shoved whatever it was in his pocket and smiled. "Hi."

"Hi." Gray smiled back, pleased to see him, if not somewhat perplexed. "How did you get in here? More to the point, why are you here and not at work?"

"Day off."

Gray bobbed his head in an exaggerated fashion, looking Will over. "And you love your uniform so much you wore it anyway?"

"OK, I'll confess." He held up his hands. "I had an appointment, and I'm done, so I thought I'd come and see you. I'm your number one fan—I've watched all your shows."

"Shopper in crowded marketplace, passenger in crowded train carriage..."

"I could pick you out of any crowd." Will grinned.

"Somehow I doubt that." Gray moved off, and Will fell in step alongside. "You didn't tell me how you got in here."

"Delivering mail."

"This isn't anywhere near where you deliver mail."

Will shrugged, tilting his head at the reception desk. "They don't know that."

"Someone needs to have a word about security."

Gray stopped to sign out, a simple task made complicated by being unable to keep his eyes off Will. He was rather partial to a man in uniform, cheesy as that was, but he'd seen him in his postie get-up plenty of times and that wasn't why he was watching him—as was the receptionist. In fact, she was watching them both, and no doubt wondering why Gray was escorting the postman from the building. Gray offered her a quick smile and ushered Will towards the door.

"Obviously, you weren't just passing by," he said once they were outside. Will unhooked his sunglasses from his hair and slid them down over his eyes. It was a pleasant spring morning—positively Mediterranean in contrast to the studio's communal dressing room, which had no windows and an enormous air-conditioning unit that turned the space into a walk-in refrigerator—but it was overcast and not that warm. In other words, not sunglasses weather.

"I kind of was. I've got a couple of cats to pick up."

"Did you drive in?" Gray scanned the multistorey car park opposite the studio, on the lookout for Will's van.

"No, I caught the train."

"How are you going to transport them?"

Will tapped his post bag. "Foldaway carry boxes."

"On the train?"

"Cats aren't big or heavy, are they?"

"I suppose not." Now it dawned on Gray. "You need someone to help carry them home."

Will's lips pursed, but the taking of offence was fake, or that was Gray's impression. "That's a terrible thing to say. I knew you finished around twelve, and I thought it'd be nice to go for a coffee."

"Really?" Gray still wasn't convinced.

"Really." Will moved off slowly and glanced sideways over his glasses to make sure Gray was still with him, which he was. "Where to?"

"Chain store or independent?"

"Independent, preferably."

"OK. There's a place round the corner. Their almond-milk latte is excellent."

"Sounds good to me." Will was distracted, and fidgeting with whatever was in his pocket. As soon as he noticed Gray watching, he stopped and smiled innocently, or his mouth did. He could have been giving him evil glares behind those dark glasses. "Do you go to this place often?"

"Original. At least once a week. I keep thinking I might try somewhere different, but why bother when I've found something I like?"

"Not really into new experiences, are you?"

Gray laughed. "Not anymore. I mean, I love spontaneity—like having coffee with you on the spur of the moment—but that's about as adventurous as I want to be these days. Alas—" he turned his head so he could see Will's face "—adventure won't relinquish its hold on me, so if you do want a hand with those cats, we'll have to take them back to my place. Rob's coming over."

"Your surveillance paid off, I take it?" He was fiddling in his pocket again.

"It did," Gray answered distractedly. "What have you got in there?"

"In here? Oh, it's...a pager."

"A pager?"

"Old tech."

"I know what a pager is." They'd reached the café; Gray held the door open for Will to go in first. "Find us a table, I'll get the drinks."

"OK."

Will walked off, his lack of protest confirming he was up to no good. Gray ordered their drinks and joined him. He wasn't sure what he could safely say to break the uneasy silence that billowed between them, and was grateful for the intervention of the barista delivering their lattes a few minutes later. They both thanked her and picked up their cups at the same time. Will inhaled, sipped and sloshed his drink around his mouth. He swallowed and hummed his approval. Finally, the sunglasses came off.

"Do you really want to know?"

Gray shrugged. "Do I?"

With a sigh, Will leaned back, extracted the small, black gadget from his pocket and placed it next to Gray's drink. "It's—"

"A wireless jammer. Put it away." Will did so. "They're illegal."

"To use, not to own."

"You wouldn't have it if you didn't intend to use it." The penny dropped, although it felt more like a whole bagful had landed in his lap with no warning. "Tell me again about the cats."

"Gray..."

"Do you need my help?"

"Yes, but that's not why I'm here."

"Am I your alibi?"

Will's laughter camouflaged what he really thought of that question, and Gray couldn't figure it out.

"Come on, Will. Give me something."

"The cats are strays, trapped in a building that's protected by a wireless security system. The woman who reported them thinks they've been in there since the building was vacated two weeks ago. I called the letting agency and asked if I could go in, but they've been locked down by the Inland Revenue. So...I'm going to break in and jam the alarm system."

"In broad daylight."

"Concealed entrance."

"You still need to shut it off first," Gray pointed out, which earned him a smirk.

"Payback for my 'old tech' remark?"

"Something like that." He forgot...or intentionally overlooked that Will had the skill set of a cat burglar—a fitting pun on this occasion—and not that different from Gray's own talents. He also had some very clever friends who owed him. "Aaron?"

"Yep. He's going to shut down the system, but it's got a failsafe that sends a reboot signal. The jammer should give me enough time to find the cats before the alarm company turns up to do a manual reboot."

"How big's the building?"

"Not huge. Four storeys plus the basement. That's where I'll start—the cats must have a food source."

Basement...food source...rats... Gray shuddered, and yet... "What can I do?"

"Well, like I said, I came here to see you, but it would be a lot easier with the two of us, particularly if there are kittens to get out."

"It's almost as if you planned the rescue for when I had a car," Gray joked. He hadn't known himself that he'd have a car this week.

"You could keep watch, alert me when the alarm guys arrive."

"How? Exotic bird call?"

Will's nose wrinkled in a grimace. "Good point. We usually do these kinds of rescues as a two-man team, but it's outside of Tie's tag radius."

"How would Tie have alerted you?"

"He'd be inside the building."

Gray picked up his cup. Filling his mouth with coffee might stop him volunteering.

"Never mind," Will saved him. "If you're still up for being my getaway driver—"

"Gee, that sounds so much better..."

"Or I go with my original plan."

"Transport a family of wild cats on the Tube?"

"I've done it before."

"Wasn't that chickens?"

"Same difference," Will muttered obstinately.

Gray couldn't help it; he laughed. It was almost worth sustaining the argument to see Will riled, but he really did want to help. "OK, how about this. We'll park somewhere out of sight. I'll stay with the car, and as soon as you're clear, call me and I'll pick you up."

"If they report it to the police—"

"I was giving a friend a lift back from the vet's. I had no reason to suspect a crime had been committed."

"I've got previous."

"How would I know? I'm a civilian."

"What about Hedley?"

Gray thought back to Rob's leaving do, when Martina had failed to put two and two together, and not just because she'd been on the brandy. The night of Freddie Berringer's arrest, she'd assumed Gray was there on SIU business and gladly handed off the corporate investigation into the Berringers' business dealings. The Met Police were only interested in getting father and son on their respective murder charges, although there was a good chance Charles's would be reduced to involuntary manslaughter for putting a drunk Hector Laird-Browne behind the wheel and Freddie would get off on the grounds of self-defence.

"Gray?"

"Sorry, I was thinking. Where is it?"

"Acton."

"That's out of Hedley's area. Even if it wasn't, I'm not convinced she knows we're an item, and, you know…it's only been five months, and I'm a former police officer. You're worried that if I find out you have a criminal record, I won't want anything to do with you."

Will raised his eyebrows. "I am?"

"Stands to reason."

The familiar, warm smile returned. "You're good at this."

"Don't know what you mean." Gray hid behind his cup. Will laughed, but there was something more. Something else. Gray finished his coffee and put his cup back on its saucer. "OK, now you've convinced me you didn't come to talk me into doing what you talked me into doing, why are you here?"

"Headaches," Will answered without hesitation, following up with a hard swallow and the nodded equivalent of *there, I said it*. All the while, he held Gray's gaze. Gray tilted his head in query. "I've been getting them since just after Mum passed."

"How bad are they?"

"Bad enough for me to go to my doctor. She sent me to a specialist."

"That's where you've been this morning?"

"Yep. I had a scan while I was there."

"How long till you get the results?"

"Next week." Will didn't need to say anything else; his fear carved deep lines across his forehead, and Gray felt awful for not noticing before. Then again, Will would have distracted him any time he came close. No doubt, the stress was further exacerbating the headaches.

"OK. Let me know when your appointment is. I'll come with you—if that's what you want."

"You don't mind?"

Gray smiled and rested his hand on top of Will's. "Not at all."

"Thank you."

"No thanks needed. That's what friends…boyfriends…are for. And yes, you can tell Suzannah I used the B-word."

Will laughed. "You can tell her yourself."

No matter that Will's daughter had been calling Gray 'Dad's boyfriend' since she'd first known of his existence—understandably, given they'd been introduced at Will's mum's funeral. Gray had learned early on that whilst Will was sociable and outgoing, at times of emotional vulnerability he became insular and went off on his own—surfing or hill-walking or some other physical means of working through his feelings. It made it an even greater privilege for Gray to have been invited to the funeral, and for Will to have confided in him about the headaches.

"Deal," Gray said. "When shall we do it?"

"Well, I've got a week's leave before Easter. I was gonna pop up to see her."

"I could come with you."

"You want to visit Suzannah and Shelley?"

"We can make a holiday of it. It's time I got to know them better, but it's up to you—you don't have to tell me now, or tell me at all." He peered into Will's half-full cup. "We should make a move. I told Rob I'd be home by two-thirty."

"OK." Will finished his coffee as he got to his feet and walked ahead of Gray, looking back at him to say, "That was to both suggestions."

Outside, Will put on his sunglasses once more, and they walked back to the multistorey, where Gray had parked the tiny hire car that was costing him a not-tiny fortune in congestion charges and parking fees. From there, Will directed him through back streets to North Acton.

"That's the place." Will pointed as they passed a dilapidated 1970s prefab that looked like every local government building of the era.

Gray read the faded 'To Let' sign's boast of '100,000 sq ft of Office Space'. "Not huge, he says..."

"I'm pretty sure they'll be in the basement."

"I hope for your sake they are." Gray continued along the street, looking for a parking space or a side road, but there was nowhere.

"What about that pub?" Will suggested.

"It'll have to do, I guess." Gray indicated and turned into the technically full forecourt. There was a gap between the row of cars and an advertising board that he could just about squeeze the hatchback into. "You'd better get out now. I'll go in and buy an OJ or something."

Will got out and went around to the back of the car for his bag. "I'll be as quick as I can," he promised, slamming the boot shut. He sped off in the direction of the office building.

Gray parked up and eyed the pub in dismay. It seemed a decent establishment, but he'd have stayed in the car if he thought he'd get away with it. Alas, the person watering the hanging baskets kept casting suspicious glances his way. Gray checked the time on his phone—12:56—and unmuted the ring tone, locked the car and went to join the other three punters enjoying an early afternoon pint.

"Alright?" the barman greeted him.

"Hello." Gray put on a show of inspecting the counter mounts before he ordered. "I'll have...a Coke, please."

"Not Newcastle Brown?" The barman collected a glass and filled it.

Gray smiled. "Later, maybe." The accent was only half-intentional, though he doubted the cloak-and-dagger routine was necessary.

"D'you live down here or...?"

"Just visiting a friend—he asked me to meet him here." Gray looked around the bar room. "It's quiet, like."

"Always is weekday lunchtimes. Gets mad later."

"I bet."

The barman handed over Gray's drink. He paid and, seeing as he wasn't stopping long, decided to stay where he was. The other customers were dotted around the bar, all eyes trained on the large TV screen. Curling. Too sedentary, intriguing but not very interesting, other than the time in the corner of the screen that permitted Gray to subtly keep check—currently 13:04. In his experience, alarm companies' 'rapid response' would give Will around thirty minutes from when they noticed the system was offline. Was that long enough to catch a couple of stray cats? Gray had no idea, although the old adage about herding the wilful little monsters sprang to mind.

Meanwhile, the curlers bowled and brushed on. It wasn't quite as relaxed a sport as Gray had first thought, and he winced and puffed along in frustration when a stone didn't quite go where it was meant to. Those shoes looked great, though. He hadn't been ice-skating since high school, and he wasn't awful, but curling shoes looked a lot easier to control than ice skates. Would they allow them at the rink?

Time check: 13:25. The alarm company might already be on the premises. Gray crossed his feet in an effort to stop his knee jigging and timed his pulse between 13:26 and 13:27. Since knocking cocaine on the head, he was a steady 70 bpm guy, but it was up at 90+, and it was all about Will. If he got caught, he wouldn't implicate Gray; no-one would ever know he was the 'getaway driver'. If he stayed put. Which he should. Will could be on his way to the pub right now.

Right now being 13:29. He checked his phone in the impossibly unlikely event he hadn't heard the alert. The Norwegians won the curling match; the clock ticked over to 13:30. The last half inch of Coke slid from the glass onto Gray's tongue, and he endeavoured to savour the too sweet, no longer effervescent liquid before it drained away down his throat.

"Another?" the barman asked.

"No, thanks. I'm going to call my friend, see where he's got to. I might be back in a bit."

"See you."

Gray left the pub, looking towards the car, waiting until he was in the driver's seat before he chanced a glance along the street. He saw the security firm's van at the same time as his phone chimed.

Too many cats. Police on way. Call Tie. Sorry. x

16: Footage

THE TURN INTO the road was almost a hairpin, and Rob missed it on a first pass. He'd never been to Gray's home before and hadn't known what to expect, although Gray had always struck him as a minimalist-loft kind of guy—not the sort to live in a two-bed mid-terrace with a front door that opened pretty much onto the pavement, and it wasn't even in a nice neighbourhood.

However humble it looked, property in NW2 cost a packet, and if Rob was honest, his judgement was tainted by jealousy. He'd had a place better than this with Zoë and Lucas, although her parents had paid the deposit, so it was never really his, or even theirs, which meant Travis had no stake in it either. That didn't appease him as much as he'd thought it would.

The front door opened as Rob climbed off the bike. There was no cheery smile to greet him.

"Alright, mate?" He advanced, removing his helmet.

"Hey, Rob." Gray shook his hand. "How was your long weekend up north?"

"Not long enough, but I got to see both my nieces, so it wasn't a dead loss."

"That's good to hear. Come on in. Coffee? I've just made some."

"Yeah, cheers." Rob closed the door and waited for an indication of whether he should follow Gray into his kitchen, go find the living room or stay right where he was, admiring the décor. The hallway was spartan—bare wood floor, plain white walls—apart from the poster-size silent movie stills following the rise of the stairs. A man smoking a pipe, a woman posed behind a microphone, and—the only actor Rob recognised—Charlie Chaplin scowling face-to-face with another guy in a hat. It was like a movie studio reception, or how he imagined one would be.

Gray reappeared with two mugs. "Sorry, I'm a bit distracted this afternoon. We'll go in here." He nodded at the doorway on Rob's left, which turned out to be the living room and, thankfully, a bit more lived in than the hallway. It was still in keeping with the black-and-white theme, other than the sofas, which were green, pink and cream—like weathered apples—and a blue envelope on the coffee table. The solitary picture on the chimney breast—there was no fireplace—was a splat from a giant fountain pen.

"Sit down, Rob," Gray invited, looking up and around as he sat himself. "The white walls aren't my doing."

Rob nodded. "I'm not judging. I know nothing about interior design."

"Same here. These—" Gray patted the sofa he was sitting on "—were the designer's idea. He sketched the entire room for me, put together a swatch and everything, but I never seem to get around to it."

Rob nodded, empathising. Zoë had made all the decorating decisions in their house, mainly because Rob had been doing so much overtime he was never home, although they had picked out the sofa together. He leaned forward to pick up his coffee from Gray's smear-free glass table, peering through it at the floor. "Oak?"

"Yes," Gray confirmed. "Now that *was* my doing. Two layers of carpet on top of lino on top of terrible floorboards. It all had to come out. The rest of the house was as it is now."

"It's got a lot of potential."

"I quite agree—in the right hands. I don't know..." He sighed as he looked around again. "I can't muster the enthusiasm, not when it's only me looking at it. Believe it or not, you're my first visitor this year. That's your leaving card, by the way." He gave the blue envelope a push, and it slid across the table. "I forgot to take it with me."

"Sixth sense." Rob picked it up and slit the top open with his key, laughing as he pulled out the card: *Good Luck – hope your new boss is less of a bastard.* "Depends who you ask," he said. "Cheers, Gray." He stood the card on the table and picked up his coffee again. "It's still a bit unreal. I keep going to check what shift I'm on and then remember I'm not. How long does that last?"

Gray tapped his finger against his lips, thinking, and then gave a resigned nod. "At least eleven months," he admitted. "And we didn't even have a shift pattern."

"You mean aside from if it was a day ending in Y?"

Gray chuckled. "That's the one. OK, to business. I was at Zoë's until around nine last night, and there was nothing going on. It's a very quiet street."

"Yeah, it is." Rob had never been fond for that reason. Where he'd grown up, everyone knew everyone else and kept an eye out for each other's kids. The South East was different, London especially, so it was only his northern roots showing.

"Typically, when I played back the video, I discovered if I'd stayed another ten minutes, I'd have got a good look at the van that stopped across the street—unless they were waiting for me to leave, of course—but it could've belonged to a resident."

"What kind of van?" Rob asked.

"A white Transit." Gray picked up a remote control and pointed it at the TV.

"Sounds like Bish's van."

"One of the guys from your regiment?"

"Yeah. I was gonna tell you...never mind. It can wait." A fuzzy image filled the screen—a perspective that was unfamiliar to Rob but wouldn't be to Lucas. "Where did you put the camera?"

"Under the bay window, next to the gas meter."

"That explains the kneecap view." Rob was looking through the gate at the street, empty apart from an occasional flash of movement as a car drove past.

"I'll fast forward." Gray skipped the video to nine minutes and forty seconds, when a white van slowed to a stop opposite the house. If they'd been parked a few inches further back, the camera would've picked up the cab. As it was, Rob could see only the driver's right shoulder, along with the side of the van.

"That's not Bish's," he said.

"Are you sure?"

"Yep. For starters, that one's in better nick, and his has got a sliding door. I was shoved through it on Friday night."

"Was the side bump rail missing?" Gray asked.

"Yeah."

"And the nearside headlamp was dipped?"

"I wouldn't know about that. Why?"

"I saw it outside the restaurant. I assumed it was a delivery van of some sort." Gray increased the playback speed; they watched an hour of video footage in fifteen minutes, during which the van remained stationary, and then the screen went black. "No movement for the sensors to pick up," Gray explained.

"So they could've been there all night?"

"Possibly. Have you ever noticed a van there before?"

"Not that I recall, but I wasn't looking for one. People keep to themselves and have no time for nosey neighbours."

Gray hummed thoughtfully. "I hadn't realised how frustrating this PI business is. All that information we had at our fingertips in the SIU—I could've been straight into the DVLA database to check if one was registered locally."

"I was thinking the same this morning," Rob said. "A blue Mondeo tailed me from my mum's to the motorway."

"An unmarked car?"

"Yep. I asked Aitch to run the plates to make sure."

"They might've been after a nick," Gray reasoned.

"If it had happened just the once, I'd agree. But I saw them on Sunday after footy too—actually, that's the other thing I want to ask you. The Strang case is still ongoing, yeah?"

"To my knowledge. Why?"

"Dan Jeffries mentioned an auction sting."

Gray nodded. "Comco Glass, yes. I'm not privy to the ins and outs of it, but it's part of the SIU investigation."

Rob drank his coffee while he absorbed the information. They'd known before they brought down the inheritance scam that it was only a tiny part of a massive operation, but Rob had left the SIU straight after. Even if Jess Lambert was the brains behind that part of it, once he had confirmation she hadn't been involved in anything worse, all he'd cared about was seeing Anders Folden put behind bars. Folden was devious and dangerous—the perfect hitman—and Rob regretted not killing him when he'd had the chance.

"What's on your mind, Rob?"

He looked up from his cup to find Gray watching him intently. "Do you think this could be anything to do with it?"

"I couldn't say for sure, but I doubt it." Gray remained cool and passive, but he was well-practised in that regard, and it meant nothing.

"The Mondeo's registered to the Met," Rob said, holding eye contact, looking for a reaction.

"What was it doing two hundred miles north of London?"

Absolutely zip. "Well, unless it's one big coincidence that someone's watching Zoë's place and my mum's..."

"They're keeping an eye on you," Gray finished.

There went Rob's last futile hope he was being paranoid.

"We can come back to that. You were going to tell me the full story."

"Yeah, I was." Rob swallowed a mouthful of coffee for lubrication, aware that Gray had intentionally shut him down. "Right, from the beginning...I joined a REME unit in Germany as an apprentice, and when I qualified, I took over from the motor mechanic. There were five of us: Lieutenant Yvette Parker aka Tonka, Sergeant Ethan McGrath, Sergeant Olivia Simpson—she was the mechanic before me, they called her Lisa—Corporal Harry Wilson aka Jock, John Garvey aka Bish, and me."

"Aka...?"

Rob sighed. He'd thought he might get away with it. "Sharon."

"Sharon?"

"Sharon Stone. It was that or Bart, but we already had Lisa. Yeah, don't think I can't see you smirking."

Gray was doing a bit more than smirking. "How did I not know this? Sharon Stone..." It had really tickled him. "I always wondered where your...unconventional interrogation technique came from."

Rob would have been laughing too—if he hadn't heard it all before, and if he wasn't stressing about Zoë and Lucas. To be fair, stress was probably causing Gray's giggles, and he got them in check pretty quickly.

"Sorry," he said, dabbing his eyes. "Keep going."

It was hard in the face of Gray's mirth, but Rob forged on. "We were home on leave when Tonka received a call to say Ethan was in police custody. He'd caught his wife cheating on him and took a cricket bat to the pair of them, put his wife in hospital for six weeks. The bloke she was with...when the military police found him, he was naked, tied to a chair, and so badly battered they couldn't even identify him by his tattoos."

"Jesus."

"Yeah, it was bad. But it wasn't really a shock to any of us. Ethan went down for manslaughter on a defence of diminished responsibility due to PTSD, which is bollocks. I'm not disputing he's got PTSD—occupational hazard and all that—but he'd always been a liability. Him and Jock were at each other all the time, although Jock's a piece of work, so I could sort of understand why Ethan wanted to smash his face in."

"Where's Ethan now?"

"In Brookhurst secure hospital."

"So he's not the reason for the surveillance on Zoë and Lucas?"

"Indirectly. Last Friday, Tonka—" Rob spotted Gray's inquisitive frown and explained. "She grew up on a massive farm and is a bit nifty in a tractor."

"Fitting."

"Fits better than Yvette, that's for sure. Ethan didn't have a nickname—I don't know if that was his doing." Rob had never been interested enough to give it any thought. "Anyway, Tonka told me he was coming up for release and she knew someone who'd wipe his record for half a million quid. She asked me to contribute, and I told her I couldn't help. It would've cleaned me out, but even if I had that kind of money going spare, I wouldn't waste it on Ethan. As far as I'm concerned, he deserved everything he got and more, and Tonka knows that's how I feel."

"What did she do when you said no?"

"She got a bit shirty but let me leave without further argument. I should've realised something was off—now I think about it, she doesn't back down easily—but I just wanted to get out of there and back to the Quarterhouse."

"Did you get lost?" Gray asked dryly.

Rob managed a chuckle. "I couldn't be arsed, to tell the truth. They'd have taken the piss if I'd turned up, and I wasn't exactly in the mood for partying after I left Tonka's. Sorry."

"No, don't apologise. I understand. If I could've given Dom the slip, I wouldn't have gone to my leaving do either. Have you spoken to Hedley yet?"

"Yeah, on Saturday. She was all right—more worried than annoyed. I told her enough to assure her I wasn't in trouble. I hope I didn't speak too soon. Did she enjoy herself?"

"I think so. She had a good drink, anyway. She'll miss you."

"Yeah." Rob would miss her too, but after seeing Lois and Amber over the weekend, he knew he'd made the right decision. "So, this investigation Bish and Jock want us to do..."

"They want us to find out what Tonka's up to, I assume?"

"That's what Jock said, but I don't buy it. The thing about him and Bish is they did twenty-two years, and they're unquestioningly loyal—I have enough of a problem disobeying Tonka myself, and I got out well before the rest of them. According to Jock, she did a bunk on Saturday morning, and it dawned on me on the way here.

If she's under surveillance, I'd have been seen at her place on Friday night. The Met will suspect I'm involved."

Gray looked pained. "That's down to me. I hassled Petridis into sending out the troops. Traffic cameras picked up your bike on the M40."

"Shit. So they could've traced back to when I left Tonka's."

"It's possible. I'm really sorry, Rob."

"Why? It's not your fault." His anger was surfacing, but Gray wasn't the target. "Right...let's think about this..." He needed to get it straight in his head. "After Jock told me about the investment Tonka tried to sell them, I thought the bit about Ethan had to be a red herring, which is why I asked you to keep an eye on Zoë and Lucas. We both know the lengths people will go to for money, and Bish and Jock would have no qualms about doing the necessary to help Tonka out. But with that van at the house and the Met tailing me...I'm not sure Tonka wanted money at all. I think she used me as a decoy."

"That's one interpretation," Gray said.

"You don't agree."

"I don't necessarily disagree." He leaned over the arm of the sofa, retrieved a folder from the floor and handed it to Rob. "After we spoke, I contacted a couple of brokers to see what I could find out about Eastern European property investment. It's a burgeoning market."

Rob flicked through the sheets inside, such good as it did him—the hard sell condensed down to numbers, graphs and stock-broker-code bullet points for busy investors. "This doesn't prove Jock was telling the truth."

"No, but...sorry if I'm speaking out of turn here. I get the feeling there's no love lost between the two of you."

"You could say that."

"And presumably, Tonka's aware, so she'd know she stands more chance of getting money out of you by asking directly than by getting Jock to do her dirty work."

"She did ask, and I said no."

"That's what I mean, because I think you were on the right lines. This isn't about money."

"Then they're both red herrings."

"Or red flags. If she's in the kind of trouble we're familiar with, she's going to be watching what she says."

Rob thought back to the conversation in Tonka's garage, trying to remember the exact words. "I'm shit at decryption."

"Aye, that's why we make such a smashing team." Out came the fake Geordie accent, and Rob had no comeback, seeing as the brainy stuff was why he'd asked Gray to come in on the PI business.

"All right. I'll talk to Jock again, see if he's got any bumph on the investment."

"If you can get that information, I'll do the rest."

"Cheers." That saved Rob wading through reams of indecipherable financial jargon. "I'll see what else I can find out about Ethan's situation. What shall I tell Jock? Are we taking the case?"

"It's up to you. I can afford to keep us afloat for a while."

"You're already forking out for surveillance equipment," Rob argued.

"You paid for the website."

"Well...I paid for the domain name and bought Dan Jeffries a pint for setting it up."

"Which saved us money."

"And now I'm going to earn us some. I'll just make sure Jock knows he's only the handbag and we're calling the shots."

"Tell you what, why don't you organise a formal meeting, and we'll both go?"

"Yeah, that might be better." Rob drained the last of his coffee and got up, ready to leave. "I'm going to pop over to Zoë and Lu's, make sure they're all right and see if there's any sign of that van."

Gray followed him to the front door. "Let me know how you get on. I'll leave the camera running for now, but I won't bother going over there, unless you want me to."

"Let's see how it goes. I'll alert Zoë and Travis to be on the lookout for anything suspicious, but if the police are keeping an eye, they don't need us amateurs to protect them."

"Amateurs? We're highly skilled, experienced private investigat—oh!"

Rob turned back to see why Gray had stopped and found him frowning at his phone. "What's up?"

"They've released him. Huh. I wasn't expecting that."

Rob raised an eyebrow rather than ask.

"Will was arrested earlier."

"What was it this time? Abandoned alpaca?"

Gray laughed. "He broke into a building to rescue some stray cats, and he had a wireless jammer on him. Or maybe not, if the police let him go."

"Didn't you give up the SIU for a quiet life?"

"That was the idea. Best-laid plans of... Alpaca?"

Rob shrugged. "First thing that came to mind."

"I'm sure they'll feature at some point."

"More than likely. I'll email you any info I get out of Jock and let you know about the meeting."

"OK. Take it easy, Rob."

"You too, mate."

Gray waited at the door and raised his hand as Rob rode off.

On to the next job, and not one he was looking forward to.

17: Due Care

AFTER ROB LEFT, Gray backed up the video footage to an encrypted external drive and then watched it again on his computer's high-res monitor, pausing and zooming in on the van and its occupant. Or occupants, as he discovered when he advanced, frame by frame, and a second head briefly popped into view. Neither was identifiable, not even by so much as gender or build; at a distance and in the dark, the picture quality was awful.

For the time being, he concentrated on the van, comparing the shape of the side panel and door to images online. It didn't take him long to narrow down the make and model, and it was one used by the Met...and by thousands of UK businesses. Gray shut the browser window and returned to staring at the blurry still.

"This is so frustrating."

If he'd gone for the streetlamp-mounted camera, or stayed longer...but he hadn't, and there was nothing else he could glean from what he'd got. He'd review whatever footage he collected tonight, and if need be, tomorrow, he'd go and see Paddy again.

***

"Rob. Hi."

"Alright, Zo?"

She was already eyeing him with suspicion—understandably when all he'd told her was he needed to speak to her and Travis together. First time for everything. As he stepped into the house, a door slammed upstairs, followed by the heavy, muted thud of a football bouncing on carpet and Lucas's appearance at the top of the stairs. He spotted Rob, yelled, "Dad!" ran halfway down and jumped the remaining steps, grabbing Rob around the middle while the football thunked its way to the bottom of the stairs.

"Alright, Lu? How you doing?"

"What did I say?" Zoë warned. Lucas peered up at Rob and slow-blinked.

"What's this? No football in the house?" Rob guessed. Lucas burrowed into his jacket. "Oy. Don't think I'm gonna take your side, mate." No response to that, Rob put his hands on Lucas's shoulders and took a step back. His son grinned sheepishly.

"Can you play in your room for a bit, Lu?" Zoë's tone turned the suggestion into an order.

"Why?"

"Your dad needs to talk to us."

"I'm us!"

"Travis and me," Zoë clarified, though Lucas understood perfectly the first time. He huffed about it, but he turned around and started back up the stairs. "Take the ball with you, please," Zoë said wearily and gave Rob a slow blink identical to their son's.

With another giant huff, Lucas collected his football and plodded, at a rate of a step every three seconds, back to his room.

"Kids," Zoë muttered.

"He's just going through a naughty phase," Rob defended with a wink.

"Yeah, it started seven years ago. I'm going to pour some wine. Do you want anything?" She was already moving towards the kitchen.

"I'm fine, cheers." Rob watched her a moment longer before entering the living room, where the low-volume TV was tuned to a news channel and Travis was working on his laptop, which he immediately abandoned.

"Alright? How's it going?" He half rose to shake Rob's hand.

"Not bad, mate," Rob said, as always distracted by the difference between his memory of this room and the reality. The big, cosy sofa he and Zoë had bought together was long gone, in its place an enormous leather L-shaped grey boxy thing like the seating in a doctor's waiting room.

Zoë came in carrying a glass big enough to take a bottle of wine, and it was almost full. She kept hold of it as she sat next to Travis, leaving the shorter limb of the L to Rob. It was comfy enough, he supposed, and she'd given him first refusal on the old sofa, so he couldn't complain. Unfortunately, his flat was pre-furnished—cheaper rent—and he had nowhere to store a sofa until such point as he could afford a better place, so it had gone to a furniture recycling warehouse. At least somebody, somewhere was getting use out of it.

Travis kept shifting his eyes between Rob and Zoë. If he had one redeeming feature—well, he had quite a few, Rob was slowly beginning to accept—his politeness had stood out from the get-go. He was waiting for someone to speak, and Rob was still trying to come up with a way to explain without worrying them. There wasn't one. Rob opened his mouth at the same time Zoë did, but she got there first.

"Is everything all right with your mum?"

"Yeah." And now he felt like a thoughtless bastard. His mum and Zoë got along brilliantly, so of course she'd have thought he was here to deliver bad news.

"Sorry. Mum's fine. Same as always, really. Tough as old boots. Harvey's not doing great, though."

"Oh?"

"Cancer of the prostate. He's starting treatment in a couple of weeks. The doctor's confident the radiotherapy will kick it into touch."

"Thank goodness." Zoë put her palm to her chest and exhaled heavily. It was a dramatic reaction, but Rob didn't think she was putting it on. He needed to tread lightly.

"What I came to talk to you about..." He sighed. "However I put this, you'll worry, but everything's OK."

Zoë lifted her wine glass to her lips, her eyes growing wide above it. She swallowed down a couple of large gulps, gripped Travis's hand and nodded for Rob to continue.

"Gray and I think the Met have surveillance on the house."

"Our house?"

"Yeah. That visit you got the other day from Jock?"

"He's the guy who came to the door on Saturday," Zoë explained to Travis.

"The geezer who looked like he'd had a frying pan in the face?"

Rob chuckled. "That's the one. As I told Zo, he's one of my old army mates. I say mates—we're not, but Jock and one of the other lads have hired Gray and me to look into our old CO." The events weren't quite in the right order, but it didn't sound as bad this way around. "They think she's in trouble of some sort, and it looks like the Met have already picked up on it."

"Why are they watching this place?" Zoë asked. "Are they expecting Jock to come back?"

"No. They're watching me."

"Oh, no. Don't tell me you're in trouble again."

"Again?"

"I'm joking, Rob."

He couldn't see the funny side, not after the con he'd had to pull on them all for their own safety. Zoë knew the truth now and said she'd accepted it, but joking or not, the accusation still stung.

With perfect timing, Lucas shouted from upstairs, "Are you finished yet, Dad? I wanna show you my new game."

"All right, Lu. Be up in a minute." Rob turned his attention back to Zoë and Travis. "I just wanted to give you both a heads-up." He decided to skip 'there's a spy camera mounted on the front of the house'. "If you spot anything you're not happy about, let me know, OK? I'll have a chat with Hedley tomorrow, anyway, see if she can shed any light on what's going on. I also wanted to ask if you've got any plans over the spring break. I was thinking of taking Lu up to my mum's."

Zoë shook her head. "I don't think we have—Trav?"

"I might've looked for something last minute, but no. Nothing planned."

"Is that all right, then?" Rob asked them both.

Travis raised his hands. "It's between you two."

Zoë shrugged. "A week without 'Mum, can I have...', 'Mum, can we go...'? Sounds good to me."

Rob pushed up from the sofa, as did Travis. There were bum-shaped impressions where they'd been sitting.

"Memory foam," Travis said. "Comfy, eh?"

"Very." It wasn't a lie, but it had nothing on the old sofa.

"D'you want a drink, Rob? Beer?"

"No, I'm fine, honestly. I'm ready to flake out, but I'd best go have a look at this game first."

Travis nodded enthusiastically. "It's awesome."

"Yeah?"

Zoë tutted. "I knew it! You didn't buy it for Lu, you bought it for you."

Travis scowled. "Did not. I ain't got an Xbox."

"Aw, poor baby. Santa might bring you one if you're very, very good."

"Always," Travis replied with a grin.

Rob unclamped his teeth long enough to say, "See you in a bit," and made a swift retreat upstairs to Lucas's room. In fairness to Zoë, she usually avoided acting lovey-dovey in front of him. He kind of wished she wouldn't. He needed to get used to it.

"Oh, wow. Those graphics!"

Lucas was sitting on the floor, leaning his back against his bed, and didn't look away from the screen. His arms were up in the air, hard left, hard right, moving with the controller as he steered an unbelievably realistic Koenigsegg around a racetrack.

"You're good at that, Lu."

"Cheers." That was all Rob was getting out of him until the current race came to an end, at which point Lucas sighed despondently. "Third again." He held up the controller. "Your turn."

"Can I?" Rob grabbed the controller before his son changed his mind and sat next to him with knees bent; the gap between the bed and chest of drawers wasn't wide enough to accommodate his legs. "Right, what do I do?"

Lucas reached across and pressed buttons until he was back at the start screen. "Choose a car."

Rob scanned the list of supercars, his heart skipping a beat when he reached 'Lamborghini Aventador'. He hoped Tonka hadn't done anything silly.

"My other car's the Ferrari," Lucas said helpfully.

"Yeah? I wish mine was." Rob opted for the 1997 Lamborghini Diablo and ignored Lucas's disapproving 'huh'. "What do I do next? Choose a race? Is that Rio?"

"Yeah. That's the one I just did."

"That'll do me." Rob pressed what he thought was the start button, but nothing happened. Lucas came to his aid.

"D'you want me to teach you the controls?"

"Nah," Rob said bravely. He didn't mind making a fool of himself in front of Lucas, which was exactly how it panned out. It wasn't cool driving a Diablo at forty miles an hour, but once around the track and he thought he'd nailed it...until he was rammed from behind by a McLaren and left wheel-spinning on the verge. Travis was right; it was an amazing game that made Rob's old favourite *Gran Turismo* look like a 1980s 8-bit video game. Eventually, the digital mechanics arrived to tow his Diablo off the track, and Lucas patted his thigh.

"Never mind, Dad. You'll be better next time. Want another go?"

"Tell you what, I'll watch you. Learn from the best."

Grinning, Lucas took back the controller and whizzed through the start-up screens, off to Monaco, his Koenigsegg in pole position. It was better than watching TV, but distracting—helicopters, passenger jets, camera flashes, skid marks appearing on the road—Rob was in awe of Lucas's ability to concentrate with all of that going on.

"So, d'you fancy going up to Nan and Grandad Harvey's?"

"Yeah! When? This weekend?"

"School holidays."

Another race finished in third place. "Are we going on the bike?"

Rob laughed. "Nope."

"Aw, Da-a-ad. But I'm nearly eight!"

"Nearly eight..." Rob tutted. Lucas had not long turned seven. "I told you. When you're big enough to ride a bike of your own..." With a struggle, Rob pulled his knees almost to his chest so he could put his feet flat on the floor. He got up stiffly. "Right, I'm going."

"'Kay, Dad. Swimming on Saturday?"

"I'll check with your mum, but yeah, probably. Be good."

"I will. Bye, Dad."

"Laters, taters." He left Lucas to his racing and returned downstairs to the living room, where Travis was watching out of the front window and Zoë was pretending to watch TV. She was still worried about what he'd told them. "You OK, Zo?"

"I think so." She put her wine down and beckoned him close, holding up her arms for a hug. She always did it, and it had always felt awkward in front of Travis, but not so much this evening. Rob's animosity had taken a back seat; all that mattered was Lucas and Zoë's safety. How could he begrudge Travis when the guy cared for them as much as Rob did? He'd look out for them.

"See you Saturday?" Rob slowly eased out of the hug and braced for hearing they'd made other plans because he should've been at his mum's.

"Yeah," Zoë confirmed. "Please be careful."

"Promise."

Her eyebrow lift was as instinctual as the word tumbling from his tongue. Rob smiled to himself as he left the room. He wasn't the same guy anymore—the one who used the job as an excuse to break promises he should never have made in the first place.

As he neared the front door, he slowed for Travis to catch up. "Thanks for this."

"No problem." Travis opened the door and then followed Rob outside. "If there's anything I can do..."

"Cheers, but I don't think there is."

"If that changes..."

"I'll let you know."

"Alright, mate. See you." Travis went back inside.

Rob stopped at the gate, looking along the road: no white van, no blue Mondeo, as far as he could tell. Behind him, the key turned and the safety chain slid across. He glanced back at the house, scanning the vicinity of the gas meter until he located the camera. The relief that stole the last of his energy confirmed he'd done the right thing.

***

Rob's old army mates certainly put their money where their mouths were. An hour after Rob's text arrived confirming he'd arranged a meeting for the following morning, Gray received a second message notifying him of a deposit from 'Sequrco' into their business account. Gray stared at it until the pound sign morphed into a miniature dinosaur and chomped its way through the numbers. £5,000. It was enough to secure their services for at least the next two weeks—unless Jock was expecting twenty-four-hour surveillance.

It seemed they had their first clients, and it was, potentially, a much bigger and more interesting case than Gray had anticipated, which would have been more along the lines of spying on 'sick' employees or running background checks for investors.

But 'potentially' was key; Tonka might simply have cut Bish and Jock out of an investment opportunity, hoping to maximise her return. It didn't explain why she'd told Rob something else—strictly speaking, that had nothing to do with the investigation they were being paid to undertake—and Gray wondered whether their clients would expect a refund if it turned out to be a cut-and-run.

He'd have to check the situation with Rob tomorrow morning, ideally before their breakfast meeting. He reloaded the text confirmation just so he could scowl at it.

Nine-thirty in Gatwick—'halfway' in terms of travelling time rather than distance. Much as Gray appreciated it was closer to them than it was to Bish and Jock, it still meant having to be out of the house by seven, and it was almost midnight. Sleepy or not, he needed to go to bed.

Up in his room, Gray undressed in the dark and sat in his boxers on the side of the bed. His mind kept flitting from the case to Will's arrest to Rob being tailed and back to the case. He couldn't see how the Met watching Rob—assuming they were—was linked to Tonka, and that worried him more, because he couldn't think of any other reason Rob would be under surveillance. Unless Zoë's new partner was shady? In which case, Rob's visit would've done more harm than good, although, given his feelings towards the guy, if Travis was involved in anything, Rob would've picked up on it a long time ago, and he wouldn't have kept it to himself.

"OK, not Travis, then," Gray confirmed aloud. He switched on the bedside lamp and just about got his pyjama top on before his thoughts wandered again.

The other possibility—which he wasn't going to mention until he knew more—was that Tonka had told Rob the truth, and the rest of it—Jock's investment story and hiring PIs—was a ruse. It would mean Rob was right about being used as a decoy. What Gray needed to establish was whether Bish and Jock's loyalty to their former CO extended to stitching up one of their own, and he could glean a sense of that from how they operated their business. It gave him the impetus to finish putting on his PJs and get into bed. Pillows propped, he grabbed his laptop and opened the web browser.

Flash website, very healthy end-of-year accounts, dozens of positive reviews from staff and customers alike, Sequrco's clients were big, important companies—banks, pharmaceuticals and a couple of the cruise lines. They must have been raking it in, and while they stood to make a tidy sum out of investing in overseas property, it wasn't lucrative enough for them to go to the lengths of hiring PIs to track Tonka down. On Bish and Jock's part at least, Gray could safely conclude it wasn't about the money. He went back to the review site containing testimonials from their staff.

Excellent rates of pay, great working conditions, paid leave, health insurance, company vehicles, approachable bosses—give or take the occasional one star from 'dismissed and disgruntled', the comments were all much the same. Sequrco was good to its staff; it was a successful and well-respected company, all of which indicated Bish and Jock weren't in on Tonka's scheme, if indeed it was a scheme.

Whatever was going on, Gray had seen enough to be confident their clients were completely above board. He was ready for sleep, and sent a 'good night' message to Will, who would've been in bed for hours already, but apart from his text to say the police had released him, Gray hadn't heard from him all evening.

It was possible—probable—Will had gone back to the building after dark to collect the jammer from wherever he'd hidden it, or even to make a second attempt at rescuing the cats, hopefully not on his own. He and Tie were only two of a network of activists, some of whom came to the farmhouse when Gray was staying over. They all seemed decent people, even if a lot of them did look like ex-cons, stare at his boots—in judgement, not admiration—and ask too many questions about what he did for a living. He kept his answers current: *I'm a postgrad student, part-time lecturer and extra in a soap opera.*

That was usually sufficient to throw them off his ex-copper scent; somehow, he didn't think Will would've shared that detail with them, if he talked to them about Gray at all. Animal libbers were a lot like undercover officers; they went by pseudonyms and used informal code when discussing cases. Unless their significant others were also 'in the job', at best they'd be the anonymous 'other half', 'the wife' or 'the husband'. Still, it was comforting to think that Will might've mentioned him in those terms.

18: Briefing

THE BUZZ OF Rob's phone vibrating wouldn't normally have woken him, but he'd slept lightly all night. He picked it up, opened his eyes long enough to confirm who was calling, hit the answer button and closed his eyes again. "Morning, Ma'am."

"Rob, is everything all right?"

"Yeah. Other than it's bloody early."

"I just picked up your voicemail from last night."

"It wasn't six a.m. urgent."

"It was eleven p.m. urgent..."

"Fair comment." Rob yawned and threw off the duvet. There was no point pretending he'd get any more sleep. He grabbed his bathrobe and talked as he walked to the bathroom. "Any idea why the Met are on my tail?"

"Are they? It's not our lot."

"I didn't think it was."

"Are you sure it's the Met?"

"Yep. Got the reg on a Mondeo up at my mum's. There's also been a van outside Zoë's—not sure on that one, though."

"That's...odd." She fell quiet for a moment. He could almost hear her mentally checking through the department's current case load. Apart from anything that had come in since Friday, which wouldn't have involved him anyway, Rob had already done that. "I wonder what the Berringers are up to," she said.

"Why?"

"Well, I don't know that they're up to anything, but I had a call from the prison yesterday. Naomi Silvestri and Wilfred Richards planned to visit Berringer Junior next Monday."

"What the hell? Richards—"

"Is our lead witness. I know. And...I've just realised that's who Gray Fisher's seeing."

"Yeah, it is," Rob said, not that she'd asked for confirmation. "Can you order them not to visit?"

"I've spoken to the both of them and advised against it, but I can't stop them, not that I can think of any good reason why they'd want to visit Berringer."

"You think he's still pulling the strings from inside?"

"It wouldn't surprise me. When I get to the office, I'll have a look and see what I can find out. Text me that reg."

"Will do, Ma'am."

"Ahem."

"Martina."

"Better. Of course, if it is related to the Berringers, it'll be—"

"The SIU," Rob finished. He didn't try to hide his aggravation.

"At least they're looking after you."

"I guess." Small mercies. "I can't wait for the trials to be over."

"You and me both." She wanted it for his sake, not her own. After Rob had left the SIU, he'd told her as much as he could about what he'd had to do. She knew what it had cost him and how desperate he was to put that part of his life behind him once and for all.

"Can I ask you something, Rob?"

"Sure."

"Are you having a pee?"

Rob cleared his throat and flushed the loo. "No, Ma'am."

"Ugh. That's... Just go away."

Rob laughed. "Have a good one, Ma...mate."

"I'll take that over Ma'am every time. You too. Bye."

***

Gray had fallen asleep with the light on, and his laptop, which had been on his chest, was on its side next to him. He was lucky he hadn't flipped it off the bed in the night—luckier still he'd woken naturally at 6:30, seeing as he'd forgotten to set his alarm. He righted his laptop and reactivated it so he could shut it down. The screen brightened on the open message window; Will had read his 'good night' but hadn't replied, which wasn't like him. It usually produced at least a smiley, more often a comment of the 'don't you mean good morning?' variety. He'd be at work now, so calling him would have to wait until after the meeting.

In the shower, Gray contemplated the journey ahead. During peak times, there was little to choose between driving to Gatwick and taking public transport. Rush hour on the M25... But he had a car. Only a budget hatchback, admittedly, but still a car. And he loved driving. He didn't even mind sitting in traffic, although if he was going to do it, he'd need to leave within the next ten minutes.

"Who am I kidding? There is no if."

It was a little more than ten minutes later that he programmed the satnav with the postcode for the hotel and set off for their 'breakfast meeting'. The chain was listed on the clients page of Sequrco's website, which Gray took as further indication of the company's good standing. He usually avoided preconceptions, but on this occasion, he hoped they'd offer some much-needed balance. He'd experienced Rob's hostility firsthand and, irrespective of what had gone on between him and Jock in the past, the old wisdom applied: the customer was always right...until proven otherwise.

For the time of day—coming up on eight o'clock by that point—the motorways weren't too bad. He knew how to drive in heavy traffic; even at the busiest junctions, he mostly managed to keep moving, arriving at the hotel at 9:10—twenty minutes early, and time enough to squeeze in an espresso and the trip to the bathroom that would surely ensue.

The espresso was fast acting as well as excellent, and he was halfway through a second cup when Rob's bike pulled into the car park. It was one hell of a machine, and at 1000cc, not really a road bike, but Rob knew how to handle it. He stopped in a narrow space directly outside the window next to Gray's table and looked in, nodding an acknowledgement.

"You must be Rob's business partner."

So much for talking to Rob before their meeting. Gray turned to face the man who'd spoken and rose to shake his hand—the left one. "Mr. Garvey?"

"Yeah, well...I prefer Bish."

"Bish. And—"

"Jock to you." Jock leaned in as he gave Gray's hand a rough pump up and down. "Did he put up a fight?"

"Sorry?"

"Shaz, erm...Rob. About taking the job on."

"We haven't formally agreed yet that we will, Mr. Wilson."

Jock pulled his top lip between his teeth; the likeness to a British bulldog was uncanny. "You got the deposit, didn't you?"

"Yes, thanks, and we appreciate the prompt payment. Rest assured, if we can't help, you'll get it back in full." Gray was starting to understand Rob's reticence. Jock was the sort of guy who bullied to get his own way, but he was also an ex-squaddie with a long service record, used to following orders whether he agreed with them or not. "Let's get settled and order breakfast. I'm not a fan of doing business on an empty stomach."

"A man after my own heart," Jock said with a wide grin, less bulldog, more emoticon. He and Bish sat in the chairs on the other side of Gray's table. A moment later, Rob joined them.

"Sorry about that. I had to move the bike. Security kicked up a stink."

"Who was it?" Jock asked.

"Dunno. His badge was flipped. Five ten, light-brown hair, beer gut."

"Alan," Bish and Jock said together.

"He's a decent bloke," Bish defended, "just a bit of a jobsworth. D'you want me to have a word?"

"Nah. It's done now." Rob smiled quickly and picked up a menu. The other three men followed his lead. "How was the drive here?" he asked generally as he perused the selection.

"Clear for us," Bish answered.

"Yes, much the same," Gray said.

"Good stuff."

"Why do they have to do all this foreign muck?" Jock grumbled. "Continental breakfast...if I wanted a continental breakfast, I'd hop on a fucking ferry." He clapped the menu shut and sat back, arms folded. "Full English and a cuppa. That's proper breakfast."

Gray kept his eyes lowered and made a show of studying his menu, aware of Rob bristling on his left and the arrival of a member of wait staff on his right.

"Good morning. Are you ready to order?"

"I am," Bish answered. "A Full English and a pot of tea for me, please."

"Toast or fried bread with that?"

"Fried bread, please."

The waiter noted it down on their tablet and looked expectantly at Jock.

"Same here, ta."

That, too, was jotted down. Rob was next.

"Bacon toasted sandwich and coffee, please."

"Filter, cappuccino..."

"Filter, cheers."

"OK, and for you?" The waiter smiled at Gray. "Another espresso?"

"Lovely as they are, I'll be flying if I drink any more. Please can I have two croissants, butter and jam, and...a glass of orange juice?"

"Of course." The waiter scribbled once more and departed.

"What was *that*?" Jock watched the waiter leave and muttered something under his breath that sounded a lot like 'poofter'.

Gray decided to get the ball rolling rather than wait for their food to arrive. He wasn't sure how long he could tolerate Jock's bigotry without taking him to task. "OK, can we start from the beginning? Rob's given me all of the information he has, but I'd like to hear it from you two, if you don't mind?"

"Not at all," Bish said. From the way he adjusted in his seat, making himself comfortable, Gray had the feeling this was going to be a long story. "We all came out of the army at the same time—me, Jock and Tonka—five years ago, and until a month back, we hadn't seen her in a good while. What d'you reckon, Jock? Three years?"

"Yeah. She was down our way for her dad's funeral, wasn't she? We met up after."

"That's right," Bish confirmed.

"Did you stay in touch by other means?" Gray asked.

"We talked on the phone a few times—I couldn't give you dates and whatnot. She's not on social networks, so nothing like that."

"You said she got in touch last month. Was that by phone?"

"Yeah, she called Bish," Jock answered. "And—"

"Maybe Bish should explain," Rob cut in.

Jock did the lip-suck again but stayed quiet. He outsized Bish in all directions and, from what Rob had said, he'd been a higher rank than him in the army, yet Jock readily deferred and let Bish continue.

"She left a message on my mobile, short and sweet. How are ya, pop over next time you're up this way, et cetera. As it happened, we were up for a gala in Blackfriars the following weekend, so I called her back and we arranged to get together for Sunday lunch. We went to some pub not far from her gaff—three courses for twenty quid or whatever it is, you know how those places are. We were there an hour, if that, before we left and went back to the house. I was driving, but Jock and Tonka were on the beer. She gets all dewy-eyed when she's had a few, starts talking about how she's thinking of moving to Germany, how much she misses Siggy and all that jazz."

"Who's Siggy?" Gray queried.

"Her bird," Jock said.

"Not exactly," Rob argued and explained, for Gray's benefit, "They're romantically involved, but they've never officially been an item."

Jock scoffed. "They've been banging each other for twenty years. I'd say that's pretty fucking official."

"Let's leave that for now," Gray interjected before Rob retaliated. Their breakfast also made a timely arrival, and the conversation was put on hold while they sorted out cutlery and poured tea, coffee and juice.

Jock nodded at Gray's plate. "How d'you keep going off a couple of airy bread rolls?"

Gray smiled disarmingly. "I don't, to be quite honest. I'll be starving by eleven."

"Should've gone with the Full English."

"I would've done if there'd been a vegetarian version."

"One of them salad tossers, are you?"

"I am," Gray confirmed. Beside him, Rob turned his angry growl into a clearing of the throat.

Jock picked up the HP Sauce bottle, shook it to within an inch of its life and liberally doused his breakfast. "It's meant to be healthier for you, that veggie malarkey. Low fat and all that."

"Very true." Croissants with butter and jam probably contained as much fat as the fry-up on Jock's plate, but nothing further was said about it. "So, you had drinks with Tonka," Gray prompted.

"Mmm." Bish had shoved a full rasher of bacon in his mouth and chewed at speed to get it down to an amount he could talk over. "She asked us how Ethan was doing—one of the lads who ended up in the nut house—and we didn't know." He swallowed, chasing it with a mouthful of tea and a satisfied sigh. "We hadn't visited him for ages, and she only said it to put us on a guilt trip. She'd seen him a couple of weeks before and knew good and well how he was doing."

"It worked, though," Jock said.

"Yeah, it did." Bish jabbed his fork into the other bacon rasher and lifted it from the plate. "We went to see him the week after. He'd just got out of the isolation unit, attacked one of the nurses." In went the bacon.

Jock gave Rob a supercilious nod. He'd already imparted that information, obviously. Gray heard the loud crunch of Rob tearing a chunk from his toastie. Keeping his mouth full—a wise move.

"The other thing Tonka wanted to know is if we'd seen Shaz...Rob. She'd heard you'd left the police a while ago and wondered if you'd gone back up north."

Rob swallowed in a hurry. "Where did she hear that?"

"Dunno. She didn't say."

Rob didn't do well at hiding how much that troubled him, but they could look into it later, once they'd extracted everything they could from Bish and Jock.

Gray continued. "Tell me about the investment. When did she first mention that to you?"

"Beginning of last week. Her brother put her on to it—he's got money in land overseas and said we needed to move fast. If we could buy while the price was still under ten euros, guaranteed we'd quadruple our investment."

"What's the name of the company?"

Bish shrugged, as did Jock.

"Yet you were prepared to risk a quarter of a million?"

"Tonka wouldn't screw us over," Bish said assuredly.

"No, she wouldn't," Rob agreed.

Gray turned and studied him in amazement. He'd thought Rob mistrusted everyone. "Is it an army thing?"

Rob laughed ruefully. "When it's life or death, you find out quickly who your friends are, and you stick together, come what may. There's no room for mistakes. Well, small ones…" He nodded at Bish, who wiggled his arm stump, funky-chicken style.

"I understand," Gray said.

Jock puffed air. "Don't let him fool you. He's no bloody hero. Just a cut, he said." He nudged Bish sharply with his elbow.

"It was just a cut!" Bish grumbled.

"What happened to it?" Gray asked, nodding at Bish's arm.

"Necrotising fasciitis and sepsis."

Gray grimaced without comment. Judging by the way Rob and Jock were acting, it was as gruesome as it sounded. He quickly moved on, or back, at least. "Did you give her blank cheques?"

"No, they were for a hundred and twenty-five grand each."

"Sorry. I meant was there a payee's name?"

"Ah. No. Tonka said she didn't know which of her brother's accounts it was going into. But she ripped them up—" Bish nodded at Rob "—right after you left."

"Right. So we need to look into her brother's business," Gray said.

"You're taking us on, then," Jock stated.

"Depends. What's the end goal? Find out what Tonka's up to, or find her?"

Bish shrugged; his stump bobbed and dunked into his egg yolk. He wiped it off with a napkin. "She'll have covered her tracks. You won't find out what she's up to until you find her."

"We don't investigate missing people," Gray said.

"She's not missing, she scarpered."

"Where do you think she's gone?"

"Germany—to Siggy's."

"Have you tried getting hold of Tonka? Or Siggy?"

Bish nodded. "Yep, both. Tonka's phone is out of service, Siggy says she's been in touch but she doesn't know where she is."

"Could she just be upset about the investment falling through?"

"If there was an investment to start with…" Bish replied cryptically.

"What makes you think there wasn't?"

"The way she ripped up our cheques, dramatic, like. That's not Tonka's style. If she was hacked off, she'd have told us so and sent us on our way, not put on a show."

"OK. What about her brother? Where can we get hold of him?"

"Not sure. He's away a lot on business. Try his secretary."

"And who's that?"

Bish's nose wrinkled. "Dunno that he's got one for sure, but he must have. So, are you gonna do this for us? We can pay you more if need be. Just name your price."

"That's a generous offer, Bish, but unnecessary at this stage." Gray glanced Rob's way. "Do you want to discuss it further in private?"

Rob shook his head but left it a good minute before he turned to Bish and Jock and said, "We'll take the case."

***

After they'd had another pot of tea each and availed themselves of the hotel's facilities, Bish and Jock departed, leaving Gray and Rob to discuss their next steps.

"I'm gonna have to go myself," Rob said. He was out of his seat and heading for the Gents' before Gray could confirm that was where he'd meant rather than home. With a few minutes to fill, Gray checked his phone for messages and tried to convince himself the absence of such from Will simply meant he was having a busy morning, not that he'd been arrested again. He didn't succeed and called Will's mobile.

It rang on but didn't go to voicemail, and reached the point where Gray thought he ought to hang up before Will answered with a neutral, "Hey."

"Hey, are you OK?" The question came out in a rush with the breath he'd been holding.

"Yeah, I'm fine." Will was distracted, offhand, probably in company. "What are you up to?" he asked.

"Just had a meeting with our first clients. How about you?"

"Stuck in traffic." Not in company, therefore. "How did it go?"

"Very well. It's an interesting one."

"Good. I'm glad it's working out for you and Rob."

"Thanks." Any less heartfelt congratulations Gray had yet to hear. "What's up?"

"Nothing. Why?"

"You sound...angry."

"Do I?"

"Are you angry?"

"Could be."

"Why?"

"No one reason. Crappy week, that's all."

"With work?"

"Work's fine."

"Headache?"

"It comes and goes. Nothing I can't handle. It's all the other stuff."

Gray floundered. He wanted to ask about the cats but wasn't sure if he was asking out of concern for their welfare or merely to avoid the patently obvious:

Will's anger was directed at him, and he had no idea why. There was only one way to find out. "Does that other stuff include me?"

"You're a part of it, yep."

"What've I done?"

"You tell me."

"I genuinely don't know."

"Really? Then you'll be surprised to hear Detective Chief Inspector Hedley called yesterday and barred me from going to see Freddie."

"Did she?"

"Huh. OK, you do sound surprised."

"That's because I am. I haven't seen Hedley since last Friday."

"But you have seen Rob," Will pointed out.

"Yes. But I didn't tell him you were going to see Berringer."

"Come on! You two have been working closely all week."

"Rob only got back from his mum's yesterday. We met for an hour and then again today—with our clients. The only time you've come up in conversation was when I got your text about being released without charge."

"So how did Hedley know?"

"Maybe Aaron or Naomi told her?"

"They didn't. You realise they're gonna have to go on their own now?"

Gray was starting to lose his cool. "I didn't tell Rob, or Martina Hedley, or *anyone at all* that you were going to see Berringer. If I had, I'd have told you."

"OK," Will accepted but his tone made clear he still didn't believe Gray.

"What's happening with the cats?" It was a lousy attempt to change the subject.

"Long story. I'll tell you at the weekend...if you're still coming over."

"Fine. I'm going. I'm sorry you're upset, Will, but you're taking it out on the wrong person." Gray ended the call without waiting for a reply. He was angry too, although not so much that he couldn't see the situation from Will's point of view.

19: Aftermath

I TELL YOU WHAT, you're lucky you didn't have the bacon." Rob resumed his seat and immediately chugged down a full glass of water.

"Salty?" Gray asked.

"Just a bit." Rob poured another glass and knocked back half of it. It had taken the edge off his thirst enough for him to notice Gray's mood had gone for a Burton. "You OK?"

"Yes, thanks." He covered whatever it was with a smile. "Productive meeting, I thought?"

None of Rob's business. "Definitely. So, plan of action?" He unlocked his phone and loaded the notes app.

"You still want me to look into the investment side?"

"If that's all right with you. I'm gonna get in touch with Siggy, see if Tonka will talk to me, assuming she's there and Siggy's covering for her. I'll try and contact her brother as well. Their mum died a long time ago—I didn't know about their dad. Tonka was very close to him."

"That's sad," Gray said somewhat perfunctorily. "OK. While you're doing that, I'll see if I can find out what Tonka's brother's up to business-wise. Do you know his full name?"

"Philip Parker. Not sure on a middle name."

"That should be enough to pull him up on the national..." Gray sagged and stuck out his bottom lip. "Bugger."

Rob laughed. "Google?"

"I suppose it'll have to do. I'd say it's like losing an arm, but Bish manages all right. Aside from table manners."

"Ha, yeah. I almost offered to cut up his breakfast."

"I wish you had. He seems a nice guy, though."

"He is. And Jock's mellowed."

Gray raised an eyebrow. "He gave you hell, didn't he?"

"To be honest, he was no worse than anyone else—outside of our unit. The army's rife with racism, or it was when I joined up. It's better now, but Tonka never tolerated his bullshit. When it comes down to it, he's all mouth, and he stuck up for me when it mattered. By the way, have you always been veggie?"

"No."

"Thought not. Will's doing?"

"Hmm. There's only so long you can keep enjoying lamb chops and sirloin steak when you've heard enough about the inner workings of a slaughterhouse to write a thesis."

"I don't think I want to know."

"Neither did I," Gray said glibly. "Anyway, where were we?"

"Tonka's brother."

"Right. If he's actively trading, he shouldn't be too hard to track down. Even if he's not, he should show up in Companies House listings."

"I wonder if he took on the farm?" Rob thought aloud. "I know their parents weren't happy about Tonka joining the army, and I'm sure she said Phil was still involved in the family business."

"OK. I'll look into that too."

"And I suppose I'd better talk to Ethan," Rob said reluctantly. "If she really was planning to clear his record, I doubt he'd tell me, but he might let something else slip."

"If it's easier for you, I could talk to him," Gray offered.

"Nah, it's all right. It's not like I've got to take the guy out for a pint and fake civility. And haven't you got enough to do already?"

Gray nodded in acquiescence. "We have a couple of avenues each to explore. Any theories at this stage?"

"I dunno. It all feels like a bit of a wild goose chase, or is it just me?"

"No, I agree. Like you say, the investment and ID might only be to throw us off her scent."

"Or they're trails to our next set of clues," Rob suggested. "Nice hunting analogy, by the way."

Gray laughed. "The joys of having a hunt saboteur for a boyfriend."

"Yeah. You know, before dealing with the Berringers, I hadn't realised it still went on. I'm amazed Will didn't take them down a long time ago." Of course, Rob knew why Will had stayed quiet. Freddie Berringer claimed to have photos of Will leaving a lab seconds before it was destroyed by explosives, but the photos had 'mysteriously' vanished between Berringer's arrest and the full search of his apartment—Rob had an idea he knew where to. "I don't recall you referring to him as your boyfriend before."

"It's a recent development—on my part." Gray's eyes became distant, and for a while he was lost in thought. He shook himself out of it and smiled wistfully. "How is it that as soon as you acknowledge the emotional commitment, it all goes to pot?"

Rob nodded sagely. He knew that feeling.

"I called Will while you were visiting the loo. He..." Gray hesitated then raised his hands in a shrug. "You'll find out sooner or later, anyway. He was intending to accompany Aaron-Naomi to visit Freddie Berringer. Somehow, Hedley caught wind of it and ordered him not to. He accused me of ratting him out."

"Harsh."

"And false. I haven't said a word to anyone."

"The prison told Hedley," Rob said. "I spoke to her this morning."

"I thought that was the case, but Will wasn't listening to reason. The truth is, he's a bit of an anarchist—very anti-establishment. He forgets sometimes who he's talking to and goes on a full-scale rant about the extent of corruption within the criminal justice system."

"He's got a point."

"He has, but he also thinks we're all in cahoots. Since last weekend, he's shared his plans with me twice. Before that, he only told me what he'd been up to after the event, and idiot me thought it was because I'd finally made my commitment clear. Now I realise he was testing the waters to see if you and I could be trusted to not go running to the police."

"Sounds like it's me he doesn't trust, not you," Rob contended, although he was thinking Gray had been closer to the mark the first time.

"As that may be, you and I are working together. I'd like to think one day we'll be friends, if we're not already. I'm not seeking reassurance, just being honest. I consider you a friend. I trust and respect you, and it's important to me that Will does too."

It was as well Gray had added the part about not seeking reassurance; in all good conscience, Rob couldn't offer it. As a colleague, yes; the trust and respect were mutual. As a friend? That would take a bit longer. "Any idea why they were going to see Freddie?"

"Unfinished business, so Aaron said. Or so Will said Aaron said."

"You're second-guessing, Gray."

"It's hard not to. You saw the way he was at Berringer's apartment. Smooth, assertive, putting words in people's mouths—he's a con man."

"He's never used those skills to break the law."

"To our knowledge, but he uses them in court. I was at his friend's trial a couple of months back. They called Will as a witness, and he effectively lied through his teeth. Tie got community service—for a fourth offence—and Will's in exactly the same boat. He should've had at least one custodial sentence by now."

"It's all mind games, Gray. You really can't judge him badly for that. Lawyers do it and get paid handsomely for the privilege. You've got to admit, it bodes well for Berringer's trial."

"There is that, I suppose. Do you want me to see what else he knows?"

Rob eyed Gray, gauging his motive. "Are you intentionally trying to cause a rift?"

"Don't you mean widen it? I'm not, as it happens. I wasn't planning to coerce him. In fact, I'll tell him I'm asking on your behalf. How's that?"

Rob was no expert on relationships, but if he'd ever tried something like that on Zoë, he'd have been out the door carrying his balls in his helmet. "If he tells you anything else, and he's happy for you to pass it on..."

Gray grinned. "I'll see what I can do."

"Lunatic."

"In remission."

"Yeah, if you like," Rob said drolly. "Is there anything else we need to discuss?"

"No, we're done, I think." Gray unhooked his jacket from the back of his chair and shrugged into it. He left a tip on the table—Bish had paid the bill earlier—and the two of them walked out together. Gray pointed his key fob and clicked; the car closest to them beeped and flashed its lights.

Rob gave the car a brief once-over. "That's dinky...for you."

"For surveillance purposes—I was aiming to blend in. Where's your bike?"

Rob pointed to the far side of the car park. "I'm gonna catch up with Hedley on my way home. I'm not happy that Tonka and Jock were able to get hold of my info so easily. I don't mind either of them having it, but it needs to come from me."

"OK. I'll email you."

"Likewise. See you later." Rob moved off. "Oh, and Gray?"

"Yeah?"

"Don't do anything stupid."

Momentarily, Gray looked stunned, but then smiled. "I might be able to manage that."

***

"Here he is, the waster."

"They seek him here..."

"They seek him there..."

"Who is that helmeted man?"

"Yeah, yeah." Rob dismissed the jibes and asked generally, "How's it going?"

Tang nodded noncommittally as he wandered past, empty cup in one hand, scratching his backside with the other.

Miller lifted the topmost sheet on his desk, scowled at it, and slammed it back onto the pile. "Same as ever."

There were a few other officers about, but Tang, Miller and Hedley were the only ones left from 'the old days', before Rob had joined the SIU—almost five years ago. Times like this, bantering with his former colleagues, it was the same feeling as coming back from leave—the permanent stacks of long overdue paperwork on Miller's desk, the dead coffee machine shoved in the corner to make way for the all-new-and-unimproved coffee machine, Tang's Itchy and Scratchy performance—even the new faces bore some resemblance to the officers whose places they'd taken. Rob felt like he'd never been away.

Then he pictured the toddler who could barely string three words together yet almost every combination included 'Daddy', who became the five-year-old wary of the stranger who knew his name. Lucas had never forgotten him, not entirely, but schoolfriends, footy and hating homework had filled the hole his dad had left. Rob knew what it had to look like through his son's eyes: a short eternity.

"Are you hanging around a bit?"

It took a moment for Miller's question to filter through Rob's bleak reminiscence. "I popped in to see the DCI, but I will do if she's due back soon. Where is she? Do you know?"

"Interview suite, talking to that Naomi Tanner."

"Oh? What's she doing here?"

"You'd have to ask Hedley that. What d'you make of her?"

"Hedley?"

"No, Tanner, you balloon."

"I don't understand what you're asking." Rob understood *exactly* what Miller was asking, but hedged his bets in case he was wrong. No point kicking off without good reason.

"I mean her being a tranny. Well...him, I suppose. Like RuPaul. Mind, I won't deny he looks hot in a frock."

"Miller..." Rob wasn't sure how to handle the remark, but he couldn't let it pass. "You're out of order."

"Why? It's the truth."

"Apart from the fact it's a derogatory term—"

"Transvestite. That better?"

Rob sighed, his patience already depleted. "Just shut up, will you, Miller?"

"What's wrong with that?"

"If you're describing yourself, nothing. Otherwise? It's none of your business."

"He's not a transvestite," Tang said on his way back with two mugs of coffee. "He's like that officer with the two warrant cards." He handed one of the mugs to Rob, who did a quick recap to confirm he wasn't taking it from the hand Tang had been scratching with.

"Exactly. So he's one of those—" Miller started.

"With all due respect, Sarge, shut the fuck up." Tang turned his back on Miller and lowered his voice, addressing Rob. "We were talking about it, Aaron Tanner and me, when we were sat outside the court. He says that's what it's like for him and Naomi."

Rob's coffee was too hot and tasted like crap, but drinking it saved him from having to give a response. He'd had the same conversation with Naomi about the Met's first openly gender-fluid PC; Tang bringing it up outside the courtroom before Charles Berringer's remand hearing had given Aaron a panic attack. Freddie Berringer's hearing had been the following day, but it was Naomi in attendance, and she brought it up with Rob, not the other way around. She was excited, knowing there was someone like her and Aaron, and impressed by the Met's support of the officer in question. It went without saying that the old guard blamed the public's lack of faith on what they saw as another crazy scheme of 'political correctness gone mad'. There again, they took issue with change of any kind, even when it was to their benefit.

Rob had to wonder if he hadn't met Aaron-Naomi whether he, too, would have considered the two separate warrant cards a step too far. It was hard to imagine a completely sane person having two entirely distinct personas, yet he'd seen it for himself. Aaron and Naomi had little in common beyond their height, build and complexion, and even those seemed to morph, retuning themselves to match the person inside. Beyond Aaron's social anxiety, they were both compos mentis.

"You can't keep away, can you?" Hedley murmured close to his right ear.

"Apparently not."

She sidled past him and propped on the corner of Miller's desk. "Social visit?"

Rob frowned, weighing up the value of an honest answer.

"No, then," Hedley concluded. "What's up?"

"My old army mates know stuff about me they shouldn't. I want to know how they found out."

"What sort of stuff?"

"My resignation...I think. It might've been when I was undercover. And one of them reckons someone at the station gave him my phone number."

"That's highly unlikely."

"I thought that."

"Any mutual acquaintances? Former REMEs in the job?"

"Not that I know of."

"OK. Well, we can check out his story." Hedley reached across the desk for Miller's phone, knocking his papers askew. He grunted. She flashed a not even a little bit apologetic smile and dialled an internal number. "When was it?" she asked Rob.

"Last week sometime. Friday, possibly. He phoned in."

She nodded, listening to whoever had answered her call. "Hi, it's DCI Hedley. Can you do me a favour? Check the incoming call record from last Friday to see if there were any relating to Rob Simpson-Stone?" She put her hand over the receiver to say, "He's checking. I'm not sure about the resignation leak. Grapevine?"

"I'd only told family and friends up north."

"So it would've had to come from HR—hello, yes. Still here. ... OK, thanks. What about earlier in the week?" Hedley asked and then told Rob, "Not on Friday."

The pause that followed was worryingly long. Rob really hoped Jock hadn't lied to him. The implications for their investigation were enormous.

Finally, Hedley said, "And that was Thursday...1809. Got it. Thanks for your help." She hung up. "Miller?"

"Yes, Ma'am?"

"Did you phone last Thursday to get Rob's mobile number?"

"What do you think? I was sitting right here!"

"With the same paperwork in front of you, no doubt." Hedley shuffled around to face Rob. "Whoever took the call assumed it was Miller. Any thoughts?"

"Yeah," he confirmed with undisguised relief. "Jock and Miller sound pretty similar. It backs up what Jock said." It didn't answer the question of how Tonka had known about Rob's resignation or his undercover work—Bish had been vague—but it could've made it onto the gossip mill, he supposed. "Cheers for chasing it up for me."

"You're welcome. On the other matter...you could see if HR have had any reference requests. That's the only way I can think an outside agency could leech info like that."

"I'll call them later," Rob said. "Naomi Silvestri's been in to see you, I hear?"

"Yeah. Just. Oh! That's what I needed to ask you. What name did she sign on her statements?"

"Naomi Silvestri, also known as Aaron Tanner, and vice versa on Aaron's."

"I thought so. The Berringers' lawyers are having a field day with them, as we expected. They're claiming Naomi's is a false statement intended to draw attention away from Tanner's misdemeanours."

"Is that why she's going to see Freddie?"

"She wouldn't divulge. I told her there's nothing he can do from where he is—I even threatened her with contempt of court. She didn't fall for it."

That made Rob smile. Aaron and Naomi were unbelievably intelligent, and savvy, and they were testifying against Charles, not Freddie. Thus, whilst there were plenty of common-sense reasons why they shouldn't visit Freddie, there was nothing legally stopping them.

"Right, I'll let you get on, Ma'am. Martina." Rob gave himself a smack on the head. "I'll get it eventually. See you, Miller."

"Detective Sergeant," Miller corrected with a cheesy grin.

"In your dreams. In a bit, Ste," Rob called to Tang, who waved without looking up from his sloth-like, one-finger typing.

"Don't forget you owe me a pint," Hedley called after Rob.

"At least," Rob agreed, ignoring the chorus of 'and me's as he disappeared through the door and went downstairs to sign out. He reached the bike and looked back at the station; it was a much nicer place to visit than work. He flipped his helmet to put it on, and stopped.

"Naomi?" He hadn't meant to say it out loud until he was sure. His pulse quickened as he ran through the mental checklist—dark-brown straightened hair longer than the last time they'd seen each other; tall, slender; designer clothes cut to accentuate curves; skin like creamy caramel—to confirm it was her.

At first, it appeared she hadn't heard him. She glanced behind her and took a step or two more before she turned and walked back, smiling all the while. He left his helmet on the bike seat and walked to meet her.

"Rob, hi! I thought it was your day off."

"Nope." He grinned, thinking he should say more but not quite sure of the order in which to say it. So he didn't look like a complete twerp, he asked, "How are you?"

"Very well, thanks." Her lightly glossed lips parted, deepest pink against whitest white teeth. He stared at her mouth; he couldn't help it. She noticed and laughed, then bashfully bit down on her bottom lip. "I just had them whitened."

"Sorry?"

"My teeth?"

Rob shook his head, bamboozled, catching on a second later. "Oh! They're... great. I mean, they look good on you." He squeezed the key in his fist until it hurt. "What are you doing here?" Tact of a brick through a plate-glass window.

Naomi's smile faded, her eyebrows drawing together in a sudden and surprisingly angry frown. "What is this? Some kind of good cop, bad cop routine to talk me out of it?"

"Talk you out of...going to see Berringer?" Rob guessed.

"See? You *do* know."

"Well, yeah. And I can't say I get why you're going, but I'm not here to stop you."

Naomi's breathing was fast and harsh, her folded arms tight against her chest. She'd been expecting a fight, and Rob wasn't sure why.

"What did the DCI have to say about it?" he asked.

"She suggested an officer escort me."

"Sounds like a decent compromise."

"I told her I'd only agree if it was you, and she told me you couldn't, so it looks like I'm going on my own." She smiled swiftly, sarcastically.

Rob mirrored her pose and shifted his weight to one foot, reducing his height by a couple of inches—enough to bring him down to Naomi's eye level. "I'm not happy about that," he said.

"What can you do?"

He shrugged. "Not a lot." She and Aaron had ignored his advice before—even when they'd asked for it—knowing full well he was trying to keep them safe. They were strong-willed and acted on impulse when under duress. It didn't bode well for a lone meeting with Freddie Berringer. "I could come with you. When are you going?"

"Next Monday. But...won't DCI Hedley have something to say about it?"

"More than likely." Hedley had something to say about everything, but he was on his own time now. She could like it or not. "Look...can we go for a coffee or something?"

"I'd love to, but I need to get home and change. Aaron has an online conference in an hour."

"Fair enough," Rob said cheerily to hide his disappointment. "Have you still got my number?"

"I have."

"Good stuff. And I've got yours. Give me a call or something and we'll sort out arrangements for Monday, yeah? If you want to. It's up to you."

Naomi studied him carefully, gauging his intent. "I'll give it some thought," she said, already turning away. "Speak soon."

"I look forward to it." Rob watched her hurry away towards the Underground station.

It was only when she disappeared into the crowd of other passengers that it dawned on him she didn't know he'd left the police. He took out his phone to text her, then changed his mind. It might influence her decision, and there was no predicting the direction. It could wait until Monday.

20: Troubleshooting

GRAY WAS MAKING progress. Slowly. Less than snail pace. In the better part of two days, the only fact he'd established for certain was that Parker Farms was a remarkably successful company limited by guarantee, of which Tonka and her brother Philip were two of six guarantors, the rest extended family members, individually wealthy and more than capable of coming good on their financial commitments to the company should it ever go bust.

Not that it was likely. There were no shareholders and no debts; the accounts were up to date, and all reports had been submitted to Companies House. Indeed, Parker Farms was so squeaky clean, Gray was instantly and enduringly suspicious, despite having read through every report, every annual statement—every single last document he could find. No bad press, no unhappy customers or employees, no complaints from neighbours about noise or light pollution, the smell of cow muck, mud on roads, too many Land Rovers... Nothing.

That was two for two on the perfect business front, and Gray was beginning to wonder if he should be looking behind the scenes for a PR company working with both Sequrco and Parker Farms. It wasn't...*normal*, and not just by SIU standards, which, admittedly, negatively skewed his expectations. Every company had some financial skeletons in the boardroom closet.

As for Philip Parker's Eastern European investments, Gray had found no evidence of investment activity, which begged the question of whether there was any credibility whatsoever to the yarn Tonka had spun Bish and Jock.

Something didn't fit. Two siblings running an honest-to-goodness family business worth £100m seemed an unlikely duo to be ripping off their friends for a relative pittance. That or it was a long con with thousands of victims, except Gray had seen the accounts, and there were no irregularities, as far as he could tell. Added to that, Rob had spoken with Philip and Tonka's neighbours, both in London and the Southwest, who had only good things to say about the Parkers.

With every last avenue exhausted, Gray quit all open windows, got up from his chair, sat down again and switched off his computer lest he was tempted to waste what was left of the evening looking over the same information duplicated elsewhere. It was Friday, almost seven p.m. Yesterday evening, he'd forgotten to eat—no surprise there. The argument with Will had played on his mind every time he stopped thinking about the investigation, and his appetite was non-existent.

He wouldn't have cared to estimate the number of times he'd almost called Will, only to abandon the idea at the last second. It would be better to wait and talk face-to-face—less chance of misunderstanding—or that was the theory at war with his desire to resolve their differences posthaste.

Now to while away the hours until bedtime. He had essays to grade, but he was mentally exhausted. He could visit the local pub, but that didn't appeal, so he made a cup of tea and sat down to watch TV. After ten minutes of flicking through the schedule and finding nothing that took his fancy, he relented and went to bed. It wasn't even nine o'clock and had to be his earliest night since his teens.

Alas, early to bed went hand in hand with early to rise, and with his brain replenished, his thoughts raced ahead of him, from the shower back to the bedroom and downstairs to the kitchen for coffee, forming new questions he could've answered in a jiffy if he'd still had access to the SIU's resources.

He supposed, in a way, it was more fun doing it without those tools at his disposal—more of a treasure hunt, a mystery to be solved. Or, at least, it would be if Gray had half a clue what he was doing. He thought back to his final SIU investigation, and how Josh—almost to spite Gray's refusal to give him access— had uncovered so many facts from so little information.

It was the complete opposite to Gray's established method of gathering every piece of information at his disposal and trawling through, discarding the irrelevant until he'd narrowed it down to a set of testable possibilities. In contrast, Josh dug into the minutiae, sifting out the smallest, inconsequential snippets and turning them over and over like a competitive gardener preparing his seedbeds. He cross-checked, trawled for more to corroborate, and re-examined his evidence, from which he conjured a conclusion.

Perhaps 'conjured' was the wrong word; Josh was no sorcerer, but from Gray's vantage point it looked like advanced magic, and he needed to know how Josh did it. Was it something he could learn? Would Josh be prepared to give away his secrets? There was one sure way to find out.

"Graham! I was just thinking about you."

"Should I be worried?"

"Potentially. How is everything?"

"Yes, good," Gray answered straight away, knowing even the slightest hesitation would be subjected to rigorous analysis. "And with you?"

"As well as one can hope. So...what do you want?"

"Charming! I could have just called to see how you are."

"At seven o'clock on a Saturday morning?"

"It's possible."

"You didn't."

"No, you're quite right. I want to tap into your expertise, if I may?"

"Aren't you still seeing your regular therapist?"

"Your other area of expertise."

"Profiling?"

Gray laughed. "The *other* other one."

"You've lost me."

"Research."

"See, it would've been much easier if you'd been less...elusive."

"Sorry, but you will have such a wealth of skills."

"Flattery will get you nowhere, or no further than simply asking outright. What do you want to know?"

"Rob and I have our first case, and I'm struggling to isolate the finer details. I want to know how you do it."

"You're a former police officer and a postgrad student. You know how."

"I read old books, analyse and critique. You're a social scientist."

"The principles are the same. If not in your literary work, then your detective work."

"And herein lies the problem. I'm so used to having the info at my fingertips, I've forgotten how to detect."

"I see. Well, contrary to where you began this conversation, I'm no expert, but I can tell you how I do it if you feel it would help."

"It's not a trade secret?"

"Hardly. I teach a simplified version to my students to help them elaborate their arguments."

"What's the process?"

"I begin by assigning every piece of information its own cube."

"Cube?"

"Six-sided, three-dimensional—"

"You can skip the geometry lesson."

"Testy this morning, aren't we?" Josh tormented. "Are you having trouble sleeping?"

"Josh, please?"

"You can tell me afterwards. My technique will make perfect sense if you allow me to explain." Josh paused, expecting an interruption, but Gray had his lips tightly sealed. Josh continued. "I visualise writing each piece of information—established facts, theories, intuitive feelings—onto the front faces of blank cubes, or, rather, a mental representation. Any new information is added to the relevant cube or allocated a new one."

"Wouldn't Post-its do the same job?"

"Not exactly, although they might work better for you."

"As a novice, you mean?"

"Your words, Graham, not mine. The benefit of cubes is they can be shaken and thrown like dice, which randomly brings up different combinations. Of course, it's not random at all. It's a mental representation governed by unconscious choice."

"I don't think I have the right kind of brain for this."

"Perhaps not. Do you possess any Post-its?"

"I believe so." He knew so. "Hold on." Gray went up to his office, to his 'teacher's bag'—a thing he'd hoped never to own—and rifled through the dry-wipe markers and other sundries until he found a dog-eared slab of Post-its. "OK. Got them."

"Different colours, perchance?"

"Stock yellow."

"How about coloured pens or pencils?"

He only had the dry-wipe markers. "Will red, green, black and blue do?"

"Perfectly. Now, write down one piece of concrete information about the case."

"Colour?"

"Pick one."

"OK. I'll go with...blue. The pens are quite thick."

"Use shorthand."

Gray stared at the blank yellow square and tried to think. He had the gist of Josh's method already and would have been happy to have a go at flying solo but played along and wrote *Parker Farms - wealthy, solvent.*

"Have you ever used a memory palace?" he asked, pulling off the top sheet and sticking it to the desk so he could write on the next: *shell company?*

"Method of loci—yes, and this isn't the same. Repeat the process until you've recorded all of the established facts."

Gray screwed up *shell company?*—very much not an 'established fact' when it had just popped into his head—and thought back over his research of the past two days. What else did he know for sure?

Bish and Jock are loyal, he wrote and then screwed that up too. He only had Rob's word for it, plus his perception, which was nothing more than a strong inkling. Or was it? Bish and Jock had been prepared to go in blind on Tonka's say-so; that struck him as very loyal. He switched the blue pen for the green and jotted it down again to come back to later. On the next sheet, he wrote: *Overseas property investment - money laundering?* He wasn't sure where that had come from. It hadn't occurred to him until that moment.

"Are you done?" Josh asked.

"Hold on." His thoughts were tumbling out faster than he could write, resulting in barely legible scribble of the highlights from the meeting with Bish and Jock until his entire desk was covered in yellow paper squares. "I'm done."

"OK. Next, jot down what you think you know—any theories or ideas for which you have no evidence yet."

"Done that already."

"In a different colour?"

"Yes."

"Excellent." Josh's praise always sounded condescending, though Gray liked to think it was genuine. "Is there anything you've put down that, at first glance, seems irrelevant?"

"All of it?"

Josh laughed. "Come on, Graham. This isn't hard."

"It'd be a walk in the park if I had access to the PNC."

"But you haven't. Don't think about it, just pick one."

Gray sighed and scanned the notes, homing in on *Overseas property investment – money laundering?* "OK."

"Put a tick next to it."

"Why?"

"Because it means something."

"This is getting ridiculous."

"You asked me to show you how I do it…"

"Fine, fine. What's next?"

"Focus on that note."

"Focusing…" Gray didn't mean to be flippant, but he couldn't see the point. "I don't hold much stock in intuition."

"What about policeman's intuition?"

"Application of stereotypes—not the same, but equally unreliable."

"He sees!"

"I don't."

"That's precisely the point. The key is to examine the root and establish whether it's reliable. If it isn't, you can discard the information. Probably."

"Probably? That doesn't sound very scientific."

"Something gave this particular note primacy."

"Or I'm hankering after my old job."

"It's a possibility. What does it say?"

"Overseas property investment as money laundering."

"Why did you write it?"

"The majority of money laundering cases I worked involved funds crossing national borders. But there's no evidence the target is investing in anything outside of their legitimate business. Although..." He hit the power button on his computer.

"You've thought of something," Josh said.

"It's a long shot. They used the same firm of accountants for twenty-five years, and then switched to another company a few months into the last recession. Before that, the estates expenditure consisted of multiple entries. The more recent accounts record it as one lump sum, and I didn't check if it was in line with previous years. I'm just waiting for the computer to start up."

"While we wait, you can tell me about your argument with Will."

"My..." The word fell away with the chin drop. "What makes you think we've had an argument?"

"We've been on the phone for half an hour and you haven't so much as uttered his name."

"Because we've been otherwise occupied."

"Am I wrong?"

"I didn't say that." When Josh didn't quip back at him, Gray relented with a sigh. "Yes, we kind of had an argument. I told you about the murder trial, didn't I?"

"The toff who killed a hunt saboteur?"

"That's the one. Will had plans to visit him in prison, but the police intervened. He accused me of telling them."

"And did you?" Josh asked.

Gray bristled. "Thanks for the vote of confidence."

"OK, you didn't."

"No, I didn't, and I'm hurt he doesn't trust me."

"Do you trust him?"

"Of course I do!" Gray winced at how defensive he sounded, but it was true. Mostly true. His computer was up and running, giving him a chance to cool down. He opened the folder containing the downloaded spreadsheets of Parker Farms' accounts. "We're still getting to know each other," he reasoned.

Josh didn't say anything—not that he needed to when Gray could see for himself.

"I'm going to talk to him about it later."

"Good."

"OK, these figures..." Eager to move on, Gray ran a few quick calculations and scratched his head. "It's not a significant change. Twenty-five thousand—a five percent increase, on average. That's not enough to purchase real estate."

"Do you think you can safely discard that information?"

"It looks like it." He felt quite despondent, but he had a whole desk full of Post-its to work through yet, and there was still something niggling him about that change from multiple to single entries. "I think I've got this now," he said.

"Are you sure?"

"Yeah. I hit a mental block. Thanks for helping me push it out of the way."

"Any time, Graham. I hope you fix things with Will."

"I'm sure we'll be fine. I'll see you...soon, hopefully."

"How soon?" Josh asked suspiciously.

He'd had a brainwave about popping across the Pennines to visit while they were up that way for Will's daughter, which rolled into *I should ask Will first*, and from there into wondering if Will was really OK with Gray's admission of his feelings towards Josh. "Summer, perhaps?" he bluffed.

"Hmm. Until the next time..." Josh hung up.

Gray stared at the monitor, or through it. If they were still off with each other in a fortnight, Will would be visiting Suzannah alone. Better to take it day by day and then decide. He refocused on the document and scanned the figures again, absently running the cursor back and forth over each spreadsheet entry. As he did so, it changed from an arrow to a pointing finger. Gray clicked, and his email programme opened. He broke into a grin.

"Well, hello, Hilary Gelling. What are you doing here?" It was too easy, but at least he had a jumping-off point.

***

"Anyone home?" Gray closed the door and took a couple of steps into the kitchen. "What on earth...?" There was an enormous glass tank, complete with sand, rocks and a chunk of tree, taking up most of the kitchen table.

"Tie?" Will appeared in the hallway. "Early fin— Oh, hey." He continued into the kitchen with his head down. "I didn't expect to see you today."

"It's Saturday. Haven't you been to work?"

"Called in sick."

"Headache?"

"Yep."

Gray pointed at the glass tank. "What's that?"

"Bearded dragon."

"A *dragon*, did you say?"

"Yeah. It's a kind of lizard. Holly found it in the woods earlier in the week. Turns out she's a terrific little terrier."

"Not the fire-spitting creature of myth and legend, then?"

"Nope, she's definitely a dog." In spite of his joke, Will remained solemn.

Gray took a cautious step closer and peered through the glass, though he couldn't see much. "Is it injured?"

"No. I don't think so." Will frowned and came over to look for himself.

"Where is it?"

"Behind the rock."

Gray squinted and thought he saw movement, but it could have been his eyelashes. "Are you going to release it?"

"Release it?" Will clearly thought Gray's suggestion was absurd, but then something must have clicked, and he *almost* smiled. "No, it's not a native species. I put a call out online to see if one had escaped from anywhere nearby. No-one's claimed it—they probably turned it out on purpose when it got too big."

"A dragon is for life..." Gray mused. He'd yet to lay eyes on it but imagined he'd only be disappointed when he did. "You're still sulking about Monday, aren't you?"

"A little bit. I'll get over it." Will sighed and rubbed his temples. "My head's banging."

"Have you taken anything?"

He laughed ruefully, wincing with the motion.

"Would a massage help?"

"It can't make it any worse."

Gray pulled out a dining chair, and Will sighed again as he sat. Freeing his hair from its ponytail, he flicked it back over his shoulders. Gray caught a whiff of lavender. "You'd rather smell like my gran's wardrobe than take paracetamol?"

Will's answering chuckle was little more than a deep hum in his throat.

"OK, let's see what's going on here..." With his palms on either side of Will's neck, Gray pressed his thumbs lightly against Will's nape and alternated between circling and smoothing upwards along the tight muscles.

"That feels good."

"Does it?"

"Yeah. It's um..." He breathed out heavily. "It's starting to get me down."

"Are they always this bad?"

"The past couple of weeks, they have been. Usually, they come and go, but this has been more or less constant for days."

"The muscles are very tight."

Will's shoulders tensed, and Gray eased off a little.

"Sorry," Gray said.

"I'm sorry too."

"Don't be. To tell you the truth, I've been so caught up in the case, I completely forgot about you going to see Freddie or I would've mentioned it to Rob—not to tattle." Gray worked his fingers into Will's hair, slowly travelling up his scalp to his crown and around to his temples.

Will leaned back with his eyes closed and a contented half-smile. "Because you trust him."

"Yeah, but if I'd told him, he'd likely have told Hedley, so your assumption was reasonable."

Will slid down the chair. "Don't stop, will you?"

"Is it helping?"

"I don't care. It's nice."

Gray laughed. "Then I'll keep going." He worked his way back down to Will's neck to give his arms a rest. "Have you spoken to Naomi?"

"Yep. I asked her not to go and see Freddie on her own. She made no promises." Will's neck muscles tightened again. Gray went back to circling and smoothing.

"What do you think this business is between them?"

"I'm not sure there is any—well, other than that they're still in love with each other."

"Wasn't Freddie and...I can't remember her name..."

"Carrie."

"That's it. Weren't they getting married?"

"Until he got locked up. Carrie's family won't want anything to do with the Berringers now, but she's always known about Freddie and Naomi—ouch!"

"Hmm...perhaps we should change the subject."

"Yeah. How's the case going?"

"Not well. What do you know about property prices in Eastern Europe?"

"Very low before the banking crisis, though it varies by country. Some have lost value, some have gained."

"What would twenty-five thousand get you?"

"Stirling or euros?"

"Stirling."

"Are you looking to buy a holiday home?" Will turned to grin. Gray pushed his cheek to get him to face front again.

"Is it enough to buy a house?"

"At a push, but it's not a good investment. You'd make very little from reselling, and timeshare is dead. Agricultural land is where the money's at. It's dirt cheap. A lot of Western-European farmers upped sticks before Bulgaria, Slovakia, Lithuania and a few others imposed legal restrictions. The EU have threatened sanctions."

"Agricultural land..." Gray echoed. "That's it!" He leaned down and planted a firm kiss on Will's forehead that made him flinch. "You are brilliant."

21: Out of Water

"HANG ON," ROB called as Lucas made for the stairs to the bus's top deck, but he was already out of sight. Rob waited in line to board, flashed their travel passes at the driver and set off after his son. The bus from the swimming pool back to the house was almost always a double-decker, yet Lucas acted as if it were a novelty every time. Rob couldn't really complain when he'd been the same himself at Lucas's age.

With his shifts over recent weeks and being at his mum's the previous weekend, it was a month since they'd been swimming—longer since he'd been to the gym—and he was feeling it. Funny how the football match hadn't been a stretch, yet climbing those steep, narrow stairs to the top deck was like hiking up Hay Bluff.

By the time he made it to the seat—at the front of the bus, naturally—Lucas had already scoffed his half of the KitKat from the vending machine. He handed over the remaining two fingers, part-melted, and declared, "I'm starving."

"Are you?" Rob knew what was coming next.

"Can we go to McDonald's?" Rob opened his mouth to reply, but Lucas followed straight up with a whiny, "Pleeeease, Dad."

"You don't like cheeseburgers."

"What? I do!"

Rob ruffled Lucas's hair and grinned. He was pretty sure if Lucas had to choose one food at the expense of all others for the rest of his life, it would be cheeseburgers. He'd probably choose them over contact with other human beings, parents included, especially if they came with gallons of tomato ketchup. "Yeah, OK. Seeing as you said *pleeeease*."

"Yesss!" Lucas turned to watch out of the front window, clinging to the safety bar as if it steered the bus. "Was it about my Christmas present?" he asked.

"Was what about your Christmas present?"

"When you came to see Mum and Travis the other day."

"It's April, Lu. It's another eight months till Christmas."

"So?"

"So we're not going to be discussing your presents yet."

"Oh." Lucas frowned in deep concentration—long enough for Rob to finish the KitKat—and then grinned victoriously. "Have you got a new girlfriend?"

"Nope."

He sagged. "Boyfriend?"

"Nope." They'd had a conversation some time ago—along the lines of some people liked girls, some liked boys, some liked neither, some liked both—and Rob had said he was in the 'liked girls' category. He'd been figuring out how to explain that some people were neither girls nor boys—something he'd never really considered before meeting Aaron-Naomi—when Lucas beat him to it. His school had toilets—not boys' or girls' toilets, just toilets—because, 'Not everyone is a boy or a girl, Dad.'

"What were you talking about, then? Grown-up stuff?"

"Serious stuff, yeah." Rob nipped that one right in the bud. He'd really hated it as a kid when adults dismissed him from discussions that had something to do with him by saying it was 'grown-up stuff', and he wasn't about to pay the same discourtesy to his son. "I was telling your mum and Travis about someone I used to be in the army with. I think she's in trouble."

Lucas gasped. "With the police?"

"She might be. Not sure."

"Did she ask you and Fish to help her?"

Rob chuckled. "Gray, you mean."

Lucas narrowed his eyes. "You called him Fish."

"You misheard, mate. I called him Gray Fisher, because that's his name."

"No, you never." Lucas adamantly shook his head.

"Yeah, I did."

"Did not."

Rob refused to argue with a seven-year-old who was stubborn and...correct, although the actual phrase was 'slippery fish'. Rob figured it would work in his favour to *not* remind Lucas of that. He had a knack for serving up honesty at the optimum moment, and never forgot things he shouldn't have heard to start with.

"Are you going to have a girlfriend one day, Dad?"

"One day..." Rob joined his son in staring out the window to distract from the image of Naomi that popped into his head. Even after the Berringers' trials were out of the way, he'd be on dodgy ground pursuing anything more than friendship. It didn't matter that he was out of the police; threats of disciplinary action or dismissal had nothing to do with it. As lead officer of an investigation for which she was a key witness, he'd held a position of power over her, and that power wasn't readily neutralised by his resignation. Maybe he'd feel less uneasy if she made the first move. He had mixed feelings about whether he wanted to be put in a position to find out.

Lucas stood up, bringing Rob to his senses. He almost told him to sit down again before he realised they were back in Kilburn and nearing the stop outside their local McDonald's. Sliding his legs around to the end of the seat, he let Lucas out so he could ring the bell and then followed him downstairs. The bus stopped, the doors opened, and Lucas jumped down to the pavement.

"They were at the pool," he said.

Rob looked around to see who he was talking about. A few other people had got off the bus with them, none of whom looked like they'd been swimming.

"In that 508 GT." As Lucas pointed, the car signalled, pulled out and sped past the bus. "Aw...they could've given us a lift—they live in our road. You would've, wouldn't you, Dad?"

"Guess so." Rob's chest tightened; the half a KitKat threatened a repeat appearance. He took out his phone and acted as if he were casually checking for messages. "What number do they live at?"

"Dunno. Think they just moved in."

"Gotcha." Rob typed the Peugeot's registration number into a text message, along with 'reg check pls', and sent it to Gray. He put his phone back in his pocket and held out his hand. "Come on, then, mate. Let's get those cheeseburgers."

Lucas pushed Rob's hand out of the way and marched off towards McDonald's. Still reeling, Rob followed him in and joined the queue. It took ten minutes to reach the counter, which was long enough for Rob's heart to slow to something closer to normal, and for Lucas to decide on which half of the menu he was ordering. Rob didn't usually let him get away with it, but it was a good distraction tactic.

It proved both expensive and unnecessary. Cars in general were Lucas's current obsession, and he swiftly moved on from the Peugeot to a long list of his favourite supercars, as test-driven in his racing game.

Rob struggled to keep up with the high-speed gabble as Lucas barely paused to shove food in his mouth and swallowed without chewing. It was astounding how much he knew, most of it stuff Rob wouldn't have had a clue about at that age. He hoped it would be enough to steer Lucas's interest away from bikes and didn't care if that made him a hypocrite. Much as Rob wouldn't be without his, the idea of his son riding one terrified him, so much so that when Lucas pointed out Bugatti rhymed with Ducati, Rob told him about Tonka's Lamborghini just to keep him talking about cars.

"Wow! Does she let you drive it?"

"I wish!"

"Is she rich?"

"Not, like, mega-rich." Meeting the Berringers, Sharstons and Strangs of this world had given Rob new insights into what real wealth looked like, and Tonka wasn't even close to owning that kind of fortune. More likely, the half-a-million car was why she lived with her brother instead of buying a place of her own. Rob wasn't criticising. One night at Siggy's, when they'd all been a bit the worse for wear, they'd shared their 'when I leave the army...' wish lists.

Top of Rob's had been the bike he now owned—a crazy expensive wedding present from Zoë that he wouldn't have bought for himself and never got the chance to reciprocate. Jock's was a Honda Gold Wing, predictably— cumbersome, expensive, might as well own a car, but it attracted attention. A Lamborghini had been at the top of Tonka's, and Bish...

Bish was driving a van that looked like it had never seen better days.

"Will you be all right there a minute, Lu?" Rob asked, already on his feet.

"Are you going for a crap?"

"Excuse me? Language?"

Lucas lowered his eyes and mumbled an apology around the last of his fries.

"I'm just going out to make a phone call."

"Please can I get an ice cream?"

Rob fished some change out of his pocket. "I dunno how you've got room." He slapped the coins down next to the heap of scrunched-up wrappers and blobs of ketchup. "I'll be right outside that door, OK?"

"'Kay." Lucas had darted off to order his ice cream before Rob made it out of the building.

Rob placed the call and turned back so he could keep an eye on his hollow-legged son. "Alright, Gray?"

"Hey. I was about to call you. That reg number. Were you expecting it to belong to a van?"

"Ah, no. Sorry. I didn't have time to explain. It's off a Peugeot 508."

"Yes, it is—one of the Met's."

"Crap. I asked Hedley to chase up the Mondeo. It's used by a specialist unit, but she couldn't find out which one."

"Are we thinking the same thing?" Gray asked.

"SIU?" The possibility didn't bother Rob so much now he'd reasoned it through. "Can we get it confirmed?"

The silence betrayed Gray's reluctance to agree, but he relented. "I'll give Dom Hooper a call."

"Cheers. And sorry." Rob didn't like putting him under pressure, but for his own peace of mind, he needed to know.

"Don't worry. It's disappointing when I've done everything by the book so far. It's not easy, but the sense of achievement is tremendous. How are you getting on?"

"Not well. I've got two numbers for Philip Parker. One's unrecognised, the other goes through to Parker Farms' voicemail."

"That doesn't surprise me. Based on the company profile, I doubt they have a staffed office. I did, however, manage to trace Philip Parker's overseas investments."

"Nice one."

There was a mumble in the background at Gray's end of the line, followed by, "Yeah, OK, Will helped me. Accordingly, Parker Farms financed the purchase of thirty hectares of agricultural land in Bulgaria, bought for cash in eight separate lots over several years."

"Blimey. When Tonka said it was a big farm, I didn't realise it was that big."

"It's a lot of land, but relatively cheap and well within the company's budget, which is why I didn't notice it on a first pass. I was looking for larger transfers of funds when it's less than they spend per year maintaining the boundaries on their UK land."

"Any dodgy business going on?"

"Clean as a whistle so far. They're limited by guarantee, so there's no share trading, and the guarantors are all minted. Parker Farms is, essentially, a hundred-million-pound leviathan steered by half a dozen well-to-do Lilliputians."

The analogy mostly went over Rob's head, but the value didn't. "You know, Tonka and her brother aren't exactly living the high life. D'you reckon they're being extorted?"

"It's possible, I suppose, although there's nothing in their company accounts to indicate that's the case, or not that I could find. Will's helping me crunch the numbers."

"See, now, *that's* commitment," Rob teased. Gray laughed. "We could afford to pay him."

"We could. Have you arranged to visit Ethan yet?"

The change of subject was subtle as a well-aimed axe, and Rob couldn't really throw it back when he wasn't pulling his weight. "I'll sort it after the weekend," he promised. "I also had a thought about Bish's van. Why's he driving a clapped-out old heap when he could afford a decent motor?"

"I assume that question's rhetorical, although I can think of a couple of reasons."

"Go for it."

"It could be adapted for his arm."

"He just sticks it between the steering wheel spokes."

"OK, in that case, personal experience would have me believe he's emotionally attached to it."

"Yeah? What did you have?"

"Ford Fiesta, one-litre, went through a gallon of oil a month and the driver's side window dropped if I went over thirty."

Rob chuckled. "Mine was a Honda c50 and the throttle used to stick."

"My sister had one of those for a few months. She gave it up for a boyfriend with a big, warm car."

"I don't blame her."

"Nor did I, even if he was a bit of a poser. The van could be Bish's runabout—a case of 'my other car's a Jaguar'. He strikes me as a Jag kind of guy."

"That's not a compliment, is it?"

"No comment," Gray said, opting for diplomacy.

"I'll give him a call after I drop Lu home, and I'll let you know." Rob hadn't been watching as closely as he'd meant to, but all was well—for now. Lucas was scraping the last dregs out of his McFlurry pot and probably working up to asking for a cookie to take with him. "I can't shake the feeling there's something Bish and Jock aren't telling us—if I can catch one of them on their own, I could push them a bit harder."

"Give it a go," Gray encouraged, which was also Rob's cue to wind up the conversation.

"OK. I'll catch you later, mate." Rob moved his phone away from his ear and eyed the 'call ended' notification in amusement. Gray obviously had better things to do with his Saturday afternoon. Rob put his phone away and went back inside. Had he not just looked at the time, he'd still have known it was half past one from Lucas's sprint for the toilets; the kid's bowel movements were regular as an atomic clock.

While he was waiting, Rob cleared the rubbish from the table and drank the last of his Coke with a grimace. The ice had melted, and the only thing going for the flat, tasteless liquid was that it was wet. He threw the cup in the bin and moved closer to where the toilets were, hoping if he could collar Lu on the way out, they'd avoid spending yet more money Rob didn't have to spare on junk food.

His mind returned to his conversation with Gray. It looked like he and Will had sorted out whatever was going on earlier in the week, and Rob was pleased for them. No two ways about it, Gray was more laid-back these days—a change that could mostly be attributed to getting rid of the stress of heading up the SIU, but Will must've played his part. Rob had only met the guy a handful of times and couldn't say he knew him that well. However, his judgement of 'smooth-talking slacker' was corroborated by Gray's snipe about him being a con man, albeit in a strictly legal sense. Freddie Berringer and Aaron Tanner were both also of the opinion that Will could've made a killing in investment banking if he'd wanted to, and neither could understand why he'd bowed out for a simple life with his family and other animals.

Rob got it, though. If he had the choice, he'd set up a bike workshop for the sole purpose of tinkering. He'd buy up old Harleys and the like so he and Lu could spend hours taking them apart and putting them back together again, sell them to collectors or even start their own collection, go to rallies, live in their overalls. Nearly all of Rob's happiest moments saw him covered in oil, and not always of the engine variety, although those were *not* the kinds of memories he wanted to build with his son, who appeared directly with a 'just had the best poo ever' grin on his face and a tp streamer stuck to his shoe.

"Lu?" Rob pointed to alert him. With a huff, Lucas stamped on the toilet paper with his other foot, net result: it was now stuck to both shoes. Laughing, Rob beckoned him closer and gave him a hand. He chucked the paper in the next bin they passed and put his arm around Lucas's shoulders, guiding him towards the exit.

"Can I have—"

"I'm spent up, mate. Sorry."

"Ohhh." Lucas plodded sulkily at Rob's side.

"Don't you think you've had enough?"

"No." That was the last Rob heard from him until they reached the corner of their road, at which point he asked, "Can I go and call for Adil?"

"See what your mum thinks."

"'Kay." Lucas shoved his swimming bag at Rob and ran ahead. It was easier to let him, plus it gave Rob a chance to case the street. There were lots of cars and no way of knowing which belonged to residents. Lucas had been right, though; one of the cars was a Peugeot 508 in the same flint grey, but it wasn't the one that had overtaken the bus. Nor was it the GT model, but with all the raving about cars Lucas had been doing, Rob couldn't imagine he'd get a detail like that wrong.

Still contemplating cars as he opened the gate—Lu dodged past him on his way out—Rob turned towards the house at the last second and startled. "Alright, Zo?" She was standing in the doorway, frowning and looking where he'd been looking a second ago. She smiled swiftly.

"Travis has something to tell you. He's upstairs."

Rob followed her in, and she gestured for him to go up ahead of her, which he did, dragging his feet and dreading he might be about to enter Zoë and Travis's bedroom for the first time. It was one thing to accept they were a couple, another entirely to have their intimacy shoved in his face. At the top of the stairs, he vented a sigh of relief.

Travis was a few feet along the landing, on his hands and knees, and peering into the gap left by a raised floorboard. He glanced up long enough to notice Rob's arrival. "Alright?"

"Yeah. What you up to?"

"Installing an alarm. If...I...can...jussst—" There was a heavy, metallic *thunk* below, followed by Travis's hiss of, "Shit." He sat back on his haunches. "I need to feed the cable back to the fuse box." He scowled at Zoë.

"That scary magic called electricity," Rob said knowingly. Zoë punched him in the arm. "Ouch!"

"Don't you *dare* make fun!" If looks could kill... Luckily for Rob, they couldn't, but electricity could, and Zoë was legitimately terrified of it.

He ducked his head contritely. "Sorry. That was out of order."

She glared at him until he had to break eye contact, returning his attention to Travis. "You've got something to tell me, Zoë said?"

"I have. It might be nothing, but when we got back from school yesterday, there was a silver van stopped across the road."

"What time was that? About half-three?"

"Yeah, it would've been. My mate was here before that, and he'd been parked where the van was. I wouldn't have thought anything of it, but the driver and passenger—such as I could see them, it had dark windows—were just sitting there, not talking to each other or getting out. I stuck my iPad on the windowsill with the camera running—they drove off about ten minutes later."

"And it was silver, you say?" Rob asked. "Not white?"

"It was silver, definitely. A Mercedes. I could only see one end of the reg, but it was this year's plates."

"Right." Rob automatically went to his pocket for his notebook and then closed his eyes, laughing at himself. "I'll stick the info on my phone in a bit. D'you want a hand?"

"I wouldn't say no."

"What d'you need?"

"If you can go down to the fuse box and pull the cable through..."

"Sure." Rob edged past Zoë—still glaring—and went back downstairs. He knew why they were installing an alarm, and he wanted to tell them it was unnecessary but wasn't sure it was true. Besides, he'd sleep better himself for knowing they had an extra layer of security between them and whoever it was who'd taken an interest in all of their lives.

22: Worms

DOM WASN'T ANSWERING his phone. The first attempt, it rang before it went to voicemail; the second, it didn't ring at all. Gray left it for the time being and reopened his browser, wishing he'd brought his tablet or laptop with him—either would have been an improvement—but he hadn't come to Will's with the intention to work. Alas, he had them both at it, and so far, Will was in the lead. They now knew the exact location of Parker Farms' overseas acquisitions, and that their accountant—Hilary Gelling, retired—undertook pro-bono work for non-profits, which was interesting but not especially helpful.

As for Gray's progress: he'd made none.

"I bet you're playing FreeCell," he muttered enviously at Will, across the table. Only Will's eyes were visible above his laptop screen, and the corners crinkled in amusement.

"I haven't played that since uni. It's boring."

"Yes, I can see how winning all the time would be a terrible bind."

Will chuckled without taking his eyes off the screen. The tensing of the tendons in his forearm and the dull click of the trackpad gave away that he was still doing...whatever he was doing. "I was no Hector," he said. "He could deduce from the opening deal whether it was possible to win—the same strategy he used with the Alternative Investment Market." Will sighed wistfully. "If only he could've applied his skills to reading people..."

He'd still be alive, Gray finished in his head. He hadn't had the privilege of meeting Hector Laird-Browne, and what he knew of the guy was what Will and Rob had told him. By their accounts, Hector had been a profoundly gifted mathematician, autistic, and naïve in his professional dealings with the Berringers. He'd also been in a relationship with Naomi, and asking how she was coping with her loss was a pertinent in-road, but Gray was reluctant to take it. No matter how hard he'd tried to convince himself he'd be asking on Rob's behalf, his desire to know more about Will and Aaron-Naomi was driven by curiosity, and it was his alone.

"Got 'em!" Will spun his laptop around.

"Who?" Gray didn't like the victorious smile beaming his way. He coolly pulled the laptop closer and read the answer onscreen. "GP Investments. The G is Gelling, I presume?"

"Yeah. Want to know how I found them?" Will was evidently going to tell him anyway.

"Only if you can multitask." Gray tilted his head in the direction of the kettle.

"*More* coffee?" Will teased but got up and switched on the kettle, talking as he prepared two mugs. "To be fair, I wouldn't have made the connection if we hadn't started out with the accountant's pro-bono work. There are very few truly benevolent individuals and corporations these days." He leaned back against the counter, ankles crossed casually. "My undergrad diss was on the history of friendly societies in the UK since 1875. That's when the legislation came in, but the big changes came with the introduction of state welfare in the mid-twentieth century. Most of the friendly societies still in existence are in the insurance sector, and hardly any operate on a purely non-profit basis—even fewer in the finance sector."

Gray pointed at the screen. "Am I correct in thinking GP Investments is a friendly society?"

"Yep."

"That's interesting." Gray scanned their scant homepage—no reference to the names of individual associates. "It doesn't explain how you made the connection."

"I'm getting to that." The kettle switched itself off, and Will paused to make their drinks. He was deliberately stringing out his explanation.

While Gray waited, he watched the glass tank for its alleged occupant. His eyes were accustomed to the light now, but he still couldn't see anything other than a big dead log.

Will put the mugs on the table. "You don't believe it's in there, do you? Want me to get it out?" He reached for the lid of the tank.

"No!" Gray shoved his chair away, ready to flee if it proved necessary.

Will resumed his seat, laughing. "It's—" he measured about twelve inches with his hands "—including its tail, and cute in a reptilian kind of way."

"I'm happy to take your word for it—unless my compliance is required in order to get an answer out of you."

"Not at all. Is there another tab still open?" Will nodded at his laptop.

Gray checked the screen and clicked on the tab in question. The result was a mess of form fields, most empty, some unlabelled, black Verdana text on a pale-grey background. "It's like Web 1.0 all over again."

"Yeah. Aaron doesn't exactly have an eye for design. Function all the way."

"This is Aaron's work?" Gray leaned closer and tried to extrapolate from the acronyms. "What does it do?"

"In simple terms, it's a search engine. You give it some parameters to work within—keywords, databases to search, Boolean operators—and it does the rest."

Gray scrolled through the endless list of checkboxes. "IR? DWP? Are those what I think they are?"

Will coughed and picked up his coffee.

"Search engine, you say..." Gray scrolled back up until the list was no longer in view. "You hacked a government database."

"I cross-referenced Companies House and the Charity Commission—both public listings, no hacking required."

"Truthfully?"

Will looked Gray dead in the eye. "Truthfully. I heard what you said to Rob, about doing everything by the book, and I respect that. It was something that never sat easy with me in the banks, and not just Berringer's."

"An honest con man," Gray mused.

"Ha. I'm not sure about honest." Will directed Gray's attention back to the screen. "You can see what Aaron's algorithm is capable of, but I assure you, on this occasion, I only used it to make our search more intuitive. I'll show you." Will waited for Gray to turn the laptop so they could both see it. "This box, where I typed 'Hilary Gelling', searches for exact and partial matches. I check this box to tell it to also match company names by their initials, and the checklist identifies which sources to search. There are other variables we could provide, such as annual turnover, trading partners, and so on. I left those empty, hit submit and..."

"GP Investments," Gray read off the screen again. "Only one match?"

"The only 100% match. Closest after that is 92%. You'd have to ask Aaron how that bit works."

Gray stared at the company names until they blurred to a dark smudge. He blinked and refocused, and opened a new tab. "What about the 'P'? Can we extrapolate outwards?"

"Why don't you have a go? Ace is really easy to use."

"Ace?"

"Aaron's Search Engine."

"That's clever." But nowhere near as clever as the engine itself. "This would've taken us days, you know, in the SIU." He clicked in a field near the top, but had no idea where to start, not with Will watching. He relinquished control of the laptop and picked up his coffee. "Thanks for this."

"Not a problem," Will answered vaguely. He typed and clicked, and typed and clicked, inhaled, exhaled...

"Can I ask you about...the cats?" Not the question Gray had intended to ask, but a better one, although Will was only half listening so he could probably have got away with asking anything. "Where are they?"

"RSPCA."

"Oh. Is that good?"

Will peered through his eyebrows at him. "What do you think?"

Gray shrugged. "I thought they might still be stuck in the building."

"The police went in with an inspector and got them out. Three litters, at least four adults—they had to euthanise most of the kittens, *apparently*." Will's voice strained; there was a lot of anger and sadness there.

"I'm sorry."

"Thanks." Will smiled and shrugged philosophically. "That's how it goes sometimes. We did what we could." He continued clicking and typing. "One positive, though. When the inspector called to update me, I told her about my most recent house guest, and she offered to take it in."

Gray looked around the room at the various pets in residence. "I'm surprised you're willing to let it go to a new home at all, let alone with an RSPCA inspector."

"She's already got a beardy...and doesn't have an issue feeding it live insects."

"Ah." That explained it. "Still, how many live insects can an invisible dragon eat?"

Will cracked a smile. "In all honesty, I won't be sorry to see it go. And the inspector seems to be one of the good ones."

"Well, when it comes down to it, you are both fighting for the same cause."

"Like Germany and Japan."

Gray laughed. "More the Allied Forces and the Resistance." A movement from within the tank startled him.

"Told you it was in there," Will said.

Gray didn't answer, dumbfounded by the creature now perched regally on top of the log. He'd expected it to be duller, not the shimmering pale gold it was. With the mass of soft-looking pointed scales covering its chin and neck, the name made perfect sense. "It's beautiful," he uttered.

"Do you think so?" Will asked doubtfully.

"You don't?"

Will eyed Gray suspiciously and leaned his chair back on two legs, reaching for a plastic box from the dresser behind him. He tilted forward again and set the box down next to Gray's mug.

"What's this?"

"Worms."

"*Live* worms?" Gray peeled back one corner of the lid and peered inside. "Oh." He nodded. "Live worms."

"Drop a couple in the tank," Will instructed with his eyes closed.

Unperturbed, Gray pulled the lid off the box and picked out two of the short, fat worms. He rose slowly and stepped towards the tank, all the while watching the bearded dragon, which scurried to the closest end of the log and was, in turn, watching him as he lifted the mesh to drop the worms in. The dragon snapped the first one out of the air, and within seconds had gulped down the other. "Can it have more?"

"Yeah, but not too many. They're a treat." Will's voice was thick and muffled by tight lips.

Gray glanced over and stifled his laughter. "You really can't deal with this, can you?"

"I'm horrified you can."

"I used to go fishing when I was younger," Gray said, quickly adding, "before I knew any better." He dropped a few more worms into the tank and put the mesh back in place. The dragon devoured the lot. "Fascinating."

Will grunted.

Gray closed the tub and pushed it back across the table; Will returned it to the dresser. He looked like he might cry or vomit, or both. "What else does it eat?" Gray asked.

"Veggies. Food pellets. And crickets. Moving swiftly on...I haven't found out who the 'P' is yet, but I have found GP's portfolio."

Gray went and stood next to Will, reading over his shoulder. "Wow, that's quite a list of clients." He recognised a few of the names onscreen. "Scroll down—oh, hold on." His phone vibrated across the table. "Can you copy and paste that into a document, please?"

"Sure."

"Thanks." Gray answered the call. "Dom, you busy, busy man."

"I was driving. Is everything all right?"

"I was hoping you might be able to tell me. Rob's picked up a couple of followers."

"Right?"

"Unmarked, registered to a Met specialist unit."

"And?"

"Any idea why?"

"If I have, I can't tell you. But you already knew that."

Gray's scalp prickled. He tried to contain his irritation, reminding himself that if their positions were reversed, he wouldn't have told Dom, either.

"OK," Gray accepted finally. "Forget I asked."

"Asked what?" Dom replied.

"Yeah, yeah. Talk to you soon."

"Be safe, Gray."

"Dom—" He'd already ended the call.

Gray stared at his phone screen for a long time after it had gone dark and only looked up because several sheets of printer paper fluttered down in front of him.

"That didn't sound like a particularly illuminating conversation," Will said.

"It wasn't." Gray's agitation was mounting rapidly, not entirely under his control. "My old unit's watching Rob. I'm sure of it."

"To do with the Berringers?"

"I think it's bigger than that." He scanned the printout, but he'd lost his focus and switched to watching Will, back on Aaron's search engine.

"I'm going to add a few more options, if that's OK with you."

"Yeah, fine," Gray answered vaguely. He was pissed off with Dom and for no good reason. Trust—or lack of—had nothing to do with it. Keep it simple and on a need-to-know basis was how the SIU operated; not even those involved in an investigation had access to all the information. That was the privilege—and burden—of the unit leader.

"Yes!" Will punched the air and startled Gray yet again. He wasn't usually so jumpy.

"What've you got?"

"The 'P' of GP Investments."

"Nice work!" That broke Gray out of his trance—briefly, until he saw the name. The familiar itch in his brain started up, impossible to ignore, making his pulse race. He had to think to breathe normally. The craving, stronger than he'd felt in months, threatened to overthrow his resolve as his worst fears rose to the fore.

"Gray?" Will was suddenly in his space, observing, frowning...worried.

"I need to go." Gray bolted from the room. He was in his jacket and halfway to the door before Will intercepted.

"Whoa! Go where?"

"Home. I'll call you, OK?"

Will spread his arms, barring the exit and cranking Gray's urgency up to desperation. "What's going on? Who's Raymond Perlett?"

Gray moved to push him aside, but thought better of it and instead attempted to stare him down. "Will, I *need* to go."

Will lowered his arms but maintained steady eye contact. "I understand, but there's no immediate rush. You won't make the next train, so take a few minutes, put a plan together—"

"Excuse me, please."

Will rubbed his chin, slowly, thoughtfully—or faking it to hold Gray long enough that he had no chance of getting that train. "If you really must go, fine. I won't stop you." He spoke quietly, without challenge—the voice of reason. The voice of a negotiator. "I'd rather you stayed, even if you can't tell me what that name means. This is our time together, and I'd like for us to make the most of it. But it's up to you. All I'm asking is you consider before you do anything rash."

"Tell me about Naomi and Freddie."

"I beg your pardon?"

Gray tried to cajole the words into the right order. The pain registered—his fist bashing against his forehead. He stopped. "I messed up, Will. Big time."

"How?"

"With the SIU. My recklessness has put Rob in danger."

"Did Dom tell you that?"

"He told me nothing."

"Then you can't be sure what's happening has anything to do with whatever you did."

"I *know* it does, Will. That name...I can't explain, and I can't do anything to jeopardise..." He bit his fist to stop himself from saying more.

Will continued observing him. "You want me to tell you about Naomi and Freddie?"

"Yeah, I do," Gray said obstinately.

"What do you want to know?"

"Why you always shut down the conversation when they come up. Is it jealousy?"

"Absolutely not." There was no defensiveness in Will's answer, just a statement of fact.

"OK. Is he abusive?" Gray shook his head. "Scratch that. I know he is. I mean, is he abusive to Naomi?"

"No...well...kind of."

"Meaning?"

"More so to Aaron. Ironically, it's one thing I can say in Freddie's favour. He accepts the dichotomy between Aaron and Naomi. What he can't accept is their co-existence. Aaron comes between him and Naomi."

Briefly, Gray forgot about cocaine and Raymond Perlett. It was for no more than a second or two, but the distraction seemed to be working, so he stayed with it. "It sounds like Freddie sees Aaron as a love rival."

"That's exactly it."

"Did Freddie feel the same way about you?"

"Far from it. He told Naomi I was using her to get at him, and he honestly thought that's what I was doing. She asked me if it was true." Will chewed his lip, guilt creasing his brow. "I told her it was, hoping it would make the decision easier for her... It would've been a safer lie to say I wanted a serious relationship. It might've kept them apart."

"Instead, you pushed them together."

"Yes, but it's not as callous as it seems. When I said they're in love with each other, I was simplifying, and it's not how you think. Freddie's besotted—has been since uni. And Naomi...she's a wily one. She knows how to play him, giving him just enough to get what she wants. Money, cars, clothes, sex—the house. Were it not for Aaron, I'd say she and Freddie deserve each other."

"But they're the same person," Gray argued.

"Spend any amount of time with them, and you'll see how wrong you are, which is why I offered to go to see Freddie with them. Naomi can handle him, no problem at all. Aaron is a different matter. Is that enough distraction? Or do you have further questions, Mr. Fisher?"

"Do you feel interrogated?"

"Not really." Will smiled and held out his hand. "Come and sit with me?"

Gray glanced behind him at the door, and then at the clock. If he didn't leave in the next couple of minutes, another train would have come and gone. But really, there was nothing he could do. He had to trust the SIU had his and Rob's backs.

"I'll let you feed the beardy more worms," Will offered.

Gray's eyes flitted to the tank. His newfound friend was still perched on the log, and still watching him...he liked to think. "OK." He took Will's hand and permitted him to lead them back to the table.

"Do you want another coffee?"

"No, thank you. And thank you for sharing."

"Thanks for listening, and staying. I'm not deliberately hiding anything, Gray. You only have to ask. You know that, don't you?"

"I'm getting there." He was trying, but not being able to reciprocate Will's honesty reminded him how much he missed being with someone in the job—how much he missed Jean. "Can we just sit and watch TV, forget about all of this?" He indicated the laptop and printout. It would drive him crazy if he let it.

"Sure," Will agreed. "We should eat too. Are you hungry?"

"I could eat, as they say."

"What d'you fancy?"

"Hummus?" Gray suggested and even managed a grin.

"Huh. I should've let you catch that train after all."

23: Networking

After watching Travis's footage of the silver van, which told Rob no more than Travis had already told him, he connected wirelessly to Gray's camera. It turned out to be even less use but at least meant he could come clean about the surveillance. He wasn't comfortable spying on Zoë and could understand why she was upset he hadn't said anything—even if he did have Lu's and her best interests at heart.

It made for a tense atmosphere, and as soon as he'd finished helping Travis with the alarm, Rob gave his excuses and got his leathers on to leave, though he had nowhere better to be. Unexpectedly, Travis was on his side, which only served to aggravate Zoë further, and as the door closed behind him, Rob heard her say, "Why do all men think we need looking after?" If she thought he was doing it simply because she was a woman, she was sorely mistaken.

"Dad!" Lucas came tearing up the street to intercept. Rob quickly pulled his visor over his face and pretended he hadn't seen his son slump, dejected. "I thought you were staying for dinner."

"No, mate. I don't want to get under your mum's feet, and I've got work."

"But you're not a policeman anymore."

"I still have to work."

Lucas sighed heavily. "'Kay." He turned around and plodded back the way he'd come.

"Laters...taters." The words fizzled out pointlessly. Rob glanced back at the house, wondering if he could stand to swallow down a slice of humble pie for Lucas's sake. Zoë was watching from the front window, arms crossed, chin jutting defiantly. Lu would pick up on the bad feeling between them, and Rob had already said he was going. He straddled the bike, took a last look along the street, and took off.

Back home, he put his phone on charge and called Bish, who stammered some bullshit about his car being in for a service, laughed way too enthusiastically when Rob asked if his other car was a Jag, and then claimed he owned a Prius, which was about as likely as Rob swapping his two wheels for four. Due credit to the guy, no matter how much Rob probed, he didn't change his story, but it was a puzzle for another time.

Next, Rob called Martina, first and foremost to ask if she fancied going for that pint, but she was away with Erica for the weekend. Even so, she got Miller to check the partial plate from the silver van; Miller called back, confirming it was a possible match for a couple of Met Police vehicles, but without the full reg, there was no way of knowing for sure.

Best guess: each time a search registered on the system, the unit in question switched vehicles, but Rob couldn't see why they'd go to the trouble when he'd sussed he was being tailed a week ago. If it was to prevent potential retaliation from the Berringers, it wouldn't matter if he knew they were watching, and if they thought he was involved in whatever Tonka was up to, their surveillance was a bust. It made no sense, and Rob was sick of thinking about it. He'd cut his holiday short, missed out on dinner with Lois and catching up with the rest of his family to spend half a week chasing a seemingly non-existent threat. Now it was the weekend again, and he was still working.

Hypocrite much? Remembering Lois's comment raised a smile, at least. Surely, Bish and Jock wouldn't begrudge him a night off…if he could think of something to do with it.

Hoping it would shake off his post-swimming weariness, Rob put on his running gear and headed out to pound the streets. The evening was cool but dry, the daylight dimming as he found his groove. He wasn't a regular runner; he normally only ran to the gym for a workout and then back again, and in retrospect, running hadn't been the best choice. With no phone, he couldn't listen to music, and the area was too familiar to offer up any distractions.

His mind kept turning over the unanswered questions. Was he barking up completely the wrong tree in thinking it was to do with Tonka? Had something happened to her? In his first stint under Hedley, there'd been two attacks on young women, and they'd kept a lid on it, knowing the attacker would strike again if he thought he was getting away with it. They'd caught him as he moved in on his third victim. If something had happened to Tonka… Except her neighbours had seen her leave home the previous weekend, the house was secure with no signs of a struggle, and Siggy claimed she'd heard from her. It all pointed to Tonka being alive and well. Besides, he was certain—almost certain—Hedley would've told him if there was an investigation underway.

Twenty minutes of churning thoughts later, Rob decided to cut his losses and go back to the flat. He nodded an acknowledgement at his upstairs neighbour, who was putting his rubbish out. Rob had an open invitation to go up and share a spliff—a particularly tempting prospect this evening—but it had the potential to put him on a major downer, and he'd delayed dealing with Ethan long enough.

A quick shower first, order in a takeaway, check out Brookhurst's visiting protocol—Rob was starting to question his decision to leave the police. He could've just turned up and demanded Ethan talk to him. Instead, he was still working antisocial hours and with none of the benefits of instant access to witnesses. He could only hope the PI business would get easier with practice.

He emerged from the bathroom to the ringing of his landline phone and the thought that he needed to set some boundaries on his working hours because his mobile was also vibrating. He answered it and let the landline go to messages.

"Alright...Naomi?" Calling from that number, it usually was.

"Yes," she confirmed. "Good evening, Rob. I hope I haven't caught you at a bad time."

"Not at all. How are things?"

"Oh, everything's fine. I've been thinking about your offer to accompany me to see Freddie. Does it still stand?"

"It does. What time do you need me?"

"Visiting is from nine-thirty. Connections allowing, it should take less than an hour to get there. Aaron's around, though, so we may need to ditch public transport at the last minute."

"I'll sort something out," Rob offered. "About eight-fifteen?"

"Perfect. Thanks so much for this. I really appreciate it. And perhaps we might get a chance to—oh, there's your phone. I'll talk to you on Monday."

*A chance to...*what? "OK, mate. Take care." Rob quickly ended the call, at the same time picking up the landline cordless. He didn't recognise the number, but it was a Watford code, most likely Gray calling from Will's place. "Hello?"

"Rob?" And that was definitely a sigh of relief. "Is everything all right?"

"Yeah. Everything's fine. Why wouldn't it be?"

"No reason. Just...I've been trying to get hold of you. I wanted to give you an update."

"I've not long been back from a run, and my phone was charging. What's up?"

"OK, firstly...the Mondeo and Peugeot are SIU."

"You've spoken to Dom, I take it?"

"I have. He more or less confirmed it."

"More or less?"

"By omission."

"Gotcha." Rob recalled Gray being much the same when he was unit leader. It was a case of asking the right questions and reading between the lines. "And the bad news?"

Gray gave a hollow laugh. "Still as astute as ever. How d'you fancy a working lunch tomorrow?"

"Sure. At your place?"

"We've come up with a way to shift our investigation along without stepping on SIU toes."

"Who's their targ...never mind." Rob knew better than to ask questions like that over the phone. It could only be Tonka or her brother if it was related to their investigation. "What time?"

"Sigma-SMS."

That was the secure service they'd used in the SIU, and Rob hadn't re-installed the app on his new phone—it was something else to fill his empty evening. Gray's precautions seemed a bit over the top, but he'd have his reasons. "I'll keep an eye out for it. See you tomorrow." He hung up and started the app download then switched to the browser to search for a number to call to request a visit with Ethan, thinking he'd be able to delay making that call until Monday. Instead, the hospital website had a form: seventy-two hours' notice, and it had to be approved by the patient. It was over to Ethan now.

Soon after, Rob's takeaway arrived, followed by Gray's message confirming their lunch arrangements—midday at Will's house—along with instructions to turn off his phone's GPS and leave his bike at Croxley station. Gray had usefully included directions to get him from the station to Will's house on foot. Rob saved the message without any further thought, more than ready for some downtime. Grabbing a beer from the fridge, he stuck on the first movie that took his fancy and settled in for a couple of hours of escapism.

***

"I should've checked—are you OK with veggie?" Gray asked, inviting Rob to step into the warm, herby kitchen.

"Yeah, I'll eat pretty much anything." He was about to acknowledge Will—back turned, hard at work at the stove—but was distracted by the cacophony of barking from beyond the door Gray opened. Rob had met Will's dogs before, and they seemed a friendly bunch, but he was on their patch, so he kept his head up and ignored them as far as was possible when they were running circles around him and bumping his legs.

Will glanced away from the pan he was stirring and gave a short, rising whistle. The dogs turned and dashed over—all except one.

"Alright, mate?" Rob peered down his nose at the big dog intent on sniffing every inch of his jeans—it seemed respectful to leave his leathers off for today.

"Jesus, Kenny, where are your manners? Give the man some space." Will clicked his tongue, and the dog slithered—there was no other word for it—away.

"He's paralysed," Gray explained. Rob hadn't planned on asking.

"And he's a tart for a good-looking copper," Will added.

Rob raised an eyebrow. Gray's pink-cheeked smirk was a sight to behold. He cleared his throat and indicated the old pine table tucked into a wide alcove. "Have a seat. Would you like a drink?"

"Please, if it's not too much trouble."

"Tea, coffee, squash...or there's some beer?"

"Coffee, cheers." Rob pulled out a chair as much as he could when there was a large glass tank on the floor behind him. He sat and peered in. "Is that a bearded dragon?"

"Yep," Gray confirmed without looking. "Will hates it."

"He doesn't," Will said.

Gray's blush had subsided, and his smirk became a grin. "I stand corrected. He hates feeding it."

"Two more hours..."

"It's going to a new home."

Rob nodded, entertained by Gray and Will's domestic bliss routine. He'd never seen Gray fully off-duty, padding around in socked feet, so completely at ease. And this felt nothing like a working lunch.

The back door opened, and another man walked in, also shoeless—and sockless—wearing board shorts, sweatshirt and a head of messy blonde dreadlocks. He acknowledged Rob with a nod and sniffed. "Is that roast dinner?"

"Yep," Will confirmed. "You staying?"

Gray delivered Rob's coffee and tilted his head towards the newcomer. "This is Tie—Will's lodger. Tie, this is Rob, my business partner."

Rob made it part way to his feet before Tie lurched across the room, extending a hefty arm. "Alright, mate?"

"Alright? Good to meet you."

"You too. Another copper, then?"

"Former copper."

"Right." Tie stepped back and scratched his head. "If you're here on business, I won't impose."

"Actually, it would be a good idea for you to stay," Gray said, warily meeting Rob's gaze. "There's a chance what's going on will affect you."

"Fair enough. I'll just go feed Benj and get some feet on. Won't be a mo." Tie went to the fridge, grabbed a handful of leaves and left the same way he'd come. A chilly rain-damped draught wafted across to the table, but it wasn't the cause of Rob's goosebumps.

Gray edged past to reach a Welsh dresser and retrieved a wad of A4 paper, which he handed to Rob.

"What's this?" He glanced over the first page. "GP Investments?"

"Philip Parker's broker." Gray was watching him carefully.

"I thought you said Parker was legit." Rob flipped the page, and then again, not sure what Gray was expecting of him. He skimmed over the lines of text—arrangement fees, transfer of money for purchases on behalf of Parker Farms, confirmations of purchases. "What am I..." Rob flipped the page and froze.

"Shit." He re-read the name to check he wasn't seeing things. "That's not a coincidence, is it?"

"Unfortunately, no. He was on the hit list at the start of the Strang investigation, but he wasn't involved, so I took him off."

"You think—"

"Lunch is ready," Will said, cutting off Rob's question. "Let's eat and talk." He set down a glass dish in the middle of the table. "Gray, can you get the plates, please?"

Gray edged past Rob again and collected plates and cutlery from the dresser while Tie returned and gave Will a hand with bringing over the rest of the food— roast potatoes, courgettes, orange and purple carrots, red peppers—as colourful as Rob's mum's dinners, and it smelled fantastic.

"Help yourselves," Will invited once everyone was seated; Tie sat opposite Rob, Gray sat to his right, opposite Will. Tie offered Rob the serving tongs, but Rob gestured for him to sort himself out first.

"You should've made a bigger loaf," Tie said, transferring two steaming slices from the glass dish to his plate. "You a meat-eater, Rob?"

"Err...sometimes." In the present company, he didn't want to admit that pretty much his every meal included meat of some sort.

"You're not missing out with Will's nut loaf, I tell you. It's the dog's..." Tie broke off with a laugh. Will shook his head, laughing too.

"It's definitely not the dog's bollocks. But it is tasty. My mum's recipe."

"Yeah?" Rob accepted the serving tongs and helped himself to a couple of slices. It looked a bit like fruit cake, but once he'd loaded his plate with roasties and veg, topped off with a good dollop of thick, dark gravy, there was no distinguishing it from a traditional roast dinner. For the most part, it tasted like one. Will was right, the nut loaf was good—a cross between sage and onion stuffing and date and walnut bread—but a bit odd to Rob's meat-eater taste buds.

Were it not for the discussion looming on the horizon, lunch would've been a very chilled affair. Will's house had a great atmosphere; Rob had picked up on it on his last visit, and he tried to soak it in, watching the activities of the kitchen's various non-human inhabitants. His mum would go nuts if she were here now. *What are all these dogs doing in the kitchen? It's unhygienic!* But sooner or later, they needed to get down to business.

"So, what's going on, Gray?"

Gray put his fork on his plate and finished his mouthful of food before he began. Rob prayed it wouldn't be a Windbag Fisher Special.

"Briefly, for your benefit, Tie, and you need to keep this to yourself..."

"Of course," Tie agreed—too easily for Rob's liking. Will must've noticed his caginess.

"Before you continue, Gray, can I just assure you, Rob, that Tie's involved in the same...undercover work I am."

Rob chuckled at Will's choice of description, as did Gray.

"If it was still my unit, I'd have had them both working for us months ago."

"That good, eh?"

Will was positively beaming at the compliment.

"You were saying," Tie prompted Gray to continue.

"Yes. A couple of years ago, Rob and I investigated a group of lawyers who were defrauding their terminally ill clients by amending wills so they named deceased or contested beneficiaries, which put them intestate. We knew our targets were working with corrupt court officials in order to push the wills through. What we hadn't realised was the extent of that corruption.

"The lawyers involved in the inheritance scam are either dead or in prison, but what they were doing is part of a much bigger scheme that's the subject of an ongoing investigation, the details of which we're not privy to. I left the unit running the investigation last year, and Rob left the year before that. However, in light of recent events, it would appear that we have attracted the attention of associates of the criminals we put away, and our old unit is also aware of that."

"Hang on," Rob interrupted. He couldn't fault Gray for his brevity on this occasion, but either he'd missed a few steps along the way or he was jumping to conclusions. Rob seriously hoped it was the latter. "The Mondeo and Peugeot 508—"

"Are SIU. The vans outside Zoë's?" Gray shrugged.

Rob sighed rather than swearing. "What's Tonka got to do with it? And Jock and Bish, for that matter."

"You're not going to like it, Rob. I'm sorry."

"Why?"

"Because...as far as I can tell, they're using Tonka to get to you, and Raymond Perlett's involved somehow."

"I'm lost," Tie said. "Who's Tonka?"

"My old CO," Rob answered.

"Oh, really? Regiment?"

"REME."

"Fusiliers. Four years."

"Same." Rob was mildly surprised that the vegan animal-libber new-age-traveller type sitting across the table from him was ever a squaddie. The bloke clearly hadn't had a haircut since he came out.

"And Raymond Perlett?" Tie asked.

"Tonka's brother's investment broker," Gray said.

"Raymond is Michelle's brother?" Rob guessed. Tie mouthed *who?*

"Father," Gray corrected. "Michelle was one of the lawyers we put in prison."

Tie nodded in understanding. "And you reckon her dad...what? Made the connection between Tonka's brother and the copper who put his daughter away?" He thumbed in Rob's direction as he said it.

"That's the bit I'm not sure about, but it looks like serendipity had a hand. Parker Farms took their business to GP Investments, and Perlett made the connection during their background checks."

"It's a bloody long shot, Gray," Rob said.

"I know. It's a gut feeling, and we need confirmation. Which is where Will's plan comes in."

Rob was uneasy with the entire setup, and he wanted to discuss it with Gray in private, but short of kicking Will and Tie out of their own kitchen, he couldn't see a way to do that.

"May I make a suggestion?" Will asked. Gray gestured for him to go on. "After we've eaten, Tie and I will take the dogs out so you can fill Rob in."

For a moment, Gray looked like he was going to refuse but conceded with a reluctant nod, after which they resorted to small talk, or Rob and Tie did. It was the same old, same old—where they'd been based, tours of duty, bland brushing over of the grimmer details, especially in Tie's case. He'd served in Afghanistan, whereas Rob had come out a few months before the first troops were sent over. He'd been lucky; Bosnia was bad enough, but 'keeping equipment serviceable for peace implementation' was an all-inclusive holiday by comparison to what the lads endured in Afghanistan and Iraq.

That conversation took them through to the end of lunch, which Rob enjoyed, though perhaps not enough to consider giving up his mum's curry chicken or the medium-rare T-bones he treated himself to when he had time and remembered to buy one. While they'd been eating, the dogs had quietly stayed out of the way, but they must've picked up on what was happening because as soon as Will set down his knife and fork, they started pacing between him and the back door.

Rob watched, fascinated, as Will affixed wheels to the big dog whose back legs didn't work while the other five milled around with none of Linford's lunacy at walkies time, although it got a bit raucous when Tie opened the door and they all tried simultaneously to charge out into the rain. Sadly, they seemed to have taken the relaxed atmosphere with them, leaving only tense silence.

Gray cleared the serving dishes from the table. "Want a coffee?"

"Sure. I'll give you a hand." Rob stacked the plates and carried them across to the sink, not sure where to start with either the washing up or his questions. He didn't want to throw accusations around.

"Leave those." Gray advanced with the kettle, and Rob stepped aside. "I'll wash them later." He filled the kettle and returned it to its base. "What's on your mind?"

"How much did you tell Will?"

"Everything."

Rob frowned, processing the meaning of 'everything'. Before today, and despite knowing far more about each other's private lives than either would've voluntarily shared, Gray had always been a little remote, maintaining a distance congruent with his former role as Rob's superior. The difference was palpable, leading Rob to conclude Gray really did mean *everything*. "I don't know if I'm impressed or pissed off."

"I was thinking over what you said, among other things. Is coffee OK? Or would you rather have tea?"

"Coffee's fine, cheers." Rob wasn't much of a tea drinker.

Gray set out two mugs. "May I ask you a personal question? It's about you and Zoë."

Rob shrugged his assent to the question, not to answering it. He'd decide once he knew what it was.

"Did you ever confide in her?"

"About work?"

"Yeah."

"The bare bones. How long I expected to be away, whether I'd be able to keep in touch..."

"And after you'd finished a job?"

"I'd give her the general gist, not the ins and outs. If the case was in the news, maybe I'd mention that was what I'd been working on, but she didn't ask, so it didn't come up. It was the same with the army. If my mum or dad asked what I'd been up to, I'd give them the sanitised version, but otherwise?" Rob shook his head.

"See, I think that's the difference, and it's key." Gray finished making their coffees, and they took them back to the table. "With Jean being in the job too, we talked about work all the time. I'm not sure we talked about much else, to tell you the truth. Even my friends, family—those I'm still in contact with—are either in the police or involved in police work in some way."

"I didn't realise your sister was."

"Yeah. Well, sort of. Part-time special constable. Obviously, George isn't, and I doubt we'll ever be close for lots of reasons, not just that. But it's part of what got me thinking. Up until last year, I lived to work, and I loved it. I really did. I hated going on leave, I worked all the overtime I could get. I went for promotions to sink my teeth into something new, not for salary or status. My job was my life, and it was great. Then Jean died, and I couldn't find my footing again. People kept telling me I needed to take a break, give myself time to recover, and I believed them.

"I didn't follow their advice, as you know. I kept going, and with hindsight, I admit there were times I wasn't up to the job. But I wasn't wrong to keep working. I was wrong to not ask for help. I should've delegated more, stuck to admin for a while. Anyway, I'm not intending to do a full post-mortem. I fucked up, and that's why we're in this situation now.

"The bottom line is, I can't have a proper relationship with Will unless I trust him with my work, because it's me. It's integral to who I am, and Will's work—not the delivering post bit, that's a means to an end, but his activism—is integral to who he is." Gray picked up his cup, smiling as he lifted it to his lips. "I think we've cracked it, Rob."

On the balance of what he'd seen and heard, Rob was inclined to agree. "OK. I wouldn't have done the same, but like you say, that's how we're different, and if it's working, fair play to you. What's this plan you mentioned?"

"GP Investments—we need to confirm whether they're involved. However, if they are, they'll know who you are, and possibly who I am too. I've exhausted all avenues, and we need inside information."

"Are you talking about sending Will in undercover?"

"Only as a prospective client. He's meeting with Perlett tomorrow afternoon—subject to your approval."

Rob's mind reeled. That was a whole new level of Gray trusting Will with his work. And risky. "Surely if they've connected Tonka to me—"

"They'll have connected Will to me? It's possible." Gray paused as the back door opened to admit five wet, muddy dogs, followed by Tie, then the dog on wheels, and finally Will.

"What if they have?" Rob asked.

"I doubt they'll recognise him," Gray said, far too casually, but he went on before Rob could call bullshit. "At your leaving do, Martina asked me if I was involved with anyone. She didn't even make the connection when I mentioned him by name."

"That's...interesting." And extraordinary, though it explained her remark about Gray and Will being an item. Martina was a damned good detective; not much got past her. "Have you ever considered becoming a spy, Will?" Rob asked, tongue-in-cheek.

Will laughed but didn't pass comment. He kicked off his wellies and left the room.

"OK. What's this plan?" Rob still needed convincing.

"Will's going to pose as an investor working on behalf of Berringer's bank. His documented track record should be enough to get him through the door."

"If we discount the fact that Berringer's is defunct," Rob pointed out.

"Well..." Gray fidgeted cagily.

"They're still operating?" Rob asked even though the answer was right there on Gray's face. "They liquidated their assets."

"And both Berringers are in prison, yes. But you know as well as I do, they won't be there for long."

"And in the meantime, their lackeys are holding the fort so they can pick up where they left—" The pieces all fell into place at once. Rob put down his coffee lest he was tempted to launch it. "That's why Naomi's going to see Freddie."

"I doubt it," Will called from outside the door, then reappeared, half in and half out of his sweater. He tugged it over his head and chucked it on the back of a chair to re-tie his hair. "But you're on the right lines. Freddie only needs one person on the outside to facilitate running his business from where he is."

"Aaron, you bloody..." Rob stopped short of calling him an idiot. Aaron was far from it, but the Berringers were bullies. Rob had hoped, with Freddie in prison, Aaron and Naomi would be safe from his constant threats to expose Aaron as a hacker. All it had done was lengthen the puppet strings. Of course, it would help if they kept their distance instead of running to Freddie on a whim.

Will patted Rob's shoulder. "Thanks, by the way, for offering to accompany them tomorrow."

"No worries." He was disgruntled Will had followed his train of thought. Rob was doing it for Naomi's benefit, and his own, if he was truthful, but Will obviously felt guilty for letting Naomi down. He'd put his neck on the line to protect her and Aaron, and he was about to do it again for Gray and Rob. The risks were tremendous, unacceptable. These people were ruthless; Rob had seen it for himself. They weren't just fraudsters and embezzlers. They were murderers. "Wouldn't we be better leaving this to the SIU?" he said. It was a last-ditch attempt at persuading Gray, and utterly pointless, knowing the man as he did, but he had to try.

"I get where you're coming from," Gray said amenably. "And I'm sure Dom's doing what he can to protect us, but if it comes to the crunch and it's us or jeopardise the whole operation..."

"We're on our own," Rob finished. He'd witnessed Gray do exactly the same 'for the greater good' on more than one occasion and dismiss the risks as collateral damage. "All right. What d'you need from me?"

"Did you manage to arrange a visit with Ethan McGrath?"

"I put in a request. There's no guarantee he'll accept."

"If he doesn't, see if Martina can get you in."

"I'm not happy—"

"I understand, but Tonka gave us two trails to follow."

"I could go back to Bish and Jock..." But then, Bish wouldn't even come clean about his clapped-out van. "Fine. I'll give it another twenty-four hours."

"Thanks," Gray said. "One last thing. You need to prime Freddie, in the event that Perlett goes digging."

"You think Berringer's going to corroborate Will's story?"

"If it's in his interests." Gray looked Rob dead in the eye until it sank in.

"Oh, for fu... You've got to be joking. You're not really going to let him get away with murder? Will?"

"From what Gray's told me, we don't have much choice."

"We don't have *any* choice," Gray said. "This is war, Rob, and I put you in the enemy's sights. I'm sorry."

Rob breathed through his nose, slow and steady, working to keep his cool. He didn't like it—any of it—but Gray was right. This *was* war, and they were outside of the system that had once protected them. They were going to need all the allies they could get. "OK. I'll talk to Berringer."

24: Journeys

GRAY CAME TO with a half-conscious remnant of his ring tone decaying in his ear and an arm that felt like it belonged to someone else. The arm flopped off the edge of the bed as he rolled and squinted at the clock.

"Ah, hell." He threw the duvet aside, got one leg out, his sleep-deprived brain clutching at reason—*7:15, alarm not set, not a workday, no need to rush or panic*—and quickly shut his eyes against the sudden illumination of his phone screen. Grappling blindly, he picked it up and chanced a painful glimpse at the caller before he answered.

"Good morning, Dom." Those were not the words in his head. His previously dead, now pain-spiked hand instinctively curled into a fist.

"Morning, Gray. Apologies for the early hour. I hoped to catch you before you left for the day."

He hadn't planned on going anywhere until he'd heard from Rob, which would be another three hours at the soonest. Now fully alert with no chance of going back to sleep, he contemplated letting Dom know precisely how unimpressed he was with his rude awakening and Dom's attitude in general. Instead of any of that, he offered a heavily self-censored, "I'm not at home. It sounds urgent."

"It is. After you called on Saturday, I got in touch with the superintendent—you know O'Rourke retired?"

"I do." At least, he'd known O'Rourke planned to retire. He'd said as much the previous spring, when he'd visited Gray in rehab and advised him to resign.

"Well, the new guy's a jobsworth, but he has his moments. I explained the situation to him, and he arranged an emergency meeting with the assistant commissioner. That meeting happened yesterday."

On a Sunday. It was some consolation to know the high-ups were taking the matter seriously. "Still AC Jackson?" Gray asked. It was irrelevant and he wasn't interested. He knew where the conversation was going. Delaying the outcome wasn't going to change it.

"Yeah," Dom confirmed. "I formally requested permission to share sensitive information with select non-police personnel, i.e., you and Rob. Jackson wanted to know the ins and outs of a duck's arse, as per. I told her as much as was needed for her to understand the necessity. She agreed to my request, but she's bringing in one of her trusted minions to keep her apprised."

"Good," Gray said neutrally though his heart was in overdrive, and he was sweating like he had a fever. He was angry, beyond the point of being able to express it in any coherent form. Dom was brandishing his professionalism, telling Gray by omission that the mess he'd left behind had finally caught up with him when he was already acutely aware. "What's next?"

"We need to meet. I'd suggest we come to you..."

"No, it's fine. Do you need me to get in touch with Rob? He was heading down to Sussex first thing, but I could ask him to come back." It would mean abandoning Naomi, unless Will could ditch work and revert to Plan A.

"Visiting's at nine-thirty, isn't it?"

"As far as I know," Gray confirmed curtly. He hadn't said where Rob was going, but Dom's question confirmed what they'd both suspected: the SIU was doing more than tailing Rob if they had that kind of information.

"You can feed back to him later."

"That urgent, is it?" Gray left a pause which Dom didn't fill. "OK. I'll come on my own."

"I'm here all morning. See you when you get here." A lighter clicked a split second before the beep of the call ending.

With the greatest of care, Gray put his phone on the bedside table and covered his face with both hands, rubbing hard at his eyes until yellow dots appeared in the darkness.

***

Leaning against the wall next to the ill-fitting door, Rob held his phone higher than necessary so he could watch Naomi buzz around the room without her realising. It was a tiny studio flat—about ten feet by twelve—with a sofa bed in one corner and Aaron's desk and computer diagonally opposite. A narrow, combined wardrobe/drawers took up most of one wall. The counter at the end holding a kettle and toaster wasn't even enough to call a kitchenette, and the small, off-centre window in the other wall, had it not been covered by a closed blind, would have offered a view of the side of the run-down B&B next door.

The bathroom—shared with the other first-floor tenants—was at the end of a grim corridor that stank of something as unpleasant as it was unidentifiable, and the carpets—where they existed—were stretched, crumpled and scarred by the tongue-and-groove joints beneath. Rob wasn't one to judge—he'd lived on a shoestring himself—but this was a very steep drop from the lifestyle to which Aaron and Naomi had been accustomed when Aaron worked for Berringer's. The fact he was *still* working for Berringer's made it an even greater injustice. They deserved so much better.

"I'm ready," Naomi said brightly with a smile to match as she turned away from the mirror.

Rob locked and lowered his phone, pressing his lips together to cover his reaction.

Her smile faltered. "Do I look OK?"

"Yeah, totally." With the pale-cream short blazer held together by one button over a plain white shirt, café-au-lait straight pants and mid-heel shoes that put her close to Rob's height, she could've stepped straight off a catwalk. She was absolutely stunning—too stunning for a prison visit, or was that the point? Rob had no idea why she was visiting Freddie Berringer. He supposed he'd find out soon enough.

"Rob, you're staring."

"Sorry." He scratched his nose, his hand covering his smile, though there was little point. She'd caught him out good and proper. "You look great, Naomi."

She bowed her head demurely. "Thank you. Shall we get going?"

"Let's do that." Rob stepped back to give her access to the door and quietly vented a breath, glad she hadn't taken offence. The attraction was still there, as undeniable as his loathing of the Berringers for making it possible for him to meet this incredible woman and impossible for him to do anything about it.

Once they were outside, Naomi double-locked the Yale, affixed a padlock to a hasp and then turned a deadlock, pulling the door tight into the frame.

"Aaron," she said, by way of explanation.

Rob nodded his approval. Regardless of Aaron's anxiety, there was a lot of valuable equipment—and clothing—in that room, and most of the tenants were the type who would help themselves if they got the chance. Not that they saw any of them on the way downstairs. It would've been nice to imagine he was stereotyping and they were all out at work, but behind those closed doors, with TVs constantly rumbling, were spaced-out junkies and prostitutes on downtime.

When they reached the street, Naomi stopped and leaned out into the road. "No bike?"

"I didn't think you'd be up for that, so I borrowed a car." Rob pointed a key fob at Martina's Renault.

"That's not a CID car, is it?"

"No. Actually, I need to tell you something."

"You've left the police?"

"Yeah. How did you know?"

"Just a feeling when we were in court. I thought you'd see through Freddie's and Charles's hearings first, though."

"Are you disappointed?"

"About you leaving the police?" He couldn't decipher the look she gave him but bottled out of probing further.

"That I borrowed a car for today," he blagged. That raised a knowing smile. She had him well sussed.

"A little. I've never ridden a bike."

"We can rectify that at some point if you fancy it?" Rob unlocked the car and held open the passenger door. Naomi smiled in thanks, her shoulder brushing his chest as she slid past him and into the seat. It didn't strike him as accidental.

***

Gray emerged from the Underground station and strolled casually, taking in the splendour of the old buildings. Art deco glazed redbrick and an inordinate quantity of satin-smooth sandstone. He'd rarely had the luxury to pause and consider the beauty of this part of the city; the times he'd worked 'at the office' had been few and far between, and always hurried in-and-outs to present cases, pick up briefs, attend disciplinary meetings or, on the last occasion, to officially hand over his department to Dom Hooper.

Dom Hooper, his oldest friend, the one colleague with whom he'd stayed in touch throughout his career. The only people Gray had known longer were his mother and sister, and they knew less about him. His work had been his life, and Dom his right-hand man. Yet, in the face of Dom's secrecy over the ongoing SIU investigation—one which Gray had set in motion—he was questioning the extent of his trust.

The reason: Gray had trained him, and if Dom was doing the job right, a couple of civilians, irrespective of their personal importance, should be far down his list of priorities. Nevertheless, he was going out of his way to give them a head start, and it was more than a gesture. Just how much he'd told the new superintendent was unclear, and Gray knew nothing about the guy. John O'Rourke—his predecessor—had left Gray to run the SIU as he saw fit. While on the one hand, he'd enjoyed that level of autonomy, on the other, nobody stepped in when his decision-making went awry.

He assumed that was why the assistant commissioner was keeping tabs this time, and it bothered him, but not for that reason. The more non-SIU personnel involved, the greater the chance they'd be silenced, shut down before they reached the source of the corruption. Gray had sacrificed everything for this operation, his sanity and Rob's safety included. If bringing it to a conclusion required lying down with dogs, so be it.

The SIU was housed on the third floor of an ordinary commercial building with signage indicating it was a Metropolitan Police administrative base, which was mostly the case. The constant drone of air-conditioning, computer fans and polite murmurs of conversation filled the cool, modern offices on the upper floors in stark contrast to the familiar sights and smells that greeted Gray as he stepped out of the century-old, well-oiled revolving door at street level. Originally a bank, the lobby still presented an expanse of gleaming-white marble floor and the unguarded oak counters from the 1920s, along which, interspersed at wide, regular intervals, were three receptionists. All three looked up when Gray was still several feet away and on a trajectory for the smiling woman to his left.

"Good morning, Mr. Fisher."

"Good morning, Belinda. How are you? You're looking very well."

"Thank you." She asked no questions, simply handing him a pen to sign in and watching him the entire time. His face burned under her scrutiny, but he couldn't help smiling at her customary appraisal. He handed the pen back. "Do I pass muster?"

She chuckled but gave no answer as she reached under the counter to collect his visitor's pass from the printer, expertly feeding it into a holder. "DCI Hooper is in conference room two." She held out the pass; he took it and clipped it to his shirt pocket.

"Thanks. See you shortly," he said and set off for the lift up to the third floor.

***

"How's Lucas getting on?" Naomi asked. They were fifteen minutes into their journey, and the roads were quiet for the time of day. There was a possibility they'd reach the prison early enough to stop for a coffee somewhere nearby. "Have I got that right?"

"Yeah," Rob confirmed. Perhaps he shouldn't have told her about Zoë and Lucas—they'd engaged in small talk to pass the time spent sitting around in waiting rooms at the station and in the courts—but with Naomi, conversation came easy. Too easy. "He's doing great. He had me playing this racing game last week. The graphics were out of this world."

"Which one was it?"

"Haven't a clue, mate. It was all the supercars and Grand Prix tracks— he kicked my arse."

"You're not a car man, are you?" Naomi's voice had the thickness that came with a smile. Rob chanced a glance her way. She still hadn't responded to his offer of a bike ride, but maybe it was better this way.

"My driving's that bad, is it?"

She laughed. "Not at all. I feel very safe in your capable hands." She reached over and lightly squeezed his arm. The contact lasted a second at most, but the tingles it sent through his entire body took a good minute to dissipate. "I loved those racing games when I was a kid."

"Did you?" Rob concentrated on the road ahead—and keeping his capable hands firmly on the wheel. He was picking up the signals. That or it was wishful thinking.

"Before Aaron and I parted company. Even back then, he was far more interested in the workings of these things. That was how he got into programming—decompiling software. He can't enjoy something for what it is. It's a man thing, isn't it?"

"I dunno about that. Computers have never interested me."

"But I bet you spend a lot of time fine-tuning your bike."

"Err..." Rob laughed. "You might have a point there."

"And you enjoy your sports."

"Not as much as I want to, but yeah. I love a good game of footy. I wouldn't say it's a man thing, though. My mate captains a Sunday league team, and their striker's a woman. She used to play for England."

"Oh, wow! I'd ask who, but there'd be little point."

"Charlie Davenport," Rob told her anyway. "She still coaches for them."

The conversation reached a natural lull, and he thought about putting on the radio, for Naomi rather than himself. He preferred to hear what was going on around him, even if it was only the quiet hum of the blowers. He stopped at a red light and watched his passenger. She, in turn, was watching out the side window, unaware, giving him the first proper chance he'd had to look at her since Berringer's remand hearing. She hooked her hair behind her ear revealing a delicate bare shell, no earrings. No jewellery at all, in fact, and he couldn't recall if she normally wore any, although she was beautiful with or without. The spring morning sun cast a pale glow across her cheek and chin, accentuating her perfect complexion. He wanted to reach out, feel her soft skin under his fingertips, an urge that became stronger each time he was in her company.

She turned and met his gaze, her expression questioning, concerned, but then her cheeks lifted and dimpled with her smile. A car horn sounded, and Rob startled back to the reality of the green light ahead. He moved off, blinking to clear the dizziness from holding his breath, getting a little hotter under the collar at Naomi's quiet laughter.

"You're still searching for Aaron," she said.

"Sorry?"

"When you look at me like that."

Rob chuckled self-consciously. "That's definitely not what I'm doing."

"It's perfectly fine. I'm used to it." She said it so carelessly, he almost believed her, but she was wrong—about him, at any rate.

"Can I be honest with you, Naomi?"

"Always."

"I never see Aaron when I look at you, though I do sometimes see you in him."

"You mean when you met at the Science Museum? Those under-table lights..."

Rob nodded. "That's what Aaron said. But...you know that."

Naomi shifted in her seat to face him. "You really do see us as different people, don't you?"

"Because you are."

"Most people can't. Even Will struggles at times."

"I noticed that the night we arrested Freddie. Will didn't realise it was you."

"Yet you did."

"Yeah. About two seconds before I decked Berringer, when Carrie admitted Charles killed..." Rob grimaced. "Shit. Naomi, I'm sorry." He should've stopped at decking Berringer.

The journey continued in silence long enough to get them out of the city, broken by a message alert on Naomi's phone. She sighed as she took it out of her bag, her actions indicating she was typing a reply. Rob waited until she was done before he asked, "Are you OK?"

She nodded. "I think so. You're right, though. I hadn't planned to be at that meeting at all. It was the shock, I think. Aaron wanted to face Freddie, negotiate terms, and he was doing so well until..."

"Until we arrived," Rob finished for her.

"Yes. Don't get me wrong, I'm glad you were there. It gave us the answers we needed, about Hector's death, and Carrie double-crossing Freddie."

Rob suspected the 'we' incorporated Freddie, and that the terms Aaron had negotiated that night were for the deal currently in place. At some point in the next couple of hours, he'd be able to confirm if he was right.

***

Never had a three-storey ascent seemed so rapid. Gray had been fine until the lift doors had closed with him on the inside, but in the few seconds it took to reach the third floor, he successfully worked himself to the brink of a panic attack. Every sensation—the inertia, the smell, the slight flicker of the dull light, the scratch on the control panel—rammed home that he was here again, in this place that had almost destroyed him once. With hands gripped tightly together, he stayed absolutely still as the lift eased to a stop and the doors opened.

"Hey, Dom." One foot in front of the other, controlled, measured steps, hand out...

"Gray." Dom shook his hand, brow furrowed, the combined aromas of cigarette smoke and mint gum ratcheting Gray's physiological arousal to nausea. "You all right?"

Gray shook his head slowly, yet perceived it as a rushed, jerky side-to-side that tilted every flat surface in sight before catapulting them upwards and outwards as if the entire corridor had quadrupled in size.

"Here. Sit a minute," Dom instructed, pushing Gray into a chair next to a vacant desk and then perching on the edge of said desk with arms folded. He looked past Gray, into the distance of the ogre-capacity corridor. "Did you see Belinda downstairs?"

"I did."

"Chatty as ever?"

Gray managed a smile. "Couldn't get a word in edgeways." Belinda only ever said what was required to do her job—in words. She could hold an entire conversation in facial expressions.

"Better?"

"Getting there." The corridor had shrunk back to almost normal size.

"You can take another minute—you might need it when I tell you who the AC's sent."

Gray chanced lifting his head so he could see Dom's face. "Who?"

"Assistant Chief Constable Martin Winstanley."

It was the mental equivalent of a hard shove in the chest, and the impact jolted Gray back in his seat. "He's not internal affairs anymore. He has no jurisdiction here." Gray's protest was feeble, and pointless.

"Joint ops. I didn't even know myself until he showed up this morning. Eight o'clock, sharp. You know how he is."

"Yeah, don't I?" Gray muttered. If he had a nemesis, Martin Winstanley was it. Before Winstanley made assistant chief constable, he'd been part of internal investigations and had outed more corrupt officers than Gray had had hot dinners—or certainly vegetarian ones. He was a stickler, even more so than Rob, and he'd been there, loitering in Gray's peripheral vision throughout his career, waiting for that one moment to occasion when Gray screwed up.

He'd been in for a long wait. Until the Strang case, Gray's record had been exemplary, but Winstanley was tenacious. He'd begrudged Gray's every promotion, even if he had admitted—after Gray had tendered his resignation— that he respected him. It had been a vendetta motivated by jealousy and a rightful sense of injustice. Winstanley had been passed over for promotions that should've been his, but he was far too good at what he did.

Ultimately, that was how Gray had attracted his attention when he'd needed his help to bring down a senior officer in his very last case with the SIU. Martin Winstanley had a nose for corruption, and had no doubt been sniffing around the SIU's operation since the very beginning. He was going to be a major nuisance and would try to block Gray and Rob's investigation. Even so, Gray couldn't think of anyone else he'd rather have on their side. Because if there was one officer he knew for sure wasn't corrupt, it was Martin Winstanley.

25: Pay the Reaper

Two and a half years ago

WHAT ARE YOU doing here?”

He'd expected a door slammed in his face; this was marginally better. Last he knew, looks couldn't kill.

She spun sharply and marched away. He pushed the door to, not quite closed, and pursued at a distance.

“Jess—” And stopped when she whirled around.

“How dare you! After everything we had, you...”

In two steps, she closed the space between them, her glare impaling him like cold steel rods, pinned to the spot, frozen to the core. The pain was physical, a clenching in his chest that cruelly mimicked his deception. In another life, he had loved her. In this life too.

“We were friends.” She spoke in a desperate whisper of disbelief, and he fell for it again—the lie that it was he, not she, who was the betrayer. “Whatever else happened between us, we were friends.” Her eyes shone with hatred, with anger, with the threat of tears.

He nodded, in thought. In deed, his body failed. “That's why I'm here. I need—”

“You set me up.”

He couldn't dispute it. He had set her up, and for that, he was sorry. For that, he hated himself more than she ever could.

“The bullshit heart condition, the shitty fake reunion... Why, Rob? Why didn't you just ask if you needed money? I'd have given it to you without a thought. I wouldn't even have expected it back.”

“There's more to it than needing money. I'm sorry.”

Her shrill laughter rang in his ears long after it had ceased, echoes of this new Jess, the one he'd refused to believe existed until he'd seen and couldn't deny it.

“You're sorry? For...what? Lying to me? Or screwing me first? What was that? Something to remind me after you'd gone?”

“Don't be—” Her slap stopped him from finishing, and perhaps it was as well. *Don't be like this*. Why was he pleading for her forgiveness when she'd set this in motion? His cheek stung, his vision blurred, and he remembered then; she'd slapped him once before, back in sixth form. No recollection of his crime on that occasion, perhaps the same as on this—that he had loved her. "Yeah, I lied to you," he admitted. "But what I say now—what I need to tell you—is the absolute truth. You're in danger, Jess. Your life—"

"No!" Her hand shot up again, and Rob braced for another slap, but she reared, shaking her head, as beautiful in fury as in passion. "I don't believe you. I can't, after..." She gripped her hair as she turned away, moaning like the bereft she had left penniless, blonde silk tangled in her fists. When she turned back, the glisten had become fully fledged tears, tiny glass beads cascading over pale-pink cheeks. Still beautiful in sorrow and disappointment. "Have you any idea what you made me do? I neglected Ellie for you." She was his ten-year-old desk mate again. *You didn't put the lids back on properly and now her felt-tip pens are ruined—because of you.* "Her hen night, her wedding, her fucking honeymoon... I fucked it all up for you, because I thought you were going to die!"

Still beautiful in her lies.

"I know about the wills," Rob said. Her shocked gasp was so well covered he'd have missed it if he hadn't seen it in their love-making more often than he wished to admit. He could tell when she was faking, when she wasn't. But she was proud, and she cared. She faked to protect his feelings, when he got carried away and didn't care enough. She still cared. He had to believe that. She'd never intentionally cause harm. Not his Jess.

He couldn't stand the deception, on either part. Say his piece and leave as quickly as possible. Never come back.

When his thoughts released him again, he found she'd moved away and was leaning against her desk, arms folded, expression hard, unreadable. "What are you talking about?"

Not a wrinkle, nor a twitch. No tells to give her away as she lied through her teeth.

"Fraud, forgery..." he began.

"Just go."

Her words crossed with his, and once she processed what he'd said, she laughed as if it were a ridiculous notion, but he'd unnerved her. He wasn't done yet.

"Biddiscombe, Campion..." There were dozens more names going back four years, possibly longer, but those were the most recent, the ones that would bring her down. The ones that gave him hope she wasn't as evil as the others. She was still the Jess he had crushed on since high school. "I know about all of it."

She swallowed, lost it a little, recomposed, her smile an attempt to disarm him, but there was no need. He was shooting to incapacitate, not kill.

"How?" she asked.

"I needed a job. You know how things are at home…"

"No. You told me how they allegedly are. I don't trust a word you say. Not anymore."

"It's true, I swear. Zoë and I separated. She's petitioning for a divorce."

Jess's right eyebrow arched and returned to resting. She refused to release him from her gaze, pushing him to continue his explanation, but he was giving it willingly. Lying to save her.

"I decided to look for a job that'd get me out of the way for a while, give us a fighting chance. There was an ad for a bike courier, carrying legal documents between London and Newcastle."

"You're working for a law firm?"

"You know which one."

"Newcastle, did you say?" Her eyes became distant in thought—more faking. "I haven't worked with any—"

"Don't you think I can recognise counterfeit IDs? I saw Jennifer Campion's passport." Or it had borne Jennifer Campion's details…along with Jess's photo.

"Right. At least I know where we stand. You've turned grass and you're giving me a chance to run. Is that it?"

She'd admitted it too easily, but then, who was there to hear? It was her word against his—respected family lawyer versus lowly document courier.

"I haven't told them, and I'm not going to." There was every possibility someone had ears on this conversation, and not those of her co-conspirators. Sharston Strang's offices were bugged; Yarrow and Perlett's too. What he was doing now was the reason he'd been kept in the dark. He was 'too close to the target', and he couldn't walk away without warning her. "I'm not in as deep as you, but I've done enough to go down."

"Your fake reunion…"

"I had to prove my worth."

"Well, I was impressed," she spat. "You didn't have to come back to gloat. To remind me what an idiot I was, trusting an old boyfriend."

Old boyfriend? He was never that. She'd never permitted him to be. "I'm not here to gloat. I'm here to warn you about Simon Yarrow. Or, should I say, Anders Folden."

"I can handle him, don't you worry."

Perhaps she hadn't seen what Folden was capable of, but Rob had. "They're suspicious, Jess. Someone tipped off the police about Campion's inheritance."

"We don't know for sure anyone did tip them off."

"*Your colleagues* don't. Not yet. But *you* do."

Jess's eyes narrowed dangerously. "And you're going to be the one to tell them it was me."

Now Rob laughed. His anger would've got the better of him if he hadn't been so close to breaking down. "You don't know me at all, do you?" He lifted his helmet, studying the lining, preparing to say goodbye for the last time. "I still love you, Jess. In spite of everything." Her eyes were on him, imploring him to look at her, and he fought against it. "It doesn't matter what you've done, I don't want you to get hurt, and right now, the safest place for you is in police custody. You could turn Queen's evidence—"

"Are you insane? I'm not handing myself in!"

He lost the fight and met her gaze, less cold but still hard as steel. Resolved. "Then walk away while you can."

She held him there a moment longer then turned and went around to the other side of her desk, picked up a file and flicked through the sheets within. "Goodbye, Rob."

***

"Naomi. So glad you could make it."

She rose to her feet as Berringer approached them in the visiting area, and they embraced like lovers reuniting after a lifetime apart. Over Naomi's shoulder, Berringer locked eyes with Rob and sneered. Rob looked away, studying the low tabletop, permitting their murmured conversation without eavesdropping. They weren't the only ones who had yet to sit, a requirement of which a guard imminently reminded them. Berringer and Naomi released each other and joined Rob in the blue and yellow plastic seats around the small Formica table.

"Well, well, Mr. Simpson-Stone. Fancy seeing you here."

"Freddie. How are you?"

"I've been better."

The niceties weren't reciprocated, and that suited Rob just fine. He wouldn't have engaged Freddie at all if he'd had a choice. The way Freddie caressed Naomi's hand had Rob feeling like a sleazy voyeur.

"Are you keeping well?" Freddie talked as if he and Naomi were alone. "You look...beautiful, as always."

"Thank you. Yes, I am quite well."

"Have you been to Roger lately?"

"Last week. He sends his regards."

Freddie leaned forward to cup her chin in his hand, looking into her eyes like a vet examining a much-loved pet. "And was everything all right?"

"Everything's fine, Freddie. Please don't fuss."

"Of course I must fuss, sweetcheeks." He let his hand drop, trailing his fingers over the line of small round buttons fastening Naomi's shirt. "There's little else to occupy my time. Do you miss me? I miss you."

Naomi nodded but otherwise didn't answer. She broke away from Freddie's gaze and looked down to where he was once again toying with her hand.

"This is new." He spun the ring, easing it past her knuckle and sliding it back into place. The weight of it caused it to twist to the side. He straightened it and did it again, and again...

Rob averted his eyes, and not out of courtesy. The sexual overtone made him want to knock Berringer out cold, more because it wasn't entirely for show. So there was still something between Naomi and Freddie, at least on his part, or Rob had misread how she'd been with him in the car, but he hadn't been wrong about the lack of jewellery. The ring was too big to miss—big enough to conceal tech of some sort—and when Rob looked again, his suspicions were confirmed. Naomi's fingers were bare once more, and Freddie was sitting back, smiling at Rob like the proverbial cat that had got the cream.

"Will's newest beau talked some sense into him, I presume?" His lazy drawl was like the sensation of walking through spider webs, and apparently the question wasn't rhetorical.

"Sorry?"

"Why are *you* here?" Freddie asked slowly, accompanied by that smarmy half-smile, as if Rob were an idiot, but it was water off a duck's back. Rob had heard the same and worse from the lawyers to whom he'd played courier, with the exception of Folden, who'd had no need to belittle people to maintain the upper hand, which was why he was their hitman. He could murder in cold blood over and over without breaking a sweat while Rob stood by unable to intervene, sickened to the core by those dead eyes that lit up only when Folden snuffed out the life of another.

"Or was it Martina who sent you? She's such a doll. My father and hers are well acquainted."

"Small world," Rob remarked coolly. It was the same flashback he'd experienced on the night they'd raided Berringer's apartment, the hint of Folden in Freddie's absolute belief he was in control, the lack of regard for those he'd hurt. Yet watching him now, clutching around for bargaining chips, Rob realised he'd been wrong. Berringer was nothing more than a spoilt brat who stamped his feet until he got his own way.

As for Martina and her dad...they were close enough for their relationship to be usurped by privileged arseholes like the Berringers, but any sway Charles had over Hedley Senior would be rendered unnecessary in the next five minutes.

"Have you spoken to Will recently?" Rob asked.

"He writes to me on a daily basis." Freddie gave a short, false laugh and then cut it dead. "Why? Does he have something to say to me?"

"You'd have to ask him that."

"The chance would be superb."

"It might come sooner than you think."

"Oh?" Freddie sat up straight again. "Do tell."

"I'm afraid I can't."

"Robert, you're such a tease." It was a flippant comment, flamboyant even, but Rob had Freddie's full attention—and Naomi's. "My lawyer hasn't mentioned the hearing being brought forward."

"It's got nothing to do with the hearing. It's about—" Rob shifted his eyes in Naomi's direction "—the bank." Barely a flinch; she was good.

"Which bank?" Freddie asked innocently—another flawless performance.

For a second, Rob wondered if Will had merely been speculating and their entire plan was about to go west. "Yours."

Freddie crossed his legs and straightened his prison-issue trousers as if they were tailor-made—a force of habit that gave away his ill-ease. "If you're after a loan, you've come to the wrong place. As you may recall, we went bust—thanks to your old cronies."

"I know you're still in business, Freddie, but I don't need your charity."

"What *do* you need?"

"If anyone asks, Will Richards still works for you."

"Anyone being...?"

"I can't tell you." Rob maintained eye contact, hating himself for what he was about to do.

Freddie's expression rolled through disbelief, bemusement, infuriation and finally acceptance. He gave a wide shrug, like he didn't care. "What's in it for me?"

"Will thinks he may have omitted a few details from his statement."

Naomi whirled in her seat, eyes blazing. The colour had drained from her face, leaving stark flashes of rouge on suddenly sharp cheekbones. "What?"

He'd wanted to warn her. The second she'd opened the door and invited him to step in while she finished getting ready, it had been there, like over-chewed, tasteless gum that he needed to spit out and instead swallowed down. Seeing her reaction now... She wasn't afraid, she was outraged, and Rob was pleased. It suggested whatever was going on between Naomi and Freddie, the feelings were one-way. Freddie still loved her, but she didn't love him.

Freddie clicked his fingers a couple of times, and Rob snapped to attention, his face heating at Freddie's knowing sneer. "I'll take it under advisement. If my barrister agrees, we have a deal. But tell Wilfred Richards if he thinks he can double-cross me..."

"It's time to go." Naomi brusquely rose from her chair, as did Freddie, stepping around the table to block her exit route. This time, when he embraced her, she remained rigid and refused to look at him. He kissed her cheek and murmured into her ear. Whatever he said, Naomi didn't react. He released her, and she marched to the door where she waited with her back turned, her shoulders narrowed and tense.

Freddie watched on like a groom jilted at the altar but quickly covered up and looked Rob in the eye, extending his arm. "I'm relying on you to take good care of her...until I get out of here."

Rob almost shunned the handshake—Naomi's business was her own—but he couldn't risk Berringer changing his mind. Reluctantly, he shook Freddie's hand and went after Naomi.

26: Defiance

GRAY HANDED THE form back to Dom—the third non-disclosure he'd signed in the past five minutes. His phone was in a locker in a room along the corridor, and he'd been body-scanned before being allowed through the biometrically protected portal to the 'inner sanctum' of the SIU—where the case files were kept.

"Like I say, it's procedure," Dom explained again as if Gray were a first-time visitor. He countersigned all three agreements and put them back in the folder. "As Rob isn't here, there's only limited information we can permit you to share with him—the rest is at your discretion."

Gray nodded, distracted by ACC Winstanley's antics. A catering assistant had delivered a tray with a coffee pot, cups and associated sundries, and Winstanley had insisted on 'being mother'. With a swift, nervous, "If you're sure, Sir?" the bamboozled catering assistant had taken him at his word and darted from the room, leaving her trolley, over which the ACC loomed, weeping-willow-like.

"Are you listening?" Dom asked.

"Hmm?" Gray endeavoured to concentrate. "Sorry. Yes. Selected information at my discretion." Winstanley stalked over with a first cup and saucer—like doll's house crockery in his spidery hand—and set it down next to Dom.

"Thanks, Sir." He waited for line of sight before he continued. "I presume you've figured out this relates to Operation Tabula Rasa?"

Gray nodded again, which was to say he'd figured out it was to do with *an* operation.

"A clean slate, Mr. Fisher," Winstanley explained loftily as he swayed back to the trolley, collected a second cup and delivered it to Gray.

"Yes, thank you, Martin, I'm well aware of the meaning of that particular phrase. As for the operation to which it applies…"

"The can of worms you upended when you went after Strang and Folden," Dom muttered and shot Gray a warning glare over the top of the cup, but Gray wasn't deliberately playing silly buggers. When he'd resigned, that 'can of worms' was still known as the SAP case—based on the initial targets and the filename suffix. Given Strang and Partners were but few of many involved, the acronym had ceased to be accurate almost as soon as it came into being, but Gray had seen no reason to complicate matters by changing it; they all knew what they were talking about. Evidently, on that score, Dom didn't agree, and it was of no concern to Gray, or it shouldn't have been.

Winstanley finally made it to the table with his own coffee and folded his elongated self into a chair. "I took the liberty of reading the files on Strang et al. while I was engaged in your disciplinary investigation. Impressive work, Mr. Fisher. Very thorough indeed."

"Thanks," Gray graciously accepted Winstanley's backhanded praise. The man never could deliver a compliment without a criticism, as if it were crucial to keeping the balance of the universe, and the supercilious expression that went with it was laughable. Or perhaps it was the gravity of the situation. Either way, Gray shifted in his chair so he was facing Dom more than Winstanley. "You were saying..."

Dom exchanged his coffee cup for a pen to fiddle with, which predictably he held like a cigarette. "Without giving you a full blow-by-blow of the last eleven months, all you need to know is the operation has expanded significantly. Our initial focus on legal and financial firms was the tip of the iceberg, and we're now working in partnership with colleagues in multiple departments, including the Ministry of Defence and the Home Office.

"We have operatives in strategic locations—some SIU, some insiders. We're looking at corruption on a massive scale, Gray, and at every level all the way to the top. They've attempted to shut us down twice. Officially, Rasa ended six months ago when MI5 took it off our hands. They reviewed our evidence and concluded it was too costly to pursue further. Then our funding was cut. However—"

"Mr. Hooper..." Winstanley warned.

Dom exhaled heavily, eyes rolling as he rephrased on the hop. He tried again. "In short, our funding was reinstated, and we were instructed to continue our investigation—unofficially." He was clearly itching to give Gray the full story, but there was no way Winstanley would stand for it. Frustrating. Someone high up—Cabinet or judiciary, maybe—had a vested interest in the SIU and the investigation, and Gray would have loved to know who, but he didn't need to.

"Perhaps, Mr. Hooper, you could skip forward to the details most salient to Mr. Fisher?"

"Of course, Sir," Dom accepted with a forced smile. "One of our operatives in the MoD alerted us to a situation concerning Yvette and Philip Parker. Rob's told you who they are, I take it?"

"He has," Gray confirmed. "MoD...this is about Yvette rather than her brother?"

"In a roundabout fashion. The system logs all searches of personnel data— where they originate, what they search for—"

"They were looking for Rob," Gray said, hoping he managed to conceal the sudden spike of anxiety.

Dom nodded. "Predictably, when we tracked down the login ID, the person in question was on annual leave, but we know it came from within the Inland Revenue..." Dom glanced Winstanley's way, as did Gray. He'd procured a clipboard from somewhere—perhaps one of his colossal jacket pockets—and was scribbling furiously with a scratchy pencil. He paused without looking up and flicked his fingers at them to continue.

Dom's surprise at the lack of objection matched Gray's own, but he eventually picked up where he'd left off. "They searched Rob's contact info and hopped from his record to Yvette Parker's—she's listed as his last commanding officer. He's still on the electoral roll at his old address, which is also what's on his army record, so we assumed they were trying to get a current address for him. We checked other government agencies and made two discoveries. One, he hasn't updated his address anywhere, which means they haven't found him yet. And two, there have been multiple searches on both Rob's and the Parkers' records going back several months." Dom paused, eyes narrowed beneath his deeply lined forehead as he studied Gray. "What's on your mind?"

Gray had only been half listening; there was a lot on his mind, at the forefront a burning and seemingly obvious question. "I'll wait to hear what you think first."

"Well, with all Rob's previous undercover stints and the high profile Met cases he's worked, he's got a fair few potential enemies—"

"You don't need to soft-soap me," Gray cut in. It earned him a derisory sniff from Winstanley, and it riled him. The trail Gray had left was entire bread slices, never mind crumbs, and he'd come clean, put it all on record and accepted the consequences, because there had been more at stake than his reputation. Besides, Winstanley got a promotion out of it, so he had absolutely no right to be up there on his very high horse.

Nevertheless, this time they were on the same side and a spat would be counterproductive, so Gray gave himself a minute before he said, "I appreciate that you're trying to protect my feelings, Dom, but we all know how badly I screwed up. It's why I'm wearing this." He flicked his visitor's badge in disappointment. Strangely, it hadn't bothered him until now, as he finally, properly acknowledged his regret for his actions, not just for the damage he'd done to Rob, but to his own career.

"Dom, you asked me why I agreed to go in with Rob on his private investigation venture, and I've given it a lot of thought. Was it guilt? At first, yes. But I think what it comes down to is this. I asked for Rob's help. He knew what it would cost him, yet he still gave it. When he asked for mine, I reciprocated, because it's the right thing to do, and because this is who I am. A former police officer with years of specialist training and experience.

"After rehab, I made a conscious effort to box it away, leave it in the past, but I couldn't. I knew, as soon as Rob came to me about the Berringers. Too much of me still resides here." Gray looked around the room they were in; he'd rarely used it, preferring to meet his team 'in the field', but the ambience, the décor, the heavy scent of ancient teak—there was no ignoring where he was. "More to the point, I no longer want to put it behind me, and I can't come back, which means sticking with the private sector, and I can deal with that.

"Rob and I work well together, but we're still building trust. I threw him under the bus, for which I accept full responsibility, but it'll be a sight easier to live with if I can make sure it doesn't get a second chance to flatten him."

Dom sucked hard on his pen and slowly withdrew it from his lips. "All right, Gray, I'll cut to the chase. We believe what's going on with Rob and the Parkers is related to Rasa. Someone's trying to get to Rob via the Parkers—who, and for what purpose? We don't know, but we're doing everything we can to find out."

"And if he gets in the way of the operation?" Gray asked. Dom steadily held his gaze. No false assurances. "Thank you for your honesty."

"It's all I've got, Gray." Dom peered past him to Winstanley; still scribbling. "I'll give you a brief overview of recent events, so you've got a better sense of what's going on." Winstanley flipped to a clean page and continued. Dom mouthed, "Catching up on paperwork."

Gray had to agree. They hadn't said enough to fill one sheet, let alone the three dangling over the top of the clipboard. "Should I take notes?" Gray asked, straight-faced.

Dom chuckled silently and cleared his throat. "Not a good idea, but I don't envisage you'll need to. Our first task was to establish whether the Parkers were unwitting victims or willing accomplices. We received that confirmation three weeks ago when Philip Parker checked in for an investors' meeting at the Royal Chester Hotel and didn't check out."

"Interesting." Gray had cottoned on now. This wasn't Dom briefing him; it was an exchange of information. "According to his sister, he's away on business."

"But you haven't been able to get hold of either of them," Dom pointed out.

Gray bristled. "Are we bugged?"

"Do you honestly want me to answer that?"

Gray didn't care for Dom's sarcasm, although he deserved it for asking a daft question. "Go on."

"We couldn't get past hotel security. UAE royalty, diplomatic envoys—it was tight. Parker attended the first hour of the presentation, went to the lounge for coffee and vanished."

"Yet you're still sure he's above board?"

Dom shrugged. "Your guess is as good as mine. Better, I imagine."

"Now why would you imagine that?" Gray was starting to get a very clear sense of what it was like to wear the boot on the other foot. It wasn't the violation Josh and others had reported when he'd informed them they'd been subjects of surveillance. More like being a rookie again, with someone constantly looking over his shoulder.

Dom wagged his pen in Gray's direction. "If you haven't already trawled through every bit of Parker's paperwork you can lay your hands on, I'll be a monkey's uncle."

"I knew there was a reason I recommended you, suck-up."

Dom dipped his head demurely, and Gray laughed. The more that was out in the open, the less tense they both became.

Dom continued, "As far as we can tell—you'll correct me if I'm wrong, I'm sure—both Parkers and their corporate interests are legitimate and fully above board. They even pay their taxes."

"I concur..." Distracted by the grating sound, Gray caught a jerky arm movement out of the corner of his eye. Winstanley made a few more brisk turns of his pencil and withdrew it from the self-contained sharpener, which he returned to his pocket. He offered Gray a grim smile and went back to his scribbling.

Gray ignored Winstanley's oddity and asked, "Do you think Parker's dead?"

"No," Dom said. "We know he's still alive and, as far as we can tell, so is his sister. We switched all surveillance to Yvette, yet somehow she's managed to disappear too."

"If you know Parker's still alive, what are we talking about here? A kidnapping?"

"Yes," Dom confirmed.

"Right. That explains why his sister was trying to get a large sum of cash together."

"No, it doesn't."

"Oh...hell." On impulse, Gray picked up his coffee but was struck motionless before it reached his mouth. He clung to the cup, focusing on the feel of it in his hands, its shape, its size, and begging internally for Dom to tell him he was wrong. An impossibly long time passed before Dom said anything at all, and it wasn't what Gray wanted to hear.

"The exchange was supposed to happen on the night of Rob's leaving do. Parker's sister turned up with a couple of heavies and bundled him into a van, as per her arrangement with the kidnappers."

"I didn't see any of you lot lurking outside the restaurant."

"Not knowingly," Dom said. "But you spoke to one of us."

Gray shook his head, dismayed. All those months of constant self-chastisement for his hyper-vigilance and the one night he'd needed it, it had failed him. "I'm losing my touch."

"No, mate. I'm just an expert at dodging you."

"Is that right?"

"I've had a lot of practice." Dom winked. Winstanley sniffed. Dom got back to it. "Needless to say, she didn't deliver him but took him to her dead aunt's place in Hampstead Heath instead—we discovered later. We lost her en route. Next thing, we were getting Traffic reports that Rob was headed up north. Then you called asking me to look into his phone..."

Gray absently sipped his coffee as he merged the various accounts of the evening together in his mind. Either Bish and Jock were damn good liars or Tonka hadn't told them about the hostage exchange. Given their conversation the other day about loyalty, Gray was inclined to think they were in on her plans, but something had gone wrong and now the kidnappers had two hostages. The question was, had Bish and Jock hired Rob to find Tonka because they were worried about her, or were they intending to make the exchange themselves?

"What do you know about John Garvey and Harry Wilson?" Gray asked.

Dom shrugged. "Not a lot. Stationed with Yvette Parker and Rob in Germany, now run a security firm...that's about it."

So much for his honesty. If Dom hadn't known who they were before they'd abducted Rob, he'd have done a full workup on them since, never mind that he kept glancing towards the door, desperate for a smoke, to escape, or both. He settled for taking his empty cup over to the coffee pot and refilling it.

Gray turned his attention on Winstanley, who was no longer scribbling; he was watching Dom with interest. A blink and his eyes were on Gray's, where they lingered briefly, narrow and perceptive. Another blink and they were back on Dom.

"We should take a break soon," Dom suggested and resumed his seat, acting as if he wasn't aware of Winstanley following his every move. When he could pretend no more, he said, "Sorry. Does anyone else want a top-up?"

Winstanley waved his hand, dismissing the offer. Gray watched him for a few more seconds before turning back to Dom.

"No, thanks." He weighed up the prospects of a straight answer in return for a straight question. Minimal, he envisaged, and headed around the houses. "You followed Rob up to his mum's and you've had surveillance on him ever since."

"That's right," Dom confirmed. He was still on edge, aware he wasn't off the hook. "We wiped next of kin off his records when he was with the unit, and he's bloody nippy on that bike. We only caught up with him because we knew where he was going."

"OK." Gray smoothed his palm down over his mouth and chin. However 'nippy' Rob's bike was, it was conspicuous, which meant the SIU had intercepted their targets' attempts to pursue him, but if they'd had line of sight... "Why haven't they just taken him out?"

"If I was a gambling man, which I am, I'd lay my money on Rob having information they need, or at least, they think he does."

It was a reasonable theory. Rob had played courier for three years, during which he'd transported millions of pounds' worth of counterfeit documents around the country. He'd likely been privy to all kinds of meetings, just a lowly grunt awaiting his next order, until the final few weeks when he'd stuck to Folden like glue. When the SIU brought in Folden, Perlett, Sharston and Strang, Rob should've been fully debriefed, and the reason he hadn't been was Gray's reluctance to put him under further strain. If he had, they wouldn't be in their current predicament, because whatever Rob knew—assuming he knew anything at all—would be as valuable to the SIU as it was to their targets.

"Are you sure this has nothing to do with the Berringers?" Gray asked. "We did royally piss Freddie off."

Winstanley snuffed air out of his nose, and Gray fought the urge to smile. It was an intentionally ludicrous question. True, the SIU romping around Berringer's bank had curtailed trading for a few days, but the damage had already been done—by Freddie's father—and it was old news. But Dom answered anyway.

"Put it this way, Gray. If it did, I wouldn't have allowed Rob to visit Berringer Junior this morning."

"You're talking about dodgy investors, the Berringers were investment bankers..."

"Oh, they move in the same business circles, I grant you, but by comparison, the Berringers are good, honest businessmen. Decent sorts, as they say."

"Aside from the murder of innocent men."

"I'm not so sure they murdered anyone. The guy in the Merc, for instance— the Berringers get chauffeured everywhere. I doubt it would've even crossed Berringer Senior's mind that Laird-Browne would get behind the wheel drunk. As for the hunt sab, I haven't seen the video, but...well, let's just say that boyfriend of yours is no Saint Francis of Assisi."

Dom's analogy was flawed, but Gray got the gist and was wise enough to let it pass. "This investors' meeting Philip attended..."

"Yeah, money laundering. They're using their spoils to make legitimate overseas property purchases on behalf of investors. The purchase goes through, they bill their investors, et voilà! Clean money with a track record. We've managed to shut down several firms—there are others. Unfortunately, we lost our source."

Gray was torn. He'd been intent on withholding what they'd discovered, at the very least until he'd heard from Will, but it was currency, and they were, allegedly, all on the same side.

"GP Investments," he said quickly before he changed his mind.

Dom shook his head. "Never heard of them." He was telling the truth.

"The G is Hilary Gelling—Philip Parker's accountant. The P is Raymond Perlett."

"Michelle's father?"

"The very fellow."

"Wasn't he on our original SAP list?"

"Yes, and he was clean, so it might be a dead end."

"I'll get someone on it." Dom moved to stand.

"If you can wait a couple of hours, I should have the answer for you."

Dom sat again, his knee jigging. Gray recognised the symptoms, the withdrawal kicking in.

"I think it might be time for that break, Sir," he said.

Winstanley set his clipboard on the table and checked his watch. Dom was already at the door.

"Just one more thing." Gray casually rose to his feet and straightened his shirt, drawing out the motion before he glanced up at Dom. "How long have Garvey and Wilson been reporting to the SIU?"

Dom turned puce. He looked from Winstanley to Gray and back again. The silence loomed large; Dom was waiting for Winstanley's permission. It took a while—at least a minute—before he nodded once to give it.

"Since we confirmed someone was going after the Parkers," Dom said.

"And you instructed them to hire Rob and me...why? To send us on a wild goose chase?"

"Not at all." Dom pulled out his cigarettes. "I did it because I needed extra eyes on Rob...and your help."

"You could've just asked. Did you think I'd refuse?"

"No. I was confident you'd agree. This way, you don't have to lie to Rob."

"But you don't want me to tell him about Bish and Jock—sorry, Garvey and Wilson."

"I'm familiar with their nicknames. I see no problem with you telling Rob now. Even if he pulls out of the investigation—"

"I can't," Gray finished, as impressed with Dom's cunning as he was infuriated by his solipsism. "You're a devious sod, Hooper."

Dom shrugged nonchalantly. "I'm merely following the rule book written by my predecessor. See you in twenty." The door closed.

Gray stared after him, no idea what to do next. Now he knew for sure there was a target on Rob's back, he wanted as much information as he could get his hands on, but he doubted Winstanley would permit him access to the case files.

"If I may offer a word to the wise, Graham..."

He still had his back to Winstanley but noted the change of address along with what sounded suspiciously like empathy or concern. Gray gave him the go-ahead.

"There's nothing to be gained from bringing Simpson-Stone up to speed on Garvey and Wilson."

Gray had been thinking the same. There was no telling how Rob would take the news that his old army mates had lied to him by omission. It may even hinder their efforts to keep him safe, but Gray had to go back with something or Rob would seek his own answers.

At such times, and in the present company, humility was his friend. Of course, Winstanley would see straight through it, but he might play along if Gray buttered him up enough.

"Thanks, Martin. I appreciate the advice. It's been good to see you again."

"Likewise."

"I had my reservations when Dom told me our meeting would be supervised."

"Quite," Winstanley said, his attention seemingly back on his note-taking. He knew what Gray was playing for, and he was making him work for it.

"Yes, I was relieved to discover it would be you."

"I'm sure."

"Of all the officers I've come into contact with in my career, and it runs into the hundreds, you're the only one I trust."

That stopped him, albeit for only a few seconds. Nor was he entirely successful in hiding his pleasure at Gray's admission. "All right," he said, "let's have it, Fisher."

"I want access to the Tabula Rasa files. No notes, no copies, I'll read them here, today, under your eagle-eyed supervision."

"That's all you want?"

"Yes, Sir."

Winstanley slowly inhaled, the air whistling its way up his nostrils. Gray waited with breath held for as long as he could, but the man had the lung capacity of an ox, and Gray had to give up before he passed out.

"That seems acceptable." Discarding his clipboard, Winstanley rose from his seat. "More coffee?"

"Yes...please. And thanks."

And *still* he didn't exhale.

27: Double Crossing

R OB SLOWED AND dropped a gear as they passed a pub with 'food served all day' signs. "How about there?"

"Fine by me," Naomi replied in the same couldn't-care-less tone she'd used since they'd left the prison, such as either of them had said much at all, which was why Rob had suggested stopping somewhere for lunch to clear the bad air between them. Understandably, she was angry. The Met had put serious pressure on her and Aaron to testify against the Berringers, but it only worked because they'd wanted to be free of Freddie. That or they'd just wanted to bring him down a peg or two.

Either way, Rob was sure Naomi didn't want Freddie out on the prowl again. Beyond that, he had no idea what she wanted, not when she'd flirted with him and then let Freddie fawn all over her. He was jealous, and aware of the parallels to the accusation he'd levelled at Jess all those years ago—*you led me on*—the difference being Jess *had* led him on, for sex, not the relationship he'd craved. With Naomi, he couldn't even be sure she was flirting. It wasn't the first time, but it hadn't mattered before Gray suggested brokering a deal with Berringer. It had been clear-cut, or clearer than the muddy mess it was now. Whether the trial went ahead or not, Rob was still a former police officer, and he'd met Naomi while on the job.

The pub's wait staff must have assumed they were a couple and showed them to a secluded table in a dark corner screened off from the rest of the dining room. Menus appeared in front of them, from which they both made an arbitrary choice and ordered soft drinks. The waiter took back the menus, returned briefly to deliver their drinks, and then left them to their silence.

Rob wanted to know about the ring Naomi had smuggled to Freddie. He could ask straight up—that was what he'd normally have done—but the last thing he wanted was for her to think he was accusing her of wrongdoing. She'd broken the prison's rules, which could have a bearing on her reliability as a witness if Berringer still went to trial *and* it came out, but Rob was increasingly apathetic towards the whole situation.

He'd done his job thoroughly, knowing the Berringers' QC would trawl every document and analyse every word for any means to have the case dismissed, and it had all been for nothing, so what did it matter if Naomi had broken a couple of petty prison rules? Freddie had wielded power over Aaron too long to uphold the illusion that Naomi was acting of her own volition, although the longer Rob spent in her company, the less certain he became that it was an illusion.

They sipped their drinks; their meals arrived. The silence continued, finally broken by Naomi's request for ketchup and Rob's unchecked reaction.

"What?" She was immediately defensive. "I like ketchup."

"I didn't say a word."

"You didn't need to. Your face said it for you." She deposited a large dollop on the side of her plate, clicked the lid shut and set the bottle down. There was a smile lurking behind that moody scowl.

Shaking his head, Rob tucked into his gammon and chips. "You and Lu would get on like a house on fire."

"How so?"

"United in your love of ketchup. The kid puts it on everything—chips..."

"What are chips without ketchup?"

"Fry-ups..."

"The perfect accompaniment."

"Carbonara." Rob nodded at Naomi's plate. Almost to spite him, she swirled her pasta-loaded fork in the ketchup, covering it completely. Rob laughed, relieved the ice was starting to melt. "I'm sorry," he said. "I should've warned you."

"Was it an option?"

"Yeah. I bottled out."

"Were you worried I'd jeopardise your success in talking Freddie round?"

"No, nothing like that. I didn't want to upset you. And for the record, it wasn't my idea."

"I'd gathered as much." Naomi exchanged her fork for her glass. "It has Will Richards written all over it."

"Does it?" Rob thought it had come from Gray—contrary to his claim it was Will's scheme—because it was a DCI Fisher tactic too. Clearly, they were well suited.

"What's it about, or can't you tell me?"

"I can't say much as it relates to an ongoing investigation."

"The PI business?" Naomi guessed.

"Yep."

"Mmm." She wanted to say more, and Rob wanted to tell her more. Regardless of what he'd witnessed at the prison, he trusted her to keep it to herself, but it wasn't solely his decision.

"You've got ketchup..." He subtly indicated her chin. She wiped with her napkin, but the ketchup stayed put. She tried again. Rob shook his head. She gave her chin one more broad wipe, to no avail. It was the tiniest spot, and he'd only used it to redirect both of their attention, but this was possibly worse. "So what have you been up to?" he asked, attempting to move the conversation on again.

"Are you really going to let me go through the rest of lunch with ketchup on my chin?" She held out her napkin and leaned forward. "No spit," she warned.

With a smile, Rob took the napkin and rubbed at the offending spot, but the ketchup was stubborn as anything.

"Everything all right with your meals?" A waiter stopped at their table.

Naomi quickly leaned her chin on her hand. "Yes, thanks."

"Great, cheers," Rob said. "Could I trouble you for a glass of water?"

"No trouble," the waiter said and left, soon returning with the water. Rob offered thanks and waited for them to move on before he dipped a corner of the napkin into the glass and used it to successfully clean the ketchup away. The cool wetness amplified the heat radiating from Naomi's skin, and Rob was once again fighting the urge to touch. Carefully withdrawing, he dropped the napkin onto the table and sat back in his chair, fingers locked and steepled above his plate.

Naomi frowned in concern. "What's wrong?"

"Nothing." Rob clasped his hands tighter together, not yet safe from temptation. "Can I be honest, Naomi?"

"Twice in one day?"

"Actually, it was the same point, but I got sidetracked."

"Oh, now I'm intrigued." That smile...if that didn't mean what Rob thought it meant...

"All right. Cards on the table. I'm very attracted to you. I have been since I met you."

"When you thought I was Aaron's wife," she said. Her smile faltered, and there was a hint of worry there, but it made her no less beautiful. "He told you we were separated."

"Yep." Rob briefly got lost in reminiscing the night she'd called him over to her mother's flat. He'd thought back on it a few times and couldn't recall if she'd claimed to be Aaron's wife, although Aaron had referred to her as such, probably because Rob had put him on the spot. If he'd known about Aaron's anxiety, he'd have taken a gentler approach. "The thing is...there was this girl back in high school I fancied like mad, and we ended up going out a couple of times, slept together quite a few more over the years... I thought she wanted what I did." He hid behind his hand and laughed at himself. "Turns out I'm really shit at interpreting signals." He peered over his fingers. Naomi smiled back at him. "Am I way off, or...?"

"No, but I have to ask. How on earth did you get with Zoë?" She was tormenting, Rob thought, but also interested to know.

"She's pretty blatant about what she wants." She hadn't changed in that regard, which was how Rob had known he was ready to move on. He was OK with Zoë loving Travis. "Anyway, it's all academic. I can't do anything about it."

"Because I was a suspect?"

"Suspect, witness, makes no odds. My hands are tied—at least until the Berringers' trials are over, maybe even beyond."

"But those won't go ahead if your plan comes to fruition," Naomi argued.

"Freddie's won't. However, we're both prosecution witnesses against Charles. That aside, seeing you and Freddie together today—"

Naomi held up her hand, no trace of the smile now. "OK, I need to explain."

"You don't."

"I do, Rob. Because if the only obstacle to our friendship becoming something more meaningful is Freddie's and my little game..."

"It's not a game to Freddie."

"Oh, it is. I know how it looks, but you have to get into his mindset. Freddie's all about acquisitions, trophies." She tapped her finger to her chest. "That's what I am to him. I'm not saying he's lying when he claims he's in love with me. I'm quite sure he believes it's true. But if he did *acquire* me, then what?"

She paused. Rob couldn't decide if it was for effect or if she was expecting him to respond, but he had nothing to say so was relieved when she answered her own question.

"It would be over, and that's the last thing Freddie wants."

"It's the chase," Rob said.

"More...a Victorian collector of exotic species. Freddie naively imagines I could survive in captivity, but he'd soon tire of me and grow neglectful. Roger—a doctor friend of his—insists Aaron and I will converge if we submit to gender alignment and psychotherapy when, in truth, Freddie will either lose me—his *exotic bird*—or he'll lose Aaron."

Rob nodded slowly. He sort of understood what she was saying. "That's who Freddie mentioned earlier—Roger?"

"Yes. He's an endocrinologist—prescribes my HRT and gives me a check-up every once in a while."

"HRT?" Rob's mum had been on it during her menopause, and if he'd given himself a minute to reason it through, he wouldn't have repeated it aloud. "You agreed to the treatment? I thought Aaron said—"

"He doesn't want it? You're quite right, but we compromised. Freddie and me, that is. You might have noticed Aaron has little regard for his appearance." Naomi smiled and bit her lip. "I must tell you about the time Aaron went clothes shopping. It wasn't long after I'd come out to our friends—Will, Hector, Carrie and a few others—not Freddie at that point. The first time Freddie met me, he didn't know who I was, other than Will's girlfriend, but that's another story."

"Touchy subject?" Rob asked. It wasn't news. Will had mentioned he and Naomi were an item back in university, but she hadn't spoken about it before. Again, Rob was struck by a touch of jealousy—mixed in with his desire to know everything there was to know about Naomi Silvestri.

"A little," she confirmed, and then, responding to whatever signal he was giving off—he hoped it was curiosity—added, "Nothing sinister. I'll tell you sometime. So, this one morning, Aaron got up and immediately flew into a fury because I'd spent all his—our—student grant on clothes, mostly for me, although I did buy him a suit, shirt and tie. He'd rather slouch around in jeans and T-shirts, and they were tatty and old, so…"

"You threw his clothes out, didn't you?" Rob guessed.

She laughed. "Yes, I did. Not all of them, mind you. I saved a couple of the less faded T-shirts and—don't you shake your head at me."

Rob *was* shaking his head, but he was laughing too. "Zoë did that to me a couple of times. They're only faded because we love them and want to get our money's worth."

"Aaron got more than his money's worth out of that lot. Some of those T-shirts went back to his high school days. Anyway, to cut a long, arduous story short, he asked Freddie to pay some of what he owed him and replenished his wardrobe. Bear in mind this was eighteen years ago, and he's still wearing those same jeans and T-shirts now."

"They're timeless," Rob reasoned, which earned him a light smack on the arm. "That was the last time he went clothes shopping?"

"Sadly, yes."

"Good for him."

Naomi narrowed her eyes. "I was starting to rather like you."

Rob laughed. He didn't actually mind buying new clothes and always tried to dress well, but it was fun winding Naomi up. Fun spending time with her, full stop. He was losing his resolve, and they'd both finished eating some time ago. "Do you want to stay for dessert?" he asked.

"Are you in a rush to get back?" she countered.

"Not especially, but there're things I could be doing, and Hedley will expect her car back at some point."

"Then we should make a move." Naomi waved to catch the waiter's attention. "Bill, please?"

The waiter acknowledged the request with a nod and left to get it.

"My shout," Rob said, pulling his wallet from his pocket. Before he could open it, Naomi's hand landed on top of his.

"Why?"

"Why not? I suggested we stop for lunch. It's only fair I pay."

"Consider it a thank-you for accompanying me to the prison."

The plate with the bill appeared on the table between them; Naomi got to it first.

"I'm not happy about this," Rob grumbled. Still intent on at least paying his share, he pulled a twenty-pound note from his wallet and dropped it onto the plate.

"Rob, you really don't have to. Aaron's bringing in a regular income." She sifted through a stack of cards and withdrew a gold one.

"From Freddie?"

She hesitated—very briefly—as she put the card down on top of his note. No denial, but he'd let her play ignorant so far; now he needed to know if she trusted him with the truth.

The waiter returned with a card reader, and Naomi paid the bill, leaving the twenty-pound note on the table. Rob exchanged it for a more sensible tip, and then they were in the car again, heading for home. They were almost outside Naomi's place before she broke her silence.

"Will you come up for a coffee? I'll tell you everything."

"What did you give to Freddie?"

He heard her draw breath as if to answer and then release it.

"Please, Naomi." Her response—or lack of—would decide where they went next, and Rob couldn't force it.

She fidgeted with her seat belt, tugging it away from her neck. "Are you obligated to report back?"

"To who? Gray?"

"Your former boss."

"You mean Hedley? No." He indicated and pulled into a space outside Naomi's building, watching her and waiting.

"An encryption algorithm."

"He's not planning to break out, is he?"

"No, nothing like that. He has restricted internet access, and it's monitored. The algorithm bypasses the restrictions and encrypts Freddie's data. He's not using it for criminal purposes, only bank business."

"How do you know?"

Naomi smiled. "The prison might not be able to monitor what he's up to…"

"But Aaron can," Rob finished.

Naomi unfastened her seat belt. "So, about that coffee…"

It was too tempting. "Some other time, yeah?"

She studied him for several seconds and then nodded. "Some other time," she said and leaned across to kiss his cheek. "Take care, Rob."

"You too," he replied, still facing forward and refusing to look as she got out and shut the door behind her.

***

"Rob. I left you a voicemail."

He startled. He'd been checking the car to make sure it was clean and tidy and hadn't heard Martina come up behind him.

"Did you?" He handed her keys over and took out his phone, tutting at himself as he turned it back on. He'd switched it off at the prison. "What's up?"

"The Quarterhouse sent us their security camera footage from the week of your leaving do."

"I know who abducted me."

"This is from earlier in the week." She moved off, expecting him to follow, which he did, into the station, pausing to sign in, and up to her office, where she logged in to her computer while he checked his other messages. All junk other than one from Brookhurst hospital to say Ethan had approved his visit— tomorrow at 1800—although Rob wasn't sure it was necessary anymore.

"Ready?" Martina asked.

"Hmm? Sorry. Yeah."

She pressed play and stepped back to give him an unobstructed view.

The footage was a wide shot of the restaurant's interior which also took in the front entrance and half of the window next to it. Rob watched the staff going about their preparations—vacuuming floors, laying tables. "What am I looking for?" he asked.

"Keep your eye on the window."

Rob shifted focus, glancing at the date and time in the top-left corner of the screen—Tuesday afternoon, three days before his leaving do—and then he saw it. A white van, sliding door on the nearside, a line of rusty holes where the rubber bump rail should've been. "What the hell? How long was it there?"

"Only a few minutes," Martina said as the time changed again and the van magically disappeared.

"The bastards. They knew I'd be there. The whole setup was bullshit. Any idea what they were up to?"

"I was hoping you might be able to shed some light."

"Nope. I haven't the foggiest, but I'm gonna bloody well find out." He was tempted to get straight on the bike and head down to Brighton. He could be there in an hour.

"How did it go with Berringer?" Martina asked. He wouldn't have put it past her to have caught on to what he was thinking and delay him on purpose, although it was a reasonable question.

"All right," he said neutrally, hoping to shut down further enquiry. No such luck.

"Nothing untoward?"

"Apart from the two of them getting all lovey-dovey?"

"Sorry to hear that."

Rob frowned. "Why?"

"I know you've got a soft spot for Naomi."

By the time he'd recovered from his shock, it was too late for him to convincingly deny it, although there was no reason for him to do so. As Martina kept reminding him, she was no longer his boss, and they were still friends...for the time being. "Yeah, well, even if there was nothing between them, I can't act on it."

"Not at the moment. Once the Berringers' trials are over, there's nothing to stop you pursuing something more."

Rob's pulse rate shot up, and he was glad he had the cover of his crush on Naomi because when Martina found out what he'd done, she'd be gunning for him.

28: Answers

THE CONFERENCE ROOM table should have been bowing under the weight of the multiple stacks of files over which ACC Martin Winstanley presided like a praying mantis.

"Reference number?" He licked the tip of his pencil and poised it above the clipboard balanced on one spindly arm, waiting to record the requested information as he had done for every file Gray had touched so far.

Gray suppressed a sigh and flipped the cover shut. "It's—"

There was a knock at the door. Martin held up his hand as if Gray were still talking. "Come!"

The door eased open, and another stack of files appeared, followed by a female officer.

"Well blow me down," Gray muttered and laughed at how obvious it was—now he knew. It was the woman he'd seen in the metro supermarket on the night of Rob's leaving do. "You were tailing me."

The female officer set down the files and brushed her palms together before offering her hand. "Dee Knight. Good to meet you, Mr. Fisher."

Gray shook Dee's hand. "And you. So that spiel about the missing partner..."

She grinned sheepishly. "DCI Hooper told me to draw attention to myself or you'd get suspicious."

"Ah, he knows me too well. You did an excellent job, incidentally, although a few times I've wondered if you ever managed to track him down."

"Yeah, sorry."

"No problem. You do what's necessary to get the job done. So, how long have you—"

"Mr. Fisher? If we may continue?" Winstanley rapped his pencil against his clipboard.

Seeing as he had his back to Winstanley, Gray took the opportunity to pull a face before he answered, "Of course, Sir. My apologies."

"That's the last of the files, Sir," Dee said, grinning at Gray's antics. He approved of Dom's decision. He liked her.

Winstanley nodded and flicked his fingers to send her on her way. "Reference number?" he repeated once the door had closed.

Gray pursed his lips but then decided to just come out and say it. "I thought promotion might make you less bitter."

"I'm not bitter, Graham."

"That's not quite the right word. Resentful?"

Winstanley placed his clipboard on top of the new stack of files and pulled out a chair but didn't sit. "Yes," he said, exaggerating the 'e' and keeping the 's' short and sharp. His focus was on the files, not Gray. "I resent having to play over-attentive nanny to an impetuous child."

"Then leave me to it. I can't go anywhere without you or Dom letting me out."

"That's precisely my point. You shouldn't even be here."

"Fine, I'll go." Gray unclipped his visitor's badge and started towards the door.

"Don't act the fool, Graham."

"I've taken up enough of your precious time. Can you let Dom know—"

"Stop!"

The hairs on the back of Gray's neck prickled. It was never wise to take on Martin Winstanley, but he was tired of hearing it—same overture, different movement. Still, he couldn't walk away; there was too much at stake. Taking a couple of slow, deep breaths, he turned around and retraced his steps until he was only a foot from Winstanley, whose face was thunder. "Look, Martin, it's done. If I could go back and fix it, I would, but I can't. The sooner you and Dom accept—"

"For God's sake, man, this is no longer about your misconduct, nor even the devastation you left in your wake. My resentment for your involvement now is that it's come too late. Have you any idea how much evidence I've gathered in the past ten years on the very people you threatened to expose?"

"You're telling me there was already an internal investigation underway?"

"I'm telling you I've known for a long time both who they are and what they're capable of, but, as the old adage goes, fools rush in..."

"If I'd had access to that information two years ago—"

"I could not have given you that information two years ago nor at any point prior, and my personal feelings toward you had nothing to do with it. We may have had our differences in the past—" Winstanley's vacuous nostrils flared wider still at Gray's disbelieving 'ha'. He inhaled—slowly, steadily—and started again. "We may have had our differences in the past, however, I would suffer your company for all eternity before I let my *resentment* stop me from doing my job."

"Suffer my company? I didn't choose to be here, nor did I request your presence."

"No. I volunteered."

"Why? Because you don't trust me?"

"Quite the contrary, Graham." Winstanley's right nostril twitched so violently it mobilised his cheek and ear, yet his tone remained as droll and irritatingly nasal as ever. "I volunteered because I cannot watch from afar when your life, and Simpson-Stone's, is in danger."

***

It wasn't often Rob was too hyped to focus on his riding, but he'd arrived home on autopilot. Still livid, he slammed his front door and didn't bother taking off his leathers before he called Bish. No answer, he tried Jock instead. He got no answer there either and dug out Bish's business card.

"Sequrco, Mr. Garvey's office."

"Hello. Put me through to Mr. Garvey, please."

"May I ask who's calling?"

"Rob Simpson-Stone."

"One moment, sir."

The line went quiet. Rob used the time to unzip his jacket and walked through to the kitchen, absently checking the fridge for beer.

"Mr. Garvey's not here at present."

"Bullshit." No beer. He kicked the fridge shut.

"Excuse—"

"Sorry, I know you're only following orders, but I need to speak with him right now."

"Please hold the line, sir." She was curt to the point of rudeness—no less than he deserved.

Rob switched his phone to speaker and left it on the counter so he could get out of his jacket. He'd walk to the off-licence once he was done with this phone call.

"Shaz, mate..."

Not Bish. "What the fuck's going on, Jock?"

"I dunno what—"

"You knew I was leaving the police."

"Yeah. You told me." He sounded suitably puzzled by the accusation, but Rob was having none of it.

"You acted ignorant about my leaving do even though Bish's van was parked outside the restaurant three days before. You *know* what's going on."

"I swear—"

"Cut the crap, Jock. Now's your chance to talk, because if you don't, I'm gonna come down there and beat it out of you."

"For fuck's sake. We're trying to save your neck here."

"Who's 'we'?"

"I can't tell you."

Rob balled his fist but stopped short of hitting anything. He was still in half a mind to get back on the bike. "Where's Tonka?"

No answer.

"Where is she, Jock?"

"I can't tell you."

"But she's safe?"

"For now, yeah. It's not her you need to worry about."

"Her brother?"

"It's—"

Rob heard Bish going nuts in the background. The bloke could swear for England when he was on one. He snatched the phone from Jock. "Rob, alright?"

"Far from it."

"What's up?"

"You and Jock are in on whatever Tonka's up to."

"Need to know." Bish wasn't kidding around, but Rob wasn't taking any more crap.

"*I* need to know," he said.

"It's better you don't."

"You're not gonna deny it?"

"There's not much point when you're right. But it's not what you think."

"No? Why don't you put me straight, Bish?"

No quick-fire response this time, Bish's noisy nose-breathing crackled against the mic until, finally, he relented. "OK. But not over the phone."

"Fair enough. Where d'you want to meet?"

"Tonka's gaff. Two hours. Bring your partner with you."

***

Gray was much more comfortable with the abundance of information heaped all around him—albeit largely irrelevant—than he'd been with Josh's approach of picking through sparse facts and following gut feelings. Nonetheless, it would've been far easier to find what he was looking for if the evidence had still been computerised, but the SIU had been ordered to destroy all files associated with Tabula Rasa after MI5's review, so he was stuck with archive copies—which included the evidence he'd collected during the SAP investigation—and handwritten records of everything since the review.

As Dom returned from his fourth smoke break of the afternoon—just after two o'clock, which Gray only noticed because it was also the time of Will's appointment with GP Investments—Gray finally found the file on Michelle Perlett and her law partner Simon Yarrow. It dated back to the beginning of the investigation, when the two first set up shop in Newcastle. Before that, Yarrow had been operating in London; the Met Police alerted the SIU when they received a complaint about Yarrow's conduct and discovered the real Simon Yarrow was dead.

For a long time, Gray was unable to identify the imposter, largely because his attention was on an insider-trading scheme that had coincidentally led him to a company in George's hometown. The coincidences didn't stop there; Yarrow's former partner in London was Terence Strang, the brother of a named partner in the law firm representing Campion Holdings—the company Gray had been investigating.

Campion's was a well-respected, benevolent firm which offered community service placements to young offenders. While Alistair Campion—founder and CEO—had been a great believer in criminal rehabilitation, Gray's experience didn't afford him the same faith in people's capacity to turn over a new leaf, so when the CEO turned up dead, rather than waste time going after Campion's competitors, Gray dug deeper into their personnel records and, by chance, discovered Simon Yarrow's real identity.

From that point on, the investigation only got stranger, and there were times Gray had wondered if he was seeing connections that simply weren't there. After all, his decision to pursue Campion's had been an excuse to get closer to George—on a conscious level, at least.

Unconsciously? Perhaps Josh's point about intuition was valid because, with the full body of evidence stacked before him, Gray was back in his SIU mindset—with a new twist. He saw...not cubes, but a map like the London Underground, and there, amid the tangle of links and terminals, one line stood bright and stark against the rest.

***

Rob had a sharp sense of foreboding about this meeting with Bish and Jock, so much so he decided to use the time before he'd need to leave for Tonka's to pick Lucas up from school. And then immediately changed his mind. Taking Lu out of class before the end of the school day would get Rob in hot water with both the headteacher and Zoë, not to mention that Jock's warning—'it's not Tonka you need to worry about'—on top of Gray's theory that someone was after them, had Rob's imagination working overtime, and he was no longer sure whose side Bish and Jock were on. Paranoia or justifiable caution?

If he'd believed it was all hot air, he'd have refused outright to go along with Will's scheme. Giving Freddie a get-out-of-jail-free card went against everything Rob believed in—same for Gray, for that matter—yet here they were, descending the rabbit hole with no idea where they'd land. To add to that, it was looking increasingly likely that Rob would have to go it alone at this meeting—Gray must still have been with Dom as his phone was going to voicemail—and he couldn't shake the feeling he was being set up.

At two-thirty, he tried Gray one last time—still voicemail—before he got on the bike and headed for Hampstead Heath and Tonka's place, keeping a close eye on his mirrors, but if he had a tail, it was someone who knew what they were doing. Once he was off the main road, he pulled over next to one of the bathing ponds, powered down the bike, removed his helmet and took out his phone.

For several minutes, he stared at the screen, re-activating it each time it went dark. His decision was already made, but putting it into effect felt like sealing his fate. In the near distance, he heard the rev of a diesel engine. A second later, a van rounded the corner—a mint silver Mercedes with dark-tinted windows. The driver's window lowered, and Bish and Jock visually acknowledged Rob as they passed him on the way up to Tonka's. Time was up; he hit the call button.

"Hello?"

"Travis? It's Rob."

"Oh, alright, mate?"

"Yeah. Well, no, actually. Listen, I need to tell you something, but you'll have to keep it under your hat for the time being. Can you do that for me?"

"OK."

"There's something going down this afternoon. I'm not sure what it is, but if it comes to the worst, there's a guy lives upstairs from me—Shammy, an old Rasta, decent bloke. He's got my spare key, and Lois, my niece, is my executor. She's got a copy of my will."

"Whoa. This is some serious shit, Rob."

"I know, and I might be way off, but if I'm not..."

"Yeah, I'll sort it, mate. Don't you worry."

"Cheers, Travis."

"Be careful."

"I will. You...too." He stopped short of saying 'look after them for me'— he knew Travis would—and ended the call, sending Martina a quick message along the same lines before he tucked his phone away and put his helmet back on.

Eyes on the road ahead, he restarted the bike and set off, prepared for the worst. Anything else would be a bonus.

29: Up the Junction

"REMEMBER THE INQUEST into Biddiscombe's death?" Gray was already thumbing through the file and continued reading without waiting for a response from Dom. Patricia Biddiscombe had been a terminally ill client of Yarrow, QC—aka Anders Folden. Her doctor had ignored an advance directive when her relatives noticed her will had been changed. Following Biddiscombe's death, the doctor's medical licence had been suspended, and in the midst of the General Medical Council's investigation, Folden had disappeared.

Gray had ordered his team stay on the trail of the will, confident it would give them their lead on which court officials were involved in the scam and that Folden would, as inevitable as the bad penny, turn up somewhere. Fortunately for the SIU—but not for Biddiscombes, who never received their inheritance— he'd been right. Perlett and Folden, still using Yarrow's stolen identity, moved to pastures new, separately. That was when Gray ordered Rob to go deeper and gain Folden's trust by any means necessary.

"Perlett and Folden were having a relationship," Gray said and continued in response to Dom's predictable 'where did you conjure that from?' frown, "They left the Biddiscombe residence together."

"That's right," Dom confirmed. "In a BMW registered to Perlett's father."

"Who was driving, do you recall?"

"Folden."

"You sound sure."

"Yeah. They had a hoo-ha over him moving the seat back before they drove off. I was going to follow them, but you told me not to. That was when we lost them."

Gray took the knock on the chin. In retrospect, letting Folden go had been a big mistake. "The thing is, Dom, now I'm looking at this with fresh eyes—" both knew he meant 'without cocaine' "—it strikes me Folden used Perlett to infiltrate the fraud ring, because he ditched her once he was in. He did the same with Terence Strang and Angela Sharston."

"Didn't we establish Folden was their puppet?"

"That's what he wanted them—and us—to think." Gray was up on his feet and moving around the conference table, sifting at speed through the stacks of files. He glanced up at Winstanley, who was twitching like he had his fingers in a power socket. "I'll give you all the references once I'm done, Martin."

That seemed to satisfy him for the time being, but Gray was on a deadline. If Winstanley cottoned on to what Will and Rob were up to today, he'd immediately rescind Gray's access to the evidence.

"OK." Gray held up the half-dozen files. "This is where it gets interesting."

Dom raised an eyebrow.

"Shut it, Hooper."

"Didn't say a word."

"Your briefings are a laugh a minute, I bet."

Dom folded his arms and held his smirk while Gray cleared a space at one end of the table and laid out the files he'd selected, one by one, in a line, identifying each in turn.

"Clarkson, Biddiscombe, Campion, Black Hole, R v Hogarth, and the Parkers. What do they all have in common?"

"Well, the first four make up the original SAP case," Dom said. "Hogarth..." He thought about it but then shook his head. "I'm not seeing a connection, or nothing that makes those specific files stand out from the rest."

That surprised Gray. Dom was sharp as they came, but, he supposed, that was the disadvantage of working in a close-knit unit and constantly sifting through the same evidence. A theory rose to the surface and there it stayed, blocking all other potential explanations. With the benefit of a year's distance, Gray could see it clear as day. "I haven't looked in the file, but I read the newspaper reports. Hogarth's husband was a senior civil servant shot dead by her lover, I believe."

"Correct."

"Was he one of yours?"

Dom waited for the nod from Winstanley before he answered. "Stephen Hogarth was a section manager in Revenue and Customs. All the overseas investment intel came from him. That's why we don't know which firms are involved currently."

"And the lover?"

"Never found. Victoria Hogarth's looking at ten years, secondary liability."

Gray studied the files again, giving himself a moment to put his narrative in order. "There are points of commonality in these six files. Mind if I share them with you?"

"Fill your boots," Dom invited.

"OK. First, we've got Clarkson's forged will—the complaint that kicked it off. Somehow, Strang and Folden caught wind of the Met's investigation and moved on before their offices were raided. Then there's Biddiscombe, same offence, but this time, Folden slipped the net during the GMC's investigation.

Similarly, with Campion's murder, by the time we'd figured out Folden was responsible, the CPS had already prosecuted an innocent man."

"And the Black Hole hostage situation?" Dom asked. "We got Folden then. Well, his trial was adjourned twice."

"Hold that thought," Gray said. "These last two cases are key. Hogarth's murder and the abduction of the Parkers, both within two days—"

A knock at the door interrupted his presentation, and Dee Knight poked her head into the room.

"Sorry to disturb you, Sir," she addressed Dom and then looked at Gray. "Mr. Fisher, I thought I should let you know your phone keeps vibrating."

"Thanks. I'll come and deal with it in a moment." It would be Will or Rob calling to update him.

Dee backed out of the room. The door clicked shut, but before Gray could continue, Winstanley cleared his throat with a loud, fake 'ahem'. Gray gestured for him to speak, though he'd have done so with or without the invitation.

"Mr. Fisher, every file you see before you—" he swept his arm over the entire conference table "—shares *commonalities*, as you call them."

"Yes, Sir, they do." Gray figured he'd wound the man up enough for one afternoon, but patience was running low on both sides. "I don't have time to go through every file, and it may well be I'm seeing a connection that isn't there."

"Which is?"

"Has anyone checked in on Folden recently?"

"He's not the only assassin on their books, Graham. Folden's of no consequence to us."

Which was precisely what Gray had thought during the original investigation, but Winstanley's attitude was starting to piss him off, the way he spoke to him as if he were a little boy telling tales to teacher. It was nothing new; indeed, it was why Gray had never had any qualms about shoving Winstanley aside on his way up the career ladder. They had no time to waste on another round of tit-for-tat, however, so Gray battened down the urge to retaliate and smiled amenably.

"Just humour me, Martin, OK? You're right, of course. To a network of this size with this much power, Folden's kind are ten a penny, but I've seen how he operates. He sidles his way in, gets close to his target. He doesn't do it for the money. He does it because he enjoys watching people suffer and die at his hands. Now, you know I'm not a gambler, Dom, but I would bet everything I own that Victoria Hogarth's lover—the man who shot her husband—is Anders Folden."

"He's still locked up," Dom said with a confidence that implied he received regular updates on Folden's status, but Gray had to ask anyway.

"You're absolutely sure?"

"We'd have heard about it if he wasn't. A patient on the run from Brookhurst would've been all over the news."

"Brookhurst?" Gray slapped his forehead as if his oversight was a matter of stupidity rather than due to only having half of the riddle until that moment. "When was he transferred to Brookhurst?"

"About six months ago. Looks like his lawyer finally found someone who believed that bullshit about a personality disorder."

It was the reason Folden's hearing had been adjourned—first to await his diagnosis, then to bring in psychiatric expert witnesses to testify—but the court ruled his actions were premeditated, and he had full mental capacity. Personality disorder or no, Folden should've been serving three consecutive life sentences. There was no reason for him to be transferred to a hospital.

"That's what Tonka was trying to tell Rob," Gray realised.

"Who?"

"Yvette Parker. The night she picked Rob up, she asked for his help." Gray hadn't met the woman and was reluctant to incriminate her, but one way or another, she'd led them to Folden. "There's a former REME in Brookhurst. Yvette asked Rob for a financial contribution towards a new ID for the guy, claiming he's up for release soon. She knows Folden's in there."

"Or it's a coincidence," Dom reasoned. "Brookhurst is the only high security hospital in the South East."

"True, and it's plausible it could have been the only one with a bed available. Even so—"

Again, Gray was cut off by Dee's knock at the door. "Sorry about this. Mr. Fisher, there's a call for you, on our system this time. He said it's urgent."

"Who is it?"

"He didn't give his name."

It had to be Rob. Will didn't have the SIU's number. "Excuse me a moment." Gray followed Dee out and across the corridor to Dom's office—what had once been Gray's office.

"I transferred the call here to give you some privacy."

"Thanks." Gray entered and paused to take in the familiarity—same desk, same computer, same tower in the in-tray. It was a lot tidier than he'd expected. Dee's doing, because Dom was a messy—

The door closed behind him, setting him back on track. He went over to the desk and picked up the phone. "DCI Fisher. How can I..." He sighed, exasperated at the instant slip, and started over. "Gray here, but you knew that already."

"Gray, it's Tie."

"Oh! I was expecting Rob."

"He gave me this number. I think Will might be in trouble."

"Why? What happened?"

"We got here early, and I hung back at the train station. He sent me a text once he was in, and I walked down—I've been watching from the park across the street. The place looks empty from the outside. Blinds down, nobody coming in or out until a couple of minutes ago when an older guy came out, locked up the building and drove off. I did a quick internet search, and I'm pretty sure it was Raymond Perlett."

Gray glanced up at the clock: 3:20. "Could Will have left another way?"

"Not that I can see. It's one of those one-storey buildings that looks like a glorified Portakabin. I could always jemmy the door."

"Yeah, don't. If you get caught, you'll go to prison. You're already out of your tag radius."

"Well, I figured the police turning up wouldn't be such a bad thing."

"I'm not so sure of that." There had always been corruption, but if it was endemic—and the way Winstanley talked, it sounded like there were only one or two decent officers left—there was no predicting how it would turn out. But doing nothing wasn't an option when Will might be in danger. If Gray took a cab, he could be at GP Investments in half an hour, but he didn't know what he'd be facing when he got there. Another hostage situation?

"I'm going to request backup," he said. "Can you stay put for now?"

"No problem."

"Thanks, Tie. Update me if anything changes. I'll be with you as soon as I can."

"OK, mate. See you shortly."

***

"Did she ever live here?" Rob asked as he returned to the living room, having completed a search of the Parkers' house that confirmed the car was gone, as were Tonka's clothes and, of course, Tonka herself.

Neither man answered. Bish kept his back turned, labouring over making three mugs of tea, while Jock loitered and snarled like a steroid-enhanced bodyguard.

"You know what? I am so done with this bullshit. One of you needs to start talking, and soon, or—"

"Or what, Shaz?" Jock side-stepped to block Rob as he moved towards Bish, getting right in his face. It was the same old trick. He was too close for Rob to take a swing at him without backing up first, and it was tempting. So very tempting.

"Pack it in!" Bish growled and slammed a mug down on the counter closest to Rob. "Punching each other's lights out will solve nothing."

Rob was still staring Jock down, waiting for him to back off. It took a smack on the arm from Bish before he did.

"You didn't answer my question."

"Yeah, she lives here," Bish confirmed. "Temporary arrangement. Phil was trying to raise the capital to buy her out of the family business so she could move to Germany."

"To be with Siggy," Jock added.

"I gathered," Rob said. He really wanted to knock that smarmy smirk off Jock's face.

"As you were, lads." Bish glared at them and took a slurp of his tea. "Yeah, so, Tonka and Phil discussed selling the business years back. They were only waiting for their dad to die."

"That's morbid," Rob remarked.

"They expected him to go a lot sooner. After their mum died, he sort of gave up, which was when the rest of the family stepped in. They wouldn't let them sell, and all the capital's tied up in land, so Phil had to look elsewhere. His accountant put him on to the overseas investment, and it was a good move to start with. He was buying thousands of acres of Bulgarian agricultural land for next to nothing and selling them a few months later for four times what he'd paid."

"You weren't spinning me a yarn, then, about the Eastern European investment?"

"Half a yarn," Bish said with a shrug. "We weren't going in on it, but we wanted to give you and your partner enough that you'd figure out what was going on."

"I knew it was bollocks. Why didn't you just tell us?"

"We couldn't, but if you'd shut up..."

Rob raised his hands and let Bish continue.

"The last lot of land Phil acquired was just before they changed the law in Bulgaria, restricting the sale to nationals only, and Phil's broker couldn't get shot. A massive firm had been buying up from Parker Farms and the like, and they'd taken the matter to the EU. Apparently, what Bulgaria are doing is illegal, but Phil wanted out anyway.

"Some farmers' collective had been in touch wanting to buy the land from him for half of what he'd paid. Well, we know what it's like in the old Eastern bloc. They had nothing to start with. With all this going on, they've got less than fuck all. But Phil wasn't aware, and I think the collective must've hit him with a few home truths because he accepted their offer.

"Then, a few weeks ago, there was this investors' meeting where they were reporting back on what happened with the EU, and Phil had only gone to inform the broker of his decision. He called Tonka from the hotel to tell her it was all sorted, and that was the last she heard from him." Bish stopped talking and started rooting through cupboards. "Why does she never have biscuits in?

I blame you, you fat bastard." He tossed an empty Jaffa cake box at Jock.

"Oy! You ate them all last time we were here, you cheeky c—"

"Enough!" Rob barked, instantly silencing both men. "What the fuck are you doing, looking for biscuits? What happened to Tonka's brother?"

"He was kidnapped," Bish said, no messing about this time.

"Who by? The Bulgarian farmers?"

Jock laughed. "You're bloody hilarious, Shaz."

Rob turned his back on him and addressed Bish. "It was a serious question."

"Not the farmers. We don't know who's got him."

"What do they want?"

"They want..." Bish swallowed hard. "You, Rob. They want you."

Rob shook his head, muttered, "What?" then, "I mean, why? Are they expecting me to do something in return for Phil's release?"

"I dunno, mate. It was meant to be an exchange, the night of your leaving do. Tonka was told to pick you up and take you to the drop-off location."

"But she brought me back here instead."

"Yeah. There's not many people know Tonka and Phil live here. It belonged to their mum's sister, and she was a bit of a black sheep. We figured it was the safest place to bring you while the police were tracking down Phil's kidnappers."

"They didn't find them."

Bish shook his head.

"Why the hell didn't you tell me any of this?"

"Like I said, we couldn't, not without disobeying a direct order."

"She's not your superior officer anymore." The irony was laughable when Rob was experiencing the same struggle with Hedley.

"If we'd told you, what would you have done? Gone after them yourself."

"With backup, yeah." No way would he have gone in alone. "It doesn't make sense. Why didn't they just pick me up?"

"Maybe they couldn't get close enough?" Bish suggested, and Rob got the feeling it was more than mere speculation.

"Who are you working for?"

"We don't work for no-one, Shaz," Jock said.

"No. You said it yourself, Jock. You're trying to save my neck. Someone's paying your firm to keep tabs on me or else it'd be me sitting wherever Phil is. Do you know where?"

"No," Bish answered. "But Tonka does."

"Then you'd better get in touch with her, right now." Rob downed his tea and dumped his cup in the sink on his way past.

Jock stepped in front of him. "Where d'you think you're going?"

"To call Gray, bring him up to speed. Not that it's any of your business."

Jock moved aside. "Off you go, then."

With fists clenched to his sides, Rob dodged around Jock and went to the garage, where he took his rage out on the stack of tyres in the corner before he placed the call.

30: Jammy

"ANYTHING?" GRAY ASKED when he finally found Tie in his hideout: a wooden igloo-shaped hut in the kids' playground.

Tie shook his head without taking his eyes off the GP Investments building across the street. "I thought you were bringing backup."

"I wanted to see how the land lay first." It was an outright lie. He'd told Dom and Winstanley he needed fresh air and then grabbed the first cab that passed. Thanks to a nifty cabbie who assumed he was with the Met, he'd been whizzed through back streets and reached Tie in well under twenty minutes. "Are you sure Will's still in there?"

"Unless he's burrowed his way out…" Tie muttered sarcastically. "You didn't report it, did you?"

Gray drew breath but thought better of continuing the deception. "No. We're already jeopardising an investigation."

"And you care more about that than Will's safety?"

To his shame, Gray had no immediate answer. The situation was too complex for a simple 'no' to suffice, because it wasn't just Will's safety here and now at stake, but it *was* Gray's current priority. He ducked inside the igloo and scrunched down next to Tie on the narrow, curved seat, trying—and failing—to contain his anxiety under the constant bombardment of second thoughts. He should've talked Will out of coming here, shouldn't have made a deal with Freddie Berringer. If anything happened to Will, or Rob, or Naomi—

Tie's hand landed heavily on Gray's and squeezed. "He'll be all right."

Gray panned up to Tie's face, surprised by his sudden tenderness. He'd expected the guy to give him hell for putting the operation before Will, knowing how close the two of them were. They shared a long history, at some point lovers and, more importantly, friends who fought for the same cause. Tie knew Will better than anyone; Gray really hoped his faith in Will was justified, and contagious. They were sitting close enough for him to catch it—also close enough for them both to startle when Gray's phone vibrated against the plywood seat. He took it out and checked the screen before answering. "Looks like we might have backup after all. Yes, Dom?"

"Where are you?"

"Play igloo." Gray ducked to peer out of the opening as a black Transit van turned the corner, slowly drove past and parked twenty yards or so along the street.

Dom jumped out, rotating on the spot until he found his target and strode in their direction, still with phone clamped to ear. "Bloody hell. How did you fit in there?"

"Found a bottle labelled 'drink me'."

"You'll never learn, will you?" he joked and hung up. It was a little close to the bone and the situation was as serious as they came, but Gray still managed a chuckle.

Dom arrived at their hut and leaned on the top, talking through the little round window. "Cosy in there?"

"Never been cosier," Gray deadpanned. There was no point asking how Dom knew where he'd gone.

"Seeing as you're sitting comfortably... The good news. I've spoken to one of the nursing managers at Brookhurst. Folden's accounted for."

"Thank God." Gray would've sagged in relief if there'd been space to do so, even though it meant he'd been way off with his analysis of the files. "And the bad?"

"We'll deal with that later. Including Winstanley."

"Threat or promise?"

"Devil and deep-blue sea, mate."

Only ninety-nine other problems to worry about, then. "This is Tie, by the way. Will's lodger."

Dom nodded. "Brian McIntyre..."

"That's right, sir," Tie confirmed. It wasn't the first time Gray had seen him defer to authority. In court, he'd been a model citizen—polite and well-spoken, hair tied back, clean suit, shiny shoes—nothing like the dreadlocked anarchist animal-libber who bunked in a damp caravan in Will's backyard.

"So you say Richards is in that building?" Dom tilted his head to indicate GP Investments.

"Yes, sir."

"Are you sure it's locked?"

"No, sir. I didn't try the door. I thought it would be better to keep my distance, but I saw a man leave and lock up on his way out."

"How long ago was that?"

"About two minutes before I called Gray, so...twenty-five minutes ago?" Tie looked to Gray for corroboration.

"It would have been."

Dom straightened up and scanned the vicinity, chewing his bottom lip in thought. If it had been Gray's call, he'd have sat tight and waited to see if Perlett came back. Or that was what he'd have done as head of the SIU. Right now, he was hoping promotion hadn't destroyed Dom's gung-ho streak. Either way, Dom had come up with something. "We're gonna try and keep this on the down-low. You two stay put."

"Yes, boss," Gray said.

Dom patted the roof of the igloo and strode back to the van.

"He's the guy who took over your unit?" Tie asked once he was out of earshot.

"Yeah."

"Seems to know what he's doing."

"He does. I hope he's quick, though. I've got more cramps than a marathon runner at the finish line."

"Surely that should be the Great North Run?"

Gray smiled self-consciously. Every time he went incognito, the damned Geordie accent resurfaced. He wouldn't have minded if he did it on purpose.

On the plus side, the weather was lousy, so they had the tiny hut to themselves with an unobstructed view of the officers getting into position—three of them. One entered the park and crouched behind bushes a few feet from Gray and Tie's location. Another—Dee Knight—rounded the corner on foot, carrying a briefcase. She crossed the road to GP Investments, tried opening the door—Tie muttered a choice word or two when the door stayed shut—and then knocked. She gave it another thirty seconds before she continued along the street towards the van.

"He's armed," Tie murmured, pointing.

Gray shifted his gaze to the guy hidden in the shadows, the butt of an MP5 just visible against his dark jacket. Tie had gone still, his breaths coming short and fast. "Are you all right?"

He nodded. "Yeah, but this is mental. He only went in there to ask some questions. How the fuck did it turn into an armed siege?"

"It's precautionary," Gray said, fairly sure he was right but aware it could all change in the blink of an eye, particularly as a second van had arrived, and this one wasn't SIU. It stopped outside GP Investments, blocking their view of the building, and two burly guys in security-guard uniforms climbed out. Judging by the lumpy bulk of their gilets, they were both armed too. Tie moved fast, but Gray was faster and threw his arm out, shoving Tie back down. Tie's head thudded loudly against the igloo's curved wall. "Stay," Gray commanded.

"Those guards—"

"Have guns. I know. Dom's got it under control." Gray's confidence was absolute. The officer in the park had changed position, giving him a clear shot if he needed it. Dom and Dee were also on the move, now both in uniform.

"Keep it on the down-low?" Tie said, incredulous.

"They're covering their tracks. Called out to a burglary..."

"So much bullshit. You need to be straight with Will, if he gets out in one piece—" Tie began, but Gray cut him off.

"You changed your tune."

"Yeah? That would be all the fucking guns. He thinks you've got a future together."

"As do I."

"No. This, happening now, is your future. Catching the bad guys. You're not bothered who gets hurt in the process."

"It's no different than you, Will and the rest in your cell." It was a low blow, but Tie had hit the raw nerve Winstanley had been twanging all day.

"Of course! We're terrorists...according to you lot."

"Take a look where I'm sitting, Tie," Gray hissed, but their argument was brought to an abrupt end by the loud crack of a door giving way, immediately followed by the wail of GP Investments' alarm. Dom and Dee broke into a run and disappeared behind the security van.

Minutes passed. Gray watched the armed officer, who, in turn, was watching whatever was happening across the road through his gun sight. Other than the constant, ear-splitting warble of the alarm, there was nothing to hear or see until, finally, someone stumbled into view. Will—uninjured as far as Gray could tell, and cuffed—with Dee right behind him. She walked Will to the SIU van while Dom dealt with the security guards. There was a lot of posturing and gesticulating on their part, but whatever Dom said appeared to do the trick, as he gave the nod to the officer in the park, and the two of them returned to the SIU van, which took off soon after. It was several minutes more before the alarm fell silent. Tie moved to get up again, and once again, Gray stopped him.

"Did they just arrest him?"

"Or made it look that way. We need to wait for the all-clear." Gray's phone was already vibrating. He took it out and hit answer.

"You're a mercenary son of a bitch, Fisher."

"Why, thank you," Gray replied drolly. "Is he all right?"

"Ask him yourself." Dom's phone crackled and then Will's voice came on the line.

"Hey."

"Hey, are you OK?"

"I'm fine. Is Tie with you?"

"Yeah, he's fine too. What happened?"

"Perlett got a phone call, cut our meeting short, but he wasn't saying anything useful. He saw me out, and I dodged back in, stayed out of sight while he set the alarm and locked up, then I called Naomi and got her to shut it off."

"The jammer..."

"Don't know what you're talking about," Will lied. "Anyway, I thought she'd have to hack into Perlett's computer, but he hadn't logged out. I managed to copy most of the hard drive before your friends arrived."

"Nice work." Gray was grinning with pride and had a shocking urge to brag. *Have you met my boyfriend?*

"I'll hand you back," Will said. The phone crackled again. This time, Gray didn't wait for Dom to speak first.

"Can we get out of here yet?"

"Yeah, but one at a time. We'll be at the gate on the other side of the park."

"OK." Gray hung up and relayed the instructions to Tie, letting him leave first and wincing along with him as he straightened up and hobbled away. Once he was clear, Gray followed in much the same fashion, checking his phone rather than returning it to his pocket. It was as well he did; he'd missed an encrypted message from Rob.

> En route with Bish and Jock. Tonka's staying in a B&B 2 miles from Brookhurst hospital. She knows where her brother is – will call when I know more.

***

No satnav necessary, Bish was evidently familiar with the locale and barely slowed to turn off the road onto the gravel driveway leading to the hotel—a moderately large Edwardian detached property with gable-end thatched roofs and modern double-glazing. Bish reversed into the space between a hefty SUV and a four-by-four—the only two vehicles in the hotel's car park.

"Where's the Aventador?" Rob asked.

"She sold it." Bish got out, slamming the door behind him.

"She what?"

"You heard," Jock said and got out of the other side. He stomped away, leaving the door open.

Rob slid across the seat and jumped down, sinking an inch or more into the gravel and rocking on his heels, a little off-balance. It had been a crazy day—prison visit, lunch, a mad dash to Hampstead, and now this—with no sign of it letting up anytime soon. He pushed the van door shut and followed Bish and Jock towards the building. He needed coffee. That or to pay for a room so he could get his head down for a couple of hours.

"Afternoon, gentlemen," a woman greeted them the second they stepped through the door. The place was much as Rob had expected. Cream walls and thick red carpets, a staircase directly ahead, dining room to his left, small bar room and lounge to his right, a muted TV playing within.

Bish approached the woman at the reception. "Good afternoon. We're friends of Yvette Parker's."

"What's your name?"

"Garvey."

The receptionist walked around to their side of the counter. "This way, please." She led them down a passage that ran alongside and under the stairs, slowing as she reached the door at the end. She knocked and turned the handle; the door dragged on the carpet as it opened. "Ms. Parker..."

Bish and Jock marched in without hesitation. Rob held back a moment to get a sense of what he was walking into—a small function room, by the looks of it, but set out for a conference with tables in a U, around which five people were seated, all in combats.

"Are you OK for refreshments?" the receptionist asked.

"For now, yes, thanks," Tonka replied, although Rob couldn't see a coffee pot or even jugs of water. Nor had he yet set eyes on Tonka, as Bish and Jock were in the way. "Let the dog see the rabbit, eh, lads?" she said. The two men did as they were told and went to sit with the others.

Tonka rose to her feet, holding Rob's gaze as she advanced on him, faltered briefly, and then hugged him. He reciprocated, perplexed—or, at least, he had a good idea what was taking place, but he was having a problem believing she'd do something this risky.

"Ma'am? What's going on?"

She didn't answer him and withdrew with a smile that fooled no-one. Murmured conversations started up around the room as she put her hand on his arm, guiding him to one side. "It's good to see you."

"And you." Still no explanation forthcoming. "Tonka, talk to me."

"They've got Phil," she said.

"I know. Bish told me about the investors' meeting and the exchange. Who are 'they'?"

"I don't know."

"Surely you must've spoken to them."

"They call from Phil's phone and use a voice synthesiser."

"Did you record the calls?"

"A couple." She already had her phone in her hand and swiped the screen a few times before she gave it to Rob. "The top one is from the night of your leaving do. It came just after you left my aunt's house. Did you ever find your phone?"

"A colleague did, but I'd already ordered a replacement."

"I'm sorry, Rob. I should've told you what was going on."

"Yeah, you should, but it's done now." He hit play and listened: *It's not too late. No more games.* "Did they set a new time and place?" Tonka shook her head.

"It's been two weeks," he said, but he wasn't going to spell it out. The chances of a hostage still being alive after that long, and with no further demands, were slim to none.

"To be honest, Rob, I accepted it as inevitable, but I've spoken to him. He's drugged up, but he's alive."

"When?"

"In the last seventy-two hours."

"Bish told me the family stopped you and Phil selling the business."

Tonka frowned. She'd already cottoned on to his line of inquiry. "That was a few months after we lost Mum, and she's been dead eleven years."

"What about the land Phil bought? How much did he have tied up in that?"

"He had a buyer lined up. Rob..." She sighed in exasperation. "There's absolutely no reason Phil would voluntarily disappear. Listen to the other message. If you don't believe me after that, well..." She was angry and upset, and Rob's low-level interrogation was making it worse.

"I'm sorry. I had to ask."

"I know." She shifted her eyes to her phone. Rob played the second message. *Why are you soldiers so stupid? Why haven't you delivered Simpson-Stone? Time's almost up.*

The message sent a chill down his spine. Not the demand itself, something about the tone, and he couldn't figure out what it was. "When did you get... never mind." The date was on the recording; it was two days old.

"They called again a few hours later, but I didn't realise who it was until after I'd answered. They said the deal was off and they'd collect you in person."

Yet they hadn't...so far. Rob would've preferred to believe it was because the kidnappers were inept rather than the truth that kept smacking him around the head. Between SIU tails, Sequrco and the squaddies in this room, the kidnappers hadn't been able to get near. "And Phil?" he asked.

"That's why we're here. We need to get on." She turned away, blocking any further questions. "I believe you know Olivia Simpson?" She gestured to the only other woman in the room.

Rob nodded and, despite his reservations about what was taking place, grinned. "Alright, Lisa?"

She rolled her eyes and laughed. "Nobody called me that in years until a fortnight ago. Now this lot have picked it up. How are you doing, Rob?"

"Not bad, cheers. You?"

"Much the same."

"This is Olivia's unit," Tonka explained. "Private military contractors."

"Gotcha." Now he knew why Tonka had asked him for money and given him that bullshit about buying Ethan a new ID. If she'd told him what she planned to do, he'd have gone straight to Martina. "Is this a rescue mission, Ma'am?"

"Phase two. Phase one is still ongoing. It's been a success so far." She squeezed his arm.

"Yeah." Rob glanced over at Bish and Jock, both with their heads bowed in contrition. To give them their due, they'd convincingly kept their cover, but there were discrepancies, too many things they knew that they shouldn't. By now, they'd have updated their contact at the SIU, and Rob really needed to pay Gray the same courtesy, but he was prepared to hold off a little longer and hear what Tonka had to say first.

31: Decoy

I**N THE BACK** of the surveillance van, Gray was still trying without success to get hold of Rob, who wasn't answering his phone, and he'd turned off GPS, so they couldn't get a fix on his location either. Working only with his message that he was heading for a B&B in the vicinity of Brookhurst hospital, Dom made a quick stop at SIU HQ to arrange transport home for Will and Tie but was unsuccessful in his endeavour to persuade Gray to go with them. Bizarrely, Winstanley sided against Dom and suggested Gray's understanding of the operation made him a valuable asset, along with a reminder that he was there in a consultative capacity and he'd have to remain in the van for the duration.

Winstanley agreed to stay back and coordinate with the team going through the data Will had copied from Perlett's hard drive, while Gray joined Dom, Dee, Tarquin—the firearms officer from the park—and Isobel—who had been part of Gray's old team—for the forty-minute drive out to Berkshire.

With Dee behind the wheel, Dom sacrificed riding shotgun to Isobel and joined Tarquin and Gray in the back. Once they were underway, he called his contact at Brookhurst to warn them to be on the lookout for suspicious activity. It was a precautionary measure; the hospital was near a large military base with a forest and an abundance of varied sports and leisure clubs between. Philip Parker could be virtually anywhere, yet the closer they came to Brookhurst, the more certain Gray was that he'd been right in the first place. It was giving him stomach cramp, not helped by sitting sideways on a none too comfortable bench seat, on top of a wheel arch and sandwiched between Dom and a tower of equipment crates.

"She's taking Rob to Folden."

His statement drew everyone's attention, including Dee's via the rear-view mirror. They were all looking at him like he'd lost the plot.

"Folden's in isolation," Dom said. "No visitors. No contact with other patients."

"You think he can't manipulate the staff to do his bidding?"

"They're trained professionals. They're used to dealing with the likes of Folden."

"I don't mean directly. He knows a lot of powerful people."

"I'm sorry, Gray, you're wrong, and not just about Folden. If Yvette Parker intended to hand Rob over, she'd have made the exchange on the night of his leaving do."

"Unless she'd discovered Garvey and Wilson were working for you, in which case, the story about McGrath's new ID was her second attempt—a ruse to get Rob to Brookhurst."

Dom sighed and rubbed his temples as if staving off a headache. He was the only one paying attention; everyone else had gone back to whatever they'd been doing prior to the conversation. "Look." He leaned in close and spoke so quietly Gray could barely hear him over the road noise. "When we're done with this, do me a favour? Talk to someone, I don't care who—even Josh Sandison-Morley—"

"Yes. Fine," Gray agreed to shut Dom up. There was no point arguing with him or showing his anger. Had anyone else dared to dismiss Gray's concerns as post-traumatic paranoia, he'd have given them hell. If they'd been anywhere but the back of an SIU van, he'd have given Dom hell too. He was prepared to concede Folden might not be the man at the top, but it didn't make him any less dangerous nor alter the fact that sixteen months ago, Rob had put Folden behind bars. Their proximity *could not be* coincidence.

Whoever wanted Rob wanted him alive, and if it *was* Folden...well, they might as well ditch the entire operation right now because once he'd broken Rob, he wouldn't stop until he'd squeezed every last bit of information from him about the fraud ring, his police work and his colleagues past and present.

And when he was done with Rob, he'd come after the rest of them.

"Update from Garvey," Dom announced. "How close are we?"

"Five minutes, Sir," Dee said.

"Pull over the next chance you get. We need to put together a plan of action."

"Will do, Sir." Dee indicated and dropped a gear.

In his peripheral vision, Gray saw Dom watching him. His pulse went into overdrive. He hadn't been wrong.

***

Rob sat through the briefing in a half-dazed state he blamed on lack of caffeine and the increasing surrealness of his day. Olivia detailed the plan and doled out tasks; her team asked questions—good questions—and came up with strategies for multiple scenarios. None wore rank insignia, yet Rob felt like a fly on the wall of the officers' mess, although the situation was more reminiscent of the police briefings he'd attended, bar the fact they were acting illegally. Granted, working undercover, Rob had crossed more than a few lines himself, but never outside the confines of an investigation.

Tonka had given him the option to join the mission, which he'd flat out refused while also aware his continued presence signified his tacit agreement to keep schtum. No problem on that score; Bish and Jock looked as shocked as Rob felt, and perhaps it was cowardice on his part, but there was no need for him to further dirty his hands when the details would already have been relayed to the SIU.

In spite of everything that had gone before, he empathised with Bish and Jock. Whether it was for the greater good or to save a life, betraying someone you loved and respected terminally damaged something inside. Every lie uttered was like watching them swallow down another mouthful of poison, and it hurt almost as much as losing them through death.

Needless to say, they willingly agreed to play their part in the mission. Jock didn't even kick off when Olivia assigned them to a lookout post half a mile from the target, with Bish's van serving as a secondary escape vehicle should Tonka's four-by-four be compromised. Rob's impression was they were being kept out of the way. After all, if he'd sussed them, Tonka would be on to them too.

He didn't blame her for taking the matter into her own hands. She'd been a brilliant CO, although he'd always been lucky in that regard. Martina Hedley was easily up there, and even Gray had had his moments, but with Tonka, the one strength that stood above all the rest was her sheer grit. The phrase 'it can't be done' wasn't in her repertoire, and from what she'd told them today, she'd tried going through official channels, but either the powers-that-be were rotten through and through, or whoever was behind Phil's disappearance had them by the balls.

On the balance of probability, Rob thought it was a combination of the two, and it put him in a major quandary. On the one hand, the SIU and Tonka's private army were on the same side, up to a point. On the other hand, the mission to rescue Phil Parker could screw up the official operation.

There was a reason Rob had been left to fend for himself. Dom was deploying the same strategy Gray had with the Black Hole heist. Rob had warned him in advance of Folden's plan to take hostages—and that there would be fatalities—but Gray had let it run its course, confident it would lure the rest of the fraud ring out into the open. That he'd been dead right was small consolation when Rob was a sitting duck.

With the briefing over, they all began to move out, and Rob went to the hotel bar, watching through the front window as the rest of them climbed into their vehicles. He was safe here, or no less safe than he'd be anywhere else, but once again, he was caught in the middle, under pressure to pick a side. Did his loyalty lie with his old army mates or with his former SIU colleagues, by default, because that was where Gray's lay? Their first case, farce that it was, was solved. They'd found Tonka and knew what had happened to her brother. By rights, he could go home and crack open that beer he'd been craving earlier. Or he could if his bike wasn't locked in Tonka's garage.

"What can I get you, sir?" the bartender asked.

"Never mind," Rob said and sprinted out to the car park, shouting, "Ma'am!" as Tonka shut her car door. She heard him and rolled down the window. "Mind if I join you?"

She studied him intently, considering his request for several seconds before she nodded and said, "Go with Jock and Bish."

"I'm in the doghouse too, am I?"

A half-smirk, half-smile was her answer as she started the four-by-four and reversed out onto the road. Bish had also fired up the van, and Rob quickly jogged around to the passenger side and hauled the door open.

"Budge up, Jock. I'm coming with."

Grunting, Jock shuffled along the seat. Rob climbed in and fastened his seat belt.

"We need to hang back for five," Bish said.

Rob nodded and took out his phone. It was the first chance he'd had to check it since he'd texted Gray. Still no reply to that, but there was a message from Martina Hedley—*stop being so bloody morose*—which made him laugh. Maybe he had jumped the gun a little with the text he'd sent her and the call to Travis. His part in the rescue mission should be danger free. Just sit tight and leave Tonka, Olivia and her unit to break Phil Parker out of a high security hospital. Piece of cake.

***

Gray stared over Isobel's shoulder at the stationary dot marking Bish's GPS tracker on the onscreen map, as he'd been doing for almost all of the ten minutes since they'd pulled into a lay-by on the main route between the hotel and the hospital so they could intercept Tonka and crew. While they were waiting, Dom and Tarquin had popped outside for some 'fresh air'. Gray could've done with stretching his legs and a warm-up—the air con was brutal—but he was doing as he'd been told...for now.

"Are you all right, Sir?" Isobel asked without taking her eyes off the screen.

"Yeah, thanks. You?"

She nodded but didn't continue the small talk, and Gray realised he was drumming on the back of her chair. He stopped.

"Sorry, Iz."

"No problem, Sir. I get a bit restless in here myself."

He'd have been a lot less so if he could've forewarned Rob. He resumed his spot on the bench seat, making a concerted effort not to fidget, and then startled when, a moment later, Isobel bolted from her chair and opened the van's side door.

"They're on the move, Sir. Heading for the ring road."

442

Dom followed her back in, along with the stink of smoke. He checked the screen. "Right. Let's see which way...yep. Dee?" She'd already started the engine and waited just long enough for Tarquin to get back in before she put her foot down. Dom jammed his hand against the roof. "Iz, have you managed to find out anything about these private soldiers?"

"Only the CO, Sir. Olivia Simpson, former REME, served with Parker, Wilson and Garvey in Germany before she transferred to a specialist unit in Kuwait. Rob was her replacement. Garvey didn't recognise any of the others."

"Ah, well. I don't suppose it matters. Soldiers are soldiers, and we know they're aiming for a quick in and out. I'm inclined to leave them to it." Dom was watching Gray, like he was waiting for him to say something.

"It's your decision, Dom."

"I've told Garvey he's to keep Rob away from Brookhurst, whatever it takes."

"And?"

"It's no great loss, is it? If they take a pop at Folden."

So that was what he was waiting for. While none of them would shed a tear for Folden, if they didn't intercept Tonka's team before they reached the hospital, there would be other casualties. The alternative, or the one that didn't involve saving Folden, required overt intervention from the SIU. If Gray's interpretation was correct, Dom was prepared to blow up Tabula Rasa on his say-so.

"I'm as sure as I can be," he said.

Dom nodded. "That'll do for me." He made the call. "It's Hooper. Evacuate your staff from the isolation unit and tell security to stand down. There's a BMW SUV and a Jeep in convoy about five minutes away. You need to let them through—we'll be right behind them. Understood?"

***

"Can't see fuck all from here." Jock hoisted his foot up on top of the dashboard, knee stuck out and encroaching into Rob's space. On the plus side, he didn't fart, and he wasn't wrong. Tall trees lined the road—more a dirt track—on either side, and the view was much the same across the T-junction ahead. In short, it was picturesque, but useless as a lookout point, not that it mattered with the hospital's twelve-foot-high perimeter wall. As long as at least one of them was in contact, they could be at the hospital's east service entrance in under two minutes.

Aside from having Jock's knee in his face, Rob was fairly chilled out. He'd seen the black van tailing them through the town centre. Even if he hadn't recognised it, he'd have known from Bish and Jock's shifty looks at each other that it belonged to the SIU, although they played ignorant admirably when he asked whether Gray had talked Dom into letting him come along for the ride. His gut said the answer was yes, but it was by the by. When Bish had turned off to head around the back of the hospital, the van had gone straight on, following Tonka and Olivia to the front entrance. If the combined expertise of six soldiers and however many SIU officers couldn't break Phil Parker out of Brookhurst, no-one could.

Jock dropped his foot to the floor and put the other one up, earning him a noisy backhander on the thigh from Bish. This time, Jock pushed out a retaliative fart and laughed like a loon. Bish wound down the window and let rip with an equally offensive stream of insults, and Rob tuned them out. Lucas could've taught them a thing or two about appropriate behaviour, like he'd done with Rob and his attitude towards Travis. He was a good kid with a sensible head on his shoulders, albeit one preoccupied with cars and junk food.

And ketchup. Rob's thoughts drifted to Naomi and their talk over lunch. Even though she hadn't said straight up she was interested in him, the lengths to which she'd gone to dismiss her relationship with Freddie spoke volumes. He'd wanted so much to stay for that coffee, and that was before Martina gave him her blessing, so to speak. If he'd accepted Naomi's invitation, it would have been a very different day, that was for sure.

"...fantasising about what he's gonna do to Lisa this evening. What d'you reckon?"

"Oh, shut up, Jock."

Rob sighed and turned away from his travel companions, staring out the side window. Up close, the trees were much more sparse and deadly still. *Could be an omen...* He should have been more worked up about what was going on. Now he thought about it, he hadn't heard from Tie since he'd called for the SIU's number, although, with the change in Gray over the past few weeks, he'd have been over to GP Investments like a shot. Will would be fine. They'd all be fine.

"Shaz, mate. You're off with the fairies."

Rob blinked and stretched his eyes wide open. "Sorry. Knackered." He felt stoned. "What's up?"

Bish released the handbrake and put his foot down. The wheels spun against the loose road surface as the van took off, flinging Rob's head back sharply and jolting his neck. He muttered a muted, "Fuck," and straightened up, supporting his neck with his palm.

"We're needed on-site," Jock said. "They've cleared the service entrance."

"What's happened to Tonka and Olivia?"

"I don't fucking know! I'm just following orders."

Rob leaned across Jock to reach the air-conditioning dial, turning it up to full and opening the vent on his side, angling it towards his face. He needed to clear his woolly head before they reached the hospital.

***

There wasn't a lot of room for pacing in the back of a fully loaded surveillance van. Gray noticed he was doing it again and stopped, quite sure he was getting on Isobel's nerves. She'd stayed behind to monitor the team's activity, and to keep an eye on Gray even though he'd sworn, hand on heart, short of earthquake or nuclear explosion, he wouldn't leave the van.

"Where are they now?" he asked, squinting at the map from afar rather than moving closer and getting in her way.

Isobel pointed at the dots onscreen. "Tarq's in an office building opposite the main entrance to the isolation unit. The DCI is...on the move. He's just gone in. And—"

"Gone into the isolation unit?"

"Yes, Sir."

Dom was deviating from his plan. "Something's not right. Where's Dee?"

"Also on the move, heading towards us."

Through the windscreen, Gray saw Dee sprint around the end of a building. She made it back to them, clambered behind the wheel and started the engine. The door slammed shut as they moved off.

"Folden's on the loose," she explained breathlessly. "The DCI needs us around the back. Get a vest on, Sir."

Gray looked behind him at the crate of vests. He'd fall flat on his face if he tried to reach it before they stopped. Isobel gasped and blanched.

"Garvey's just come through the service entrance."

Gray flung himself a few feet along the van and grasped the computer bench before he flew right past. Bish's dot jumped a few millimetres closer to their location. "We need to stop him."

"But the DCI—" Dee began.

"I know!" And Gray was a civilian. Irrespective of their acknowledgement of his former rank, they had to follow Dom's orders. Luckily, Dee had done exactly that and screeched to a halt on the other side of the building. Gray made it the rest of the way to the crate and fought his shaking hands to get a vest on and fastened. "Do we know where Folden is?"

"No, Sir. Just that his room's empty."

"Where's Parker's lot?"

"All over the place. Yvette's on the first floor with Philip. He's not mobile and the lifts are locked. They're having to carry him down."

At least they'd have one success today. "OK. What are our orders?" Gray asked.

"Watch the back doors in case Folden comes this way."

There was only one way to stop him getting to Rob now. Paying no heed to the voice in his head reminding him his firearms licence was no longer valid,

Gray loaded the Glock from Tarquin's AFO kit, ready to do what he should have done two years ago.

***

"Where am I going?" Bish asked as he took another speed bump at 40 mph and all three of their heads hit the roof. A swerve to the right and Jock crushed Rob against the passenger door, a lecherous grin on his stupid moon face as he hoisted himself upright again.

"Jock!" Bish yelled. "Where the fuck am I going?"

Jock got his shit together and refocused on the road ahead. "Next right."

"Fuck's sake." The van took the corner on two wheels and ran straight over a tulip-covered roundabout. "Flowerbeds in a prison hospital. Whatever next?"

"Good to know our taxes are being well spent, eh, Shaz?"

Rob ignored them, his attention on the view ahead: a box-grid-covered access area, and the SIU van.

"Cavalry's here," Jock spat. Bish slammed on and reversed back, having another go at the tulips.

"What are you doing?" Rob asked. "That's the isolation unit."

"Wrong side," Bish said, spinning the wheel hard right. As they took off, Rob caught sight of one of the SIU waving both arms, Semaphore-style.

"They're trying to get our attention. We need to go back." He turned in his seat to look behind them.

"There they are," Jock said.

Bish hit the brakes before Rob had a chance to turn around, and his seat belt almost decapitated him. He unclipped it, but Jock didn't wait and instead clambered over the console and followed Bish out of the driver's side. They made it over to the small group struggling from the building as the siren went off, and suddenly there were people everywhere. Rob got out and stood, leaning on the door, watching security staff armed with batons jog past as if they weren't there, all heading into the building.

"Rob! Get back in the van!"

He spun in the direction of the voice. "Gray—"

"Get back in the van. Folden's out."

"Folden...what?" Rob replayed Gray's garbled statement, but it still made no sense.

"He was transferred to Brookhurst six months ago."

"Shit."

"They brought you here on purpose."

"No. Bish and Jock are undercover."

"I know. Dom can deal with them later. You need to get in the back and keep your head down, all right?"

"Yes, Sir," Rob answered automatically, only realising because Gray smiled and patted his arm.

"Stay safe, Rob. I'm going to bring this bastard down if it's the last thing I do." With that, Gray sped off towards the building and Rob went around the back of the van, but neither reached his destination.

At some point, Dom had arrived on the scene and was walking and talking with Tonka behind two of Olivia's team, who were carrying Phil over to Bish's van. Without looking away—and with no sense of urgency whatsoever—Dom waved his arm, flagging Gray down, and then stopped next to Rob, who stepped aside and held one of the van doors open while they lifted Tonka's brother in. Phil was doped up to the eyeballs but otherwise appeared uninjured. As the soldiers pulled the door shut, Rob noticed a stretcher and other medical equipment in the back of Bish's van. It had been part of their plan from the beginning.

"Dom, with all due respect..." Gray marched over, red-faced and looking ready to thump him. Dom raised his hands in surrender.

"Cool it a minute, all right? Folden's long gone."

"What?" Gray glared at Dom and then Tonka. She nodded, and Dom gestured for her to explain.

"The ward plan—you know, the chart of which patient is in which bed, who their doctor is, and so forth? The room they had Phil in was listed as Anders Folden."

"Jesus." Gray clamped his hand over his mouth, inhaling through his fingers. His horror was genuine, and Rob shared it.

"So...he's been out for three weeks?" Rob asked.

Dom nodded. "Looks that way. We've requested access to all security footage to see if we can pinpoint exactly when it happened and how. Obviously, we'll question the staff in the isolation unit over the next couple of days, and the hospital's press officer's going to inform the media ASAP. I'm sorry, Rob, but as of now, you're a protected person."

32: Interim

I'M NOT PUTTING him back in hospital," Tonka snapped when Dom asked, again, if she was sure she could cope with looking after her brother. "Someone making tea?" she threw over her shoulder on her way up the spiral stairs. Getting Phil up those when he could barely stand had been an absolute bugger.

Bish obediently refilled the kettle. They'd been stuck at Brookhurst for a further hour while security confirmed Folden wasn't on-site, during which Dom had spoken briefly to several of the senior staff before they convened an emergency meeting to try to establish how Folden had escaped and what they were going to do about it. When they were finally allowed to leave, Olivia had taken her team back to the hotel, and the SIU, plus Rob and Gray, had followed Bish's van back to the Parkers' place so they could check it was secure.

With Tonka's insistence that she'd nurse Phil at home, Bish and Jock had agreed to hang around for the next forty-eight hours, more for the Parkers' peace of mind than anything. Dom and Gray were in agreement that Folden was done with them, and Dom had told Dee, Tarquin and Isobel to return the van to HQ then go get some shut-eye—"Full team briefing, 0800."

It was while they were waiting for Phil's GP to arrive, and Gray had gone outside to call Will, that Dom broached the subject of protection again, but Rob was as adamant as Tonka; he wasn't moving to a 'safe house'. Too long spent in bedsits up and down the country and living out of his panniers had taught him the value of privacy, of having a base. His flat was small, basic, not in a great area, expensive for what it was, but it was his own space where he could come and go as he pleased and do whatever the hell he liked.

"To be honest, I'm glad," Dom said, nodding thanks at Bish for the fresh cups of tea that appeared in front of them. "It's a pain in the arse to set up, and your flat should be safe enough, seeing as you haven't even told the council you're living there."

"I wasn't banking on staying more than a few months," Rob justified.

"Well, we'll keep an eye on you, obviously..." Dom paused to take a drink. "My bigger concern is Zoë and Lucas."

"Yeah. Mine too." It was all Rob had thought about for the past two weeks, and that was before he knew Folden was at large.

"We could get them into the women's refuge until we sort out something more long-term."

"What about Travis?"

"Yeah. Tricky one, that." Dom rubbed his eyes and yawned. He'd aged considerably in the past sixteen months. He was a couple of years younger than Rob, and smoking wasn't doing him any favours, but he looked bone-tired, like he might keel over at any second.

"Hey, Bish, what the hell's in this tea?"

"You what?"

"I've been spaced out all afternoon and poor Dom's nearly in a coma."

Bish looked at the kettle, then at his own cup, then shrugged. "It's just ordinary tea, isn't it?"

"Passion flower," Tonka said. Rob hadn't noticed her come down. She walked over to the window and peered out into the almost-darkness.

"Everything OK?" he asked.

She nodded but kept her back turned. "He's only half with it. Says he can't remember much, other than arguing with the staff over his name. How do you convince doctors you're sane when they think you're delusional? You could rot away in a place like that."

She fell quiet, and Rob wondered if she'd been talking about Phil or Ethan— or both. The story about getting Ethan a new identity might have been bull, but her fears for his future were genuine and, after what Rob had witnessed today, with good reason. Every building inside those high walls had been windowless, the atmosphere eerily oppressive, and then chaotic and dangerous.

Rob assumed secure hospitals, like prisons, locked down after an incident, so his visitor's pass probably wasn't valid anymore. Nor did returning to Brookhurst appeal, particularly as he didn't *have to* visit Ethan now. But still, he was considering it.

"What are you doing?" Tonka's question jolted Rob out of his thoughts, and he opened his mouth to answer, but she wasn't asking him. He followed her bemused gaze across the room to the kitchen area.

"Is it an aphrodisiac?" Jock asked, peering into his cup.

Tonka laughed. "You wish! Passion flower aids relaxation and eases anxiety. I've needed it of late, but there's ordinary tea in there as well." To prove it, she went over and took a box of Tetley out of the cupboard. "Try these next time, lads."

"An aphrodisiac?" Bish repeated and slapped Jock upside the head.

"Passion flower! Should do what it says on the tin."

"Idiot."

"Fuck off."

Dom turned away and mouthed at Rob, "They'd drive me round the bend."

Been there, done that.

The front door opened, and Gray came in—Rob had almost forgotten he was out there—along with Phil's GP. Tonka went to greet her and took her up to Phil while Gray joined Rob and Dom on the sofas.

"Will and Tie are both fine," he said before either could ask. "At the pub."

"All right for some," Dom grumbled.

Rob nodded in sympathy, knowing Dom still had a good few hours of work ahead of him, although Rob was well past his beer craving. He just wanted to go home and watch crap telly in bed, but he had a few things to sort out first. "What shall I tell Zoë and Travis? The refuge would be OK. Travis'll do whatever's best for Zo and Lu."

"Leave it with me. I'll have a chat with witness protection. We should be able to sort something for tomorrow. In the meantime, the surveillance is still in place." Dom yawned again and stood up. "Right. I need to head back, get the paperwork done, for what it's worth."

"You won't lose your job," Gray asserted. Rob hadn't been aware it was a possibility, as Gray had yet to brief him on what he'd found out earlier. "Not with Martin Winstanley in your corner."

"We'll see." Dom sounded far less confident than usual. "Rob, I'll be in touch."

Rob got up and shook his hand. "All right, mate. Thanks for everything."

Dom forced out a smile and moved on to Gray. No handshake for him; they hugged, and it wasn't a short one.

Rob switched his attention to Bish and Jock, sitting at the kitchen counter and figuring out their duty rota. However much they got on his nerves, Rob was grateful for all they'd done and no doubt would continue to do until this was over. They were good people to have onside, and he knew he could count on them, one hundred percent. Even Jock.

**

Gray handed the debit card reader back to the driver and chastised himself for once again wasting a small fortune on a cab. He'd got in it with the intention of going home to pack a few things and then driving the hire car—which he should have returned a week ago—to Croxley. But when the driver had asked 'where to?' he'd made a split-second decision. Surely he'd left enough items of clothes at Will's over the past few months to have a full change. If not, he'd stick the same ones back on in the morning.

Either way, there he was, standing outside Will's local, as were Will and Tie but on the other side of the building, evidenced by the sound of Will's hot-chocolate laughter drifting on the cool breeze that blew across the waterways and golf course beyond the pub, bringing with it the distinctive aroma of cannabis and tobacco.

Gray sighed. Not the welcome he'd hoped for, but it was his own fault for not sharing his plans. He entered the pub, muttering, "They're shitfaced," to himself and preparing to find out exactly how shitfaced they were.

Not very, it turned out. As he came through the front entrance, they walked in the back and, despite the sizeable mid-evening crowd, Will saw Gray at once. His face broke into a broad, definitely pleased smile. "Hey. I didn't know you were coming over."

"Surprise?" Gray smiled back coyly, and Will laughed.

"BRB," Tie said and set off in the direction of the Gents'.

"Wheat beer?" Will suggested, already moving towards the bar.

"Need you ask?" Gray followed him over and stood next to him, leaning heavily on the counter as the tension of the day seeped away. It wasn't over yet, not by any stretch, but he had to keep it in perspective. They were in a better position than eighteen hours ago. Phil Parker was safe and well, and there was an entire force of police and ex-army personnel making sure he—and Rob—stayed that way.

"How's everyone doing?" Will asked, sliding Gray's pint to him. He picked it up and drank thirstily, half-emptying the glass before he found the wherewithal to move it away from his lips. He glanced around him before he answered. No-one was close enough to overhear.

"OK. Rob's gone to see Zoë and Travis. Dom's arranging a safe house."

"For all of them together?"

Gray raised an eyebrow. "Much as Rob seems to be getting along with Travis these days, they're far from best mates. No, Rob's staying in the flat." Gray wasn't sure how Rob had talked Dom into agreeing and couldn't say he was happy with the arrangement, but it wasn't his call. "Dom's worried about his job."

"Really? After what he did today, he should be up for a medal or promotion."

"I couldn't agree more." Gray nodded an acknowledgement at Tie, who joined them at the bar and tapped his pint glass to Gray's in a silent toast. "I can't say much, but the long and short of it is he disobeyed orders from on high."

"Will he lose his job?"

"Honestly, I don't know, but he'll almost certainly be suspended." Someone on the Tabula Rasa roster would have the authority to make Dom pay for his insubordination, but at least he had Winstanley on his side.

"What happened with that Perlett guy?" Tie asked.

Gray had been hoping—unrealistically—they wouldn't bring it up. "Believe it or not, he's innocent, but you still both did great work this afternoon."

"In other words, it was a waste of time." Will winked at Tie.

"Not at all. Perlett recognised Rob's name from his daughter's trial when he was doing the background checks on Parker Farms, and he told her when he visited her in prison. She passed it on to Folden. All her dad did was break a few data protection laws, and not on purpose."

"Doesn't surprise me," Will said. "His computer was wide open. And a mess. Worksheet one, worksheet two...worksheet five thousand, four hundred and sixty-one..."

"That's what my hell will be like," Gray said.

Tie was listening to them and grinning into his beer. Will pointedly ignored him. "He seemed a nice old guy."

"He was very cooperative, apparently, and a great believer in the justice system." He'd also said Michelle deserved to be in prison, which was probably why Winstanley had gone lightly on him.

"Well, I'm glad he's in the clear," Will said. "We need to look after companies like GP Investments."

Gray picked up his pint and drank to hide his smirk, noticed Tie doing the same and laughed, spurting beer all over his face.

"What?" Will protested. "Friendly societies are an endangered species."

"Only a merchant banker..." Tie muttered.

"Did you want another beer or a smack in the teeth?" Will threatened.

"My round," Gray said. "Then I'm going home to bed."

"I thought you were staying over."

"Well, when I say home..." Gray left it open for Will to interpret however he saw fit.

The conversation moved on, or, rather, Tie chatted away to another guy who came in with a German shepherd while Will fussed over the dog. He was too quiet—he usually held full-on if one-way conversations with dogs—and Gray was beginning to wish he'd dismissed his error with 'you know what I mean' or blatantly stated that what he was really saying was he wouldn't mind taking their relationship to the next level.

The guy with the dog moved away to sit at a table, and Will straightened up, lifting his glass to his lips as he said, with no more than a glance Gray's way, "Whenever you like."

***

"Hello?" The crackle of the intercom made it impossible to distinguish who had answered.

"Hey, it's Rob."

With a buzz, the lock released, and he stepped in, trudged across the scruffy foyer and up the creaking stairs to the first floor, as he had fourteen hours ago.

It felt like days, and he was dead on his feet, but his heart put on a final sprint when he reached the room and the door swung open. *Still Naomi.*

She smiled and beckoned him inside. "I wasn't expecting to see you again so soon."

"I hadn't planned on stopping by..." He didn't know what else to say and it left him dumbstruck and defenceless. The way she was watching him... He saw the moment she registered something was wrong, a flicker of fear across her face, a fleeting glimpse of Aaron, and then she smiled. Confident, flirty Naomi was back.

"How about that coffee?" she suggested.

"I'd like that." He chanced moving further into the room, drifting closer as she filled the kettle and switched it on, slid two mugs in front of it.

"Instant OK? I can make filter if you..." She turned, her gaze holding his briefly as he took the final step and their torsos made contact.

He leaned in, murmured, "Instant's fine," against her cheek, traced her jaw with parted lips. A remnant of his resistance whispered *stop* then was silenced by the warm pressure of Naomi's palm on his back. She rolled her head to the side, a soft sigh escaping in response to the kisses he scattered over her neck, slowly working his way to her mouth.

"Are you sure you want this, Rob?" she asked, closing her eyes as he mirrored her, pressing his palm to her back and pulling her body tight against his.

"Do you?" he countered. Their lips bumped with his words, then met in mutual response.

They kissed deeply, passionately, continuing long after the kettle had clicked off, neither willing to stop. It would've been easy to take it further—the bed was just across the room—but for now, the kiss was enough.

When they finally eased apart, breathless and giddy, still in each other's arms, Naomi said, "I've wanted this for so long."

"Me too," Rob admitted. No point denying it anymore.

The intensity of the moment had passed, and he released her. She switched the kettle back on and resumed making the coffee.

"What made you change your mind?" she asked.

"The shit that's happened today." He wasn't sure how much he should tell her, or what effect it would have on Aaron.

"You're in danger, aren't you?"

Rob stared at the floor, suddenly ashamed of his selfishness in coming here, driven only by his need to see her before he was forced into hiding, or worse.

"Talk to me. Please, Rob?"

He nodded. "Yeah. I'm in danger."

"I'm so sorry." She reached for his hand, weaving her fingers with his. She understood his fear. She'd been there too. "Can I do anything? Can Aaron?"

"I don't think so." Rob lifted his head so he could see her, acknowledging the sincerity of her offer with as much of a smile as he could muster before he pulled her to him again, needing someone to hold him, someone to hold. "I just had to see you tonight. I hope you don't mind."

"Of course not."

"I can't stay, though."

"I know. You need to check in with Lucas and Zoë." She kissed him gently, squeezed his hand. "Do what you have to, Rob. I'm not going anywhere."

***

The safety chain rattled, keys jangled, and the door swung open on Zoë in pyjamas. "Rob," she said, stony-faced, making sure he wouldn't miss her displeasure.

"Hey. Sorry. I thought I'd be here sooner. Were you in bed?"

"No." She plodded back along the hall, leaving him to shut and re-lock the door. "Lu is, though," she warned and disappeared into the living room.

Rob followed her in, and he and Travis gave each other a nod in both greeting and confirmation that it hadn't 'come to the worst'. Not yet.

"I need to talk to Lu too."

Zoë reached the sofa and about-turned, muttering, "I'll go make coffee," as she dodged past him and back out to the hallway, where she shouted upstairs, "You still awake, Lu?"

The answer came in the form of a heavy thud and the scrabble of bare feet overhead, down the stairs...

"Dad!" Lucas tumbled to a halt in front of him. "What're you doing here? Is it to do with the police?" He looked towards the window. The curtains were drawn, but Rob had seen the car outside.

"Yeah, mate, it is."

Lucas's mouth opened in a big, wide 'o'. "Why are they watching us?"

"I'll explain when your mum comes back."

"I'm back." Zoë stepped past again with three mugs. She deposited one on the table at the free end of the sofa and the other two on the table at 'her' end. "D'you want a drink, Lu?"

He shook his head without taking his eyes off Rob.

"Are you going to sit?" Zoë asked, more prompt than question.

He didn't want to—he'd been sitting for most of the day—but reality kicked his feet from under him. This was what nightmares were made of. A real-life bogeyman was out there. He was coming after them all, and he'd take Lucas first just to watch Rob suffer. That twisted smile, that singsong snide tone, it was a game, a sick game, and Rob could've stopped him, could've—

"Rob?"

Zoë's voice shoved the image of Folden's face aside, in its place the sight of Lucas, staring up at him, frowning, puzzled, not yet afraid. Rob smiled and ruffled his son's hair, but he couldn't stretch to the lie that it would be OK.

"You need something a bit stronger than coffee," Travis said. He left the room before Rob could reply.

"Sit down," Zoë commanded. He did as he was told.

Travis returned with a tumbler of Scotch. "Here you go, mate."

"I'm on the bike," Rob protested but took the glass anyway and gulped down a mouthful, relishing the unfamiliar burn in his throat.

"Leave the bike here. We'll call you a cab, or you can kip on the couch." Travis looked to Zoë for support, which she gave without hesitation.

"You can use Lu's sleeping bag," she said. "I've never seen you this shaken up."

There was no point playing it down, but he'd keep it to the bare bones for Lucas's sake. Lu was sitting so close he was almost on Rob's knee. "Have you seen the news this evening?"

"Local or national?" Zoë asked.

"Either. The patient who escaped from Brookhurst?"

"Yeah," Travis confirmed. "It was on the radio. Someone you know?"

"I put him in prison."

"That'd do it. D'you think he'll come after you?"

"He might." Rob held eye contact until he was sure Travis understood there was no 'might' about it.

Travis nodded. "What do you need from us?"

"The head of my old unit is arranging temporary accommodation for the three of you, in case the escapee gets hold of this address."

"Is that really necessary?" Zoë asked and then glowered when Travis interjected before Rob could answer.

"Tonight?"

"Tomorrow," Rob said. "Not sure what time it'll be."

"No problem. We can pack a few things before we go to bed so we're ready."

"Hold on!" Zoë held up her hand. "What about Lu and school?"

"Isn't spring break next week?"

"Yep," Travis confirmed.

"It'll be sorted before they go back."

Lucas groaned.

"It had better be," Zoë warned. "He's already behind with his work."

"Can we still go to Nan and Grandad Harvey's, Dad?"

With everything else going on, their trip had slipped Rob's mind.

"Pleeease, Dad?" He was doing it again, the big wide pleading eyes, and Rob didn't know how to answer. He looked to Zoë and Travis for guidance; they both shrugged.

"I think we'll have to leave it till the next holiday, Lu."

Lucas slumped in disappointment but said, "'Kay. Can I go back to bed?"

"'Course you can."

He got up, calling, "Night!" as he hurried from the room, on the brink of tears.

"Laters, taters." Rob's heart was breaking. He couldn't let his son down. Not again. He glugged the rest of the Scotch and accepted a top-up, waiting until the thumps overhead ceased, signifying Lucas had made it to his bed. "I'm gonna get a car," he said, then clarified, "I'm not selling the bike, but it's too easy to recognise."

"If you need somewhere to store it, you can leave it in my warehouse," Travis offered.

"Cheers, but I should be OK." He'd already arranged to leave it in Tonka's garage, but he appreciated the offer. "And if it's all right with you both, I'm still gonna take Lu up to Mum's next week."

Travis thumbed at Zoë. "It's the boss's decision."

She locked eyes with Rob. "No, it's your decision. I trust you."

"Thanks," he said. He vented a long, exhausted breath and downed the second glass of Scotch. "Right, where's that sleeping bag?"

Epilogue

I'M STILL BLOWN away they didn't notice their patient had changed identity," Gray said. Indeed, he'd said the same thing, with minor variations, at least a dozen times in the week that had lapsed since they'd discovered Anders Folden's body-swap trick. Theorising how he'd conned an entire team of medical professionals was an excellent and necessary distraction from the horrifying reality of Folden being out there, somewhere, enacting the next stage of his plan.

A doctor emerged from one of the two doors on the other side of the waiting room and strolled over to the admin desk. He looked so confident, so sure of his abilities, Gray wondered if he'd have fallen for Folden's ploy. What would it say of his competence in treating the sick?

The doctor picked up a patient's file from the desk and called, "Joan Ogilvy?" The woman sitting in front of them gathered her belongings and hurried after the doctor. The door closed.

"Why would they question it?" Will asked rhetorically, which was a new development. Every time Gray had brought it up, Will had listened but made no comment, and that was fine. Gray was only thinking aloud. But they both needed the diversion today.

"Why wouldn't they? Parker's twenty years older than Folden, and completely grey."

"Ah, but there was that psychological study, wasn't there?" Will said.

"Was there?"

"Yep." He was on his phone, playing a game that consisted of repeatedly poking the screen to land a blob of bright-green jelly with eyes on a tower of neon-pink blocks. He mistimed a poke, and the blob splatted against the side of the screen. Will locked his phone and put it in his pocket. "The participants thought it was a job interview. Halfway through, the interviewer left, and a different person came back in. Most of the participants didn't notice. It's called change blindness or something."

"After months, though?"

"Maybe they were all in on it."

"They weren't," Gray said.

Will shrugged. "Why don't you ask Josh? He'll know."

Gray felt his face warm and glanced sideways, spotting the wicked glint in Will's eyes. He bumped Will's thigh with his own. "How's your head?"

"Fine today, typically." He took a breath to say more but didn't—another instance of the unspoken fear rising almost to the surface.

Will didn't talk about his mum's illness, only her life before diagnosis—the protest marches and sit-ins, her amazing vegan meals, all the skills she'd taught him, the knowledge she'd imparted, her unconditional love—so Gray didn't know if genetics had ever been mentioned. Whatever the outcome of today's appointment, he was sticking around for as long as Will would have him.

"Wilfred Richards?" It was a different doctor, but she made the same slow scan of those waiting. Will got up, and the doctor gave a polite almost-smile, directing him towards her consultation room. As he reached the door, Will glanced back, his chilled confidence supplanted by nerves and panic. Gray was right behind him and met his gaze, transmitting good thoughts and reassurances that Will wasn't doing this alone.

"Mr. Richards, I'm Miss Crawford, consultant orthopaedic surgeon. Please, have a seat." She indicated the plastic chair closest to her desk for Will and then the one next to it, casting a cursory glance at Gray before she seated herself in a comfy-looking swivel chair and opened Will's file. "You've been having headaches?"

"Yes."

"For how long?"

"About six months."

She hummed, her eyes still on his notes. "Debilitating... No blurred vision... No dizziness..."

"No," Will confirmed.

"What do they feel like? Are they in one particular place, or...?"

"Mostly here." Will touched the area behind his right ear, holding position until she looked his way. "It feels like something's squeezing my skull."

"All of it, or just that region?"

"Just that bit."

Wheeling her chair closer to Will, the doctor leaned forward and cupped the side of his head, pressing her thumb and fingers into his hair and working her way down and around to his nape. "Any pain in your neck at all?"

"Sometimes, maybe? It's hard to tell."

She rolled her chair back and flicked through the rest of the pages in Will's file. "You came for an MRI scan two weeks ago?" Will nodded. "It's clear." She must've heard him exhale—she'd have needed to be in a different room to miss it—because she asked, "What did you think it was?"

"I hoped it was migraines, but...my mum died last year. She had a glioblastoma."

"I see. Well, glioblastomas are not inherited, unless they're a secondary symptom of something else, and even then, it's rare. I think what's happening here is what's called a cervicogenic headache, caused by an impinged nerve in your cervical spine. The nerve pathways are very close, and they interact. The brain can't discriminate, so it makes a best guess. The pain in your head is referred pain—the problem is in your neck. Before the headaches started, were you in an accident of any kind, or did you change your lifestyle?"

"Yeah." Will laughed and rolled his eyes. "It was when I started working for Royal Mail."

"Lots of lifting?" the doctor guessed.

"Yep, and getting in and out of the van."

"OK." She put the file on the desk and focused on Will, properly, for the first time. "I can give you an injection now that will see off the headache, possibly for good. I also want you to attend physiotherapy for a few weeks and sort out your posture, get some pointers on how to lift without injury. The important thing is there's no underlying medical cause."

Will sighed and reached for Gray's hand, squeezing it hard. "Thank you. That is a huge relief."

"For both of us," Gray said.

The doctor's smile was more convincing this time. "I'll get that injection for you now. It—"

Will gave a tentative cough. "Sorry to interrupt, but I don't want the injection."

"It's very quick and no more painful than a tetanus jab."

"I'm OK with needles, but I don't take medication."

She leaned back in her chair, her eyes coolly judgemental. "It's your choice, Mr. Richards."

"I appreciate you taking the time to see me, Miss Crawford. You've lifted a massive weight from my mind. I can handle the pain myself, now I know it's nothing serious, but I would like to take up your offer of physio."

"I'll make the referral today. You'll get a letter within a couple of weeks with a number to call to arrange an appointment."

"Thank you."

"Any further questions?"

Will shook his head. "Gray?"

"None from me."

"All right. I'll see you for a follow-up in three months." Miss Crawford picked up a pen and started writing, offering another almost-smile to send them on their way.

***

"How long now, Dad?"

"About quarter of an hour."

"You said that last time."

"Because you only asked two minutes ago."

Lucas huffed, jiggling in his seat. "Are we stopping at the services?"

"Not unless you're gonna pee your pants." Rob indicated to overtake a truck. The drive up north had been uneventful—no hold-ups, normal traffic—but five hours on the road had him fidgety too, and he resisted the temptation to put his foot down, indicating to pull back into the inside lane. The motorhome drifted in behind him and flashed its lights twice. Rob watched the speedometer, laying off the gas until the needle returned to hovering on sixty.

Lucas twisted in his seat to look out the back window. "Does Nan know they're coming?"

"Yeah." He'd had to tell her—the same version he'd told Lucas—seeing as she'd be stuck with that motorhome in the drive for the next week. "Sit properly, Lu."

That earned Rob another huff, but Lucas turned to face the front again and started fiddling with the blowers. "Are you keeping this, Dad? Once the crazy man's back in hospital?"

"I dunno. D'you want me to?"

"If you like."

Lucas fell silent, and Rob briefly glanced over, laughing when he saw his pinched-lipped expression. "What car d'you reckon I should get?"

"An Agera."

"How much are they?"

"Two million."

"That all? I could get you one while I'm at it."

"Will you, yeah?"

"Oh, yeah," Rob said, nodding solemnly.

"Or a Veyron. They're not as much."

"We don't want to cheapen our image, Lu."

"True, that. What about a Veneno?"

"I thought you didn't like Lamborghinis."

"The new ones are all right, I s'pose. Will your mate get hers back?"

"I hope so." Now the Parkers' relatives had agreed to sell the company, there was no reason why Tonka couldn't buy back her Aventador, or a Veneno even.

"How about a Lykan Hypersport?" Lucas suggested.

"How much are they?"

"Guess."

"Hmm...two million?"

"Nope. More."

"Two and a half?"

"More."
"Blimey. Three?"
"Nope..."

***

"I think I'm going to buy another car."

A catering porter stopped next to their table and held open a rubbish bag. Will dumped their empty cups in it and smiled in thanks. "The journey's been all right," he said.

"Yeah, it has," Gray agreed. "But the cost of train tickets...I could lease a car for that. Actually, I might look at leasing instead."

"Just a little runabout?"

"I was thinking more along the lines of an Audi. Something with a bit of oomph."

"You're a speed demon," Will teased.

Gray weighed it up. "I don't push the engine beyond its limits, but—" He paused to listen to the announcement that they were arriving at Leeds. Other passengers were already out of their seats and moving along the carriage. In the next gap, Will stood to get their bags down from the overhead lockers, and he and Gray joined the slow flow towards the doors.

"But?" Will prompted, glancing back.

"Yes. I'm a speed demon," Gray admitted. Will laughed. "I'm nervous."

"You'll be fine."

The train stopped, and the queue edged forward. Will stepped down onto the platform, waiting for Gray to clear the door before they moved off again, side by side, close enough they could've held hands but settled for the safer contact of knuckles brushing together, parting briefly to pass through the ticket barrier.

"It bothers me," Gray said.

"Seeing Suzannah again?"

"Not exactly. How reckless I was. Sometimes I almost forget, but then we do something like this, and my thoughts immediately default to the worst-case scenario."

"Everything in life carries risks, Gray. It's unreasonable to believe you can mitigate all of them."

"I know, but I have to exercise more caution." Gray spotted Suzannah up ahead, waving frantically. He waved back, even more astounded by her and Will's alikeness than the last time he'd seen her. She was a beautiful young woman and, judging by her smile, as happy to see Gray as he was her. "Especially now I have responsibilities."

***

"You all right, Mum?"

She was standing, arms crossed, staring out of her living room window at the motorhome taking up all but an eighteen-inch-wide strip of driveway and blocking most of the daylight, leaving the front of the house unusually dark.

Rob drew up next to her. "Mum?"

"Yes, dear. Just daydreaming." She nodded at the motorhome. "Does it have all the mod cons?"

"You mean a fridge and cooker and stuff? Yeah. It's even got a shower."

"A toilet?"

"Yep."

"Mmm." She nodded thoughtfully. "Would your friends like to come in for a coffee?"

They were there as a deterrent, a show of force, so it wasn't as if they were aiming to stay hidden.

"I'll ask them," Rob said. With a quick check what Lucas was up to—playing with Linford in the back garden, under Grandad Harvey's supervision—he opened the front door and almost walked into Dee Knight. He startled and stepped back.

"Sorry!" Dee grimaced.

"No worries. Everything all right?"

"Yes, thanks. And in here?"

"Same," Rob confirmed.

"Great. I just came to let you know I'm heading out to the local supermarket. We forgot sugar."

"Fair enough, but my mum'll have some, I'm sure, unless you needed to pick up other things? I was actually coming to invite you both in for coffee."

"Oh, fab! We don't want to impose, though. Are you sure your mum won't mind?"

"It was her idea. Believe me, she wouldn't have invited you if she minded."

"OK. I'll go get Tarq and we'll be right in."

"See you in a minute." Rob left the door on the latch for them and went upstairs to use the bathroom before he joined everyone in the garden.

It had been a hell of a week. Between getting Zoë, Travis and Lucas settled in their temporary home—a ground-floor flat in St. John's Wood—and telling Dom Hooper and Martin Winstanley everything he could remember from his work on the original investigation, Rob had barely had a minute to himself. His flat was full of surveillance equipment, and the car he was driving—not his choice—was a basic Ford Fiesta bought by the SIU and registered under the pseudonym 'Steven Radley'.

The rest of his paperwork was being processed and would be ready by the time he and Lu were back in London, which would be about when the Freddie Berringer shit hit the fan. Not that Rob had anything to do with it anymore. With no leads on Folden, Rob was out of circulation indefinitely, and he was also out of the loop.

Not surprisingly, Hedley hadn't been in touch since Will amended his definitive statement that 'Berringer attacked the victim without provocation', which would have resulted in a murder conviction, to 'the victim had a hammer in his hand when Berringer attacked', which would more than likely lead to a complete acquittal. Rob felt terrible for his part in sabotaging the case, but it was all horses for courses at this point, and he had bigger things to worry about than Freddie Berringer getting away with murder, or whether Martina ever spoke to him again.

He finished up in the bathroom and walked along the landing, pausing at the window that overlooked the back garden. Lucas and Linford had stopped chasing around in circles and were crashed together on a picnic blanket while Harvey was giving Dee and Tarquin the guided tour, which made Rob chuckle. Either they were really into their bedding plants or they were great actors. Fortunately for them, it wasn't a big garden, and in any case, Rob's mum imminently came to the rescue with a coffee pot and mugs.

Turning from the window, Rob took his phone from his pocket and checked it, purely out of habit. He wasn't expecting any calls, and there was just one notification: he opened the message on his way downstairs, smiling at the caption '*your gorgeous nieces xx*' accompanying the photo of Lois and Amber enjoying a rare night out together. By the looks of it, they were in the wine bar in the town centre. Too much black and white, too many lights, it attracted the younger, trendy crowd and was not somewhere he'd choose to go. There again, they didn't like his choice of social venue much either.

He re-locked his phone and made a mental note to give them a call later, see if they fancied having a pint with their Uncle Rob. He'd even put up with the wine bar if they insisted. The 'where' didn't matter, only the 'who'.

Rob almost made it to the garden before it hit him, stopping him dead in his tracks and turning his blood to ice. The image of Lois and Amber, smiling into the camera...

It wasn't a selfie.

DISTRACTIONS

A year has passed since Rob Simpson-Stone received a photo of his nieces enjoying a night out, unaware their photographer was one Anders Folden: a psychopathic hitman Rob helped to put away while working undercover for the Met Police Special Investigations Unit.

Only Gray Fisher—Rob's former boss, now his business partner—is taking Rob seriously. The powers-that-be insist Rob and Gray are being paranoid: there's no proof the photo came from Folden, who's stayed off the authorities' radar long enough to have assumed a new identity and fled overseas. It takes a significant threat to Rob's son's life for anyone to question that assertion, but police protection is worth nothing when the target has friends in high places to bend and break the law to his will.

Folden won't stop until he's completed his mission: to fulfil a contract or end a personal vendetta, Rob and Gray are no longer sure which. What they do know is they need to find him before he finds them—with or without help from the authorities.

Distractions Playlist:
https://is.gd/DistractionsPlaylist

For all of us who will never know what it's like
to live with a 'normal' dog.

"Two traits are essential in a criminal: boundless egoism and a strong destructive urge. Common to both of these, and a necessary condition for their expression, is absence of love, lack of an emotional appreciation of (human) objects."

Sigmund Freud

1: Virtual Danger

ROB STOPPED THE car at the kerb, engine idling, and went through the motions of checking over his dashboard controls as he scanned the vicinity, alert to any and every movement. Tree branches shifted in the spring breeze; a neighbour deposited folded cardboard in their recycling bin. Otherwise, the street was dead quiet. Every parked vehicle was empty; no blinds or curtains twitched.

Satisfied all seemed in order, Rob switched his attention to the house: the home of his former in-laws. It was a decent-sized property in a well-to-do suburb but smaller and humbler than the foreboding representation in his mind, which said more about him than them. They might not have always got along, but Zoë's parents were decent people. The kind who stepped up without a second thought.

Unfortunately, acknowledging that wasn't enough to stop Rob showing off, and as he reversed the car, he oversteered and barely missed the gate post. Cussing, he stopped, repositioned...and reminded himself his services were only needed because Zoë's fiancé was away on business. No-one else would be impressed by his posturing.

Still, he had to compensate somehow for the base-model used blue Fiesta bought and registered on his behalf—or on behalf of 'Steven Radley'—when the two cars parked in the drive both carried this year's licence plate. One was Zoë's, the other her mum's, both compact hatchbacks but with pretty much every optional extra. Custom alloys and paint jobs, body kits, lowered suspension...and a wide space between them where Zoë's dad's car would have been if he weren't at work. Rob could've parked his car *and* his bike in that space.

Then again, had he been on the bike, he wouldn't have given a toss. For the time being, the Suzuki was still in storage, and for no reason, if he believed DCI Tant, which he didn't. One brief 'out of courtesy' phone call to say nothing had changed was never going to cut it. *Twelve months* their lives had been on hold, waiting for Anders Folden to make his next move. Twelve months since Rob received the photo of his nieces enjoying a night out, smiling at the camera, unaware their photographer was a psychopath out to reap revenge on their uncle...

Twelve months since he'd promised his youngest niece his life would be less dangerous now he was out of both the army and the police.

Tant was right about one thing, though: there was no proof Folden had sent the photo. It had come from a now-dead pay-as-you-go number, but who else would have sent it? At least Gray believed him, as did Dom Hooper, for what it was worth when Dom was still on a suspension. Without him on the inside, and with 'no contact in over a year', the police were no longer actively investigating Folden's escape or trying to track him down. They'd circulated their intel to Interpol and border control and washed their hands of him, insisting Rob and Gray were worrying over nothing, and Dom Hooper should know better than to buy into their conspiracy theories about systemic corruption when it had already put his career in jeopardy. Anders Folden had no 'friends in high places', according to Tant, and anyway, he was someone else's problem now.

A sharp rap on the Fiesta's side window startled Rob out of what had become an ever-repeating replay that brought no answers. His ex-mother-in-law peered down at him in pinched-lipped puzzlement. With lively blue eyes, light freckles across her nose and wavy shoulder-length black hair that hinted at her Gaelic heritage, she hadn't aged a day in the five years since he'd last seen her. He shut off the engine and pulled the key from the ignition but had to wait for her to move before he could open the door.

"Alright, Dora? How're you doing? You're looking well."

"Good afternoon to you, Rob." She reciprocated his embrace and stepped back but kept her hand on his arm. "I'm very well, thanks. You?"

"Same."

"We were expecting you this morning, weren't we?" She squeezed and released him. "The motorways were bad, I heard on the radio."

"Yeah." Rob turned away to lock the car. Like his mum, Dora had an in-built lie detector, and apart from a minor snarl-up at Birmingham, his route had been clear. The delay was his own doing—a voluntary detour into the city affording him a congestion charge and not much else. If he could stay focused, he might get through the rest of the day without any more idiocy.

"Are you coming in?" Dora's voice sounded distant, and when Rob turned back, he discovered she was at the front door to the house.

"Sorry." He got his act together and followed her inside, waiting for directions on which room they were headed for. The Cliftons weren't minted, but they weren't scraping around for pennies. Like Rob, Zoë's dad was a child of the Windrush generation, and her mum's family had arrived from Ireland during the same era. Both had followed their parents into the NHS, albeit flipping the typical gender roles along the way, given Dora was the doctor and David was the nurse, or these days a general manager of nursing services in the private sector. Both earned decent salaries, reflected in the top-rate education they'd secured for their daughter, and in their commuter-belt detached house with double garage, tasteful modern décor and furniture, newly fitted kitchen...

"Coffee, Rob? D'you still have it black?" Dora was already filling a mug from a push-button machine topped by a bean reservoir.

"I do." He turned his ear toward the door and listened over the sound of running coffee and furniture muffle, just making out a voice, an indistinct, one-way conversation, possibly a radio or TV. "Is Lu's tutor here?"

"Not today. He'll be playing that ridiculous game, no doubt." She handed him the mug.

"Cheers." Rob accepted and took a sip. "Good coffee, that. I've been looking at getting a machine myself." Another deflection. Rob didn't bother much with coffee at home—he hadn't even kept a jar of instant in the flat—but he was gutted Lucas hadn't come racing down to see him.

"They're handy," Dora said, following up her sideways glance with a smile that told Rob she'd fully got the measure of him. She finished filling a second mug and gestured to the stools at the centre island. "Sit yourself down. I'll let them know you're here."

He'd been in the car for most of the day and would rather have remained standing, but he obeyed out of politeness, listening on as Dora bustled from the kitchen and up the stairs.

All the times he and Zoë had visited, before Lucas was born and after, Rob had never been upstairs. Zoë's parents weren't overly formal, but they weren't overly friendly either—towards anyone, not just him—although Dora was a hugger. Rob didn't measure up to their expectations. They weren't happy about the ten-year age gap, his police background, the fact his parents were separated, the bike... It was all pretty damning, yet Zoë insisted they were 'fond of him', which sounded like a placation. Still, he supposed, they'd permitted him to marry their daughter.

At the jangle of bracelet charms signifying Dora's return, Rob glugged at his coffee, not wishing to seem ungracious or draw further attention to his wandering concentration.

"Zoë's on her way down." Dora brought her mug over and propped on the stool opposite his, vocalising a sigh as she adjusted her position. "So how're your mum and stepdad doing these days? Zoë tells me your stepdad's been having radiotherapy."

"Yeah, he has, for prostate cancer."

"What age is he? Seventies?"

"Just turned seventy. They caught it early, though."

"Oh, well, that's good news."

"Yeah." For Rob, his stepdad's optimistic prognosis was more than good news; it was a life-changer. Since losing Jess, he'd been stuck in the mindset that all cancer was terminal. Accompanying Harvey to Clatterbridge for his treatments and chatting to the other men there for the same reason, even some of their wives who'd survived cancer themselves, had changed his outlook. If they'd found Jess's earlier, she might have recovered...and gone to prison with her associates, where she'd have died of shame. He could just see her, without all her designer gear, cycling through the same three outfits—

"She's almost done."

Rob blinked and refocused. At some point, Dora must have left the kitchen again because she was on her way back. She resumed her seat, and for a fleeting second Rob was certain she was going to ask what was on his mind, but he must have sent a shutdown signal.

"Are you sure you're going to fit everything in the cars?" She tilted her head back, indicating the rooms above.

Rob chuckled, relieved, although it was still a loaded question. Zoë had survived two months in the two-bedroom apartment—the 'safe house' Dom Hooper had arranged—before she'd packed up and moved in with her parents. She'd left the furniture behind, but no way would ten months' worth of clothes, toiletries and personal belongings fit into two small hatchbacks, which Rob had known all along.

"My mate's coming with his van. Should be here in—" he fished out his phone and checked the text "—half an hour, he reckons."

"Right." Dora nodded and sipped her coffee, her gaze settling on a point somewhere between the island's top and the low-hanging overhead light. A few minutes passed, the silence leading somewhere. Rob waited, admiring the white-porcelain-tiled walls, granite counters, glossy doors...back to Dora's expectant, calculating eye contact. "What d'you make of Travis, then?" she asked.

For a moment, he was too stunned to answer, his brain taken over by the realisation that if she was asking his opinion, she liked him more than she liked Travis. *Get in there!* It went some way towards compensating for Lucas's lack of interest. Fighting a grin, he said truthfully, "I didn't like him at first, but he's a good bloke, and he loves Zo and Lu."

"What more could you ask?" Dora remarked. She had the kind of dry Irish sense of humour that made it impossible for Rob to tell whether she was being sarcastic. "Still, now everything's settled, they can get on with planning the wedding."

"Yeah, I suppose," Rob agreed.

Dora cocked her head. "You're not happy about that, are you?"

"I am, as it goes."

"But?"

Everything isn't settled. "No 'but'. I'm pleased for them."

"Pleased for whom?"

Zoë's hands pressed down on Rob's shoulders as he jumped. She laughed, stepping to his side, barefooted, hence the silent approach, and beckoned for a hug. He obliged.

"It's so good to see you," she murmured against his cheek.

"You too." Rob reluctantly released her. He meant everything he'd said: he was happy for Zoë and Travis and well past wishful thinking about what might have been. But he still missed her and Lucas, and, if he was honest, after a year of camping out in his mum's spare room and keeping a low profile, the loneliness was getting to him.

Zoë went and poured herself a coffee. "Hasn't Lu come down to see you?"

"Nope."

"The little..." She marched out of the kitchen again and shouted up the stairs, "Lu, your dad's here!"

"'Kay. Coming now."

Zoë returned, shaking her head. "He's obsessed with that game."

"Still the racing?"

"No, some online game—the one everyone's playing."

"Not me," Rob said, clueless. He'd played his fair share of computer games as a teenager, but he was more into his sports—footy, rugby, the occasional game of cricket—and wasn't up on technology.

"Nor me," Zoë said. "But Travis plays it. Drives me mental."

Dora cleared her throat and twiddled with her earring.

Zoë rolled her eyes. "Mum and Dad don't like him."

"That's not true!" Dora claimed even though everything Rob had seen and heard so far said Zoë was right.

"Then what?" she asked.

"Well..." Dora fussed with her blouse, tugging it away from her throat. A mottled rash raced up her neck to her face. Her eyelids fluttered and then she sighed. "He just seems to spend an awful lot of time working away."

"Would you prefer he ran his business from here?"

"Not really, but...I don't know. You'd think he'd want to be with his wife-to-be and stepson. You know what I'm saying, Rob, don't you?"

Zoë put up her hand. "You don't have to answer that, Rob."

He'd had no intention of doing so. Travis owned warehouses in Heathrow and could manage them remotely from anywhere, which was handy for

Zoë's work, or it had been. Before Folden's escape, Travis had spent a lot of time with Lucas, picking him up from school, taking him to football practice and matches, ferrying him to and from mates' houses and so on. 'Stepdad of the Year', Rob had dubbed him bitterly, even though Travis had always respected Rob and Lucas's relationship and the activities that were Rob's to do with his son. And when it came to getting Zoë and Lucas to a safe house, Travis had sided with Rob to persuade Zoë it was necessary.

For all of that, Rob wasn't going up against Dora to defend Travis when she was already contrite and keeping her eyes down to avoid Zoë's angry glare.

To get out of their way, Rob finished his coffee and took the empty mug over to the sink. "Should I go and chase Lu?" he suggested.

"Good idea," Zoë said, still glowering at her mother.

"Give me a clue."

"Hmm?"

"Whereabouts in the house is he?"

"Oh!" Zoë turned his way. "Up the stairs, second door on the left."

"Gotcha." Rob left the kitchen, quickening his steps as the argument started behind him, Zoë's and Dora's raised voices carrying all the way up the stairs. Zoë's accusation that her parents never approved of her choice of partners rang true to Rob's experience, although now he was a parent himself, he recognised a good deal of that was protectiveness. Zoë was an only child, like Lucas—that may well change once Zoë and Travis were back under their own roof—and, same as Rob, they would kill to protect his child.

He stopped on the landing outside Lucas's room and raised his hand to knock, delaying to listen to the simulated machine-gunfire coming from within, along with Lucas's laughing boast that he'd taken someone down. Before the flashback took hold, Rob knocked and turned the handle.

"Alright, Lu?"

"Dad!" Lucas tugged off his headset, chucking it as he hurdled a box in the middle of the floor. His foot snagged in a cable and sent him stumbling into Rob, who caught him and lifted him into the air. Lucas clung on, both arms, both legs. "When did you get here?"

"About twenty minutes ago. Didn't you hear your nan and your mum shout up?"

"N...yeah. Sort of." Lucas wriggled to break free. "I'm not a baby, Dad."

Rob released, letting Lucas slide down onto his feet. "You're eight, I know. But what's this game?" He nodded at the computer display of a dark city street, armed avatars running around and shooting at one another, weapon fire and shouts coming from the headset. At that volume, it was a miracle Lucas wasn't deaf already. "Are you old enough to play that?"

"Aw, it's well good, Dad. Come and see." Taking the safer route around the box, Lucas plopped down onto his beanbag and picked up his game controller. The display changed to a weapons inventory, which he flicked through, exchanging his submachine gun for an assault rifle. "I've got to get to the other side of the building and rendezvous with Tempest."

"Who?"

"Online friend. We're doing a campaign together."

"Right." Rob was none the wiser. "Listen, mate, you need to save your game and get packed up. The van'll be here any minute."

"'Kay. Hold on." Lucas picked up his headset and shouted into the mic, "Got to go. I'll be on later." He peered back at Rob, who nodded and mouthed, *Who you talking to?*

The answer came not from Lucas, but from the cold, horrifying recognition that gripped Rob like hands around his neck as the words came through the headset. "No problem, Lucas. Be seeing you."

"That's Tempest." Lucas shut down the game. "Not sure where he's from, but his English is really good."

"Yeah?" Rob said, half listening and pulling his phone from his pocket, trying to keep his cool as he opened a new encrypted message to Gray Fisher.

"Yeah. I've got loads of mates from all over the place."

"Have you?" Rob answered, typing at the same time.

Folden's in contact with Lucas.

2: Near-Distance

"I THINK I MIGHT have the soup." Gray tapped his finger midway down the gatefold menu and glanced up at his companion: an attractive woman, late twenties, straight brown hair past her shoulders...a dancer. She was too flexible not to be.

She nodded enthusiastically. *"I hear it's really good."*

"What are you having?"

Frowning, she returned her attention to her menu. *"I might have the soup too."*

"Copycat." Gray's words merged into a smile.

His companion's eyes widened, but she smiled back. *"I like soup!"*

Gray laughed—silently. Take Nine of the restaurant scene: romantic date/marriage proposal ending in rejection, a fallen chair and the proposee fleeing, the proposer in hot pursuit. But those were not Gray's and his silent companion's roles. They and the rest of the 'supporting artistes' were the backdrop: ordinary diners on an evening out, the afternoon's darkness courtesy of half a dozen blackout blinds across the restaurant's front window. Those were cheaper than paying both the restaurant to close for an evening and the SAs unsociable-hours rates.

The chair went over a ninth time, and the female star, enraged by her on-screen boyfriend's poor timing, stormed off. She made it halfway to the door before the call came from the director: "Go again."

The female star shrieked, nothing fake about her enragement now, and retraced her steps to the table where she stood by, snarling, while the chair was righted. One of the make-up girls swooped in to daub powder on both the leads' faces, the crew reset the scene, and the director and assistant producer huddled with backs turned to discuss where it had gone wrong. Like good little props, the SAs sat still and silent, awaiting the countdown to Take Ten. All this for a scene which, in the final cut, would last about thirty seconds.

Five minutes passed. Murmured conversations broke out and were shushed. The stars ran their lines without the cameras rolling, and again, and again. Gray relaxed against the wall, his thoughts on fast-forward to the real evening of folk music that awaited at the end of his working day. Every so often, a wave of noise washed over him and he tuned back in. A writer was on set; they were reworking the scene. Gray tuned out again.

Growing up in the Southwest, he was no stranger to folk music and quite enjoyed the occasional open-mic night at their local pub, but he wouldn't have gone there specifically for the purpose, as they'd be doing this evening. A forty-five-minute drive up to Hitchin to watch a gig which, Will had insisted at every given opportunity since he'd made the suggestion the previous weekend, would change Gray's opinion of folk music forever. Well, he'd enjoy the drive if nothing else.

He was drawn back to his surroundings this time not by the cyclical noise levels, but by his table companion's hand waggling in front of his face.

"You!" the director called above the din. "In the blue shirt."

It took a second for Gray to connect the description to his attire, and a further second for his heart to sink. It had arrived: the moment every soap extra longed for—every one other than Gray. A man condemned, he rose from what was, in fact, his very comfortable chair and wove between the people and equipment to reach the director and writer, the latter turning her laptop so he could see the screen.

"Two lines," she said, indicating the same. "To fix the pacing."

Noting the writer's sour sideways glance at the director, Gray took the laptop and read the section of script on-screen.

> *Waiter: Is everything all right with your meal?*
> Matt: [impatient] Yes, yes.
> Jen: [distracted] May I have a glass of water?
> *Waiter: Of course. [bows head and departs]*

"Can you do it?" the director asked.

"I can," Gray confirmed.

The director nodded once at Gray and clapped his hands for everyone else's benefit. "Positions."

The writer stepped off set, and a wardrobe assistant signalled to Gray. He went over, unbuttoning his shirt on the way and exchanging it for the proffered white shirt, black waistcoat and black bow tie, all the while aware of the director's attention. As he turned to meet the man's gaze, his line of sight was broken by a hand wielding a make-up brush, and he stayed put to have more powder applied before once more establishing eye contact with the director. With a singular jerk of the head, the man beckoned Gray back to him. *Like a lamb to the slaughter.*

"Where d'you want me?" Gray asked, consciously pushing down the fake Geordie accent which, through habit, came to the fore whenever he had to go into role. Incognito. Undercover.

The director's eyes narrowed. "Do I know you?"

"I don't think so."

The man scrutinised him for several excruciating seconds before he dismissed the notion with, "Obviously just seeing you around here," then went on to explain what he wanted him to do.

Take Ten: Gray was in position, off camera. The leads and SAs sat ready at their tables. Action. At the appropriate juncture, Gray advanced, passed the silently conversing extras, delivered his lines, retreated—it was fortuitously straightforward, given he'd only half-heard his directions—and at last they'd nailed the scene.

Gray returned his costume and pulled on his shirt, buttoning it on the move, still doing so as he grabbed his jacket from the pile at the back of the restaurant and made his getaway through the kitchen, only slowing when he was out in the open. He took a deep breath, its release a sigh of resignation.

He'd been an extra on the show for over eighteen months, and of course he'd recognised the director straight off the bat, but Gray was one of thirty-plus anonymous actors, 'walking props' whose job it was to blend into the background. Thus, he'd escaped attention until today. If he'd stayed even a minute more, the director would've remembered how he knew Gray, of that he was quite sure.

It had to be at least ten years ago because Gray hadn't long been out of uniform when he and his colleagues, back then common or garden CID, took apart Cordial Productions' studio, trying to establish whether the actor who had fallen to his death had been murdered. Gray's old boss thought so, but the evidence pointed towards involuntary manslaughter. Either way, director Richard Pritchard was unapologetically responsible, the extent of his negligence obliterating the attending officers' amusement concerning his name. Pritchard had sent the actor up onto a high platform knowing it hadn't been risk-assessed but too impatient to wait. The platform support collapsed, and the actor dropped twenty feet, head first, onto bare concrete.

In court, Pritchard claimed he'd been told the platform was secure and ready for use, and he had witnesses to corroborate. The jury came back with not guilty—infuriating but not a surprise. Pritchard was as good an actor as any of his cast, present or past, and had turned the courtroom into his stage for the duration of the trial.

Gray's ire at the injustice had lessened with time. That and the experience of watching more brutal, self-serving men than Pritchard walk free. And 'Rick Hubbard', as he was now known, seemed to have learned his lesson, these days less inclined to risk actors' lives in order to meet production deadlines. As a former leader who'd taken the same liberties with his team's safety and paid the price, Gray empathised, but he didn't want to be around when Pritchard figured out who he was. This was it: the end of his stint as a soap opera extra, and he was fine with that.

He hadn't gone into it for the money. Nobody did. Nor had he been chasing fame. After so long working undercover, he'd needed to step out of the shadows, be seen. His family and friends—even his therapist—thought his approach drastic, but it had worked. Eighteen months on, he finally had something resembling a normal life: a house, a boyfriend, half-ownership of an investigative agency, his postgrad studies. He didn't need this gig anymore.

Gray fished his phone from his pocket, planning his text to Will as he waited for it to switch on. He needed to tell his agent too. *Maybe I should talk to Will first, sleep on it a day or two.* He doubted it would change his decision, but they weren't filming over the weekend, so there was no rush.

The phone's screen lit up, the signal flatlining for a few seconds while it located and connected to a network. Gray tapped in his PIN and thumbed the 'messaging' icon as a call came in, accidentally answering it, although he'd have answered it anyway. He caught sight of the 'Sigma-SMS' icon in the menu bar as he put the phone to his ear. His heart skipped a beat.

"Hey, Rob."

"Alright, Gray? Did you get my text?"

"Only just. I—" Gray's throat was suddenly too tight to get the words past. Rob wasn't a man for small talk, but the complete absence of pleasantries rang deafening alarm bells and triggered an all-too-familiar craving. Within the panic time warp, Gray had no concept of how many seconds passed before he pushed out, "I haven't read it yet. What's going on?" He already knew but clung to a sheer thread of hope he was wrong until that one word came back, almost knocking him off his feet.

"Folden."

***

Adrenaline had powered him to the station, through the short train journey and the five-minute walk to Reardon House: on paper a Metropolitan Police administrative base but also headquarters of the Special Investigations Unit. Rob had arrived before him and loitered impatiently while Gray exchanged his shaky signature for a visitor's pass. The comedown had hit as they stepped into the lift.

Half an hour on, the nausea had dwindled to the occasional stomach cramp and dull ache behind his eyes; Gray was well into the exhaustion stage. He hadn't called Will yet to pull out of their plans for the evening, and he didn't want to, but it was looking increasingly like he had no choice.

If there was one point he could make in DCI Chris Tant's favour, it was that she made no secret of where her loyalties lay. Suffice to say, they were not with the SIU, which, given she was acting head, was problematic at best. She flipped through the printouts of cached text chat between Lucas and 'Tempest', lingering for less than a second on each before she slid them back into the folder and clapped it shut, pushing it across her desk—*Dom's* desk. She sat back, contemplating Rob then Gray over the top of her glasses.

"There's nothing we can do."

"Ma'am—" Rob began, but Gray jumped in.

"Why not?"

"We can't confirm this *Tempest* is Folden—"

"It's him," Rob said with dead certainty.

"I only have your word for that, Mr. Simpson-Stone."

"With respect—" Gray said, and this time she cut him off.

"Save your breath, Mr. Fisher. I know what you're going to say." She took off her glasses, chewing the earpiece as she studied Rob at length. He was in Gray's peripheral vision, but he'd be holding Tant's gaze, attentive, deferential, reading her intent. Finally, she put down her glasses. "Let's assume, for now, you're right that it's Folden. He's using a VPN, and we have no means to trace him. He could be anywhere in the world."

"Or he could be in a house across the street from Rob's son," Gray argued.

"The Clifton residence is Thames Valley."

"The SIU has national jurisdiction."

"Under the current structure, the SIU is restricted to MPD operations." She ploughed on with her point, flattening potential opposition. "The Cliftons' internet is a protected connection. It's unlikely anyone could pinpoint Lucas's location from that alone."

"So that's it?" Too late, Gray realised he'd raised his voice. However angry he was, in police service or out, he could usually keep his temper in check. Tant was a mere pen-pusher, there to ensure the SIU faded out of existence with a *poof!* rather than a bang, and not worth getting het up over.

To her credit, she responded reasonably to Gray's outburst. "I understand how worried you must both be, and I take your son's safety very seriously, Robert."

Rob stiffened at the use of his full first name.

Tant picked up the folder of printouts. "The best I can do is ensure this gets to the right people."

"Thank you, Ma'am," Rob said.

Her eyes flicked to Gray—he looked away, thanking her for nothing—and back to Rob. "If you feel your wife and son need alternative accommodation, I can look into it."

"We've already made arrangements, Ma'am."

"All right, then. Is there anything else?"

"No, thank you."

"Mr. Fisher?"

Gray shook his head and pushed out his chair. "I'll have the Scheiffer report back to you first thing tomorrow."

"Oh? I wasn't aware you were still consulting for us."

"Only accounts ledgers."

"Good to know we're giving you the fun jobs," Tant said. "Well, I have a meeting in—" she glanced at her bare wrist "—damn. I keep forgetting I didn't put my watch on. What time is it?" She was already on her feet and striding across the room.

Gray and Rob both glanced at the clock above the door and made eye contact. "Quarter to five," Gray said.

No acknowledgement from Tant; she opened the door and waved them past. "I'll find someone to escort you back to reception." Before Gray could tell her they'd make their own way down, she called, "Excuse me!" to DS Isobel Barnes, who'd emerged from the storeroom opposite with a box the size of a microwave oven. "See Mr. Fisher and Mr. Simpson-Stone out, please."

"Yes, Ma'am." If Isobel's weary, apathetic tone were purely for effect, it was wasted on her current boss. Tant's door—*Dom's* door—clicked shut against Gray's back.

Isobel gave a resigned sigh, though there was determination in her eyes. Gray sensed her readiness to escape from the drudgery of the new SIU.

"Can you give me a sec, Sir? I'll just stick this on my desk."

"No rush," Gray assured her with a smile that he hoped hid his devastation at what was happening to the SIU. In most respects, the office appeared as it had in its heyday, with the few officers onsite engaged in admin duties, the difference being that in Gray's time, the rest would have been out in the field whereas those present constituted the entire staff. The SIU was dying before his eyes— right when they needed it most.

"Gray?"

"Hmm?" With some effort, he clicked back to reality. "Sorry, Rob. Did you say something?"

"Yeah...I'll tell you later." Rob nodded to indicate Isobel was on her way back, empty-handed. She continued past them, gesturing that they follow her. She, too, looked as if she had something to say but couldn't safely do so in the office. She called the lift and kept her eyes on the doors.

Gray opted for functional small talk. "Are Zoë and Lucas staying put?"

"For the time being," Rob confirmed.

"How did Zoë take it?"

"Not well, and I had to log Lu out of his Xbox account—told him to stay off it until further notice. I'm not very popular just now."

"I can imagine. Was he able to tell you if he'd let anything slip?"

"He says not, but when he's in the zone he chats rubbish."

The lift arrived, and the three of them stepped inside. Isobel pressed the button for the ground floor; the doors closed. She stood at ease, staring dead ahead. Gray cleared his throat, and she looked his way—eyes only.

"Permission granted," he said.

"Is this about who I think it is, Sir?"

"Gray," he corrected. She smiled apologetically, but he doubted she'd ever feel comfortable calling him that. They'd worked together too long. "Yes," he said, "I'm afraid so."

She held her position, the only tell a slight clenching of her jaw. "Is there anything I can do?"

There was plenty, but it wasn't the time, and the lift was slowing down. It stopped and the doors opened. The people waiting to get in moved aside, and Gray and Rob got out, as did Isobel. She led them over to the reception desk, waited while they returned their visitors' passes and signed out, then walked with them to the external doors.

"I think we can manage from here," Gray said, standing by while Rob shook Isobel's hand; when it came to Gray's turn, he delayed releasing her and held her gaze. "See you soon, Iz—take care."

"You too, Sir." Her voice remained neutral, though her solemn expression made clear she'd understood his words were more than a nicety. He couldn't risk saying more until he'd established the seed he'd planted had germinated. He followed Rob outside, only then registering the absence of crash helmet. "How did you get here?"

"Tube. The bike's still in storage."

"You didn't fancy driving in?"

Rob smirked at Gray's tongue-in-cheek question, and they set off together towards the Underground station. "I'm gonna give it a run out tonight."

"Not the Fiesta."

"No." Rob managed a chuckle but quickly became serious again. He was a cool operator who rarely shared his thoughts or feelings unless someone asked for them—other than his loathing of the entry-level Fiesta, of which Gray had heard plenty over the past year. Dom hadn't involved Rob in the decision beyond justifying his choice as the car that would give Rob the best chance of blending in and living a normal life without drawing Folden's attention—the very opposite of the big, roaring Suzuki that was Rob's pride and joy.

Now, after months of resisting the temptation, he was talking about taking the bike out on the road, not coincidentally on the day he'd discovered Folden had been talking to Lucas, and nothing Gray could say would stop him. He couldn't order Rob to leave the bike where it was; nor would he insult him by pointing out the obvious risk. If the only way Rob could clear his head was through spending a couple of hours zooming up and down the North Circular in the dead of night, then the best Gray could do was pray Folden wasn't hiding close by.

They were almost at the station before either of them said anything else, and it was Rob who spoke first.

"We need to figure out what we're gonna do. If the SIU won't intervene..."

"It's more a case of they can't."

Rob bristled. "I should've known you'd stick up for Tant." It was a defensive blow, and Gray flinched at the truth of it, but he knew better than to take it personally.

"Believe me, Rob, I don't like this either, but she's been given a job to do, and it isn't leading the SIU. Six months from now, there'll be no SIU."

"Did Dom tell you that?"

"Dom's out of the loop, but I've seen it before, the first time I applied for promotion. Customs and excise secondment—there was some hoo-ha that ended in the team leader resigning. They appointed Martin Winstanley over me."

"That must've stung," Rob said.

"At the time." Gray hadn't long finished his probationary period and was being primed for greater things, but he hadn't known that then. "It was a sideways move for Winstanley, and he was just there to oversee the operation winding down. After that, he came back to CID, and we worked one more case together—Scheiffer the diamond smuggler, we never caught him—before I got promotion and Martin moved to internal affairs.

"Scheiffer..." Rob frowned. "Hold up. The case you mentioned to Tant? She acted like she knew what you were talking about."

"And then promptly sent us on our way."

After a beat, Rob's frown lifted as he figured out what Gray was up to. "You're dangling a hook."

Gray grinned. "Now all we have to do is wait for the wily shark to notice the interim head of the SIU is sticking her nose into his old cases."

"Wouldn't it be easier to phone him?"

"I already tried after you called, but his old number's out of service. He's gone up in the world since we last saw him. Getting hold of a deputy chief constable by phone without a direct line involves talking to half the police officers in the country, and I don't want to alert anyone. On which note..." Gray took out his phone and unlocked the screen. "I still need to call Will. We were going out this evening."

"Don't change your plans, Gray—unless you're looking for a get-out."

Am I? Will's number was on-screen, but he hadn't yet clicked the call button. "No, I'm not," he confirmed for the both of them and put his phone back in his pocket. "Keep me updated, though."

"Will do."

They arrived at the station and went through adjacent ticket barriers, slowing as they approached the stairs down to the platforms; they were going in opposite directions.

"So are we hanging fire until you've talked to Winstanley?" Rob asked.

Gray nodded. "That's step one. I'm still in touch with a couple of Jean's colleagues in Interpol. I should be able to talk them into sharing anything they've got on Folden. Other than that...we're on our own."

3: Highway to Hell

A RE YOU SURE you'll be all right, now?" Dora asked. She cleared the table without checking everyone was done eating, which they were—even Lucas, whose king-sized sulk didn't seem to have affected his appetite. Rob wasn't sorry Dora had brought an end to the tense staring at food the three adults had been enduring.

When she reached across for Zoë's plate, Zoë gave her a playful smack on the arm and took over. "We'll be fine, Mum."

"Like I say, I can get someone to cover for me tonight."

"Rob's staying until Dad gets home." Zoë looked his way for further confirmation. He nodded.

Dora took Zoë at her word and moved towards the door, although she was still fretting. She paused and drummed her nails on the doorframe. "I'll just pop up and change, but promise me you'll call me if...well, just keep me updated, all right?"

"I will," Zoë promised, sighing once her mum was out of hearing range. She carried the plates to the dishwasher and opened it but got no further than that, sucked into her own cycle of worry.

Rob collected the glasses from the table and took them over. "OK?"

"Hmm?" Zoë rubbed her forehead. "Yeah, just stressed."

Rob offered her an apologetic smile. He hated seeing her like this. It wouldn't have been as bad if Lucas were old enough to understand and comply instead of fighting them over why he couldn't just set up a new Xbox account and use a pseudonym—"like you've got, Dad." The argument ended in Zoë sending Lucas to his room and then breaking down in tears while Lucas screamed "*It's not fair! I hate you!*" from the top of the stairs.

Lu was right. It wasn't fair, and Zoë told him so over dinner. They'd never used sending him to his room as a punishment, and he was already without his Xbox, but it had been a hell of a day for all of them. Of course, Lucas took the explanation as permission to start over, and if Zoë hadn't been there for backup, Rob would have caved to his son's pleas. He seemed to be doing that a lot of late. Since Folden's escape, he hadn't been able to take Lu swimming or to footy or on that camping trip he'd been promising for almost two years, and he had no other way to make it up to him.

"I'm off," Dora called from the doorway, her troubled frown fixed on her grandson's back. "Good night, Lucas."

"Night, Nan," he mumbled.

Dora shook her head and looked over at Zoë. "See you in the morning." She shifted her gaze to Rob. "See you whenever."

"Soon, I hope. Thanks for dinner."

"My pleasure. Take care now." No hugs for Zoë or Lucas, she turned and hurried from the house, but Rob had seen it: her desperate fear for her family that would have ended in tears and Dora ditching her night shift to stay with them if she'd delayed any longer.

"Hey." Zoë rubbed his back, and he forced out a smile. "Don't beat yourself up."

"It's my fault, Zo."

"No, it's not. This is on Anders Folden. Don't lose sight of that."

"You didn't sign up for this."

With an exasperated slow-blink, she shoved him aside with her hip and started loading the dishwasher. Rob helped, or tried to; he put two glasses in and she moved them somewhere else. He raised his hands and backed off, looking around to see what else needed doing.

"Sorry," Zoë said. "A place for everything..." She glanced over her shoulder at Lucas, still sitting at the table, still sulking. "Get ready for bed, Lu."

His scowl deepened.

"Now, please."

Lucas huffed and stomped out of the room, thumping his feet all the way up the stairs. A door slammed, and Zoë made a small sobbing sound. "He's going to be a nightmare without his Xbox."

Rob nodded. They'd even tried to compromise: Lucas had plenty of games he could play offline, but they weren't *the* game, and the ensuing tantrum was why Rob had banned him from the Xbox completely.

"Was I too hard on him?"

"No. He was being a little shit."

"True, but it's not like he can go out and play."

"One evening won't kill him."

If it *was* only one evening. Bottom line: Rob didn't trust Lucas to not defy them and set up a new account. He felt terrible for thinking it, but that was what he'd have done in Lucas's position. "What about you?" Rob nodded to indicate Zoë's phone.

"With no internet, you mean?" She reached over and tapped it, bringing up the lock screen, which displayed the time against a lava-lamp animated background. "How about that? Zero notifications!" She grinned.

Rob laughed. "Serves you right for being so popular."

"It's only ever work or junk mail—no great loss. But what you said before about me not signing up for it? You wouldn't have taken on the undercover jobs if I hadn't pushed you, and you warned me there were risks."

"Not like this."

"It's an extreme situation. How could you know?"

"I did know. Going after Folden—"

"And Jess..." Zoë pointed out, no spite. Rob hadn't admitted to everything that transpired between him and Jess, but he'd given Zoë enough for her to understand he'd acted under duress for the most part.

"We should've found another way to get them," he said.

"For God's sake...Rob! You have to stop blaming yourself. And you have to stop blaming Gray too. It's neither of your fault."

Easier said than done. His mind kept going over the same events—nights with Jess, torn up by guilt for entrapping her and for 'cheating' on Zoë, the times he'd had to turn a blind eye to Folden's brutality, Gray coercing him to stay the distance, constant promises it was nearly over—

Zoë's arms came around him, dragging him from his thoughts. "Stop it."

"Sorry." He hugged her back, pressing his lips to the top of her head. It was automatic, instinctual almost, and platonic. He still loved her—as the mother of his son, the woman who'd married him when he'd thought a bachelor's life was all that lay ahead. He could still cherish what they'd had together and what they were now.

But not for long. The doorbell sounded the death knell on their moment of tenderness, and they froze. Zoë's dad would've used his key, and they weren't expecting visitors.

"I'll get it!" Lucas shouted, already racing down the stairs.

"No!" Rob and Zoë yelled in unison, both sprinting for the door and somehow getting there before him. Rob stood to the side while Zoë took a couple of deep breaths before peering through the spyhole.

"What the...?" She reached for the door latch.

"Zo..." Rob warned. The look she gave him was filthy, which was fair enough—why would she answer the door to a dangerous stranger? Even so, he stayed where he was and at the ready. The door swung open, and Lucas charged forward.

"Travis!"

"Hey, Lu. Missed me, did you?" Bemused, and with Lucas clinging to his legs, Travis heaved one foot then the other over the step and into the hall. "Alright?" he acknowledged Zoë and Rob.

"Alright?" Rob echoed, moderately disgruntled by Lucas's delight at Travis's arrival. It was as much about Lu building an alliance against the parental enemy as having missed his stepdad.

Zoë shut the door. "What are you doing here? You aren't due back till Sunday."

Rob tactfully retreated a few steps while she greeted Travis with a hug and an unhurried kiss.

"Wasn't gonna leave you to face this on your own, was I?" He grimaced at Rob. "If you know what I mean."

Rob smiled. "No worries." He tapped Lucas on the shoulder. "Come on, you. Let's give your mum and Travis a minute, shall we?" He led Lucas towards the stairs.

"What we doing, Dad?"

"Bedtime story."

"Boring."

"You don't know that."

"All books are boring."

"Who said anything about books?" At the top of the stairs, Rob glanced back at Zoë and Travis, still arm in arm, watching his and Lucas's progress. "I'll put this one to bed and be back down. I have an idea how to get your internet sorted."

"Yessss!" Lucas cheered and raced off to his room, all of a sudden on his best behaviour.

***

Gray didn't know what to do. His knees were aching, his feet had gone to sleep, and he was no closer to a decision. His new boots were comfortable, stylish, though he doubted anyone would notice let alone care about his dress sense at a folk gig. But his old boots...they were more than footwear. They were memories, cracked and scuffed, repaired and reheeled, and they were his favourites, not just in his current collection; of all time.

"Decisions, decisions..." Will came into the bedroom, his smile evident before Gray looked back over his shoulder to be dazzled by full-beam happiness. Dressed but also shoeless, Will plugged in the hairdryer and bent over, flipping his hair forward, revealing the darker brown beneath the natural blonde streaks and blowing shampoo-scented hot air in Gray's direction. Doris the terrier, who'd been asleep on Gray's pillows, commando-crawled to the end of the bed, sticking her head in the perfumey gust and panting and blinking. The rest of the dogs had stayed downstairs and would be crashed out wherever they felt like it, probably end to end on the sofa.

Will said something else, inaudible above the hairdryer's drone, and repeated himself when Gray said, "Pardon?" but Gray still didn't catch it. Knowing it was pointless to ask again, he turned back to the wardrobe and his decision, the difficult made impossible by the intoxicating aroma of warm, sweet shea butter. The temptation proved too great, and he sprang to his feet, drawing breath through his teeth as he hobbled over and set to work on combing Will's hair with his fingers, getting tangled on his first stroke. "Did you brush this?"

"Nope. Why bother when you'll do it for me?"

Gray caught that well enough. "Damn cheek." He tugged a little harder.

"Ow! Don't punish me! You love it!"

"I wasn't! And I do, but it's like mattress stuffing back here." Gray pulled his fingers free and opted for the hairbrush, doing his best to separate the matted clump. "You're making it worse," he complained, scooping the stray strands blown by the hairdryer, intent on joining their brethren. Will angled the nozzle away. "That's better." Progress at last, but Gray took his time.

With the tangle gone, he made one last run-through with the brush then went back to using his fingers, smiling in response to Will's knowing smirk. Of all Will's assets he'd fallen for, the least expected was his long hair, and he was making the most of the opportunity to play with it before it went back in its ponytail.

"Are you done?" Will switched off the hairdryer and straightened up.

"I suppose so," Gray grumbled. "Do we have to go out tonight?"

"*I* do. I promised Jed, but you don't have to come."

"No, I want to." He stopped playing with Will's hair, laughing when Will moaned and lolled against his shoulder. "Unless you're open to persuasion that I need you more?" Gray teased.

Will put his arms around him and kissed him. "Joking aside, I know you're worried about Rob, so if you need me here, I'll call Jed and make my excuses."

"No."

"Really, it's not a..." Will trailed off at Gray's eye-roll. Gone was the time when Gray blindly accepted Will's agreeableness. It wasn't an act; Will would do anything to avoid conflict in their relationship, other than talk about why.

Gray eased out of the embrace, trailing his hand over Will's arm as he moved past him, back to the wardrobe. "Thanks, but I'll dwell on it if I stay here." He took out his new vegan boots and closed the door. "I can't do anything until I've heard from Martin Winstanley anyway. *If* I hear from him."

"Put the others on," Will said.

"These are comfy enough." Gray sat on the edge of the bed and picked up a boot.

"Yep, but the others are your favourites."

Gray stopped to stare at him. "How do you know they're my favourites?"

"You used to wear them all the time when we were dating."

"We never *dated*."

"When we were first seeing each other, before you went veggie. Just put them on—I know you want to."

"But they're leather," Gray pointed out.

"And the cow's already dead. The least you can do is make it a worthwhile sacrifice."

"Hmm. Think I might stick with these." Although...there was a logic to Will's argument that changed Gray's mind before he'd put the second boot on. "Are you going to berate me all evening?"

"Not a word, Scout's honour." He even saluted.

Gray got up again and exchanged the faux-buckskin boots for the leather ones. "If it's any consolation, I left my suede jacket back at the house."

Will nodded once. "I'll wait downstairs." He turned and left, but not before Gray glimpsed his expression. There was a whole paper's worth of subtext to that hasty exit.

"I'm coming now," Gray called and went after him, boots in hand.

***

It was going on for nine o'clock by the time Rob had explained his idea to Zoë and Travis and driven back into the city, to the Parkers' place in Hampstead Heath, where his bike had been stowed since the previous spring. He stopped at the gates, the car's headlights skirting the dark, empty house owned by Tonka— aka Lieutenant Yvette Parker, his former CO—and her brother. It hadn't surprised Rob that after last year's ordeal they'd both moved away, in Tonka's case to end her lonely retirement in England and join Siggy—her long-term, long-distance love—in Germany. She'd told him they planned to get shut of the house at some point, but he was welcome to use it in the interim.

As he toyed with the fob that unlocked the gates, the long day caught up with him, the pressure building in his head until he wanted to yell. Frustration, fury and too much time on the road, he was dog-tired and done waiting for others to move into position. When he'd left his mum's that morning, the only blot on his day had been trying to manufacture an excuse to call Naomi. Now he had a reason, his desire had been overwritten by a single thought: he was going to find Folden and beat the fucker to death.

A darting dot of light caught Rob's attention—a torch wielded by a neighbour walking a dog. The man veered around the back of the car, eyes averted: Rob's cue to move. He clicked the fob and drove through the gates as they opened, squinting at the sudden brightness of the security light. Keeping clear of the garage door, he parked up, made sure he had the correct key in his hand and got out of the car.

The beep of the house alarm sent him into a mild panic as he tapped in the memorised code, exhaling in relief when the silence resumed. For a moment, he remained in the hallway, shielding his eyes from the eerie green glow of the panel's standby LED, and contemplated heading straight back out on the bike. Packing his leathers for the drive down, he'd almost convinced himself that he and Gray had it wrong and everyone else—the SIU, Martina Hedley, even Zoë—was right. Folden was dust in the wind, and it was time to resume their lives, or in Rob's case start over. He'd given up his flat in Kilburn, commuting down south as and when he and Gray had a case when they were both needed in the field, but Zoë, Lucas and Travis could have returned home. Travis wouldn't be sleeping in his warehouse, and he and Zoë could finally have the wedding Lucas had been harping on about for the past eighteen months.

Finding out Folden had been talking to Lucas wasn't enough to change Rob's mind, only his purpose. Switching on a couple of lamps, he conducted a quick reccy of the house, leaving his bag upstairs in the master bedroom before returning to the open-plan ground floor, pleased to find the fridge partly stocked with beer and long-life milk. There'd be teabags in the cupboard, a few odds and sods in the freezer. Maybe later, he'd crack open a beer, try to wind down a bit. It was the only way he'd be getting any kip tonight. He shut the fridge and turned to survey the space, aware of every creak as the building cooled in the evening, the slow tick of the clock on the wall to his left, the shadow of a tree branch shifting across the floor, the restlessness he couldn't shake without getting out on the bike, and the danger of doing so.

Rob had spent three years in Folden's company. He knew how Folden got his kicks. He'd be close by, watching, enjoying every moment of their suffering, and Rob would be damned if he was going to sit back and wait for him to move in for the kill.

***

Enough was enough. After thirty minutes of silence bar the 'getting into the mood' music blasting from the car stereo and Will drumming along on his thighs, Gray lowered the volume and took in breath to speak...and held it. Will's hands stilled and he turned away, watching out the passenger side window.

"Sorry," Gray said, "but can we discuss this?"

Will affected a convincing carefree tone. "Sure. What's up?"

"You tell me."

Will turned back. "I don't know what you mean." The lie tripped off his tongue with confident innocence, but Gray wasn't fooled.

"Earlier, when we were talking about my boots—"

"I told you—I'm fine with you wearing them."

"No. Something's bothering you." Gray replayed their conversation, or about three words of it before Will turned up the stereo, louder than it had been before.

"This is a great track. It's about Greenham Common. Jed co-wrote it with his mum—I told you she and Mum were there together, didn't I?"

"You mentioned it," Gray said. It had been Will's winning argument for why they should go to the gig, but Gray stayed quiet while Will recounted it again. Accordingly, Jed's mum and Will's had been close friends since their days at Greenham Common, and from what Gray could hear of the song over Will's babbling, it was a fitting tribute. However, the significance was all in the timing. Will was deploying misdirection, meaning Gray was right to worry.

"My jacket," he said when Will finally stopped talking. "That's what it was. When I mentioned my jacket—"

"Bernie—Jed's mum—lives down in Cornwall now, not far from where I surf. She said we're welcome there anytime."

"Great," Gray said but he refused to be derailed. "When I mentioned my jacket, you glared and walked off."

"I didn't walk off." Still the calm, peaceable tone. "We needed to leave."

"Will, please!" For the briefest moment—as long as he dared—Gray looked Will's way, making eye contact before attending to the road again.

It was some minutes and miles later before Will relented and switched off the stereo. "It's about the house."

"Yours or mine?"

Will laughed joylessly. "And ain't that the rub?"

Gray frowned, wishing he could properly see him. They'd been living together for a year, and other than the usual tiffs any couple had, perhaps a few that were unique to them, there had been no indication things were going irretrievably awry. "Do you want me to move out?" he asked.

"Of course not! But that would require you to have moved in, Gray, which you haven't."

"Meaning?"

"Your suede jacket?"

"I don't follow."

"It's still at *your* house, along with the rest of your stuff."

"Stuff I don't need anymore," Gray argued. Aside from the clothes he wore on a regular basis and any new ones he'd bought since he'd moved in, or semi-moved in, as Will would have it, the only other belongings he'd brought with him were his toiletries and computer. Everything else—furniture, kitchen appliances, linens—were still in the house he'd bought with Jean's money and put to as much use as he would a bed-and-breakfast. It was never home. *Will's* was home. "I can't wear that jacket," he blustered, "and there's no point taking up what little storage there is in the farmhouse."

"There are two empty bedrooms."

"Do you really want to fill them with my old junk?"

"We could put some of it to good use."

"Like the sofas?" Gray asked facetiously.

"Yes, I'm sure *the mutts* would have the time of their lives sprawling and leaving mud and hair all over your three-grand sofas."

"It's really not a pr—"

"Don't!"

Gray pressed his lips together, anxiety fluttering in his stomach as he accepted he'd taken the 'not a problem' mockery too far. This was the most honest Will had been with him in a long time, possibly since the start of their relationship, and the last thing he wanted was to shut him down. "Sorry."

"Apology accepted."

"I love those mutts. You know that, don't you?"

"Yep."

"Would it help if I sold the house?"

"You're missing the point, Gray. I just want you to properly move in rather than keeping your options open."

Keeping my options open? Suddenly it all made sense. "That's what you think I'm doing?"

Will fiddled with the glove box, opened it, flipped it shut. "Are you?"

"No!" Gray indicated and changed lane to come off the motorway, frustrated by the misunderstanding and that he hadn't challenged Will sooner. As laid-back and confident as Will Richards was, he was not secure about *them*. That was a painful revelation but not really a shock, given Will changed the subject any time they talked about past relationships. He was hiding some deep wounds, and Gray didn't feel qualified to go poking around, but he could give Will the reassurance he so clearly needed.

"I've been delaying dealing with the house to give Rob first refusal on renting it. He wants somewhere bigger so he can have Lucas over more often, and I can afford to keep the rent low." That was before Folden made his most recent play, but Gray was in no rush as long as Will was OK with it. "What do you think?"

Will shrugged. "It's your house."

"And our future. It should be *our* decision. If you'd rather I sold it..."

"No." Will's palm landed, warm and heavy, on Gray's thigh. "Prices are still rising, and the market should stay buoyant for a while yet. It's a good investment."

"Are you sure?"

"About it being a good investment?"

"Will..."

"One hundred percent," he confirmed.

"And I promise, I have properly moved in."

"I believe you."

Gray slowed and stopped at the junction, resting his hand on top of Will's. "I'm not sure I believe you...yet. But as soon as this Folden situation is resolved, I'll get the house cleared and talk to Rob, OK?" He met Will's gaze, the confirmation coming in the form of a wide smile that radiated across Will's features, and which Gray would have mirrored but for a further realisation that hit him like a charging bull.

Will's smile vanished. "What's the matter?"

"Rob. I've just figured out what he's up to. I need to stop him."

***

Fully fuelled bike, tyres up to pressure, not a speck of dust—all Rob had to do was open the garage door and he could ride off into the night. He had the route mapped in his mind, not one that would allow him to put the bike through its paces—he was fairly sure most of the roads these days were capped at 20 mph—and it needed a good run out as much as he did, but Lucas's safety was paramount.

It wasn't easy walking the heavy bike from the garage along the drive and down to the T-junction. Other than a couple of passing cars—big, executive models no doubt driven by city high fliers for whom getting home before nine was an early dart—the neighbourhood was deserted. When he reached the main road, he started the bike but kept the revs low while he waited for the lights to change and then joined the flow of traffic, tucked behind a bus and in front of a Transit van. The bus signalled it was turning right at the next junction, which was the opposite direction to where Rob needed to go, but he kept following it until he was clear of Hampstead, then took the Finchley Road, past Hyde Park and almost down to the river before zigzagging back to Holborn. If London had a barristers' quarter, this was it.

Pulling into a motorcycle bay—a new instalment since his last visit—Rob dropped the kickstand and peered up at the sash windows above the Clough Chambers' signage as he took out his phone, looking away only as long as was necessary to hit the right number in his contacts. It rang out twice before it was picked up; the line remained silent. A shadow passed one window and then appeared at the next.

Rob said, "We need to talk."

4: Fire on the Mountain

H OW LONG?" Rob kept a casual stance as he gave the barrister's office a once-over. It looked no different than the last time he'd been there.

"Just over a month," answered the man, who was not Benjamin Clough, QC but his once junior partner—*something* Heyes, if Rob recalled correctly. Heyes picked up the cigarette packet on his desk and offered it to Rob, who shook his head. "Mind if I do?"

"Go ahead." He was already breathing as shallowly as he could. Smog hung around the maroon-shaded lamp on what was formerly Clough's desk, and the air was thick with stale smoke.

Heyes lit up and drew on the cigarette for a good five seconds before releasing a noxious cloud, dusky purple against the oak-and-books backdrop. "Bloody Europe." He indicated the chair on the other side of his desk, waiting for Rob to sit before he sat himself and expanded on that statement. "Can't smoke until everyone's buggered off home for the day." He held up the cigarette. "It's the only way I get any work done."

It was all bull; like Clough, Heyes pretty much lived in his chambers, but Rob listened impassively, waiting for the barrister to take the lead, though he seemed in no rush to do so. Propping his cigarette in the ashtray on his desk, he opened a drawer and took out a Courvoisier bottle and two fat, crystal brandy balloons. This time, he didn't ask before he poured an inch of cognac into each glass and pushed one across the desk.

"Thanks." Rob lifted it to his mouth, swirling and sniffing, briefly enjoying the festive feelings evoked by the rich, warm fumes. He rarely drank spirits but did the decent thing and took a small sip.

"All right, let's get to it." Heyes settled back in his chair, crossed feet propped on the corner of his desk. Clough would be turning in his grave. "What did you come here for?"

"A private matter. How did he die?"

"Electrocuted himself." Heyes held up his glass, studying the golden liquid within. "Drunk in his Jacuzzi—toppled the heater." Tilting his head back, he looked Rob in the eye. "Perhaps I can help?"

Rob ignored Heyes's offer. "An accident?"

"So they say." Heyes didn't believe that any more than Rob did.

Rob nodded, took another sip of cognac. He didn't know Heyes well enough to trust him—not that he'd trusted Clough, but they'd had an understanding.

Benjamin Clough had been as corrupt as they came, bribing opposing counsel and judges, terrifying jurors and silencing witnesses. He'd been the fraud ring's go-to for counterfeit documents, although he never dirtied his own hands. He was merely the middle man, taking an unseemly wedge of the pie for his minimal troubles.

He was also the only one to suss Rob was an undercover officer—thanks to good recall skills, as opposed to his powers of deduction. Clough had been barrister for the defence on a trial up in Stratford-upon-Avon and had cross-examined Rob—the arresting officer. When they'd come face-to-face during the SIU operation, Rob had expected Clough to throw him to the dogs. Instead, he'd agreed to keep Rob's cover if, in return, Rob omitted Clough's involvement in the scam from his reports. Both had kept up their end of the bargain, even when Folden had retained Clough for his murder trial.

If Folden had tried to flee the country, he'd have come to Clough for fake identity documents. Maybe Clough had threatened to turn him over to the authorities; 'accidental electrocution while drunk' was a good fit with Folden's preferred MO of making it look like natural causes or a fatal mishap.

Heyes extinguished the cigarette and picked up the packet, considering a second. "Is there anything else I can do for you?"

"No—thank you. And thanks for this—" Rob set the barely touched brandy on the desk "—but I'm on my bike." He stood, aware of Heyes watching his progress across the room.

As he reached the door, Heyes murmured, "Godspeed."

Rob turned back, meeting the barrister's impenetrable gaze, briefly, before it was obscured by new smoke.

***

"What d'you think?" Will shouted directly into Gray's ear when the band took a brief break. The words puffed sweet, cidery breath across Gray's face.

"I'm really enjoying it," he said without hesitation but with some surprise at his admission. He'd anticipated having to pretend for Will's benefit, and his attention wasn't fully on Jed's band. On the whole, though, since Gray had made the call regarding Rob's antics, he was fairly relaxed. That could well have been down to the marijuana haze that lingered like low cloud, defying the draughtiness of the enormous converted barn in which they were standing, along with at least a hundred other people. Still more reclined on the stacks of hay bales lining both side walls.

A low, wide, makeshift stage took up most of one end of the barn, a barrel bar at the other—a 'bring your own drinking vessel' affair where people took their various mugs, tankards, glasses and flasks for a refill as and when they needed one, all included in the entry fee. There were nibbles too—vegan, spicy concoctions like Bombay mix and spinach pakoras, Sheese crackers and soybean hot dogs—and a whole lot of the hippie equivalent of secret handshakes. Gray had figured out this was an animal-libber crowd a few seconds before Will confirmed it, explaining it was a fundraiser to help out with legal expenses for some guys who were being prosecuted on what was essentially a civil offence of trespassing, but they'd done so on government property. Specifically: an MoD research laboratory for testing chemical weapons...*allegedly.*

Whatever the benefit, everyone was on their best behaviour—soft drugs and lack of alcohol licence notwithstanding. Gray had been to his fair share of festivals in his younger years—actually, not that much younger, as the last time was with Jean—and here, as with those, was evidence of the argument put forth by campaigners for legalising the use of recreational drugs. There were no sudden surges of unrest common to the average weekend evening in the city, almost all of which were fuelled by alcohol. Indeed, the atmosphere in the barn was so chilled, Gray hadn't thought once about cocaine, not beyond acknowledging he'd been craving-free all evening.

And the music...it was like no folk music he'd heard before. Electric guitars, fiddles, accordions, heavy bass and drums, the beat thrummed through him, zapping his negative thoughts and dispersing with no after-effects. The lyrics, mainly political in nature, were cleverly put together and charged with emotion—anger, frustration, none of it mindless or inciting violence; the first choice for Will and his kind was peaceful action.

To think, eighteen months ago, if Will had brought him to a gig like this with songs of revolution and anarchy, Gray would've run as fast as his little establishment legs could carry him. His political views hadn't shifted much since then. He still saw the value in rules and some sense of social order, still believed change had to be effected from within the system; but for all of that, he couldn't think of any place he'd rather be.

Will had wandered away and returned shortly with a very murky pint of scrumpy—Gray's regional brew growing up, and he'd have liked nothing more than to indulge this evening. Alas, he'd had his designated-driver single pint not long after they'd arrived, so he settled for appreciating it vicariously, turning his attention back to the band, and not a moment too soon. Jed beckoned to someone in the audience, and a woman climbed up onto the stage. She must have been used to performing as she accepted without hesitation the acoustic guitar someone handed her, positioned the strap around herself and stepped up to the mic next to Jed's.

"I'd like to introduce you all to my mum, Bernie," Jed announced to much cheering, taking the moment to switch his electric guitar for an acoustic also. "This next song is one we wrote together to commemorate and celebrate the women of Greenham Common. Tonight—"

Jed had to stop again, drowned out by the cheers coming from everyone in the barn—Will included. He glanced Gray's way with a huge grin and very wet eyes. Gray smiled back and took hold of Will's hand. He almost wished he hadn't when Jed finally finished his announcement with, "This song is dedicated to Judy Richards, much-missed mum of my good buddy Will." Gray clenched his teeth through the squeeze and kept his eyes on the band, aware that Will's tears had fully broken free, although with what came next, Will would need a whole lot more of that scrumpy to rehydrate and recover.

"Are you gonna help us sing the chorus?" Jed asked.

"Yes!"

"Smashing! I'm sure you all know the words already, but in case you don't..." Jed gave his mum a nod and started strumming. After a couple of chords, she sang a line, and the audience sang it back to her, repeating for the four lines of a song Gray had heard only once but would never forget.

> You can't kill the spirit
> She is like a mountain
> Old and strong
> She goes on and on and on...

It was the song they'd sung at Will's mum's funeral—her family, friends and women from Greenham—the song the women had sung when they'd formed a human chain around the base. The recorded version of the song Jed and his mum had written didn't have that chorus thus had not prepared Gray for the power of the live performance—of Jed's fast-paced, spiky lyrics about war and pollution and death and the end of times, which felt as if they were running at double the speed of the chant led by his mum, one against the other, sometimes in harmony, sometimes clashing horribly.

Inevitably, Jed reached the end of his final chorus, but the chant went on for several more rounds. Gray wasn't counting. When, finally, it finished, the barn was dead silent for a beat and then erupted in cheers, and at last Gray's hand was his own again. He joined in with the applause, watching Will clap and cry, cider sploshing from the glass clamped under his arm. He noticed Gray watching him and smiled, no words, but Gray nodded, understanding the unasked question: *What did you think?* Overwhelming, powerful, beautiful.

Above the buzz of the still-applauding crowd came four clicks of the drumsticks followed by an instantly recognisable opening fiddle riff, the reaction to which near blew the barn roof off.

"You know this one, then?" Will asked, smirking as he made it obvious he was looking down at Gray's feet, alerting him to the fact they were shuffling of their own accord. Gray grinned and shrugged.

"Who doesn't?" he said as Jed talked the opening line: "The devil went down to Georgia..."

***

"Mr. Simpson-Stone. I've been expecting you."

"Damn it." Rob flopped into the back seat and slammed the door shut. He'd turned off his phone after he'd left Clough's office, so he knew he hadn't been tracked. "Gray put you up to this, didn't he?"

Dom didn't deny it, nor did he admit it, but why else would he be in the back of the police car that had pulled Rob over? "To be honest, Rob, I'm surprised it took you this long, and I get it—"

"Do you?" Rob cut in angrily.

"I've got kids too, mate!"

The statement came as a bit of a slap in the face. Rob hadn't known that.

"I'd give my life for them, same as you."

Rob shook his head, too riled to respond, and stared at the Traffic officer's back, pressed against the closed driver's door. He'd stayed out to give them a chance to talk, but Rob didn't have time for this.

"What d'you want, Dom?"

"Nothing. Apart from your safety."

"You normally ride around in the back of a unit on a Friday night?"

"That's on a—"

"Never mind." Rob had already sussed that whatever Dom was doing here—beyond following up on Gray's call—it was some kind of undercover work. Officially, Dom was suspended from duty pending a gross misconduct hearing. Unofficially...

"Can I go now? Or are you impounding the bike?"

"Not this time," Dom answered with no humour. "But have a think, Rob. Sacrificing yourself isn't going to protect Lucas, is it?"

"You think I'm baiting Folden."

"Whether that's your intent—"

"It's not."

Dom shrugged. "The end result's the same. We haven't spent a year keeping you under the radar for you to walk right up to him without backup."

"*We?*" Rob asked, even though Dom wouldn't tell him, but at least he'd know Rob had picked up on it.

Dom sighed. "Do me a favour, all right? Don't do anything stupid. Stay safe."

"That's what I was trying to do, Dom. Now, if you're done with me?" Rob gestured at the door, and Dom reached forward and rapped on the window. The Traffic officer let Rob out. Without a backward glance, he returned to the bike and took off into the late-evening traffic—too late now to do what he'd intended.

A few miles on, still livid he'd been held up, Rob jumped a red light. Luckily, the only traffic coming across the junction was turning left, but it gave him enough of a scare to accept he was in no fit state to 'stay safe'. At the next junction, he turned off into the industrial park and headed for a twenty-four-hour café—not quite the lone customer. There was a young couple, huddled close, occasionally sharing a smile or a kiss. A new relationship, possibly an illicit one, given their location. The café wasn't part of a chain, and it was pleasant enough, but it needed a lick of paint and some up-to-date fixtures if it wanted to attract more than a teenage couple keeping away from the crowds and an idiot who'd got so worked up about friends looking out for him he'd almost killed himself.

The more Rob thought about it, the more he could see Dom's point, which was no doubt shared by Gray. To them, it would look like he'd gone out on the bike purely to attract Folden's attention, and he'd be lying if he claimed he hadn't considered it might happen. However, he'd convinced himself it was a calculated risk. He *was* trying to flush Folden out, but by making contact with Folden's former associates. And if Folden had caught up with him this evening? It would have brought his search to a timely and successful conclusion.

The young couple were leaving. One of them went into the Ladies' whilst the other stood by the door, checking their phone, prompting Rob to do the same. There was a missed call and a message from Lois: *Did you get lost on the way? Your favourite eldest niece, asking for a nan who's giving her hell. x*

"Shit." He should have called hours ago to let them know he'd arrived safely.

The youngster at the door looked over, and Rob smiled in apology as he hit reply on Lois's message. He typed and backspaced through 'Hey Lo' and decided to make a move so he could get back and call her. The other youngster came out of the toilets, and Rob followed the couple out, pausing to put his phone away and zip up his leathers. As he stepped off again, one of them called, "Oy, mate, is that your bike?"

"Yeah, why?" Rob asked, looking from the kid to the bike, catching sight of movement around the building, a shadow cast by someone moving away at speed. Rob ran to the corner, but whoever it had been was nowhere in sight. When he turned back to ask the young couple what they'd seen, they were gone too.

5: Trust No-one

G RAY LAY ON his side, watching the LED colon flash on his bedside clock. Quarter to eight on a Saturday morning: Will had booked the day off, knowing he wouldn't be up to an early start after their night out, although it hadn't been too late. They'd been home before two, which was within Gray's realm of normal bedtime but a late one for a postie like Will, with multiple pints of strong scrumpy for good measure. Then they'd had to deal with the animals, doling out pills, getting Kenny into his wheels so he could go for a pee—it had taken a fair few treats to persuade the daft dog he wasn't going for a walk and to come back inside. It was going on for three by the time they made it into bed.

Given all of that, quarter to eight was probably too early to wake Will and definitely too early for Gray to be wide awake, making plans, eager to move forward now he was seeing their relationship a little more from Will's perspective. This morning, contrary to his 'once this is over' suggestion, he'd search for a removal firm that would pack up his house for him and cart everything to Will's, or everything he wanted to bring. The appliances could stay; the sofas and bed, they'd need to discuss, and it was nothing to do with the value. Gray wouldn't have cared if they'd been designer one-offs, but the furniture in the farmhouse had belonged to Will's mum, and he might not want to replace it for sentimental reasons. For as much as Gray was tempted to keep quiet about his plans so he could surprise Will, assumptions about what the other wanted or expected out of their relationship had scuppered them too many times already.

First task, then: discuss his plans with Will, *after which*, if Will was agreeable, Gray would contact a removal firm.

Now it was a case of waiting for Will to wake up. Gray's thoughts had taken him to 7:59, giving him a full minute to conclude eight o'clock was a more than decent lie-in for someone who was usually up and out the house by five-thirty. He rolled onto his back, stretched an arm behind him... and sighed.

"I should've known," he murmured into the quiet stillness of the dark room, which told him not only that Will was up, he was already out with the dogs. Perhaps that was what had woken Gray fifteen minutes ago, in which case he had about half an hour to shower, dress, make coffee and—if he was feeling confident

DEBBIE MCGOWAN

he knew what needed to be done—prepare the dogs' breakfasts. Or maybe he'd leave those to Will.

While he showered, Gray reflected on whether he was using lack of confidence as an excuse, but no. Since moving into the farmhouse, he'd learned how complex the needs of rescued animals were, particularly those liberated from labs or equally horrific situations. He paused, soapy sponge in hand, realising the connotations of his thought process. Of course he'd known illegal dog fights went on, and he'd loathed hunting for as long as he could remember, but before Will, he'd viewed animal research as vital to medical advance. He'd certainly never have described animal research facilities as 'horrific', but having witnessed Benjy bunny endure his baths so his genetically modified skin didn't erupt into cysts, Gray could think of no more accurate word.

He also realised how easy it was for a person to become radicalised. The anti-terrorism training he'd undertaken with the Met had framed radicalisation as something that happened to vulnerable individuals or those with an axe to grind. He was neither, yet he turned a blind eye to the stuff Will, Tie and their associates did, and was prepared to go along with the agreed 'going to see a man about a dog' code for anything Will judged Gray wouldn't want to know about. Often, Gray had thought they should specify some rules for that judgement: as it stood, it covered everything from Will protecting Gray against the trauma of the worst kinds of animal abuse to never putting him in a position where he'd be compelled to report that a serious crime had taken place.

Noises from downstairs brought Gray's wondering to an immediate conclusion with no decision on whether he should broach the subject. He quickly finished up in the shower, throwing the towel around him as he exited the bathroom, coming face-to-face with Will, still in his coat and boots.

"Hey," Will said, keeping his voice low. "Rob's downstairs."

Gray was too surprised to even utter a redundant 'is he?'

"He looks pretty hacked off. Thought I'd better warn you."

Gray nodded. "Thanks."

Will turned and went back downstairs, calling at normal volume, "I'll make coffee."

"OK," Gray replied and dashed into the bedroom, straight to the window, confirming Rob had come in the car, not on his bike. Either he'd been intercepted or he'd seen sense of his own volition. Gray had a good idea which it was. Not wanting to infuriate Rob more than he already had, he dried off as much as necessary to get his clothes on and gave his hair a scrub with the towel, finger-combing it on his way down to the kitchen. He stopped in the doorway to gauge the situation and figure out his next move.

Will had made the coffee in record time and was presently tackling animal breakfasts. Rob was sitting at the kitchen table, his attention ostensibly on the dogs' antics, his jaw set, brow furrowed, shoulders wide and rigid. 'Hacked off' about summed it up. Bracing for the worst, Gray entered the room.

"Good morning, Rob."

"Gray." Expression unchanging, Rob panned to Gray's location.

"Social call? Or have I forgotten—"

"You had to interfere, didn't you?"

Gray raised his hands in a shrug, affecting puzzlement. He wasn't owning up until he knew for sure that was why Rob had turned up first thing on a Saturday morning. Judging by the humourless 'ha' carried on a breath, Gray wasn't dodging it that easily.

"What? You're gonna tell me you didn't call in a favour last night? Come off it, Farrar, I know how you operate."

Farrar. So that was Rob's current mood—back in the SIU mindset. "It was for your own good."

"Is that right?" Rob asked, softening his tone to thank Will, who'd dodged across the firing line to deposit coffees on the table and then made a beeline for the door. Gray caught Will's gaze, beseeching him not to leave.

"Still got my boots on," Will said, assuring Gray he was coming back.

While Will dealt with that, Gray tentatively approached and sat in the chair diagonally opposite Rob's, waiting for Rob to say more, but evidently he was waiting for Gray to explain.

"They stopped you, I take it? I only asked them to keep an eye on you."

"Pull the other one."

"That's the truth. You said you needed to let off some steam."

"And you decided I had an ulterior motive."

"Well, didn't you?" Gray asked, continuing before Rob could answer. "You say Folden's out there somewhere, yet it didn't occur to you he might see you last night?"

"Hold up." Rob's shoulders seemed to widen by a good six inches, his fingers curling against the tabletop. "I *say* Folden's out there?"

"Now, Rob, don't—"

"You think I *imagined* it was Folden talking to Lu?"

"Of course I don't." Gray kept his tone as peaceable as he could manage when he'd put himself on a back foot. At no point in the past twelve months had he doubted Rob, or not consciously, but they couldn't prove Folden had sent the photos of Rob's nieces, and he only had Rob's say-so that it was Folden he'd heard through Lucas's Xbox.

"It *is* black coffee for you, Rob, isn't it?" Will waited for confirmation before he joined them. The question prompted both Rob and Gray to pick up their untouched mugs—Gray registered the defusion at the same moment Will said, "Sorry if I'm butting in where I'm not wanted, but Gray, didn't you ask your colleagues to keep a lookout for Rob?"

"Yes."

"Because you were worried for his safety."

"Well, yeah..." *Ah.* Therefore he must've believed him.

Rob's anger was still at the table, but he toned it down and took a mouthful of coffee. Gray did likewise and then nearly spat the coffee out again when Rob said, "At least it was only Dom Hooper."

"You saw Dom last night?"

"He was in the back of the unit that stopped me. I didn't even make it out of Holborn."

And the shocks kept on coming. "So you *were* trying to lure Folden out."

"Christ, Gray. I've got to wonder why you recruited me in the first place if you think I'm that much of a bloody idiot. If Tant's right and Folden's gone OS, he'd have got himself a passport and all that jazz."

"Ah! You went to see his barrister...Clough, is it?"

"That's him. Or it was. He's dead."

"Murdered?"

"The coroner says not, but yeah. My guess is Folden went to see him and Clough couldn't or wouldn't help him. Clough was a decent bloke—for a bent lawyer."

"Sounds like you were on friendly terms."

"Let's just say we had an understanding."

Gray didn't want to know, or not now Rob was admitting to having done something he'd kept from the SIU, but he'd thought it odd that all those dirty lawyers had secured themselves clean counsel, so much so he'd tried to dig up something on Clough, QC and found nothing. "Folden could've got a passport elsewhere," he reasoned.

"Or bypassed the border," Will chipped in. Gray gave him a sideways glance. Will pursed his lips.

"You're both right," Rob said, "which was what I was trying to establish last night. Clough didn't deal directly with the forgers, but he knew the bloke who did. I was trying to track him down when Dom pulled me over...on your orders."

"I didn't call Dom," Gray said and decided to temporarily dodge the bullet of telling Rob who he had called by following up on what he'd said he'd do. "Let me see what my Interpol guy knows." He brought up the number on his phone, still listed as *Jean's Nicolas*, and went through to the living room to make the call. A slight delay told him it was routing internationally before the not-quite-the-same ringing tone and then Nicolas's voice.

"Hello?"

"Bonjour, Nicolas. Ça va?"

"Oui, bien. Graham, good morning! How are you?"

"I'm very well, thank you."

"It's been a while."

"It has." Pre-leaving the SIU, in fact, so at least two years. "What's new with you?"

"Que du vieux," Nicolas said—effectively *same old, same old*—and they both laughed. That was pretty much the extent of Gray's conversational French, though, so for the most part the call continued in English. Gray managed a few more pleasantries, conveniently avoiding mentioning he was no longer in the police, but social calls really weren't his forte and he quickly came to the point.

"May I ask a favour of you? It's work-related."

"Sure, if I can help."

"There's a Red Notice on a patient who escaped from a secure hospital last April. I'd like to know if he's attempted to leave the UK."

"Name?"

"Anders Folden. I'll send a text with the other details—date of birth, known aliases."

"I'll see what I can discover."

"Thank you, Nicolas—merci."

"À plus." Nicolas ended the call. Gray returned to Will and Rob in the kitchen.

"He's getting back to me."

"So you were saying—about Dom," Rob said. "That you didn't call him?"

"Right. Yeah..." So much for dodging a bullet. Gray resumed his seat and picked up his coffee. But perhaps if Rob knew how many people were on their side, it might stop him flying solo again. "I called Martina Hedley."

Rob flinched, though barely. "Hedley owes no-one."

"Indeed not. But she didn't do it for me." Gray let that settle for a moment before he asked, "When did you speak to her last?"

"A while back. Do you reckon she told Dom?"

"Hard to say." More likely Dom had pulled in a favour so he could still keep tabs on them. "You should arrange to meet up with her, socially, while you're down here."

"Yeah, I might do that," Rob muttered with no indication he intended following through. He shifted on his chair, still frowning, although it was less angry, more pained. "To be honest, I had reasons other than Folden for going to see Clough last night. It was Travis's suggestion..." Rob's gaze lost focus momentarily. He shook his head. "I couldn't have been more wrong about him."

Gray glanced sidelong at Will, in this instance to see if it was just Gray being dim. Will did a kind of shrug with his face. Gray turned his attention back to Rob.

"What did Travis suggest?"

"A new start for the three of them. New town, new identities..."

"And his business?"

"He's already sounded out his nephew about taking over on a temporary-might-become-permanent basis."

"That's..." Gray tried to think of a suitable word.

"Mental?" Rob provided. "I told him that."

"You can't fault his commitment to Zoë and Lucas."

"But what if I *am* wrong, Gray, and none of this is Folden?"

"You were sure yesterday."

"Yeah, and if Dom hadn't caught up with me, I'd have set the wheels in motion. Now...I dunno. I'm not superstitious, don't believe in karma and all that crap, but maybe this isn't the right way to tackle this."

"It's drastic, I'll give you that. Did you delete Lucas's online account?"

"No, I just banned him from logging on—Zoë's mum turned off the internet just in case."

"OK. I've got an idea. You won't like it."

"Gray, if you're gonna say what I think you are, don't bother."

"We need proof it is actually Folden—record his voice—and we need to do it without him realising you're on to him."

"That would mean telling Lu what's going on."

"I'm sure you said you'd told him about Folden last year."

"No. Only that someone I put in prison had escaped and might come looking for me. As far as Lu's concerned, Tempest is a friend, nothing else. If I tell him it's Folden, not only do I risk scaring the crap out of him, I'm telling him this person he looks on as a mate is using him. I won't do that."

"Fair enough," Gray said, accepting Rob's reasoning. "Then we need to come up with another way." He sat back, nursing his coffee cup, no solutions immediately coming to mind.

Like a kid waiting to ask a question in class, Will put up his hand, which made Rob laugh in spite of the gravity of their discussion.

"Yes, Will?" Gray demurely nodded permission for him to speak. Will grinned and then addressed Rob.

"Aaron might be able to help you."

"He's got a lot on his plate already, with working for Freddie Berringer and what-have-you."

"Knowing Aaron, he's done with all the bank stuff before Freddie's even lifted his ugly mug from the pillow."

"It's not legal, though, is it? Aaron would ghost them or whatever it's called."

Will laughed. "Aaron break the law? The last time he did that, he landed Freddie as a forever friend."

"A life sentence, more like," Rob muttered bitterly.

"No argument here," Will said. "But I meant ask Aaron if he'd help you trace Tempest and maybe get him to batten down Lucas's Xbox at the same time."

"Right, yeah." Rob nodded. "That's a bit less extreme."

"Still illegal," Gray said out of the side of his mouth. Will ignored him. Rob didn't appear to have heard, and his next question gave away his thoughts.

"How is Aaron, Will?"

"Doing OK. We spoke a couple of weeks back—they asked after you too."

"Aaron did or Naomi?"

"Mmm..." Will tilted his head from side to side. "Hard to say for sure. They're very fluid at the moment."

Gray quietly observed the two men as they talked. Will was not in the least self-conscious discussing Aaron-Naomi, which was reassuring. In the past, he'd changed the subject any time Naomi came up, which had roused Gray's suspicion that Will still had feelings for her that ran deeper than friendship.

While Will was unperturbed, the same could not be said for Rob, who somehow retained the relaxed posture he'd worked so hard to achieve earlier, but what he'd said about Aaron having a lot on his plate was piffle. Rob had gone above and beyond in supporting Aaron-Naomi through the Berringers' trials and hadn't taken much persuading when it came to accompanying Naomi to see Freddie Berringer in prison. Until this morning, Gray had put it all down to Rob being a decent human being, which he was, but he was a decent human being carrying a torch for Naomi. Her continued involvement with Freddie must have been a real kick in the teeth.

"Anyway," Gray said when he'd heard enough and they weren't letting up, "I'm going to give Dom a call in a while, try and get him to talk to me."

"I can hear him now," Rob said with half a smile.

"That's on a need to know?" Gray guessed—not a wild stab in the dark. SIU leaders said it so often, almost two years on, Gray sometimes had to stop himself from saying it to students, although these days, Will merely rolled his eyes when Gray said it to him because it was entirely automatic and past being embarrassing.

Rob had finished his coffee and was making a move. "Any word from Winstanley?"

"Not yet," Gray said, but he was confident it would come within the next couple of days. He waited while Rob shook hands with Will and then followed him to the door. "Did you manage enough of a ride to get it out of your system?"

"Not really, but it'll have to do." Rob stared morosely at the blue Ford Fiesta. "Like Dom said, I wouldn't want to deprive Lucas of his dad. I just lost my head for a bit yesterday."

"Understandable. We'll get him, Rob."

"Yeah, we will." Rob strolled out to his car, raising his hand in a wave.

Gray waited to see him safely set off and then shut the door, tripping over the lead to the vacuum cleaner. He followed it into the living room. "I only did that yesterday," he complained.

"Did you see the state of Rob's jeans?" Will brushed a clump of dog hair off his thigh in demonstration of the problem.

"He won't care."

"Well, I do. Look!" He scooped another handful from the sofa. "How Holly isn't bald..." He reached for the switch on the vacuum cleaner, but Gray covered it with his hand.

"Before you do that, how attached are you to that sofa?"

"Attached? Emotionally?"

"Yeah. You know, with it being your mum's. Is it an heirloom?"

"Hair trap, don't you mean? It's been a good sofa, but I wouldn't mourn for it. Why?"

"I was thinking I could contact a removal company sooner rather than later—get them to bring the sofas here. And the bed, if you're agreeable, that is."

Will raised an eyebrow. "You're actively trying to make me say it, aren't you?"

Gray replayed what he'd said, for a moment missing what Will was getting at. He figured it out, though, when Will postponed the vacuuming briefly in favour of wrapping his arms around Gray and giving him an uncomfortably tight hug, but it was worth suffering for the smiley kiss and the murmured words that tingled his lips.

"Not a problem."

6: Nowhere Man

R OB DIDN'T WANT to go back to Tonka's, where he'd spend the rest of the day stewing in his thoughts, but he didn't know what else to do. He had a list of people he needed to see, and it remained the same post-discussion with Gray, who'd texted to say his contact at Interpol hadn't found any evidence Folden had left the country, but every one of those interactions was going to be tough, and Rob was drained.

That was the best part of being back up north: his friends were nearby and there was always someone happy to meet up for a pint and a game of pool, watch the footy or even just chat. He'd been able to rebuild his relationship with his sister and his youngest niece, support his mum and 'keep Harvey company' while she was at work, which had grim moments when Harvey got caught up in his own mortality—moments which gave Rob a chance to work through his grief for Jess and finally see her for who she'd really been, to lay the ghost to rest.

Maybe that was why he was low—a touch of homesickness. When he was up north, he was always going down south, not going home. London had never felt so lonely. The past year, living away from Lucas and being out of the police, had been like a holiday, albeit one where the knowledge that Folden was out there somewhere had constantly worried away, never too far from the front of his mind.

For that reason more than any other, Rob was no longer sure it had been Folden's voice coming out of Lucas's Xbox, and as Gray had said, there was only one way to confirm it. If Rob was wrong, then maybe he'd been wrong about the photo of Lois and Amber too, in which case the entire year of life on hold, missing Lucas, losing Naomi—all of it had been unnecessary. But if he was right...

"There's no other way," Rob confirmed aloud. The car stereo drowned his words, not that he could recall a single song that had played in the half an hour since he'd left Gray and Will. He cranked the volume another notch and tried to listen, focusing on the insubstantial bass coming out of the tinny factory-fitted speakers—yet more evidence of the stopgap his life had become or else he'd have pimped the sound system if nothing else.

Now he was resigned to using Lucas to confirm 'Tempest' was Anders Folden, Rob started figuring out what needed to be in place first to protect his son—himself too—and switched route accordingly, making the call, hands-free. At least this crappy little car had that functionality.

The line rang out once before it was picked up.

"Miller got it bang on with Scarlet Pimpernel."

Rob chuckled. "Guilty as charged, Ma'am."

"Christ, Rob, you've been out a year and you're still calling me that?"

"Nah, mate. Just winding you up. How's it going?"

"Not bad. Where are you? Still up north?"

"You know I'm not."

"I do," Martina admitted straight up. "What the hell were you thinking?"

"I wasn't."

"Like a compulsion with you, that bloody bike—a biological need."

"Something like that." Exactly that, in fact. "Listen, are you free anytime today?"

"All of it for you, Rob." Martina's tone turned sultry—the usual wind-up, to Rob's relief.

"Does your wife know about us?" he bantered back, and Martina laughed.

"Not yet. What time are you thinking?"

"Whenever suits. I'm about twenty minutes away from the station, thirty from your gaff—unless you fancy meeting for lunch?"

"Yeah, let's do lunch. I'm at work—should be done around twelve. How's that?"

"Perfect," Rob said. He'd forgone breakfast to go and see Gray; an early lunch suited him just fine.

"Shall we meet here or...?"

"Works for me. I'll see you at twelve."

"See you then. Oh, and Rob? Don't do anything stupid."

"I'll do my best." Rob was smiling as he ended the call. He'd spoken to Martina just once in the past year, a couple of weeks after he'd played his part in sabotaging the case against Freddie Berringer—for no good reason, as it turned out. She'd have every right to hold a grudge, but she didn't, and Rob couldn't have been happier. Sure, she'd give him hell over lunch; it was no less than he deserved. But their friendship had survived. More than that, as Gray had said when they'd hatched the plan to get Berringer released, they needed all the allies they could get—*if* Folden was as close as Rob believed.

He had a couple of hours to kill before he met up with Martina, and he still didn't want to go back to Tonka's, even though he'd slept like a log in Tonka's whopper of a superking-size bed, and the shower was top-notch, as was everything else in that house, but being on his own, he'd be tempted to 'do something stupid'. Instead, he went with the lesser of two evils and headed for Marylebone: where Freddie Berringer resided when he was 'in the ton'. *Arsehole.* He wasn't even being pretentious.

As he had the previous morning, Rob parked opposite Berringer's apartment building—a red-brick half-block of West End real estate protected by spiked black iron railings at ground level and pointed arches reminiscent of crenellations across the roof. Unlike the previous morning, when he'd sat, phone in hand, watching Berringer's apartment windows, he got out of the car.

Even as he locked up and crossed the street, he was asking himself if it was worth it. If he was wrong about Folden, then no, it wasn't worth it. Yet curiosity egged him on. Curiosity along with an almost unbeatable urge to follow his heart instead of gut instinct. And then he was pushing the doorbell next to the art deco door, his gaze drawn to his fragmented reflection in the polished brass inlay and to the concierge eyeing him from the desk across the foyer. The door buzzed to admit him; Rob inhaled deeply and passed through the portal of the Filthy Rich.

He approached the desk under the constant scrutiny of the older and rather stately uniformed man behind it. "Good morning. I'm here to see Aaron Tanner."

The concierge glanced down under the desk and frowned. "Is Mr. Tanner expecting you, sir?"

"No, he isn't."

"I see. One moment, please." The man picked up an old-fashioned phone receiver and put it to his ear but didn't place a call. "Can I see your badge, please?"

Automatically, Rob reached inside his jacket, slowly easing his hand out again when his brain checked back in. *How to get out of this one without looking even more of an idiot...* Lying crossed his mind. "I'm not here on police business," he said, which was ambiguous enough, should the concierge be under orders to turn away strangers. "Tell Mr. Tanner that Mr. Simpson-Stone's here to see him, please?"

The concierge snuffed air from his nose and pushed some buttons on the phone. He must've been hard of hearing as the ringing out was easily as loud as a phone on speaker. Thus, Rob heard someone pick up at the other end and say "Hello?" Whilst he recognised the voice as belonging to Aaron-Naomi, he couldn't have identified which with any certainty. Whoever it was, they gave the instruction to send Rob up to the apartment.

The concierge offered Rob a forced but polite smile as he put down the receiver. "Have you been here before?"

"I have, yes. Number three, first floor?"

"That is correct." Still reluctant, the concierge pointed to a door across the foyer. "I'll let you through." The door release was already buzzing.

"Thanks." Rob strode away before the man changed his mind.

As minted as the occupants of the building were, it was bloody draughty, and it took a fair bit of effort to pull the door open. The gust coming down the stairs hit Rob in the face so hard he blinked against it. The stairs, too, he'd noticed last time, were worn smooth to the point of precariousness, and he kept hold of the cold, brass banister up the two flights to the first floor, pausing on the landing to get his bearings while the old adage about places looking different in the dark played out in real-time because in daylight, he couldn't for the life of him remember which of the four doors was Berringer's. None of them bore a number, and were it not for one opening, he'd have had to knock on them all.

"Rob, hi." The greeting was accompanied by a wide smile—pleased possibly. Surprised for sure.

"Hi," Rob replied, playing it safe as he couldn't work out who he was talking to. He'd spent time with Aaron; he'd spent time with Naomi; he'd seen them shift from one to the other. *Sometimes we're whole...we interlock.* "It's good to see you."

"And you," they said. "Come on in." They moved aside and gestured, more expansive than Aaron, less self-assured than Naomi. "Freddie's not here."

Rob nodded, unseen, and accepted the invitation.

"Coffee?"

"Yeah, that'd be great, cheers."

Again, there was that smile and then an inquisitive frown. "Are you all right?"

"Yeah..." Rob began but decided to come clean. "I'm sorry. What do I call you?"

"Oh." A self-conscious laugh. "Aaron? That's probably easiest for you."

"Not Aaronaomi?"

"You remember."

"Of course I remember."

They chewed their lower lip in thought and after a moment shrugged. "I prefer Ari."

"Ari. Got it."

"I'll make that coffee."

"OK."

Ari left Rob standing in the hall and disappeared through a doorway, calling back as a clear afterthought, "You can join me or go and sit in the lounge." They reappeared. "Sorry. I'm not used to entertaining visitors."

"No worries," Rob assured them with a smile. At least they were feeling equally awkward.

"Coffee," Ari said and disappeared again. Rob followed them into the very modern, blindingly bright kitchen.

"No housekeeper?" he asked.

"She's gone to collect Freddie's dry-cleaning." Ari pushed a button on top of an enormous coffee machine and turned their head only, enough to make eye contact. "So stereotypical, isn't it?"

"Yeah," Rob answered vaguely, admonishing himself for analysing their every gesture. He switched to taking in the room. It was much warmer than the stairwell had been, but it felt unlived in, unloved. Granted, not every kitchen was filled with the welcoming spiciness of his mum's or the chilled vibes of Will's, but Berringer's was clinical and superficial, like an IKEA demonstration.

"How did you know?" Ari asked, still with their back to Rob.

"Hmm?"

They turned around, leaning against the cupboard, arms loosely folded. "You recognised I wasn't Aaron."

"Right, yeah." Rob couldn't explain. Ari was wearing a T-shirt and jeans, socks, no shoes, no make-up, just-got-out-of-bed hair. To all intents and purposes, Rob was looking at Aaron, but there was something that wasn't Aaron, and it was more than the absence of social anxiety.

"The new T-shirt?" Ari suggested with a coy grin.

Rob chuckled. "Maybe." There was still more, but it eased the tension between them. "I've missed you," he admitted.

"Naomi, you mean?"

"No." Perhaps he'd been too open. Certainly, he hadn't meant to say it, but he did miss them, not just what might have been with Naomi. Circumstance had screwed any chance he had at that. Circumstance and Freddie.

The coffee rescued Rob from sharing that bit with Ari too, or it would've done if he'd let it go. They handed him a cup and led the way through to the lounge—a room Rob had turned over in the search for evidence to substantiate Berringer had killed a hunt saboteur even though he'd already admitted it—'in self-defence'—and they had video footage. However, Berringer hadn't just got Rob's back up; he'd royally pissed off Martina, and she'd made his life as miserable as she could, within the confines of the law. If London still had village stocks, she'd have stuck Berringer in them and left him to the crows. Given all of that and Rob's part in setting Freddie free, it was, frankly, astonishing Martina was talking to him at all, never mind meeting him for lunch.

"I hope we're still friends," he said, his thoughts about Martina, Naomi and Aaron converging. "I should've called." Getting Lucas and Zoë to safety, searching the wine bar where Folden took the photo of Lois and Amber, ferrying Harvey to and from the hospital, keeping up his side of the business...he'd hardly had a minute, but he'd thought about Naomi often. "It's been a hell of a year," he said. "I'm sorry."

"It's OK, Rob. I told you I wasn't going anywhere."

Except you did. Rob went with the less spiteful, "The last time I saw Aaron was at Charles Berringer's remand hearing, and we couldn't really talk. And Naomi...well..." He shut up. He'd always seen Aaron and Naomi as two different people, to the extent he had to remind himself that anything Aaron told him, Naomi already knew, which didn't stop him telling her, then having to follow up with, "But you already knew that." They'd laughed about it enough for Rob to no longer worry he'd offended her—she'd said she appreciated his sensitivity to who she and Aaron were—but faced with Ari, Rob was thrown off his game. It was like meeting up with an old friend, all the ways they'd changed over the years mingling with the familiarity of the person they'd been way back. With Ari, Rob didn't know how to act.

"I should've done better at keeping in touch, but I kept putting it off," he said.

"Because of Freddie."

Rob nodded. "To be honest, I didn't expect you to leave him. You've been together a long time, and wanker that he is, he looks after you."

"Rob—"

"As long as we're still mates..."

"We are."

"Good." Rob took a mouthful of coffee, drawing a line. He hadn't come here to rekindle what had almost been. He and Naomi had shared one kiss and a promise that when it was all over, they'd come back to whatever was happening between them, but nothing had changed. She was still with Freddie and Folden was still at large.

For a few minutes, they sat in silence, like ex-lovers waiting for the same train, trying not to see each other, to acknowledge their shared history. The silence took on a substance of its own, thickened, became stifling.

"Nice space," Rob said, giving the lounge the same treatment he'd given the kitchen, and heard Ari exhale, venting their tension.

"Yes. Although I don't often come into this room. Nor does Freddie." They smoothed the arm of the large, modern chair in which they were sitting. "When he's here at all."

Rob wasn't sure what to do with that statement so he chose to ignore it. "Where's your tech gear?"

"In the office—a closet, essentially—at the back of the dining room. I can show you if you like."

"Why?"

They smiled and shook their head—more Naomi, less Aaron. "I don't know. Rob...I don't wish to be brash, but what is it you want?"

"I need your help. Or advice, at least."

"With?"

"Tracing an online gamer. A dangerous man."

"This is to do with what happened last year, isn't it?"

"Yeah, it is. I need to find this guy before he finds me...or my family."

"Don't the police have them in some kind of protective custody?"

"Not anymore." How to explain? Rob hadn't told Naomi about Folden, purely because there'd been no opportunity to do so. He wanted to tell her now, or tell Ari, which amounted to the same thing, but if he so much as cracked open the floodgates, it would all come rushing out—his barely contained anger at Gray, his fear for his son's safety, the jealousy and regret for leaving Aaron-Naomi at Freddie's beck and call, the desire to hunt down Folden...

A warm hand grasped his, pulling him back from the brink.

"Tell me as much as you feel able," Ari said, keeping hold of Rob's hand—more a fist—as he took a few slow, deep breaths, focusing on bringing his emotions under control.

"I don't know where to start."

"What brought you here today?"

"Well...I came down yesterday to help Zoë and Lucas move back home. Zoë hated the flat the Met sorted out, so she's been staying at her parents' place with Lu, and her fiancé has been kipping in his warehouse. When I got there, Lu was on his Xbox, playing some multiplayer online game. The guy he was talking to...I recognised his voice. It's someone I put away."

"Is he still in prison?"

"No. He was transferred to a secure hospital—some bullshit mental illness. He's a psycho, but he knows what he's doing. Remember the night I came over, just before I went back up north?" No point playing coy. "The night we kissed."

"Yes, I remember," Ari said. "Fondly."

Rob smiled, briefly. "That was the day I found out he'd escaped. A week later, he sent me a photo of my nieces on a night out, then nothing for twelve months, now this. I've got no proof it's him—even Gray's doubting me—but I know it is. I just know." As sure as he knew he still had feelings for Naomi and, it seemed, Ari.

"What do the police say? Your old boss—Detective Hedley—have you spoken to her?"

"Not yet. I'm seeing her today—for lunch."

"Ohh...good luck!" Ari grimaced on Rob's behalf. They'd experienced Martina in battle mode.

"Thanks. I'm gonna need it. She's still gunning for me over screwing Freddie's trial."

"OK." In one graceful move, Ari uncrossed their legs and rose from the sofa. "Let's see if we can find this man." When Rob didn't move, they tugged his hand. "Are you coming or staying here?"

"Can I bring my coffee?"

A raised eyebrow was all the response he got. Rob took a quick gulp of his coffee and abandoned the rest. He didn't want to waste a second of Ari's company.

They'd taken no more than three steps along the hall when the apartment door opened, admitting one dishevelled, unsteady Freddie Berringer. Jacket over his shoulder, tie knot halfway down his chest, large stains on the front of his shirt—wine, if the alcoholic through-draught was anything to go by—he bumped the door shut when he rocked back against it, squinting in their direction.

"Mr. Simpson-Stone? What an unexpected and absolute pleasure!"

"Freddie," Rob acknowledged nasally. The man stank to high heaven, and not just of alcohol. Of sex.

"It's been a while." Freddie bounced off the door and tumbled towards them. "Where've you been hiding?" He stopped a foot in front of Rob and acted out looking him up and down, but his eyes were playing helter-skelter.

"Up north."

Freddie nodded, wobbled and stepped off again, knocking into Rob as he passed him. "I'm going to bed." He stopped next to Ari and leaned in until his lips were against their ear. "Coming, sweetcheeks?" He stumbled on, calling back, "Bring him if you want."

They both watched him go.

Ari swivelled slowly to face Rob, utterly horrified.

Not in a million years, Rob mouthed, and they both laughed—silently, such as it mattered. Within seconds, loud snores rumbled from the doorway through which Freddie had fallen. "Should I go?" Rob asked.

"No. He'll be out of it for the rest of the day."

"Are you sure?"

"I'm sure." Reinstating their grip on Rob's hand, Ari steered him past the dragon's den and onwards through the dining room to the 'closet' that served as Aaron's office.

7: A Good Thing

I T'S DONE." GRAY came back into the kitchen and tossed his phone down on the narrow sliver of table that wasn't covered in paperwork.

"What is?" Will asked without looking up.

"I've booked a furniture removal firm."

"Uh-huh."

"For Tuesday."

"OK."

"Are you listening?"

"Yep."

"Then can you give me a hand clearing some room for my collection of fur-lined smoking jackets? I say collection—it's only two, but they're quite dense and take up a lot of space."

"Sure."

"Will?"

He sighed and looked up. "There's space for them in the furnace."

"Oh, so you were listening."

"Yep, but I'm also trying to keep numbers in my head."

"In that case, I'll get out of your way."

"Thanks."

Disheartened, Gray picked up his phone and ambled away to the living room where he was no more welcome than he'd been in the kitchen and had to balance on the edge of the chair because Holly was in it and the rest of the dogs were taking up the entire four-seater sofa. The sofas Gray was bringing were both three-seaters, which would give them one more sitting space—for one more dog, knowing Will. Of the six he had currently, only three were from the five he'd had when Gray first met the pack. Within weeks of 'Nev the Naughty' staffy passing, 'Bailey the Obedient unless another dog tries to mount him' staffy arrived, went to a new home, came back, went to another new home, came back...stayed.

Then there was Holly—a tiny, timid terrier with half an ear and one seeing eye, and with whom Gray spent the most time sharing chairs and beds. She was the sweetest little thing, second only in Gray's heart to paraplegic Kenny, a large brownish-black mongrel, part Irish wolfhound and by far the biggest member of the pack. Monster the collie cross had passed the previous summer, leaving Kenny, Dotty Doris the Patterdale terrier and Fido the Heinz 57 the three from the original pack. The other newbie was a lunatic border collie who'd been with them less than a month and would presently be out under the caravan. Will was gently teaching her she was allowed inside, but she'd been a working dog for all of her ten years. It was a lot of training to undo—if it could even be undone.

Gray's new reality hit him then, not like a sledgehammer; more a soft pillow around the head. He was giving up a newly refurbished house in central London for a somewhat tumbledown cottage in the commuter belt, sharing a bed with a postie/animal rights activist/former investment banker, six dogs, four guinea pigs, a psychotic parakeet, half a dozen chickens and a genetically modified rabbit. Granted, he usually only shared the bed with Will and the dogs, sometimes the rabbit, but for someone who'd never even had a pet goldfish, it had taken some getting used to. While he wouldn't give it up for anything—would give his life for Will and his menagerie—he was starkly aware he was surrendering the only place to which he'd been able to escape for a few hours' peace.

In light of all that, Will's disinterest was bothering him a lot more than it ought. Or perhaps it was the absence of a call from Winstanley, plus the fact that every time Gray's phone buzzed, he jumped, as did the more skittish members of the pack. As if to prove the point, his phone vibrated in his hand, and Holly leapt over the arm of the chair and sprinted from the room. Gray watched her go and then frowned at his screen.

Not Winstanley; a text message from Rob.

> Followed yours and Will's advice. AT locking down XB – can trace the target. Lunch with MH. TTYL.

Gray was still trying to decipher the abbreviations when Will came into the room, sat on the sofa arm closest to the door and said, "You look smug."

"Do I?"

"Was that Winstanley?"

"No. Rob. He's with Aaron—or he was. He might be having lunch with MH by now, whoever that is."

"Martina?" Will suggested.

Gray tutted at himself. "Obvious, now you've said it. I guess he really did follow our advice."

"Good on him. How'd it go with Aaron? Did he say?"

"Very well, if I've interpreted correctly. Aaron's securing Lucas's Xbox and thinks he can trace Folden."

"Tempest," Will corrected. "You don't know it's Folden."

"Potato, pot-ah-to."

"See? I knew you believed Rob."

"I didn't doubt him for one second, smarty pants."

Will smirked and said nothing.

"Now who's looking smug?"

"Are you going to tell me about this removal van?"

"Have you written down your numbers?"

"Nope. I don't need them anymore."

"What were you doing?"

"Seeing if I've got enough in my savings accounts to pay for Suzannah's Sweet Sixteen. She wants a beach party—surfing, fire dancers, barbecue, lights, music..."

"Sounds expensive."

Will nodded noncommittally and looked along the length of the dog-loaded sofa. "Do we need to move this before Tuesday?"

"Depends. Do you want to rehome it?"

"It's knackered, Gray." Will bent down and lifted the corner of the fabric across the sofa base where the stitching had come away and continued to do so with an ominous ripping sound. "Recycling centre for you, my old friend." He patted the cushion, sending up a plume of dust and dog hair.

Gray was struck by the sudden, wholly imagined sensation of having a hair in his mouth. "I could ask the guys to take it away with them," he suggested, pinching at his hair-free tongue.

"Great," Will agreed immediately.

"I can also contribute to Suzannah's birthday."

"You don't need to."

"I want to."

"Are we keeping both beds? Which is more comfortable? You've slept in them both."

"And he deflects again."

Will sighed and slapped his hands on his thighs, pressing down hard enough for his feet to slide across the floor. "I don't want to talk about it."

"Why?" Gray asked. Paul the psychotic parakeet chipped in with, "Why? Why? Be quiet! Hello, Paul."

Will scowled at the bird. "Because...I have a problem with it, and it is my problem, not yours."

"Because she's your daughter, not mine? We're cohabiting. Sharing the load."

"You already pay more than half of the bills. And you're still paying the bills on your place."

Gray unlocked his phone and scrolled through the apps until he found the one that connected to the smart meters in his house. "Look." He turned the phone to show Will the digital dial representing his electricity usage, the needle hovering around the number two. "It's pennies a day. I can afford to cover my share here."

"That doesn't mean I have to be happy about it," Will grumbled. "I was thinking, maybe I should apply for another job in the city."

"Really?" Gray couldn't decide if this was still deflection from the real issue, although he couldn't figure out what that was. It seemed unlikely Will was unhappy with Gray doing something for Suzannah. He'd said them getting along was more than he could've hoped for. "It's an option, I guess," Gray said.

"I'll make a few calls on Monday while I'm off—pity it's not Tuesday or I could've come into the city with you and gone hobnobbing while you're overseeing your furniture guys."

"I won't be overseeing them. I need to email them a list of what needs moving, and they'll pack it up and bring it."

"How are they going to get into your house? Won't you need to go over with the keys?"

"They're sending a courier to pick them up."

"That can't have come cheap."

"It wasn't extortionate," Gray argued. This was definitely deflection, but as he'd discovered in the car the previous evening, if Will couldn't physically escape, Gray could whittle away at him, keep bringing the discussion back to the point at which Will had derailed it, and eventually he'd come clean, or he had about his feelings on Gray keeping his house. It was worth persevering. "So how much is this party going to cost?"

"Not sure, but it'll be in the thousands. Shelley's asked Suzannah to write down who she wants to invite, as it depends on how many are coming."

"And will you tell me once you know?"

"Sure," Will agreed too easily. Gray didn't like the nonchalance one bit, and now Will was on his feet. "I'll make lunch. What do you fancy?" He reached for the door, but Gray was ready for it. He leapt from the chair almost as quickly as Holly had and dashed across the room, blocking the exit. Will dangled his arms like a huffy teenager. "Gray, I'm hungry!"

"OK. I'll let you go and make lunch on the proviso we sit and we talk, and you tell me what's on your mind."

"Do I have any choice?"

"Yes. But as my therapist says, honesty is a good thing."

Will's eyebrows rose by the tiniest fraction, and his eyes changed, pupils dilating, his normally relaxed posture stiffening visibly. "Doctor Josh or your *actual* therapist?"

Gray relented. "Forget it. Let's just eat lunch." He stepped aside, expecting Will to leave. When he didn't, Gray shrugged in query.

"Honesty?" Will said. Gray nodded, still prepared to let him off the hook. "This thing with Rob and Folden—what if it's still going on in August? I can't ask Suzannah to hold off on celebrating her sixteenth birthday."

"I'm not suggesting you should."

"You're not going to be at the party, are you, if Folden's still on the loose?"

"Oh, I am, Will. She's only sixteen once."

"So...what? You'll leave Rob to fend for himself?"

"It's only one day—"

"Plus a day's travel—"

"Two days, then—"

"—and back."

"Three days, five, a week—I'm sure Rob can manage without me." Just as sure as he was that this had nothing to do with him missing the party. It was about him choosing someone or something else over Will. Of course he wouldn't leave Rob to fend for himself, but he wouldn't let Suzannah down either, or Will. If it came to the crunch...he had no idea, but he'd find a way.

***

"Click the 'connect' button now, Zoë."

Rob had watched her via the smaller screen to the left of the two massive monitors, executing Ari's many instructions. They were straightforward enough that Rob thought he could have followed them too, but Zoë's frown persisted. He'd noticed yesterday that she had more lines around her eyes, dark shadows beneath them, a few grey hairs. He wanted to believe they were normal signs of ageing and tried to recollect when he'd spotted his first grey hair.

"It's connected," she said. "What next?"

Ari tapped a few keys, eyes on the text scrolling up one screen, then tapped a few more. They nodded. "That's it. The Xbox is now connected via a VPN."

They'd already explained how it worked, not that Rob could even pretend to understand, but he'd got the gist. Unfortunately, Ari had confirmed that 'Tempest' was also using a VPN, and they could hack it, but it would take time. Rob wasn't sure how much of that they had. He'd seen how Folden operated: he'd set his sights on Campion's inheritance long before the SIU caught up with him, and it had been another two years before he'd murdered

Campion, but that was only phase two. Phase three—getting his hands on the money—had taken a further year. Folden played the long game, and there was no predicting when he'd strike.

"What do I tell Lu?" Zoë asked. "He's going to notice Tempest is never online when he is."

"There's no need to tell him anything, Zo."

"Or if Tempest sends him a text message?"

"I'll intercept and respond to it," Ari said.

Zoë looked pained. "You've already done so much."

"It's nothing." They turned, meeting Rob's gaze.

"Zo's right. This is above and beyond."

"Anything for Lucas." Ari's smile—Naomi's smile—made Rob's heart skip a beat. He couldn't look away. Things could've been so different.

"It's not nothing..." Zoë said, and Rob snapped out of it, glimpsing her curiosity before she shut it down. "Thank you."

"You're welcome." Ari made busy, escaping Zoë's sizing up of the situation.

Rob had no such luxury. She tilted her head in an unspoken question she'd no doubt be asking later. "Travis and Lu will be back soon."

"Yeah, I need to make a move too."

"Do I just logout?"

"Yes," Ari answered.

"OK. Thanks again. See you later, Rob."

"You will."

Zoë's face disappeared from the small screen, and Rob vented a long breath. "I'm going to get the third degree."

Ari nodded in agreement, still typing away.

Rob switched his focus to the strings of text and numbers. "I did computer studies at school."

"So did I."

"I bet you didn't spend three months inputting thousands of lines of BASIC from a magazine only to get the message 'syntax error at line whatever'."

"No, I spent three months inputting my own code—same end result."

Rob chuckled, enjoying the effortless conversation. In this tiny, air-conditioned cupboard filled with tech, where the slightest muscle twitch resulted in contact, he was at ease for the first time in months and in awe of Ari's talent. They'd set up Lucas's Xbox account so he wouldn't show as online when Tempest was, effectively blocking him on a temporary basis, unblocking him at random intervals when he was offline so it appeared as if they kept missing each other. Folden wasn't stupid; he'd figure it out, but this would buy them a few more days while they waited for Winstanley to make contact, if he ever did. In the meantime, Lucas's connection was encrypted, making it almost impossible for someone to pinpoint his location from his online activity. Of course, Folden could already know where to find Lucas and was simply waiting for the optimum moment to make his move, but Rob couldn't think about that.

"I guess I'd best make tracks or I'll be late for my lunch date."

The tapping stopped. "A date?"

"With Martina Hedley."

"Oh, yes. You mentioned it earlier." The tapping resumed a little more jerkily than before.

"Problem?"

"You didn't say it was a date."

Rob grimaced, unseen. Ari's back was fully to him. "It was a figure of speech. Look, Nao—Ari…" Rob rubbed his hands over his face, the tension returning. "OK. For one thing, Martina's happily married, and she's gay, so that's a non-starter whichever way you look at it. For another, you and Freddie—"

"Are the same as we ever were—the same as when you and I kissed."

"Freddie was in prison," Rob argued, backtracking slightly with, "but I get what you're saying. It's like a business arrangement."

"Mostly it is precisely that."

"You don't sleep together."

"Are you asking, Rob?"

"What would be the point? We still can't take this anywhere." But he wanted to. So much. The images in his head right now…if only Ari knew. Skin on skin, goosebumps and nipples erect from the cool air and arousal, hot breath, soft lips, grinding against the wall, falling to the floor…

"Until Folden's back behind bars," Ari interrupted the fantasy as Rob's imagination presented him with a vision of Freddie swinging the door open and leering down at them, lip curled. That got Rob's libido in check pretty damn quick.

"Yeah," he confirmed, cheeks burning, heart still pounding. "I need to go."

"You go. I'll keep cracking at Tempest."

"Cheers." Rob stood and stretched his back. Ari stood too but kept their distance. "Keep me posted. In fact…do you use Sigma-SMS?"

They made a *pfft* sound and shook their head. "Five years ago. May I have your phone?"

Rob compliantly dug it out of his pocket and handed it over, impressed but no longer surprised by how deftly Ari thumbed through different screens. They leaned down to their computer and clicked a couple of keys. A progress bar zipped from zero to full, something pinged, and they handed Rob's phone back.

"Secure IM. I took the liberty of sending it to Gray and Zoë too. I hope you don't mind."

"I don't. I can't speak for them, but I'm sure it's fine. Thanks. Again. I owe you one, big time."

Ari smiled and kissed Rob's cheek. "I'll be here, waiting to collect."

8: Upping Gears

"WOULD YOU ADAM and Eve it? He actually turned up!"
Martina slid her phone into her blazer pocket and took a couple of steps towards Rob, who didn't dwell on the whys or wherefores before he hugged her, right there outside the police station—his former boss, a friend he'd been sure he'd lost. She returned the hug swiftly and patted him on the back, a little cool with him.

"Where are we going?" she asked. "Have you decided?"

"Is that Chinese place still open? The one with the lunch buffet?"

"Under new management, but yes, it's still open."

"Then let's go there—unless you've got a preference?"

"I'm easy," Martina said breezily, following up with, "Don't say it," as they moved off.

"I wasn't gonna say anything."

"But you thought it."

"As if I'd dare!" Rob protested, laughing. If she hadn't mentioned it, it wouldn't even have entered his head. "Your car or mine?"

"No bike? Damn."

"You're bloody hilarious. For that, you can drive."

Martina grinned. "I'm pleased you said that. Wait till you see my new car."

"Oh?" Rob was intrigued, but she wasn't telling. She adjusted their course towards the staff car park. "Oh!" Rob said again when he saw it, gleaming red amid a sea of black, silver and mute blue. "Nice!" Cars had never been his thing, but Martina was a bit of a petrol-head on the sly, and she'd landed herself a top motor: a spanky new Mercedes Roadster. "Must've been a decent pay rise this time around," he muttered in jest.

"That and a dead dad," Martina said. She opened the driver's door and bobbed out of sight.

Resisting the urge to bang his head on the roof, Rob climbed in beside her. "I'm sorry. I didn't know."

"How would you? 'Keep in touch, Rob.'—'I will, mate. I promise.'"

Rob had no defence, or none worth offering. Visiting Ari had confirmed he hadn't shoved them into the shark's mouth and lifted some of Rob's guilt for his part in getting Freddie Berringer out of prison, but he'd compromised his principles. Martina was about as likely to forgive him for that as he was to forgive himself.

"He was a heavy drinker, my dad," she said, and Rob got the impression she'd done it to save him from self-damnation. "We knew it was coming."

"But still, I should've known," Rob said. He fastened his seat belt. "When did he pass?"

"Last July. To be fair, he'd stopped drinking about five years before, but the damage was already done." She started the engine, shifted into reverse and arced smoothly out of the space. "And it's better for Mum, or it will be once she ditches the old widow weeds. She put up with it a long, long time—I don't know how she didn't divorce him." Martina paused briefly in thought, gave a quiet laugh and shook her head. Back into drive, she moved off, seemingly unaware of the gaggle of admirers loitering outside the station. "Anyway, enough of that. How's Harvey doing?"

"OK. He had his last lot of radiotherapy a couple of months ago, but he's still suffering with fatigue—that's normal, apparently—so my mum's gonna be walking the dog until…" Rob had almost said 'until I get home', but there was no telling when that would be. Despite the oncologist's reassurance that Harvey *should* make a full recovery, Rob hadn't wanted to leave his mum on her own. More selfishly, he'd almost had a life during the past year, one that didn't revolve around working all hours only to barely cover his rent and maintenance for Lucas. He'd reconnected with his old buddies and finally got back to playing footy.

Maybe it was time to think about relocating. True, he'd see less of Lucas, but it would also give him a reason to get out on the bike for a few hours every other weekend, and he'd need to seriously consider the logistics of keeping the investigation business running. They'd been lucky in that they'd had a string of jobs involving internet research and virtual spying, and Rob had been able to pull his weight by working on those while Gray dealt with the face-to-face stuff, but that wouldn't always be the case, although, again, he could commute as and when.

It dawned on him he'd been weighing up the pros and cons of moving back up north permanently for some time—not just today—and the pros had been winning until he'd seen Ari. Now he wasn't sure he wanted to go back at all.

The car stopped at a junction, and Martina glanced at him. "Penny for them."

"Nah. They're not worth that much. I'm digging the ambient glow, by the way." Rob ran his fingertip over the red strip along the underside of the dash. It had been a blatant and poor change of subject, but Martina didn't push him. "So how much did Gray tell you?"

"That depends what's gone on."

"Did he tell you about Folden cyber-stalking Lu?"

"You're sure it's Folden?"

Rob's temper flared, but he quickly got it in check. "I'm getting sick of people asking me that. I was stuck with the bloke for three years." He still heard him sometimes, an echo lingering in the dark that mercifully faded with the nightmare. "I know his voice."

"I believe you."

"Thank God. That's one of you."

"Is that a spot of paranoia there, Rob?"

"The new head of the SIU didn't want to know."

"I heard it's being shut down."

"From Dom?"

"Dom...?"

"Seriously?" Rob shook his head.

"Seriously, who the hell's Dom?"

"DCI Dom Hooper—he took over from Gray."

"I'll take your word for it." Martina scowled at the still red traffic light.

"Then how do you know about the SIU shutting down?"

"And I was kidding about paranoia. Jesus, Rob. I'm married to the woman who holds the Met's purse strings, and the SIU's in the next round of cuts. They don't have the resources to go after Folden. But Dom Hooper—I never even met the guy, or not that I recall."

"That's interesting because he was there last night, in the back of the Traffic unit."

"Maybe Gray told him."

"He says not."

"Well, I'm telling you—all I did was asked Traffic to let me know if they saw you." Martina turned on the stereo, ending any further discussion on that topic.

At last, the lights shifted to green, and Rob attempted to chill out, listening to the music—piano and a woman's voice, determined, mesmerising—pretty powerful stuff.

"Who's this?" he asked.

"Mary Lambert."

It wasn't the sort of thing he normally listened to, but he was enjoying it enough to be disappointed when Martina stopped and switched off

DEBBIE MCGOWAN

the ignition, taking the music away. He made a mental note to look up Mary Lambert later and unfastened his seat belt. "We could've walked it."

"We could," Martina agreed, "but then you'd have missed out on the ride."

"Fair comment." He reached for the door handle.

"Before we go in…" Martina said and waited for his attention. "The Berringer shit show—was it worth it?"

He'd hoped she wouldn't ask, and he was tempted to tell her they wouldn't have known Folden had escaped without Will's intel, which he couldn't have got without Berringer's assistance. She'd never know it was a lie, but Rob would. "I wish I could say it was."

"Well, if it's any consolation, Berringer would likely have walked free anyway. Expensive lawyer, friends in high places…" She turned so she could make eye contact. "There's something else you should know." She left him a 'chance to prepare' pause, and Rob braced. "Charles Berringer also walked free."

Not as shocking as he'd expected. "Your dad's doing?" he guessed. At the prison visit, Freddie had hinted his father had something on Martina's—they were former Etonians or some such—but Rob hadn't pushed for details. He wasn't sure he wanted to know now, or certainly not enough to interrogate Martina. He appreciated her telling him she'd bent a few rules too, not in so many words, but it was there between the lines, and it put them on an even keel as regards going against their morals.

"We've got to let it go, Rob. Scum like the Berringers always get away with murder. Literally."

"True enough. Can we eat now?" Rob's belly gave a loud grumble in support of that idea. Martina blinked at him like he'd done it on purpose. He gave her a cheesy grin.

"Come on, then," she said. "I'm paying."

"Yeah, right." Not if he had anything to do with it, but she was already out of the car. They could fight it out when the bill arrived.

The restaurant was busy but not crammed, and they were taken to a table right away, where they ordered soft drinks. Once the waiter delivered their plates and cutlery, they raided the buffet.

"Oh, look at that." Martina nodded to a section of counter separated from the rest. "We could've invited Gray and…what's his name again?"

"Will Richards."

"That's it. I can never bloody remember. I don't know why."

Rob didn't know why either, considering Martina had interviewed Will twice and she was one of the best detectives on the force, in Rob's humble opinion. "So, apart from a declining conviction rate and budget cuts all over the shop, what's the latest?" he asked, loading up with spring rolls—from the veggie counter because they looked tastier than the non-veggie version.

"Not a lot—oh! Actually, have you heard about Miller?"

"What's he done this time?" They continued along the counter as they talked.

"Enough to get him suspended."

"Blimey. Sounds serious."

"It's typical Miller, nothing out the ordinary. He used a racist slur when he was bantering with Tang, but we're cracking down on casual discrimination, so I hauled him in. It's wrong of me, I know, but if I'd thought about it, I'd have just kicked him up the arse. He was already on a written warning after calling Aaron Tanner...well, you know what, and I sent him on the diversity training, but it doesn't work on Miller's type. So now we're waiting for a formal disciplinary hearing. Serves him right. Bloody dimwit."

"Yeah, maybe not, Ma...Martina. Crap. I thought I'd nailed that." Martina gave him a look. "I'm not saying Miller should get off with it, but... well, you just used a slur without realising."

"What did I say?"

"Dimwit?"

"Shit, yeah." They'd reached the end of the counter, which was as well, as their plates were full to capacity. "But that's what I mean," Martina continued when they got back to their table. "These terms are entrenched in our culture, and of course we have to challenge it or it'll never change, but it doesn't seem fair to punish someone like Miller, who's been in the job thirty-five years. If I can't get it right, it's got to be like learning a whole new language to him. But the federation are aiming to get him out on retirement before we get a date for the disciplinary."

"And he'll spend the rest of his natural calling a spade a spade," Rob said, trying not to sound bitter. He'd had a few run-ins with Miller, who was of the same ilk as most of Rob's old army buddies—'You're a coon, what d'you reckon to this?' in response to every anti-racist initiative. 'It was a black youth, no surprise there—no offence, mate', 'Is Jamaica a decent holiday spot?' How would he know? The only time he'd been abroad was on active service—in Germany and Bosnia—nowhere near Jamaica. To Rob's mind, the anti-discrimination policies never went far enough, but when he and Tang had been the only non-white officers in a twenty-strong department, speaking up was more trouble than it was worth.

"What's the solution, Rob?" Martina asked.

"There isn't one. Or not a quick one, at any rate."

"Just keep at it." Martina loaded a pancake with duck and hoisin sauce, took a bite and chewed thoughtfully. "I'm considering early retirement," she said.

"Yeah?"

She nodded and swallowed. "Erica's due to go in October, and I don't want to hang on another ten years to join her."

That was a big change of heart, and it had to be losing her dad that had brought it on because the Martina Rob knew, they'd have been carting her out in a body bag before she stopped working. Now she was talking about coming out before she'd done her thirty years. Either her dad had left her a very wealthy woman or given her a mortality jolt. Perhaps both.

"Do you miss it?" she asked.

Rob shook his head. "Not even a little bit."

"But you're still doing it in a way, aren't you?"

"I guess. Most of the time, it's nothing like police work. Like, the last job we did was a PPI claim firm where the customer service staff were scamming the boss—not just a few of them. The whole workforce. It had been going on for years. He was so minted he didn't notice until the claim deadline passed and he was winding down the company, and it was fraud, but he didn't want to bring charges against anyone. I reckon he had a few dodgy skeletons lurking, and if it'd been an SIU investigation, we'd have taken him down too."

"Which is why there's a demand for what you offer," Martina said.

"Yeah, totally. Plus we're getting the kickback on the stuff the police can't follow up. The business is solid. But I don't see me doing it forever."

"Still clinging to your bike workshop dream," Martina mused.

Rob smiled at her having remembered that. "One day, eh?"

"One day," she echoed wistfully.

That was the last thing either of them said for a while. The food was tasty but not out of the ordinary, and there was plenty of it; they both went at the same time to load up with main courses, noticing a group of police admin staff at a large table towards the rear of the restaurant, celebrating one of their number's birthday. Otherwise, the diners were in ones and twos, all in office attire.

Back at their table, Rob and Martina discovered their empty glasses had gone; they ordered more drinks the next time the waiter passed their way.

"I don't know how people do wine at lunchtime," Martina remarked, eyeing the people on the table across from theirs, who were on their second bottle.

"I know what you mean." Rob didn't drink often, but Sundays after footy, he'd been having a couple of pints and then losing the afternoon to a prolonged nap, so he'd stuck with Coke today, as had Martina.

The waiter came with their refills and set them down just as Rob's phone vibrated, rattling his unused knife. He frowned at the screen as he picked it up and hit answer. "Alright, Travis?"

"Dad! Can you come and get me?"

Rob met Martina's gaze, puzzled but not panicking...yet. "I thought you were with Travis, Lu."

"Yeah. We went to the games shop down from Nan and Grandad's, and... hold on. The man'll tell you."

There was a rustling sound at the other end of the line, and Martina mouthed *what's going on?* Rob shrugged and sipped his Coke, trying to ignore the heavy weight that had settled in his stomach.

"Hi, I'm the manager at Gamez," a male voice said at Lucas's end. "We're not sure what happened, but—what's your name again? ... Lucas, right. Yeah, Lucas said some guy was talking to him, and then...well, we're checking the security cameras now—"

Lucas shouted in the background, "He knocked Travis out, Dad."

"What?" Rob was gripping his phone so hard it creaked.

"The paramedics have just arrived," the manager said. "Would it be OK to hand you back to Lucas—"

"Give me the postcode."

The manager reeled it off, and Rob repeated it to Martina.

"OK. Put my son back on for me, please."

More rustling, and then, "Dad?"

"I'm on my way, Lu. I'll be about half an hour. You should call your mum."

"I can't. It's really bad, Dad." Lucas was crying, and Rob was losing it.

Martina waved to get his attention. "Keep talking to him," she instructed as she got up and hurried after the waiter.

"It's all right, mate," Rob said, fighting to stay calm. "What happened?"

"I dunno. I was looking at controllers, and this man started talking to me, asking me which Xbox I had. I thought he worked there."

"Don't they have a uniform?"

"Yeah. I think he was wearing one."

Martina was paying the bill.

"So he was talking to you," Rob said. "Then what happened?"

"He said they had the new controllers behind the counter. Next thing, Travis full-on tackled him from behind, and then he was just sprawled on the floor. There's loads of blood." Lucas's sobbing was ripping Rob to pieces.

"You're doing good, mate. Really good."

Martina grabbed her bag from under the table and waited until Rob was on his feet before she speed-walked ahead of him to the door. He followed her out.

"Can you remember what he looked like?"

"I couldn't see. He had a cap on."

"Was he white, black...?"

"White, yeah. He had short sleeves."

"OK." Rob got in the Merc and was thrown back in his seat as Martina took off. One more question. Just one more. It stuck in his throat. "Lu..." He coughed and swallowed. Too much saliva. "Did the man have an accent?"

"A bit. Not a strong one or anything."

"What was it like? Was it like Nana Dora's, or...?"

"No, it was sort of like Oscar in my class."

"Where's he from?"

"I dunno. It was a bit like Tempest's, but I don't know where he's from either. I'm sorry, Dad."

"It's all right. We'll sort it out." Rob's head was going to explode. "One sec, Lu. Just gotta put my seat belt on." Balancing his phone on his knee, he dealt with his seat belt, grabbed his phone again, hit mute and said, "Floor it."

Martina didn't need telling twice.

9: Too Close

G RAY CAUGHT UP with Rob in the A&E waiting room where he sat, harrowed to the point of haggard, with his very subdued son snuggled at his side. Gauging by all the empty sweet wrappers stuffed in Lucas's pockets, they'd been there long enough to buy out the vending machine. Neither noticed Gray's cautious advance and startled as if he'd materialised from nowhere.

"Sorry." He sat on Rob's other side, leaving a seat between them—physical space to avoid invading Rob and Lucas's cocoon—and time for either to speak first before he asked, "How are we all doing?"

"Travis is fine," Rob said.

"That's good news."

"He regained consciousness in the shop. No concussion—they're just gluing his head." Rob sipped a breath through pursed lips—a clear afterthought that he shouldn't say what he'd planned to. He'd only partially answered Gray's general enquiry into their well-being and was giving off a definite 'leave it alone' vibe. Meanwhile, Lucas stared into the distance, lost in a daze.

"Any idea what happened?" Gray asked.

"Travis...overreacted." Rob was playing it down for Lucas's benefit. "Grabbed the bloke from behind and got thrown back into a metal shelving unit. It's all on the shop's security video."

"That's something."

"Yeah. Martina's dealing with it. Well, she's liaising with the local police. Anything from Winstanley?"

Gray got in half a head shake before Lucas asked, "Dad, please can I have another Twix?"

Rob sighed and dug in his pocket. "Your mum's gonna have my guts for garters." He handed over a pound coin. "I want the change."

Lucas scurried away to the vending machine against the far wall.

As soon as he was out of earshot, Rob leaned closer and murmured, "It was Folden. And yeah, I'm sure."

It would have been too great a coincidence for it to not be Folden. Yet Gray's stomach somersaulted at the confirmation.

"I don't think the video footage is enough to prove it to anyone else, mind you," Rob added. "There isn't a clear shot of his face. He tried to lure Lu away, and..." Lucas was coming back. "I've told him," he finished quickly.

"Probably for the best," Gray said and smiled at the frowning little boy. "You like Twixes, eh?"

"No kidding!" Rob said. "They're your favourite, aren't they, mate?"

"Yeah." Lucas flopped down onto his seat, half-heartedly tugging the Twix wrapper in two directions and kicking his feet.

"He's worried about his mum," Rob said, winking at Gray. Lucas kept his head bowed, his heels banging against the metal chair support, still playing with the wrapper without opening it. "It's gonna melt, Lu."

Lucas shrugged and put the Twix in his coat pocket. Rob patted his son on the back, keeping his hand there, too far gone to disguise his own worry.

Gray forcibly switched role. He couldn't be there as Rob's friend and business partner and support him effectively when their worst-case scenario was unfolding in front of them. On the drive over, he'd prayed Rob was wrong—about everything, not just this. It had escalated without warning, discovering Folden had been talking to Lucas online one day, an attempted abduction the next. It had happened so close to Zoë's parents' house, Folden had to have known Zoë and Lucas were staying there. Who knew how long he'd been watching, waiting for the right opportunity to make his move?

"Where's Zoë?" Gray asked.

"With Travis."

"Has anyone talked to them about accommodation?"

"Another safe house, you mean?" Rob shook his head. "We'd have heard about it."

Gray smiled grimly at the truth of it. Rob was expecting another fight from Zoë, but last time, the 'safe house' had been a purely precautionary measure. This time, the threat was clear and present, and Gray doubted she'd resist.

"Are you OK here for now?" he asked.

"Yeah." Rob pulled Lucas closer, pressing his lips to the top of his son's head, making it clear—consciously or not—that Gray had intruded their circle of trust.

"I'll find out what's going on."

As Gray walked away, Lucas said, "Fish'll catch him, won't he, Dad?" If Rob answered, Gray didn't hear. He only half heard the receptionist tell him which room Travis was in. His brain was processing at double-speed, back in the mentality of head of the SIU, calculating risks as he ran through what needed to happen: get Zoë, Lucas and Travis somewhere safe—Rob too, ideally; check the security footage from the shop to see if it yielded any further clues; interview the staff; go back over the logs from Lucas's Xbox in case Folden had let anything slip—he might even have bragged about his plans, as he'd done in the past. Lucas wouldn't have picked up on it, but Gray might.

Gray stopped outside Travis's room but didn't enter. There were already two CID in there, and it gave him a much-needed pause for thought. None of this was in his jurisdiction nor formally his responsibility. He was a private investigator and postgrad student, no longer the head of the SIU, and an attempted child abduction guaranteed a speedy and thorough police response. They'd be crawling all over the town centre, interviewing potential witnesses, reviewing that video footage. But they didn't know Folden the way Gray did. More to the point, nobody knew Folden better than the man sitting in the waiting room, comforting his son.

As a police officer, Gray had played by the rules. Admittedly, when it came to sending in undercover operatives, those rules left a wide scope for interpretation. It was the only way they could get the job done, and Gray's superiors had known that, which was why they'd given him carte blanche to fulfil his duties as he saw fit and never questioned his decisions. Even at the end, when Gray had wandered far off-piste, it wasn't his superiors who'd brought him back into line; it was Winstanley. A lesser man would've run Gray through the gross misconduct wringer, yet Winstanley let him clear his desk, as it were, and close his final case, then seconded Gray's recommendation for Dom Hooper to succeed him.

Through the glass in the door, Gray watched two undoubtedly accomplished police detectives garner useful information from Travis, which they would take back to their commanding officer, who would brief a team with decades of experience, and they'd set out in earnest to find their would-be child abductor. With the best of intentions, they'd haul in the usual suspects—known paedophiles and mad men who flouted social boundaries—and they'd waste days and precious resources looking in all the wrong places.

Anders Folden wasn't a child abductor. He was a psychopath who'd put his skill set out to tender, and he had a score to settle. He'd spent years defrauding the rich and murdering on demand entirely undetected. Even when the SIU had caught him, he'd evaded a prison sentence and escaped from a secure hospital. A year on, they only had an inkling where he was because he wanted them to know. If they were going to capture him, they'd need a team with a unique combination of knowledge and experience—

a team who knew him intimately, who could predict his next move. They needed Gray's team.

He knocked on the door and entered, smiling at the two detectives, both of whom stopped talking to coolly regard him. That they'd let him enter the room without throwing him face down on the deck told him they'd sized him up while he'd been standing outside, which boded well in terms of their capability for protecting Lucas, Zoë and Travis. One less thing to worry about.

"Can I help you?" the closer of the two asked.

"Yes, you can. I'm Rob Simpson-Stone's business partner and a family friend." He glanced at Zoë, sitting next to Travis's bed, and was relieved when she nodded, confirming his statement. "Is there anything I can do?"

"We have everything under control, Mr...?"

"Like what?" Zoë asked Gray, talking over the police officer. "Because I've already told *them*—we're not moving."

"Zoë—"

"No. I know that's why you're here, Gray, and I'm—*we're* not uprooting Lucas again. He's missed months of school—learning, football, time with his friends—because it was supposedly safer to keep him at home, but nowhere's safe."

"Folden knows where you live."

"And what? Don't you think if he was clever enough to find us here, he'd find us wherever you put us? At least here, police officers are guarding us twenty-four seven. I'm sorry, Gray. I know you're trying to look after us, but we're staying put."

Gray inhaled deeply, not to argue with her. She was resolute, as Rob had known she would be.

"OK. Then what can I do?"

"Find him." Zoë's gaze hardened, her tears glinting splinters of ice. "Find him and make sure he never hurts my family again."

***

The streetlights came on as Gray joined the M25, merging into the flow of traffic. It was moving at a decent speed, but he was in no rush and stayed in the inside lane. Driving took the edge off his stress and let him concentrate, make lists and prioritise, plan operations—get the job done.

He'd been driving for about fifteen minutes when he suspected he'd picked up a tail, but at that stage he wasn't overly concerned. New drivers often tagged behind other motorists; it gave them an excuse to trundle, safely blaming the guy in front for their lower-than-average speed, although Gray was driving at the speed limit. He put his foot down—not by much—

and indicated, pulled out to pass a camper van then moved back into the inside lane. Sure enough, a minute or so later, the other car likewise indicated and pulled in behind him and in front of the camper van.

There were services a mile ahead. Still giving them the benefit of the doubt, Gray came off and crawled around the car park once before he followed the exit signs back onto the motorway, checking his rear-view mirror for the dark hatchback. And there it was. Gray hit the call button on his stereo. "Call Will." It rang out twice and connected.

"Hey," Will answered. "You OK?"

"Yeah. Sort of. I need you to call Aaron for me. Get him to look up a car reg."

"OK. Hit me with it."

Gray eased off the gas, reducing the distance between him and his follower. Unlike Will, he didn't have a knack with numbers and double-checked he had it right before he passed it on.

"Got it. I'll call you back."

"Thanks."

The call ended, and Gray's radio resumed. He hadn't noticed it was on earlier, caught up in slotting all the pieces into place as his tentative scheming became a solid plan. Now, if he could lose this tail...

Two hundred yards to the next junction and holding, one hundred yards, fifty yards...he swerved across the rumble strip onto the slip road and dropped from sixth to third, the negative G-force pulling him forward, arms locked straight and a big grin on his face from the sheer exhilaration of the chase and—he hoped—getting away from his pursuer. The lights at the top of the slip road changed to green as he reached them, same for every set on the roundabout. He stayed in the right-hand lane until he'd passed the second exit, drifting over as if to go back on the M25 anticlockwise, checking his mirror and whooping as the hatchback, too late to change course, headed down to the motorway. Gray stopped abusing his engine and made a nice, leisurely second circuit of the roundabout, back to the second exit onto the A3. Fifteen minutes later, he re-joined the M25 and Will was returning his call.

"Not sure if this is good news," Will began.

"Unmarked police car?"

"You got it. Registered to the Met."

"I thought it might be."

"Are you on your way home?"

"Yeah. Thirty minutes, according to Waze."

"See you in twenty then," Will said.

Gray chuckled. "I have a plan."

"Uh-huh?"

Gray couldn't decide if he was miffed or pleased at Will's lack of surprise. "I'll tell you when I get home."

"In twenty minutes..." Will said.

"Or thereabouts."

The car stereo kicked in again. Gray turned it up, switched to cruise control and wriggled into a more comfortable position. He had a feeling this might be his last opportunity to relax for a while.

***

He wasn't wrong. Nor did Will have a chance to warn him before he walked into the living room and discovered they had a guest, although the only element of surprise was that he'd beaten Gray back to the house.

"Well, well, Mr. Hooper! What brings you to this neck of the woods?"

"I wonder!" Dom stood so they could greet each other properly with a hug. It had been a good six months since Gray had last seen him, but Dom was the same as ever: creased and worn out as old jeans.

When they finally released each other, Gray stepped back, venting a breath. He'd been functioning on adrenaline, and he was, all of a sudden, as exhausted as Dom looked. "You know about this afternoon, I take it?"

"Yeah." Dom rubbed his hand over his heavily stubbled grey chin. "I have something to tell you."

Gray examined him, top to toe, noting the rigid stance, the uneven hang of his arms at his sides. He was carrying a firearm. "Who are you working for?"

Dom's eyebrows rose, and Gray put up his hand.

"Forget I asked. I'm just glad you're on my side."

"You think," Dom said, and for a moment Gray wasn't sure he was joking, but then Dom barked a laugh that startled Holly from the couch and set Kenny off growling. "You daft bastard. I'm always on your side."

"I appreciate the reassurance. To be honest, Dom, it's getting hard to tell."

"In general?"

"In particular quarters. I dropped in on Tant yesterday."

"I heard."

Gray sniffed, wondering if he should bother saying anything else when Dom seemed to know everything already.

"Look, Gray, I can tell you some of it, but is there somewhere I can pop out to make a call first?"

"Lean-to in the yard," Will said, moving towards the door and beckoning Dom to follow.

"Cheers."

The two men left Gray standing in the middle of the living room. There was space for him on the sofa without having to evict one of the mutts, but he was restless, nervous, thinking about cocaine. He registered Will filling the kettle—after the fact, as Will was in front of him, smiling but concerned. "You look knackered."

"I am. I was fine driving," Gray said through a yawn that caught him entirely unawares. He groaned. "God, I need an early night. When did Dom get here?"

"Five minutes before you. I told him you were due home and invited him in. That was OK, wasn't it? I've only met him once."

"Have you?"

"When he fake-arrested me last year."

"Oh, yeah, of course."

"But from the way you talk about him, he seems more than a former colleague."

"He's a good friend—the best I've ever had. Present company excepted."

Will smiled and put his arms around Gray. "You don't need to butter me up."

"I beg to differ."

"OK. You don't where Dom's concerned."

"Has he said anything?"

"Nope. He just came in and sat down. Well, he said 'nice bird' because Paul was warbling like the sweet little psycho he is, and then he made a fuss of Kenny for a bit."

"And Kenny let him? The rotten cheat."

"I told you—he's a tart for a good-looking copper."

Gray kissed Will's cheeky grin.

"Talking about me?" Dom asked first, knocked on the door *and* coughed second, to announce his presence.

Both grinning now, Gray and Will broke apart; Will left to make drinks.

Gray moved over to the sofa. "Still smoking, then?" he asked, checking he wasn't about to sit on a dog. Thus, he didn't see Dom's reaction, and Dom didn't answer, but when Gray looked his way again, he was sitting in the chair, ready to explain. "I'm listening," Gray said.

"There's not much I can tell you at this point, other than what you've worked out for yourself, but what I will say is this. Trust *no-one*. Since I've been on this operation...Christ, Gray, you wouldn't believe some of the shit that goes on. And it's not your everyday corrupt officers taking backhanders or lying to save a colleague's neck when a complaint comes in. This is the sort of abuse of power that could bring down the establishment."

Will brought in the coffees, left two on the table and turned to leave.

"You can stay, Will," Gray said.

"Are you sure?"

Gray looked at Dom, who shrugged. "Makes no odds to me."

Will accepted the invitation and sat next to Gray on the couch, or next to Doris, who was next to Gray on the couch. Gray stroked her absently, struggling to connect the dots. Good friend that he was, Dom wouldn't have tailed Gray up the motorway in an unmarked car just to check he got home safely, and whatever task force he was part of had no obvious connection to the attempt to abduct Lucas.

Of course, the benefit of having worked together for so long was that they could follow each other's line of reasoning, and Dom's next words solved that puzzle.

"Remember I suspected the head honcho at Brookhurst had something to do with Folden escaping? I was wrong, or at least that's only the half of it. He had help from someone on high, and I do mean on high."

"Government? Judiciary?" Gray asked. Dom kept his poker-face. "Are they still helping him?"

"We think so, which is why I'm warning you."

For someone sharing on a need-to-know, Dom had given Gray a lot to speculate over. However, he knew better than to push for names.

"What did I say about that dog?" Will nodded at Kenny, who had shuffled closer and closer while Dom had been talking and was lying in front of the chair, half-rolled onto his back with Dom's foot rubbing his belly.

"You're a handsome lad," Dom complimented.

"Yeah, he's really not," Will said.

Gray shook his head. "Call yourself an animal lover?"

"Mmm...not a label I've ever worn, but whatever. He's ugly as sin."

It was what Will always said—a running joke between them because Kenny was Gray's favourite and vice versa—but he didn't mean it.

"He's mellowing, though," Will observed.

"He is," Gray agreed, "although Dom's good with dogs."

"I can see that."

"Yeah, that was what I was going to do before I joined CID—train as a dog handler."

"Another career I ruined," Gray muttered.

Dom grunted. "Don't start that bollocks again."

"It's true."

"No point wallowing now."

"Oh, believe me, I wallowed myself dry in the rehab clinic."

"Should I get out the violins?" Will asked.

Gray and Dom both chuckled. What they'd said was mostly true: Dom had gone into the police with a view to working with one of the canine units, but it was his decision to apply for CID at the same time as Gray, and to join Gray's teams as he moved up the ranks. Aside from recommending him for the SIU, Dom's career trajectory was not on Gray's conscience, although it had been. A month in rehab had given him plenty of time to reflect and come to terms with his guilt for the lives he'd destroyed, or so he'd believed back then. Intensive clinical counselling followed by eighteen months of therapy and no coke had allowed him to separate the things he was responsible for from the rest, and to accept he couldn't change what was in the past.

"So, Dom…" Gray leaned forward and picked up his coffee, settling back in his seat, continuing casually, "I was going to call you tomorrow."

"Yeah, of course you were."

"Business matters," Gray said, as if the clarification were needed.

"What kind of business?"

"I had a job for you, but there's no point in asking, is there? If you're still working for the Met."

"I'm still suspended," Dom said. "Officially."

"But you are still working for the Met."

Dom's lips were sealed, but his heavy in-out breath was as good as a 'yes'. "What do you need?"

"I'm putting a team together. I want you on it."

"You're going after Folden."

"I am."

"There's already a man hunt underway."

"At least one, according to Tant."

"The powers-that-be won't like it."

"When has that ever stopped me?"

"Or hesitate in prosecuting should you step outside the law."

"I wouldn't have it any other way."

"I don't have to remind you how dangerous Folden is."

"I'm aware." Gray sighed. Attrition by tedium was one of Dom's oldest and most-practised tricks. However, valid as his arguments were, Gray couldn't back down, as well Dom knew.

Dom shifted his gaze from Gray to Will. "You're not surprised by any of this."

Will shook his head. "How long have you been out of the police, Gray? Nearly two years?"

"Twenty-two months," Gray confirmed.

"And at what point during those twenty-two months would you say you stopped being a police officer?"

Gray frowned as if he were working it out.

Will laughed, a deep rumble, warm and familiar, and reached across Dotty Doris to squeeze Gray's knee. "It was always going to come to this."

Gray nodded, a little self-conscious that Will had revealed how well he knew him in front of someone else, but it was only Dom. Smirking Dom, the smug swine who one day might just get to be Gray's best man.

"Right then, Mr. Fisher." Dom straightened his face. "Who else is on this team of yours?"

10: Keeping it Brief

B Y MONDAY MORNING, Rob was running on empty. He'd stayed at Zoë's parents' for the weekend, on Saturday night top-and-tailing with Lucas, which was like sharing a bed with a giant, hyperactive worm, and Sunday night on the sofa, mostly staring into the darkness. Every ordinary nighttime noise—and the less ordinary, like a vixen screaming at four in the morning—reminded Rob his family was asleep upstairs while their police guards watched from across the street. He felt no happier for knowing they'd had as little sleep as him, and he couldn't stomach breakfast but could have kissed his ex-mother-in-law for the travel mug of coffee she'd pressed into his hand on his way out the door.

"He'd better not do a Windbag Fisher Special," he muttered to himself an hour later as he pushed open the pub door and swallowed a retch brought on by the pungent aroma of citrus furniture polish and last night's beer.

The woman brandishing the spray can glanced over but continued buffing a hole in the counter. "They're in there, love." She nodded towards the pool room.

"Cheers." Rob sidestepped between the tables, powering on through the déjà vu. This was where he'd met Gray for the first time, on the same kind of morning five years ago—the kind where the pale spring sun was blinding yet gave off next to no heat, and Rob was still shivering from the walk from the station. Such was the nature of sleep deprivation. When this was over, he was booking a holiday to somewhere hot—Mexico, Lanzarote, the Costa del Sol—anywhere would do.

As he reached the door, he heard the clack of pool balls colliding and stopped to watch Will make his shot. He missed, and Dom moved in, positioning his cue and glancing up.

"Morning, Rob."

"Morning. Isn't it a bit early for that?"

"Never too early for pool. Bollocks." Dom missed too.

"You're not on the beer already, are you?"

"That's the only reason I'm here!" Will said, although he wasn't drinking. None of them were.

"It's his day off," Gray explained. He was leaning against a bar table, arms folded, surveying the room as if it were a crime scene. Rob recognised that stance. This was the all new improved unofficial SIU, and he was going in with eyes wide open. Gray added, "She said she'd serve us if we wanted it."

Rob mentally recapped to remind himself what they were talking about. "No beer for me today." Or for the foreseeable future. He needed a clear head even if he had caught the train that morning, which he'd regretted the moment he called Ari to check what time they were arriving and got Aaron instead. The chances of him making it there on public transport were slim.

"Is this everyone?"

"We're still waiting on a couple of people. The formal introductions shouldn't take too long—you know everyone already anyway."

"Fair enough," Rob said, the end of which was cut short by Gray cracking his knuckles. Rob cringed.

"Sorry. I'm going for an orange juice. Anyone want anything?"

"Any chance of a cup of tea?" Dom asked.

"I'll see what I can do." Gray went back out to the bar room. The pool game continued. It had to be said, Will and Dom were evenly matched— in other words, both crap—and Rob soon lost interest. He couldn't decide if Gray was being deliberately vague about who was on this team, and he tried to come up with a list of the most likely suspects, but he didn't get very far. He didn't care especially; mavericks that they were, Gray wouldn't have recruited them if they couldn't get the job done.

"This is quite the incident room."

Rob did the fastest about turn of his life. "Josh? What the…?" He laughed, astonished. No messing about, they embraced. Four days ago, they'd been in a pub up north with the rest of their mates, and Rob had won the mini pool tournament. The prize: everyone else paid for his kebab on the way home. Four days. It felt like a lifetime.

"Put him down, Rob," Gray said. "You don't know where he's been."

"On the crack-of-dawn express," Josh complained.

"First-class," Gray pointed out.

"Yes, I suppose free coffee went some way towards making up for leaving the house at five a.m."

"Was that a hint?"

"Was it too subtle, Graham?"

"Be right back."

Gray left, and Rob released Josh—or they released each other. "It's good to see you, man."

"You too, Rob. Gray told me what happened with Lucas. How is he?"

Rob shrugged. "He's a little tough-nut. He's coping. Zoë…"

"Not so much?"

Rob shook his head. "I tell you what, when we catch that bastard, we should just hand him over to her."

Josh smiled, acknowledging Rob's dark joke. "And what about you? Are you coping?"

"Got to, haven't I?"

"You haven't, and none of us can know how you're feeling, but you're not doing this on your own."

"I know." For which Rob was immeasurably grateful. "Don't take this the wrong way, but *why* are you here?"

"I'm wondering myself," Josh said, smiling sweetly at Gray, who delivered a cup of feeble-looking coffee into his hands and departed again. Josh braced, nose wrinkled in anticipated disgust, and sipped the beige liquid. "Not as bad as I expected." He put the cup on the shelf behind him. "I'm drawing up a psychological profile for the unsub—that's what the FBI call them, isn't it?"

"No idea, mate, but I can tell you plenty. What do you want to know?"

"Everything, but I'll come back to you, if I may? I should probably say hello to the others."

"Sure," Rob agreed, not that he had a choice, seeing as 'the others' had almost doubled in number with the arrival of Dee Knight and Isobel Barnes.

"Alright?" Rob greeted them, less surprised by Isobel's presence than Dee's.

Isobel acknowledged him with a nod and made a beeline for Dom. She'd been around when Rob was working for the SIU, but he only knew her in passing. She was one of Gray's staunch supporters, so it made sense he'd recruit her for this mission—for that reason and because it gave him a woman on the inside.

As for Dee...she was grinning at him like they weren't here to figure out how to catch a psychopath who'd attempted to abduct his son. Yet Rob couldn't help but grin back. "It's been a while." A year, to be exact.

"It has," she said. "I hoped I'd never see you again."

"Yeah, thanks for that." Rob chuckled. They'd got to know each other fairly well in those two weeks Dee had camped out in his mum's driveway on the off-chance Folden decided to show his face. The male officer who'd been with Dee snored something chronic, and Rob was too stressed out to sleep, so they'd kept each other company, watched Freeview, played Scrabble— she'd kicked his arse—and had a few too many on more than one occasion. By the time her stint was over, they were friends with an inkling they could have been more. They'd exchanged mobile numbers and hadn't used them.

"How're you doing?" Dee asked, the grin gone.

"I've been better."

"I bet. And how's the main man?" She meant Lucas.

Like a lump of dry biscuit, the words stuck in Rob's throat. The overtime, the undercover secondments, staying away so no-one could trace him back to them—he'd done it all for Zoë and Lucas, to give them a good, secure life, and he'd failed anyway.

Dee touched his arm. "I'm sorry. Is there anything I can do?"

Rob looked around the room, for what, he wasn't sure. Inspiration maybe? While everyone had been chatting, Gray had returned to his spot by the table under the frosted window, his attention switching between them and his phone. He must've been running a timer because, after a seemingly arbitrary number of minutes, he put down his phone and stood up straight. Without him uttering a word, the conversations petered out and they all gave him their attention.

"Your job, I guess," Rob murmured in answer to Dee's question.

She smiled. "I think I can manage that."

With all eyes now on Gray, he brought his hands together in a single, soft *clap* and kept them clasped as he began to speak.

"Thanks, everyone. Be assured, I'll do my best not to turn this into a *Windbag Fisher special...*"

Most of them laughed quietly and politely. Dom glanced over at Rob, both raising their eyebrows doubtfully.

"Watch it, Hooper," Gray warned, still keeping it light and banterish. It didn't do much to ease the tension in the room, but Rob appreciated Gray's efforts. "OK. I really am going to keep this short. I realise some of you don't know each other, which we'll rectify this morning, but you all know why Dom and I have brought you in on this."

This time, Rob looked over at Dom, but Dom kept his focus on Gray.

"On paper, it's a straightforward job with one goal: to neutralise the target with as few casualties as possible. We know he's well connected. We've seen him slip the net three times. We know he's an accomplished con artist and a hitman. We know he's close by, and that he's playing with us. What we don't know is what his next move will be.

"That's our first task. Dom or I will brief you individually in full, but so you all know who's doing what, I'll run through it now.

"Isobel is our person on the inside. She'll keep an eye on Detective Chief Inspector Tant and report back any new intel on the target.

"Dee is on security detail. She'll stick close to Rob..."

Rob side-eyed Dee, and she winked at him. It could've been worse, he supposed.

"...while he liaises with our tech person. They couldn't make it this morning. They'll be monitoring online activity—the target's finances, social media and so on.

"Josh is our profiler and has already started putting together a psychological portrait of the target.

"Dom and I will coordinate the operation, and you'll check in with us every eight hours at the absolute outside. Iz and Dee, you'll report to Dom. The rest of you will report to me. Got that?"

There was a rumble in the affirmative and lots of nodding heads.

"Good stuff. Now, we have the pub to ourselves for the next couple of hours. After that, it's a virtual briefing room for us, I'm afraid. You should have received a link from Ari—our techie—to an ultra-secure messaging service. Download and install the app and follow the onscreen instructions, and you'll be good to go. Any questions?"

Dee put up her hand. "What do we do if we make contact with the target?"

"If you're able, take him down."

"Understood, Sir."

"And if we're not?" Josh asked.

"When you install Ari's app, it'll prompt you to set a keyword or phrase that will trigger an alarm and switch on GPS."

"Very clever."

"We'll all get the alarm call and converge on your location. Keep in mind everyone other than you is licensed to carry a firearm."

"I'm not," Rob said.

"Correction. Everyone except Josh has *trained to use* a firearm."

"I'm not carrying a gun, Gray," Rob insisted.

Gray looked at Dee, and she shrugged.

"I won't let him out of my sight." She grinned at Rob. "Not even to shit."

"Nice."

"Any other questions?" Gray asked.

"I have one," Will said. "What happens if the real police go after you?"

"Run?" Dom suggested, tongue-in-cheek.

Gray nodded. "Seems reasonable to me. Joking aside, if you see any coppers around, abandon whatever you're doing and get out of there. If you get arrested—"

"Call Simon Yarrow, QC," Josh finished. Rob couldn't help himself; he cracked up laughing, as did Dom and Gray.

"Who's Simon Yarrow?" Dee asked.

"One of the target's false identities."

"Good to know."

"It's unlikely he'll use it again," Josh said. "In my humble opinion."

"Humble?" Gray repeated with a slow blink. Josh shot him a sardonic smile. "As I was saying, *if* you get arrested, call your liaison contact. We'll arrange your release or, failing that, legal representation or whatever else you need. One more thing—Ari will be monitoring your communications, so behave yourselves, all right?"

People didn't look too happy about it, but they all nodded.

"Josh—you mentioned wanting to talk to some of us?"

"Yes. Anyone who has any information about Folden—even hearsay—I need to chat with you one-to-one."

"We'll sort out a space for that. Dom—anything you want to add?"

Dom shook his head.

"OK. That's it from me. Grab yourselves a drink if you want one. Josh will let you know when he's ready for you, and if you're hanging around for lunch, I'm paying."

A small cheer went up.

"Caviar and Champers all round, then," Dee joked.

"Truffles for me," Will said.

Gray ignored them and dodged past, on a direct path to Rob, saying as he reached him, "Sorry about that. I didn't have a chance to tell you. Dee was a last-minute addition to the team."

"No worries." Rob felt a million times better than he had earlier. "You're paying for all this, aren't you? I don't just mean drinks and lunch. The whole operation."

"A couple of consultation fees and some hotel rooms."

"Weapons, surveillance, legal counsel..."

"I can afford it, Rob. It's the least I can do."

"Well, thanks." Rob was more grateful than he could convey when he was close to tears and took a few seconds to look around the room again while he composed himself. "You brought in the A-team."

"The best of the best. I made you a promise, Rob, that I'd take that bastard down, and I will. Whatever it takes." Gray was emotional too. "Enough of that. Are you staying for a while?"

"I dunno. Am I?" he asked Dee.

"Defo," she said. "I'm bloody starving, and I've been on the road two days straight." She rocked back and forth, eyes comically wide. "Still moving."

Rob laughed. "Yeah, all right, then. I'm up for fish and chips in a bit. In the meantime, I'm gonna have a beer, seeing as I've got a chaperone. Dee?"

"Coke for me."

"OK. Gray?" Rob was already on the move.

"I'm buying."

"You're not. Guinness and black, yeah?" Rob made it to the bar and smiled at the woman who'd been cleaning earlier and was midway through returning glasses to the rack above the counter.

"Won't be a sec, love."

"No rush." Rob turned and looked back. Through the archway into the pool room, he could see one end of the table and Gray and Dee standing where he'd left them, deep in discussion. Dom stepped into view, his hand resting on Gray's shoulder as the two of them laughed at whatever had been said, followed by a nod from Dee, who looked Rob's way and pointed two fingers at her eyes and then at him. He gave a 'what you gonna do?' shrug, but he couldn't have given her the slip if he'd wanted to.

"What can I get you?" the woman asked behind him, and he turned to face her again.

"Lager, Guinness and black and a Coke. All pints. And one for yourself."

The woman gave a nod and set to work. Rob took out his phone and opened the app, bringing up Aaron's number, watching the Guinness slowly fill the glass while he waited for an answer. The call connected and then the line went dead. Not two seconds later, a text message came in—*I'll call you*—and then an incoming call. Rob hit answer, mimed *one minute* to the landlady and stepped outside. The door didn't even close before Dee appeared, glaring. He pointed at his phone, now clamped to his ear.

"Hey."

"Hello, Rob. It's Aaron. I couldn't answer until I'd disconnected your mic."

"Eh?"

"I was listening to the briefing."

"Through my phone?"

"Yes. Sorry."

"How...never mind. There's no point to this call, then, as that's what I was gonna tell you."

"Do you trust all those people?"

"I am doing—with my life."

"Josh is one of your friends from up north, isn't he?"

"Yeah. We've known each other since high school."

"Is he a proper psychologist or one of those fake experts?"

Rob huffed a laugh. "He's a proper psychologist. Are you gonna vet the whole team?"

"No. I'm making sure my records are complete."

"O...K." Rob generally overlooked Aaron's quirks, but even for him, it seemed a bit over the top. "I'm sure you could find him online. He publishes academic papers."

"I have records for everyone except Josh and Dee," Aaron explained as if he hadn't heard what Rob had said. "What's she like?"

"She's..." Rob frowned at Dee. "She's standing right next to me."

"Is she pretty?"

"I guess."

"You find her attractive."

Bingo! Rob was in no doubt that he was talking to Aaron, but here was a reminder that Aaron, Naomi and Ari were the same person after all. That, or he was way off and the interrogation was courtesy of Aaron's anxiety, *not* Naomi's/Ari's jealousy—talk about a piss-take when they'd gone waltzing straight back to Freddie the second he was out of jail. Either way, Rob couldn't talk about it with Dee there, which was how it was going to be until they caught Folden.

"Is there anything else you need to know?" he asked.

"No, thank you, Rob. You've been very...helpful. Goodbye." Aaron hung up.

"Crap." Rob sighed and put his phone away. "I've upset them." He still wasn't sure who, specifically.

"What was that about me?" Dee asked, holding the pub door open and waiting for Rob to enter first.

"Ari doesn't have records for you and Josh."

"Oh. Well, we can sort mine out, no trouble at all."

"And they wanted to know if I found you attractive."

"That's...weird."

Rob spotted the drinks he'd ordered lined up on the bar. "Best pay for those."

He went over, wallet in hand, but the landlady shook her head.

"Already paid for, love."

Holding in a sigh, Rob left a tip on the counter and put his wallet away. He handed Dee her drink.

"Cheers." She took a sip, smacking her lips as she swallowed. "So do you?" she asked, looking Rob dead in the eye.

"Do I what?"

"Find me attractive."

He was well and truly caught in her gaze and had already given himself away, but so what? There was no reason to lie about it. "Yeah," he said. "I do."

11: Interview with a Friend

As per Dee's 'not even to shit' promise, when Rob said he wanted to sit at the bar, she pulled up the stool next to his, positioning herself between him and the exit. Glad as he was for her protection and her company—even if it did come with a gun—he couldn't set aside his fear that everything they were doing was playing into Folden's hands.

Over the past thirty-six hours, Rob had watched the footage from Gamez too many times to count, and the opportunity was there: Folden could have taken Lucas. But he hadn't. He'd waited for Travis to intervene, or that was how it looked to Rob, and if he was right, Folden was sending him a message: he was ready to make his move, and he'd had a whole year to prepare, while they had days—at best—to figure out what he was up to and track him down.

For now, everyone was safe. There were no plans to end the police presence outside Zoë's parents', and Rob's mates on the force up north were unofficially keeping an eye on the rest of his family. In the unlikely event that Folden walked into the pub, three armed officers were ready to shoot him on sight. But that would be too easy.

"D'you reckon Ari's still spying on us?" Dee asked out of the blue, or so it seemed to Rob, but he'd been away with the fairies. "On me and him, I mean." She nodded to direct Rob's attention to Josh and his temporary interview room: a laptop on a corner table surrounded on two sides by a bench seat, a third side screened by a half-wood, half-glass panel. He'd already spoken to Dom; presently, he was questioning Isobel Barnes. Rob was next. "He's not giving anything away, is he?" Dee observed.

"No. He's..." How to describe Josh without insulting him?

"Uptight?" Dee suggested.

Rob chuckled. "I was gonna say guarded, but yeah, uptight. Though he's not as bad as he used to be."

"How long have you known him?"

"Twenty-five years or thereabouts. We went to the same high school but didn't speak until sixth form. I was going out with one of his friends and accused him of trying to split us up. He told me she was seeing someone else."

"What an arsehole!"

"Him or her?"

"Both, now you mention it, but who rats out a mate?"

"He wasn't being vindictive, and to be fair, I started it. He and Jess were study buddies—proper little swots, the pair of them."

"Yeah, he looks like a swot," Dee remarked.

"He might, but Jess didn't. She was a stunner." *Tall, blonde, all boobs and cleavage*...although she'd meant a lot more to him than eye candy. She'd been his first full-on teenage crush and held him in thrall. Sadly for him, he wasn't the only one.

Dee's face appeared an inch in front of Rob's. "Where've you gone?"

"Sixth-form study room..." The vision faded, and Rob laughed off his embarrassment. "Jess kept disappearing on me. I thought she was with Josh, and he thought she was with me. Turns out she had a few lads on the go."

"Good on her!" Dee held up her pint in a toast.

"Yeah." Rob could smile about it now. Jess had made him no promises, then or ever. "Josh did us both a favour in the long run."

Josh had finished talking to Isobel and signalled for Rob to go over. He took a swift glug of his pint and left it on the bar. "Keep hold of that for me?"

"Watch your back," Dee warned. She wasn't entirely joking.

Rob smiled. "There's a lot more to the story—maybe I'll tell you sometime." He went over to join Josh, glancing back at Dee. She'd spun her stool so she could watch them, eyes narrowed and judgemental.

"I see I've made my usual impression," Josh remarked.

Rob shook his head at Dee and turned to face Josh. "I was telling her about Jess and sixth form. She thinks you're an arsehole for taking my side."

"For which I make no apology. Let me just save this..." Josh squinted at his laptop screen, tapped away at his keyboard for a few seconds and sat back. "Are you ready to tell me about Anders Folden or do you need time to build up to it?"

"I'm ready," Rob confirmed. "Though I'm not sure where to start."

"I've read the statement you gave to Winstanley last year, and Dom's granting me access to the SIU case files, so that should cover all the facts. What I'm more interested in—and what would be more useful—is your reading of Folden. Did you know that experienced police officers are at least as accurate as psychologists when it comes to drawing up an offender profile?"

"No, I didn't know that."

"It's well substantiated by research. You are *the* expert here, Rob—years of police experience plus prolonged direct contact with the target. However, that's a vast amount of information to dig into. It might be easier if we start with a critical incident—one specific event that comes to mind when you think of Folden."

"When he shot Neil," Rob answered straight away. "I don't know why it sticks out—I guess because it was the first time I witnessed him kill someone, and there was no reason for it. Folden could've just hit Neil, knocked him out—he was close enough—but he shot him, point-blank, and walked away smiling and splattered in blood." The scene at Black Hole Studios was as vivid in Rob's mind as if it had happened minutes ago, but where he normally sought distractions to shut it down, he took the time to explore, to look around—the stark dazzle of white spotlights on steel, the otherwise eerie lack of reflections off the matt-black walls, the absolute deadness that swallowed every sound, the horror-stricken hostages—and suddenly he understood why it was significant. "Sharston was as shocked as the rest of us. Folden wasn't following orders."

"Did he usually?"

"Yeah. He'd complain, but he'd do as he was told. This time, though, he acted off his own bat. I remember now—Sharston asked him why he'd done it, and he blamed Neil for playing the hero, trying to protect Campion's son, like he had no good reason to do so."

"Could he have been following someone else's orders?" Josh asked.

"It's possible, but who'd have wanted Neil dead? He was a harmless old stoner. This was more impulsive—no. I don't mean impulsive. Folden hadn't planned it, but he didn't lose control."

"Why do you think he did it? Did he know who Neil was to Alice?"

"I'm not sure. He knew Alice was Jason's mother, and obviously he knew Campion was Jason's father, but Neil wasn't even supposed to be there. He was staying at Alice's..." Rob's guilt smashed into him like a knee to the balls, and his instinct once again was to curl protectively around it, but he wanted to go on. To confess. "Sharston sent me to get Jason from home and deliver him to Black Hole. I sat outside, delayed as long as I could—I was waiting for the go-ahead from Gray. He should've been moving the team into position.

"Then Jason left, took a taxi to Alice's, and I followed him on the bike. She wasn't there, but Neil was. I told Sharston I couldn't get to Jason because he had company. She ordered me to ditch the bike and bring them both in. I should've held on..." He tried to recall why he hadn't. "I took the long route back to Black Hole, but I still hadn't heard from Gray. He was waiting for proof they planned to kill Jason and Alice, but the SIU's surveillance equipment couldn't get past the studio's soundproofing. I was on my own, and I couldn't do anything without blowing my cover."

"Do you need a break, Rob?" Josh asked, sensing it before Rob did: his stress level was through the roof, but it wasn't full-on PTSD. He'd been there a few times over the years, all rooted in his time in the army, not his undercover work for the Met. After what he'd done with the SIU, it should've been the other way around.

"I'm all right," he confirmed. "But cheers."

"Just say if it gets too much, OK?"

"Will do."

"I interviewed Alice yesterday. As you'd expect, she also found it difficult to talk about what happened at Black Hole."

"Yeah? She was a bloody wonder that day. She always struck me as this timid, mouse-like person who let people walk all over her, but she was totally zen. She kept the other hostages calm and tried to talk Folden down. Maybe that's why he killed Neil—because Alice was getting through to him and he needed to shut her up. I dunno. Maybe he had sussed that her and Neil were lovers."

"Alice believes Folden is motivated purely by financial gain."

Rob shrugged neutrally. "She's known him a long time. I'm not sure I agree, but I guess it's easier to think he's doing it for the money, not because he gets off on hurting people."

"You don't seem to have that problem," Josh observed.

"I've met a few nutters like him. Psychopaths or sociopaths—whichever it is. They don't give a shit about anyone but themselves, not even the people they claim they love." Rob was thinking about Ethan—his old sergeant in the REMEs—who'd murdered 'for love'. Ethan and Folden were from the same mould. "Which is it, by the way?"

"Both psychopathy and sociopathy are associated with antisocial personality disorder. Based on Folden's callous aggression towards Neil, and you implied he's quite calculating, he exhibits some psychopathic traits. However, I'm still puzzled over his motivation for killing Neil. From what Alice said, she has some emotional attachment to Folden. Did you ever see evidence that he cared about her?"

"I only saw them together that night, but he didn't talk about her, or not the way he talked about Campion."

"How did he talk about Campion?"

"Like he was his dad. That's what I couldn't get. He mourned for Campion, properly mourned, to the extent I thought we were barking up the wrong tree and Folden hadn't murdered him after all. Then there was the whole thing of claiming Campion's fortune was rightly his. At his trial, the prosecution treated it as a bullshit defence, but I reckon Folden really believed it."

"Interesting." Josh leaned forward and did something with his laptop. "I just want to make a note of that, as Alice said much the same."

"I figured you were recording the audio seeing as you weren't taking notes."

"I am."

"Fair enough." Rob stayed quiet while Josh typed at speed for a minute or so, thinking he should've brought his pint over.

"Nearly done," Josh said, which made Rob smile. He was long past wondering how Josh read people so accurately without even looking at them.

"OK. My final few questions are about you and Folden."

"What he wants from me?"

"Yes, but before we get to that, how would you characterise your relationship with Folden, seeing it through his eyes?"

No way was he getting inside Folden's head to answer that question. "I haven't a clue."

"Did he consider you equals?"

"I doubt he even knew my name until the last few months of the operation, so no. He never saw me as an equal, more like a threat to his position. A couple of times he sniped that Sharston had only brought me in because I'd been shagging Jess, but I'm not sure whether he meant it was out of pity for me or out of respect for Jess."

"Would you say he considered you a friend?"

"Folden doesn't make friends."

"But did he trust you?"

"No more than he trusted anyone. Sometimes he'd tell me stuff like he was confiding, but it was all manipulation."

"What sort of stuff?"

"We're back to that question, aren't we? What does he want from me?"

Josh looked a little shame-faced. Gray must have put him up to asking, but Rob wasn't dodging the question for that reason. Folden had shared his sicko fantasies about torturing people before he killed them—including Josh. Rob would rather come across as hiding something than dump that burden on someone else, especially one of his closest friends.

"I honestly don't know what he wants," he said. "I'd tell you if I did. Dom and Winstanley are convinced I know something or Folden thinks I do. But the last twelve months of the operation...losing Zoë and Lucas...Jess passing... there's blanks all over the shop. I'd already told Gray I wanted out. He put me in a position where I had to take the assignment, and I still hated him for it, but I can't fault how well he looked after me at the end. As soon as we'd taken down the fraud ring, he released me, said he'd use the evidence from surveillance so I didn't have to give a statement and relive it all.

"Now I wish I'd made that statement because I'd gladly tell Folden what he wants to know if it would get him off my back once and for all. This'll sound egotistic, but the photos of Lois and Amber and making contact with Lu—I think Folden's taunting me. Don't get me wrong—he's capable of hurting them to reach me or just because he feels like it. But it's me he wants, and the second I know why—"

"You'll give yourself up?" Josh said. "That would just be plain stupid, Rob."

"Why would it? My life's been on hold for a year, and I'd barely got it back on track after the SIU. I'm tired, Josh. I need this to be over, and nothing you or Gray can say will stop me going after him if the chance presents itself." Rob recoiled at his accidental admission. "Sorry. I don't know where that came from."

"I do," Josh said, "and I'm almost certain it's why Graham asked for my input on this."

"Not because you're top of your field?"

Josh laughed modestly. "I'm not at the top of any field, certainly not offender profiling, but I don't do so badly at supporting my friends. Irrespective of whether it's the reason Graham wanted me on board, it *is* the reason I agreed. I saw you with Folden at Black Hole. I know how much he's taken from you, and I promise I will do all I can to bring this to a timely conclusion—without you going kamikaze on us."

"Thanks," Rob said, though he was making no promises on the kamikaze front.

"Any time." Josh pressed a couple of keys and shut his laptop. "Now, I don't know about you, but I'm ready for my free lunch."

"Likewise," Rob said, receiving loud and clear. He returned to Dee, giving her a brief nod of thanks for looking after his pint and the new one she'd lined up behind it. He downed the warm beer and leaned on the bar, emotionally drained, listening to Iz taking lunch orders, the low hum of conversation between Gray and Dom. His eyes closed; it couldn't have been for more than a second, but when he opened them again, he had company.

"Will," he acknowledged.

"How're you doing?"

"Coping. You?"

"Fine." Will tracked Gray's progress over to Josh. "Just standing by while he does his thing, you know?"

"Yeah." Rob watched long enough to establish Josh was reporting back to Gray, then picked up his pint. "Are you feeling like a spare part?"

Will didn't answer and instead asked, "How did it go with Josh?"

"I told him as much as I was able." He and Josh talked often and frankly but never about Folden, or not since Rob's partial confession that night at Black Hole Studios, while Neil was carted away in a body bag and SIU and local police officers moved around them in a muffled, surreal blur. Josh had saved Rob's neck then too, cutting him short before he spewed the lot and checking there were people he could talk to. The support had been second to none, and Rob had left the SIU, satisfied at a job well done but glad to put it behind him and move forward with his life. Then the system had screwed him over.

Rob's phone buzzed his thigh. "That'll be Ari," he said, unlocking the screen and confirming he'd been right: *Josh will ask you if he needs more, I'm sure.*

"Any news?" Will asked.

Rob showed him the message.

"The seal of approval," Will said wryly but quickly switched on the charm when he spotted Gray and Josh coming over. Isobel and Dom arrived soon after.

"Everyone's staying for lunch, Sir," Isobel reported. Rob spotted Gray's fond eye-roll at the term of address. "I've put in the order."

"Thanks, Iz. Anyone need a drink?"

Josh and Isobel answered in the affirmative.

"I've got one," Dom said.

"So have I." Rob held up his barely touched pint. In truth, he'd have gladly abandoned it and the fish and chips to go home and kip, except he wouldn't have slept. He'd have replayed the video from Gamez and beaten himself up over all those missed chances he'd had to kill Folden—to end this before it began.

"Oy." Dee nudged him with her shoulder. "Get that beer down you."

"Are you trying to get me hammered?"

"Nope. I'm saving myself from having to spend the next however long looking at your face."

"What's wrong with my face?"

"Nothing usually. Right now, you'd give what's-his-name a run for his money—that big bloke you were in the army with. Jock, is it?"

"You cheeky..." Rob laughed in disbelief that she'd made the comparison. Jock had the sort of face even a mother would have trouble loving.

Dee grinned. "Better?"

"Yeah."

"Good. Now then, where are these fish and chips?"

12: Intuition

AFTER LUNCH, AS Gray had expected, Josh shunned his suggestion the three of them work on the profile together at the farmhouse, insisting he needed to 'acclimatise', and in any case Gray knew he worked best on his own. Gray, in turn, insisted on escorting Josh to his hotel, waited while he checked in and then accompanied him up to his room. No funny business—Will was with them. Not that Gray would even consider making a move on his brother-in-law, irrespective of his unyielding adoration for the man.

Will and Josh chatted amiably on the way up in the lift, although Will was on edge, refusing to let a single moment of silence pass unfilled. If Josh had picked up on it too, he didn't react in any way Gray could discern; had their interchange been a high stakes poker game, Josh and Will would have been the last two players at the table.

With Josh safely ensconced in his rather grand temporary accommodation—he didn't react to that either—and connected to the net via Ari's VPN, Gray and Will left him to it. The dogs weren't used to being on their own for more than a few hours at a time, and Gray wondered if that was the reason for Will's chatty behaviour on the way up because he was a different man on the way back down, leaning with his chin on Gray's shoulder, breathing a steady swing rhythm into his ear.

"Are you OK?" Gray asked.

"Yep."

"Are you sure?"

"I love you," Will said and kissed his cheek. No build-up, no charged moment of anticipation, no passionate pounding of hearts. Just a simple statement of fact, albeit a statement he'd never made before. Gray watched their reflection in the mirrored lift wall—Will's lazy smile and his own flushed cheeks.

"What brought that on?"

"Seeing you in action this morning."

"That impressive, am I?"

Will dug his chin a little deeper into Gray's shoulder. "You *are* impressive, but that's beside the point. You're doing this for Rob."

"Don't suggest it's out of kindness. It's not."

"Really? You think this is still all about waylaying your guilt?"

"Maybe not all. But I can't sit back and do nothing when I have the power to do something. You do the same. In fact, what you do is so much more selfless. You save lesser creatures, and you get no thanks for it.

"Agree to disagree," Will said.

"Which part?"

"They're not lesser creatures, and have you met Kenny?"

Gray pictured the big old dog, not on his wheels but shuffling around the kitchen on his bottom, play-fighting with Bailey and knocking over chairs. Will was right: those 'lesser' creatures expressed their thanks through their abundant joy for a life they wouldn't have without Will.

"I love you too."

"You don't have to say it because I did."

"I'm not. I'm saying it because I do, and because I've never said it before."

"Ever?"

"Not to you."

The lift stopped. Gray lifted his shoulder to gently nudge Will's chin away.

"It was the right time," Gray justified.

"Yeah, it was." Will stared wistfully at—more like through—the lift doors. "My mum would've loved you."

Gray squeezed his hand. "I'm glad I was able to meet her."

"Same."

The doors opened onto the busy foyer, and Gray released Will, instantly on alert, which was no different than any other day, but he was overly aware of every step they took, every person who walked by, every obstacle between them and the outside world. Nothing out of the ordinary happened; they bade the doorman a good afternoon and stepped out onto the street, moving close to the kerb, ready to flag down the next taxi. Gray inspected every vehicle that passed. Commuters, delivery drivers...

"You miss it," Will said. "Working for the police."

"Very much." Gray had admitted it to himself some time ago—within a few months of being discharged from the rehab clinic—and to Dom and Winstanley last year when they'd been going through the Tabula Rasa case files. If he could turn back the clock, he'd make different choices—better choices. Ones that didn't destroy his career or recklessly shove his people out of the bunker and into the enemy's sights.

A cab stopped to drop someone at the hotel, and Gray and Will grabbed it before anyone else could.

"Where to, fellas?"

"Croxley," Gray said.

"Stepney Green station," Will said. "We've got Travelcards, Gray."

"OK." He supposed it was a bit frivolous getting a taxi door-to-door, and they were coming back into the city to meet Josh for dinner, assuming they could persuade him to put down his research for an hour or two. If they saved the money now, they could take a taxi home later and Gray could have a couple of glasses of wine.

They must've picked the only non-chatty cabbie in London, which made for a very quiet ride to the station, as Will was engrossed in thought, which Gray didn't want to interrupt. They were on the train before they resumed their conversation.

"Did you ever say it to Josh?" Will asked without elaborating, but Gray knew what he meant.

"Not 'I love you'. I told him I was in love with him."

"His response?"

"He shouted at me, I think. I can't really remember. We were on our way back from visiting a crime scene, and I was jacked up. I took him to Jean's grave."

"A crime scene, cocaine and a cemetery. That's a terrible first date."

Gray laughed. "Believe me, I've had worse."

"You and me both!"

"What was your worst?"

"Kira." Will smiled in thought, his gaze distant. "The girl I went out with in sixth form. She asked if we could do something exciting. I suggested ice-skating. I don't know why. I'd never been before."

"Was it exciting, though?"

"It was eventful. I fell over and took her with me. She landed badly and broke her wrist."

"Ouch!"

"That's what she said, among other unrepeatable things, but it wasn't terminal. We went out for a few months afterwards. What about yours?"

"With you," Gray admitted without qualms, aware on a deeper, indefinable level that their relationship was undergoing a rapid evolution.

Will put his hand on his chest and gasped dramatically. There was some real hurt hidden behind the ham. "It wasn't that bad...was it?"

"It was awkward."

"Because you unwittingly fed me meat."

"See, now that doesn't sound like a bad first date," Gray said, flirting with the double entendre, "but that was our second. The first was dinner with the Sandison-Morleys."

"I classed that as more of a meet-the-family kind of thing."

"You'd already met them," Gray pointed out. He was gearing up to asking Will what he'd wanted to ask all day, but every time he'd tried, he'd bottled it. He just needed to spit it out. "I know you said you were OK with me bringing Josh in on this, but are you really OK with it?" *There. That wasn't so bad.*

Will shrugged. "He's the best person for the job."

"Yes, he is, but—"

"Can we talk about it at home?"

"Sure." Gray could hardly refuse, and their timely arrival at their connecting station nipped off any chance of awkwardness developing. They stood single file on the escalator with commuters sprinting past, but they were in no rush and made it to the platform as a train departed, leaving them standing alone.

"I wanted to ask you something too," Will said. "About this morning."

"Go ahead."

"Why didn't Dom tell them he was still gainfully employed?"

"They didn't need to know."

"There was more to it than that. I was picking up a vibe from him."

"What kind of vibe?"

"I'm not sure. It was the way he was watching everyone while you were talking. I might've imagined it, or maybe it's just you undercover cops and your secretive ways."

"You could always ask Josh later. If you picked up on something, he will have too."

"Competition, huh?" Will mimed pushing up his sleeves and made a beckoning motion with both hands. "Bring it on." He grinned, and Gray sighed, mildly exasperated. One more reason to hope they caught Folden sooner rather than later.

***

"Great ride, Kit." Rob patted the dash and tilted his head as if listening. "Guess she's not talking to me." He looked down to unclip his seat belt. When he looked up again, he met Dee's not-impressed scowl. "What?" he asked innocently, like he didn't know he'd worn out the *Knight Rider* joke before they'd left the city centre.

"You're only jealous," she said.

"Got it in one. I'd totally swap my bike for an electric hybrid." He opened the door and got out, eyes on the unmarked police surveillance van parked across the street as he waited for Dee to lock the car.

"A *Porsche* electric hybrid." She drew up alongside. "All quiet here. That's good."

They moved off in step, almost quick-march pace, crunching their way up the gravel driveway.

"Lu will like it," Rob said as he reached for the doorbell.

"At least I get to impress one Simpson-Stone man," Dee grumbled.

Rob turned to check he was reading her right but promptly turned back when the door opened.

"Alright, Travis? This is Dee Knight. She's my security detail."

"Oh, alright! Come on in!"

"How's the head?"

"Sore but nothing I can't handle. I've got a thick skull." Travis knocked on his head—on the opposite side to the crusty, red-black stripe through his buzz cut—and grinned broadly at them both, flashing a gold molar Rob hadn't noticed before, which didn't mean it was new. It was about time he properly got to know this man who'd risked his life and was prepared to give up his business and start over with a new identity to protect Zoë and Lucas. Acknowledging that took some of the shine off Dora's switch from glib tolerance of her future son-in-law to overplayed 'pleased to see you' at her former son-in law when Rob and Dee entered the kitchen. Slippers shooshing over the tiles, she scurried to greet them with hugs, all smiles. Travis made a tactical retreat.

"It's a relief to see your face," she said, lightly pinching Rob's cheeks and pulling him down to kiss him—on the lips. Dee looked slightly alarmed, and Dora laughed. "Rob's used to me, aren't you? It's just my way, but I'll leave you be, sweetheart. Would you like a drink? Tea, coffee? Something stronger?"

"Coffee's perfect, Mrs. Clifton," Dee said.

"Dora to you." She shooshed back across the kitchen to the coffee machine. "I've made a big stew—I hope you're both hungry."

Rob and Dee shared a sly grimace. They'd had fish and chips in the pub, same as the rest of the team, but when everyone else had gone their separate ways, they'd stayed for dessert. Being a typical British pub, it was a choice between cheesecake, sticky toffee pudding or chocolate fudge cake; they'd both opted for a huge chunk of sticky toffee pudding that stood like a volcanic island erupting toffee sauce into a sea of custard, and they were stuffed. However, rejecting Dora's stew was out of the question.

She delivered two mugs of black coffee to them. "I'll fetch you the milk," she said to Dee, then to Rob, "I know you don't want any."

"None for me either, thanks," Dee said.

"God, I don't know how people drink it without milk. Looks like you've found yourself an ally, Rob."

"Yeah, looks like," Rob agreed lightly and stuck his nose in his mug before Dora dug him any deeper a hole. His and Dee's shared tastes extended well beyond black coffee to food, music, politics, sense of humour, sense of injustice. Dee also owned a bike—a nifty Triumph Tiger in matt black. Rob had fawned over the photos in the pub, aware of the sparks flying between them and cringing with guilt whenever Aaron's reaction popped into his head. The timing was off for a relationship of any kind with anyone, but wasn't it just bloody typical? Three years of being single and now there were two people he was attracted to, whom he was confident were also attracted to him.

"Dad!" Lucas skidded into the kitchen, saving Rob from further damning introspection with the quickest hug ever when he realised who else was there. "Dee!"

"Hey, dude!" They bumped fists. "Alright?"

"Yep. Are you still in the camper van?" That was Lucas—no beating about the bush.

"Better! D'you wanna see?"

"Yeah!" Lucas dashed off again. "Getting my trainers," he shouted as he thumped up the stairs and then back down again with said trainers in his hand. He dropped them on the kitchen floor and shoved his feet into them.

"You're going to ruin those!" Dora chastised, at which he bent down and poked his finger in the back of one whilst wiggling into the other.

"Ready!" He beamed, victorious.

Dee put down her barely touched coffee and went after Lucas.

"Oy! What happened to not even to you-know-what?" Rob protested.

Dee glanced back over her shoulder. "Priorities and all that."

She followed Lucas down the hall—Rob knew the exact moment the front door opened by the shrieked, "Whoa! A Porsche Cayenne!"

"That child..." Dora rolled her eyes.

"Has he been playing up?" Rob asked.

"No, just miserable. It's nice to see him smiling instead of dragging his chin on the floor. He doesn't really understand, which is a good thing. If your man had..." Suddenly overwhelmed, she turned away, clearing her throat as she swiped a cloth over the counters.

"But he didn't," Rob reminded her. With Dee's assistance, he'd managed to stop thinking about it for a while in the pub, and dwelling on it now would only send him back into a blinding rage. "I need to give you a heads-up," he said to Dora's back. She was checking the stew on the stove. "Dee's armed."

Dora gasped and whirled around, pan lid in hand, dripping condensed steam onto the floor. "A gun in my house? Rob! Your son's staying here!"

"I know, and I feel the same. But she's a licensed firearms officer. It'll be stored in a locked case when she isn't carrying it."

"I'm not happy." Dora put the lid back on the stew. "Not at all."

She didn't say anything else, keeping busy with mopping up the puddle, tidying around the already tidy kitchen, refolding tea towels and straightening the serving utensils hanging from a magnetic strip above the cooker. Rob drank his coffee in silence, wishing Dee and Lucas would hurry up.

"What time's David home?" he asked.

"Twenty minutes."

The silence resumed. He drew breath, not sure what else to say, and then his phone buzzed. He let the breath go and checked the screen.

"Excuse me a moment, Dora." He hit answer on his way out. "Alright, Martina? Gimme a sec..." He dodged into the living room and pushed the door mostly shut. "Everything OK?"

She launched straight in. "I don't know how to put this." And then paused. Rob waited it out. He heard Lucas and Dee come back in and pass the door, Lucas in the throes of high-speed supercar gabble. Finally, Martina said, "I heard a rumour private investigators are going after...a person of interest to you."

"Oh? Where did you hear that?"

"I can't say. Is it true?"

Rob had tried not to involve her in the Anders Folden drama, and he didn't intend to now, but he couldn't lie to her. "Yeah, it's true."

"Have you got a death wish?"

"If I did have, I wouldn't be able to act on it." Right on cue, the door bumped Rob's shoulder. Dee popped her head into the room, saw Rob's phone and frowned in question. He mouthed *Martina* and gave her a thumbs up so she'd know it was nothing sinister. Dee mouthed back an 'oh' and was going to leave, but Rob signalled her to stay. She came in and shut the door. "Honestly, Ma'am...balls. *Martina*. You don't need to worry about me. I'm only along for the ride." Or that was how it seemed to him. Will could just as easily have been Gray's liaison with Aaron/Ari.

"Gray's keeping you in the loop," Martina said. "Would you want it any other way?"

"I guess not. Was it Aaron?"

"I *can't tell you*!" Martina repeated. "But it's someone with your best interests at heart. Anyway, I'll leave you in peace."

"Ha. Not much chance of that. I'm at Zoë's parents'."

"In that case, I won't add to your woes. Take care, Rob."

"You too, mate." Rob ended the call and raised his eyebrows at Dee. "She knows about the operation."

"How?"

"She wouldn't say."

"To be honest, I'm surprised Gray and Dom didn't bring her in."

"Why would they?"

"A DCI in the Met is a useful source of intel."

"*Limited* intel. She's hardly ever out of her office. I mean, I get why Gray's brought Isobel Barnes in—"

"Interpol took over the man hunt from the SIU."

"As far as we know."

Dee hummed noncommittally but didn't argue the point. "Maybe Gray told Martina—you know? A test to see if he can trust her before he doles out her real assignment."

"Bloody hell." Rob chuckled. "You didn't even work for him and you know his MO."

"He might have a *tiny* bit of a reputation." Dee measured about half a centimetre with her finger and thumb. "I'm gonna pop over and have a chat with the lads in the van. Give 'em their due, they were on me before we made it to the gate, and they called in my number."

"That's good to hear." Rob huffed a sigh. "I wish I knew where that bastard was hiding."

"We'll find him."

"Will we?" he asked dubiously.

"He's not gonna stay in the shadows for long. He's too much of a narcissist." Dee squeezed his shoulder. "See you in a bit. Go spend some quality time with your son."

13: Shifting Goalposts

"H E'S NOT A narcissist." Josh set down his soup spoon in the half-empty bowl and picked up his napkin, dabbing his lips. At his request, the three of them were dining in the hotel restaurant—extortionate prices for a mediocre selection of dishes, of which honeydew melon was the only vegetarian starter. Not a fan of melon of any kind, Gray had skipped it, and Will had finished his some time ago whilst Josh and Gray debated the merits of analysing Folden's personality as part of his psychological profile.

"Convince me," Gray challenged, feigning confidence in his assertion that personality type could predict criminality. He'd read up, but if he'd considered himself any kind of expert, he wouldn't have needed Josh.

"I can see where you're coming from," Josh said amenably—a sure sign he was building up to shooting Gray down in flames. "He displays a significant number of narcissistic tendencies—a sense of entitlement, an obsession with power and control, no fear of being caught—"

"A lack of empathy," Gray added, "surrounds himself with sycophants..."

"All of which are also consistent with psychopathy," Josh argued.

"Other than the sycophants," Gray argued back.

"He doesn't collect sycophants, Graham. He establishes relationships with people who can get him closer to his victim."

A waiter came and took away their starters, eaten and half-eaten.

"Then how do you explain his involvement in the fraud ring?" Gray sounded supercilious to his own ears, so he probably deserved Josh's sanctimonious rhetorical response.

"Is it not obvious?"

"Let's assume not."

"All right." Josh sat back, toying with the stem of his empty wine glass. Will refilled it. "Thank you." Josh took a sip and continued, alternating eye contact with Gray and Will, though it was Gray he was telling. "Strang et al. were Alistair Campion's lawyers, yes?"

"Yes," Gray said, checking their proximity to other diners. None were close enough to hear, but it was an unnecessary risk. "Can we keep it anonymous?"

"As you wish," Josh said. "The target was at the law offices on work placement after he graduated, meaning...?" He waved his hand, encouraging Gray to respond, and Gray was sure—*relatively* sure—he could provide the right answer, but he was enjoying being regaled far too much to speak up.

Josh sighed. "Meaning he had access to all of the company's legal documents—privatisation, investor information, the CEO's assets and will—and that was when he decided he was going to take it all."

"See?" Gray said, his tone cocky. "Sense of entitlement and extreme ambition. *Classic* narcissism."

"Then he bided his time for eight years."

"Pure conjecture."

"Read the witness statements from the company's former employees. Several mention that the target's sudden turning over of a new leaf coincided with his stint in the law offices. He was scheming all that time. If he were a narcissist, he'd have cleaned the CEO out back then, but he didn't. Impulse control—*a key trait of psychopathy.*"

"Well, I'm convinced," Will said. Up to that point, he'd sat with a permanent half-smile, quietly watching and listening to the verbal table tennis. Gray was glad to have him back to his usual chilled self after what had turned out to be a very brief discussion of how he felt about bringing Josh in as a profiler. Yes, Will had admitted, it bothered him—not because Gray had asked Josh, but that he'd done so without checking Will was OK with it first and delivered it as *fait accompli*. In their new spirit of openness, Gray owned up to having done it on purpose, certain Will wouldn't have approved of his decision and determined to bring Josh on board—for the right reasons. Halo effect notwithstanding, Josh was the best profiler Gray had ever worked with.

Their main courses arrived, all vegetarian, seeing as Gray had chosen for Josh after five minutes of watching him pore over the menu with an expression suggesting it listed rats' curried entrails, deep-fried maggots and the like.

"Of course, it's irrelevant," Josh said, winding tagliatelle around the prongs of his fork. "The association between personality and offending is tenuous at best, and if our target is a hitman, conventional profiling doesn't apply. However, we should factor in that he started out as a white-collar criminal, so one question we need to ask is at what point did he shift from white to red collar, as Frank Perri coined it. If you haven't done so already, his work is well worth a read." He blew on the pasta and put it into his mouth.

"I have," Gray interjected.

Josh blinked, surprised, maybe even a little impressed, and quickly swallowed. "Then you'll know that in most cases, the offender turns violent to avoid detection or to access their victim's money. Not so for our target."

"He murdered the CEO and attempted to murder the only surviving heir to get at the money."

"That's only one of the target's offences and insufficient for any meaningful inference. When I go back up to my room, I'll conduct a thematic analysis of all the data from the crime scenes, or as much as there is in the records your former colleagues sent over. Until I've done that, I'm afraid I can't tell you anything of use."

"Can't you extrapolate from his personality type?"

"You might as well ask the waiter when he comes to collect our plates. This pasta is delicious, incidentally. An excellent choice."

"Thanks." Gray revelled in the praise, regardless of its offhand delivery, which had Will keeping his head down in an effort not to laugh out loud. Gray shifted in his seat so he couldn't see him. "There's something else I'd like you to do for me, and I need to keep it between us."

"I'm listening," Josh said.

"Can you take another look at the video footage from the games shop?"

"Yes, I can do that. With a view to what?"

"Two things. One, if there's any way to confirm it's our target—"

"Gray..." Will warned.

"What's wrong with seeking a second opinion?"

"When the person providing it is personally acquainted with your witness and you've sworn them to secrecy?"

"I see," Josh said. "You think 'R' misidentified him."

"No," Gray protested. "I don't think that at all, but why upset the apple cart? I've watched the footage so many times I've lost perspective. I'm almost certain it's our target. However, I need proof."

"I can't give you proof, only probability."

"Then give me that."

"OK. And two?"

"Tell me if you think it was a real abduction attempt."

Josh pulled the face that meant he was chewing the inside of his cheek, as he always did when he was pondering a dilemma. "I'll do it," he said. "On one condition."

"Name it."

"Neither you nor 'R' take on the target on your own. Whether you agree with me or not, and irrespective of its lack of validity in terms of predicting his future behaviour, he *is* a psychopath, capable of inflicting tremendous pain without breaking a sweat."

"I can't make any promises, but I'll do everything I can to avoid that eventuality." Optimistically, Gray took out his phone and brought up the video.

"That will suffice, thank you." Josh propped a pair of barely visible glasses on his nose and took Gray's phone.

For the next ten minutes or so, Gray and Will waited patiently, finishing the last dribble of wine while Josh watched and rewatched the thirty seconds of footage, pausing on specific frames, occasionally nodding and humming. Finally, he said, "I can't confirm with certainty that it's our target, but the lack of hand gestures and the distance he maintains from his would-be victim strongly indicate the appropriate gender and cultural background. Idiomatic of our target is that roll of the left shoulder. I noticed he did that during our prior contact, when he was boasting. I've cued it for you." He handed the phone back to Gray, who held it so Will could watch too and hit play.

"Oh, yes, I see it," Will said. "That's subtle."

"Where?" Gray asked in patent disbelief. He played the segment again, still not seeing anything in the grainy, too-small image.

"There!"

"Dear me. All that training…" Josh tormented.

"He's suggestible," Gray argued, tilting his head towards Will, who looked affronted but recovered quickly, seeing as it wasn't true.

"As regards whether it was a real abduction attempt, I don't believe so, and neither does 'R'."

"You didn't mention that earlier."

"I wasn't sure it was relevant. He was under duress, and my impression was that he was voicing his fears rather than imparting useful information."

Gray locked his phone and returned it to his pocket. "Whatever, it's confirmation enough for me."

"Glad I could oblige," Josh said. "Now, if you don't mind, I have a lot of work to do." He pushed his chair back.

"You're not staying for dessert?" Will asked, nay, pleaded. It was a bit pathetic but at least as sweet as anything on the menu.

Josh made a face. "I'm not big on dessert." He was trying to let Will down gently.

"How about a coffee? An espresso, perhaps?"

Josh ummed and ahhed a few seconds longer and then pulled his chair back in. "OK. I'll stay for coffee. Then I really do need to get to work."

***

"Josh is brilliant, isn't he?" Will said much later, when they were back home and settled in bed.

Gray turned on his side and propped on one elbow, staring down at Will's relaxed features. "How much of that wine did you have?"

Will laughed. "Three, maybe three and a half glasses."

"Did you drop a pill of some kind before we went out? Have a sneaky toke in the Gents'?"

"None of the above." Will rolled to face Gray, resting his hand on Gray's hip. "It was fun listening to you two slug it out. I love intelligent people." His voice had descended to a sultry rumble. "It turns me on."

Gray fought his smile. "You still have a crush on him."

Will closed his eyes, blushing furiously but with no shame. "So bad."

"I'm appalled!"

"Not jealous?"

Gray slid his arm under Will's neck and moved closer, talking against Will's lips. "Whose bed are you in?"

"Mine? For one night only." Will's kiss was slow and seductive, but Gray's thoughts had wandered ahead. "Not in the mood?" Will asked.

"It's not that. I'm just thinking...I should've cancelled the furniture removal company. I wonder if I can get hold of them first thing."

"It's very short notice. They'll still charge you."

"But it could all kick off tomorrow."

"Or it might not," Will reasoned. "And you chose a company who do everything for you. Couldn't you let them get on with it?"

"I suppose so. I'll have to bring Josh back here so I can oversee delivery. That or leave him on his own."

"What time will they be here?"

"Around two."

"I'll be back from work by then, and Tie's coming over. I'll get him to give me a hand shifting the sofa out."

"You don't mind?"

"Of course not!"

"So I won't cancel then. And I'll get up with you at five, catch the first train—"

"Won't that be a bit early for Josh?"

"Oh, he won't sleep tonight. He'll stay up working on the profile."

"All night?"

"All night."

"That's dedication."

"That's insomnia, but if it gets us to Folden quicker..."

Will moved in again, pushing Gray onto his back and nuzzling his neck. "You're so mercenary," he murmured, working his way across Gray's chest. "I like it."

"Hmm. I can tell." It was having the desired effect on Gray too, and he lifted his hips, pressing up against Will's erection, but Will moved away. "Where are you going—ah!" he said as Will stripped off and jumped back into bed.

"If you're getting up with me, you'd better get your kit off."

Gray was already on it. In seconds, they were rutting and rolling, the covers heaped half on the bed, half on the floor as they took turns getting each other off with hands and mouths and an urgency that afterwards had Gray wondering if it came from the near-threat to their mortality or their shared attraction to the same man, concluding the latter and, as he drifted off to sleep, thinking what a good thing it was that psychologists couldn't actually read minds.

***

Perhaps he had been a little ambitious. The five a.m. world of early spring was a cold, frost-coated place and altogether too bright for Gray's night-owl sensibilities, but get up with Will he did. He even made the coffee and took Kenny out for a pee while Will washed and dressed for work. It wasn't the first time Gray had been up with Will and the lark, but it was rare. Yet for whatever reason, this morning it was a comforting routine as familiar as if they did it every day.

"You made coffee." Will strode into the kitchen still buttoning his pale-blue postie shirt. When Gray didn't answer, Will asked—and it was only then Gray registered he'd spoken at all—"Are you OK?"

"Yes, I am." He handed Will his coffee. "I want to marry you."

"Shit!" Will held the mug away from him, a brown streak forming down his front. "That's hot!"

"Oops!" Gray ran a tea towel under the cold tap, wringing it out and wishing he'd kept his mouth shut. "I'm sorry."

"No! Don't be. Hold on, let me put this down." Will offloaded his coffee and held his arms aloft, an unresponsive statue as Gray pushed the wet tea towel up inside his shirt and dabbed at his chest.

Aware Will was watching him, Gray refused to look up, instead lifting the front of Will's shirt to examine his skin. "No scorch marks."

"It didn't have time to soak through. Gray..."

He was back at the sink, rinsing the cloth, which he used again to dab at the stain before swapping for a dry cloth.

"Would you stop?" Will requested gently.

Gray stopped. "I think I left my common sense in bed."

"What are you worried about? The day ahead or what you said?"

"A bit of both, but mostly what I said. Can we start over?"

Will laughed. "Absolutely not. I can't do another eighteen months of fumbling for words to reach where we've come to these past few days. But if you want to take it back to the point after you handed me my coffee...and...action!"

"Will—" Gray's tongue jammed up against his teeth, refusing to budge. What he'd said he meant with all his heart, but the words had leapt free with no conscious effort.

"How about if I turn away?" Will suggested.

Gray laughed, the sound juddering with his nervous jitters. Will had indeed turned away, but it didn't make it any easier. "Turn back." Gray circled the air with his finger, unseen.

Will turned back, smiling. "I love it when you get flustered like this—makes me wanna hug the life out of you."

"One murderer on the loose is quite enough, thank you." Gray scowled, but he was fighting two muscle impulses because Will's smile was infectious—and fading.

"Should I leave it alone?" Will suggested. "I'll leave it—"

"No. Will, I want to spend the rest of my life with you. Will you marry me?"

"In a heartbeat."

"Yes?"

"Yes. God, yes!"

Gray's relief escaped in a small burst of laughter, cut short by a gasp as he was gripped in a hug so sudden and energetic his feet briefly left the floor. Will kissed him, many times over, only stopping when Gray hiccupped.

"I gave you those, didn't I? Sorry."

Gray shrugged away the apology and hiccupped again.

"Believe it or not, I was going to ask you yesterday," Will confessed. "In the lift."

"Why didn't you?"

"If you'd said no—"

"I wouldn't have said no."

"If you had..." He shook his head, pain hijacking the laughter lines, eyes tearful. "It would have ended us."

"I'm not so sure about that, but I wouldn't have said no, Wi—ll." The hiccups were driving him nuts, and he needed to stop talking to slow his breathing, but he finally understood the source of Will's insecurity, so he persevered. "You asked Shelley to mar—ry you."

Will nodded. "Twice. The first time, she said it was for the wrong reason. She was pregnant with Suzannah, and I told her that wasn't why I was asking, but I thought...maybe she's right. So I let it go. Then we had Suzannah, and

I was working city hours. It was the only way we could afford a place, and our mums were amazing. Shelley's used to come down from Leeds for two weeks at a time just to give Shelley a break, and my mum childminded for us when Shelley went back to work. But she wanted to be home with the baby, and she hated it.

"Suze was nearly two before I got up the nerve to ask again. I suggested we move to Leeds. That way, Shelley could give up work and she'd be near her mum and dad. In the short term, I could commute at weekends, stay with my mum during the week—she'd given me her blessing even though it meant missing out on seeing her granddaughter. I think, sooner or later, she'd have probably followed us up there.

"Shelley turned me down again—on the marriage proposal. She said yes to moving to Leeds. She said I was still asking for the wrong reason, that I was doing it for her, not because I wanted us to be married. This time I couldn't let it go. I kept bringing it up, and we had the same argument over and over, where she'd say she didn't understand why getting married was so important to me, it was just a bit of paper, no big deal, and I'd say if it's no big deal, then why are you so against it?

"It was juvenile and stupid, but as one of my mum's friends used to say, I was like a pit bull with a small child—before you get on your high horse, it was back when the media were hyping up the whole dangerous dog thing, and my mum's mate had just rescued an abused pit bull. The way the tabloids were telling it, Rotties and pit bulls were savaging kids left, right and centre, and that dog *was* a maniac, but she was gentle as they come."

"You've sidetracked," Gray said, surreptitiously reining in his high horse and noting with some relief that his hiccups had stopped.

"You know the rest. We lasted another six months before Shelley did the grown-up thing and moved back to Leeds with Suzannah. It still hurts, but it worked out for the best and gave us both a chance at being good parents. The end."

"What did you do with the engagement ring?"

"Gave it to Suzannah for her thirteenth birthday. It's the one she wears on a chain. That was your only takeaway?"

"No, but I've always wondered what happens to the ring after a rejected proposal."

"OK, I suppose I'm not really surprised by that, but now do you see why I thought you'd say no?"

"I do. Thank you for telling me."

Will smirked. "Not a problem."

Gray shoved him lightly in the chest, making contact with the cool, damp patch surrounding the coffee stain.

"I'd better change." Will moved to leave.

"Before you go…" Gray said and waited for Will to look back. "The other thing I took away was that you might worry, given what's going on, that I asked for the wrong reason."

"It hadn't occurred to me."

"But it might later, while you're stuck in traffic or waiting for someone's signature, or…it doesn't matter. All I want to say is I'm not retracting my proposal, but when this is over, when Folden is back behind bars or six feet under, I'm going to ask you again. I love you."

Will's smile was easily as bright as the sun that had peeked over the horizon, spilling golden light into their kitchen. He leaned in and kissed Gray once, softly and slowly. "Same," he said, backstepping and laughing while Gray tried to prolong the kiss. "I'm going to be late for work!"

Will cool-cat-strutted away, leaving Gray with the image of a swaying bottom and a grin to last the day.

14: Boxes

GOOD MORNING!" GRAY stopped a few feet away from the sofas in the hotel foyer, where Josh was working on his laptop, an empty coffee cup on the low table in front of him.

"Morning," he responded without looking up.

"I expected you'd be in your room."

"Temporarily evicted by the chambermaid."

"Oh?" Knowing how Josh was about privacy, Gray had picked this hotel specifically because it wasn't the kind to kick its guests out of their rooms for housekeeping.

"I asked her if she'd do mine first," Josh qualified. "I fancied a change of scenery." He key-commanded a 'save', closed his laptop and finally looked up at Gray, tilting his head to one side, eyes narrowing. "A good night's sleep?"

"A short night's sleep, but yes, I slept well, thank you." There was more to that question, Gray was sure, but he went along with the charade. "You?"

"I was working." Josh leaned forward and peered into the empty cup. "Are we venturing anywhere imminently, or shall I order coffee?"

"Coffee would be good," Gray said. "I'll go—"

"No need!" Josh leaned to the right to see past him, held up two fingers, smiled and mouthed a thank-you.

Gray looked over his shoulder at the reception desk—one of the two young men staffing it left—and then back at Josh. "You've settled in quickly."

"I ran out of coffee in my room and had to call down for more." He nodded towards the desk. "Those two have been here all night."

"Did you sleep at all?"

"I napped around four. Are you going to sit?"

Gray edged around the table to reach the sofa at right angles to Josh's, taking the seat closest, and joined him in watching the other residents come and go—mostly businesspeople, no doubt heading off for a day of back-to-back meetings.

The man from the desk arrived with their coffees and a smile for them each, Gray first, then Josh, whom he addressed. "You asked me to remind you about breakfast, sir."

"Yes, I did. What time do you serve until?"

"Nine o'clock."

"OK. Thank you."

The man bowed his head and marched back across the foyer.

"How do you forget breakfast?" Gray asked.

"By having a coercive brother-in-law."

"I asked if you'd help us."

"You said R—"

"No names, remember?" Gray interrupted.

"You said the target's..." Josh scowled. "The target's target's life—Jesus, this is going to get wordy. As per the last time we worked together, given the circumstances, I couldn't refuse. But I think I've established the target's motivation for picking 'R'. Well, one of two possible motivations, potentially both valid."

"My goodness, you're a fast worker!" Gray gushed.

Josh smiled demurely. "Insomnia is a trusty sidekick."

Which had been the second deciding factor in Gray's decision to ask Josh rather than any other profiler. Once he'd set his mind to something, he wouldn't stop until he'd completed his task. Even so, Gray hadn't expected anything close to a working profile so soon.

"I spoke to A—" Josh amended "—*the techie* last night." He was back to people-watching but afforded Gray a brief moment of eye contact.

"That's...astonishing."

"Because of their social anxiety? We talked about it briefly."

"Did you Freud them?" Gray asked.

"Don't you start. I get enough of that from..." Josh vented a frustrated sigh. "Seriously, how do you people communicate?"

"Acronyms, mostly. I didn't mean it as an insult, by the way. You're a Freudian psychologist."

"I respect the man's body of work and the undeniable role he played in putting our discipline on the map, but I'm no Freudian. I say this knowing you'll call me a liar when I tell you my theory later. But in answer to your question, no, I didn't *Freud* them. They called because my connection kept dropping out, and it just came up in conversation. I hadn't realised they were a friend of your better half's."

"Since uni," Gray confirmed. "Sounds like you had a good chat."

"Yes. It was...insightful," Josh said. "I might have some breakfast after all. Care to join me?"

"Sure, why not? Room service or...?"

"I thought we could eat here, although I'm not giving you my progress update in spy code."

Gray chuckled. "OK. How about we eat first then you can brief me up in your room?"

"If you like." Josh waved at his personal receptionist, who dutifully headed over.

Gray threw in casually, "I'd also like to pop to my house to see how the furniture removal guys are doing."

The receptionist had pre-empted Josh's request and handed them each a breakfast menu. "Signal when you're ready to order."

"Will do, thank you."

The man departed again, and Josh opened his menu, studying it as he asked, "Where are you moving to?"

"Nowhere. I'm moving my stuff to Will's."

"I thought you'd already done that."

"Not the furniture."

"Why? Did you think it wouldn't work out?"

Gray bristled. "I'm not even deigning that with a response."

"It was only a question, Graham."

"Nothing is 'only a question' with you."

"Surely that's why I'm here."

"Don't be smart."

"I touched a nerve. I'm sorry. I didn't do it on purpose. It's just...you have trust issues."

"Trust issues? I don't have trust issues."

"Then why are we going to check on the furniture removal guys? Is there a problem?"

"Hopefully not. They called earlier to confirm access to the delivery address, claiming I hadn't indicated it on the form. I'm almost certain I did." Gray visualised the website, but the more he thought about it the less sure he was that he had provided the information. "Anyway, it's a good excuse to check everything is in order."

"See? You don't trust anyone."

"Not true!"

"Prove it."

"I trust you."

"Hmm. I've no idea why."

"Oh, you do," Gray quipped but wished he hadn't when Josh turned red and hid behind his menu. "And I'm almost there with trusting my SO," Gray added quickly.

Josh lowered the menu and closely observed Gray for several moments, effectively transferring the blush from one to the other. "Good for you." Not the slightest hint of sarcasm or condescension this time.

Gray waited until they'd ordered their breakfasts—poached eggs and wholemeal toast, both—before he shared his other news.

"I asked him to marry me."

"Aha! I *knew* something had put a spring in your step!" And now Josh was back to being smug, but it lasted three seconds, if that, before he held up a finger and asked, "Did he say yes?"

Gray laughed. "Yes."

"Thank God! Congratulations to you *and* your SO."

"And to you!"

"Why?"

"You set us up."

"Erm...yes, I did, but not so I could brag about my matchmaking capabilities, even if they are second to none." Josh peered down his nose, checked his cuticles and tugged his shirt sleeves straight, but he couldn't keep up the act. "I won't pretend I'm not inwardly cheering at being proved right about you two, but it's because I want you to be happy, and I can see that you are. Really, congratulations. It's wonderful news, as I'm sure our nearest and dearest will agree."

"Thank you." With that out of the way, Gray relaxed back against the soft leather of the well-worn chesterfield to drink his coffee and await his breakfast. His day had been perfect so far, but he was taking nothing for granted. He still needed to tell his family, of whom George was the easiest call. Becky would demand 'the deets' and want to know when they were coming to visit, and whether he'd told Mum/planned to tell Mum/wanted Becky to do it. Becky had only met Will twice, which was enough for him to charm her socks off and convince her that he could win their mum around. Gray wasn't so naïve.

Someone in blacks-and-whites—overworked and apparently not on 'Josh's staff', judging by their super-cool efficiency—delivered their breakfasts and more coffee, and the hotel foyer quietened as, beyond the doors, the city day began in earnest, making for a pleasant atmosphere with just the right amount of hustle and bustle to occupy their minds while their mouths were otherwise engaged. The sleepless night must have burnt off the meagre calories Josh had consumed the previous day, and he'd cleared his plate before Gray had started on his second egg and slice of toast, which was tasty, although perhaps not proportionate to its price tag. It had taken almost five years, but Gray had finally put a dent in Jean's money. Well, more a wing-mirror ding than a fully fledged dent.

Still, he thought he should perhaps ease off on his spending, shift some to his savings account or have Will find him a decent portfolio for investment. After all, he had dependants to consider now, both hairy and non-hairy varieties, and although that had been true for the past year, the marriage proposal formalised his commitment to Will, Suzannah and the pack. He wondered, too, what Jean would have made of his proposal—would he have delighted in Gray seizing the moment? Teased him for his lack of romance?

"What are you thinking about?" Josh asked, hooking Gray and holding him with a deep, mind-probing stare that lifted the memory of last night to the surface and reignited his flaming cheeks. Josh raised an eyebrow.

"About money. And my previous SO."

Josh nodded but said nothing, or not about Gray's sidestep, but he had to have noticed.

"Shall we go?" Gray suggested.

"Whenever you're ready." Coffee in hand, Josh turned, resting his arm along the back of the sofa, feet crossed, uncharacteristically casual. It was safe to say he'd successfully 'acclimatised' and was in no rush to go anywhere.

Gray followed Josh's lead and picked up his cup, swirling the remaining half inch or so of liquid, eyes on the motion as he remarked, "I thought you'd be eager to share your conclusions."

"We can just go straight to your house if you prefer."

"I wasn't trying to hurry you."

Josh didn't believe him, and rightly so. It wasn't a blatant lie, but Gray had selected the removal firm on the bases of their excellent reviews and that they would do all the packing for him. Missing access information aside, there was no reason for him to stick his nose in, but something kept niggling at him—a forgotten memento maybe?

"They won't be there for another hour," he mused aloud but left his concerns unvoiced.

"OK. I need to make a phone call. Can you follow me up in five minutes?"

"Will do."

Laptop tucked under his arm, Josh was up and heading for the lift. It arrived as he reached it.

"Are these finished with, sir?"

Gray panned from the lift doors—closing with Josh on the inside—to the member of hotel staff waiting for a response on their empty plates and cups. "Yes, thanks."

The woman deftly stacked the crockery on her forearm and left.

Gray checked his phone for calls and messages—both the ordinary kind and via Ari's app. They were abundant but not new: the last message was from Rob for his four a.m. check-in—Gray really hadn't thought through the implications of 'every eight hours, max'. Rob had reported *AOK*.

The message before that was from Josh—*Nothing of concern to report*. A dodgy wi-fi connection probably wasn't 'of concern', but Gray made a mental note to clarify what needed reporting and what didn't and began typing a message to everyone to change the call-in schedule, getting no further than 'Adjustment to...' before his phone screen switched to incoming call. Gray hit the answer button.

"You can come up now."

"On my way." Gray backspaced the message, reluctantly extricated himself from the comfortable hollow he'd carved into the sofa and went up.

"Were you watching through the spyhole?" he asked when the door to Josh's room opened as if triggered by a sensor.

"I heard the lift stop. It squeaks. Coffee?"

Gray stepped in and closed the door. "Not for me, thanks." Eighteen years in police service and academia, and he'd never met anyone else who consumed the ungodly amount of coffee Josh did. He crossed the spick-and-span room, nary a sign someone was staying in it, and sat in one of the easy chairs. "That was a quick call."

"Yes. George is communicating in grunts this morning."

"He's worried."

"Of course he is. We're chasing a serial killer."

"Did you tell him about me and Will?"

"No—should I have done?"

"Not at all. Just checking."

Coffee made, Josh sat in the other chair but then got up again and retrieved his laptop—"To refresh my memory," he explained as he resumed his seat.

"Right," Gray said wryly. It was a prop, nothing more. "Let's hear what you've got."

"I'll start with a brief overview of the 'facts' as they're recorded. I read through the police reports and witness statements for every offence in which Folden was directly implicated as well as those for which he was under suspicion but the evidence was insufficient to arrest him. That's a total of twenty-three separate incidents, the first of which took place in Bergen, Norway."

"Folden's hometown," Gray said. "Impersonating his father to buy alcohol—not exactly the biography of a psychopath."

"Nor enough to warrant his parents sending him away," Josh remarked.

"Agreed. We said at the time—when we were preparing for the CPS on the Strang case—there had to be more going on than a string of cautions for juvenile delinquency. Something was the final straw for his parents."

"If you would permit me to enlighten you..." Josh gestured grandly. Gray chuckled.

"Oh, do!"

Josh leaned closer to his laptop screen, scanned back and forth a few times and read aloud, "Clausen, Tom, sales clerk, Vinmonopolet. Admitted with three wounds, two to chest, defensive wound on right hand, consistent with a knife attack."

Gray was momentarily lost for words. "How did you get hold of that?"

"Ari excavated it from the hospital records."

"And you're confident Folden was the assailant?"

"Clausen's emergency admission was the evening before Folden was arrested and cautioned, and the Vinmonopolet is the only place one can buy alcohol in Norway—legally, at least. But Folden wouldn't have been flashing false ID to buy it on the black market."

"Why wasn't he prosecuted? The police must've known what he'd done."

"I'd speculate his parents negotiated a deal. Folden's grandfather is a politician, so his family must hold some sway, and the Norwegian system is more inclined than most towards restorative justice for young offenders. Folden's parents may have offered to send him somewhere for rehabilitation."

Gray nodded slowly, processing the information. It was a sound theory, but it was no more than that without evidence. "We need to talk to Folden's aunt, the problem being she was very badly affected by his conviction and moved away—she might even have gone back to Norway."

"Then let's go through this first and see if you still think it's necessary," Josh suggested.

"OK."

"Folden's next known offence occurred after he moved to England. He was caught in possession of and admitted to selling counterfeit passports, for which he received an eighteen-month custodial sentence. At twenty-one, he was released on licence with extensive support from the probation service. He'd completed the first year of his law degree in prison, and his probation officer sent him to Campion Holdings PLC for his community service, where Alistair Campion offered him legal work in the firm."

Gray interjected, "And by way of saying thank you, Folden murdered him."

"Now, now, Graham. A little patience, if you please. There are two more implicated offences before Alistair's untimely demise."

"My apologies."

"Accepted. While Folden was at university—funded by none other than Alistair Campion—one of his lecturers claimed he was being extorted by a student, but he refused to name them. The lecturer later confessed to an affair with a female undergraduate who dropped out because she was pregnant."

Gray was suddenly nauseous. "I see where this is going."

"Yes, I felt much the same at two o'clock this morning."

"What was the other incident you mentioned?"

"If I'm right, it's the point at which Folden's criminal career diverged. Campion's lawyers were, as we know, Sharston Strang and Partners, and Campion arranged for them to take Folden on as a paralegal. Given the seriousness of his prior offence, he could never practise as a solicitor, yet Alan Strang agreed to mentor him. Alan's older brother was also a lawyer, working at the same London firm as deceased barrister Simon Yarrow, whose identity Folden stole and whose death was recorded as natural circumstances. A few months before Folden started work for Alan Strang, Yarrow had made a report to the Bar Standards Board of potential misconduct—financial irregularities in Terence Strang's practice. Then Yarrow died—anaphylaxis, allegedly, though he had no known allergies—and the inquiry into Strang went away."

"Was Yarrow having an affair, by any chance?" Gray asked—hardly a wild stab in the dark, given both Campion and the lecturer had affairs.

"No. Yarrow was single, no known romantic associations."

"So where is this pattern?"

"Bear with me, Graham. All will become apparent. The next two definitive offences are the ones on which you were lead investigator—Clarkson's and Biddiscombe's counterfeit wills. Ronan Harper—"

"Clarkson's son," Gray provided.

Josh nodded. "Was estranged from his parents. Specifically—"

"His father," Gray finished.

"Oh, good. You've caught up." Josh tossed Gray a smile befitting a primary schoolteacher praising a struggling pupil who'd guessed the right answer. "Harper was a heroin addict in recovery, but his illness was cited in his parents' divorce, and they'd both cut contact with him—until his father was dying and reached out."

"Addiction is so destructive," Gray said, flashing back to those first days in the rehab clinic when he'd have sold his sister to get his hands on cocaine. He'd been fortunate enough to have a supportive employer and the money to pay for top-notch private treatment or else he didn't care to think which road his life would have taken—presuming he hadn't accidentally overdosed and killed himself, which would have been his lot some time ago were it not for Josh. "So you're saying Folden has two psychological profiles?"

"Only one profile, but there are two distinct patterns to his crimes." Josh turned his laptop towards Gray. "Do you recognise this man?" Gray shook his head. "Kevin Callaghan? Your testimony put him behind bars."

Gray stared hard at the smiling thirty-something on the screen. To his shame, he couldn't reconcile the image with his memory, yet he'd shadowed Callaghan for months.

"To recap, for the scatterbrained," Josh said, "Callaghan was Biddiscombe's doctor and refused to follow his patient's advance directive when her stepsister noticed something was wrong with the will. The malpractice suit was a smokescreen so Folden could make his getaway with Biddiscombe's money, except he didn't. He pursued Callaghan and threatened to kill him. The stress of that, coupled with the fear of punishment from his physically abusive father, led to Callaghan's psychotic break and—to cut short a long story we're both familiar with—eventual death in prison."

"Are you suggesting Callaghan's suicide was staged too?"

"Oh, no. It was definitely a suicide. But Kevin wasn't Folden's victim."

"His father was," Gray realised.

"Précisément! For Folden, it's a double reward—punishing fathers who abandon their sons and—"

"What's that? Some kind of Oedipal complex?" Gray asked in all seriousness. Josh pointedly ignored him.

"*And* getting paid for the privilege. I'd even go so far as to say he picks and chooses the contracts he accepts on that basis."

"God, if we'd known back then..."

"You wouldn't have caught him, Graham. There's a strong probability you won't catch him now."

"That's not what I want to hear."

"I'm sorry. I won't lie to you. Folden conned Sharston, Strang and countless others in the criminal justice system—including the SIU—into believing he was just a puppet, a paid-for hitman, torturer or whatever was their bidding. But he wasn't working for them."

"We know he had help from someone higher up."

"I concur. More worrying still, whoever's paying him knows he doesn't do it for the money. Folden earns his living through criminal gains, but his motivation is the thrill he gets out of watching men suffer at his hands."

"Men?"

"Whether business or personal, every one of Folden's targets was male."

"He tried to kill Alice Friar."

"No. Angela Sharston tried to kill Alice Friar."

"But he didn't do anything to stop her."

"I'll concede that," Josh said. "However, my point remains. Folden didn't escalate the way the classic profilers suggest. By every account he had a normal childhood. Even as an adolescent his misdemeanours were on a par with what George and other boys I knew got up to. Indeed, the only remarkable thing about Folden's development is the complete absence of any precursors to the onset of a personality disorder or criminal behaviour. There's no evidence of abuse or self-harm, no family history of mental illness, yet his attack on that sales clerk in Norway sparked the beginning of an industrious and brutal criminal career. Folden found his raison d'être—a tool to punish those who'd wronged him and a trade he toiled to master."

"Which of those is his motivation for targeting Rob?" Gray asked, adding before Josh could offer an 'insufficient data' rebuttal, "An educated guess."

"It's of little consequence. Killing is as fundamental to Folden's identity as investigating is to yours or theorising is to mine. He couldn't stop if he wanted to, and he doesn't want to."

"Then there's only one option."

15: Something in the Air

ROB TROD CAREFULLY and kept hold of the banister as he descended Tonka's spiral staircase. The steps were too narrow at any time but especially when his balance was off, thanks to half a dozen beers and a very late night—so late he'd sent his four-a.m. check-in text as he'd got into bed. He'd crashed out before putting his phone on charge, so he didn't know what the time was, but he wasn't first up.

"Afternoon," Dee greeted him from the far side of the downstairs room where she sat, cross-legged, smack-bang in the middle of one of the massive, white sofas, laptop balanced on her thighs, a pile of paper to her left, her phone, water bottle and a discarded sweatshirt to her right.

"Is it?" Rob thought it was late, but not that late.

"Nah—half ten, just gone. Coffee?"

"Yeah, but stay there. I'll make it." He stepped down to ground level—his equilibrium caught up a second later—and staggered across to the kitchen area...straight into the breakfast bar. He swore under his breath and rubbed his hip. "Was that beer super-strength?"

"Just common or garden pilsner. Still smashed?"

"I dunno." Rob wobbled again on his way to the sink with the kettle. "It doesn't usually get me like this."

"Did you sleep OK?"

"I think so. My last recollection was texting the group."

"I saw that. You can't have been that pissed—there wasn't a single typo. Ear infection?"

"Not that I know of." Rob switched on the kettle and went over the sofas, thinking he'd be wise to sit down before he fell down. "How are you doing this morning? Did you sleep?"

"Yeah, I'm all right. Been up since eight. Had a shower, wasted some time on social media, watched a video of a dickhead politician talking about how the police need more powers. More money is what we need, mate."

"You sound like my old boss."

"Gray?"

"Martina. The SIU was never short of a bob or two."

"I remember—I used to process the expenses claims." Dee set her laptop aside and turned, stretching her legs along the sofa. "It's out of order—the elite units always getting the lion's share."

"Not anymore. Gray reckons the SIU's on its way out."

"It wouldn't surprise me. The unit I'm working for now has had its budget slashed to free up more money for recruitment."

Rob nodded. "That's all Martina's missus talks about—recruitment. She's even tried to persuade me to go back." The kettle came to a boil, and he went to deal with the coffee, still unsteady on his feet. It had to be the stress.

"Are you tempted?" Dee asked.

"Nope." Rob didn't even leave a beat, but he considered his answer as he made the coffee. No, he wasn't tempted to go back into the police, nor did he regret leaving, or not in any significant way beyond the barriers he and Gray faced in conducting their private investigations. They both still had contacts on the force whom they could've tapped for information; failing that, Aaron could've found a back door into the national computer, but they'd agreed from the start: no dodgy dealing, they'd do everything by the book; apart from a couple of car registration searches, they'd stuck to it.

Rob gingerly carried the coffees over to the sofas. "Nothing going on then?"

"Dead quiet." Dee took one of the mugs from him. "Where's your phone?"

"Upstairs on charge."

"At least it's stopped you watching that video footage."

Rob looked away, shame-faced. She had him on that one. He wasn't even sure why he kept watching it. It just made him mad. Gray and Dom might've put him out of action, stopped him acting on the instinct to protect his son, but it didn't take that instinct away.

"I want to go see Lu today."

"We can do that," Dee said.

"And go for a run. Bloody typical. I'm not really into running."

"But now you can't, you want to?"

"Pretty much." More that if he didn't find an outlet, he was going to end doing something dangerous.

"We can always work out here," Dee suggested. "There's plenty of space."

"What? Aerobics or something?"

"I think you might be being a bit sexist there, Rob."

"I didn't mean to be."

"Who does aerobics anymore, anyway?"

"My mum, and my nieces do Zumba. Isn't that aerobics?"

"Dunno, mate. I've never done it."

Rob recognised that tone—the one that said 'watch it, sunshine, or you're for the high jump'. His mum used it too. "So how do you keep in shape?" he asked—a much safer bet but also a genuine observation. Dee's snug-fit grey top and pants contoured an athletic physique and toned muscles. She was super fit.

"Kickboxing, stamina training, weights, cardio, spinning. I run sometimes, usually on the treadmill. Horseriding..."

"Yeah?"

"Well, I used to. I stopped years ago—before uni."

"Did you have a horse?"

"Yep, although it was more of a timeshare, and it's not like other sports where you train and you do the sport and that's it. You're responsible for mucking out, taking her out in the morning, putting her back again in the evening. It takes up a huge amount of time. Are you still playing footy?"

The sudden switch back to Rob said it all. Dee missed riding, no doubt missed her horse too. After walking Linford for a year, Rob understood that attachment well enough. He acknowledged her sadness with a sympathetic smile and answered the question. "I *was* playing, back up north. I told you some of my mates run a Sunday league team, didn't I?"

"I think so."

She didn't sound so sure, and Rob honestly couldn't remember what he'd told her a year ago. He'd only officially joined the Lions the past season, so he might not have mentioned it.

She smirked. "Sunday league, old blokes with beer bellies... I bet that's a fast-paced, action-packed game."

Rob laughed. "I guess I deserved that for the aerobics and Zumba, but it's a good team—the best in the region. Most of our players are in their thirties and forties. And we've got a female striker."

"Oh, I take it all back then." Dee rolled her eyes, but she was smiling too. "So when d'you want to go see Lu?"

"I'm in no rush. I like your workout idea, if you promise to be gentle with me."

"Ha! No chance!"

He scowled, and she mirrored it, exaggerating the pout until Rob couldn't help but smile.

"Tell you what," she said, "you go get some kit on and I'll shufty these sofas out the way. Then we'll play it by ear. What d'you reckon?"

"Sold."

***

Forty minutes later, Rob had upgraded his assessment of 'super fit' to 'bionic'. Kickboxing, stamina runs from one wall to the other, skipping with a rope Dee had found in the garage—he'd been knackered before they'd finished warming up while she still looked like she could've run a marathon.

"Hang on," he panted and stopped two minutes into the five of alternating scissor jumps and squat-thrusts. He bent, resting his hands on his thighs, sweat dripping off him. "Gimme a minute."

"No worries. It's a tough routine," Dee said, though she was coping with it just fine.

"How often do you work out?"

"Every day."

Rob straightened up, still breathless. The sweat trickled back down his face. Dee was watching him. "I'm an old man," he joked self-consciously. Dee was ten years younger than him—around the same age as Zoë.

"I probably shouldn't tell you I already did a bit of a workout first thing."

"Bloody hell. I think I might give it up as a bad idea." He glanced longingly at the sofas.

"Come on!" Dee encouraged. "Another ten minutes and we're done." She'd kept up the jumps and squat-thrusts while they'd been talking. It was some consolation she was also breathless and sweaty.

Rob picked up the rhythm and resumed, saying, "I need you as my personal trainer."

"I'm up for that—if you're serious."

"While we're stuck here, you mean?"

"And after. I'm moving back to London in a few weeks."

"Oh?"

"The job up north is secondment."

"Didn't know that." He could hardly get the words out between breaths, and his legs were past jelly, heading for liquid.

"We'll do another five minutes," Dee said. "All right?"

Rob managed to nod as they switched to squat-thrusts again, eyes locked with Dee's. Down...up...down...

She grinned. "Yeah, I'm well up for it."

***

"You're quiet," Dee observed some way into their journey to Zoë's parents' place. When Rob didn't reply, she lowered the volume on the car stereo and glanced across at him. "I thought you'd nodded off."

"Just daydreaming." That was about all he could articulate. His head was a mess. When she'd finished running him ragged, he'd gone up to shower and stayed in his room for a while, taking time to process the undeniable chemistry between them. Then he'd switched on his phone and seen the message from Ari—*Is it because of Freddie?*—timestamped halfway through their workout, confirming firstly that Ari was spying on them, and secondly that yesterday's interrogation was, as he'd suspected, fuelled by jealousy.

Rob hadn't responded to the message. He wasn't sure what to say when Ari was right, or half right. Rob had stayed up north to keep an eye on his nieces and help his mum and Harvey, but he'd only stopped returning Naomi's calls after Freddie was released from prison and she'd moved in with him.

The thing was, Rob got it. With Freddie, Ari had the perfect setup: Naomi liked the finer things in life, which Freddie supplied in abundance; Aaron could work from home, and regardless of how it seemed, he stood up to Freddie when it mattered most, refusing to go down the gender reassignment route, which was what Freddie wanted. As Aaron had said when Rob first realised they—Aaron/Naomi—were gender-fluid, it was a death sentence for Aaron, but Freddie couldn't see that.

Much as it pained Rob to admit it, now he'd met Ari, he could understand why. To Freddie, Ari was an amalgamation of Aaron's and Naomi's best features, not part of the whole person, and in a way, Rob was as bad, seeing them as two separate people. One thing or the other. Binary thinking. Rob's mind filled with *The Matrix*—the strings of green numbers, which his memory insisted were zeroes and ones. He took out his phone and searched for an image from the movie—to prove the point to himself. *Not zeroes and ones.*

Another text message:

~ *I shouldn't have asked. Sorry.*

Rob stared at the notification hovering over green and black. He clicked on 'reply': *No chance to text back. Can we talk sometime?*

"What's happening?" Dee asked.

"Nothing. Just text-chatting with Ari."

~ *The Matrix?*

Rob smiled as he typed: *Binary.*

~ *It's a jumble of nonsense letters and kana characters.*

There was a brief delay, then:

~ *Not binary.*

Rob typed back: *I know that...now.*

He waited. After a few minutes with no response, he locked his phone. "I wish I'd had breakfast."

"It's past lunchtime," Dee pointed out.

Rob's belly grumbled. Dee laughed.

"Want me to stop at McDonald's?"

"You read my mind."

Dee's smile lingered a second before it was lost to concentrating on navigating across three lanes so they could double back to the drive-thru.

"Thanks for this," Rob said.

"Anytime."

Rob's screen activated.

~ *Yes. We should talk. x*

***

"Do you all have to be in here?" Dora lifted Rob's arm to wipe the kitchen island. Only half an hour previously, she'd shouted up the stairs to ask if they planned on spending the entire day cooped up in Lucas's room. To be fair, all the Cliftons were going a little stir crazy, other than Lucas, who didn't have a single care now he was back on his Xbox, playing some world-building game—with Ari.

"We should check in with the team," Dee suggested and gave Rob a nudge.

"Good idea." He slid off his stool and sidled towards the door.

"Hold on!" Zoë called. She grabbed Travis by the arm and towed him across the kitchen. "We need to talk to you."

Rob frowned, but Zoë shook her head, waving him on, so on he went. "Where can we go and be out the way?"

"The cellar?" Travis suggested.

"Dad's down there," Zoë said. "The garage." She marched ahead, still towing poor Travis and unimpressed when Dee blocked their route with her arm she could enter first and make sure there were no intruders lurking.

"Clear," she confirmed, granting them access to the chilly, grey space three-quarters full of tidily stacked furniture.

"Look, there's even somewhere to sit." Travis pulled the top garden chair from a stack and set it down, repeating three more times. He sat and nodded in satisfaction. "If we got a beer fridge, we could stay out here all day."

Zoë gave him a look. "It's the middle of the afternoon."

"So? What else are we gonna do?"

"No beer," she said sternly.

Travis stuck out his bottom lip. Zoë wavered but remained resolute.

"What did you need to talk to us about?" Rob asked. The question came out more curtly than he'd intended. Upstairs, he'd realised Ari had been playing games with Lucas at the same time as they'd been texting each other—was he reading too much into the delayed response? Whatever, they did need to talk, if for no other reason than to clarify where they stood.

"Come and sit," Zoë prompted.

Rob leaned conspiratorially towards Dee. "I hate it when people say that."

She nodded. "Serious shit's about to go down."

"Rob!" Zoë snapped.

With an overplayed sigh, he went over and moved a chair so it was opposite hers. Dee stayed where she was.

Zoë exhaled shakily and reached for Travis's hand. "We wanted to tell you first..." She looked ready to cry, and Rob's imagination took off. *They're gonna emigrate, and I don't blame them, but Lu—*

"I'm pregnant."

"Right," Rob said, but the news took a bit longer to sink in, and longer still to hit him emotionally. "Blimey. I mean, congratulations." He was stunned, but he was happy for her. Happy for them both. And terrified on their behalf.

"Thank you," Zoë said with a sniff. A pair of tears rolled down her cheeks.

"Zo?"

She laughed and shrugged. "Hormones."

Rob smiled, remembering now how much she'd cried when they were having Lucas. At first, he'd worried she was depressed; she'd assured him she was fine, but the smallest things would have her sobbing—favourite TV series coming to an end, baby birds learning to fly. In those nine months they had to have bought a lifetime's supply of Kleenex.

"So you haven't told Lu yet?"

"Not yet."

"He's gonna be over the moon."

"Do you think so?"

"Yeah, definitely. Wasn't that why he wanted us to get back together?"

"Err, yeah." Zoë glanced at Travis, who didn't react at all to Rob's comment, which was a bit insensitive in retrospect. "So, we were thinking..." Zoë continued, "we should bring the wedding forward."

"To when?"

"A month. That's the legal notice period."

"We don't know what the situation will be a month from now."

"It's been like this for a year already, Rob. How much longer are we supposed to wait?"

"Until it's safe."

"And when will that be?"

"We could find Folden tomorrow—"

"Or it could take another three months. Or three years!"

"No," Rob said. This was the end game, he was certain. If Folden was true to form, they were talking days, weeks at a push. Always the long, slow torture, like trapping a spider and pulling off its legs, one by one, watching it skitter with seven, six, five, four, three, two...down to a body exhausted, immobilised and afraid. Then, in a frenzy, he'd crush it and squeeze it and stamp it into the ground, loving every second.

First the photos a year ago, then the online communication with Lucas and the alleged attempted abduction within a couple of days of each other—Folden was building up to the frenzy.

"Shit." Rob was on his feet and tugging his phone from his jeans.

"What is it?" Dee asked.

"Folden's about to play his next move." The line rang out. "Come on, Gray! Answer, damn it." Rob let it ring twice more and tried calling Dom. Same result. "Why the hell aren't they answering?" He hung up again and called Ari. "Hey, it's Rob. Can you tell me where Gray and Dom are?"

"Yes. One moment. Gray and Josh left the hotel fifteen minutes ago, heading for Gray's house. And Dom is...*was* in a Met Police building in E1."

"That's the SIU," Rob said, thinking aloud. "What the hell's he doing there?"

"I'm afraid it's a bit of black spot," Aaron/Ari said. Rob wasn't sure which. "I can try and hook in to their security cameras."

"No, don't worry about it. I'll try Gray again. If he's driving, he might not be able to answer his phone. Can you let me know when Dom's back on the grid?"

"Of course."

"Cheers..." Rob stumbled over which name to use, although Aaron wouldn't have said he'd *try* to hack the cameras.

"Ari," they confirmed, then, "Call me when you can." They weren't asking for an update on Gray and Dom.

"I will," Rob promised.

16: Lost in Transit

"WHY NOW?" JOSH studied the front of the house as if he were a prospective buyer while he waited for Gray to lock the car.

"I beg your pardon?"

"You and Will have been living together for almost a year. Why is it only now you've decided to officially move in? Because that decision must have come before the marriage proposal."

"Yeah, it did," Gray answered vaguely and checked the time. He had three missed calls, and the furniture guys should have been at his house already—even allowing for heavy traffic—but none of the calls were from them. They were from Rob, and Gray got no answer when he returned them.

"Is there a problem?" Josh was observing him closely, head tilted like a curious dog.

"I don't know. They're late."

"Or maybe they were early?"

"It's possible." They'd have needed to be very early to have finished, unless they'd just chucked all Gray's stuff into boxes, in which case he'd be unpacking broken plates later. "There's only one way to find out."

He took out his spare key and stepped around Josh to access the front door. "I must admit, I'm not impressed. That company was far from the cheapest." He put the key in the lock and twisted to the left. The key stopped at the forty-five-degree mark without engaging the mechanism. Gray pushed on the handle; the door opened. "Looks like you were right, and they've been and gone."

"Lucky you were so insistent on coming to check up on them."

"Isn't it?" The house was in a relatively nice area, and he'd installed shutters on the rear-facing windows when he'd 'unofficially' moved to Will's, but an unlocked, empty property would soon have been noticed by thieves, squatters or both.

The puzzle became more complex still when Gray opened the living room door and discovered all his furniture exactly where he'd left it.

"Did you employ cowboys?"

Of course Gray had checked the company's credentials, but now he was wondering if he'd been thorough enough. The only reason he could come up with—or the only reason he was prepared to entertain—for why his house had been left unlocked and unattended was that they'd downed tools for lunch before they'd even begun; a quick tour around the ground-floor rooms confirmed nothing had been packed.

"Maybe they started upstairs," Gray said, though he unholstered his gun on the way up. With every step, his unease ratcheted another notch. When they reached the landing, he stopped and called, "Hello?" listening for any indication of activity.

"What?" Josh said. "You think they forgot to bring packing tape and one stayed here while the other went to get some? There's no-one here, Graham."

Josh was right: the house was dead silent. But someone *had been* there because Gray kept the doors shut, and most still were—all bar one: his bedroom.

Taking no chances, he whispered to Josh to stay back and moved stealthily along the landing to the open door. He paused again, breath held, but heard only his pulse. Using his foot, he pushed the door fully open, gun trained on the widening gap, his gaze fixed on a point across the room so he'd be able to pick up even the smallest movement in his peripheral vision. The half of the room he could see was all in order, right down to the jacket and boots he'd chosen then discarded the last time he'd set out from his house to meet Will. Gray switched on the light and panned right. From his current position, only the foot of the bed was visible, the duvet ruched where he'd sat to change his boots—no. He was a compulsive duvet straightener. He wouldn't have left it like that. One step forward would confirm if he was right. One step...

"Ah, hell."

Gray advanced into the room far enough to confirm there were no intruders, or none other than the man in grey overalls sprawled face down on the bed, blood splatter framing his upper back and a bullet hole between his shoulder blades. Gray watched for the rise and fall of the man's torso and checked for a carotid pulse, noting the man's body temp registered as within normal range, but there were no breaths and no pulse.

"Dead," he whispered to Josh as he passed him and continued along the landing to check the rest of upstairs. Satisfied there was no-one else in the house, he returned to the dead man. "Can you call the emergency services?"

Josh moved out of sight but not out of hearing distance, and Gray listened to his side of the call, using it to ground himself as the horrific realisation slotted, piece by jagged piece, into order in his brain. This was Folden's work, it had to be. He'd either been watching Gray's house for some time or somehow found out the removal firm was coming. Alternatively, the removal guys could've disturbed a trespasser—an armed trespasser. Unlikely as that was, Gray exercised diligence, drawing on his training and years of experience in an effort to distance himself.

Rolling the guy to check his uniform for a logo would further contaminate the scene, so instead, Gray took out his phone and loaded the furniture company's site, going straight to their gallery page. There was only one staged photo of two smiling men lifting a sofa into the back of a van, and both wore the same grey overalls as the man on the bed.

"Police and ambulance on their way," Josh said from the doorway.

Gray nodded, unable to articulate over the jumble of thoughts. He needed to alert Will and Tie before they got back to the house, except...

"The animals!" He almost retched in his panic.

Josh advanced into the room, but Gray held up his hand to stop him coming any closer. "To preserve the scene. Come on." He led the way back downstairs, gun in one hand, phone in the other. "I need to get hold of Will. Can you hit the alarm button and call Dom? Tell him Folden's hijacked the furniture van." They stepped outside, and Gray locked the door, only then looking at Josh. "OK?"

Josh nodded, his ghost-white visage belying his calm compliance as he made the call.

Gray wasn't faring much better; his hands were shaking to the point he mistyped his PIN twice before he brought up Will's number, repeating in his head *please answer*, but Will was still at work and the call went to voicemail. Gray hit end call, tried once more, to no avail, and thumbed at speed through his contacts, down to Tie's number. Again, it rang out unanswered and went to voicemail, and again, and again. Gray hung up, retried, hung up, retried—

"Jesus, Gray!" Tie finally answered on the first ring. "I only popped upstairs for a piss! Where's the fire?"

"Sorry, Tie. This is urgent—I'll explain later. Get the animals out and take them somewhere safe then stay away from the house."

"Roger that." No questions, no wasting time. That was the beauty of the animal rights network.

Gray hung up and took a moment to breathe—slow, deep breaths. He'd assumed Tie was in his van—Will's van, in actuality—but even if he wasn't, he'd sort something out, and he and the animals would be safe.

Next: to intercept Will, who generally didn't return Gray's calls until he'd finished work, and that would be too late. He tried calling again. Still voicemail.

"Dom's sending a car for us," Josh said.

"We've got my car." Gray redialled—

"He said to leave it here. He'll get someone to drive it back to my hotel. And the police helicopter's going out for the removal van."

—and hung up. "Damn it. I can't get hold of Will." He jabbed the call button again.

"Dom's dealing with that too," Josh said.

"How?"

"I don't know, but he's a senior police officer. He'll find a way."

Gray gave up and stared back at the house, as if he could glean from it what Folden's game was, and trying to convince himself that Dom would reach Will in time. "Where's Rob?"

"With Dee."

Gray nodded, grateful they were safe. "Let's wait in the car," he said, joking glibly as he crossed the pavement, "George is going to kill me."

"Never mind George! You've just completely messed up my profile!"

Gray's laughter escaped in a burst of hysteria. He clicked the key fob; the car unlocked, and they both climbed in. "I'm sorry I put you in danger."

"I know you are, but we're both at fault. All that discussion of narcissism last night and still we were too arrogant to take a step back so we could see the full picture."

"I'm glad you're here."

"I'm not sure I feel the same."

"I can't believe all this time Folden's been using Rob to get to me."

"It's a possibility," Josh said, although his tone said *wrong again!*

"Enlighten me."

"I need to go back over the data—"

"Forget the data. Gut feeling. What's Folden up to?"

"I don't—"

"Just go with it. Please?"

Josh sighed. "Fine, but you might as well ask a psychic. As far as I can tell, Rob's still the target."

"So it *is* personal."

Josh shrugged but didn't get around to answering, as an unmarked SUV pulled up outside Gray's house. Dom and Iz got out, both in Kevlar vests, and waited for Gray and Josh, not a word spoken until they were all safely inside the vehicle with Dom behind the wheel. He put his foot down, catapulting Gray and Josh against the backrest. Soon, they were moving at speed, dodging through traffic.

"Where are we going?" Gray asked, still battling to buckle in.

"Oh, bugger this!" Josh released his seat belt and it retracted violently.

"Berringer's," Dom said, tapping on his earpiece to answer an incoming call. "Hooper. ... Yep." He met Gray's gaze in the rear-view mirror. "That's good news. Keep me posted." He tapped his earpiece again. "Will's safe."

"Thank God." Gray slumped in relief. "Where is he?"

"On his way to McIntyre...Tie. He asked me to tell you that everyone got out and they're going to ground."

"OK."

"I take it you understand what that means."

"Kind of." Gray knew it meant Will, Tie and the animals would be with their own kind. Where, specifically, he had no idea, but they were safe, and that was all he cared about. "Is Berringer aware we're RV-ing at his apartment?"

"I didn't ask. Ari suggested it. The building's deceptive. Looks like it's got a part-time retired concierge and fuck all security when it's armoured up like the Bank of England."

"I'll take their word for it," Gray said, wondering how Will had managed to talk his way in the night he'd confronted Berringer if it was as secure as Ari claimed. But then, it was Will. He could talk his way in or out of anywhere, quite possibly including the Bank of England.

Twenty-five minutes to Berringer's, according to the satnav; Dom drove like a boy racer let loose at Brand's Hatch and they made it in eighteen. When the concierge let them in without checking their credentials, Gray almost said 'I told you so' but hastily swallowed his words at the sight of the firearms officer guarding the stairs. Another stood sentry outside Berringer's apartment, only stepping aside when an officious-looking woman opened the door and thrust her hand, palm up, at Dom.

"Your identification," she demanded. Dom took out his warrant card and held it up for her to see. She frowned at it but, seemingly satisfied, let them in, explaining in the same brusque tone, "Sofia Selkirk—Mr. Berringer's assistant."

Her self-introduction summoned the man from wherever he'd been, and he sauntered to a stop dead centre of the hallway, hands stuffed in pockets, chin up, beady eyes wandering. It became apparent why as they moved closer. Berringer was drunk and deliberately standing in their way, although he looked like the slightest breath of a breeze would knock him over.

"Take them through, Sofia," he slurred, turned and endeavoured to swagger back whence he'd more than likely come—a sitting room, Gray discovered as they passed by. Berringer poured himself another whisky and ignored them.

"This way," Sofia said, directing a stern look at Gray, and led them into the dining room, a long, relatively narrow space with windows at one end, the Venetian blinds partly closed, hence it was dim despite the plain white walls upon which hung a few vibrant, modern paintings. It looked no different now than when Gray had first met Aaron Tanner and Freddie Berringer—when Will and Freddie had their showdown. Ultimately, it had all been pointless hot air: Will had changed his statement so Berringer would walk free because this cause—finding Anders Folden—superseded all others.

"Have a seat," Sofia invited. "I'll let Mx. Silvestri know you're here." She marched off towards another doorway at the far end of the back wall, trusting them to do as they were told, which they did.

It was at that point Gray noticed a third officer standing near the windows with his back to the room. His armoured attire padded out his tall, thin frame to almost average width, but there was no mistaking his identity.

"Martin."

"Graham," he acknowledged without turning around.

Next to Gray, Josh muttered, "And today was going *so* well," which put a bit of a smile on Gray's face even though he wanted to go over and give Martin Winstanley a smack in the teeth for keeping him firmly out of the loop because, now he knew Will was safe, Gray was seeing if not the full picture, a decent proportion of it.

"Excuse me one moment," he said—to Josh only—pushed his chair back and walked the length of the room, stopping next to Winstanley. "What took you so long?"

Winstanley didn't answer and continued gazing through the blind slats at one particular spot, prompting Gray to look what was there: a marksman, plus guards all over Berringer's building. This wasn't an emergency meeting; it was a fully fledged operation.

"Dom's working for you, isn't he?"

"Well done, Mr. Fisher. As are you now."

Gray turned his head sharply, about to bite back, but instead clamped his lips together, silencing a gasp. Winstanley looked ill: sallow, wrinkled skin, dark-ringed eyes, his nose, already on the large side, drooped like a turkey's snood over his thin lips, almost down to his chin. "How long?"

"That's hardly important."

"So all your bluster last spring about me seeing connections that weren't there—"

"You jeopardised my operation then, and you continue to do so now, despite my warning—my efforts to *protect* you. What in God's name were you thinking? Putting your face in front of a TV camera."

"What's that got to do with what happened this morning? It won't air for weeks yet."

"As that may be, your *debut* put you on the payroll, ergo in the Inland Revenue system."

Gray was so taken aback he stuttered out a few nonsensical syllables but couldn't form a single, coherent sentence. He couldn't believe how stupid he'd been, how complacent. All those years of undercover investigations, never attending court to protect his identity. Not only did Folden now know what he looked like, he also knew Gray's Equity name—essentially his legal name—and could trace him in public records.

To their left, Sofia reappeared with Ari, who tapped at a tablet on the move. Gray waited until they were at the other end of the room, keeping his voice low to say, "After we're done here, you and I need to talk."

"Agreed. But first, I require your assistance with this conference."

"Assistance?"

"More...your trust and cooperation."

"That's rich!"

"Graham—"

"No, I'm sorry, Martin, but perhaps if you'd kept me informed, I wouldn't have *jeopardised your operation* or put people's lives on the line." So saying, Gray returned to his seat next to Josh, who narrowed his eyes but kept whatever opinion he might have—and he would have one—to himself.

Something clicked to Gray's left and up; he spotted the red indicator light a second before the projector cast a blue square onto a stretch of white wall between two portraits, one of a woman Gray vaguely recognised, the other of Freddie Berringer that made him look a sight more handsome and sober than he was in real life.

"Hello," Ari offered as a general greeting and smiled, and Gray realised it was them in the portrait, or Naomi at least. He, Josh, Dom and Isobel mumbled the same in response.

Winstanley came over, his deep-lined eyes locked on Gray's. Gray stubbornly stared back, but his anger was a fragile shield barely capable of protecting himself, let alone Will, Rob, Josh and everyone else he'd endangered, and Winstanley was not the enemy. A single nod was all Gray offered, no promises, but it was enough, as Winstanley nodded back.

"Is everything ready?" he asked Ari.

"Yes." They handed Winstanley the tablet and took a seat next to Gray. The four of them had automatically clustered around one end of the table; typically, it was the one which meant they weren't fully facing the projection, and they had to shuffle their chairs back so they could see.

"Sofia's arranging some tea," Ari said.

"Many thanks," Winstanley acknowledged, somewhat distracted by what he was doing, or trying to do, and after a minute of struggling, he beckoned for Ari's help. Rather than hand over the tablet, he waited for them to walk around the table to him. The projection changed to the messenger app homepage and then switched to a video conference with two windows, both blank, but they didn't stay that way for long.

"Hello, Rob," Ari said. "Can you hear me?"

"Yeah, very clearly," Rob confirmed, now in the right-hand window. Dee—sitting next to him—gave a thumbs up to confirm she could hear too.

A woman appeared in the other window—forties, possibly early fifties, bobbed brown hair, no make-up, glasses—whom Gray didn't recognise, but judging by the sarcastically muttered "Great" from Josh, he did.

"Can you hear me, Professor Holt?" Ari asked.

"I can," she replied.

"Thank you, Mx. Silvestri," Winstanley said. "I'll take it from here."

Rather than walk back to the other side of the table, Ari pulled out the closest chair and sat, leaving Winstanley the only one still standing.

"Introductions, briefly," he said. "I'm Deputy Chief Constable Martin Winstanley, Internal Affairs," then, gesturing to each person in turn, "Mr. Graham Fisher, formerly head of the Special Investigations Unit, now a private investigator. To his right, chartered psychologist Mr. Joshua Sandison-Morley and Detective Sergeant Isobel Barnes, SIU. To my right, technology specialist Mx. Ari Silvestri and, of course, you know Detective Chief Inspector Dominic Hooper."

He paused for the murmured exchange of greetings before directing the attention of those present to the projection. "Via video link two, we have former Metropolitan Police Officer Robert Simpson-Stone, also a private investigator and Mr. Fisher's business partner, and Detective Sergeant Dee Knight, presently on secondment with Project Servator. Lastly, on video link one is Professor Trudi Holt, a forensic psychologist from King's College, London."

"Gosh! What a team of experts," the professor gushed, her smile warm and a touch smarmy. "I believe Mr. Sandison-Morley and I have already met."

"Yes, we have," Josh confirmed.

"I wasn't aware you were a forensic psychologist."

"I'm not."

"Oh, I'm sorry. I misunderstood—"

"Quite the contrary," Gray interjected. "I brought in Mr. Sandison-Morley to profile our target. He undertook consultations with my former unit—with great success, I might add."

"Mmm-hmm." Professor Holt was singularly unimpressed. "I look forward to comparing notes."

"Yes, indeed," Josh said with unseemly and phony enthusiasm.

Gray winced, as did Rob. They'd both had the same thought about the inevitability of Josh telling Trudi Holt how he really felt about them working together, and she didn't look like she'd hold back any punches either. But they'd only be expressing how they all felt about this impromptu collaboration.

"If I may..." Winstanley said, pausing for less than a second to ensure he had everyone's attention. "We have a lot to cover this afternoon. First, to recap events from earlier today.

"The body found in Mr. Fisher's empty property has been identified as Keith Thompson, an employee of Brentford Furniture Removals. Thompson was shot once at close range. His assailant hijacked the furniture removal van and forced Thompson's co-worker, Sanjay Khanna, to drive him to the van's destination—Mr. Fisher's current residence. The suspect absconded as we moved in on the van, leaving Khanna severely traumatised but uninjured. From Khanna's description and the suspect's motivation, we're almost certainly looking for Anders Folden. As I speak, a team is processing the crime scene and securing Mr. Fisher's property.

"All other relevant information pertaining to this investigation, up to and including last week's attempted abduction of Mr. Simpson-Stone's son Lucas, is in the e-dossier Mx. Silvestri has copied to your secure inboxes.

"Second, I must thank Mr. Fisher for putting together, as the professor noted, an exceptional team. It is, shall we politely say, unorthodox and compromises every principle I have upheld throughout my career. Alas I have no choice but to come humbly before you and request your cooperation.

"As some of you may have already discerned—" Winstanley's appraising gaze swept to Gray "—DCI Hooper and I have been working together for some time. Our operation is deeply covert to the extent that it does not officially exist. I cannot over-emphasise the necessity of maintaining that state of play. Suffice to say, this is more than a hunt for a murder suspect. It is a matter of national security."

17: Too Many Chiefs

WHILE WINSTANLEY DRONED on, Rob quietly opened the top drawer of Dora's desk—she'd let them use her home office for the video conference—and searched by touch for something to write with and on. Eventually, he found a wad of Post-Its, a broken pencil and an electric pencil sharpener that screamed like a pneumatic drill when he put the pencil in it. Startled, he let go of the pencil, the machine spat it out, and it rolled away under the desk. He stretched his leg, trying to reach it with his foot but only succeeded in knocking over Dee's water bottle and pushing the pencil further away.

Dee must've realised he was up to something as she improvised an Oscar-winning performance of a loud coughing fit and swiftly muted their mic, keeping her hands up to hide her mouth as she spoke.

"Get my water for me." She booted the bottle across the room. "What are you doing?"

"Writing you a note." Rob went to retrieve the bottle and checked the view on-screen to confirm he couldn't be seen. "How well do you know Winstanley?"

"Not very. He came to SIU HQ last year—the day we discovered Folden had escaped. That's the only contact I've had with him."

"Yeah. Same here."

"Is there a problem?"

Rob watched the video feed, the suspicious glances aimed in their direction. Dee coughed and spluttered some more.

Something about the setup bothered Rob, and he couldn't figure out what. After all, getting Winstanley's attention was exactly what Gray had angled for, and Rob had gone along with it, even though he knew the man no better than Dee did and internal affairs was the enemy within.

Winstanley's jobsworth rep was infamous; he was the very last person anyone would expect a slippery player like Gray to be pally with. Yet Rob trusted Gray's judgement. Even when it had put him in Folden's sights, the end had justified the means. The sticking point this time was that Gray had deferred to Winstanley, no questions asked, although Rob didn't know what had been said before he and Dee had joined the meeting. What was clear was that Winstanley hadn't come to their aid; he'd come because he needed their help, and he was going all around the houses and sucking up to get it.

Perhaps it was nothing more than Rob's 'paranoia', and he had to trust someone in all of this. The question was, did he trust Dee more than he trusted Gray?

"I've got to turn the mic back on," Dee warned, reaching for her laptop.

"Wait!"

She froze, her finger millimetres from the button.

"I think Winstanley's stalling us," Rob said.

"Why?"

"Maybe we're getting too close to catching Folden."

"You think Winstanley wants the glory for himself?"

"No, what he said before about national—"

"Your thoughts, Mr. Simpson-Stone?" Winstanley asked the question at close quarters to whatever device he was using, and the sound distorted and crackled.

"Later," Dee said. "OK?"

With a shrug, Rob returned to his seat. He handed Dee's water over and unmuted the mic.

"I couldn't hear you, sorry, Sir. Could you repeat that?"

Gray interrupted before Winstanley could say another word. "No, Martin. It's absolutely not acceptable."

"We'll monitor him constantly, and there'll be a tracker implanted in his shoe. Of course there are risks, but—"

Gray slammed his hands on the table. "Enough!"

"If you have any other ideas for how we reach Folden—"

"We don't need to. We have two experienced profilers in our midst, either one of whom could extrapolate from the evidence you've amassed if you'd damn well let anyone at it, man."

"I'm alarmed by your insinuation, Graham. It was always my intention to grant you access to my case notes. However, if the information were in there, I assure you I'd have already found it. This is the only way—"

"*If* it's the only way, then you do it, or Dom."

Rob caught Dee's glances out of the corner of his eye. While both had missed what Winstanley had started with, they'd heard enough to pick up the gist. Winstanley wanted Rob to make contact with Folden.

"Excuse me, Sir," Rob interjected. "Could I ask for a quick recap? What do you need me to do?"

"What you were attempting to do when DCI Hooper intervened. Let Folden catch you and then let him talk. Professor Holt will brief you on how to interact with the target to maximise the chance of getting the information as quickly as possible. As soon as you do, we'll pull you out."

"Understood," Rob said, pretending he hadn't noticed Gray's angry head-shaking all the while Winstanley had been talking. "I'll do it."

Gray and Josh nearly gave themselves whiplash with the speed they turned to look at him. The protest was inevitable.

"It's not happening."

"Graham." Winstanley leaned right across the large table, his height putting him within touching distance of Gray, who didn't so much as flinch. "Unless you intend to volunteer—"

"I volunteer."

Winstanley made a sound somewhere between choking and laughing. "I admire your tenacity. However, Simpson-Stone—"

"*With all due respect,*" Rob said forcefully. "Gray, I appreciate what you're doing, but it's me he wants, and I know him better than anyone."

"Which he'll use to his advantage," Josh said. "Don't forget he knows you too."

Rob cussed—in his head—hating Josh for interfering. Winstanley didn't look too impressed either and rounded on him.

"In your *learned opinion*, Mr. Sandison-Morley, what is our best course of action?" He hovered, waiting for Josh to respond.

For a minute, maybe two, Josh sat dead still, his occasional blinks and Winstanley's tics the only signs that the video feed hadn't frozen. Then, at the point where Winstanley's twitching reached tremor proportions, Josh said, "Detective Sergeant Barnes is." He turned as if to look Rob in the eye, but didn't—was so far away from looking him in the eye he couldn't even have passed it off as being down to communicating via video camera. "If the SIU's records are accurate, Folden and Isobel have never interacted directly."

"The same is true for me," Gray argued.

"He knows who you are, Graham. He knows your weaknesses and he'll use them against you. But he knows nothing about DS Barnes, and—again, assuming the SIU's records are accurate—he's never targeted or killed a woman."

Rob was ready to lose it. If at any point they found themselves in the same place without some half-cocked vigilante ex-Met-Police task force listening to their every word, he'd give Josh hell. As it was, Rob had only one trick up his sleeve, and it was dirty, but he had to speak up.

"Josh, you've met Folden."

"I have."

"Gentlemen!" Winstanley enunciated loudly and slowly. "This is not up for discussion. My question was rhetorical. I believe Mr. Simpson-Stone is the best option we have, and Professor Holt concurs."

Up to that point, the woman in the little window on Dee's laptop had looked like she was taking a nap, but at the mention of her name she sat up straight and said, "The deputy chief constable is correct." No way had she heard what he'd said, but Josh was on the ball.

"I *do not* concur, *Sir*, and I believe if you permit Rob to continue, you will see why."

Winstanley didn't move for a long time, but eventually he stepped back, slowly pulled out the chair next to Ari's and sat. "Get on with it, Mr. Simpson-Stone."

"Josh, as a psychologist, have you ever worked with anyone like Anders Folden?"

"As a *psychotherapist*...I've counselled numerous clients who manifest personality disorder characteristics to varying extents. Would I consider any of them psychopathic? Potentially. However, I'm not qualified to offer psychiatric diagnoses."

"When you were treating them, did you ever feel unsafe?"

"On occasion, I have treated clients whose potential for violent or aggressive behaviour has made me feel unsafe." *Now* Josh looked Rob in the eye—a plea for him to stop the interrogation, because that was what it was.

"Three more questions," Rob assured him and waited for Josh's nod before he went on. "The Black Hole hostage situation—you volunteered to go in so the SIU could establish the location and status of their targets, one of whom was Folden. Is that correct?"

"Yes."

"Were you aware of who Folden was before you volunteered?"

"I'd conducted my own investigation into one of his aliases, so I was aware of what he was capable of."

"Yeah, you're dodging the question, mate," Rob accused as lightly as he could. "Let me put it another way. Did you know he was a psychopath?"

"No, I did not."

"And if you'd known, would you have volunteered to enter Black Hole?"

"Yes."

That was not the answer Rob had expected, and it threw him for a moment. He'd been trying to make the point that no person in their right mind would knowingly hand themselves over to a psychopath who'd murdered before, although he'd be ruling himself out if he did that, and perhaps he'd been way off in thinking Josh was 'in his right mind' that night at Black Hole. Still, it made no odds to where Rob had been heading with his line of questioning.

"In your learned opinion," he deliberately borrowed Winstanley's words, "would Folden attempt to kill Isobel?"

"I do not believe so."

"Would he attempt to kill me?"

Josh closed his eyes and inhaled deeply before answering. "Yes."

"We're wasting time," Winstanley snapped.

"Isn't that the point—" Rob glared at him "—*Sir*?"

Winstanley reared like a cornered scorpion. "I don't appreciate your tone, Mr. Simpson-Stone."

"And I don't appreciate being volunteered for a suicide mission. Because, let's be honest, you wanted me to do this all along."

"I'm not sure how you reached that conclusion."

"You let Folden escape."

"Again, I can't see—"

"Then I'll spell it out for you. Folden murdered one man and took another hostage, then drove off in a furniture removal van, which has to be a seven-and-a-half-tonner, minimum, with a speed limiter. Yet he was able to stay ahead of the pursuit cars—"

"As you acknowledged, he'd taken a hostage."

Rob shrugged. "Collateral damage. If you'd wanted to take him out, you'd have done it."

"That might be how it works in the armed forces, Mr. Simpson-Stone—"

"And in the police, particularly if we're talking about neutralising a threat to national security, but Folden isn't the threat, is he? You're after whoever's pulling his strings, and you still think I have intel on *your* target even though I gave you and Hooper everything last year."

"Not quite everything," Dom said. "You failed to mention your little arrangement with Folden's barrister."

Rob's heart leapt into his throat and then buried itself in his bowels, or it felt like, and not because he'd been caught out. The worst he'd done was turn a blind eye to Clough's activities in order to maintain his cover—actions which any SIU leader, past or present, would have condoned. However, that Dom Hooper knew about the arrangement confirmed they'd been watching Rob for a lot longer than the past few days or even the past year, which brought a further realisation—one which Gray must've had at the exact same moment because he got there first.

"You orchestrated the entire Brookhurst Hospital incident. You broke Folden out."

"Nonsense!" Winstanley objected.

"Someone else might've set it up, but you let him get away, just like you did today."

"Last resort," Dom admitted.

"Mr. Hooper..." Winstanley warned.

"Sorry, Sir, but I think we might get further if we give them the full story. They deserve to know the truth."

Gray laughed bitterly. "The actual truth or another set of lies by omission?"

"I'm on your side here, Gray!"

"Oh, come off it, Dom. You need our help, pure and simple, but you're right. You're not getting it until you tell us everything—the full, unedited version."

Dom's jaw moved, chewing on nothing—a match for how much information he was volunteering unless he had to.

"OK," Gray said, "let's start with an easy question. How long have you been working for Winstanley?"

"Two years." Dom was looking at Winstanley, so he missed Gray's reaction. It might have been an easy question to ask, but the answer was definitely not an easy one to hear.

"While I was still leading the SIU," Gray mused. "Good to know."

"You were already on your way out," Dom tried to reason, but if Rob sensed Gray's fury over a video feed, it would've been blasting the people in that room like a hurricane. "It also had no bearing on the unit or your role."

What a bastard, Rob thought at the same time as Josh reeled. Dom was supposedly Gray's oldest and closest friend.

Gray, in contrast to Rob's and Josh's palpable astonishment, shut off any semblance of emotion, reverting fully to his Graham Farrar persona and getting down to business.

"So you allowed Folden to escape from a secure hospital to catch a bigger fish."

"Eventually," Dom agreed. "After our attempts to steer Rob to Folden failed."

That was all Rob needed to hear to finally see red. He jabbed the mute button and jumped to his feet, staring at the wall above the desk, hands on his head for fear he'd punch something.

"Hey." Dee stood too but kept her distance. "Let's take five." She signalled a timeout to the camera.

"They think I'm bent," Rob muttered. "That's why they want me to do this—not because I know Folden. They think I'm in on it! After all this fucking time, everything I've done for them and their shitty operations..." He was too mad to vocalise further, or not safely. He wanted to tell Dom and Winstanley—and Gray, for that matter—to go fuck themselves, and the only thing stopping him was that his son was in the room next door and didn't need to hear or see his dad lose it.

Almost without Rob realising, Dee guided him out of Dora's office, down the stairs and out to the garage, where he permitted himself a growl to vent some of it, but it was nowhere near enough.

"Spar with me," Dee invited and took a protective stance in front of him, fists guarding her face.

"Don't be daft."

"What—you reckon you'll be ready to go back up there and continue with the briefing in five minutes?"

"I'll have to be." Rob turned away, counting the slats of the roll-down garage door—taking *count from one to ten* to a whole new level—but all he could see was Dom's face. "I don't get it," he said. "Dom's a decent bloke."

"It's not about him, though, is it?"

"Me, bent. I mean, what the fuck?" He registered what Dee had said and turned back to her. She immediately resumed her stance and danced from foot to foot, which pushed a chuckle out of Rob. "Why aren't you mad?" he asked.

"Why would I be?"

"They're acting like you, Isobel and Ari are invisible, and Josh has basically signed Iz's death warrant."

"Oh, you noticed, did you?" Dee jabbed with her right hand, coming within a whisper of Rob's cheek. "You didn't do any better."

"I spoke up for Iz, and I wasn't ignoring you. I confided in you!"

"Yeah, but you didn't do anything to bring us into the discussion, did you, eh? Eh?" She jabbed with each 'eh' until Rob jabbed back. She blocked him with no effort whatsoever. "That's more like it." She jumped up and down, alternately in his space and at arm's length. Rob threw a few punches, none with any force, laughing when Dee grabbed him by the wrist—laughing a bit less when she jerked him forward and decked him.

"Some mate you are," Rob grumbled from the floor.

Dee grinned and offered him a hand up. "Better?"

"A bit." He was feeling calmer—as long as he didn't think about it. "Fair comment, though, about not involving you."

"It's on Winstanley more than you," Dee excused.

"Still doesn't make it right. Our Lois—my niece—"

"The lawyer."

"Yeah. She says half the fight in court is about being taken seriously, and that's before she's even tried to win the case."

"I know where she's coming from, but really, Rob, you're more savvy than most blokes."

"Only because I grew up with assertive women—my mum, my sister..." And Jess too, but it didn't feel right to mention her at that moment. "We should get back to it before they make any decisions on our behalf."

"Good idea."

"Dee?"

She was almost at the door back to the house and stopped suddenly and turned, bashing Rob with her shoulder. "Yeah?" she asked, but he'd forgotten what he'd wanted to say. Their faces were kiss-close, his reflection a dark silhouette in her eyes, blue irises, unnaturally bright.

"Contacts?" he murmured, no longer thinking, caught off guard. Her answer was a *hmm* that barely sounded before the space between them diminished and their lips met. For the briefest moment, he felt a pang of guilt for cheating on Naomi, but it was lost, along with the kiss, when someone knocked on the door behind Dee. It opened as they sprang apart.

"Hi—sorry." Zoë stepped halfway in, her phone in her hand. "It's Gray, making sure you're OK. He said he's calling 'off the clock'."

"Cheers, Zo." Rob took the phone from her. "Alright, Gray?"

"Not exactly. Are you?"

"I'll get over it. Sorry about Dom, mate. That's out of order."

"Yeah, well, I think he kept it from me for the right reasons," Gray said. Rob wasn't so sure about that. "And in fairness, you withholding info on Clough looks dodgy."

"He'd made me, Gray. I had to do something or he'd have blown my cover."

"That's what I told Hooper and Winstanley."

"Except I never told you."

"It's the only explanation that makes sense."

That knocked the remaining wind out of Rob's sails and gave him the confirmation he'd needed. He could trust Gray.

"I suggested we break for refreshments, reconvene in another fifteen minutes," Gray said. "Are you up to it?"

"I will be, thanks. And sorry for abandoning you."

"Don't worry about it. In light of what's transpired, I'm even less happy about you making contact with Folden. Winstanley's only goal is to get information, and if he believes you've gone rogue, he won't think twice about sacrificing you to get it. Which means..."

"You're going undercover," Rob finished, knowing from Gray's tone that nothing would change his mind, irrespective of any official arrangements Winstanley made. "What do you need from me?"

"Every last thing you can tell me about Anders Folden."

18: Who Swallowed a Spider

T HE LAST SECTION of their briefing was tense and not particularly productive. Winstanley was as dead set on sending Rob to make contact with Folden as Gray was against it, and so the discussion became abstract and protracted as they sought a contingency plan upon which they could all agree. Dom kept his mouth shut throughout, only speaking once they were on their way down the stairs from Berringer's apartment, when he muttered an apology and fled the building before Gray and Josh made it to the foyer.

"Desperate for a smoke," Gray justified aloud to Josh but knew that the day marked the lowest point in his and Dom's fifteen years of friendship—one from which it might not recover.

Having left Winstanley with Ari to figure out the technical requirements for the non-mission, Gray and Josh got into the same unmarked SUV that had delivered them to Berringer's and which was now taking them to the Parkers' house. Rob and Dee were picking up takeaway on their way back from Zoë's parents'. It would have made for a pleasant evening of socialising were it not for what lay ahead. Gray didn't hold out much hope that Rob's calling it a suicide mission had been an exaggeration and wished he'd spent a little more time during the Strang investigation watching Folden rather than Jessica Lambert's friends, but such was the benefit of hindsight.

There was no sign of Dee's car when the SUV pulled up outside the locked gates to the Parkers', which was to be expected, as they had further to come. Josh was deep in contemplation, and the driver, aside from being someone Gray didn't know, appeared to be using the time to catch up on paperwork. In the ensuing silence, Gray's dread swelled, crushing all other thoughts and hopes, until he could no longer keep it in. "I don't want to die."

Josh turned his head, giving Gray a look of mild amusement.

"I'm not joking around," Gray said.

"I didn't think you were."

"Then what's funny?"

"None of it. However, nobody twisted your arm, Graham. I can, therefore, only surmise that your claim of not wanting to die is either a flat-out lie or due to a lack of self-concept."

"I have no choice, since you put Isobel forward. She has family."

"And that makes her life somehow worth more than yours?"

"People depend on her. Same with Rob."

"I see."

"What the hell does that even mean?"

"What does what mean?"

"Your knowing little 'I see', like you've suddenly gained tremendous insight into the problem but it's far too complex for the rest of us to comprehend, so you sit there in arrogant silence while we flounder."

"Wow!" Josh's mild amusement became a grin. "You really are in a stinker of a mood this evening."

"What do you damn well expect? Christ, man, tomorrow..."

"Could be your last tomorrow?" Josh finished for him.

"You're not helping."

"Au contraire!" Josh wafted his hand at Gray. "Do you remember our conversation after we found out that young cult member we interviewed had committed suicide?"

"Bits and pieces," Gray said.

"You asked me if I'd rather have spoken to him alone, and I said yes, because I care about you, and I'd wanted to save you from having to go through feeling responsible for his death."

"Right. I remember. What's your point?"

"We're here again, is my point. You're beating yourself up for that furniture guy's death, but it wasn't your fault. You're taking on Folden because you can't deal with the guilt of anyone else dying instead of you. Yet in all of this, you're overlooking your own value. All the people who care about you—Will, his daughter, George, Libby, Becky, Rob, Dom—"

"Arguable."

"Martin Winstanley—"

"Scraping the barrel."

"And me. I know what you're doing, Graham. I know because I've been there and done the same. You tell yourself your life is less important than all of those around you, but what you're really doing is getting out so you don't have to face the pain of losing the people you love while blatantly disregarding their loss."

"So you agree I'm not coming out of this alive?" Gray said, refusing to consider the merits of Josh's analysis, largely because he'd felt the jab of every word.

"If that's what you go in believing. Folden is no fool, but he does lack empathy, and those narcissistic tendencies of his that you're so eagerly clinging to will be *your* undoing, not his."

Gray wasn't sure if he was relieved or disappointed when Dee's car drew up in front of the gates. Josh was kicking his arse, emotionally, but the message was seeping in, working its way through his defeatist mentality.

"We'll finish this discussion later, once we're back at the hotel," Josh said as the SUV followed Dee's Porsche through the gates and up the drive to the Parkers' house. "You will be staying the night, I presume?"

"In your hotel room?" Gray asked in disbelief.

"It's a twin. You need somewhere to stay, and we both need the company."

"If it's OK with you."

"I wouldn't have offered if it wasn't." The SUV stopped and the driver got out and opened the door on Josh's side. Josh unfastened his seat belt and put one foot out of the door. "Don't try anything," he warned and then slid out of the car, leaving Gray gawping, goldfish style.

***

"Chinese is OK, isn't it?" Rob asked. It was Hobson's Choice—'this or fresh air' as his mum would say—but Gray and Josh confirmed it was fine anyway and seemed oblivious to his attempts to make conversation for the sake of it. Things with Dee had been a little edgy since their interrupted kiss in the garage, and Rob was glad of the temporary reprieve from her exclusive company because there was only one way it was going. There was nothing awkward about the tension between them; it was a charge like static, and they were both avoiding intentional touch whilst trying to accidentally bump into each other, negotiating the kitchen area as if it were a galley on a narrow boat rather than an open-plan space that could have hosted a cocktail party for a dozen or more guests.

With the food laid out on the table—they kept it in the plastic boxes to save on washing up—they served themselves, although Rob made sure the veggie dishes were closest to Gray, who gaped as if he couldn't believe what he was seeing when Josh loaded his plate with sweet and sour pork, chilli beef, Szechuan king prawn and egg fried rice.

"What?" Josh asked, adding a spring roll to the pile.

"I'm surprised you eat this."

"I love Chinese food!" Josh bit off half of the spring roll, smiling obnoxiously as he chewed and then fanning his mouth. "God, that's hot!" He gulped the bottle of beer Rob provided him. "Thanks," he said, then, "Anyway, you can talk. How much of that is *really* vegetarian?"

"No idea." Gray mimicked Josh's spring roll chomp—having blown on it first.

"I didn't know you were veggie," Dee said.

"Yeah. I have been for about a year."

"I guess eating meat wouldn't go down well with your other half."

"Well, he certainly wouldn't have cooked it for me, but he didn't nag me when we ate out and I chose steak, and I didn't stop eating it on purpose. It just kind of happened." Gray frowned, his gaze losing focus, the half a spring roll still held between his forefinger and thumb.

"I'm sure he's fine," Josh comforted.

"I know," Gray said. "I just wish I knew where he'd gone."

"You'll be reunited before you know it." Josh still had his beer in his hand and held it up as he gave Gray an elbow nudge. "Are you going to..." He jerked his head in Rob's direction.

"What?"

"Tell him."

Gray shrugged. "You can if you like."

"What's this?" Rob asked.

Josh merely raised an eyebrow and gave Gray another nudge—hard enough to rock him sideways.

"For f..." Gray muttered, laughing and turning pink. "Will and I are getting married."

"No way!" Rob quickly armed himself with beer, as did Dee. "That's bloody brilliant news, Gray! Congrats, mate." He waited for Gray to pick up his beer and tapped bottles with him.

"Congratulations," Dee said, beaming at him as she, too, tapped their bottles together. "There is life after the SIU then. Cheers." She tipped her bottle to her mouth, grinning around it and winking at Rob.

Blood or adrenaline or whatever it was rushed down his arms and legs, and he took an extra-large glug of beer, wondering how long it be until Ari called on some pretext or other, as they'd done every time he and Dee got close, with the exception of their kiss in the garage, when they'd abandoned their phones. They could always turn them off—well, they couldn't, and that secretive nonsense wasn't Rob's style anyway. He and Ari needed to have a grown-up conversation, but he was done dwelling on it for now.

"Have you set a date?" he asked Gray.

"I only proposed this morning, so no, not yet. We need to work around Suzannah's and Libby's school terms, and I'm not sure what I'm doing about a best man." Just like that, Gray was back to looking glum. As if to add insult to injury, his phone buzzed once and switched itself off. "Damn it. I haven't got my charger."

"I can lend you one," Dee said.

"Or a toothbrush, razor, change of clothes..."

"Where are you staying tonight?" Rob asked.

"With Josh."

"And I have a spare toothbrush and a whole array of hotel toiletries," Josh pointed out.

"You're a similar height and build," Dee observed.

"I'm not sharing my underwear," Josh said.

"I wasn't going to ask," Gray retorted. "And we've got to get through a night of sharing a room first. Who's to say I'll even live long enough to need clean underwear?"

Dee's jaw dropped.

Rob nodded. "It's a fair point. Josh is inhuman before his first coffee."

"Soon's kill you as look at you," Gray added.

"How rude!" Josh acted outraged, and everyone laughed, but the real purpose of their evening together loomed ahead, and once they'd all had enough to eat, Rob cleared the table. Dee grabbed some more beers from the fridge, and they moved to the sofas.

"I doubt there's much I can add that I didn't already tell Josh," Rob said as a preamble to telling Gray 'every last thing' about Folden.

"What's his weak spot?"

"He doesn't have one."

"There must be something."

"I dunno. I only ever saw him off his game once. He was going to court, and Sharston made a throwaway comment that he looked sharp. He acted like he hadn't heard her, then later called her every name under the sun—went into graphic detail about what he wanted to do to her—in the middle of it all asking me what was wrong with his suit. Actually, now I think about it, I caught him sneering at his reflection a few times, like he was disgusted by what he saw in the mirror. Mostly he avoided looking in them. He hardly ever shaved, not that you'd notice unless you got up close."

"That's narcissism," Josh said.

Gray turned, slowly and with a good deal of undisguised surprise, and stared at him. "Come again?"

"Low self-esteem is associated with narcissism."

"But you said—"

"I know what I said, Graham, and I stand by it. Folden exhibits traits consistent with psychopathy, but that doesn't preclude him from being a narcissist."

"Dee said that," Rob interjected on her behalf. He'd taken her earlier point to heart. "Didn't you?"

"I did."

"On what grounds?" Gray asked.

"Trudi Holt's profile."

"Holt's already profiled Folden?"

"Yep. It's in the Rasa case file."

"How kind of Martin Winstanley to send it my way," Josh muttered.

"I don't believe this," Gray said. "He implied he'd just brought her on board!"

"Nope. She consulted on a couple of SIU investigations before I went on secondment. The profile's on my laptop—I'll go and get it." Dee left and went upstairs.

"I wonder what else Winstanley isn't telling us," Rob said.

"Shall we give Dom a call and find out?" Gray had his phone in his hand and attempted to activate it. "Shite. Oh, well, it's probably for the best. You know, Martin asked for my trust today."

"I thought he already had it."

"He lost it. Same for Dom, I'm sorry to say. Looks like we're on our own again."

"You're not." Dee resumed her seat next to Rob. "You've still got us." She unwound a phone charger cable, plugged one end into her laptop and gave the other end to Gray.

"Dee's right," Josh said. "You also have Isobel and Ari."

"For what it's worth."

"Here you go." Dee shoved her laptop in front of Gray. "I thought it was the full profile, but it's just the executive summary."

"Thanks." He fell silent, reading and frowning, then handed the laptop to Josh. "Nothing new there."

Dee met Rob's gaze, and he winked. They were already grinning in anticipation when Josh delivered his verdict.

"She's *obsessed* with social learning theory, but her analysis has some merit. I quote: 'Folden builds relationships with men whom he perceives as father figures, however, his concept of a father–son relationship is distorted by his parents' actions—similar offenders have a child abuse victimology. Folden has experienced emotional neglect but not material neglect and thus has learned to associate money with emotional attachment, demanding the same display of love from his victims.'"

"Sounds like someone has daddy issues," Dee said.

"Extortion and blackmail instead of hugs," Gray mused.

"Not instead of, Graham. According to Holt—and, much as it pains me, I concur—those *are* Folden's hugs. When his victims threaten to report him, he experiences rejection."

"Yeah, that makes sense," Rob said. "It all fits with the Anders Folden I know."

"Oh, good. I finally got something right on the profile." Josh flashed a sardonic smile at Gray.

"He blamed me for his original profile being wrong," Gray explained.

"In jest," Josh pointed out. "It's not your fault the furniture guy's dead."

"I know. You said. Nor is it yours for failing to predict it from your profile."

"Of course, he wouldn't have been there but for you suddenly abandoning five years of cautious living."

"May as well have fired the gun myself," Gray agreed, nodding sagely. "Given you introduced Will and me, that makes you my accomplice."

"Sidekick," Josh corrected. "Villains have accomplices. Heroes have sidekicks."

"Are you saying I'm a hero?"

"God, no. But you're no villain either. No cat for one."

"I could get a cat..."

"More beers," Rob said, enjoying Gray and Josh's smooth switch to banter even if it was all distraction. In other circumstances, they'd have made for a hilarious double act in the classic style—Abbott and Costello for a new generation. If Gray really was considering replacing Dom as best man, he wouldn't get much better than Josh.

"Can we talk strategy?" Gray suggested once Rob was back in his seat. "Unless there's anything else you want to add?"

"Not at this point," Rob confirmed.

"Josh, how much of an adjustment does your profile need, realistically?"

"Very little, now I've read Holt's."

"So your two-motive theory still stands?"

"As best I can tell."

"Does that mean Folden's motivation for targeting Rob is personal or business?"

"You keep asking me that, and it's still conjecture...yes, I'd say there is a personal element to it. However, it strikes me that Folden is playing the same game as Winstanley. Both have been tasked with obtaining information—it might even be the same information—and they believe Rob can get it for them."

"Rob," Gray said, continuing before Rob went on the offensive, "I know you went through all this with Dom and Winstanley last year, but is there anything at all you can think of that both Folden and Winstanley would want?"

"Not from my contact with Folden, but when Winstanley interviewed me last year, he kept throwing in questions about some security van heist near Downing Street or Westminster—somewhere government-related—that went down while I was undercover. I don't know anything about it, and I told him as much."

"That sounds like a lead to me. I'd ask Winstanley, but he doesn't like sharing his toys—I wonder if Ari can dig up any info."

"Let's hope so," Josh said. "Knowing in advance what Folden's after will significantly increase your chances of survival."

"Jesus. Don't hold back, will you?"

"I'm sorry, but it's true. Everything—my analysis, Rob's knowledge, even Holt's conclusion—indicates the relationship between Folden and his victims is social psychological. He constantly seeks their approval. If he gets what he wants, they live. If he doesn't, they die. Would you agree, Rob?"

"Yeah, but you make it sound easy, and I'm telling you, it won't be. You can't butter Folden up. He'll see straight through it."

"So how do I give him what he wants?" Gray asked.

Rob shrugged. "*You* can't."

19: To Catch a Fly

N IGHT CAP?" GRAY suggested when he and Josh arrived in the hotel lobby nearly two hours later, having taken their Met Police chauffeur on a detour to buy boxer shorts and socks.

Josh put on a show of pondering but predictably cried off. "Thanks, but no. I'm going to turn in. You stay and have one if you want to."

"Which would disturb you least? If I come up with you now or later?"

"Later. You trained to be stealthy, did you not? Night." Josh walked off towards the lift.

"Good night," Gray called after him and headed for the bar, where he briefly contemplated hitting the bourbon. It had once been his tipple of choice, but so had cocaine chasers, and his wagon was wobbling, a wheel about to fall off, so he went with the safer option of Guinness and blackcurrant. The Irish barman didn't bat so much as an eyelash.

Retiring to a plush corner bench, Gray spent a while observing, unnoticed by the device-occupied guests, although they likely wouldn't have noticed had they been paying attention to their surroundings, which was less to do with stealth than Gray's 'gift' of ordinariness. Neither attractive nor unattractive, average height, average build, unremarkable hair, he had no trouble hiding in plain sight, all of which went a long way towards being an exceptional detective. Alas, a year of low-level snooping in loan company offices and chasing insurance scammers, of playing it safe and colouring within the lines, was no preparation for an operation of this magnitude. He was rusty, afraid he'd lost his nerve. Afraid, full stop.

With too much time on his hands for his own good, Gray went with the crowd and took out his phone, his plan to kill an hour or two browsing mindlessly put on hold by an unread text message.

Just checking in. We're all OK. Everything OK there? Miss you. x

The message was only a few minutes old. Gray started typing a reply, changed his mind, backspaced, typed *One sec. Calling you. x* and downed his beer, leaving the glass on the bar on his way out the back of the hotel to the small, dark courtyard designated for smokers. Once he was sure he was alone, he returned Will's call, becoming unexpectedly jelly-legged as the line rang out.

"I miss you too," Gray said as soon as Will picked up. They both laughed at his lovesick outburst. "Hi."

"Hi," Will replied. "I feel a million times better for hearing that."

"Did Tie get everyone out?"

"Yep. Even the chickens. I said he should've left Paul there. Psycho face-off."

Gray chuckled. "I'd be hard pushed as to where to lay my money."

"Are you allowed to tell me what happened?"

"Yes, but..." But they were so far away from each other, and Folden had come so close to getting to Will. All day, Gray had ignored the what-ifs. He *had* checked up on the furniture removal firm. Folden *hadn't* reached Will. It was pointless going over the alternative scenario, yet he kept thinking *at least our last conversation would have been a good one.*

That was what he wanted to tell Will: not what had happened, but his distress for what could have happened and what may still happen. But who did that to someone they loved?

"Hey," Will said gently, "it's OK if you don't want to."

"I—" Gray choked up, started again. "I do, and I will, but not yet." *Not until it's over.* "I just need to hear your voice. What are you up to?"

"Chilling and enjoying a beer. How about you?"

Gray glanced through the window into the bar room where his hastily emptied pint glass had been cleared from the counter and someone else occupied the seat he had vacated. "Same," he said. "About to head to bed."

"That's early for you. Did you go back to the house?"

"No, I'm..." For a split second, Gray considered lying and saying he was staying with Rob and Dee, purely to save Will from any unnecessary jealousy, but perhaps a little jealousy was healthy—certainly healthier than later being caught out for a lie and having to rebuild trust. "I'm staying with Josh."

"In his hotel room?"

"Yeah. It's a twin—well, you know that."

"OK."

"It was his suggestion," Gray said defensively. "I was—"

"I said it's OK."

Gray sighed, hating Will's agreeableness more than ever. He didn't want to stay in a hotel room with Josh; he wanted to be with Will, wherever he was. "Are you sure?"

"What would you do if I said no?"

"Pay for another room."

"Money bags," Will teased. "It's not a problem, I promise—the opposite, actually. I'm thankful you're not alone tonight."

"Me too," Gray admitted. He wanted to ask where Will was, and Ari's app was secure enough to do so, but it was safer for Gray not to know—one less piece of information Folden could worm out of him.

For several minutes, they stayed on the line, neither speaking, both appreciating the other's distant company. Out of habit, Gray listened for clues in the silence but heard only Will's breaths and the pause in rhythm when he took a mouthful of beer.

"I should go," Gray said eventually, reluctantly, but it was gone eleven and he was shivering.

"It sounds cold."

Gray's laughter warbled. "It is."

"I'll call you tomorrow. Same time?"

"Or I can call you." The thought of Will calling him over and again, receiving no answer...

"OK," Will accepted, letting him off the hook. "I love you."

"I love you. Sleep well."

"You too. Good night."

"Night." Gray ended the call and swayed, his shoulder coming to a rest against the damp, frigid brick wall, his vision sparkling, the dim bulkhead lights dotted around the courtyard reflecting off his newly formed tears. He wanted more alcohol, to drink until he'd obliterated his fear that he'd had his share of happiness, which was never far from the surface, but he was wise enough to recognise his decline into pitch-black misery was partly down to the beers he'd already consumed. In any case, he'd need his full faculties tomorrow. Sleep, shower, get the job done, get on with the rest of his life with Will.

***

"*Bridget Jones*," Rob suggested.

Dee laughed. "No!"

"*Four Weddings and—*"

"Hell, no!"

"*Blade Runner*?"

"What?" Dee did a kind of slide-spring combo off the couch, landed cross-legged next to Rob and bent closer to the rack of Blu-rays left behind by the Parkers. "All those crappy rom coms and then an absolute classic."

"Tonka always did have eclectic tastes."

"She took the rest of the sci-fi with her, did she?"

"Dunno, but I'm leaving it to you now." Rob slid the *Blade Runner* case in with the others—not quite *all* rom coms but not far off—and scooted back until he was leaning against the couch.

Dee tilted her head to the side to read the titles on the spines, running her finger along the top row, the middle row—"There is literally nothing here I fancy."

"Nothing at all?"

"Not in the movie department." She gave him a cheeky grin over her shoulder. Rob reached behind him, snagged a cushion and threw it at her. She caught it one-handed and kept hold of it as she shuffled around to face him, hugging the cushion to her. "We don't have to watch a film," she said.

"No, we don't."

"Should I stick on some music instead?"

"Fine by me." Hands behind his head, Rob closed his eyes and listened to the flick-through of the channels, little bursts of the current hits, the classics and heavy rock, finally settling on R&B.

"I love this song," Dee said. Rob recognised it as one of the songs Lois listened to in the car, but he couldn't have named it or the artist. Dee knew it word for word and she sang along. She didn't have a half-bad voice. The song came to an end, and the channel went to an ad break. "Gonna go do a quick patrol," she said.

"All right, mate." Rob opened his eyes a fraction as she set off, barefooted, vest top, yoga pants and thick black holster strapped to her right thigh. She sprinted up the stairs and out of sight; Rob shut his eyes again and rested his head back on the sofa seat, the sound of Dee walking around the upper storey fading in and out as he drifted closer to sleep. He startled awake when she landed on the sofa behind him.

"You were out of it there."

"Just resting my eyes."

"Whatever! You didn't even blink when I moved your head out of the way, just kind of..." She bent around him, leaning off the sofa so he could see her impression of him, gawping and gormless. He laughed.

"And what? You're like the women in films when you're asleep? Perfect make-up, not a hair out of place, gently fluttering eyelids..."

"You know it!" She grinned at him, the grin softening as she bent further, bringing her face closer to his. "Or you could find out," she murmured as their lips touched. Rob turned as best he could, their heads almost at right angles, making it impossible to share anything but an open-mouthed, prolonged kiss that was wet and messy and hot as hell, and yes, he wanted to see what she looked like as she slept...as they made love...as she climaxed—

He pulled back. "Sorry. I can't do this." He picked up his beer, nursing it, shaking his head, while she didn't move, just watched him and chewed her saliva-shiny lush bottom lip.

"You're seeing someone," she said.

"It's...complicated."

"That's what they all say."

"No. It's not like that. I'm..." He was at a loss. "I'm gonna go to bed." Draining the last mouthful of beer, he got up, left the empty bottle on the breakfast bar and walked across to the stairs, pausing to look back at her. "I really am sorry."

She stared at him a moment longer. "Night, Rob."

"Night," he replied and plodded up the stairs, mentally kicking himself all the way.

***

As it turned out, Gray and Josh could have used the same bed on timeshare. When Gray made it up to the room a little after midnight, Josh was asleep, his phone propped on the bedside table auto-scrolling through a slideshow of photos of George and Libby. Gray picked up the phone to deactivate the screen but changed his mind and set it back in position before quietly undressing and climbing into the other bed, but he wasn't yet ready for sleep.

For the next three hours, he re-read the files from the SIU investigation into Strang et al., in particular the bits and pieces on Folden, and the evidence Winstanley had forwarded from his ongoing operation, which included Holt's profile. It was by no means all of the Tabula Rasa files, but it was everything of relevance to their current priority, mostly sightings of Folden, and most of those in and around London: Westminster; Holborn, near his barrister's chambers; Finchley, within the radius of Gray's house; and Kilburn, where Rob had previously rented a flat. There were also a few from up north—both east and west—from around the time Rob had received the photo of his nieces; thankfully, none were in Croxley, although there was no telling where Folden had been during the unexplained periods.

It was clear Winstanley had been keeping tabs on Folden's activities himself—as he should, considering he'd intentionally let the man escape from a secure hospital—but nowhere near closely enough, weeks at a time passing with no signs of Folden, only for him to pop up a hundred miles from his last known location. What was also clear in both the increasing frequency and riskiness of the measures Winstanley was taking was that he was getting desperate. If there was one thing Martin Winstanley couldn't abide, it was rule-breaking, yet he'd let a dangerous criminal flee twice, the second time knowing he'd murdered an innocent man.

That alone was enough to leave Gray beyond doubt that Winstanley was working for someone else, and he was curious to know who because taking Folden out of action was not enough, or else Winstanley would have left Gray and his team to get on with it.

Gray switched off his tablet and rolled onto his side, watching Josh's photos roll around again—husband, daughter, mother-in-law, pets. Gray had once coveted the life Josh and George had made for themselves. Now it was within his grasp and he was damned if anyone was taking that from him. If he had to, he would kill Folden and leave Winstanley to deal with the rest.

Resolution made, Gray closed his eyes, vaguely aware of Josh moving around the room as sleep overcame him.

***

When Rob came downstairs the next morning, the events of the previous evening were still as fresh as if they'd happened only moments ago, which they shouldn't have been. Between worrying about Gray and beating himself up over turning down Dee/cheating on Naomi, he'd had a crappy night, but it looked like he was the only one suffering.

"Morning!" Dee greeted cheerily from the kitchen and held up the coffee jug. "You want?"

"Please," Rob replied, nonplussed. He'd expected the cold shoulder or at the very least that she'd have found an excuse to leave the room. "Been up long?"

"About five minutes longer than you." She set the coffee going and turned back. "What's that look for?"

"What look?"

"The one that's as good as saying, 'Dee, mate, you're lying through your teeth.'"

"Blimey, I don't even have to open my mouth! Although you defo got up half an hour ago to put your face on."

"Told you—I wake up looking like a movie star." Dee winked, leaving Rob none the wiser but glad there was no animosity. Still, he owed her an explanation.

"Listen, about last night, I'm really sorry."

"Yep, you said that. Don't sweat it."

"I should explain."

"No need. The timing's not right or you're not interested, and anyway, I'm your bodyguard so it's inappropriate, probably."

"Probably?"

"Well, we didn't sign an anti-fraternisation agreement."

"Fair point, but not what I'm getting at. What I said about it being complicated—"

"You're not gonna let this go, are you?"

"I will if you want me to."

"Will it make any difference to us?"

"It might."

Dee studied him for a moment, and he smiled hopefully. "OK," she said. "But let me pour the coffee first."

Rob accepted that suggestion and perched on a stool at the breakfast bar while she did the honours, coming to sit next to him once she was done.

"Spill," she invited.

"There *is* someone I care about but we're not really seeing each other, I don't think. We kind of started before I went up to my mum's last year, but they're in a relationship with someone else, except I'm not sure if it's a proper relationship or exclusive, or if they expect us to be exclusive, and they're not around at the minute for me to ask."

Dee's eyebrows rose above her coffee cup.

"Told you it was complicated." Rob chuckled self-consciously.

"Hmm." Dee put down her cup. "To recap: you're possibly seeing someone who is possibly seeing someone else but you don't know and you don't want to screw up what you may or may not have with them."

"Pretty much."

"Yeah, that's complicated," Dee agreed, and Rob laughed, his face straightening in an instant when she asked, "It's Ari, isn't it?"

"Wh— How could you possibly have guessed that?"

"Oh, I don't know. The grief you got off them yesterday might have given it away."

"Yeah, tell me about it."

"So they're actually with that Berringer blurt, are they?"

"God knows. Part of me thinks it's just for convenience."

"Because Berringer's rich, you mean?"

"Yeah." It was close enough. Rob wasn't sure how Ari would feel about him sharing that both Naomi's high living and Aaron's salary came out of Freddie's pocket.

"Well, for what it's worth, I agree that you and Ari need to thrash this out. Obviously, I'm well up for us doing something—one-off sex or more—and I don't want to come between you guys if it's serious, but—no, shut up, Dee."

"What were you going to say?"

"Doesn't matter." She slid off her stool, taking her coffee with her. "Shower time." She paused as she passed him, resting her hand on his shoulder. "I'll leave the door unlocked, in case you need me." Then she sashayed away.

20: Perhaps She'll Die

THE HOTEL ROOM'S shower wasn't far off a jet wash, strengthwise, although infinitely warmer, and Gray was in no hurry to leave it behind. Pretending he hadn't heard the light rap on the bathroom door, he shut his eyes, leaning back into the pummelling cascade—then gasped and half-drowned himself when the door opened a couple of inches.

"Graham?" Josh called through the gap. "Dom and Winstanley are here."

"They're what?"

"Urgent briefing, they said. Room 521, ten minutes."

"They can have me when I'm good and ready," Gray snapped and immediately regretted it, but the door had already closed. Josh was the last person who deserved Gray's ire even if he was the one least likely to take it to heart. Still, an apology was in order...in a while. Gray wasn't rushing for anyone this morning, least of all Dom Hooper and Martin Winstanley.

Overnight, Gray's sense of betrayal had escalated to outright resentment. He had an operation to oversee and neither the time nor patience for backstabbing former colleagues whose unannounced arrival had overwritten his plan to have breakfast with his brother-in-law.

A last supper of sorts.

Before he descended too far through the cloud of black thoughts that doomed the mission myriad different ways, Gray turned off the shower, quickly dried off and struggled into a bathrobe, tying the belt as he opened the bathroom door.

"It's not you," he said to Josh's back, receiving a dismissive shrug in response. "I hoped I'd have more time to...to have a coffee, eat breakfast...and..."

"You're not ready." Josh turned around, his stern expression softening on sight. "Oh, Graham." He dodged around the end of his bed and pulled Gray into a hug. "I know I said you had to be less defeatist about this, but it's entirely reasonable to be scared."

"Is it?" Gray mumbled against Josh's shoulder and sniffed, inhaling the scent of coconut shampoo. It was strangely calming, or perhaps not that strange. Gray always felt calm in Josh's presence. "You realise the irony, don't you? This is near as damn it the same recon mission I gave Rob. I'm shitting myself."

"Figuratively, I hope."

Gray gulped a laugh. "More evidence of my poor decision-making."

"Nonsense." Josh took a step back so he could look Gray in the eye. "I may not always approve of your methods, but I admire your capacity to make the hard choices and do what you have to."

"You flatter me."

"This morning, perhaps, but I mean it, Graham. You've saved lives—countless lives—because I know as well as you do that white-collar crime is never victimless."

Gray was listening and taking in Josh's every word, but he was also aware of his phone vibrating on the bedside table. He reached it as the caller gave up. "Unknown number. They'll ring back or they won't." He slid the phone into his bathrobe pocket. "Thank you. I needed that pep talk."

"Any time," Josh said. "I have plenty more prepared."

"I bet—ah, looks like they're calling back after all." Gray pulled out his phone and hit answer. "Hello?"

"Gray, it's Martina. Sorry to cut to the chase, but is someone shadowing Rob?"

"If he's out and about, Dee will be with him."

"He's on the bike."

"That doesn't necessarily mean he's on his own." But it was likely. "Any idea where he's going?"

"The West End, by the looks of it."

"OK. Thanks, Martina. I'll see what I can find out. Keep me posted."

"Will do."

Gray hung up and threw his phone on the bed, grabbing the three-pack of boxer shorts and pulling at the top seam on the packet. "That was Martina Hedley—Rob's old boss." The packet popped open, and the boxer shorts exploded from it. He retrieved a pair and turned away to put them on. "She says he's out on the bike. Can you alert Dom?" No answer from Josh, Gray turned back and saw he already had his phone to his ear.

"Hey, it's Josh. Martina Hedley just called. Rob's— OK. ... Yes, I'll tell—" He moved his phone away and scowled at it. "He hung up on me."

"What did he say?"

"He said get your arse up to room 521 and—for goodness' sake! Graham!" Josh shielded his eyes. "Can't you do that in the bathroom?"

"It's not as if I'm starkers."

"You might as well be."

No time to cater to Josh's prudishness, Gray had acted decisively and cast aside his bathrobe. With difficulty, he wriggled into a pair of socks, donning his trousers then his shirt on his way across the room to the door. He was still pushing his feet into his shoes as they stepped into the lift.

Catching his dishevelled reflection in the mirrored wall, he gave his hair a finger comb and ruffled the top so it wasn't flat to his head. "They'd better have coffee up there."

"You took the words right out of my mouth," Josh said then sighed. "I don't know about Folden being a narcissist...your hair is *fine*."

"Says he who had the hairdryer running from four till half past this morning."

"That's such a lie!"

"Oh, really?" The lift slowed. The doors opened.

"Erm...oh, yes, all right, I was running the hairdryer for half an hour," Josh admitted. "I was cold." They stepped out onto the fifth floor. "How does Rob's old boss know he's gone out on his bike?"

"The number-plate recognition system. She'll have a flag on his reg."

"Doesn't she trust him?"

"To do the right thing, yes. As for doing as he's told..."

They arrived at room 521, and Gray raised his hand to knock, lowering it again when the door opened and Dom silently beckoned them inside.

Unlike Josh's suite, room 521 was a basic single room containing a narrow bed that hadn't been slept in, a small bedside table, a desk and two wooden chairs. Winstanley perched with notable discomfort on one of the chairs, his knees almost up under his chin, his attention on the open laptop on the desk as he acknowledged them with a cursory, "Good morning, gentlemen."

"Martin," Gray said though he was staring at Dom, who steadfastly avoided eye contact as he gestured to the empty chair. "No coffee?"

"I'll make you both coffee." Dom crossed the room to a stand upon which was a kettle and mugs so small they wouldn't have been out of place at a dolls' picnic. "You should still have a seat."

"Can we discuss the conversation I've just had with Martina Hedley?"

Dom and Winstanley looked at each other but gave him nothing.

"You know Rob's given Dee the slip?"

Tumbleweed.

"If Rob's out there on his own—"

"He's safe, Graham," Winstanley said.

"You know that for sure?"

"As sure as we can be." Dom this time. "That's all you need to know."

"Oh, come on!" Gray appealed to them both. To God too. "Enough of the secrecy—either you tell me everything or we're done."

Winstanley's expression remained passive while he considered, with no urgency whatsoever, Gray's threat. He nudged the empty chair away from him. "Have a seat, please, Graham."

Tempted as he was to tell Winstanley where to stick it, Gray sat, and as he did so, Winstanley stood, offering his chair to Josh, who stayed where he was—not even an arm's length from the door.

"As you wish." Winstanley didn't bother sitting again and instead moved closer to the window, glancing briefly out of it before perching uneasily on the end of the bed.

Dom handed one minuscule mug to Josh and delivered the other to Gray, joining him at the desk and taking over the laptop.

Gray watched Dom's face rather than the screen. "What are you showing me? Evidence that Rob's in cahoots with Folden?" He surprised himself with how spiteful he sounded.

Dom turned away from the laptop, finally looking Gray in the eye. "Rob's on his way to Berringer's. Dee heard him leave and called it in."

"And are you keeping tabs on him or leaving him to fortuitously bring your plan to fruition?"

"For Christ's sake! Of course we're keeping bloody tabs on him! How else would we know where he's headed?"

Gray shrugged wearily. "You tell me."

"I *am* telling you."

Winstanley cleared his throat. "We didn't come to discuss the ins and outs of Mr. Simpson-Stone's love life. Mr. Hooper, if you would oblige…"

"Yes, Sir." Dom turned back to the laptop but said quietly, "That's what I meant about you not needing to know. It's a personal matter."

"I'm sure Rob'll be delighted to discover you're spying on him."

"Not just on him."

Gray shot a look at Josh—still close to the door but leaning against the wall, arms folded, ankles loosely crossed, seemingly unperturbed by the revelation. There again, Gray had warned the team Ari could monitor their conversations, which led to a further realisation.

"Ari's working for you too."

"Indeed they are," Winstanley confirmed. "And they have you to thank for it."

"How so?"

"Their freelance undertakings for your company this past year have been outstanding, wouldn't you agree?"

Gray didn't care one bit for Winstanley's smug demeanour. Aside from the admission of further covert surveillance, there was an underlying threat of action if Gray didn't play nicely, because not all of their research had been 'by the book', although Gray hadn't commissioned Aaron directly. Will had. More to the point, Rob knew nothing about it.

"Internal affairs bringing in a hacker..." Gray casually tossed the grenade back. "So that's why you're here, is it? To talk me out of going after Folden? Put me in protective custody?"

Winstanley's nostrils flared then sucked in with his extended inhalation. Despite his non-existent patience, Gray waited out the eternity until Winstanley exhaled. The man used oxygen like a free diver.

"We'll see," he said and directed back to Dom.

Dom turned the laptop towards Gray. "We intercepted this an hour ago." He was using his softly-softly voice—the one he deployed to deliver bad news to victims' relatives. "It was destined for your inbox."

Two clicks and an image opened, but Gray didn't see it—couldn't when he was staring at the trackpad, suddenly paralysed by a dread-filled anticipation as he raked through the possibilities. *Folden's found Will. No. Not even Winstanley is heartless enough to inform me like this. Has he got to Becky? Or George?*

"It's OK, Graham," Josh said, mercifully clueless as to the path of Gray's thoughts. "Take your time."

Black spots splattered his visual field, alerting him he was on the brink of hyperventilating. He coughed into his fist and kept his knuckle pressed to his nose, mouth closed. It took a bit of work, but he managed to slow his breathing, then, before he could get worked up all over again because it might be nothing, he looked at the image.

Thank God.

Not Will, Becky or George. Female, late twenties/early thirties, very short blonde hair, open denim jacket over tee, jeans, sneakers; large supermarket, breakfast cereal aisle; half-full shallow trolley; alone. The woman was ordinary-looking, just someone doing their weekly grocery shopping. Gray squinted at the contents of the trolley, analysing her purchases for clues, and returned to her face. Only then did he recognise her.

Helen.

In his defence, she'd had long hair the last time he'd seen her—more than two years ago—and he'd never seen her dressed so casually. Less justifiable was the evidence that he'd succeeded in putting her out of mind, or not *her* per se; what she represented. He'd been through it over and again—in therapy sessions and on his own, post-nightmare. Intrinsically, he accepted he'd done what was necessary, but that didn't make him feel any less guilty.

He examined her shopping again—still eating the same junk as when they'd lived together, which gave him an odd sense of nostalgia and heartburn but not much else.

Was she with someone new or still living alone?

Had she continued studying after she moved back to Newcastle? She'd be close to graduating if so.

Intuitively, Dom pre-empted Gray's next question with, "A female officer is staying with her."

Gray nodded to indicate he'd heard and continued staring down the tunnel at that photo, the white noise of the room pressing in, comforting, no need for explanations in his present company. They knew who he was, what he'd done. Helen Walker: the groom's sister, maid of honour and daughter of Penny Walker, nee Strang. Gray had been angling for an invitation only—a Strang family wedding, so much champagne, so many loose tongues—and it had paid off in information gleaned. As for the personal costs...

He should have walked away after, should've let Helen down gently and just walked away. But then she told him she hadn't believed in love at first sight, not until it happened to her—did he feel the same?

It was the best cover—an ambitious police sergeant marrying into a family of corrupt lawyers. The Strangs didn't suspect a thing. It was the best cover, and the worst deception.

He'd have broken her heart either way. He had to believe that.

Gray stared at the photo until his eyes burned, and he closed them, turning his face towards the window before he opened them again, welcoming the pain as his pupils and brain puzzled out what they were supposed to do with all that light, the retinal negative of Helen superimposed on the cartoon-blue sky. A dark form registered in his peripheral vision: a marksman on top of the building across the street.

"You think Rob's safe because Folden can't be in two places at once." Gray's statement put a crack in the silence but wasn't enough to shatter it. He waited for a response, fear accelerating his rage until he couldn't contain it. "People are dying, Martin, while you trot on like the *fucking jobsworth* you are. This has to stop. Now!"

"Graham, you don't—"

"Don't you *dare* tell me I don't understand. Helen is an innocent party in all of this. God knows I already put her through enough! You've got sixty seconds to tell me what Folden wants or I'm out of here."

Winstanley wasted thirty of those seconds blinking, slow and dull-eyed, but he must've realised Gray wasn't calling his bluff. "All right," he said with deep resignation. "Mr. Hooper, Mr. Sandison-Morley, would you leave us alone, please?"

"Yes, Sir," Dom replied, nicotine-eager. "We'll go and get a decent coffee." He ushered Josh out of the room.

"My treat," Winstanley called after them.

Josh glanced back at Gray, who offered the best smile of reassurance he could muster. The door closed.

21: Misdirection

WINSTANLEY MOVED AWAY from the window, back to the chair. "I promise you, Graham. I'm doing all I can to protect Helen. Your mother, sister and brother too. Were I to know Will's whereabouts—"

"Good, then." Better Will was invisible than relying on Winstanley's trusted few to keep him safe. "So...?" Gray prompted.

Winstanley sighed and clasped his hands in his lap, his delay a sign of how deeply unhappy he was rather than believing Gray would relent on his demand. "Some years ago, not long after I took the interim post with the Met's anti-corruption unit, my superior—it matters not who—instructed me to compile a report for the Independent Office for Police Conduct. He didn't tell me why he needed it, but you know the drill—audits, budgeting projections, performance monitoring and so forth. I didn't question the whys and wherefores, simply did as requested.

"A week after I submitted my report, I received a call from one of the IOPC's directors. You see, I'd sent the report directly to them, merely intending to show initiative, and it was in the raw, so to speak. Unedited." Winstanley paused, brows raised. "You seem amused, Graham."

"I am." No point denying it. "I've read your 'unedited' reports, Martin. I find them...enlightening."

Winstanley permitted himself a small smile—demure as the Mona Lisa, but a smile nevertheless—at Gray's feedback. "My superiors rarely appreciate my candour."

"But some of us do, as did that director, I imagine."

"So it appears. They were part of a government committee investigating organised corruption of the justice system. On the basis of my report, I was invited to join that committee, and I accepted. I was honoured to have been asked, and to be acknowledged, finally."

Gray nodded, understanding where Winstanley was coming from. For all that they'd rarely seen eye to eye and often been pitted against each other in their careers, no-one deserved such accolades more than Winstanley. "Are you still on the committee?"

"Not officially. Alas, the best means of avoiding detection for those usurping the system is to poison the medicine. You would recognise the names of many who have served on that committee—John Hebden, for instance, served for two years prior to his death, and—this must go no further, Graham."

"You banished Dom and Josh before you'd speak to me," Gray pointed out. "If our most trusted associates cannot be party to this..."

"You will be tempted when I tell you who the only currently serving senior police officer is."

"Who?"

"Commander Dunleavy."

"Martina's wife is corrupt?"

"Did you not think so yourself when you declined to invite Martina onto your task force?"

"I didn't ask her because..." Gray stumbled. In truth, he'd considered it for a fleeting second but dismissed it without thinking too hard about why. "I don't know," he admitted. "Rob trusts her, but I've never worked with her."

"Better to play it safe," Winstanley agreed. "Which is precisely why I am no longer reporting to the committee."

"You're working for someone in Westminster," Gray guessed. "Government?" Winstanley remained static. "Civil Service." That set his lips a-twitching. "Secret Service?" Still not a word, but Winstanley's facial muscles were so mobile his head could have upped and left the building under its own steam. "What has Rob got to do with all this?"

"The preamble is necessary, as you shall see. A little over two years ago, an armoured vehicle was intercepted on its way to the National Crime Agency. Both guards were seriously injured, but only one item was stolen—a hard drive containing a confidential and highly sensitive dossier. From security footage, we were able to identify one of the suspects and bring him into custody. Of course, he wouldn't say who he worked for, but he did tell us the package had been handed off to a motorcycle courier."

"Rob was one of many," Gray reasoned.

"Ah, but his bike is distinctive—unmistakeable."

Gray reeled. No wonder Winstanley and Dom were so sure Rob was dirty. He briefly contemplated suggesting someone else might have been on the bike, but there was more chance of Rob being corrupt. "What was in the dossier?"

"I can't tell you."

"Martin..."

"I can't because I don't know. But what I can tell you is the intelligence agent who sent it was shot dead minutes after the package was handed off. He'd been undercover for a year, investigating Invecta."

"Invecta..." Gray recognised the name but couldn't place it.

"A prominent lobby representing big business and implicated in state capture in several other countries. We needed hard evidence—companies involved, connections with MPs, judges, transactions between interested parties—"

"And the agent found it," Gray finished.

"We believe so. Furthermore, Cameron Barnett—Invecta's CEO—was formerly a barrister and acquaintance of both Benjamin Clough and the real Simon Yarrow."

"So there's a good chance Folden's involved with Invecta."

"He almost certainly is, but again, we'd need hard evidence to prove it."

"OK." Gray wasn't liking how the pieces were slotting together. "Let's say Rob did pick up the package containing the hard drive. What happened to it after that?"

"Whereabouts still unknown."

"You're telling me a consignment that was so important it was being transported in an armoured vehicle disappeared into thin air? Surely it had some kind of tracking device?"

"Simpson-Stone disarmed it."

"Rubbish! Rob can barely use his mobile, never mind disarm a government-issue tracker."

"Technology doesn't lie, Graham."

"But people do. You claim the system is riddled with corruption, yet you'll take the word of some government tech monkey over Rob's?"

"I appreciate this is hard for you to accept—"

"You're wrong, Martin. Rob's a good man."

Winstanley nodded, not in agreement, and met Gray's gaze, eyes narrowed. "Yet you still require proof."

Gray laughed, unnerved, and stood to leave. "I think we've said all we need to, don't you?"

"Greed takes no prisoners, Graham."

"Not Rob. I'd lay my life on it."

"Would you?"

The door opened before Gray could respond.

"Sorry about this, Sir." Dom entered, followed by Josh. "There's a problem with the photo of Helen Walker."

"Really?" Winstanley muttered sarcastically.

"Yes, really," Josh retorted. "It was taken at least two weeks ago—before Easter. There's an Easter egg display at the far end of the aisle."

Frowning, Winstanley turned to the laptop and bent to scrutinise the image, nose almost on the screen.

"Then he knew who I was before we filmed the restaurant scene," Gray said.

"No," Josh answered. "He knew *Graham Farrar* was married to *Helen Farrar*."

"Why send the photo *after* he came to my house?"

"Maybe the email was delayed," Dom suggested.

Winstanley indicated the email header. "He sent it this morning. He wants us to think he's in Newcastle."

"Why?" Gray knew the instant the word left his lips. He stood and tugged his phone from his pocket, unlocking it as he spoke. "Killing Thompson, hijacking the furniture van, this photo—it's all misdirection. How the hell did I miss it? Folden's target's the same as it always was." And they'd dropped their guard. "Where's Rob now?" He was already calling him.

"I'll check." Dom took over the laptop.

With the others in the room, Gray couldn't ask for confirmation, but it would've been redundant anyway. Folden was after the same thing as Winstanley: that hard drive.

"Rob's arrived at Berringer's," Dom reported.

"He's not answering," Gray said. "Call Ari."

"You're interfering, Graham," Winstanley warned.

"Screw you, Martin. This is *my* operation! Dom, call Ari *now*. Tell them under no circumstances to let Rob leave."

Dom looked from Gray to Winstanley, awaiting further instruction. Crucial seconds ticked by and then, finally, Winstanley said, "Do it."

"Yes, Sir."

***

The concierge must have recognised Rob, as he offered him a polite 'good morning' and didn't bother asking for credentials or where he was heading before he released the door to the stairs. Rob cleared them in twos, breathless from exertion but less stressed now he was inside Berringer's building. He was safe there—safer than anywhere else—but he didn't have much time. He'd probably been clocked by half a dozen speed cameras in his haste; only when he reached the apartment door did it occur to him that he could be springing a surprise visit on Aaron, and it was too late by then. He knocked and stood back, helmet in hand, stance non-confrontational. A key turned, multiple locks disengaged, the door opened; Ari gripped his arm and tugged him inside.

"That was quick." They shut and locked the door.

"How did you—" was all Rob managed before they silenced him with a hard press of a kiss that resulted in them bouncing apart. When Rob got his senses back, he said, "You knew I was coming."

"I've been tracking you since Dee called Dom to say you'd left on the bike. Why on earth did you do that?"

"I had no choice."

"If Folden catches up with you..."

Rob shrugged. "He hasn't yet. But that's why I'm here. Is Freddie home?"

"No." Ari broke eye contact. "He's out of town for a couple of days. Business matters. Meeting with investors, I think he said. It might take longer. It does sometimes. Anyway, he's not here. Are you staying long enough for coffee? Or tea? Oh, you don't drink tea, do you? I'll pour us some coffee." They turned towards the kitchen, but Rob caught them by the shoulder, halting their progress. They turned statuesque, and Rob immediately let go.

"Sorry." Cautiously, he rounded them so they were face-to-face again, for what it was worth. Ari was looking everywhere but at him. "Talk to me."

"About what? You came to me."

Rob sighed. "What was all that about Freddie?"

"I don't understand—"

"Where is he?"

"I told you—he's away on business."

"Yeah, you did, and I'm not accusing you of lying or covering for him, but something's off."

"Are you staying for a drink or not?" Ari's tone had a forced sharpness that Rob couldn't interpret. They didn't seem anxious, but they were tense and defensive. He moved aside.

"Coffee's good," he said, holding back to give them space and following at a distance, which he maintained while they were in the kitchen, only approaching when Ari held out a cup for him to take. "Thanks."

"I didn't mean to snap. I'm sorry."

"No worries. I'm sorry for getting on your case."

Ari gave a small laugh. "Let's go sit...somewhere." They looked around the kitchen wistfully. "I have a sofa in my bedroom. Is that OK?"

"Err...sure." Rob had been under the impression they shared a bed with Freddie, which they must have done some of the time, but then he remembered what Aaron had said about living upstairs from Naomi and her former lover. Whatever the arrangement now, the room Ari took Rob into was a definite Freddie-free zone. In fact, other than the dark greeny-blue sofa where Aaron's computer had been, the setup was identical to the bedsit Naomi had rented before Berringer's prison release, right down to the kitchenette tucked in the corner.

"For Aaron's benefit," they said.

"Gotcha."

"Not just the kitchen—the entire layout." They sat, legs curled under them. "I'd prefer to see out of the window, but I've given up moving the furniture around only to move it back again—sit down, Rob."

He did so and sank comfortably into the deep cushion, putting the window above his eye level.

"Still, it suits our needs today," Ari said. "Best not to display you like a department store mannequin."

Rob laughed. That was one constant he'd noticed between Aaron, Naomi and Ari—their dark sense of humour—and right now he appreciated it more than ever. He adjusted position so he could see them; their smile threatened to knock him off course. It would be too easy in the heat of the moment to override his head and give his heart and body a chance at taking their fill, but he'd defeated those instincts twice in the past twelve hours, and he needed answers.

"So you're still spying on me," he said lightly as a way of establishing how much Ari had heard.

"Not since last night. I heard your discussion about rom coms and Dee leave to do her security check. I heard you snoring while she was gone...and the silence after it." Ari sighed—disappointed, sad, maybe both. "That was when I turned off the mic. I knew what you were doing, where it was leading." They closed their eyes, their Adam's apple giving away their heavy swallow. "I could tell you I was protecting your privacy, but it's not true. I couldn't stand it, and I have no right to feel this...*insane* jealousy about you and her. But I saw it in the videolink yesterday, and I hear it in the way you talk and laugh together. It was inevitable, and I want to hate you both for it."

"But you don't."

"How can I? I care deeply about you, and she makes you happy—happier than you'd be with me. Damn it." Ari covered their eyes with their hand. "I'm sorry. This isn't fair on you."

Rob shifted along the sofa and put his coffee cup on the floor, then eased Ari's cup from their hand and set it beside his. "D'you want a hug?" Ari nodded and shuffled closer, laying their head on Rob's chest, their arms around his waist, his arms circling them. "You're wrong," he murmured into their hair. "We didn't sleep together." Ari sniffed but said nothing. "It was a close call, though."

"You should have taken it."

"Why? So it makes the decision for us? Is that what you want?"

"No. I don't."

"Good."

Rob had come to talk—about Freddie, about Dee—and draw a line, but his resolve had been low before he'd got on the bike and was undone by Ari's kiss, short and sharp as it had been. They were wrong. *This* was the inevitable, and unless Ari pulled the brakes, he wasn't going to fight it.

They both moved at the same time. Ari straddled him, and his arms slid down until his hands rested on their hips.

"Good how?" they asked, closing in on his mouth, denying him the chance to answer. He let go of everything and dived head first, leaving behind thoughts of Freddie and Dee and his fears for what was to come. All that mattered was here and now, this kiss, Ari in his arms, the press of their body against his, so attuned to each other's needs that Ari tugged at Rob's T-shirt as he attempted the same with Ari's.

They paused only as long as it took to fully remove their T-shirts, then came back together, skin on skin. Rob's kisses trailed away from Ari's mouth to their neck as they rose, and back again as they fell.

"Is it too forward of me..." Ari murmured, delivering kisses along Rob's jawline and catching the gold stud in his earlobe between their teeth. He'd put it back in when he'd left the Met and mostly forgot he wore it, but there was something indefinably erotic in the light discomfort exuding from the pull on the metal bar.

"This?" he asked, belatedly realising Ari's question, which he'd been waiting for them to finish, might be complete.

"Nuh-uh." They lifted again, rolling their hips as they descended, making full, through-denim contact with Rob's erection as they whispered, "To want you inside me."

Rob exhaled, and a low groan escaped. "I want that too," he confirmed. "But..."

Ari slid backwards until they were standing and took his hands, pulling him up from the sofa. "But what?"

"You're not hard."

"The effect of HRT." They released his hands and looked him in the eye. "Are you sure you want to do this?"

Rob nodded. "Just making sure you aren't doing it for me."

Smiling, Ari gripped his buttocks and ground against him. "Absolutely not."

The bed was only a few feet away, but an age passed before they reached it, unbuckling belts, trampling out of jeans and socks, finally naked. The duvet plumed, creating a cocoon around them as they tumbled onto the soft mattress, kissing and writhing, urgency increasing. Ari grappled blindly for the bedside cabinet but couldn't reach, and Rob reluctantly rolled onto his side, tracing their spine with his fingertip as they sat on the edge of the bed, smiling when they shivered.

"It tickles." They turned back, condom and lube in hand, a question in their gaze.

"D'you want to put it on or shall I?" Rob asked.

Ari grinned. "Not your first rodeo?"

Rob laughed rather than answer. He and Zoë had enjoyed all kinds of sex, same with Jess, but it was hardly the time to discuss it. Or maybe it was exactly the time. Still, he'd rather not risk killing what might be their one and only chance to make love. He went to take the condom, but Ari jerked it out of his reach.

"I'll do it," they said. They pushed his hip, trailing their fingers across his groin as he rolled onto his back. Rob watched—not just what they did with the condom. The subtle flex of biceps, the smooth inverted V of a bent knee—every curve, every freckle, the shimmer of sweat that turned their skin brushed bronze... the amused arch of their eyebrows as they became aware of his attentiveness.

"What are you doing?"

"Looking."

"I can see that, but why?"

"Because you're beautiful."

Ari's smile turned bashful. "Thank you." They handed him the lube bottle. "How do you want to do this?"

"Whatever's best for you."

"Like this?" They lay on their side, their back to his front, and looked over their shoulder.

Rob squeezed lube into his palm, leaving the bottle within reach and curling around them, murmuring, "Are you OK?" into their ear.

"Yes."

He slid his hand between their bodies, smearing some of the lube over the condom then gliding his palm down the centre of Ari's buttocks, applying gentle pressure with his fingers, slowly easing his way in, pressing harder on each pass until Ari pushed back impatiently. Rob moved into a better position and rocked his hips, concentrating so hard he forgot to breathe and gasped as he slid deeper into Ari—body, mind, soul.

He kissed their shoulder. "Tell me what you want."

"This. Forever."

"I don't think I can last that long," he joked to conceal how much that word tore him apart. Arousal reinforced what he'd felt a year ago—what he hadn't stopped feeling since. He was in love with Naomi...Ari—they were the same beautiful, brilliant person, of whom he was not entirely sure he was worthy, but in this singular, transient moment, he was their everything and they were his.

Bending his knees so he could move more freely, Rob twisted to reach Ari's lips, spanning their arm and smoothing it all the way down until his hand grasped theirs, moving with it as they masturbated. He was fighting to maintain his rhythm and prolong the pleasure, and he was about to lose the battle when Ari arched, only their hand moving as they stared at him unseeing. They were still lost in their climax as Rob's hit.

By the time he came down, Ari was panting and smiling, and Rob realised he was too. He collapsed back onto the bed, no longer inside them but still maximising contact head to toe, arm draped over them, thumb brushing their nipple. Their breathing steadied, synchronised.

"I'll deal with the condom in a minute," Rob said, drunk on endorphins.

"Let me." Ari acted before he could protest. "Stay there."

"OK." Not difficult when he felt as if he weighed four times as much as before. He heard a toilet flush and lifted his head just enough to notice a second door to an en suite from which Ari emerged wearing a red kimono. The silk was chilly against Rob's chest as they snuggled back into their previous position. They breathed slowly and deeply, a pause after each inhalation as if they'd intended to speak but changed their mind. After several minutes, they said, "Freddie isn't on a business trip. We had a fight last night over his drinking."

"A physical fight?"

"No. He'd never hurt me."

That was a matter of opinion, but Rob let it go. "What happened?"

"I told him I was leaving. He interpreted it as an ultimatum. So...he's booked himself into rehab, and now I don't know what to do."

"Because he's trying to fix it?"

"Yes—not for the first time. His drinking has always been a problem—he was an alcoholic before we were at university—but it was low level, you know? A drink every day, a couple of splurges a week—it's his upbringing. It's been far worse since he came out of prison. I don't recall the last time he was sober."

"Could he be using rehab to stop you leaving?"

"Who knows? Either way, I'm trapped."

"You need the job."

"No, I don't. While he was in prison, I freelanced on a few software projects. Companies are offering me work almost every week. Between contracts and my stock portfolio, I could buy this apartment."

"Whoa!" Berringer's apartment was worth millions. "So why were you living in that shitty bedsit?"

"A year ago I *was* destitute, but it only takes a couple of well-placed investments and then selling at the optimum moment—" Ari grinned "—and I have an app for that."

Rob chuckled. "You're incredible. Do you know that?"

Ari smiled, but it faded fast. "I'm a socially anxious nerd who can only function in the real world about fifty percent of the time."

"Whatever, you don't need Freddie, Ari. You don't need anyone."

"No, you're right. But I do want you. I want to be with you, and fate keeps conspiring against us. Because here you are again, but I have to stay and give Freddie a chance. Do you understand?"

"I do," Rob said. "And if things were different, I'd be gutted right now. But I came to ask you to do something for me."

"Was the sex to soften the blow?"

Rob hugged them closer and kissed their neck. "It was an unplanned but welcome diversion."

They rolled to face him, meeting his gaze and holding it. "What do you need me to do?"

"Send Folden a message. I'm ending this now."

22: Showdown

A LL IN POSITION, Sir." Isobel indicated the surveillance van's monitor, on which were displayed the head cam feeds of the four officers stationed at various points in and around Berringer's building.

"Thank you, Barnes." Winstanley, unable to stand upright, crouched at Isobel's side and tapped his finger on thin air in front of the bottom-left image: a slightly out-of-focus view of the basement garage. "Give me another three-sixty."

"Yes, Sir." Isobel relayed the order to the officer in situ, and the camera panned jerkily, taking in all of the drab concrete expanse, empty but for Rob's bike.

Winstanley grunted in disappointment as if he'd expected it to change since he'd sent the officer down there. "Any word from Silvestri?"

Both Gray and Isobel shook their heads. Dom's calls before they'd left the hotel had gone unanswered; the app had been quiet for almost an hour; Rob's phone was going to voicemail. Everyone was prepared for the worst, the dull weight of expectancy allowing them to unhurriedly follow procedure.

"All right. Time to move in." Winstanley activated his radio and gave the order to Dom, already inside the building.

Gray watched the monitor, specifically the feed from Dom's head cam, pointing at Berringer's apartment as another officer rammed the door. On the second strike, the door gave a thunderbolt crack and splintered from its frame, and Dom, Dee and the officer with the ram entered, calling "Clear" on the rooms as they passed. Daylight flared through each doorway they left open, slicing across the grainy dark of the forebodingly quiet apartment, but there were no signs of a struggle or any kind of disturbance—until they reached the dining room at the end of the hall, at which point someone screamed and the surveillance van's monitor blanked out.

Gray leapt to his feet. "What happened?"

"Not sure, Sir." Isobel rebooted the feeds, to no avail.

"I'm going in." Gray took one step. Winstanley's arm descended like a car park exit barrier.

"Wait, Fisher!" he barked.

"It's not your—" Gray's phone pinged, interrupting his tirade, as did Winstanley's and Isobel's. He hadn't even unlocked the screen when the camera feeds came back online. He caught a flash of red in one before it jolted to the right.

"What the hell...?" Forgetting all about his phone, Gray moved closer to the monitor, trying to make sense of what he was seeing. One cam was on the move, walking the perimeter of Berringer's dining room; another provided a view of what at first glance appeared to be a cupboard but then panned across a server stack to a metal desk and two huge monitors. Whoever was wearing the third cam was looking down at a pair of bare legs, slowly scanning upwards to the source of the red flash.

"Ari?" Gray uttered in astonishment.

"It would appear so," Winstanley said irritably. "Signal jammer. Aren't those illegal?"

Gray caught Isobel's eye. They would have laughed in other circumstances, seeing as most of what Winstanley had Ari doing on behalf of whatever untouchable echelon he worked for was questionable on the legal front. But Gray's reaction wasn't to the cameras going down.

"You're clear to go in, Sir," Isobel reported.

"Thank you," Winstanley acknowledged. "Barnes—stay here. Fisher—with me." Almost walking on his knees, Winstanley proceeded to the van door and stepped down onto the pavement, hence he missed Gray's mocking salute. Isobel didn't.

"Good luck, Sir," she said.

"Thanks, Iz. See you shortly, I hope."

Gray followed Winstanley from the van and into the building, where the concierge was ready to throw in the towel and waved them onwards without so much as a glance. They reached the first floor and passed a maid standing outside the door to the apartment next to Berringer's, watching the action and reporting in Polish to someone unseen.

Winstanley pushed the top half of Berringer's door. It swung free of the bottom half and tilted dangerously on its single, straining hinge. Beyond it, Ari was a vision of red fury yelling at Dom. Winstanley gingerly pushed the bottom of the door open but didn't enter.

"I don't think you need to worry about knocking, Martin," Gray said.

Winstanley pivoted at the waist, head inclined, his expression one of alarm. In the background, clearly struggling to keep his cool, Dom said, "If you'd answered our calls or checked the app—"

"You didn't have to break the door down!"

"Mx. Silvestri," Winstanley called and did actually knock on the upper half of the door. It bounced and dropped a couple of inches, the bottom corner coming to a rest against the frame. "If I may—"

Ari cut him dead with a single glare. "I'll talk to Gray. No-one else."

A momentary stalemate ensued, during which Gray's view consisted of Winstanley's back and half of Ari's steely gaze. Eventually, Winstanley relented and stepped aside, granting Gray his first full look at Ari, which answered the question of why they and Rob had been out of contact. Winstanley was right: Rob's love life was nobody's business but his own, but his other actions were a concern to them all.

Ari didn't speak, merely jerked their head to indicate where they were going and walked off. Gray looked to Winstanley for instruction.

"Go," Winstanley said. "And be quick about it."

Gray went after Ari, passing a battle-weary Dom as he entered the dining room, where Dee and the other officer were talking quietly, heads close together. They stopped when they saw him.

"In there." Dee pointed towards the door in the far wall.

Gray made his way over, acutely conscious of the silence behind him and the hum of air-conditioning ahead. The change in temperature had him shivering as he entered the small room—home to the server stack and monitors he'd seen on the cam.

As soon as he cleared the door, Ari shut it and said, "You're too late. Rob left twenty minutes ago."

"His phone signal says otherwise."

Ari reached into the pockets of their kimono and withdrew two phones.

"Unbelievable. Where's he gone?"

"To meet Folden. I don't know where."

In truth, Gray had expected it, but not for Rob to leave his phone behind so they had no way to trace him. "Tell me exactly what was said."

"Nothing was said. Rob asked me to send a message via Lucas's Xbox account asking for a time and place." Ari went over to the desk and unlocked their computer. "This is the reply that came back."

Gray could see it from where he was standing, but he moved closer to make sure he'd read it correctly. One word: *Carabiner*. "What the hell does that mean?"

"I don't know, but Rob did."

"Did he take a taxi?"

"No. He was on foot."

"Heading for the Tube?"

"I don't think so."

"OK. So it's somewhere close by or Folden came for him, in which case he knows where you live," Gray said, adding—because Ari was being intentionally obtuse, "We'll have to arrange somewhere for you and Berringer—"

"He may have caught a bus."

Gray rubbed his eyes, gritty and sore from lack of sleep and too many bright screens, but also to express his weariness with their interchange. "Any idea which one?"

"I don't."

"But you could look it up."

"Rob said—"

"I don't care what he said. I'm going after him, so you can speed up the process by helping me or I'll take the long road and find him myself."

Ari stood defiant, arms crossed, expression hard and determined in spite of the tears rolling down their cheeks. "Please don't make me do this."

"I'm trying to save his life, Ari."

"What life? He's been in limbo for the past year. He just wants it to be over. Whatever happens with Folden, he's at peace with it."

"Well, I'm not!" Gray shouted. He was out of patience and time. "I made Rob a promise, and I'd rather fulfil it *before* Folden kills him. Are you going to stand back and wait—"

"All right! I'll do it!" Ari cut in angrily. Shoving Gray aside, they dragged a chair out from the desk and sat more heavily than their slender form should have permitted. "You're all the same." They took their frustration out on the keyboard. "Men in power, making your demands and your threats. You're all the same." The monitor display changed to the London Transport logo and a list of bus route numbers. "There!" Ari nodded at the screen. "What is your bidding now, *sir*?"

Gray leaned closer, focusing on the list and not saying what was in his mind to say. "I'd like to see the full routes for each, please."

A new tab opened—old school dark-grey background and bold Times New Roman in default Web 1.0 colours—green, yellow, cyan and white.

Gray blinked a few times and squinted at the retina-scorching text. "I can't read that."

Ari clicked a key combo, and the colours inverted. "Better?"

"Yes. Thank you." It wasn't a vast improvement, but he could at least make out the words, such use as it was. Ignoring the night buses, the five routes passing through or terminating in Marylebone covered half the city. In Gray's current mental state, he couldn't even grab a thread and begin narrowing it down to one route, let alone one location.

"Would it help if I overlay the routes on a map?" Ari asked.

"It might. Let's try."

Ari set to work, still beating the hell out of their keyboard but perhaps with a little less destructive intent.

"Thank you," Gray said.

A map filled the screen. Ari centred it and zoomed in. "What's wrong with your eyes?"

"Photophobia—hypersensitivity to light."

Five red lines appeared on the map. "From your accident, or have you always had it?"

Gray started—at the abruptness of the question rather than Ari knowing about the accident. Will could've told them, or it could've been in the police files Winstanley had allowed them to access.

"I apologise. It's none of my business." Ari stood and rolled their chair towards Gray, then pulled a second chair along from the far end of the desk.

"Thanks." Gray sat. "From the accident," he answered, examining the map. "It's worse when I'm tired or stressed...or trying to pinpoint a single location among hundreds." He leaned back and closed his eyes to give them a rest. "We need to identify any places on those bus routes Rob and Folden have in common." He blinked a few times and opened his eyes again. They were adjusting, slowly. That or Ari had turned down the screen brightness. "Don't suppose you have access to the GPS info from Rob's old courier routes?"

"I'll check." They went straight to a specific folder and opened several files, scanning and closing each in turn until one remained. "Not routes—dates, times and locations—I'll overlay them on the map." They copied the text from the file into a spreadsheet, saved it, imported it...

A heat map.

"Damn, you're good!"

Ari blushed. "I try."

"All right, let's see what we've got."

The heat map of Rob's courier drops was largely uniform in colour, but there were a couple of hot spots—one covering the part of Holborn where the law courts and most of the barristers' chambers were, therefore where most of Rob's pick-ups and drop-offs would have been. The other had nothing to do with Rob's undercover work, or not directly: it was the home he'd shared with Zoë and Lucas—the home they should currently be sharing with Travis. Rob's time with the SIU was before Travis came on the scene, and in those three years, Rob had seen his wife and son only a handful of times, yet how often must he have just parked up and watched the house for it to show as a hot spot?

Otherwise, there was no obvious correspondence between buses from Marylebone and Rob's courier routes, rendering it useless as a means of establishing where he was meeting Folden, but it might hold the key to proving Rob had nothing to do with the hard drive. However, Winstanley had made it clear that information was classified.

"Could you do me a favour, Ari? Send me a copy of that text file?"

"Of course." They switched to the other monitor and whizzed through the process in seconds. "Done."

"Thank you." His phone buzzed to indicate the email's arrival. "Can you think of anything else Rob's said that might be useful?"

For their part, Ari considered the question before they shook their head. "Perhaps Josh could take a look, do some kind of geographical profiling?"

"It'd take too long, but send it to him anyway—and Professor Holt." Gray contemplated sending an instruction with it that Josh and Trudi work together and pool their knowledge, though he doubted either would agree. Josh rarely complied unless doing so coincided with his own goals, but he was under strict orders to stay at the hotel, and the map data might keep him occupied until Gray could check in. "I need to report back to Winstanley, get the search underway."

Ari was in the process of sharing the files but gave a nod to acknowledge they'd heard.

Gray rose from the chair. "Ari, I'm sorry for the way I spoke to you. This must be hard for you."

"Yes, it is."

"Are you coping?"

"While I have things to do." They sniffed, brushed away tears, kept typing. "I'm sorry for what I said too. I know you're one of the good ones."

"You don't know that."

"I've read your personnel files and heard what they say." Ari glanced towards the door, indicating Winstanley and Dom, Gray thought. "They have a great deal of respect for you."

"And a bizarre way of showing it."

"Because they're not like you. They lead by exerting their authority over their subordinates. You lead by example. You never ask anyone to do what you aren't willing to do yourself. You have a strong conscience and a kind heart."

"If you say so."

"I do—you've compromised so much for Will."

"And he for me," Gray pointed out.

"Oh, I agree, though you left him less far to travel. He would give up almost everything if you asked him to."

"I would never do that."

"I know, as does he. I'm not sure how much he's told you about us...?"

"A little." More than a little, within the confidence of their relationship. He needed to leave, but he was also curious to hear more, so he let Ari continue.

"We sat next to each other in our first university lecture—and every lecture thereafter because something clicked between us. I'm not sure what. Perhaps it was no more than each sensing in the other how different we were from everyone else. Both working class, both from lone-parent families, both LGBTQ, though back then I only presented as Aaron.

"Will was the first person I ever told, but don't imagine it had anything to do with me feeling I could confide in him. Too much vodka and a game of Truth or Dare—he told me he fancied me—Aaron—and then locked himself in the bathroom." Ari smiled, recalling, "I thought he'd gone to throw up, and I stood outside, begging him to let me in, worried he'd aspirate. He refused, of course, so we held an entire conversation through that door.

"When I'm Aaron, I'm...I don't know...too anxious to feel an attraction maybe? When I'm Naomi, everything changes, and I *was* attracted to Will back then, but only sometimes. I tried to explain through the door and the slur of vodka, and Will was convinced I was just being nice, trying not to hurt him."

"How long did it take him to open the door?" Gray asked.

"An hour and a half!" Ari laughed, as did Gray. "He may have passed out for a time. After that—months after, actually—we became an item, mostly confined to LGBTQ society events. As far as everyone was concerned, we were a same-sex couple. Will supported me while I found the courage to be myself in public, introduced me to his friends and covered for my anxiety—even after we broke up.

"When Freddie and I started seeing each other, Will was the only one of our friends who spoke out, insisting I deserved better. Had I known then of Freddie and Will's history...well, I suppose it wouldn't have made a difference. Freddie would have found other ways to manipulate us. My point is, Will had every reason to end our friendship, but he didn't. He would move heaven and earth for the people he loves, and most—myself included—are flattered. He gives and we take without ever giving in return because we believe it's what he wants. How could we think otherwise when he tells us it's so? But you didn't fall for it."

"I didn't trust him," Gray admitted. "Not at first."

"You saw past the distractions and misdirection. It's a trait both you and Rob possess, and it's...disarming. But this—" Ari gestured around the tiny room "—is my life. Will is yours, and Rob wouldn't thank you for risking it on his behalf."

Gray let Ari's words settle awhile, appreciating their honesty, their help, their encouragement, wishing for more time to get to know each other, to pick up where Will had left off in convincing Ari they deserved better than Freddie and this life. But there was only one person who could do that.

"Thank you for everything, Ari. I *will* find him."

Ari's smile was less than optimistic as they said, "I hope so."

***

In all his years of police service, Gray had never had to inform next of kin of their loved one's demise. He'd been with other officers when they'd done the deed; he'd felt their distress, possibly as keenly as if it were his own. As far as he knew, Rob was still alive, yet Gray had that same feeling as he stopped the car outside the Cliftons' residence. He'd called ahead, so Zoë was expecting him, but he needed a moment to get into the right frame of mind.

You never ask anyone to do what you aren't willing to do yourself. Of everything Ari had said to him, that one statement was the fish bone he couldn't swallow. Gray had prided himself on leading by example, but now the boot was on the other foot and Rob had gone after Folden so Gray wouldn't have to, he saw with brutal clarity how utterly reckless his approach had been.

The blinds in the house's front window swayed, signalling it was time, and as he locked the car and walked up the path, he scratched around for a vestige of hope, a white lie he could convince himself was true before he faced Zoë and Lucas. Folden hadn't killed Rob yet, and he wouldn't until either the hard drive was in his possession or he realised Rob didn't have it. All Rob had to do was play Folden long enough for them to find him.

Gray dug deep, not for a smile—there was no good news to warrant one—but for calm and sincerity. The door opened.

"Hi, Zoë."

She exhaled. "Hi. Come in." Squeezed his hand as he passed. "I was so sure you'd come with bad news."

23: Trip Switch

Is there any chance Rob has what Folden wants?" Zoë asked. Other than shouting at Lucas for asking what a carabiner was—admittedly three times, after which he'd stomped out of the room—it was the first time she'd spoken since Gray finished telling her Rob had gone to meet Folden.

"No. I'm certain he doesn't." The statement left a space into which doubt seeped. All this time he'd insisted Rob was what he seemed: a decent, upstanding guy using his skill set to earn a living. Going to Folden was supposed to give him a chance to clear his name, but had the PI work merely been a means of maintaining his contacts within the system?

"Gray? What aren't you telling me? There's more, isn't there?"

"No, there isn't. I just zoned out for a minute—sorry. I didn't sleep well last night."

Zoë grimaced in sympathy. "I'm having the same trouble—for a different reason. I'm pregnant."

"Is that good news?"

"The timing could be better, but yes."

"Then congratulations." The word had never felt so flat and meaningless.

"Thanks," Zoë said, no celebration there either. "Travis and I agreed we'd wait until I was twelve weeks along before we shared—that was yesterday."

"You told Rob."

"We did. I was worried how he'd take it, but he seemed OK. Now I think I might've pressured him to act."

"In what sense?"

"I told him Travis and I weren't going to delay our wedding indefinitely while we wait for this to be over."

"Ah. I see what you mean, but I'm fairly sure he'd have done this regardless." Gray could think of at least two other incentives Rob had for wanting to speed things up. "When's the happy day, if you don't mind me asking?"

"We had the register office appointment booked for today."

"For the wedding?" Gray was astounded—more so that Rob hadn't said anything—and he must have looked it.

"To give notice." Zoë's laughter at his reaction rapidly diminished to a shaky sigh. "I was so adamant we were getting married in a month, come hell or high water..." She shrugged in resignation and held Gray's gaze. If she was seeking guidance, she was out of luck; Gray had none to offer. Rob might not come back from this, and the day would be marred whether she went ahead or postponed, which would also be true of his and Will's wedding. But he couldn't think like that. He had to believe they'd find Rob before it was too late.

"I'll have to cancel today's appointment anyway," Zoë said as if their thoughts had been one and the same.

"Do what feels right," Gray suggested—sound advice for them both. "I need to get back out there—I just wanted to tell you in person. Can I do anything for you, like..." He shook his head, at a loss. "I don't know."

"Thanks, but you've done enough, and I mean that in the best way." She got up, as did Gray, and drifted reluctantly towards the door. "And if I can do anything for you..."

"Thanks, Zoë. I'll update you as soon as I have any news." Gray stepped into the hall, looking up towards the sound of thumping feet as Lucas came charging down the stairs, breathless and excited.

"I know what a carabiner is!" he announced, skidding to a halt.

"Not now, Lu."

"It's important, Mum!" He grabbed Gray's hand and poked something cold and metallic into it.

Frowning, Gray looked down. "Yes, that's a carabiner."

Lucas beamed. "Didn't know they were called that. It's off the rucksack Dad got me—it's got two so you can carry your compass and other stuff. It's for camping, except we haven't gone camping yet. I put the other one on Dad's bike so he doesn't forget."

Gray's heart rate hit cocaine velocity. "When did you put it on there, Lucas?"

"Ages ago!"

"Ages as in days or weeks?"

"Nah, man. Years!"

"It can't have been that long," Zoë argued.

"It was! Remember? Cos I got my sore ear in the summer holidays. That's why we couldn't go camping."

"OK, that was nearly two years ago."

"Is it a good clue, Fish?" Lucas peered up at him, blinking big brown eyes.

"Don't be rude, Lu," Zoë admonished.

"I wasn't!"

"It's all right," Gray assured them. He knew Lucas called him Fish, and while Zoë's discomfort indicated the nickname's origin was less than complimentary, Lucas was a good kid who didn't know the meaning of malice. "It's an excellent clue. You've been really helpful, thank you." He wasn't sure how yet, but if he hadn't already been determined to bring Rob back alive, Lucas's proud smile would've sealed it. "I'll see you soon. Be good for your mum, OK?"

"I will!" Lucas promised.

Gray stepped outside, waiting to hear the door lock before he walked to his car, where he checked in with 'his' team. Isobel was back at SIU HQ doing her real job but managed to give him a quick progress update. Accordingly, with 'one of the alleged suspects' being a former police officer, Winstanley had an official excuse to interfere in the coordination of the various local police services involved in the 'man hunt'. Dom had Ari combing through Rob's phone logs, Dee had gone back to the Parkers' to oversee the search of Rob's car and his belongings, and Josh...

~We've changed tack.

"We?" Gray asked aloud as he typed the same.

~Trudi and me. Who else?

Gray stared at the text, confounded, muttering, "Amazing what he'll do for a friend."

~We're looking for Folden's aunt.

"Are you, indeed." He didn't type that; he called instead. "What about the geographical profile?"

"What about it?" Josh said. "Ari's already done most of the work."

"You can't add to it?"

"Not in any useful way. We've calculated radii based on the time Rob left Berringer's, but we don't know if Folden's in a car, on a bike, came by train, plane, boat—"

"OK. I take your point. Tell me about his aunt."

"We're still looking. Trudi's profile indicates Folden and his aunt were close, so he may be staying with her."

"Do you agree with that assessment?"

"It's an avenue worth exploring," Josh said diplomatically.

"All right. Keep me posted. I'm following a possible lead too—can you upload your map overlay?"

"We're working on it live, so you should already have access—Dom has."

"I'll check now. How are things there otherwise?"

"Better than anticipated."

"Glad to hear it. I'll let you go."

"Take care, Graham."

"You too."

Gray ended the call and opened the map with its ever-growing number of overlays, the most recent of which was like a cross-section of a tree trunk—quite possibly from entirely the wrong tree—but Folden had to have seen the carabiner on Rob's bike at some point. There was no other way a seemingly random word could convey a meeting place. The question was when and where—a year ago when he escaped from the secure hospital or during the past few days? If they could isolate the timeframe, they might be able to narrow down an area based on Rob's phone's GPS and identify potential rendezvous points. Gray started the engine and called Dom, hands-free. He wasn't sure where he was going, but he couldn't sit outside the Cliftons' any longer.

"Hooper."

"Hey. It's Gray. How are you doing with Rob's phone?"

"Nothing useful from calls and texts, and GPS was turned off until Ari set up the app. We're going through the location data now."

"Can you add it to the map?"

"It's sketchy but can do. Have you got something?"

"Possibly. The carabiner is on Rob's bike."

"No-one's been near the bike," Dom said.

"It's been on there for two years, and we know Folden was locked up for the first year."

"Then he must've seen it last Friday night," Dom reasoned.

"Or after Brookhurst," Gray argued. "There was a two-week gap between Folden's escape and Rob taking the bike off the road."

"We had eyes on Rob twenty-four seven."

"Oh, yes. So you did." Gray's scalp prickled at the reminder, but he kept his cool as he said, quite matter-of-fact, "You deserve an Oscar for that performance, Hooper."

"What are you talking about? I didn't know Folden was on the run."

"You were already working for Winstanley."

"He only gave the order to start surveillance. He didn't say why. And for the record, if I'd known he was going to let Folden slip through our fingers this time—"

"You'd have told him where to get off?"

"I would, as it goes. Look, Gray, I know you're pissed off with me and think I've betrayed you. But can you see it from my point of view? You're Rob's business partner. Whether he's bent or not, you're too close. I couldn't risk involving you. But I've never lied to you, and I never will."

"Guess I'll have to take you at your word—for now."

"That'll do me," Dom said. "For now. So...what're we looking for? Sports shops? Motorcycle dealerships?"

"Maybe." Gray gracefully accepted the step-down. "Have you got Rob's full route from last Friday?"

"Partial only. He must've turned his phone off, but we can fill in some of the blanks. He called Clough's landline at 21:42. I caught up with him at 22:14," and he was still in Holborn. He got snapped jumping a light a couple of minutes after I let him go—he could've gone anywhere after that. Where on his bike is the carabiner, do you know?"

"No, but it's about two inches long, so you should find it easily enough."

"There's nothing there now that I can see. Hold on while I get back in—before you ask, I stepped out to give us some privacy and figured I'd check the bike while I was at it. I'm on the old nicotine patches."

"None of my business. But good for you."

Dom didn't reply, and Gray listened instead to him puffing and panting as he went back up the stairs to Berringer's apartment.

"Putting you on speaker," he said. "Ari, are you able to access CCTV on or around Chapelle Court, Holborn from last Friday evening, nine-thirty onwards?"

"I would think so." The *tap-tap-tap* of rapid keyboard work was all Gray could hear and then, "Here you go."

"You're a bloody wonder. Just running forward on double-speed," Dom explained for Gray's benefit.

"OK."

"There's Rob arriving at Clough's chambers…"

Gray indicated and pulled over. There was little point heading back into the city if they were as close to figuring out where Rob had gone as he hoped.

"And there's Rob leaving," Dom said. "Timestamp 22:04. No sign of Folden."

"So if they did cross paths, it must've been after you stopped him." Two blue dots appeared on the map, close together. "I take it that's where you stopped him and where he jumped the lights?"

"Yep. We need to know what time Rob got back to the Parkers'. Ari, any chance—"

"I can hack the alarm system?" they finished on Dom's behalf.

"That's the one." His admiration was apparent in his tone, and it made Gray smile. The more he learned about Ari, the better he understood how they and Will had become such good friends, both so unassuming in their brilliance, so amenable. Little wonder, also, that Berringer was able to usurp that brilliance to build his empire.

"The alarm was switched off at 23:19," Ari reported.

"And it's a thirty-minute journey, max," Gray said. "That's our window. Rob stopped off somewhere between Holborn and Hampstead Heath." He traced the red lines of bus routes passing between those points and tried to come up with likely venues. "OK. Forget retailers—they'd have been closed. Are there any fast-food outlets near the junction where he jumped the lights?"

The map dimmed, and a text message flashed onto the screen—for Gray's eyes only. It was from Dee.

~ *They took something from his car.*

"There's an industrial park with an all-night café after the next junction," Ari said.

Nausea mounting, Gray read the message again, and again, and hit reply: *I'll call you in a sec.*

"Any cameras?" Dom asked.

~ *They're still here. Will call you when clear.*

"None I can access."

"Thoughts?" Dom said.

OK. Did you see what it was?

~ *No. Small though.*

How small?

"You still there, Gray?"

"Yeah." He watched the message window, willing Dee to reply.

"What do you want to do?" Dom asked.

~ *RF bag. TTYL.*

"I'm looking." Gray swiped the text window away and zoomed in on the map, commanding his brain to stop second-guessing what they'd found in Rob's car, but it had to be tech of some sort. The RF shield bags the Met used were about 8x11 inches—plenty big enough for a hard drive.

"Take your time, Fisher. No rush."

He let Dom's sarcasm pass and said, "That bus route's walking distance from the industrial park."

"Agreed. See you there?"

"I'll race you."

***

"Would you like anything else? A muffin or a pastry?"

"No, cheers." Rob paused his observation to pay for his espresso. He didn't even want it, but he'd had to buy something. The café was busier than it had been on Friday night, but it was still too quiet for him to lurk, particularly as there was no telling how long it would take Folden to make his move. He could already be there, somewhere he could see but not be seen, waiting for Rob to drop his guard.

His espresso appeared next to his elbow. He took it and a newspaper from the stand on his way to the same table as last time, tucked against a wall and facing the door. He flipped the paper and read the back page—end of the footy season, same old teams vying for the top spot—then thumbed the corner to turn the page.

Something clunked, heavy and metallic, pinning the paper in place.

"Hello, Robert. May I join you?"

His stomach lurched and his hackles went up, but Rob managed to stay stock-still, refusing to acknowledge the man now sitting opposite. Anders Folden, right there in the over-cologned flesh, smiling broadly as if their meeting was an unexpected, pleasant surprise. Rob's anger simmered and threatened to boil over; he picked up the carabiner and squeezed it until it dug into his palm.

A couple of minutes ticked by; Folden cased the café while he waited for his drink—an obscenely large cappuccino that made clear he was in no rush to move on. A couple more minutes. Still not a word spoken.

Rob smoothed his thumb over the wide curve of the carabiner, the warmed metal no longer registering inside his fist, and watched Folden casually sipping his coffee, his constant half-smile accompanied by an occasional sigh of satisfaction.

"So, Robert." He used his real accent—well-spoken English with a strong Norwegian flavour, pronouncing every consonant. "How have you been?"

Rob looked him in the eye, held it. "What do you want?"

Folden gave a controlled, quiet laugh. "How is Lucas?"

Rob sat back and shoved his hands into his pockets, still clutching the carabiner, his feet planted wide beneath the table, claiming space. Folden acted as if he hadn't noticed, though a slight upward twitch of his eyebrows said otherwise.

Rob asked again. "What do you want?"

"How many times did you talk about your son when we were working together?" Folden waited an overly long time for a response he wasn't going to get before he answered his own question. "Not even once. And he's such a spirited boy. You must have many stories of the things he does—the things you do together. Father and son—"

"What do you want, Folden?"

"Another for you?" He gestured at Rob's espresso cup.

That turned out to be a much harder question to *not* answer, and Rob almost shook his head but caught himself at the last second.

"As you wish." Folden picked up his cappuccino and held it, ready to drink. "You know what I want, or you wouldn't be here, but let's not talk about that now." He disappeared behind the enormous cup, tipped it and gulped, draining the rest in one go. He set the empty cup on the table. "We will leave before your clever friends figure out where you are." He rose but remained in front of his seat and stared at Rob until he got up. "There again," he murmured, herding Rob from behind, out of the café and towards a black Toyota, "if they're really clever, they will not come looking for you at all."

24: The Game

GRAY ARRIVED SECONDS before Dom, their two cars the only vehicles in the six-bay lot in front of the café, although Folden's could have been any one of those in the vast car park on the other side of the industrial estate, if he was there at all. They didn't wait for backup. Indeed, they hadn't requested any, seeing as they were there on little more than a whim. Armed and automatically falling into their long-practised routine, they entered the building—Gray through the front door, Dom through the back; they'd meet up at the counter.

Gray moved steadily, taking the time to confirm his first impression was accurate: if Rob had met Folden there, they weren't there anymore. He reached the counter as Dom appeared in the passage a few yards behind the woman serving. Dom shook his head and signalled he'd go around the front to join Gray rather than terrify the poor woman by suddenly materialising next to her.

"Morning. What can I get you?"

"Good morning. I wonder if you can help me?" Gray unlocked his phone. "Do you recognise this man?" He showed her a photo of Rob.

"Yeah. He was here earlier. Sat over there." She pointed to an unoccupied table to Gray's left. "Bought an espresso. Kept watching the door—must've been waiting for someone." Before Gray could ask, she added, "That other bloke sat with him, now I think on. Delivery got here while I was doing his cappuccino."

Dom appeared next to Gray. "Was this the other man?" He showed her Folden's mug shot.

"Might be...yeah, I think so." She frowned. "He had longer hair, sort of dirty blonde, you know what I mean?" She lifted her head to acknowledge a customer queuing behind them and then scrutinised Gray and Dom. "You coppers, then?"

"We are." Dom showed her his ID. "We'll be out of your way soon. How did they act with each other? Did they seem friendly?"

Gray prickled at Dom's word choice. However involved Rob was in this, he'd still met with Folden as a last resort.

"They sat together, so I s'pose they were."

"No raised voices or anything suspicious?"

She shook her head. "Just drank up and left."

"Together?" Gray asked.

"Yeah. Got into a black car of some sort. Don't ask me what it was. A car's a car."

"What time was that?" Gray and Dom asked in unison.

The woman shifted her eyes from one to the other. "Not sure—half an hour ago or thereabouts. Are they in bother?"

Gray and Dom bypassed the question with a police-issue smile.

"Thanks for your help," Dom said, and they both turned and dodged around the eavesdropping customer to make a swift exit. As soon as they'd cleared the building, Dom alerted his colleagues to be on the lookout for two men in a black car, make and model unknown—a description that applied to a sizable proportion of the vehicles on the city's roads and depleted what little hope Gray had been clinging to that they'd find Rob before Folden could get any distance away.

"Where do we go from here?" he asked.

Dom shrugged and took out his keys, fiddling with them as he pondered. "I don't know. Much as I hate to say it..."

"Rob went willingly?" Gray suggested, incensed, except he was no longer sure if it was with Dom for investing in Rob's guilt, or with Rob for giving him something to invest in.

"Whatever, we need to find him," Dom said. "I'm gonna head back in and update Winstanley. What are you doing?"

Gray didn't answer because he had no answer. For the first time since this all began—since Folden's escape from Brookhurst—he was at a totally loose end. Irrespective of what they'd found in Rob's car, the PI business was dead in the water. He'd given up acting, his house was a murder scene, his PhD work was on Will's kitchen table, and Will was God knew where. That left him with—

"Get a wiggle on, Fisher, or I'll be sparking up one of these fags." Dom waved a cigarette packet in Gray's face, yanking him back off the highway to hell. "Come with me if you want—leave the car here till later."

"No. I'll go catch up with Josh, see if he and Holt have made any progress."

"Are you sure?"

"I am, but thanks."

"Anytime, mate." Dom squeezed Gray's shoulder and unlocked his car on his way around to the driver's side, looking back at Gray over the roof. "Don't do anything I wouldn't."

***

The last thing Rob remembered was wishing he'd thrown himself out of the car immediately rather than waiting and hoping they'd get caught in traffic. By the time they did, he couldn't even lift his hand from his lap, never mind reach the door handle.

He'd come to, minus shoes and belt but fully clothed, on a single bed in a dark room, no idea how long he'd been there, although it was still daylight outside. Thin, flaring streaks of it leaked between the horizontal blind slats across the two slim windows. There was a sink too—a small wash basin affixed to the wall. That was as much as he could discern before he had to put his head back down. Whatever that syringe contained had been fast-acting, taking Rob from alert to unconscious in minutes, and the hangover was something else, as was the ache in his thigh where Folden had jabbed him the second he'd fastened his seat belt.

Unable to keep his eyes open, Rob listened for movement or any indication of where he was. But there was nothing. No birdsong, no passing traffic, no voices, footsteps, TV or radio. He could've been alone, but he wouldn't be for long. This was Folden's kink—locking up his victims and leaving them in the dark—a nice bit of sensory deprivation to disorientate and escalate their desperation to escape. He'd taken a great deal of pleasure from the Black Hole hostages' efforts to bargain for one another's freedom, to the extent Rob was convinced Folden's frequent visits to the toilet were to knock one out over how panicked they were in that sightless, soundless room.

Rob realised he'd drifted off when he came to a second time, and he quickly swung his legs off the bed and sat on the edge, swaying and woozy, though his vision was less blurry than before. Standing required all his concentration and two attempts before he was steady enough on his feet to risk taking a step, then he nearly went down when he tried to bear weight on his right leg and his thigh muscles went into spasm.

He waited for it and the accompanying cold sweat to pass and limped slowly across to the windows, clinging to the wall while he figured out what he was dealing with. At least now he knew why he couldn't hear anything, as what he'd thought were blinds were steel shutters on the outside of double-glazing. He edged along, holding on to the sill, and tried to twist the handle on the vent, with the expected outcome. Locked, as, no doubt, was the door. Checking would be a waste of energy he didn't have.

Rob tried again to stand on his right leg and hissed, cussing under his breath as he shuffled over to the sink. It wobbled when he leaned on it to stoop and splash his face with cold water—the only kind available—and swill his powder-dry mouth. He was almost too parched to care whether the water was safe to drink, but he spat it out anyway. He straightened up and pivoted on his good leg to take in the room from his new vantage point, holding his breath to listen again for any signs of life. Again, he heard nothing. The sedative fog lifted a fraction, letting in dread. Had Folden's plan been this simple? To lock him up and leave him to die?

Rob's bravado—or whatever the hell it was that had brought him this far—dissolved into thin air. Of course Folden wouldn't just leave him here. Watching remotely wouldn't satisfy his lust. He'd be somewhere close by, waiting for Rob to give him a reason to act. The thought solidified into an image, a series of images, a personal horror show of Folden picking off Lucas, then Lois, then Amber—every last person Rob cared about. All of them would die if he resisted in any way. It was his life or theirs.

A little more of the fog cleared, and Rob chanced moving away from the sink, back towards the bed, getting a sense of it by touch. Bare foam mattress on a timber base, no headboard, no pillow, yet still inviting in his doped-up state. He wondered how long he'd been out, not that it mattered. Even if Gray and his team of geniuses figured out he'd gone to the café, they had no means to track him from there.

The stupid thing was he'd have got away with bringing his phone. Folden had been so confident he'd turn up alone and unarmed he hadn't bothered to frisk him, and that confidence wasn't misplaced because now Rob understood what the past year had been about. The photo of Lois and Amber, getting close to Lucas, going after Gray—Folden had been laying the foundations, guaranteeing Rob's compliance and making it appear he was in on it all along. Now Winstanley and his crew would be looking for two fugitives, if they were looking for him at all. He was entirely at Folden's mercy, and the slightest wrong move could trip the switch.

He had to escape, figure out where he was, call for help, and without Folden realising.

Returning to the windows, he pressed firmly on the glass. The frame creaked, but it was rock-solid. Short of ripping the sink off the wall and lobbing it, breaking a window was a non-starter and pointless with the steel shutters. He considered the door from afar. Even if he could pick the lock, there'd likely be a padlock on the outside.

If he was escaping that way, he'd have to subdue Folden first, which would require a weapon. Standing side-on to the sink, he could make out four round marks above, where a mirror or cabinet must have hung at some point but not anymore, so that was a no-go, which left the bed base.

He was in the process of trying to work one of the legs loose when there was a clatter against the outside of the door, followed by the scrape of a key in a lock. Rob dived onto the mattress as the door started to open. The ceiling light came on, and he threw his arm over his eyes, continuing to roll as if just coming round, although there was nothing fake about his groan as he sat up, nor his sideways topple that stopped only because Folden had sat beside him.

"Don't worry, it wears off," Folden cooed. "Drink some of this."

Still dazzled, Rob squinted at the uncapped plastic bottle in Folden's hand. He took it, too thirsty to refuse, and gulped down half the water before Folden whipped it away from him.

"Now, now, greedy." Folden nudged Rob's shoulder and looked around the room as if seeing it for the first time. "So...here we are. Like the good old days, no?" He grinned at Rob, who could only laugh at the insanity of the man sitting so close to him they were touching arm to arm, thigh to thigh.

"If you'd just wanted to meet for a catch-up—" Rob started, but Folden cut him off.

"You know what I want."

Rob shook his head but kept his gaze locked with Folden's, determined to hold it in spite of his inescapable reality. "Swear you won't hurt my family."

"I have no intention of hurting your family. You, however..." Folden stood and went over to the sink, turning back to offer Rob a hopeless shrug. "You will die. But I will grant your wish. I get what I want, your family stays safe." He held the half-full water bottle above the sink and tilted it to forty-five degrees. "Think very carefully about what you say next, Robert."

Rob could barely hold himself upright, let alone think. Whatever he said, Folden would know he was playing for time.

"I'm waiting," Folden sang. He increased the angle of the bottle, and water trickled from the neck, gurgling down the drain. It was a futile threat when he was going to kill Rob anyway. "Come now, I'm giving you a chance to save your family. Don't be sad."

But that wasn't why Rob had his head bowed. His neck no longer seemed able to hold it up, and he was sliding off the bed, but he'd figured out what Folden was up to. He was using the bottle as an hourglass, and when the water was gone...

The trickle became a stream, and Rob tried to hoist himself back into a more secure position, but his arms gave out. Vision swimming, he shot one last desperate look at Folden and fell forward into blackness.

***

Gray was clock-watching. It was hard not to when every second counted. He'd now been officially informed that evidence had been seized from Rob's car, which was as much as anyone was saying. The list Ari had sent also proved fruitless, indicating Rob hadn't been on the road at the time of the security van hijack. To corroborate the information, Gray needed access to the SIU's personnel files, but Dom was radio silent and Isobel was caught in the middle, torn between following Tant's orders and her loyalty to Gray. He wasn't going to make it any more difficult for her than it needed to be.

He hadn't heard from Winstanley and was loath to call him. Gray could picture him, right now in some high-up's office, sipping expensive whisky and enjoying the big pat on the back for making significant progress in his investigation, which was no longer about rescuing a hostage but taking down two dangerous criminals. Dead or alive.

"Are you still with me?" Josh asked.

Gray nodded and glanced up, spotting Dee's quick shift of attention away from him to her phone. She'd come to the hotel to tell Gray what she'd seen, and stayed, whether to fulfil her paid-for security brief or because she had nowhere else to go, he didn't know and couldn't bring himself to care.

So now it was just the three of them: Trudi Holt had left with a promise she'd be back in the morning once she'd dropped her children at school, and Gray both admired and hated her for maintaining that normality when all the other parents on the team had put their home lives on hold to see this through.

When Rob had given up his freedom for his son.

He stood and grabbed his coat. "I could do with stretching my legs. I'll pick up the *Standard*."

"I'll come with you," Josh said. "Let me just save—"

"Never mind. I'll look at it online." Gray sat down again but kept hold of his coat.

"I can go and get you one," Dee offered.

"It's fine, really. I forget I can read it digitally. Save the trees and all that."

Josh peered over his glasses, giving Gray a doleful look. "Ari's adjusted the map. Do you want to see?"

"Is there any point? He could be in New York or Abu Dhabi by now. In fact, why don't you just stick a pin somewhere in Europe?"

"Ignoring the fact that the airports are on alert..."

"He could still get on a boat."

"In which case, he's heading for Norway, and the ferry ports are also on alert."

"It seems counterintuitive—staying in familiar territory. Folden's cleverer than that." Gray reactivated his phone screen. "When do you want dinner? It's six-fifteen—I'll pop out and get us a takeaway."

Josh took of his glasses and sat back, regarding Gray with undisguised cynicism. "No."

"Too early?"

"Too dangerous."

"Folden's got Rob. He's not—"

"Stay here, Graham."

Gray opened his mouth and closed it again. He'd been trying to escape all afternoon—half an hour would've done, not even that—but Josh hadn't let him out of his sight.

"We aren't having takeaway. Ari's invited us to join them for dinner. I accepted on Dee's and your behalf—I hope that's all right, Dee? I said we'd be there at seven-thirty."

"I thought you'd want to work through," Gray tried.

"Oh, we'll still be working," Josh assured him.

Gray sighed, no option but to relent. He unlocked his phone again. Josh reached over and pulled it from his hand.

"I'll keep hold of this for the time being."

"I was going to call Will."

"When?"

"Well..." Gray faltered.

"You can have it back when you're ready." Josh dropped the phone into his shirt pocket.

"Fine. We might as well leave for Ari's now."

"Sorry to butt in," Dee said. "I'll give dinner a miss, if that's all right. I want to head back and shower and stuff, but I'll escort you to Berringer's first."

"No problem—you can go now if you like."

"I'd prefer to make sure you safely reach your destination. That's what you're paying me for, right?"

"We really don't—"

"Let me do my job." She was already zipping her jacket.

Gray looked to Josh for guidance and received a subtle head bob.

"OK," he agreed. Her plea was a timely reminder he wasn't the only one struggling. "I'll call Dom later—see if he can get someone over here so you can take the night off. How's that?"

Dee nodded. "Thank you."

**

When Rob came to next, it was with the ceiling light glaring in his face and a killer headache. There wasn't a part of him that didn't ache, but he managed to pull himself into a sitting position, the effort of which left him snorting hard through his nose. His lips were stuck together, and he had no saliva to ease the process of prising them apart with his tongue. He braced and tensed his jaw then swore—"Uck"—in his throat as the skin ripped off his lips.

Need for both hydration and a piss drew his eyes to the sink. The neck of a bottle was visible above the rim, triggering his last memory of Folden pouring the water away.

"Bastard drugged me again," he muttered aloud, sounding like an eighty-a-day man. He remembered now, toppling face first—Folden must've put him back on the bed.

Getting off it again was no easy feat. Between the foam mattress's rubbery surface and his lethargy, Rob couldn't slide to the edge, and his right thigh muscles were still weak, possibly bruised, so he couldn't lift his own weight. In the end, he had to roll and drop onto all fours then clamber drunkenly back to his feet, but on the whole he was in better shape than earlier, and once he was upright, he made it to the sink without relying on the wall for support.

The bottle was still half-full, a sediment of white powder settled between the ridges in its base. Rob picked it up and shook it, then tipped it straight down the plughole. Whatever came out of the tap had to be safer than what was in that bottle. Except when he turned the tap, it only dribbled. The dribble became a slow drip; Rob turned off the tap and banged the empty bottle against his forehead.

He was an idiot to not see that coming. He *knew* Folden. He'd witnessed the games, the glimmers of hope in his victims' eyes, reconciling to their fate— *If nothing else, I've still got...* as Folden snatched that hope away.

If nothing else, the sink was somewhere to piss, and Rob relieved himself, quickly switching to mouth-breathing to avoid the strong stench of his deep-yellow stream. He really wished he'd had something more than an espresso.

He finished and zipped up, feeling marginally better for emptying his bladder, and turned to survey the room as he'd done earlier. The harsh, unfiltered light from the bare bulb revealed the foam mattress was clean and new-looking, as was the hefty pine bed frame, and the room was in decent shape—smooth, matt-white walls with short, neat skirting boards, blemish-free, dark-wood flooring, recent double-glazing. Rob rapped on the wall above the sink: no telltale reverberation of plasterboard. It was either a quality new build or a damn good renovation.

The internal brightness made it impossible for Rob to see if it was still light outside, although his body clock was telling him it was early evening, going on for twenty-four hours without food and around twelve without proper fluids. If Folden was intending to let him waste away, he had a couple of days in him yet—longer if he didn't exert energy unnecessarily. It might even be long enough for Gray to find him because, in spite of how difficult Rob had made it, Gray *would* look. Part of him was holding out for a successful rescue mission—the selfish part that wanted to see his son grow up, find love, pursue his dreams, the part that wanted to believe he had a future with Ari...the part that crumpled to the ground in defeat knowing the consequences of Gray finding him without neutralising Folden.

As he cried—and laughed at the fact he still had tears to shed—he pictured Lu playing on his Xbox, chatting online with his mates, moaning about being back in school. He saw him in his tux, trying not to fidget, heard Zoë and Travis exchange vows, watched Lois and Amber dance the night away, felt his great-niece's hand gripped around his finger as she toddled along, so tiny and perfect...

The price for his life was too high. He'd known that going in.

But he wasn't ready to give up yet.

25: Holding Pattern

I'M SO PLEASED you could make it!" Ari's bubbly welcome took Gray by surprise—Josh too, judging by his camera-flash-in-the-eyes expression. "Come on in!" Ari barely stopped short of dragging them over the threshold, casting a disparaging glance at the armed officer standing outside as they firmly pushed the door shut.

"They dealt with that quickly," Gray remarked, eyeing the new door— identical to the old one prior to its run-in with a police battering ram.

Ari's eyebrow lifted with their cheeky smirk. "DCC Winstanley was *deeply* concerned for the security of my equipment."

"I bet he was."

Ari laughed and padded away down the hall, glancing back to check Gray and Josh were following, which they were, into the kitchen.

"Is he giving you trouble?" Gray paused to appreciate the pleasant aroma of recently prepared vegetables. "The officer outside I mean, not Winstanley." It went without saying that Winstanley would be.

"No, but it's not easy to relax with him there. Strangers make me anxious, and, alas, my hospitality repertoire is limited to entertaining bank clients armed only with their un-PC jokes and need to impress." Ari smiled but was palpably on edge.

"You don't need to go to any trouble for us," Josh said.

Gray nodded in agreement. "Unless you want to."

"It's really no trouble, and you're hardly strangers with...everything." Another half-smile. "I made an avocado and tomato salad. I hope that's acceptable?"

"Sounds delicious!" Josh enthused. Either he really liked avocado and tomato salad or he was ladling it on for Ari's benefit.

"And chilled a Verdicchio."

"Wonderful!" Gray said, and he *was* ladling it on. He wasn't much of a wine drinker, though Jean had been and had often accompanied a salad with a glass of Verdicchio—the greener the better, he'd said.

Ari handed Gray the bottle and a corkscrew. "Would you do the honours?"

"Of course."

"Thank you." They picked up the salad bowl, of which Josh immediately took charge.

"Where do you want it?"

Ari directed him towards the dining room. "The glasses are already on the table." They watched Josh leave and then lowered their voice so only Gray would hear. "I spoke to Will earlier."

"How is he?"

"Worried. Frustrated. Missing you. He wondered why you hadn't called with an update."

"We agreed I'd call him this evening." It was a lousy justification when Gray had spent half the day chasing breadcrumbs and the other half trying to shake off his associates so he could go and buy coke. Until Josh had confiscated his phone, it hadn't even occurred to him to call Will.

"He told me you proposed," Ari said.

Gray nodded. "Yesterday." The dim, distant memory was buried beneath the hell of the last thirty-six hours, during which he'd reacquainted with Graham Farrar, that grim spectre of the past who'd slipped through while he wasn't paying attention.

"I couldn't be more pleased for you both." Ari startled him once again with a hug.

"Thank you." Warmth spread through Gray's chest, up his neck and across his cheeks—less embarrassment than relief as he reclaimed control from his imposter persona. He wondered if Ari had any idea of the timeliness of their intervention.

The craving dwindled, leaving him exposed and conscious of Ari's increasing rigidity and the fact he was still hugging them. He let go and resumed battling the wine bottle. "How are you feeling now?"

"Oh...you know." They turned away and picked up a baguette and a bread knife. "Keeping busy—with Freddie away, I have to oversee business operations."

"You're on your own?" Gray wasn't happy about that. "I could ask Dee to stay here overn—"

"No—thank you."

It sounded like Gray had hit a raw nerve there. "So what's Freddie up to?"

"Nothing exciting."

And another. He cut his losses. "The glasses are in there, did you say?"

"Yes." Ari turned back and appraised Gray for a moment. "Will also said I had to remind you to keep the faith."

"Regarding?"

"Rob. Whatever was in his car was planted to incriminate him."

"You know that for sure?" Gray asked.

"I do, but if you're asking for evidence, I can't give you any. Rob needs us to believe in him. He's been gone for eleven hours. Our memories of him may be all that's left. So let's remember him the right way."

"No!" Gray shook his head, angry Ari was already thinking like that. "No. We *will* find him."

"You know that for sure?" They turned the question back on him.

"Yes. And I can give you statistics as evidence. I'm not giving up on him, Ari."

They waved the baguette, smiling as they passed him by. "That's more like it."

***

At the clunk of the padlock on the outside of the door, Rob jumped to his feet and raised the two bed legs above his head, ready to swing. He hadn't seen or heard Folden in hours—not since the water bottle—time enough to dismantle the bed frame, using the foam mattress as a muffler, and get into position. The key turned in the lock, the door opened, and Rob put his full weight into his swing, slamming the wood into the side of Folden's head.

Folden yelled and staggered backwards, hand clutched to his cheek. Blood seeped between his fingers. "You...*fuck*!" He pulled his hand away, revealing the thick, four-inch-long gouge from a protruding bolt, and stared at his palm. One more swing would take him down, and Rob raised his arms again, but he wasn't quick enough. In a flash, Folden's shock turned to rage, and he pinned Rob against the wall by his wrists, the thick pine crushing his windpipe. "Why do you do this when I could leave right now and kill your son?"

Even if Rob had been physically capable of answering, he wouldn't have done so.

"I do not understand. You surrender to me to save Lucas and then do this stupid thing."

Rob feebly pushed back against Folden's hands. He was blacking out but managed to relieve the pressure enough to drag in a breath. "The hard drive," he rasped.

That got Folden's attention, though not in the way Rob had hoped, as he exchanged his grip on Rob's wrists for direct control of the bed legs and leaned into them. Rob's vision went from sparkling to dimming, then, just as the dark curtain descended, Folden eased off.

Rob fell to his knees, gasping for air. He didn't care that Folden was now in possession of his only weapon and didn't see it coming, but he'd expected it and put up his hands, fists balled to shield his head. *Smack, smack, smack, smack, smack.*

Folden stopped. No. Paused. Shadow arms reached for the ceiling; heat rushed to Rob's mangled fingers. "I'll take you to it!" he cried. "The hard drive."

Smack.

Another pause. Rob chanced looking up at Folden, whose face contorted in ridicule and bemusement. "What?"

"I'll help you find it." Rob snivelled, well past playing it tough.

"What are you talking about? Hard drive?"

Folden's derisive laughter set Rob's left ear whistling. He pressed the heel of his hand to it, yelling in pain as the bolts in the tops of the pine jabbed his shoulder.

"Do you want me to stop?" Folden asked.

Rob nodded meekly.

"Then don't try to escape. And don't give me any more of your bullshit. If you can't give me what I want. Well..."

Maybe it was the drugs because Rob still had no idea what Folden was after. Or maybe he wasn't after anything and it was all part of the game, in which case, it was Rob's move.

"I don't know what you want, Anders."

The lengths of wood thudded to the floor, bouncing out of reach. Folden slow-applauded. "Well played, Robert. At last. Now, get up."

Rob wondered briefly what would happen if he stayed where he was, but once again his survival instinct kicked in—against his will. Now to figure out how he was getting off the floor without leaning on his hands and with his right thigh out of action.

"*Get up!*"

"Give me a chance, for fuck's sake!" Rob rose on his knees and pressed his shoulder to the wall, slowly dragging himself up onto his feet...and coming nose-to-muzzle with a Glock.

Folden jerked his head towards the remains of the bed base. "Bring it to the door."

"How?" Rob held up his hands to make his point, nearly vomiting with the pain.

Folden plastered on that crazed smile. "You'll find a way. You have a strong incentive, after all. Do it." He waggled the gun in front of Rob's nose.

He was weak, defenceless. On his own. He couldn't afford to give Folden an excuse to abuse him further. Gritting his teeth, he straightened his fingers out of their protective fists and crossed the room. The endorphins hit, leaving him high and dizzy, almost toppling as he reached for one of the longer lengths of wood. It shot away from him and spun across the floor.

"How fucking stupid are you?" Folden roared and booted the joined slats so hard they slammed in quick succession into the opposite wall. "I don't have all night to watch you crying like a baby and taking this all—" Folden bent and acted out picking up the mattress with his elbows, mocking Rob's pain in expression and tone. "*Oh, oh*—one piece, *oh*, at a time." He grabbed the corner of the mattress and hurled it towards the door. "Hurry up or I'll shoot you."

"Go for it," Rob challenged.

"In the foot or the hand?" Folden pointed the gun at one and then the other.

Rob was counting on him not wanting to fire the gun if he could avoid it. There had to be neighbouring houses. Someone would hear.

Folden shrugged as if bored and shook his head. "Later," he said and stalked back to the door, shoved the mattress out and leaned against the doorpost, sneering. "On you go."

Rob shuffle-kicked the rest of the timber across, piece by piece, trying to see out of the door, but Folden blocked him and moved it out himself, seemingly unaware of the blood still trickling down his face onto his shirt collar.

Let him talk, Winstanley had said, but it was irrelevant now. Rob wasn't wired; there was no team waiting for his signal.

Still, Folden hated talkative hostages.

"Are you taking aspirin or something, Anders?"

Folden's sneer became a pitying grimace. "Awww. Did I hurt you?"

"Your cheek's bleeding pretty badly. It should be clotting by now."

"Be quiet."

"You should probably—"

"I told you to be quiet." Folden hadn't raised his voice, but the threat was clear, so Rob shut up and got on with shifting the last few bits of wood, inching closer to the door each time. The hallway was too dark for him to see further than the couple of feet illuminated by the light in the room. He shut one eye and continued with his head down, back and forth, slower and slower. The pain, thirst and hunger were taking their toll, and he was breathless and sweating fluid he couldn't afford, but he was almost done.

As he neared the door for the last time, he kicked the piece of wood a bit harder than before so that Folden had to move to pick it up. Rob switched one open eye for the other and, with his temporary night vision, leaned past Folden and took in as much of the hallway as he could: another door, stairs at the end, a large picture or poster on the stairwell—

The gun slammed into the side of his head, and he fell backwards, yelling when his hands hit the floor first and Folden stamped on his fingers then leered down in disgust as Rob vomited what looked like worms but were noodles, he hoped.

"You are making this harder than it needs to be," Folden hissed and stepped back into the darkness, pulling the door shut. The lock turned; the padlock clunked into place.

Exhausted and wracked by pain, Rob rolled onto his side, pulling his legs up to ease the cramp in his stomach. He was done fighting.

***

"Are you looking for the safe?" Gray asked, tongue-in-cheek. Josh had been staring at Berringer's portrait intermittently throughout their meal, which had been delectable—all the more so for being the first home-prepared food they'd had in days.

Josh frowned and leaned towards Ari without taking his eyes off the portrait. "Who painted that?"

"Darwin Forester—he's a renowned portrait artist."

"He's not very good, is he?"

Ari was taken aback. "I don't know. Isn't he?"

Gray sighed paternally and explained, "Josh's husband is a painter."

"Oh, really?"

"Hmm." Josh was still fixated on the painting. He picked up his wine glass and walked over to take a closer look, shifting between the portrait of Berringer and the one next to it. "Actually, I may have judged too soon. This one of you is a good likeness."

Ari's eyes widened further. "Do you think so?"

Josh turned sideways and alternately studied them and the portrait of Naomi. "It's photographic, although...I haven't noticed you wearing make-up."

"I do sometimes."

"And I suppose you put on your Sunday best for a portrait sitting."

"I suppose," Ari agreed. Josh must've picked up on their caginess because he blushed and returned to his seat.

"Sorry. I get carried away analysing. I hope I didn't offend you."

"Not at all," Ari assured him. "Does your husband paint portraits?"

"Not formal ones like those. He prefers to capture a person's essence—a moment unawares. I may be a little biased, of course, but I think his work is phenomenal. Would you agree, Graham?"

"I would, but I'm probably a bit biased too." He was also getting restless. The twelve-hour mark had passed while they'd been eating, along with the distressingly devoid-of-Rob eight-hourly team check-in, and there'd been no word from Dom or Winstanley either. For all Gray knew, they'd clocked off for the night, lucky bastards. He knocked back the last of his wine and stood, gathering the plates.

"Leave those," Ari said. "Sofia will be here first thing."

"I was going to make coffee—I might as well take them with me. Would anyone else like a cup?"

"Let me. I'm supposed to be entertaining you, remember?"

Gray relented and sank back into his chair.

Ari rose, leaning on his shoulder as they reached past him for the plates. "After that, we should see if we can make any headway in locating Folden's aunt. What say you?" With the lightest squeeze, they released him and left the room with the plates.

"I should call George," Josh said. "Where's the bathroom?"

"On the right—I think there's a linen cupboard first."

Josh took Gray's phone from his pocket and placed it on the table. "In case you need it. Won't be long." He also left.

Gray picked up the wine bottle, tipping it from side to side and listening to the slosh of the last inch of wine within. It should have been him with Folden. After all, that was why he'd said he'd call Will rather than have Will's call go unanswered. But the guilt that had eaten at him all day wasn't because Folden had Rob. It was because Gray was glad it wasn't him. As natural as that feeling might be, he was disgusted by his cowardice—for having pushed Rob to act. For those reasons, he couldn't call Will, no matter how much he wanted to.

"I made a cafetière so we can help ourselves," Ari said, announcing their return. They set the tray on the table. "You'll have to drink it here, though—no liquids near the tech."

"No problem." Gray forced a smile. "Josh has popped to the bathroom."

"I heard him—he's on the phone, I think." Ari laid out three saucers and shallow coffee cups.

"Yeah. Calling his husband."

"Your stepbrother?"

"Half-brother," Gray corrected. "Same dad."

"Right. I have a half-brother, or half-sibling at least. Assigned male, though I've never met them. My mum had them when she was seventeen, and they were adopted."

"Have you ever tried to find them?"

"Yes. And succeeded."

"But you haven't made contact."

"No." Ari smiled in thought as they poured coffee into the three cups. "Imagine finding out in your forties that you were adopted. Of course, they may know, in which case they've had ample opportunity to find Mum and me and chosen not to."

"I see your point," Gray said. "So you should be able to track down Folden's aunt?"

"I'd say so. I'd have looked earlier, but I couldn't with Dom watching over me. On which note...Josh can be trusted, can't he?"

"Absolutely. The worst he'll do is try to persuade you to give him access to your search engine."

"Then he'll be disappointed. Only one other person has access to Ace, and only because he helped develop it." Ari held out a cup for Gray.

"I beg your pardon?" Gray stared at them. "Will *helped* develop your search engine?"

"Ah." Ari put the cup down again and chewed their lip. "You didn't know."

Gray shook his head. "My fiancé is a hacker on the side?"

"No, not really. He has a knack for heuristic programming, but I should've said he *consulted* on Ace. He's not a hacker."

"You don't have to defend him, Ari. Not to me." Gray would have reassured them more, but Josh was back from his extended bathroom visit. "All OK?" Gray asked.

"With George and Libby, yes," he answered cryptically.

"Coffee?" Ari handed him a cup.

"And the rest?" Gray prompted.

"Aitch heard about Rob's abduction and blabbed to the Lions."

"Ah, hell." Gray had visions of them all piling down to London in cars. So Ari would know what they were talking about, he began to explain, "Aitch is—"

"Detective Inspector Henry Hartley," Ari interrupted. "One of Rob's close friends up north and fellow player on the Red Lions' Sunday League soccer team." Ari nodded at Josh. "Your husband plays for them too. Centre-forward."

"Erm..." Josh blinked, speechless.

"Yeeaah," Gray said. "Ari's *really* good at research. Speaking of..." He downed his coffee in one. "Drink up, Josh. You can't take it with you."

Still bamboozled, Josh lifted his cup to drink, spilling most of it when someone hammered hard on the front door.

"What the hell?" Gray muttered in alarm.

"I'll check the security camera," Ari said on the move. Gray followed them across to their office but didn't enter. "It's the police." Ari brushed past Gray and marched off down the hall, leaving Gray and Josh staring at each other.

The sound of voices carried from the front door to the dining room but not what they were saying—a quiet, respectful interchange—and then multiple footsteps headed their way. Gray steadied himself with a hand on the back of a chair and braced for the worst possible kind of bad news.

The two plain-clothed officers appeared in front of him. "Graham Fisher?" one asked.

"Yes."

"We need you to come with us, sir."

"For what purpose?"

"Questioning in relation to a National Crime Agency investigation."

"*Which* investigation?"

"We can't tell you that, sir."

"Will you arrest me if I refuse to comply?"

"Yes, sir."

"I guess I'd better come peacefully, then." Gray shrugged at Josh and Ari. "Sorry."

"Don't worry about us," Josh said.

Ari nodded. "We're fine. Is there anyone you need us to call? Your lawyer?"

"No. I'll do it when I get there. I'll speak to you both later." Gray pocketed his phone and addressed the two officers. "I'm all yours."

26: Access Denied

"THIS INTERVIEW IS being audio recorded. This is an interview with—state your full name, please."

"Graham Andrew Fisher."

"State your address, please."

"Bryn Cottage, Byewater Lane, Croxley, WD18..." Gray usually had to ask Will for the last part of the postcode. "Sorry, I can't remember the rest."

The officer ignored his apology and stuck to her script, which Gray didn't think was intentionally to put him ill at ease but did so regardless—to the extent he stumbled over his date of birth.

"I am Lyndsey Massey, Assistant Head of Technology, National Crime Agency, Cyber Crime Unit. Also present is—identify yourself, please."

The other officer said, "Theodore Pearce, Investigator, National Crime Agency, Cyber Crime Unit."

"There are no other persons present. The date is the twenty-ninth of April. The time is twenty-two seventeen. We are in an interview room at..."

Gray listened, trying not to nod along. The wording had changed little since he'd left the police, and while NCA officers were a different kettle of fish, it was reassuring to know they followed the same procedures. Marginally reassuring, given their designations. Massey went through the usual cautions and statement of rights—to remain silent, to legal representation.

"I must ask you why you have not requested legal advice or to consult with a legal representative by telephone."

"No comment."

Massey pursed her lips briefly, no doubt preparing for *one of those interviews*, before continuing. "I must remind you that you can ask at any time for free legal advice during the course of this interview. If you want legal advice, say so, and I will suspend the interview and arrange for legal representation. Do you understand?"

"Yes, I understand."

"Are you prepared to continue and answer questions without legal representation at this time?"

"Yes, I am." More to the point, he had no choice but to continue without legal representation, for the same reason he would be answering all questions with 'no comment' unless otherwise directed by Winstanley and him alone.

"Can you tell me what you do for a living?"

"No comment."

"According to Company House records, you are co-owner of a private investigation agency. Is that correct?"

"No comment."

"The Company House record indicates you run said agency with Robert Simpson-Stone. Are you willing to confirm this?"

"No comment."

Massey sighed out of her nose and looked over her notes. Five minutes in and already Gray was wearing her down. He felt awful about it—he'd been where she was, and she had to continue until she'd asked all her questions.

"Earlier today, our colleagues in the Metropolitan Police Service searched Robert Simpson-Stone's current residence and vehicle. Are you aware of this?"

Gray shrugged apologetically. "No comment."

"Do you recall Mr. Simpson-Stone ever using a laptop?"

"No comment."

"Our colleagues found only limited technology on the premises—a mobile phone charging cable, a laptop and an external hard drive. Do you know if Mr. Simpson-Stone owned any such items?"

"No comment," Gray replied too quickly in his attempt to avoid visibly reacting to the revelation.

"What do you know about the hard drive, Graham?"

"No comment."

"I'll tell you what *we* know. A hard drive was stowed under the spare tyre in the boot of a blue Ford Fiesta registered to a Steven Radley, which is an alias used by Robert Simpson-Stone. The hard drive was brought to my unit and on inspection established to be the property of Her Majesty's Government. Specifically, the hard drive was stolen two and a half years ago while in transit between government departments.

"I must ask you again—do you know how the hard drive came to be in Mr. Simpson-Stone's possession?"

"No comment."

Massey shared a glance with her colleague and closed her notebook. "I'm ending this interview for the time being, Graham. It's late, and I think you need a break to reconsider your refusal to seek legal advice or representation." She checked the time—"Interview ended at twenty-two thirty-one"—and stopped the recording.

"I'm sorry," Gray said.

"So am I, Graham. There are officers waiting outside under orders to arrest you if you don't tell us about the hard drive, because you do know something." Massey and her colleague rose from their chairs, as did Gray, breathing through his mounting panic as he moved towards the door.

"Would it be possible for me to make a phone call, please?"

Massey paused, hand on the door handle, and nodded. "I will put your request to my superiors. However, you're being detained on the grounds that it is necessary for us to obtain, examine or analyse information with the aim of obtaining evidence in relation to the prevention of terrorism. You will not be questioned further until you have secured legal representation."

That was straight from counter-terrorism policy and expanded a few hours of inconvenient questioning to a possible forty-eight hours of detention, with or without charge. Even if the window for cooperating were still open, Gray could do nothing, say nothing to jeopardise Winstanley's years-long operation.

As he stepped out of the interview room and was handed over to the awaiting officers, he could only hope Winstanley really did have his back.

***

Pain finally surpassed exhaustion, impelling Rob to move from where he'd been dozing fitfully for however long it had been since Folden whacked him with the gun. His internal clock was shot, but it had to be hours because he needed to pee again. How he was going to manage that he really didn't know and contemplated just pissing himself where he lay. Then he remembered the stink from last time. The vomit was bad enough.

Using his hips and feet only, it took a while, but he was able to shuffle across the floor until he was lying side-on to the wall and pushed up with his elbow, grunting through the pain. He made it as far as sitting and rested awhile to get his breath back and assess the state of his hands. They were mottled black and red, the skin distended around his useless sausage fingers. He couldn't tell if they were bruised or broken and tried wiggling his thumbs. The action shot spikes of pain up to the base of his skull, but they were functional.

When he'd recovered as much as he was going to, he manoeuvred, less than snail pace, onto his knees and, as he'd done earlier, shouldered his way up the wall. It was much less painful once he was on his feet, although reaching the sink was only half the battle.

As it turned out, Folden had done him a favour by removing his belt; his jeans were well worn, so the button popped open with relative ease, allowing him to hook his thumbs under the waistband and push them down. Balancing on his toes, he leaned over the sink and braced his forearm against the wall. A trickle of dark orange ran down the porcelain, not even enough for the smell to register.

He shook himself back inside his jeans and pulled them back up by the belt hooks but could do nothing about the button. He didn't want to think what he'd do when his bowels kicked into action. The last thing he'd eaten was the Chinese takeaway with Gray and Josh—the monosodium glutamate had done him no favours on the hydration front—but he was a crap-a-day kind of guy, after his shower every morning. He supposed if the urge did hit, it would give him a rough idea of the time.

Right now, though, it felt like nighttime, and his body wanted rest. Hoping a bit of water had collected in the pipes, Rob bent and got his mouth under the tap before he bashed it on with his arm, almost gagging on the unexpected gush. He swallowed down a couple of mouthfuls before the taste registered, then the smell, and the whole lot came straight back up. Through tears, he watched the filmy, brown slime slip down the plug hole.

Still retching from the stagnant water, he leaned his back on the wall and slid all the way to the floor.

Well played, Folden had said. That was all it was to him. Not a man's life. A crazy, dangerous game.

***

At three a.m., they let Gray go without charge and escorted him back along too-bright corridors to the lift down to street level, spewing him out into the night air, cool but still warmer than the conditioned air he'd been breathing for the past five hours. In their defence, they were following a reasonable avenue of inquiry and even offered him a lift 'home', which he declined. Josh's hotel was only a thirty-minute walk away, but Gray waved down a cab and directed the driver to drop him a couple of miles further on, then backtracked on foot via a route littered with venues—nightclubs, doorways, alleys—where he could find what he needed. He turned off the well-lit thoroughfare into a dim, grimy back street, keeping his head up and hands in pockets as he passed the prostitutes who muttered *pig*, the shadowed hookups and industrial bins' guard of honour, on towards the portal: a black, riveted-metal door scarred by the boots and knives of the desperate and greedy.

A few feet away from his destination, Gray faltered, his eyes drawn away from the door to a girl, mid-teens, crouched behind a small incinerator bin. She glanced up and froze momentarily, the underside of a tourniqueted, blue-white arm exposed, hypodermic millimetres from penetration.

At least I don't do heroin. The words flurried, became a blizzard of lies— coke wasn't addictive, he could function better with it than without, all things in moderation—the lies he'd told himself, the lies he was telling himself again. The girl's feet slid across the ground as the drug wrapped its tendrils around her, the needle still in her arm. Gray was her. She was him. He was a junkie, and he had to get away from there.

Some time later, he reached the hotel, breathless, exhilarated, and leaned against the wall to recover and take stock. He'd won on this occasion, but it had been too close a call. In rehab, he'd learned to be mindful of urges rather than push them away because they would only come back stronger if he refused to acknowledge what he was feeling. He needed time to do that. Time and a safe place.

He didn't go up to Josh's room. He didn't know if Josh was there or had stayed with Ari. Either way, Gray needed to be somewhere else. He was sober and glad Dee had given them a lift to Ari's as it meant his car was in the hotel car park. From there, he headed for the M1 and Croxley—*home*—grateful for quiet roads and effective heating but so tired he had to switch over to air-con or risk falling asleep behind the wheel. His teeth were chattering by the time he drew up outside the house.

Dark as it was—he left the lights off—and eerily quiet as it was, Gray's tension slid from him like a rain-soaked coat the moment he set foot inside. He locked the door and went straight upstairs, first to the bathroom then the bedroom, where he kicked off his shoes and, fully clothed, collapsed on top of the covers.

A couple of hours later, he awoke, shivering, his hip tingling with pins and needles. He rolled, taking the duvet with him, wrapped himself in it, inhaling Will's scent as he drifted. The tingle persisted. He rolled back and felt around the bed until he found his phone and thumbed the screen without opening his eyes.

"Graham, where the hell are you?" Josh demanded. "We thought you were still with the police, but Dom said they released you hours ago."

"Is Dom there?"

"No. I spoke to him on the phone."

"What time is it?" Gray peeped over the duvet at the clock. "Shit." Scrabbling to untangle himself, he sat up and put his phone on speaker. "I slept through my alarm." And then some. It was nine-fifteen. "I'll be with you in—"

"Never mind that. We've found Folden's aunt."

"Where?"

"Well, I say found her..."

"In Norway?"

"No. She's buried in Canterbury. She died a month ago."

"Damn it. Did he kill her?"

"Unlikely. For one, it doesn't fit with his profile. For two, she had lung cancer. She changed her name, not by legal means, after Folden was convicted, and I've just spoken to a Macmillan nurse who said a young man had been staying at the apartment. She thinks he kept it on."

"So he could've taken Rob there," Gray realised giddily; a glimmer of hope at last. "Do Dom and Winstanley know?"

"Yes—that's why I called Dom. He was going to contact Canterbury Police and get them to check the property."

"OK." Gray's body finally caught up with his racing brain and propelled him from the bed. He unbuttoned his shirt and threw it at the hamper without looking, horrified when he glimpsed his reflection in the wardrobe mirror. Sheet creases in his face, one sock hanging off the end of his foot, the other missing entirely, fingers-in-the-outlet hair, stubble bordering on a beard. "How long ago did you speak to Dom?"

"Fifteen minutes."

That vetoed the shower and shave. "You're at the hotel, I take it?"

"For the time being. Are you leaving now?"

"Pretty much." Stamping on his dangling sock, Gray tugged it off and grabbed a clean pair from the drawer.

"How long will you be?" Josh asked.

"An hour." Another call was coming in—Will's number. "I've got to go. See you when I get there." He disconnected from Josh and answered Will. "Hey. I was going to call you first thing this morning, but—"

"Gray, you need to get to Ari. They're in trouble."

"What?" After four hours of deep sleep, it was too much to take in at once. If Folden was in Canterbury, he couldn't get to Ari, and in any case they'd have hit the alarm. A little reason reinstated, Gray took a deep breath and literally and figuratively pulled his socks up. "What kind of trouble?" he asked on the move. He propped his phone on the bathroom sink and grabbed his toothbrush from the shelf where it stood alone.

"The police are there," Will said. "They're demanding Ari go with them, but they won't say why. Ari's anxiety is sky-high."

"Are they under arrest?"

"Not yet."

Gray racked his brain for options. "I'll call and speak to the officers, ask them to wait until I get there."

"Where are you now?"

"At home."

"Our house?"

"Yeah." Hearing Will call it that warmed Gray right through. "They took me in for questioning last night, and I came back here rather than disturb Josh."

"That was thoughtful of you." Will's tone was crisp—understandably when Gray hadn't called like he'd promised, not that he could have done so while in custody.

He squeezed paste onto the brush and gave his teeth the shortest clean ever—one all-round scrub, one spit. "That wasn't the only reason," he admitted. "I needed to be here."

"You're struggling."

Gray nodded but didn't answer. He wanted to pour it all out, tell Will how close he'd come to falling off the wagon, and about his conversations with Ari—how much they'd helped him—and that he was finally, *finally* OK with Will and Ari's friendship. He went with, "Better this morning."

"And the house?"

"As we left it," Gray confirmed, on the one hand aware the trip home had been necessary for his mental well-being, on the other frustrated he was too far away to help Ari. "Jesus, this is maddening. If there was a damned police officer on the force we could trust..."

"What about Dom and Winstanley?"

"Dom's following up a possible lead on Folden's location. Winstanley—your guess is as good as mine. I'd ask Dee, but I don't think Ari would appreciate it."

"Right now, I don't think Ari would care who you sent. They're locked in their bedroom."

"I'll try Dee."

"What about Josh?"

That was a better idea. "Yeah. I'll do that. I need to make a move."

"OK," Will said. "But, Gray? This being open thing has to work both ways. You know that, don't you?"

"I didn't want to worry you."

"Don't you think I was more worried when you didn't call?"

"I know. I'm sorry."

"Call me later, OK?"

"I will. I promise."

"I'm gonna hold you to that. You've got this." Will ended the call.

Gray pocketed his phone and looked up at his reflection, amazed by what a couple of minutes with Will, even at a distance, could do. "I've got this," he told the Gray in the mirror. Oddly, he believed it.

27: Shots Fired

I F ROB'S TIME in the army had given him one thing, it was the ability to grab some kip in virtually all conditions because, despite the stomach cramps, broken fingers and cold, hard floor, he had fallen asleep. He must have done or else he'd have heard Folden come in.

He was there when Rob opened his eyes. Sitting across the room, back to the wall, gun balanced on his thigh, legs splayed as if he'd fallen down drunk. Watching.

Smiling.

He tilted his head to the side, matching Rob's orientation. "Today's the day."

That taunting singsong was a tell Rob had picked up on a long time ago. *When, exactly?*

"Our time together is coming to an end. Will you miss me?" Folden paused, eyebrows raised. "Cat got your tongue?"

Another attack of cramp forced Rob's knees up towards his chest, his overworked diaphragm propelling the breath, breaking the dry seal of his lips. But he didn't break eye contact. Not even to blink.

"Here you'll be, all alone, waiting to die. Looking at you, it won't be too long. Hours? A day?"

When he delivered Alice to Black Hole. That was the first time Rob had noticed it. *What does it mean?*

"We are the same, you and me." Folden picked up the gun and twisted it perilously, his eyes following its swing from side to side. His thumb was so close to the trigger, either of them could be shot if it went off, and he didn't seem to care.

He's compromised.

"You like to think it's not so—should I tell you why it is?" He shifted his eyes from the gun's motion. "You see, I recently lost someone very dear to me."

Rob tried to swallow, to force his voice box into action. He couldn't talk Folden down, but if he could provoke him, get him to come closer...

"Such a cruel disease, cancer. Once the rot sets in, it cannot be stopped. All the power we have to give and take life, and yet nothing we do can save a loved one."

The taste of his own blood. The smallest amount of saliva—enough to swallow, possibly to speak, and say what? That Folden was wrong, they were nothing alike? Hardly the kind of statement to keep the flimsy emotional connection, possibly the only reason he was still alive. A lie, too, when Rob had been in Folden's shoes. He'd felt that powerlessness with Jess and even with Harvey.

So Folden was right, up to a point. They'd both witnessed cancer take the people they loved. But Rob's empathy was not reciprocated.

"You don't believe me," Folden said. "I can see it in your eyes—your disgust for the idea you and I could be in any way alike. But that is only one way we are. The other you will realise in time, waiting for your friends to come to your rescue. They won't come. You've convinced yourself they don't know where you are, but they would find you if only they tried."

"Who died?" Rob's voice hardly sounded, but Folden had heard him.

"What does it matter to you?"

"It doesn't."

"As you asked, I will tell you. It was my aunt."

"I'm sorry."

"No. You're not sorry." Folden put the gun on the floor and crossed his legs, no longer watching Rob. He seemed deep in thought and was humming a tune so quietly Rob had to strain to hear. He didn't recognise it, couldn't even be sure it was a real song, but he did know he'd never heard Folden sing before. Then, as if someone had hit a stop button, Folden cut off mid-phrase and said, "She loved me. Very much." He picked up the gun again, an unconscious action, and stroked it with his thumb. "She raised me."

"I remember," Rob said.

"Do you?"

"You told me."

"I don't recall, but this, you see? *This* is what had me wondering why you never talked about Lucas. All the time you and I spent together and not one mention of your precious son."

"You know why, Anders."

Folden gave no acknowledgement of Rob's statement. "She loved me," he repeated. "And I her. We speak of people we love."

"I was an undercover police officer."

Still Folden ignored him. "She had cancer before, when I was younger. She was sick for a long time, but she got better. Then she was sick again, and I went to prison, and she got sicker. They couldn't stop it, and she was so, so brave. Never let me see how she suffered..."

Folden chattered on, but it was just a background drone against the onset of more cramps, accompanied by a spiky, hot pain in Rob's lower back like being kicked repeatedly—his kidneys, he self-diagnosed. It was the same kind of pain as when he'd had gallstones. He grunted through it, staring at the gun and wishing Folden would shut up and shoot him.

"I miss her. She looked after me, forgave me everything—"

"Like Alistair Campion?"

Folden's grief-slack features morphed into the familiar sneer. "Enough chitchat." He jumped to his feet and tucked the gun in his waistband. "So you know about the hard drive, huh? My little insurance policy if your friends decide you're worth saving?" He idled towards the door. "And my parting gift—something for you to think about as you lie here dying and waiting..." At the door, he turned back, grinning. "Lucas deserves better than you. Now he has it."

***

Gray got up and walked over to the reception desk to try his luck again. He'd headed straight for the NCA—where they'd taken Ari—but of course no-one would tell him what was going on. They'd stuck him in a small waiting area, and that was what he'd been doing for the past half an hour: waiting and seething and doing his best not to take it out on anyone but Winstanley, should the man ever show his face.

The clerk on the desk sniffed sharply and put on a smile. "Yes, sir? How can I help you?"

"Sorry to bother you again. The thing is..." He had a brainwave. "I'm Mx. Silvestri's advocate, and I should be with them while they're assisting your agency."

The clerk glanced in the direction of the security guard manning the walk-through metal detector and back at Gray. "Please sit down, sir."

"Can you at least call someone?"

"Sir, I've already—"

"OK. OK." Gray raised his hands in surrender and obediently returned to his seat. He could only imagine what kind of trauma Ari was going through at the NCA's hands, although, to be fair to Lyndsey Massey, she'd been nothing but polite and professional with Gray.

There was still no news from Dom—Gray took out his phone and checked again to confirm it—but the more he thought about it, the more convinced he became. Folden *had* to be holding Rob at his deceased aunt's apartment. Granted, Folden had never been the sort to stay under the radar, hence Gray's conviction that he was a narcissist, but of all those sightings Winstanley had recorded, not one was in Canterbury or even close. Folden had wanted Winstanley to see him popping up all over the place so he didn't go looking for a base.

The phone on the clerk's desk rang, and Gray held his breath, briefly optimistic that it was the 'send him through' call he'd been hoping for, but no. Toner cartridges for the printer were apparently more important than an interviewee's anxiety, although, again, Massey would have followed protocol and checked Ari was up to being interviewed.

The toner cartridge discussion ended, and Gray sighed, seeking further distraction in his surroundings. The security guard looked equally bored—they were in little more than an alcove at the end of a short corridor off the main reception area. No foot traffic; nobody else waiting. A muted flat-screen TV played away unwatched amid the beech and grey fixtures and fake parlour palms—a bland, modern interior insultingly at odds with the building's stunning Edwardian façade.

The soundless soap opera went into an ad break. Gray's boredom cranked up another notch...and then ended spectacularly when the security guard's phone rang, followed by his own, the stuttered identical ring tones echoing eerily as each answered their respective call, eyes locked in suspicion.

"Morton here," the security guard said.

"Hello?"

"Mr. Fisher?"

"Yes."

The security guard said, "Copy that."

"This is Lyndsey Massey."

"Hello, Ms. Massey."

The guard abandoned his station and marched over to the clerk.

"I would be grateful if you could come up to room T6. It's on the third floor."

The guard murmured something; the clerk murmured in response.

"Are you still there, Mr. Fisher?"

"Yes, sorry. I'm on my way," he said and hung up.

Except he wasn't going anywhere.

"Sorry, sir." The security guard spread his arms, blocking Gray's route. "You need to stay where you are."

"I've been ordered to report to room T6."

"It'll have to wait."

"What's going on?"

"Security drill. Nothing to worry about."

Gray backed off. It wasn't a drill; that much he could tell by the shift in atmosphere and the minor commotion spilling in from the suddenly busy foyer. He watched with interest, attempting to discern what had happened, his viewing interrupted by the guard's 'ahem'. Gray returned to his seat and clasped his hands, thumbs circling, feet tapping, restless, restless...

The clerk stood and pointed a remote control at the TV. The channel changed, and the volume rose.

Main screen: FTSE.

Breaking News ticker: *Shots fired outside Met Police building... Senior officer critically injured...*

Gray's heart was in his mouth. *Which senior officer?* He knew most of them—by reputation or as former colleagues. With everything else going on, his mind made a catastrophic shortcut to *Winstanley or Dom?*

A talking head replaced the FTSE. "This just in. Shots have been fired outside a Metropolitan Police administrative base, with reports of at least one person critically injured. The area has been cordoned off and police marksmen are on site. It is believed the injured person is a senior officer. We'll give you more on this story as we get it."

Gray's phone rang; it was still in his hand and he let go of it in shock. It landed screen down. Gray picked it up, holding his breath as he hit answer on Dom's number.

"Dom?"

"Yeah."

"Thank God."

"You heard, then?"

"About the shooting? It's all over the news."

"Bloody hell. It's not even been five minutes."

"Who got shot?"

"Erica Dunleavy."

"You're kidding!"

"I wish I was. She was on her way to a meeting with Winstanley."

"Jesus! Is Martin all right?"

"Yeah, he was nowhere near. Where are you?"

"At the NCA. They brought Ari in for questioning."

"How quickly can you get to the SIU?"

"I can't. We're on lockdown."

"Balls." Dom puffed into the phone.

"Are you smoking?"

"No. Got one of them little plastic doodahs from the chemist. It's a bit shit, to be honest. I'm gonna have a word and send a car for you, all right?"

"Dom, I can't leave Ari."

"I'll sort it. Winstanley needs them for a job. As soon as they're cut loose, get your arses over here."

"That's some serious string-pulling power. Maybe I should ask Winstanley for a job too."

"Maybe you should," Dom said, as if it were a real possibility.

"I'll think about it," Gray muttered, matching Dom's sarcasm. "Have you heard back from Canterbury?"

"No, but Folden's not at his aunt's place."

"You sound very sure of that."

"I am," Dom said. "I saw him. He was here."

"Folden's the gunman?" Gray reeled. "Did you get him?"

"Not yet, but no time to explain. See you shortly."

**

The lift pinged to signal its imminent arrival, and Gray exhaled, long and slow, trying to rein in the hell breaking loose in his head. The door opened; Naomi stepped out.

"Gray, hi!"

"Hi," he replied, kissing cheeks, only moderately surprised by her gender shift and only then because she dressed like a catwalk model. "How are you doing?" he asked.

She smiled faintly. "Let's get out of here."

They fell in step, moving apart to pass through security, on towards the exit. The black SUV was parked directly outside, the same officer behind the wheel as had driven Gray and Josh to the Parkers' two nights ago. A second officer held the back door open; Naomi and Gray climbed in. The door closed, but the officer remained where he was.

"Naomi, I'm so sorry you had to deal with that on your own. They wouldn't let me come up."

"It's fine," she assured him. "They barely made it through their introductions before my anxiety attack."

"Oh, no. That's awful."

"It was, but it did get me out of a tight spot. Those poor officers—Winstanley advised me to answer 'no comment' to all their questions."

"I did the same to them last night," Gray said, his attention on the activity outside the SUV. Massey had emerged from the building and was talking to the second officer.

"She was asking about a hard drive." Naomi shifted her eyes to indicate Massey. "She claimed Rob had it. Is that true?"

Massey handed over a Faraday case, and the officer walked around the back of the car. The boot opened and shut. Massey went back inside the building; the officer continued his circuit to the front passenger seat.

Gray fastened his seat belt. "Wherever it's been, we know where it is now." The driver met his gaze in the rear-view mirror and then pulled away, into the late-morning traffic.

The journey continued in silence for a while, the everyday hubbub of the city lending an air of ordinariness to the extraordinary events of the past few days. A man was dead. A senior police officer was fighting for her life—

Rob too, if Folden hadn't killed him already. The hard drive was almost back in the right hands—

Naomi leaned her head Gray's way and murmured, "You spoke to Will?"

"Briefly," he confirmed, saved once again by her impeccable knack for interjection.

"I'm sorry if I caused trouble for you by calling him. I thought you were still in custody, and I panicked."

"No apology needed, or not from you. I should have checked in when they released me. I'm sorry. But Will was fine. Well, he's pissed off I didn't call him last night, but that's entirely on me. He and I need a good long talk when this is over. There's so much about me I haven't told him—things that might end us."

"Helen?" Naomi guessed.

Gray nodded. "And this now. The other night...Will said I was mercenary. He was joking, and it was in the heat of the moment, but I can't stop thinking about it. I pushed Rob, not consciously, but I knew. As soon as I said I was going after Folden, I knew he'd step in and take my place."

"You couldn't have stopped him."

"I wouldn't have tried to. This is the only way he can prove he isn't corrupt. But I wouldn't have sent him in without a vest and a tracker."

"Have you given up hope of finding him?" Naomi asked.

"Of course not."

"Good. Neither have I." She tilted her head back, indicating their cargo. "What do you think's on it?"

"Couldn't say," Gray lied. He watched the traffic ahead inch along. They were almost at the SIU.

"MPs' sex tapes?" Naomi suggested. Gray side-eyed her and then turned so he could see her properly. She grinned. "Oh, come on! You're no fun."

He chuckled and shrugged. "OK. I reckon it's...High Court judges playing strip poker. Everything off except the wigs."

"Matching merkins." Naomi snorted an infectious giggle, and Gray caught it. The driver's disapproving frown in the rear-view mirror made it worse.

"Oh, God. What an image!" Gray cried with laughter but then sobered in an instant, automatically responding to the environmental cues.

One: passers-by ran for cover.

Two: Gray grabbed Naomi and pulled them down low in the back seat.

Three: the rear window exploded, raining tiny cubes of glass over the car's interior.

Four: someone shouted, "Drop your weapon!"

Five: a gunshot.

28: Smart

Anders Folden was dead. A single shot in the centre of his back. No question regarding use of lethal force: he was armed and had already shot two people. Detective Chief Inspector Dominic Hooper's actions were reasonable in light of what he believed the circumstances to be. Or what he claimed he believed them to be.

"What the fuck did you kill him for?" Gray charged and slammed his hands into Dom's chest, sending him staggering backwards. Dom regained his balance, and Gray went to shove him again.

"Gray—" Dom tried to restrain him, but Gray flayed his arms evasively. "Gray, listen—"

"How do we find Rob now?" He grabbed Dom's shoulder, clasping a handful of jacket and ragging him with it. "How? Answer me, man!"

"Should I have let him shoot you?"

"You weren't stopping him from shooting us! You were stopping him from taking the hard drive." Saying it out loud catalysed Gray's rage, and he threw it into a punch, which Dom blocked and then tried to take him down, but they'd trained together, worked side by side for over a decade. They were evenly matched. Dom's elbow struck Gray's shoulder; Gray dodged left and went in low. His fist hit home and winded Dom but not enough to put him out of action. Now as mad as Gray, Dom grabbed Gray's head with his left hand and swung his right fist.

Gray's vision blurred and doubled as the shock ricocheted through his skull and down his neck, but he kept fighting, as did Dom, determined, unstoppable... until the Tasers intervened, delivering a few seconds of agonising, immobilising, full-body cramp.

Gray collapsed, no thought for Dom beyond wanting to kill him, but as he lay there waiting for the muscle spasms to stop, his rage lost its atavistic edge and he glimpsed reason. It wasn't just about finding Rob. It wasn't even that Dom had denied Gray the opportunity to kill Folden himself. It was cumulative, and it had been a year in the making. Dom had betrayed him. Winstanley had betrayed him. All that time, they'd let Gray wrestle with his guilt over the continued threat to Rob's life and Dom's suspension when Winstanley had engineered Folden's escape. And now they'd commandeered the SIU—the unit Gray had nurtured and nourished and grieved for.

So, while his anger was more or less back under control, the rest of it was red raw and wide open. This was personal, but there were greater things at stake than his ego.

With a lot of effort and no help whatsoever from Dee and Isobel, both of whom had holstered their Tasers and then heartlessly yanked the probes from their respective victims, Gray made it to his feet. Dom was larger—a couple of inches taller, more muscle bulk—and still incapacitated, but he was looking up at Gray, looking him dead in the eye. Gray shook his head, conveying his lack of remorse, and offered his hand. It took Dom a few tries, but he managed to grab Gray's arm, and between them they hoisted him off the ground.

"Gray—"

"Save it, Hooper. Do you hear that?" Gray nodded in the direction of the sirens, their source not in sight, but they were growing louder. "That'll be an armed response crew, and now I'm stuck here. If Rob dies because of you—"

"*Don't you fucking dare*—" Dom stopped shouting when Dee and Isobel reached for their Tasers again.

"He could still be alive." Gray tried to keep his volume down, getting completely drowned out by the arrival of the armed response and tactical support vehicles. The sirens stopped, and half a dozen officers piled out.

"I'll talk to them." Dom started walking over, smiling and calm, like he hadn't just taken a life, albeit that of a murderer, but it was a pointless endeavour, they both knew. There was a post-incident procedure to follow, and it could take all day. By then, it could be too late to save Rob—if it wasn't already.

***

It didn't take all day.

The post-incident manager was a no-nonsense inspector who set up an incident room in a disused ground-floor office in Reardon House and whizzed through the officers' initial accounts like she was in line for a completion bonus. Maybe she was. Gray wasn't up on current efficiency incentives. Nevertheless, an hour passed before he signed his civilian witness statement and returned to the foyer, where Naomi had been waiting for him since the shooting.

She hurried over when she saw him. "Are you all right?" She scanned his face, her shifting expression telling him he looked a state. "Your jaw is dreadfully swollen. Is it fractured?"

He'd almost forgotten about his fisticuffs with Dom and wasn't grateful for the reminder. He opened and closed his mouth a few times, shifting his jaw from side to side. "Just bruised." That was a relief. Dom had a wicked upper cut.

"Winstanley is expecting us both upstairs," Naomi said. "A briefing of some sort?"

Gray felt physically sick at the possibilities but suppressed any outward display so as not to further distress Naomi. He kept his response to a weary, matter-of-fact, "OK. Let's get this over with."

Naomi followed Gray's lead—signing in, taking their visitors' passes—and they were in the lift as Dom exited the makeshift incident room. The lift doors closed, and they ascended. Naomi took a breath as if to speak. Released it. And again. The lift slowed.

"Folden would've killed us," she said.

"Yeah." Gray wasn't so sure about that.

The doors opened, and Tant stepped forward, arm extended. "Mr. Fisher."

"Afternoon, Ma'am." Polite but indifferent, he shook her hand.

"And Mx. Silvestri, is it?"

"Yes," Naomi confirmed, also shaking Tant's hand and then shrugging at Gray as they traipsed after her.

"We're in conference room one." Tant indicated the door on her right, no mention of what had taken place earlier. "Just in here." She held the door for them.

Gray forced out a thank-you as he passed her by, his focus on Josh and Trudi, who were standing over a computer. Trudi pointed at the screen and murmured; Josh nodded and hummed. Neither acknowledged Gray and Naomi's arrival.

"Help yourselves to refreshments," Tant invited, casting a suspicious glance at the psychologists. "I'll be back in a moment." The door quietly clicked shut.

Gray blew air as he surveyed the room, the décor and furnishings no different than during his time; unwelcoming as ever, yet reassuringly tranquil. There was nothing about the situation that pointed to the bad news he'd anticipated on the way up.

"Tea or coffee?" he asked Naomi.

"Tea, please. White, no sugar."

Gray dumped his jacket on a chair on his way to the jugs at the far end of the room, where he poured tea into two plastic cups. He added a dash of milk to both and brought them back, handing one to Naomi, who had perched on the edge of the table.

"Thanks." She angled her head toward Josh and Trudi. "I thought they didn't like each other."

Gray watched them for a moment. "They don't." There was respect, certainly, but it was a tense and temporary alliance that was nearing an end.

The door opened again, and Winstanley ducked into view. Gray's hackles rose at the sight of him.

"Mx. Silvestri. Come with me, please."

Naomi handed her tea to Gray.

"Do you want me to come with you?" he asked.

"No, you stay. I'll be OK." Her rapid nod said otherwise, but her priorities matched Gray's, and he couldn't tackle those if he was taking care of her. She left with Winstanley.

Gray cleared his throat to attract Josh and Trudi's attention. It didn't work. He went over. "What are you up to?"

They both jumped and pivoted his way.

"Good grief!" Josh leaned left and right, taking in Gray's face from all angles. "What happened to you?"

"Playground scrap."

"With whom?"

Dom walked through the door.

"Ah," Josh said.

"Josh, Trudi," Dom acknowledged. "Glad you made it. Iz and Dee will be here in a minute. Probably gone to recharge their Tasers." He rubbed his side, wincing. "Those bastards don't half hurt."

"Yeah, tell me about it." Gray's leg was still tingling with the after-effects of having the barbed probes embedded in his right hip and buttock.

"DCI Tant's coming in too."

"OK," Gray said neutrally. It was her unit, after all. Nothing to do with him.

Dee and Isobel arrived, and Dee went to pour drinks.

"We searched Folden, Sir," Isobel reported to Dom. "No phone, no wallet, no keys."

"All right. Thanks, Iz."

She took a seat at the table, soon after joined by Dee, who looked sheepish and quickly diverted to her phone.

"No news?" Gray asked Dom.

"Nothing."

"It's almost thirty hours."

"I'm aware, and we're looking for him. That's all we can do."

"What about Folden's car? Did you get anywhere with that?"

"Nope. Turns out the firm who operate the industrial estate car park is a scam. The cameras are recording, but they're not connected to anything."

"How does that make them money?"

"They charge the businesses, don't they?"

"Do they?" Gray's phone vibrated: text message.

~ *Sorry about zapping you.*

Gray looked over at Dee, who put her hands together and fluttered her eyelashes. Gray smiled and mouthed *I deserved it* and turned back to Dom.

He wanted to ask how Erica Dunleavy was doing, but Winstanley had returned with Tant. Gray hung his jacket on the back of the chair and sat.

"Afternoon, all." Winstanley was chipper and smiley. Gray would have very much enjoyed doing something about that. "Thank you for joining me for this debrief. As our operation has concluded, I'm handing over to Detective Chief—"

"Hold your horses!" Gray interrupted. "*Debrief*?"

"Yes, Graham. As I was saying, Detective Chief Inspector Tant will be overseeing the task of—"

"*Your* operation might be over, Martin. *Mine* is not."

"Are you volunteering to assist DCI Tant?"

"Yeah, sure." Gray shrugged. "Why not?" He gestured grandly for Winstanley to continue. "Take your time. We've plenty of it."

"Graham, we can discuss your concerns after this meeting—in private."

"Absolutely!" He matched Winstanley's opening tone. "You carry on."

Winstanley regarded him a few seconds more and then swept his arm Tant's way. "DCI Tant, if you would be so kind...?"

"Yes, Sir." Tant swallowed nervously. "As per the Police Commission's Twenty-Twenty Vision directive, the SIU is in the process of merging into the National Economic Crimes Agency and as such is assisting in the pursuit and detention of a number of fugitives. Top of our list is Robert Simpson-Stone. Since we believe he's now working alone, we anticipate he will attempt to leave the UK. We've already alerted border authorities and will be contacting his former colleagues in the Royal Engineers to ask for their cooperation."

Josh raised his hand. "Pardon my interruption, but may I ask—has Mr. Simpson-Stone taken his motorcycle?"

"No. Sorry—forgive my bluntness, but who are you?"

"Josh Sandison-Morley. Consultant psychologist."

"Consultant to whom?"

"He's with me," Dom said.

Gray frowned, wondering what Dom was playing at, not that he was complaining.

"In that case," Tant answered, "the motorcycle is in our compound. It's unlikely anyone would risk arrest for something they could easily replace." Her smile was patronising and short-lived. She moved on. "We're also monitoring the suspect's accounts and have confirmed with the bank that there have been no transactions in the past forty-eight hours. However, given the suspect's knowledge of the system, he may have made alternative financial arrangements in advance—"

"Excuse me butting in again," Josh said. "Do you not think there might be another explanation for the lack of activity on his accounts, for instance, that he was abducted?"

"The evidence found in the suspect's car is incontrovertible, Mr...sorry, I've forgotten your name—"

"I hate to contradict you, Chris," Dom said, "but the evidence is circumstantial at best, and Josh makes a good point. Two, actually. I worked with Rob for three years. He *would* risk arrest to retrieve his bike. If not that, to say goodbye to his son, who's still under close protection."

Tant stayed perfectly still and expressionless, although Gray could hear her breathing, fast and shallow. "Thank you for your input, Dom, in light of which we'll extend our surveillance to include Mx. Silvestri's residence and that of the suspect's former in-laws."

Gray could stay quiet no longer. "Just to get this straight—have we dispensed with justice completely?"

Tant laughed. He'd riled her. "Of course not!"

"Then call Rob by his name. Not 'the suspect'."

"Simpson-Stone *is* a suspect."

"Or he's a victim whose life is in danger and you're neglecting your duty to protect him."

"You're hardly qualified to lecture on the topic of neglect of duty, Mr. Fisher. Now, if I may conclude—"

"Add breach of data protection policy to that."

"—before I hand back to the deputy chief constable..."

Tant talked over him, so Gray did the rudest thing he could without disrupting the debriefing to the extent he'd be asked to leave. He took out his phone, turned up the volume and scrolled through his apps, opened and closed them, *click, clack, click clack,* swipe-deleted emails, checked his smart meter readings—

Smart meter readings.

How—

"I know where he is!" Gray shoved his chair back and stood, yanking his jacket free. The sleeve knocked over the plastic cup, splattering his half-drunk tea across the table.

"What're you talking about?" Dom asked, already on his feet.

"Rob. I know where he is. Look!" Gray showed Dom his phone, still open on the smart meter app, the needle hovering between the numbers five and six. "It's usually around two pence an hour, to cover the standing charge, so unless forensics left a light on..."

"They might've done," Dom said, "but we've got nothing to lose by checking."

"So you're with me?"

Dom raised an eyebrow—a silent 'need you ask?' that he followed up with, "I'll bring the car round," already on the move.

"Don't forget the keys!" Gray called after him.

Dom stopped in the doorway. "To your gaff?"

"The police locksmith—"

"Said you signed for them. I'll bring the ram." Dom was gone before Gray could offer thanks, which would have been automatic, not heartfelt.

"Dee, I need you too."

"Yes, Sir." She went ahead with Dom.

"What about me, Sir?" Isobel asked.

It wasn't Gray's decision to make, and he looked to Tant, who shrugged.

"I can give you two hours, Mr. Fisher."

"Thank you, Ma'am. Iz, can you call the paramedics?"

"Yes, Sir." She left too.

"Josh, what do you want to do?"

"I'll stay here with Naomi."

"Shit." In dealing with Winstanley's circus, Gray had forgotten about her.

"She's perfectly safe, Graham," Winstanley said.

"What have you got her doing?"

"She kindly agreed to assist me with a data recovery exercise."

"Kindly agreed?"

"For God's sake, man. Stop terrorising me and go!"

"We're not done here, Martin," Gray said on his way out the door. "Not by a long shot."

***

Dom gunned the engine all the way to Finchley but slowed right down as he turned into Gray's road, bringing the car to a quiet stop outside the house. Gray was straight out and sprinted to the front door, ram in his hands.

"Wait!" Dom shouted. "We need to see what we're dealing with." He directed Dee and Isobel to the main road, from where they could access the alley behind the houses.

"We're wasting time," Gray said.

"Another couple of minutes won't matter."

Gray clamped his teeth together, knowing whatever he said wouldn't be civil. As an officer, Dom had many strengths, but caution was a long way down the list, which meant, at best, he thought they were on a wild goose chase.

Isobel returned without Dee. "No signs of movement at the back. Dee's climbed over the fence to try and see through the shutters."

An ambulance turned the corner and crawled up the road, pulling in behind Dom's car.

"I'm going in," Gray said. Before Dom could stop him, he swung the ram as the door opened, and he almost collided with Dee.

"Whoa!" She jumped out of the way and thumbed behind her. "Back door was unlocked. All clear down here. There's a dirty mug on the draining board, but that's it."

Handing the ram to Dom, Gray pointed up the stairs and moved off, stepping quietly, Dee on his heels—literally, when he stopped without warning at the top. "What the hell?" Flummoxed, he cleared the stairs, and Dee joined him in staring at the debris piled halfway along the narrow landing. "That's the bed from the spare room." There was also a high stool from the kitchen with a large, black bucket on top, a length of hose drooping down from it. Gray followed the hose into the bathroom—the site of further devastation. The cold water pipe had been spliced and the hose jammed onto it, secured by a jubilee clip.

Gray stepped back onto the landing and panned up to the door farthest from them. It was too dark to make out what it was, but there was definitely something attached to it. He switched on the light.

"I'm guessing that padlock isn't your doing," Dee said.

"No." Kicking the mattress aside, Gray edged past the bed wreckage to access the door, lifting the hefty padlock to examine it. "We need bolt cutters."

"Dom'll have some. Be right back." Dee thundered down the stairs.

Gray waited for silence then pressed his ear to the door. He heard nothing. He moved his head back and knocked. "Rob? Are you in there?" He listened again but still heard nothing.

He was contemplating kicking the door down when Dee returned with a pair of bolt cutters.

"Sorry if I damage your paintwork."

"Forget the paintwork. Have at it."

It took a couple of attempts and a lot of grunting on Dee's part, but she got through that padlock.

"There you go." She stepped aside. It was then that Gray noticed how pale she was. He opened his mouth to ask if she was all right, but she shook her head to stop him. "Please...just open the door?"

Gray nodded. "OK."

The paramedics had followed Dee up and were standing by.

Hoping he was prepared for the worst, Gray turned the handle and slowly pushed the door, meeting no resistance. He fully opened the door and stepped over the threshold. "Ugh. Jesus..." The smell was horrific—not decaying flesh, thank God. Blood, shit and vomit, and there, lying in the middle of it all, was Rob.

"Is he still alive?" Dee asked.

Given the position Rob was in—semi-foetal, swollen fists in front of his face—and the rigidity of his body, Gray thought he was but waited until he'd confirmed it for himself.

"Yeah. He's alive and conscious—just about. Rob, it's Gray." Stepping around the pool of bodily fluids, he crouched next to Rob's head. "Can you hear me, Rob?"

He watched for movement, aware of the paramedics now in the room with them. Rob's eyelids twitched, and the smallest croak sounded in his throat.

Gray exhaled. "Good man. The paramedics are here. They're going to look after you, get you to a hospital. OK? You're safe now..." The relief was choking him. "Folden's dead. You're safe, my friend."

He straightened up and moved away to give the paramedics space to work, trying to get himself together before he chanced looking at Dee, but she was one step ahead and wrapped him in a hug, tight and secure, murmuring through her own tears, "All right, mate, I've got you."

29: Two Birds

ROB HAD NO memory of being in the ambulance. He remembered the clunk of the padlock against the door, his relief that Folden had come back to finish the job—his even greater relief at hearing Gray's voice...and his shame for the mess he was in. After that, there was a bloody big hole until someone yelled in his ear and he lashed out, convinced they were chopping off his hands. It turned out they were straightening his fingers for an X-ray and the yell had been his own.

Several hours, some heavy-duty pain relief and a bag of intravenous saline later, he felt almost human again, or as human as he could in an open-backed hospital gown with his hands swathed in so much bandage he looked like he was wearing snow-white boxing gloves. And he had a killer itchy nose.

"Knock, knock!" Gray poked his head through the cubicle curtains. "Hey."

"Alright?" He sounded—and felt—like he'd swallowed half a pound of gravel. He coughed, hoping to clear his throat, and flinched in pain. Gray flinched with him.

"Can I get you anything?"

"Ice chips?" Rob indicated the plastic cup on the locker next to the bed.

Gray peered into it. "Melted."

"Give it here."

Gray brought the cup and held it to Rob's lips, dribbling the water into his mouth. It wasn't even cold and tasted strongly of chlorine, which was a million times better than the last water he'd drunk, but he wouldn't drink it for fun. He grunted to signal he was done.

"I'll go get you a top-up," Gray said.

"Of lager, yeah?" Rob joked, still husky. He could've given Satchmo a run for his money.

Gray smiled. "I'll see what I can do." He disappeared back through the curtains, and Rob caught a glimpse of someone's arm clad in blue-black uniform.

The itch was driving him mad, and he wiggled his nose, which sent a sharp shock through his eye sockets and left the itch untouched. Gingerly, he brought his hands up to his face and rubbed his nose on his wrist, inhaling bandage lint. That made it worse. A sneeze built, and he braced for it, but the urge came to nothing. He relaxed again and shut his eyes.

The curtain swished open. "Unfortunately—ah."

"I'm awake," Rob said, though it was an effort to stay that way. "What were you gonna say?"

"The nurse said you're going to theatre soon, so no more ice."

"Fair enough." He'd only been half compos mentis when they'd told him they needed to put pins in two of his fingers and hadn't registered it meant surgery.

"Also, there's someone out here waiting to—"

"Dad!" Lucas charged past Gray into the cubicle and then halted like he'd run into a wall, staring at Rob's hands, then at his face, then back at his hands.

"Alright, mate?"

"What happened?"

"Got into a fight," Rob said lightly, glancing up at Zoë, whose shocked expression matched their son's. "I'm all right, though. The doctors are going to fix me up in a bit."

"Did you fight Tempest?"

"Yeah."

Lucas was still staring. His lip quivered. "I'm sorry, Dad." His mouth turned down, and he squeezed his eyes shut. He sniffed in, trying to be brave.

"Aww, mate. Come here." Rob raised his arm just high enough for Lucas to bob under it and held him as tightly as he could, which wasn't tight at all. Lucas burrowed his face into Rob's side and sniffled. "You've got nothing to be sorry for."

"He hurt you cos of me."

"No, he hurt me because he was a bad man. You did nothing wrong, Lu."

"Is he dead?"

"Yeah, he's dead. He can't hurt us anymore."

The news helped Lucas get control of his sobbing, and he lifted his head, resolutely looking Rob in the eye. "Good, cos if he was still alive, I'd buy a real assault rifle and shoot him up bad style."

"Err, yeah. I think me, your mum and Travis might need to find you a new game to play." Rob looked up at Zoë, who was also crying. She tried to smile and shook her head. *Hormones*, she mouthed. Rob winked in understanding. "Is Travis with you?" he asked.

She nodded. "In the waiting room."

"Have you been here long?"

"A few hours."

"Blimey."

"We're heading home, now we've seen you."

"*Home* home?"

"Yeah." Zoë smiled, mixed emotions. "We've got a lot of cleaning to do before bedtime."

"I'd better not hold you up, then."

Lucas threw his arms around Rob's middle, squeezed and held on.

"Come on, Lu," Zoë cajoled. "Your dad needs to rest."

"'Kay..." Lucas huffed and reluctantly let go. "Bye, Dad."

"Laters, taters. Be good, yeah?"

"Yeah!" He said it as if he was never anything else. He moved away, and Rob caught Zoë's silent communication to Gray.

"Let's give your mum and dad a minute, Lucas," Gray said. "Want a Twix?"

"Yesss!" And off he went, gabbling—"Did you shoot him, Fish?"

"Not me, no."

"Was it Dad? I bet it was. He used to be a soldier. Not, like, a sniper or anything. He doesn't know much about guns cos he was a mechanic. Did he bash his head in with a spanner?"

"That child," Zoë said. "What are we going to do with him?"

"He'll be all right once he's back in school."

"Uh-huh." She shook her head at him and sighed. "You're an idiot. D'you know that?"

"Yep."

"You could've been killed."

"I wasn't, though. It's over, Zo. We can get on with our lives again. You and Travis can get married."

"We'll have to wait until you've recovered."

"No need for that."

Zoë glowered. "You're coming to the wedding."

"You don't have to invite—"

"You're coming."

Rob managed half a chuckle and hissed. Laughing hurt. "Fair enough."

"Now, who'll be your plus-one, I wonder..." Zoë's eyes narrowed.

"You timed that, didn't you? Waited till I couldn't do a runner."

"Don't know what you mean!" She pretended to fight a smirk. "You and Dee look good together."

"Yeah?"

"But you and Ari..." She watched his face. "Lu won't care either way. He loves them both."

"And you?"

She shrugged. "Lu explained that whole gender-fluid thing to me. I can't say I understand it—not that it matters. I want you to be happy. Don't screw it up—for my sake!"

"I'll try not to," Rob said, and he meant it.

"Good. OK. I'm done being the sassy ex-wife." She leaned in and very carefully hugged him. "We'll see you tomorrow. Good luck with the op."

"Thanks, Zo. Enjoy your bed."

"Oh, I will, don't you worry." With a smile, she slipped through the curtains.

On his own again, Rob closed his eyes, for the first time letting his mind wander back over his ordeal, or the bits he could remember. He'd witnessed a different side of Folden, something deeper, closer to the core of who and what he was, and Rob was struggling to reconcile it with the goal that had kept him going through the past year. He'd felt sorry for Folden, had understood his pain—not just over losing his aunt but the revelation of how lonely the guy was, because the waiting for friends who never came spiel was about Folden. Of course, it was also part of the manipulation. He'd wanted Rob to feel guilty for duping him. He'd wanted Rob to empathise and acknowledge the things they had in common. *We are the same, you and me.*

"Stockholm syndrome."

"Eh?" Gray was back, on his own.

"Nothing." He was getting scant recollections of black and white posters high above him as the paramedics had bumped him down the stairs. "So that was your house?"

"Yeah. Talk about hard-faced."

"How did he get in?"

"The police locksmith gave him the keys. He had ID and a signed authorisation."

"Is that how you found me?"

Gray shook his head. "Nope. By the deduction of power." He took out his phone, thumbed the screen and turned it Rob's way. "Smart meter."

Rob peered at the dial, its digital needle hovering on the number two. "Very smart meter." His mum had one and was constantly thrusting her phone in his and Harvey's faces as evidence they were wasting electricity. He was glad the message hadn't sunk in or he might've worked harder to turn off the light Folden had left on.

The curtain opened a fraction, and a doctor peered in at Rob. "Wrong cubicle. Sorry." She disappeared, leaving a gap through which he could see the corridor beyond and that same arm in uniform as before. Gray pulled the curtain shut.

"Question," Rob said.

"Go on."

"Folden's definitely dead, isn't he? I didn't imagine you saying it."

"No, you didn't imagine it. Dom shot him."

"So why have I got a police guard?"

"Ah." Gray turned and looked over at where the gap had been. He turned back, chewed his lip, took in a long breath. "What do you know about a hard drive?"

"Not much. I know Winstanley thinks that's what Folden was after. He's wrong."

"You sound very sure of that."

"I am...sort of." Rob tried to remember exactly what Folden had said. "I told him I'd help him find it—when he was smashing my hands up. I was just trying to get him to stop. He made out he had no idea what I was talking about. But then, before he left... He was really cut up over his aunt. I've never seen him like that. She must've been in remission—she had cancer."

"She died a month ago."

"He told me. The cancer came back while he was in prison, and he blamed us. Well, me, I guess. He was going on about how we had all these things in common, and I was trying to keep him talking, keep him thinking like that. Then I mentioned Campion's name, and he flipped, said something about the hard drive being his insurance policy if you found me." Gray was nodding. "What did he mean?"

"It was in your car."

"The fucker stitched me up—agh! Shit!" Pain shot up Rob's arms, and he went rigid, terrified to move. "Gotta stop doing that," he said through clenched teeth.

"Do you need me to get someone?" Gray took a step towards the curtain.

"Nah. I'll be all right in a minute." He slowly untensed, leaving his fingers until last. "Hurts like a bastard."

"I can see that."

"Can you do me a favour and sort these pillows? It might help to sit up a bit. I dunno. Can't make it any worse."

Gray came closer, looking down past Rob's head. "There's a remote control." He picked it up and pressed a button, watching the top of the bed rise. Rob grunted. The bed stopped. "How's that?"

"Better. Cheers."

Gray left the control on the locker and stood where he'd been standing before, his eyes averted.

"You don't have to stay, you know," Rob said.

"I'll keep you company until they take you to theatre. Unless you want me to go?"

"No." He'd had enough solitary confinement for one day—for one lifetime. "I'm going down for this, aren't I?"

Gray didn't answer.

"What's so important about this hard drive?"

"It holds evidence of state capture—government corruption."

"Bloody hell. Well, that's me screwed. But I swear to you, I knew nothing about it until Ari..." Rob shut up, for what good it did. Gray's eyes weren't averted now.

"Until Ari what?" he asked.

Rob wasn't up to talking his way out of that one. There again, he didn't need to with Gray. He wouldn't grass Ari up. "They listened in on your top-secret conversation with Winstanley. And for your information, I'm pretty good with a mobile phone these days."

Gray snuffed a laugh, but his expression told Rob he was right to worry.

"Great, isn't it? I survive being abducted by a psychopath and land in prison."

Gray smiled ruefully. "I'm confident it won't come to that. It's still only circumstantial. Actually..." He frowned and held up his index finger, pausing for several seconds, and then tapped it against his lips. Then he wagged it at Rob. "I don't think Folden ever intended to kill you."

From where Rob was lying, it didn't feel that way. "Then what was it all about?"

"Setting you up."

"And we prove that how?"

"It'll be difficult, especially as he was trying to get the hard drive when Dom shot him. But he left the lights on and the back door unlocked. He expected us to find you alive. If he'd intended to kill you, he'd have done it before he went after Dunleavy."

"Dunleavy? Martina's missus?"

Gray grimaced. "Shit, you don't know. Folden shot her. She's alive—"

"Why would he shoot Erica?"

"A contracted hit? Winstanley hinted she was corrupt—"

"That's bullshit."

"She's got to be involved somehow."

"No." Rob wasn't as close to Erica as he was to Martina, but he'd spent enough time with them, in and out of the line of duty, to know the kind of women they were—the kind of officers they were. "I'm not buying it, Gray. Erica's straight as a die."

"All right. So maybe she had dirt to dish on Invecta—" Gray stopped, and then laughed and smacked his forehead. "Folden's never hurt a woman."

"That we know of," Rob argued.

"We went through his file—twenty-three offences and not one with a female victim. Josh and Trudi independently worked it into their profiles. There's not much they agree on, but they're adamant about that. So either Erica wasn't the target or..."

Wherever Gray's reasoning had taken him, his face paled until it was no more than one shade darker than the bandages on Rob's hands.

He unlocked his phone and put it to his ear. "I'm afraid I'm going to have to abandon— Hello, Dee? I need you in here, now, please." He ended the call, muttering to himself. Rob caught the mention of Martina but not much else before Gray looked up. "Sorry. Thinking aloud. Dee's just—"

"Here," she said, materialising next to Gray.

"Guard this man with your life. Don't let anyone in here. And I mean *anyone*."

"Gotcha."

Gray swept the curtain aside, stepped out and whisked it back. Rob heard a murmured exchange take place between him and the officer standing outside, followed by activity on the officer's radio and brisk footsteps heading away. Rob shifted his eyes up to Dee's face. Her grinning face.

"What?" he asked.

"You had a shit without me."

"Fuck off!" Laughing turned out not to be the best idea he'd ever had, but it got him past his embarrassment. "Ow, that really bloody hurts."

"Serves you right." Dee was laughing too, but it quickly turned to tears. "You idiot."

"That's exactly what Zoë said—have you two been talking?"

"Yeah, but not about you." She shook her head at him, just like Zoë had. "I can't believe you gave me the slip!"

"I'm sorry. I had to."

"Idiot," she muttered again. She dug a tissue from her pocket and wiped her eyes and nose. "How are you doing, anyway?"

"Still breathing. Starving."

"You're nil-by-mouth."

"Yep." He raised his hands a fraction. That was as much as he could handle. "Waiting for an op. I tell you what, I'd give my left leg for a shower."

"Your left leg?"

"Well, my arms are busted, and my right leg isn't much better."

Dee nodded as if she were considering the logistics. "See, I'd offer to give you a bed bath, but Naomi might have something to say about it."

Rob's heart went into a canter. "Is she here?"

"No. Winstanley's got her working on that hard drive they took from your car. Was that Folden's doing?"

"Probably," Rob dismissed. He wanted to clear the air with her. "Dee... I'm sorry if I led you on."

"You didn't. I tried to lead you, but you weren't having any."

"I want to make a go of it with Naomi. It might not even work out, but I've got to give it a chance, you know what I mean?"

"I do know what you mean, and like I said, don't sweat it. We're still mates, yeah?"

"Yeah."

"And if things don't work out...well, I won't wait for you, but who knows, eh?"

"We can drive off into the sunset in your electric hybrid?"

"*Porsche* electric hybrid, and I don't care what you think. Lu says it's wicked. But enough of that. Who am I guarding you from now?"

"Good question. Do you know what happened with Erica Dunleavy?"

"Folden shot her."

"It was definitely Folden?"

"Who else?"

"Were there witnesses?"

"Dom Hooper."

"Anyone else?"

"Not sure. Why?"

Now Rob understood why Gray had got Dee to come in and then gone tearing off. "Because Gray doesn't think Folden shot her."

Dee frowned, processing the implication. Rob saw the moment it clicked. "No. That can't be right. It can't. Not Dom. I worked with him for a year—you worked with him for longer. What do you think?"

"I don't know."

"Gray's wrong. Got to be." Dee was still shaking her head, trying to rationalise, when the curtain whisked open. Her hand went straight to her gun. A nurse entered. Dee subtly stood down.

"Rob. They're ready for you in theatre. Are you ready for them?"

"Do I have a choice?"

"Only if you want people to start calling you the crooked man. Excuse me, please." The nurse smiled at Dee and waited for her to step aside. "You're best going home, love. He might be out of it for a while."

"I'm coming with him."

"You can't do that, I'm afraid." The nurse was very patient, but she'd misread the situation.

Dee pulled out her warrant card and held it up. "I'm here to make sure nothing happens to him."

"Oh! Sorry. I thought you were his girlfriend."

"No worries." Dee winked at Rob over the nurse's back. "I'll just have a gander." She thumbed towards the curtain as she went off to check their path was clear, returning with the same thumb stuck up to confirm it was.

The nurse released the bed's brakes and eased Rob out into the corridor, where a porter took over, and they set off, Dee walking alongside.

"Alright?" She glanced down swiftly.

"Yep," Rob confirmed, although in truth, he was a bit nervous. He'd never been under anaesthetic before.

As they passed the officer on guard duty, the officer's expression shifted to disdain. He lifted his radio and mumbled, "Accompanying suspect to the operating theatre." Rob listened to flat feet falling behind him and hoped Gray had a plan to clear his name. In prison or out, as a bent copper he was done for.

30: One Stone

I CAN'T GIVE YOU that information, sir," the receptionist repeated with heavy, don't make me call security emphasis and tilted her monitor away from Gray, as if he could have seen it anyway. She was one of several behind a long counter in the hospital's atrium, all of whom looked harried half to death as they tried, with constant interruption, to clock off for the day.

"I understand." Gray contained his frustration. A flash of a badge and she'd have told him all he needed to know, but he was a civilian and she was just doing her job. "If she's still in surgery—I'm not asking you to tell me—but if she is, where would I be most likely to find her next of kin?"

The receptionist stared at her screen, working hard to ignore him, and he hated pressing her, but it was a big hospital.

"I'm sorry. This is urgent."

"Try the hospital coffee shop. Through the double doors, turn right, follow the signposts."

"Thank you," Gray said, adding, "You're doing a great job," as he took off for the double doors, which automatically opened on his approach. He went through them and veered right, looking up at the signs indicating the various departments, thus he almost missed Martina step out of a lift some yards in front of him and merge into the foot traffic. Luckily, she was heading the same place he was and he caught up with her in the queue at the counter. In a world of her own, she didn't see him and leapt back in surprise when he said hello.

"Gray!"

"Sorry I startled you. How are things?"

"OK. Erica's in recovery, waiting to go to the cardio ward, so I'm squeezing in a quick coffee while I can. Can I buy you one?"

"Let me get them," Gray said. "I want to talk to you anyway." And ask why Erica was going to a cardio ward.

"Next, please." The counter assistant smiled at them; Martina gestured for Gray to do the honours. She wanted a latte; he opted for the same, paid and left Martina to choose somewhere to sit.

"Erica went into cardiac arrest," she said, quashing that mystery once they'd settled at an out-of-the-way table. "The bullet grazed her hand—minimal tissue damage." She rubbed at the fleshy V between her finger and thumb. "At least she's had the bypass now—she's been putting it off for a year. Never the right time to go off sick."

"But she's OK?" Gray asked.

"She should make a full recovery."

"Thank God."

Martina picked up her coffee, holding the cup as if it were a rice bowl. "How's Rob?"

"Fine apart from his fingers. He's got to have k-wires in a couple. He was waiting to go to theatre when I left."

"Will he still be able to ride his bike?"

"The doc says so. Mind, I can't see much getting in the way of that, can you?"

Martina chuckled. "Good point. So...you wanted to talk to me?"

"Yeah." He paused, trying out various questions in his head before he settled on, "Do you and Erica ever discuss your work?"

"Sometimes." Her eyes bore into his, scrutinising, wary. "Are you asking if I knew she was due to meet with Winstanley this morning?"

Gray nodded. "Do you know why?"

"Why you're asking or what the meeting was about?" She put down her cup, her latte still untouched, and sat back, for several minutes watching other patrons come and go before she leaned forward again. "This is about Dom Hooper, isn't it?"

The fact she'd gleaned that much was enough for Gray to take his concerns to Winstanley, but he was holding off until he'd heard what Martina had to say and hoping he wasn't underestimating the threat posed by doing so. "I realise what Erica shares with you, she shares in confidence..."

"But you suspect Hooper's dirty?" She was back to scrutinising him. "Friday evening last, did you get him to pull Rob over?"

"No. I thought you had."

"Is that what he told you?"

"I didn't ask." *Trust no-one.* Dom's warning was playing on repeat in Gray's head, but the conversation was heading a big, cryptic nowhere. One of them needed to take the leap. "Are you aware Dom's working for Winstanley?"

"Yes."

"And are you aware Winstanley thinks Erica is corrupt?"

"Yes. That's why she requested a meeting with him."

"To clear her name?" Gray guessed. Martina nodded. "And implicate someone else?" And again. "Dom." No confirmation necessary.

"I'm sorry, Gray. I know he's a friend of yours."

"What's he into?"

"Misappropriation of police funds."

"How much?"

"You'd have a better idea than me. With the last round of cuts, Erica was instructed to reduce expenditure force-wide by thirty percent. She's been at it for two years—going through the finances of every single department, hauling in managers on an almost daily basis to account for discrepancies. That's what happened with Dom Hooper—substantial amounts unaccounted for after he took over from you, and she asked him to explain. He pleaded ignorance. The next thing, he's officially suspended on full pay in relation to another matter and Erica's told to shelve her investigation."

"Someone covered for him," Gray surmised.

"Looks like. And there's more. The minister in charge of the select committee Erica was serving on called to say her services were no longer required, no explanation."

"The committee Winstanley was on?"

"Could well be, but Official Secrets Act and all that. She *can't* tell me everything. My point is, it happened after she collared Dom Hooper." Martina shrugged. "As I told Rob, I've never met him, but it seems to me whatever he's into, he's in deep."

"That's what worries me about this morning," Gray said. "He was there when Erica was shot."

"I know. He called the ambulance and then called me."

"He's the only eyewitness."

"Not quite. Erica saw it too."

"What did she see?"

"She didn't say, but if you want to ask her, you can join the queue—excuse me one moment." Martina extracted her phone from her inside pocket and answered it. "Martina Hedley." ... "OK. Thank you." She put her phone away and got up, cup in hand. "That was the ward sister. I need to go."

"Thanks for talking to me," Gray said.

"No problem." She knocked back her coffee and put the cup on the table.

"Do you think Dom was desperate enough to try to stop her getting to Winstanley?"

"If you're asking was he desperate enough to shoot her..."

"That's what I'm asking."

"Like I say, I've never met him, but if I were you, I'd be watching my back. Give my love to Rob."

"Will do. And regards to you and Erica."

With a nod, she strode away, leaving Gray with his latte and the greatest moral dilemma he'd ever faced.

***

The mobile signal in the hospital was lousy in general but particularly so in the visitor's toilet. That was where Gray was hiding out, wishing he only had a call of nature to make. He did that first, as a means to delay, and washed and dried his hands. Thoroughly. He wanted to be wrong—wrong about this instead of the past fifteen years—but that gut feeling, his 'copper's intuition', was unrelenting.

With his phone dipping in and out of emergency calls only, Gray accepted defeat and headed through the atrium and onwards to the exit. Half a dozen people loitered outside, some smoking, most talking on their phones. Gray passed them by and crossed the street, dodging behind a pillar at the side of the building opposite. From there, he made the call via Ari's app. It connected first time, but he had to redial twice before Winstanley answered rather than hanging up.

"Can't talk now, Graham."

"It's urgent, Martin."

"I'm heading into a crisis meeting with the deputy commissioner."

"Well, give your apologies and call me back!" Gray hung up, counted to twenty, went for a redial and hit 'answer' instead.

"London had better be burning," Winstanley muttered sourly, but he'd returned the call posthaste.

"Sorry. This can't wait. Have you watched the security footage from the Dunleavy shooting?"

"Not yet."

"Are you looking into it?"

"I have more pressing matters to attend to."

"It doesn't fit the suspect's profile."

"The victim's reason for being where they were—"

"She was on her way to meet you and someone tried to stop her," Gray said. Winstanley grunted. "But it might not be who we thought."

Winstanley didn't speak for a while. It would be no easier for him to process than it had been for Gray, but somebody needed to confirm what had really happened, and Winstanley was closest. Finally, he said, "That's a very serious allegation, Graham."

"I don't make it lightly, believe me."

Gray heard the long whistle of Winstanley's nose sucking in air. "All right. I'll look into it."

"Thank you." Gray waited to see if he was going to say anything else. True to form, he did so as Gray moved his phone away from his ear.

"You might be interested to know our technology consultant was successful."

"That's good news."

"Indeed it is. Goodbye for now, Graham."

"Bye, Martin."

The call ended sombrely. They should both have been elated. Rob was alive; Winstanley had his data. A double victory. Yet it felt an awful lot like defeat. The feeling clung to Gray, weighing down his every step as he crossed the street, back to the hospital, no real thought for where he was going or why, until someone called his name.

His heart took off as he stopped, turned and walked the few feet back to the visitor's toilet where he'd dallied before he'd made the call to Winstanley. "What the hell have you done?"

"Not out here." Dom hooked Gray's arm and pulled him inside. "I just missed you before."

Gray shook him off. "You lied to me, Hooper."

Dom calmly locked the door and stood in front of it. "When did I?"

"Folden didn't shoot Erica. You did."

"Gray...mate—"

"Don't 'mate' me. What was it you said?" From where he was standing, he couldn't tell if Dom was armed. "You've never lied to me and you never will?"

"Everybody lies."

"Not you. Not to me."

"I didn't this time either."

"But you didn't correct me." Gray paced, turned back. Yes, Dom was armed. "What you've done—it's the lowest of the low." He couldn't even raise the alarm because it would go to Dom's phone too, that was, if he could get a signal at all.

"Yeah, well. That's where I'm at." There was no anger in his words, nothing threatening about his stance. "I fucked up, Gray, good and proper."

"Of all the ways you could've fucked up—"

"It was an accidental discharge, and I only shot her in the hand, but she went and had a bloody heart attack, didn't she? I don't even know if she survived."

"She survived," Gray said, though Dom deserved to suffer.

"Thank Christ." Dom dragged his hands over his face and kept them there. Behind them he was weeping.

"Is that it? Confession over? Can I go?"

"I'm not stopping you." Dom stepped away from the door.

Gray moved carefully, keeping his eyes on Dom all the way, but it looked like he really was going to let Gray walk free.

He had the door unlocked and open a couple of inches when Dom said, "I need your help."

"How's that? A human shield so you can get out of here?"

"I'm going to make this right, Gray."

"I have no idea what *this* is."

"A long story, is what it is."

Gray shut and locked the door. "Put your gun on the floor."

DEBBIE MCGOWAN

Dom did as he was told and backed up against the wall. The emergency cord dangled a few inches to his left, too close for Gray to reach it first if the need arose. For the time being, he didn't believe he was in danger. He picked up Dom's gun and removed the magazine, set both on top of the toilet cistern, put down the lid and sat.

"I'm listening," he said.

"From the beginning?"

"It's your story. You decide."

"From the beginning, then." Dom reached over and grabbed a few paper towels from the dispenser, gave his face a rough rub and binned them. Red-eyed, unshaven, sunken-cheeked—he looked wretched. "So...about five years back, I was at the casino when this bloke gets chatty. We have a few drinks, and I'm nearly done for the night when he invites me to buy into a poker game. As you know, I'm a roulette man these days, though I dabbled a bit with cards when I was younger, and I was up a few grand, so I figured what the hell? Finish the night in style. Except it didn't work out like that. Three, four in the morning, it dawned on me why I stopped playing poker.

"See, roulette, you're just playing against the house. With the cards, there's that human element, and the job, it breeds arrogance, makes you complacent. Because you can tell when a scumbag's blagging you, you start believing you're some kind of all-seeing eye. Nothing gets past you. So there I am at the poker table, just me and the bloke who invited me left, and I think I've got him well sussed. He's bluffing, I'm holding a full house, so I go all in.

"Needless to say, I lose the lot, and I get up to go, but this bloke—Cameron Barnett, his name is—asks me if I want a chance to win back my stake, shakes my hand, says, 'Same time tomorrow?'

"The next night, we play again, and I'm losing again, and I know I should walk away, but I can't. I'm out of chips, credit card's maxed—luckily, I'd transferred the kids' maintenance already and that money's safe because by this point—"

Loud hammering on the door made Gray jump to his feet and catapulted Dom from the wall.

"Fisher, are you in there?"

"Winstanley," Gray muttered. He had to have blue-lighted it all the way to get there so fast. Dom opened his mouth to speak, but Gray shushed him with finger to lips and called, "I'll be out shortly, Martin."

"Is everything all right?"

"Yeah. Just...I'm on a long job."

After a few seconds, Winstanley said, "I'll be in the atrium."

"OK."

"Go," Dom whispered.

Gray shook his head and moved to the door, listening as the murmured voices and footsteps faded. He looked back at Dom. "That's two chances I've had to leave now. Keep going. You were out of chips, and...?"

"I staked my motor."

"Jesus, Dom." Gray had always thought Dom's gambling was an expensive pastime but well within his control. Apparently not. "You've still got the car, though. Did you win it back?"

"I wish. After the game folded, Barnett followed me out so I could clear my shit from the glovebox and do all the reg stuff, and at the last minute, when I'm trying to figure out how the hell I'm getting home, he said he'd let me off the debt but not to forget I owe him one."

"You know who Barnett is, don't you?"

"Yeah. I looked him up the next morning, found out he's CEO of this political lobby, Invecta. He's worth billions. Letting me off thirty-five grand made no odds to him."

Gray balked. "Thirty-five grand?"

"That's only the start of it, mate."

"Hence the dipping into the SIU pot."

Dom ducked his head in shame. "I've let you down."

"You have, and yet I'm still here. Tell me what happened with Barnett."

"Right, yeah. A couple of years go by, and I've forgotten all about it, or not forgotten. Out of sight, as they say...until one day out the blue, he rings me at work and says, 'I'm calling in my debt.' But he wasn't after money. He wanted that hard drive. He said if I could deliver it to him, we'd be even—I didn't ask too many questions.

"Trouble was, he wasn't the only one trying to get to it. Barnett told me where and when it was being dropped off. All I had to do was confiscate it. I was watching from the car when these two blokes in balaclavas jumped the security guards and made off with the package. I called it in and followed them—I couldn't believe it when they handed it off to Rob."

"You wiped his route off the system."

"I had to. See, that was my chance, but I couldn't take Rob down. He's one of us."

"You were singing a different tune in front of Winstanley."

"Yeah, well, he's like a bloodhound, isn't he? The slightest sniff of corruption and he's away, nose to the ground."

"Anything to lead the trail away from you." Gray had been there, done that, and was trying to reserve judgement, at least until he had all the facts. "What did Rob do with the package?"

"Delivered it to Benjamin Clough. Rob didn't know what it was, but Clough did. I searched his chambers, but I couldn't find it. In the end, I had to own up to

Barnett, and he told me to forget about it—said he wasn't worried. It'd be taken care of. I wiped Rob's route off the system so Barnett or whoever he sent after Clough couldn't trace it back.

"Fast forward to a month ago, the hard drive's on the move again and Barnett's back in touch. It turns out Folden was supposed to have dealt with Clough back then, but we took him out of action. That was when Winstanley approached me, by the way—after Folden went down. He was furious we'd screwed up his operation. Well, not his operation, per se. His big boss who's trying to topple Invecta."

"The one who let Folden out of Brookhurst," Gray said. "And got you off the hook for nicking police money."

"*Almost* got me off the hook."

"Do you know who it is?"

"Some faceless, nameless bigwig in the Secret Service. All I know is we were to keep tabs on Folden and let him lead us to the hard drive."

"But you already knew who had it."

"D'you think you and Rob are the only ones who got nice little snapshots of your family?"

Gray sighed. "What the hell did you get yourself into?"

Another sharp knock on the door. "Fisher?"

"Honest to God, Martin. Can't a man crap in peace?"

"Sixty seconds and I'm coming in."

"Talk fast," Gray told Dom. "A month ago…"

"As far as I can tell, Folden paid Clough a visit at home, used lethal force to get the hard drive, but instead of delivering it to Barnett, he used it to blackmail him—money, a passport and a way out of the country or he'd hand it over to the authorities. But Barnett's a gambling man too, and he called Folden's bluff, knowing he had me to fall back on if the hard drive came our way."

"Seems plausible," Gray said. "What doesn't make sense is Folden sticking it in Rob's car and then coming back for it."

"Right. Which brings me to this morning. Dunleavy warned me yesterday—twenty-four hours to come clean and tell Winstanley it's me not her who's been embezzling. I was ready to do it until the NCA called Winstanley to say they were getting nowhere with the hard drive and he told them to send it over to the SIU. It was my last chance, Gray. I could finally get Barnett off my back, but I needed to stall Erica. That's all I was trying to do. Stall her long enough to get the hard drive. Then I saw Folden across the street, and he'd seen me—"

"So you didn't kill him to stop him getting the hard drive," Gray accused, "you killed him to save your own neck."

"No, listen to me, Gray. Folden drew his weapon, and I was going to take him down, but Erica misread the situation—understandably. I mean, how would she have known? She went to disarm me. I didn't mean to shoot her. I swear, Gray, I didn't. I'm a lot of things, but I'm not that." Dom was starting to ramble in desperation. "He wasn't there for the hard drive. He was there for us. You. All I know is his gun was pointing right at you. What else could I do?"

"I want to believe you, Dom. I do. But shooting people in broad daylight? It doesn't fit Folden's profile."

"To hell with his profile! I'm telling you the truth!"

Dom was sobbing, barely making sense. It was out of character. Dom was always rock-solid, taking the stresses and strains of the job in his stride...or so Gray had believed.

"God, what a bloody mess." He ripped a three-foot-length of toilet paper from the dispenser and shoved it at Dom. "You know you're an addict, don't you? You can see that?"

"Yeah. I realised a while back it was getting out of hand."

"Then why wait until now to ask for my help? I could've paid your debts."

"I'd have only run up more."

Gray had to concede that one. "So what *do* you want from me?"

"I want to testify against Barnett. I'm going away for this, it's only right, but I don't want another Folden going after my kids."

"You're asking me to protect them?"

"No. I want you to build the case against Invecta...with Winstanley."

"That's a *big* ask."

"Yeah, and I've got a damn nerve making it."

Gray wasn't sure he could do it, not necessarily because he'd have to put up with Winstanley for however long it took, although he wasn't enthralled by that prospect. What concerned him more was Dom using his addiction as an excuse for what he'd done, knowing Gray would be damning himself if he took the hard line and judged Dom as fully culpable. But Gray had sought treatment of his own volition. That was key. Maybe if he could establish Dom was doing the same...

"How's the smoking cessation going?"

"One month, eleven days."

It was a good effort, showed willingness to get better. Dom wasn't a lost cause.

"All right," Gray said. "If Winstanley's on board, I'll agree to it, but first things first—"

"Hand myself in and clear Rob's name."

"That's the ticket." Gray picked up the parts of Dom's gun and moved towards the door but stopped short of unlocking it. "You're still a git, Hooper, but you've always had my back, and you saved my life today. I owe you one. Now, let's get out of here before Winstanley kicks the door down."

31: Time and Tide

N<small>O GENERAL ANAESTHETIC.</small> The surgeon had sold it to Rob like it was a good thing, but if he was ever given the choice between being knocked out or enduring a blow-by-blow account of what they were doing to him, complete with sound effects, he'd take the general anaesthetic every time. Better still, not get into a situation where he needed to make that choice at all.

A couple of hours on, the numbness was wearing off and he was in some pain, but nothing he couldn't handle. Timothy—his named nurse, who'd accompanied him back from surgery and settled him onto the ward—told him to shout if it became too much—"No point playing the hero." There was no more danger of that. Rob had well and truly learnt his lesson, although he'd taken it as a figure of speech—until the healthcare assistant who brought him lukewarm coffee and a straw stared at him for a good minute, then said, "You're better-looking in real life."

Courtesy of his ward neighbour's iPad, Rob had since seen the *Evening Standard*. They'd gone to press before Dom's arrest and plonked Rob's only social media photo alongside Folden's mug shot. For one night only, he was a fugitive on the run—incapable of running anywhere—and from the funny looks some of the other patients' visitors gave him, he had to wonder how many calls the police had received telling them the 'may be dangerous, do not approach' suspect was in the general surgical ward.

He wasn't too worried. It would sort itself out and, crucially, he had dinner in front of him. Hospital bangers, mash and beans—a veritable feast. However, while holding a sausage or a spoon between his thumb and his cast was just about doable, getting it to his mouth...

"Crap." He scowled at the puddle of beans slithering down his gown.

"Would you like some assistance?"

His heart nearly pinged the beans off his chest, and he looked up, smiling at the sight of Naomi standing at the foot of his bed. "Alright, you?"

"Hi." She was smiling too. "Yes, I'm all right." Though she looked tired. "Are you?"

"Stoned on codeine, and I don't know how to use cutlery anymore, but yeah, I'm doing OK." He followed her movement from the end of the bed to the chair next to it, which she turned so it was angled towards him before she sat.

"I'm not a very good nurse, I'm afraid." She gently eased the spoon from his tenuous grasp, using it to scoop the beans off his gown. She went to put them on the edge of the plate.

"Oy, don't waste them!"

Naomi laughed and fed them to him. "Hungry?"

"Mmm." He swallowed. "Like you wouldn't believe."

She fed him another spoonful and scraped together the remaining beans, keeping her eyes trained on the plate. "Sorry I didn't get here earlier."

"No worries. I'd have been lousy company anyway."

"I doubt that. You'd have been better company than I had, regardless. I went to see Freddie."

"Oh? How is he?"

"Fully into the DTs. Emotional, confrontational..." She raised her eyes to meet Rob's. "I told him it was over. The relationship, the business—all of it."

"Ah, mate." It had been tough, he could tell. All those times he'd wanted to hold her, now she was here he couldn't do a thing about it.

She straightened up, tears on her lower lashes shimmering gold under the ward lights. "I was going to wait until he was discharged, but when is the right time? How long before I'm confident he won't relapse? I'm not sure I ever will be, but what I am sure of is how I've felt this past two days, not knowing if you were alive. The second I heard you were safe, I told Winstanley I had to leave. He arranged a car to take me wherever I need to go for the rest of the day."

"I'm guessing you sorted his hard drive?"

"Oh, yes!"

"Easy-peasy?"

She smiled bashfully. "I appreciate your confidence in me. It was more difficult than it should've been, considering the encryption's obsolete. I managed to dump the contents of the flash chip fairly quickly, but I couldn't do anything with it. In the end, I had to copy the data literally bit by bit before I could isolate the security PIN—I'd tried half a dozen other approaches first..." Naomi stopped and grimaced. "Sorry. I shan't bore you further."

"You carry on," Rob invited. True, his eyes had glazed over, but that was down to the drugs and the afterglow of hearing she'd ended things with Berringer. He could listen to her for hours, even if he didn't understand half...*most* of what she said, which was when it dawned on him. "Hold up. *You* did the tech stuff?"

"Winstanley gave me little choice."

"But *you*, rather than Ari or Aaron."

"Oh! I see what you mean. It's not that I can't do it. I'd just rather not. It's hard to explain, but it makes me feel...out of sorts, like I'm not me, if that makes any sense at all?"

"Yeah, it does, I think."

"More beans?"

"Please."

Naomi fed him the rest, meeting his gaze once or twice but on the whole avoiding looking at him.

"Mash?" She chopped a lump off the grey potato, which was solid enough to be a finger food, but that Rob had fingers to hold it with. It was also cold and unappetising, and Naomi was still acting strange.

"No, thanks. I'm done."

She put down the spoon and stood to move the table out of the way. "How's the pain?"

"Not great," he admitted. "Gonna ask for more pills in a bit."

"Do you want me to find a nurse?" Naomi peered along the ward.

"I want to try and hold off till you've gone. They knock me out."

She resumed her seat in the chair at his bedside, her hand resting on his bare upper arm. Her touch sent a shiver of sensation through his body—pain and pleasure. "I'll be back tomorrow, Rob."

"I'll be here," he said, winking when she afforded him another fleeting glance. "What's on your mind?"

"You and me...Aaron." She shook her head. "Not Aaron now. I'm still me. Naomi. But I can only give you a part-time relationship."

"And full-time friendship," Rob pointed out.

"Is it enough?"

"How about we just try it and see?"

"OK." She took a long, deep breath and put her free hand on her chest. "Sorry."

"Anxiety?"

"Yes. It'll go away in a minute." She smiled self-consciously. "Please tell me you have some vices."

Rob chuckled. "Where do I start? Let's see...I'm incommunicative, intense, can't take a joke, a big let-down—"

"Now you're showing off."

"And that." Rob grinned but added on a serious note, "I get panic attacks too, and nightmares. A lot of them about Folden." They'd been almost prophetic. Or maybe it was as Josh said: Rob knew Folden well enough to predict what he'd do. He could've asked him, seeing as Josh had just walked into the ward with Gray.

"I'm not staying," Josh said before he reached Rob's bed.

"Nice to see you too, mate."

Josh rolled his eyes. "I mean my train departs in half an hour. I only popped in to say goodbye."

"I'm not staying either," Gray said. "Long drive ahead, but I thought I'd best warn you to expect a visit from Winstanley tomorrow."

"Great," Rob muttered. "While you're here, I want to say thanks, *all* of you, for everything you've done." He'd already thanked Dee, with tears on both sides, before she'd handed him over to Timothy and left, her mission complete. "When I can hold my own again, the beers are on me."

"I'll look forward to it."

"Coffees are on me too," Rob added in response to Josh's frown. "What's up?"

"I was more hindrance than help."

"How d'you work that out?"

"Narcissism." Josh sighed. "I was wrong."

Gray punched the air. "Can I have that in writing?"

"When's the deadline?"

"I'm kidding."

"I'm not! Nor was Winstanley this afternoon. He appears to have forgotten I wasn't working for him."

"Didn't you agree to submit a joint report with Professor Holt?"

"Yes, but that's beside the point. When do you want *my* report?"

"When it's done."

"I can't work without deadlines, Graham."

"So pick a date."

Entertaining as their bickering was, Rob interrupted before they got too carried away. "What made you change your mind about Folden, Josh?"

"His blaze of glory and what you told Graham earlier. It made me revisit my original profile. Folden was motivated by feelings of betrayal and abandonment—his parents, his grandfather, Alistair Campion, Alice, his aunt...and you. You said he didn't make friends, and I concur, but in lieu of friendship, he'd constructed a mental representation of you, to which he formed an emotional attachment."

"That's why he thought we had things in common—he was comparing himself to the me in his head?"

"That's my theory, yes. Coming face-to-face with the real you, he interpreted the incongruence as deception. To be clear, you have nothing in common with Folden, but his self-esteem rested on your rescue, which is to say, if you were worthy of being saved, so was he. At the point when he decided no-one was coming for you, he came to us."

"I think I get you. When we were in the café, he said...well, I can't remember exactly, but it was along the lines of if your friends know what's best, they won't come looking for you. I took it as a threat—if I fought back or tried to escape or did anything to alert you, he'd go after Lu, Lois and Amber."

"He may well have meant it that way," Josh said.

Gray shook his head. "I disagree. I think if we'd found you while he was still there, he'd have killed you."

"On what basis?" Josh asked. "What's your evidence?"

"Habitual grandiosity, vis-à-vis going down in a blaze of glory."

"Or, conversely, he concluded from your failure to save Rob that he too was unworthy."

"Are you two going yet?" Rob asked, and he was only half-joking. In time, he might be up for trying to get his head around why Folden had done it, but right then he wanted nothing more than a top-up of painkillers and Naomi's unassuming company.

To their credit, Gray and Josh didn't take his bluntness to heart. With guilty smiles and apologies, they said their goodbyes, promising they'd be in touch soon. Seeing as Rob would be convalescing at his mum and Harvey's, he hoped he'd be seeing Josh again very soon, although he still had to figure out how he was getting there, and he'd be relying on his friends for lifts for a while.

After Gray and Josh left, Naomi fetched the nurse, who hit him up with more codeine and left them to enjoy the remaining fifteen minutes before Rob conked out—just long enough for him to say what he needed to.

"I'm thinking of moving back up north."

Naomi perched on the edge of the bed. "On your own?"

"Doesn't have to be."

Her gaze lost focus; she was thinking it through. Her slight head-bobbing became a definite nod. "I could live anywhere and do my job," she said. "But...I need a bit of time first, and my own space. Freddie's been in my life for so long, I have to prove to myself I can keep him out." She met Rob's gaze and held it. "I hope that's OK."

"Yeah, totally. We're in no rush, are we?"

"No." She came closer, leaning down to share an unhurried kiss, and resumed her seat next to the bed, her head resting on Rob's shoulder as the codeine kicked in and his eyelids slid shut.

**

It was long past midnight before Gray awoke from his supposed-to-be-short power nap, threw his overnight bag in the car and set off. Once again, he'd failed to call Will as promised; hopefully, all would be forgiven by daybreak. In the early morning hours, the haze of light pollution, fine misty rain captured in headlight beams and plumes sprayed by larger vehicles all lent the M25 an otherworldly aura that made anything seem possible.

After so many years away at university, working in London and moving around the country, heading into the Southwest still felt as if he were going home—even more so for what waited at the end of this journey. Dawn chased him, trees and road signs throwing elongated purple shadows like arrows pointing to his destination. Black silhouettes and grey expanses slowly filled with colour and detail, farmhouses, hedgerows, lambing sheds, clusters of reclining cows.

Five a.m...passing the turn-off that would have taken him to his hometown, he slowed a fraction while he pictured his mum sleeping and imagined a different reality where he could have let himself in and napped on the couch, later surprising her with his unexpected visit and a cup of tea.

Life coaches, magazine articles, therapists—he'd read and heard it a hundred times over, how he should cut 'that toxic person' out of his life. Sure, he could walk away anytime, grieve as if she'd died. But he wasn't ready to do that, still believed they could fix their relationship without him pretending to be something he wasn't, and time was on their side. Like his craving for cocaine, his need to keep trying to mend the rift between them wasn't as strong as it had been, and there was only one thing he was craving right now.

Six a.m...the landscape changed again as he passed Stonehenge, the creeping sunrise charging the ancient stones so they glowed a deep, warm orange. As familiar as Salisbury was to him, he'd never taken its history for granted, but it had a different significance since he'd met Will: the feminine connecting past and present through Will's mum and the women who'd fought with her for peace; the campaigns for animal rights and liberation symbolised by Porton Down and the tireless work of Will and his kind. Just as he'd changed the world around him, Will had changed Gray in so many ways, and for the better. He wasn't sure if that effect worked in reverse, but he felt no need to leave his mark, claim territory or ensure his legacy. Cliché that it was, he'd played his part in making the world a safer place. He was at peace.

The drive through the night was taking its toll, and Gray exchanged the background drone of generic radio broadcasts for his streaming music account, smiling when it picked up where it had left off the last time he'd listened: on the way home from the folk gig a long, long week ago. He flicked back through the tracks to the one dedicated to Will's mum, relishing the memories of the chant at her funeral and the canon around the barn. When the song finished, he left the rest of the EP to play and drummed along on the steering wheel, glad of Jed's musical company during the toughest hour of the drive.

Dense hedgerows abuzz with spring's new life, dips and sharp turns that almost doubled back, a tractor and a campervan, no other traffic, the low sun blinding in front and then lost to another bend. The road straightened for a short time as it descended toward the coast, a house here and there, and a few more and finally the bay ahead. Gray rolled past the barriers, found a parking space, switched off the engine, lowered the window and breathed in the rich, ionised air sweeping in off the high tide.

The next thing he registered was movement in shadow form, flickering over his shut eyelids. Cautiously, he opened one eye, smiling at the vision of Will, leaning on the sill of the open window and smiling back, wisps of hair swirling around his face.

"This is a nice surprise," Will said.

"For me too." Gray stretched and brushed his fingers down Will's cheek. "It's over." The relief of being able to utter those words zapped Gray's last reserve of energy—he could gladly have reclined his seat and passed out for the next however long but for the ache in his knees and the even greater ache for proper physical contact.

"Are you getting out?"

Gray nodded. "Building up to it."

Will stepped back, opening the door, and Gray heaved his exhausted body out of the seat and into Will's arms. Neither spoke for some time, for there was no need, although Gray couldn't shake the feeling that he was missing something.

Even caught in a warm embrace, the ocean breeze sneaked into every little nook. Coming on top of sleep deprivation and the ordeal of the past seventy-two hours, Gray shivered and attempted to withdraw, but Will squeezed him tighter. Gray laughed.

"I'm only getting my coat."

Will released him; Gray grabbed his coat from the back of the seat and pulled it on, sneaking the small velvet box into his pocket, meeting resistance in the form of dog-poo bags, which was when he figured out what the missing thing was. "Where are the dogs?"

Will peered past Gray and stood on tiptoes. "Somewhere down there. Come on." He held out his hand. "They'll go nuts when they see you're here. They've missed you."

Gray took Will's hand, and together they strolled down the slipway onto the beach. As they reached the sand, Gray stopped and bent to take off his boots and socks. He got one boot off before a shunt from the front, courtesy of a big dog on wheels, toppled him and he landed on his backside. The rest of the pack soon caught on and came bounding over—all but the new collie, who was chasing waves, other dogs, seagulls, surfers—anything that moved.

"Told you!" Will said.

Around the sides and the top of many, many slobbery kisses, Gray caught Will's beaming smile, and beamed one right back. "Any chance of a hand up?"

Will reached down and gripped Gray's arm, pulling him to his feet. "So you found us."

"I did, all by myself."

"How did you know?"

"This is your sanctuary."

Will nodded. "When Suze was little, we used to come here on holiday and stay at Jed's mum's place—up there." He pointed towards the cliffs. "She loved it."

"So much she chose it for her Sweet Sixteen," Gray noted.

"Yep. You didn't call again."

"I fell asleep. Sorry."

They set off along the beach, the dogs running rings around them before tearing off, and back again, while Gray recounted the previous day's events to Will, who played along convincingly, but Gray wasn't fooled. Will hadn't even asked about the tremendous bruise covering a good quarter of Gray's face.

"Naomi's told you all this already, hasn't she?"

Will just smiled, admitting to nothing. "So it's really over?"

"Well, I need to be back in London by Monday to give my statement and hand over my evidence to Winstanley. Then there's the furniture guy's funeral and Dom's trial. And I'll have to rethink what I'm doing with the house—look into private rental maybe." He could be wrong, but he suspected murder and abduction were not strong selling features. "There's also something you should know." He'd rehearsed on the drive down, but trepidation and the wind whipped him breathless, and he found he couldn't get the words out.

"Gray, however bad it is, it can't be worse than what we've been through this week. Just say it."

"I've been married before."

"OK. Not what I expected—unless you're talking about Jean-Michel?"

"No." They reached a clutch of large rocks and stopped walking. Gray turned toward the ocean, watching the collie bounce along the shoreline, scooping up mouthfuls of sand and seawater. "It was part of my cover on the Strang case. Helen is the Strangs' niece, and she was maid of honour at her brother's wedding. I was conducting surveillance in the nightclub where they had the hen party. She came over and started chatting me up. I wanted an invitation to the wedding, so I went with it."

"And ended up marrying her? Was the wedding in Vegas?"

Gray laughed ruefully. "Newcastle, and not an Elvis impersonator in sight. I don't say this to make what I did seem any less heinous, but you'd be surprised how many undercover officers end up married or even having kids just to maintain their cover."

"What you're telling me is it meant nothing." Will wasn't seeking assurance. He was disgusted.

"No, I'm not! I wasn't in love with her, and I didn't desire her, but it meant something to her, and I won't deny that. She was innocent, and I hurt her, and then Folden went after her..." Gray swallowed hard, refusing to shed tears. He didn't deserve sympathy for what he'd done. "You have a right to know— to make an informed decision."

"Decision?" Will turned and observed him. "About us?"

"Yes." Gray swallowed again, this time to build courage. Taking a step back so he wouldn't land in the rock pool, he dropped to one knee.

"I'm not helping you up again," Will joked, but his wide-eyed expression made it clear he knew what Gray was up to.

"Wilfred Richards..." Gray pulled the velvet box from his pocket and wrangled it open. "Will you marry me?"

Will looked down at him for a long time—long enough for Gray to think the worst and start sinking into the wet sand. The dogs, all bar one, had noticed Gray at their level again and came over to join his game. Through their jostling nudges and wet, waggy tails, Gray held steady.

"You OK down there?" Will asked, a hint of a playful smirk creeping into his cool, calculating regard. Still, Gray didn't move. He wasn't sure he could anymore.

"Yes," Will said, finally putting him out of his misery.

Gray eased the promise ring from the box. "I hope it fits." There was no reason it shouldn't when he'd taken Will's grungy tungsten ring to the jeweller to get the size. Even so, Gray held his breath as he slid the plain silver band onto Will's finger, and sighed in relief when it fitted, but didn't linger for a reaction. He'd sunk to midway up his thigh; the sand squelched rudely as it released his knee.

The dogs, unimpressed by grand romantic gestures, had all gone off in different directions. Will gave a shrill whistle, and they came running back to join them as they set off once again, hand in hand, along the beach.

"What would you have done if I'd said no?" Will asked.

"Attached it to Kenny's collar," Gray replied with a smile. "That's your only takeaway?"

Will chuckled. "I wouldn't have said no. Thank you for telling me about Helen."

Gray nodded, no quips, no jokes. His life, his career—one and the same—had not inspired openness, but he was getting there, day by day.

Epilogue: Not A Baby Anymore

August

"I SMELL BACON!" LUCAS'S loud exclamation sounded from inside the tent as he half unzipped the doors and commando-crawled through the small gap, still in his sleeping bag. Like a camo-patterned giant caterpillar, he humped and slithered out into the open and sat up. "Da-a-ad! You're not supposed to do it on a stove!"

Rob shushed him. "Keep your voice down, Lu."

"But you said we'd make a real fire!"

"I'm not cooking breakfast on a campfire. We'll make one tonight, OK?"

"S'pose." Lucas flopped back on the grass in a sulk, but it didn't last long. From beyond the trees surrounding their pitch came the sounds of splashing and laughter. Lucas sat up again. "Are we going kayaking today, Dad? Can we go after breakfast? Will they let me do it on my own?" And he was off.

Rob smiled, listening to him, and flipped the bacon and sausages. They'd brought a couple of days' supplies with them—breakfast and sandwich stuff, burgers and marshmallows—so there was no urgency, but they'd need to head out at some point to find a supermarket. He'd chosen this particular campsite because it offered the best of both worlds: each pitch was in its own clearing away from other campers, giving the feel of being alone in the forest, but there was a central hub with a small shop, launderette, log pile, and toilet and shower block.

Better yet, the facilities were mixed gender—a new and unexpected consideration for the camping trip that had been two years in the making. Rob had assumed it would be just the two of them, but Lucas had insisted Ari come too because "Aaron was in the Scouts and can do that rubbing two sticks fire thing, Dad." Madly, it turned out to be true. Rob had brought matches anyway, but he was well up for watching Ari show off their firelighting prowess later.

"...so can we, yeah?" Lucas finished.

"We need to give breakfast time to go down first, and we'd better check what Ari wants to do—"

"Kayaking's fine by me," came the confirmation from inside the tent.

"Yesss!" Lucas jumped up and trampled his way out of his sleeping bag, abandoning it to fully unzip the tent. "Morning, Ar...Naomi. Dad's made bacon and sausages. Are you getting up?"

"Lu! Behave!" Rob warned.

"It's all right. Morning, Lu. Yes, I'm getting up now. Can you close that zip again for me, please?"

"Oh! Yeah. Sorry." Lucas backstepped and pulled the zip down, looking sheepish—the usual bashfulness of an almost-nine-year-old hurtling towards puberty. Due credit to his school, they'd nailed the diversity stuff; Lucas was totally unfazed by Ari's gender-fluidity. In fairness to himself, Rob had only messed up once. He stayed at Ari's every other weekend when he went down to see Lucas; one Friday night, Rob had fallen asleep next to Ari, woken up alone and found Aaron in the kitchen making coffee—having surprised him with a kiss on the back of the neck before he'd realised.

It was inevitable from time to time. Since they'd cut ties with Freddie Berringer, Ari's gender had been much more fluid, but—Aaron said—at least Rob wasn't repulsed by him. Tempted as Rob was to pay Berringer a visit on Ari's behalf, he abided by their wishes and let Berringer have the final word, which came in the form of a vast bouquet of peach-coloured roses and a card that said *you were always expendable*—good grace by Berringer's low standards.

So no, Rob wasn't repulsed by Aaron. Equally, he wasn't attracted to Aaron, nor Aaron to him, and the guy needed his own space. They were still figuring out the logistics for when they moved in together—a bit like living with someone who worked away from home, Rob envisaged.

"That bacon is *very* crispy," Naomi murmured into Rob's ear.

"Err, yeah." Crispy going on cremated. He'd been miles away and hadn't been paying attention—hadn't even heard the tent unzip. He quickly turned off the flame. "Lu, can you set up the chairs, please?"

"'Kay."

"What would you like me to do?" Naomi asked, her voice deep and silky, not just from sleep.

"Table," Rob said, getting hot under the collar—hotter still as she sauntered away in her short shorts and bent to pick up the bag containing the folded table. With some effort, and remembering they were sharing a tent with Lucas for the next six nights, Rob dragged his mind out of the gutter and dished up the food.

Not surprisingly, Lucas's barely touched the sides, and he was done almost before Rob started eating.

"Can we go kayaking now?"

"I told you—you need to let it go down first or you'll get cramp."

"That's just swimming."

"Any physical activity straight after food."

"But—"

"I have an idea," Naomi said. She got up and went inside the tent, returning with the leaflets for the different activities on and around the campsite. "Here you go, Lu."

With a huff, he took them from her and turned them over one at a time—"Boring...nah...boring...boring—"

"Give 'em here." Rob snatched up the haphazard pile Lucas had discarded. "Right, what've we got? Paddleboarding, wakeboarding, kayaking, obviously—"

"Waterskiing?" Naomi asked.

"Yep."

"Ooh! I've always wanted to waterski!"

Rob laughed. "That's tomorrow sorted."

"What would *you* like to do? It's your holiday too."

"I'm up for anything that gives me some peace and quiet." He honestly didn't care what they did, but Naomi was waiting for him to come up with a suggestion, so he flipped through the remaining leaflets—bike hire, wildlife trails, zip wires, pony treks...he got stuck on that one.

Naomi tugged the leaflet from his hand. "Is this what you want to do?"

Never mind pony trekking, Rob's heart was doing plenty of galloping of its own because his thoughts were on Dee and her horseriding. Since he'd left London, they'd spoken just once, for no reason other than they were both busy—she with her new job on some task force or other, he with physio and pottering in the old workshop behind Johnson's Garage, which he was hoping to set up as a motorcycle repair shop once his hands were fully healed.

"Rob?"

"Hmm? Sorry. What d'you reckon to pony trekking, Lu?"

Lucas shrugged noncommittally. They were getting nothing out of him until he'd got the kayaking bug out of his system, so as soon as they were all finished with breakfast, they took a quick trip up to the hub to do the dishes, use the loos and brush their teeth, then headed down to the lake.

"There they are!" Lucas sprinted off along a path signposted 'Krazy Kayakz'.

Rob sighed. "He's a bugger once he gets a bee in his bonnet."

"Like father, like son," Naomi remarked with a knowing smile.

Rob had no defence, so he kept quiet as they traipsed after Lucas, emerging a couple of minutes later at the lakeside, both shielding their eyes against the sunlight glinting off the rippled surface.

"Absolutely stunning!" Naomi uttered at his side.

Rob couldn't agree more, but he only got to enjoy it for about five seconds before his phone rang. He hit the answer button. "Morning, Gray."

"Hey, Rob. How are things?"

"Awesome. I'm on my holidays."

"Are you really? Good for you!"

"Yep. Finally booked that camping trip." And returned the carabiner to Lucas's rucksack. "New Forest. Very picturesque. What are you up to?"

"Currently enjoying a latte outside a Cornish beach-hut café."

"Nice! You're on your holidays too?"

"We are. It's Suzannah's birthday."

"Oh, yeah. I remember you saying. Sweet Sixteen surf party."

"Surf party, fire-eaters, music, dancing, barbecue—but not until this afternoon. This is the calm before the storm."

Rob chuckled. "Sounds like you've got a fun day ahead."

"I hope so. Anyway, I don't want to keep you away from *your* fun. There is a reason for my call. Have you made any plans for the tenth of April next year?"

"Not yet."

"Will and I are looking at dates for the wedding, and that's the favourite, but I wanted to check you were available before we went any further."

"I'll make sure I am." Rob was a little perplexed why it mattered. "Did you want me to dogsit while you're on your honeymoon?"

Gray laughed. "No. I wondered if you'd do me the honour of being my best man."

"Me? I mean, yeah. I'm honoured you're asking, but..."

"But?"

"Well, I figured with you falling out with Dom, you'd ask Josh."

"Ah. Can I be honest with you, Rob?"

"Of course."

"Dom and I have resolved our differences for the most part, but there's no telling when his hearing will be or whether he'll be at liberty whatever date we pick. I talked it through with him, and he suggested I ask someone else. In fact, he suggested I ask you."

Rob hadn't missed that Gray was dodging the 'why not Josh?' question, but he left it alone. "Does it look like Dom'll do time?"

"He'll definitely get a custodial sentence. There's a fifty-fifty chance it'll be suspended."

"All right, how about this? I'll be your reserve best man, in case Dom can't be there."

"That's hardly fair on you."

"If I felt hard done by, I'd have told you to take a hike. As I say, I'm honoured you've asked me, and I'll fulfil the role to the best of my abilities. But we both know Dom's your first choice, and that's how it should be. So what d'you reckon?"

"If you're sure..."

"I'm sure."

"Dad, hurry up!"

Rob shot Lucas a warning glance. "I'd best go before my son has a meltdown over these kayaks."

"All right. I'll catch up with you after your holiday. Have a good one."

"You too, mate."

***

"Did he say yes?"

"Sort of." Thrown a little by Rob's response, Gray hadn't noticed Will and Suzannah return, but there they were, standing in front of him like wetsuited bookends, matching blonde-brown ponytails dancing in the ocean breeze, surfboards at their sides. "He struck a deal with me."

"What kind of deal?" Will asked.

"He'll do it if Dom's not available."

"That's good, isn't it?"

"Well, yes, but..."

"It's what you wanted."

"It is." He wouldn't have dreamed of insulting Rob by asking him to be 'reserve best man'. Their friendship was worth more than that. But Will was right; Rob's answer had solved Gray's dilemma.

"You should come surf with us," Suzannah said. "You're all up in your head."

Will nodded in agreement. "It'll get rid of your stress."

"Who says I'm stressed?" Gray protested. Granted, in the general scheme of things he was a worrier, but he was the most relaxed he'd been in months—years, really. However, this was Will and Suzannah's time, a chance for father and daughter to catch some waves together before the partying began in earnest. He wouldn't encroach on that. "I'll join you tomorrow."

"Promise?" Suzannah said.

"Promise." As if he could do anything else while held captive by those beseeching big brown eyes. Same as her father, Suzannah was a closer.

"Deal," she accepted. Leaning her surfboard against the table, she reached behind her neck and unfastened her chain. "Can you look after this for me?"

"Of course." Gray held out his hand to receive the chain bearing the engagement ring Will had bought for Shelley, its smooth, oval gemstone like a droplet captured from the ocean beyond. Closing his fingers around it, Gray looked up at Will, sensing in that moment another shift, subtle yet vital as the changing tide.

"We'll be back soon," Will said as he and Suzannah picked up their boards and set off for the surf.

"I'll be waiting."

"I know."

"Yeah, you do," Gray murmured. He followed their progress, neither of them looking back as they waded through the waves and bobbed out of sight, two sets of footprints the only physical evidence they had ever been there, and all of a sudden, the might of the ocean was utterly terrifying to him, in its grasp two of the most important people in his life. Before that fear could thoroughly take hold, his phone rattled across the table. He didn't recognise the number but answered just the same.

"Hello?"

"Graham, hello. I'm glad I've caught you."

"Martin. Another new number?"

"Yes. Do add it to your contacts—I plan on keeping this one. I thought I'd share the good news with you. Yesterday, I presented our evidence to the Home Secretary. When Parliament resumes, he will inform the Cabinet of his intention to open a full public inquiry into the actions of Invecta and a number of other private lobbies during the past ten years. He has asked me to lead the select committee conducting the inquiry."

"That's excellent news, Martin! And very well deserved. Congratulations!"

"Thank you, Graham." Gray could almost feel the heat coming off Winstanley's glow of satisfaction.

"Does that mean you're coming out of the police?"

"No, not at all, which is as well because I have a proposal for you."

"Oh?" Gray spotted Shelley on her way down the slipway and waved. She waved back and headed over.

"I appreciate you and I are not friends, Graham, but I like to think we share a respectful, professional bond that extends beyond being mere colleagues."

"I concur," Gray said.

"As such, it is my understanding from our interchanges over the years that were the opportunity to present itself for you to re-enter the police service, you would not hesitate to seize it."

"That's a fairly accurate understanding, yes." Gray hardly dared hope the conversation was going where it seemed to be. He smiled at Shelley, who left her bag next to him and signalled to ask if he'd keep an eye on it. He gave her a thumbs up.

"The opportunity is presenting itself, Graham."

"Tell me more," he said, the picture of cool, calm and collected even though his heart was having a rave and continued to do so while Winstanley explained what he had in mind: a new unit with national jurisdiction, working in partnership with internal affairs and human resources to oversee and enhance the accountability and support of undercover officers.

"You have a nuanced perspective, Graham, as a former undercover officer, leader, and through your work in the private sector. Your insight into the unique challenges faced by undercover officers is second to none. I can think of no-one better qualified for the task."

"Thank you for saying so, Martin." Such an incredible opportunity; he'd be a fool to let it pass him by. But it wasn't solely his decision. "How soon do you need an answer?"

"I'll email the information to you in a moment. Shall we say...by the end of the month?"

That was almost two weeks. Plenty of time to ponder and discuss. "Perfect."

"Excellent," Winstanley said and then nothing else, but Gray had grown wise to it, so he waited and was finally rewarded with, "It sounds rather windy where you are, Graham."

"Yes. I'm on the beach."

"A holiday?" Winstanley sni*ffffff*ed. "I may take one myself sometime. I'll leave you to enjoy it."

"Thanks, Martin. Speak to you soon."

"Indeed. Goodbye, Graham."

Call ended.

"Looked intense," Shelley said, returning with a surfboard. She, too, was in a wetsuit but took a bottle of sun cream from her bag and applied it generously to her face and neck. She was much fairer-skinned than Will and Suzannah. "Everything OK?"

Gray nodded and smiled. "Everything's fine." His phone buzzed again with the promised email and then a text message: *Forgot to mention – it comes with a promotion, should such things still serve to motivate. –MW.*

"He knows me far too well."

"Will?"

"No. Former colleague. Will and Suzannah are already out there."

"Sorry—didn't mean to pry." It was a well-practised apology. Prying was to journalism as mistrust was to police service, not that Gray doubted Shelley's sincerity; they'd always got along well. But knowing she'd rejected Will's marriage proposal—twice—made him sceptical of her intentions when he hadn't been before. It didn't matter. She'd had her reasons, and they were none of his business.

"It's all right, you didn't. All set for this afternoon?"

Shelley nodded. "More or less." She put the sun cream back in her bag.

"Anything you need me to do?"

"Don't think so, but you've done enough. Thanks again, by the way. It helped massively."

"It's my pleasure."

"I didn't mention your contribution to Will."

"He already knows."

"And he was OK about it?"

Gray tilted his head from side to side. "Comme si, comme ça."

Shelley laughed and tucked her board under her arm. "You'll win him round. You always do. See ya."

"See ya," Gray said as she jogged away. She was right. He could always win Will round, but as with everything that made up their relationship, it worked both ways. Or everything apart from the dogs, who were back at the house with Tie, and Gray was missing them something fierce. If he were to end up in the highest echelons of the British police, he'd still have no jurisdiction over Will's many dogs, guinea pigs, bunnies, psycho parakeets or whatever furred and feathered fiends needed sanctuary. And he wouldn't want it any other way.

The End

Acknowledgements/Credits

Much gratitude to David, Bob, Amy, Nige, Al, Andrea and Jor for (respectively and respectfully) crit-partnering, alpha-reading, beta-reading, editing and proofreading, and catching me when I fail/flail/fall.

The following sources were either used for research/reference or quoted directly:

'You Can't Kill The Spirit':
The Danish Peace Academy (n.d.) 'You Can't Kill The Spirit', written by Naomi Littlebear Morena, adapted from the song/chant 'Like a Mountain', in *The Greenham Common Women's Peace Camp Songbook* [Online]. Available at https://www.antiwarsongs.org/canzone.php?id=6888&lang=en.

Suspect interview procedure (adapted):
Great Britain. Home Office (2020) *Interviewing Suspects: Version 6.0* [Online]. Available at https://assets.publishing.service.gov.uk/government/uploads/system/uploads/attachment_data/file/859218/interviewing-suspects-v6.0-gov-uk.pdf.

Offender profiling/personality disorder research:
Crowell, S. E., Beauchaine, T. P. and Lineham, M. M. (2009) 'A biosocial developmental model of borderline personality: elaborating and extending Linehan's theory', *Psychological Bulletin*, vol. 135, no. 3, pp. 495–510, American Psychological Association.

Fox, B, and Farrington, D. P. (2018) 'What have we learned from offender profiling? A systematic review and meta-analysis of 40 years of research', *Psychological Bulletin*, vol. 144, no. 12, pp. 1247–1274, American Psychological Association.

Perri, F. S. (2011) 'White-collar criminals: the "kinder, gentler" offender?' *Journal of Investigative Psychology and Offender Profiling*, vol. 8, no. 3, pp. 217–241.

Perri, F. S. (2016) 'Red collar crime', *International Journal of Psychological Studies*, vol. 8, no. 1, pp. 61–84.

Epigraphs:
Freud, S., Strachey, J., Freud, A., Strachey, A. and Tyson, A. (2001) *The Standard Edition of the Complete Psychological Works of Sigmund Freud*, London, Random House.

Gandhi, M. (1969) *The Collected Works of Mahatma Gandhi, Vol 31 (Mar 22 - Jun 15, 1925)*, Ministry of Information and Broadcasting – Government of India Online]. Available at: https://www.gandhiserve.net/about-mahatma-gandhi/collected-works-of-mahatma-gandhi/031-19260615-19261104/.

Ginsberg, A. (1986) 'The Fall of America' in *Poems of These States 1965–1971*, San Francisco, City Lights Publishers.

About the Author

Debbie McGowan is an author and publisher based in a semi-rural corner of Lancashire, England. She writes character-driven, realist fiction, celebrating life, love and relationships. A working-class girl, she 'ran away' to London at seventeen, was homeless, unemployed and then homeless again, interspersed with animal rights activism (all legal, honest ;)) and volunteer work as a mental health advocate. At twenty-five, she went back to college to study social science—tough with two toddlers, but they had a 'stay at home' dad, so it worked itself out. These days, the toddlers are young women (much to their chagrin) and Debbie teaches undergraduate students, writes novels and runs an independent publishing company, occasionally grabbing an hour's sleep where she can.

Social Media Links

Website: debbiemcgowan.co.uk
Newsletter Signup: eepurl.com/b8emHL
Blog: deb248211.blogspot.com
Facebook: facebook.com/DebbieMcGowanAuthor and facebook.com/beatentrackpublishing
Twitter: @writerdebmcg
YouTube: youtube.com/deb248211
Instagram: instagram/writerdebmcg
Tumblr: writerdebmcg.tumblr.com
LinkedIn: uk.linkedin.com/in/writerdebmcg
Goodreads: goodreads.com/DebbieMcGowan

For a full list of Debbie McGowan's books, visit:
http://www.debbiemcgowan.co.uk/?n1=publications

For more from Beaten Track, visit:
https://www.beatentrackpublishing.com

Previously, in
Hiding Behind The Couch

Three years ago, Detective Chief Inspector Gray Fisher, then head of the Metropolitan Police Special Investigations Unit (SIU), was travelling home from a wedding with his civil partner Jean-Michel. Jean-Michel was driving, and he was tired; he ended up on the wrong side of the road, and they crashed. A couple of days later, Jean-Michel's life support was switched off and he died, leaving Gray a devastated but wealthy man. In an effort to allay his grief, Gray threw himself back into his work, relying on cocaine to maintain his gruelling schedule.

Gray had already established the whereabouts of his half-brother George, whom he'd never met. As he tells George the first time they properly speak:

> I've been in the police since I left uni. I started off on the beat and applied to CID, then volunteered for an undercover team investigating white collar crime—embezzlement, money laundering, tax evasion—all very tedious, but it involved big bucks and clever thieves. I'd already looked you up and knew where your mum lived—you were in Colorado, so I didn't do anything about it, and then I met Jean, and it didn't matter so much, because I wasn't on my own anymore.

> It's incredible, now I look back on it. I was running some searches on the database for a newly floated company doing some insider trading. It was mostly run-of-the-mill stuff—nothing I could really get them on, so I started looking at their trading partners, cross-checking entries in their accounts, and this one particular entry caught my eye. It was for one of their subcontractors, and the company—Campion's—was based in your hometown.

> I dug a little deeper. I noticed there was a lawyer by the name of Strang representing the company involved in the share price fixing, and Campion's lawyers were Sharston Strang. I started to join the dots. There were some scant notes on a couple of possible fraud cases

in London, some more up in Newcastle, and another involving Sharston Strang. I got permission to do a bit of preliminary work, with the intention of getting in touch with you while I was in the area.

When he realised George was too close to the SIU's target, Gray put a hold on making contact and turned his attentions to his investigation of the fraud cases. He needed an undercover officer to infiltrate the targets: trawling through the Met Police files for officers with undercover experience, he came across Rob Simpson-Stone, who not only came from George's hometown but had also gone to school with Jessica Lambert—one of the lawyers suspected of fraud. Gray heavily leaned on Rob to take on a job as motorcycle courier delivering counterfeit documents for the fraudsters. Rob was ideally placed to infiltrate the fraud ring and later used his friendship with Lambert to gain access to the people at the top of the chain.

After Campion's CEO (Alistair Campion) was murdered, it transpired that he and his personal assistant Alice Friar had a long-term affair. They also had a son (Jason), who was adopted by Alistair's friend/silent business partner. The son inherited Campion's fortune, and the fraudsters made a second attempt to get their hands on it, holding Alice and Jason hostage at Black Hole—the music studio Jason built with his inheritance. Rob Simpson-Stone was there at Black Hole, along with Angela Sharston—one of the corrupt lawyers—and Anders Folden, a paid-for hitman employed by the fraud ring and responsible for Campion's murder. The evidence the SIU collected plus Lambert's confession was enough to take down the fraud ring, and all those involved were incarcerated.

Following Gray's career crash-and-burn and subsequent resignation from police service, he bought a house in London and restarted his life, working towards a PhD in English Literature along with occasional work as an extra in a soap opera (for therapeutic reasons, plus he studied drama as part of his first degree). He became acquainted with George's husband Josh—a psychotherapist—during the fraud investigation, and they worked together on Gray's final case with the SIU. During that time, Gray developed feelings for Josh and in admitting this to Josh, Gray acknowledged they were a sign he was recovering from his grief. Josh took Gray under his wing and introduced him to Will Richards—a surfer from London whom Josh and George met on their honeymoon.